DANIEL DEFOE was born in St. Giles, Cripplegate, London, about 1660. He went to Charles Morton's academy to study for the ministry but ended up entering the business world instead. His poem, *The True-Born Englishman*, published in 1701, met with resounding success. In 1702 he attacked the Tories in a pamphlet, *The Shortest Way with the Dissenters*, and was sent to prison. Released in November, 1704, he became a secret agent for the government and continued to write pamphlets. Between 1718 and 1723 he published *Robinson Crusoe, Moll Flanders*, and *A Journal of the Plague Year*. Forced to go into hiding to escape his creditors, Defoe died, a lonely and hunted man, in Ropemaker's Alley, Moorfields, on April 26, 1731.

HENRY FIELDING was born near Glastonbury, Somerset, in 1707. His early education was conducted by a clergyman; he later went to Eton. His first comedy, *Love in Several Masques*, was produced at Drury Lane in 1728, and over the next eight years he wrote several dramatic successes, among them *Tom Thumb* (1730-31), a burlesque. He published *Joseph Andrews* in 1742, *Tom Jones* in 1749, and *Amelia* in 1751. In 1754 he sailed for Lisbon, a journey described in detail in a posthumously published work, *Journal of a Voyage to Lisbon* (1755). He died two months after his arrival and was buried in the English cemetery where, in 1830, a monument was erected in his honor.

OLIVER GOLDSMITH was born in 1728 in County Langford, Ireland. At the village school in his father's West Meath parish, Goldsmith learned of, and became enamoured of Irish folklore, music, and verse. He entered Trinity College, Dublin, in 1744, and obtained his bachelor's degree in 1749. In 1756 he began writing newspaper and magazine articles, children's books, essays, and sketches. The publication of his poem, *The Traveller* (1764), and his novel, *The Vicar of Wakefield* (1766), raised him to the ranks of first-rate writers. His play, *She Stoops to Conquer* (1773), brought renewed plaudits. Goldsmith died on April 4, 1774.

THREE EIGHTEENTH CENTURY NOVELS

Moll Flanders

by Daniel Defoe

Joseph Andrews

by Henry Fielding

The Vicar of Wakefield

by Oliver Goldsmith

INTRODUCTION BY ERICA JONG

A SIGNET CLASSIC
NEW AMERICAN LIBRARY
TIMES MIRROR
New York and Scarborough, Ontario

NAL BOOKS ARE AVAILABLE AT QUANTITY DISCOUNTS WHEN USED TO PROMOTE PRODUCTS OR SERVICES. FOR INFORMATION PLEASE WRITE TO PREMIUM MARKETING DIVISION, THE NEW AMERICAN LIBRARY, INC., 1633 BROADWAY, NEW YORK, NEW YORK 10019.

Cover art: Detail from "Dedham Vale" by John Constable
SCALA/Editorial Photocolor Archives, Inc.

Library of Congress Catalog Card Number: 81-85139

Moll Flanders, Joseph Andrews and *The Vicar of Wakefield* are also available as separate volumes in Signet Classic editions.

SIGNET CLASSIC TRADEMARK REG. U.S. PAT. OFF. AND FOREIGN COUNTRIES
REGISTERED TRADEMARK—MARCA REGISTRADA
HECHO EN CHICAGO, U.S.A.

SIGNET, SIGNET CLASSICS, MENTOR, PLUME, MERIDIAN AND NAL BOOKS are published *in the United States* by The New American Library, Inc., 1633 Broadway, New York, New York 10019, *in Canada* by The New American Library of Canada Limited, 81 Mack Avenue, Scarborough, Ontario M1L 1M8.

First Printing, February, 1982

1 2 3 4 5 6 7 8 9

PRINTED IN THE UNITED STATES OF AMERICA

INTRODUCTION

In England during the 18th century a new literary form evolved, which was not only revolutionary in its own day, but has remained the liveliest of forms in our own. That new literary form was the novel—and like most art that sees life in a radically new way, it made its appearance on the scene in a cloud of condemnation, cries that it was not literature at all, and allegations that it corrupted the morals of women.

What things characterized the 18th-century novel and made it so different from all its literary predecessors? First, the novel was realistic. It did not use those traditional mythic plots that had been the staple of English writers from Chaucer to Shakespeare. It purported to present the actual experience of actual people. Second, it presented life not in the vacuum of timelessness (which surrounds Spencer's or Milton's created universes), but in the very timely flux of quotidian experience. (In *Clarissa* and *Tom Jones*, we can make chronologies for the action, which check out to the very last details.) Third, the novel was perhaps the first literary genre to rely on a very specific sense of place—interiors and exteriors described not in general terms, but in highly specific ones. And fourth (and perhaps most important), the prose style of the novel eschewed eloquence for eloquence's sake and adapted instead an anti-literary language so as to better reflect the ordinariness of ordinary life.

These characteristics of the novel* are so familiar to us today that we may fail to realize how revolutionary they were in the 18th century. When John Updike opens a novel (*Rabbit Is Rich*) with a detailed description of a Toyota car dealership in 1979, the year of the gas crisis, we do not find anything unusual about the sort of material he is presenting. We *expect* novels to have cars and car showrooms in them, gas crises, references to brands of toothpaste, political events—not to mention people's bodily functions, sexual longings, tastes, smells, appetites. In fact, this passion for realism is a very modern passion. It reflects an essentially individualistic view of the universe—a view of the universe quite different

---

* For a more detailed explanation of the novel's break with the past, see Ian Watt's excellent book: *The Rise of the Novel* (University of California Press, 1962), from which these ideas are abstracted.

from the one required to build the great cathedrals, write the *Divine Comedy*, or perform miracle plays. The earlier way of conceiving the universe saw the whole of human experience as elemental and unchanging—life, sin, death, redemption—usually in that order. The modern one sees the individual as having some control of his destiny through his own actions.

Nor were these the only factors that led to the rise of the novel. Economic changes were also vastly important. The birth of the middle class, of leisured, affluent wives (who did not have to toil on farms or in cottage industries), made the novel commercially viable. The spread of literacy was equally essential; before the novel could flourish, there had to be enough readers to support it. And though the reading public in the 18th century was minuscule compared to today's (in England it numbered only in the tens of thousands for a nation of six million), it was still much larger than the essentially aristocratic reading public of Chaucer's or Shakespeare's day.

The three novels in this volume exemplify different aspects of that revolutionary 18th-century form, the novel. By looking at these three novels, we can understand how flexible the novel is and how its flexibility in part accounts for its longevity.

Moll Flanders, the earliest book (1722), is essentially a rogue's biography. It purports to be the true history of a famous criminal's life. (That is another essential characteristic of the novel: it always claims for itself the distinction of truth. However seamy the life it presents, however wretched the smells and tastes, Truth, noble Truth, is said to be at fault—and certainly not a desire to alarm or titillate. Contemporary writers who create mock-autobiographies, mock-confessions, are really working in the central tradition of the English novel, that of pretending absolute veracity.) *Moll Flanders* exemplifies this strain of fictional tradition perhaps better than any other book. The non-fiction feeling of *Moll Flanders*, the concentration on ledgers, accounts, prices, quantities, has been said to reflect the rise of bourgeois consciousness—that consciousness which seeks to know life by quantification rather than by its essences. And it is true that we find in *Moll Flanders* a new way of seeing reality, which the 18th century invented (or at least perfected). Moll often appears to be a creature made up entirely of externals. We know the price of everything around her and the value of nothing. She loses husbands, gains husbands, has children, loses children, usually without more than a perfunctory tear. Yet despite her lack of psychological depth, she has the most important quality the protagonist of a novel can ever have: She elicits our sympathy and our identification. "Heartless, she is not," Virginia Woolf said of her, "nor can anyone charge her with levity; but life delights her, and a heroine who lives has us all in tow. Moreover, her ambition has that slight strain of imagination in it which puts it in the category of the noble passions."

Defoe's great device as a novelist was to put his solitary hero or heroine in the direst straits at the outset of the action so that he or she could be tested against all the hardships life had to offer. About *Moll Flanders*, Virginia Woolf points out that "the briskness of the story is due partly to the fact that having transgressed the accepted laws at a very early age, she has henceforth the freedom of the outcast."

Moll is an outcast partly because of being a thief, but also because of being a woman. And here Defoe shows himself far ahead of the brutish male chauvinism of his time. He creates a female character who is as adventurous and courageous as any man, but who is also honest and straightforward in a way we find very contemporary. Defoe's exemplary views on women have frequently been quoted:

> "I have often thought of it as one of the most barbarous customs in the world, considering us as a civilized and a Christian country, that we deny the advantages of learning to women. We reproach the sex every day with folly and impertinence; which I am confident, had they the advantages of education equal to us, they would be guilty of less than ourselves."

But his sympathy for the female sex is better shown through our response to the character of Moll than through any nonfiction tract Defoe wrote. Without writing a feminist polemic on the harsh fate of women, Defoe manages to suggest the extreme difficulty of women's lives. It is just as Tolstoy once said, "I have found that a story leaves a deeper impression when it is impossible to tell which side the author is on." We respond to Moll Flanders with feminist sympathies in part because Defoe's empathy for women is so unconscious and unpremeditated. He merely grants Moll the same selfhood he would grant a male character. In the 18th century, that was nothing less than revolutionary. Once again, Virginia Woolf appears to have said the last word on Defoe's peculiar genius: "He seems to have taken his characters so deeply into his mind that he lived them without exactly knowing how; and like all unconscious artists, he leaves more gold in his work than his own generation was able to bring to the surface."

In *Joseph Andrews* (1741) we see the 18th-century novel in another guise: the novel as comic epic. Fielding constantly claims for his narrative the distinction of the epic, and classical references abound, both in *Joseph Andrews* and in *Tom Jones.* Some historians of the novel have been duped by this into thinking that Fielding really was writing epics in prose—a claim quite as untrue as the claim that Joyce was writing an epic, not a novel, in *Ulysses* (simply because he makes abundant use of classical parallels).

In fact, *Joseph Andrews* fulfills nearly all the characteristics of the novel previously enumerated: realism of plot, place, interior, and conversation. Though Fielding is indeed more rhetorical and ornamental in his writing than Defoe, he tends to be ornamental in well-defined descriptive passages where the rhetoric almost draws ironical attention to itself *as* rhetoric. But in his characterization, comic conversation, descriptions of place and landscape, Fielding is every bit the chronicler of the quotidian that Defoe is.

Fielding claimed epic status for his novels simply because the novel was considered such a low and disreputable form in the 18th century. It had a literary status slightly above that of the comic book or "photo-novel" today. Nearly always, new art forms which appear on the scene are thought vulgar and lowbrow at first and must claim relationship with existing highbrow art forms in order to elevate their own status. In the '60s, pop-music critics analyzed Beatles' songs as if they were poems by Yeats. In the early days of the novel, there was the same impulse to dignify the medium with references to the highbrow art. The epic (and the tragedy) were the most highbrow of arts to the 18th-century reader. But by the 18th century the epic had run its course; it no longer reflected life as it was lived or the values of society. A new form that reflected those values had to be invented, and the novel was born to that destiny. Quite naturally, it paid lip service to earlier genres in order to justify its existence.

Joseph Andrews began as a parody—Fielding's response to the runaway success of *Pamela* (1740). It is safe to say that

Pamela was the *Fear of Flying* of its time: applauded for its honesty and verisimilitude by some as passionately as it was denounced for its prurience by others. Fielding was on the side of the detractors. He loathed *Pamela*—both the book and the fictional lady. He found in Pamela's insistence on preserving her virginity until she was safely (and lucratively) married, a mercantile mentality quite at variance with the classical ideals of goodness he espoused. To satirize Pamela, he invented for her a fictional brother, Joseph, who serves a lascivious lady in town (as Pamela serves a priapic squire in the country). But to Pamela's false goodness and modesty, Fielding opposes Joseph's true goodness and modesty. No minx seeking to marry upward, Joseph loves his sweetheart, Fanny Goodwill, with all his heart, and Fanny, unlike the logorrheic Pamela, can neither read nor write.

Joseph Andrews began as a mere parody, but it did not remain one for long. The characters galloped away with the author's heart. Joseph and his adoring Widow Booby, Parson Abraham Adams, Mrs. Slipslop, all came to life under Fielding's quill and took his story off into the realm of literature (when he had perhaps intended only diversion).

For here is the main point to be made about that curious 18th-century invention, the novel: It is a form that somehow never quite works unless we love the main characters. Critics will quibble and nitpick about the supposed death of fiction in our time. Trendy writers will speak of "faction," "non-fiction novels," and "docu-novels." Frenchmen will argue about novels without character or plot. Scholars will speak about "hermetic" fiction, "fabulist" fiction, and other academic inventions. But novels don't usually engage us unless somehow the main characters enchant us, win our hearts, and make us fall in love with them.

John Updike has suggested that the novel is by its very nature sentimental, and that the protagonist of a novel "Must earn our interest by virtue of his . . . *authentic sentiments*." I think this is true. I would go so far as to say that this is the *sine qua non* of novel writing. The plot may be improbable, the prose uninspired, the morality questionable, but the protagonist must seduce us and make us feel that his or her concerns are also ours.

Which brings us at last to that curious book, *The Vicar of Wakefield* (1766)—to which all of the above criteria certainly apply. The plot is improbable: Never were the wicked so wicked or the good so good. The prose is uneven; the morality, which may have been more plausible in the 1760's, seems terribly dated today. Yet generations of readers have had their heartstrings tugged by Dr. Primrose's goodness. His imperishability of spirit, his will to endure, even in the worst of times, his human and touching survival in the face of adversity, are what keep us reading and believing, even when it is almost impossible to believe.

Finally, there is another trait of the novel which *The Vicar of Wakefield* illustrates: the tendency to find human life redemptive even when the worst has happened. As Virginia Woolf says,

> ". . . Goldsmith not only believed in blackness and whiteness: he believed—perhaps one belief depends upon the other—that goodness will be rewarded, and vice punished. It is a doctrine, it may strike us when we read *The Vicar of Wakefield,* which imposes some restrictions on the novelist. There is no need of the mixed, of the twisted, of the profound. Lightly tinted, broadly shaded with here a foible, there a peccadillo, the characters of the Primroses are like those tropical fish who seem to have only backbones but no other organs to darken the transparency of their flesh. Our sympathies are not put upon the rack. Daughters may be seduced, houses burnt, and good men sent to prison, yet since the world is a perfectly balanced place, let it lurch as it likes, it is bound to settle into equilibrium in the long run."

The best-loved novelists of all periods (Dickens in the 19th century, J. D. Salinger, John Updike, or I. B. Singer in our own time) usually have in common their ability to suggest the redemptive possibilities of human life. They complete the action as the arc ascends. That it can also descend, we surely know. But we *need* the novelist to remind us of the *possibility* of ascension. And in order to feel that possibility, our hearts must beat with Moll Flanders, with Parson Adams, with Dr. Primrose. To that end, their creators must endow them with the gift of life—for no other reason than so they can pass it on to us.

Having said these things about the three novels in this book, perhaps we can understand why the novel form exhibits such strong life-force even 250 years after its birth. It has never been weighed down with pretensions of high art (as, for example, lyric poetry has); instead, it has run the gamut from trash to literature. It is beloved by readers of

Gothic romances no less than by readers of Gunther Grass and Isaac Singer. It has this amazing versatility that allows it to break all literary rules with impunity—save the rule that the protagonist must win our hearts and that we must be impelled to turn the page. Its trashy beginnings have given it an irrepressible vitality. We may wager that the novel will endure as long as it does not betray its lower-class origins and seek to become a false aristocrat. For the novel is more in danger of death by literary criticism than death by popular neglect. As long as it is read by servants as well as masters, it will remain alive. It can only perish by being received forever into the airless Temple of Art where no characters breathe, and consequently, no readers read.

—*Erica Jong*

[illegible] comparisons no less than by readers of [illegible] and Isaac Singer. It has this amazing versatility that allows it to break all literary rules with impunity—save the rule that the protagonist must win our hearts and must make the reader impatient to turn the page. Its trashy beginnings have given it an irrepressible vitality. We may wager that the novel will endure as long as it does not betray its lower-class origins and seek to become a false aristocrat. For the novel is more in danger of death by literary criticism than death by popular neglect. As long as it is read by servants as well as masters, it will remain alive. It can only perish by being received forever into the airless Temple of Art where no characters breathe, and consequently no readers read.

—Erica Jong

THE FORTUNES AND MISFORTUNES
OF THE FAMOUS

Moll Flanders, &c.

Who was Born in Newgate, and during a Life of continu'd Variety for Three-score Years, besides her Childhood, was Twelve Year a Whore, five times a Wife (whereof once to her own Brother), Twelve Years a Thief, Eight Year a Transported Felon in Virginia, at last grew Rich, liv'd Honest, and died a Penitent

Written from her own Memorandums

by Daniel Defoe

THE PREFACE

The world is so taken up of late with novels and romances that it will be hard for a private history to be taken for genuine where the names and other circumstances of the person are concealed; and on this account we must be content to leave the reader to pass his own opinion upon the ensuing sheets and take it just as he pleases.

The author is here supposed to be writing her own history, and in the very beginning of her account she gives the reasons why she thinks fit to conceal her true name, after which there is no occasion to say any more about that.

It is true that the original of this story is put into new words and the style of the famous lady we here speak of is a little altered; particularly she is made to tell her own tale in modester words than she told it at first, the copy which came first to hand having been written in language more like one still in Newgate than one grown penitent and humble, as she afterwards pretends to be.

The pen employed in finishing her story, and making it what you now see it to be, has had no little difficulty to put it into a dress fit to be seen and to make it speak language fit to be read. When a woman debauched from her youth, nay, even being the offspring of debauchery and vice, comes to give an account of all her vicious practices, and even to descend to the particular occasions and circumstances by which she first became wicked, and of all the progressions of crime which she run through in threescore years, an author must be hard put to it to wrap it up so clean as not to give room, especially for vicious readers, to turn it to his disadvantage.

All possible care, however, has been taken to give no lewd ideas, no immodest turns, in the new dressing up this story; no, not to the worst part of her expressions. To this purpose some of the vicious part of her life, which could not be modestly told, is quite left out, and several other parts are very much shortened. What is left 'tis hoped will not offend the chastest reader or the modestest hearer; and as the best use is to be made even of the worst story, the moral, 'tis hoped, will keep the reader serious even where the story might incline him to be otherwise. To give the history of a wicked life repented of necessarily requires that the wicked part should be made as wicked as the real history of it will bear, to illustrate and give a beauty to the penitent part, which is certainly the best and brightest if related with equal spirit and life.

It is suggested there cannot be the same life, the same brightness and beauty, in relating the penitent part as is in the criminal part. If there is any truth in that suggestion, I must be allowed to say 'tis because there is not the same taste and relish in the reading; and indeed it is too true that the difference lies not in the real worth of the subject so much as in the gust and palate of the reader.

But as this work is chiefly recommended to those who know how to read it and how to make the good uses of it which the story all along recommends to them, so it is to be hoped that such readers will be much more pleased with the moral than the fable, with the application than with the relation, and with the end of the writer than with the life of the person written of.

There is in this story abundance of delightful incidents, and all of them usefully applied. There is an agreeable turn artfully given them in the relating, that naturally instructs the reader either one way or another. The first part of her lewd life with the young gentleman at Colchester has so many happy turns given it to expose the crime, and warn all whose circumstances are adapted to it of the ruinous end of such things, and the foolish, thoughtless, and abhorred conduct of both the parties, that it abundantly atones for all the lively description she gives of her folly and wickedness.

The repentance of her lover at the Bath and how brought by the just alarm of his fit of sickness to abandon her, the just caution given there against even the lawful intimacies of the dearest friends and how unable they are to preserve the most solemn resolutions of virtue without divine assistance—these are parts which to a just discernment will appear to have more real beauty in them than all the amorous chain of story which introduces it.

In a word, as the whole relation is carefully garbled of all the levity and looseness that was in it, so it is applied, and with the utmost care, to virtuous and religious uses. None can, without being guilty of manifest injustice, cast any reproach upon it or upon our design in publishing it.

The advocates for the stage have in all ages made this the great argument to persuade people that their plays are useful, and that they ought to be allowed in the most civilized and in the most religious government; namely, that they are applied to virtuous purposes, and that by the most lively representations they fail not to recommend virtue and generous principles and to discourage and expose all sorts of vice and corruption of manners; and were it true that they did so and that they constantly adhered to that rule as the test of their acting on the theatre, much might be said in their favour.

Throughout the infinite variety of this book, this fundamental is most strictly adhered to; there is not a wicked action in any part of it but is first or last rendered unhappy and unfortunate; there is not a superlative villain brought upon the stage but either he is brought to an unhappy end or brought to be a penitent; there is not an ill thing mentioned but it is condemned, even in the relation, nor a virtuous, just thing but it carries its praise along with it. What can more exactly answer the rule laid down, to recommend even those representations of things which have so many other just objections lying against them? Namely, of example of bad company, obscene language, and the like.

Upon this foundation this book is recommended to the reader, as a work from every part of which something may be learnt and some just and religious inference is drawn, by which the reader will have something of instruction if he pleases to make use of it.

All the exploits of this lady of fame, in her depredations upon mankind, stand as so many warnings to honest people to beware of 'em, intimating to 'em by what methods innocent people are drawn in, plundered, and robbed, and by consequence how to avoid them. Her robbing a little child, dressed fine by the vanity of the mother, to go to the dancing-school is a good memento to such people hereafter, as is likewise her picking the gold watch from the young lady's side in the park.

Her getting a parcel from a hare-brained wench at the coaches in St. John's Street, her booty at the fire and also at Harwich—all give us excellent warning in such cases to be more present to ourselves in sudden surprises of every sort.

Her application to a sober life and industrious management at last, in Virginia, with her transported spouse, is a story fruitful of instruction to all the unfortunate creatures who are obliged to seek their re-establishment abroad, whether by the misery of transportation or other disaster; letting them know that diligence and application have their due encouragement even in the remotest part of the world, and that no case can be so low, so despicable, or so empty of prospect, but that an unwearied industry will go a great way to deliver us from it, will in time raise the meanest creature to appear again in the world and give him a new cast for his life.

These are a few of the serious inferences which we are led by the hand to in this book, and these are fully sufficient to justify any man in recommending it to the world, and much more to justify the publication of it.

There are two of the most beautiful parts still behind, which this story gives some idea of and lets us into the parts of them, but they are either of them too long to be brought into the same volume and indeed are, as I may call them, whole volumes of themselves, *viz.:* 1. The life of her governess, as she calls her, who had run through, it seems, in a few years all the eminent degrees of a gentlewoman, a whore, and a bawd; a midwife and a midwife-keeper, as they are called; a pawnbroker, a child-taker, a receiver of thieves and of stolen goods; and, in a word, herself a thief, a breeder up of thieves and the like, and yet at last a penitent.

The second is the life of her transported husband, a highwayman, who, it seems, lived a twelve years' life of successful villainy upon the road, and even at last came off so well as to be a volunteer transport, not a convict, and in whose life there is an incredible variety.

But, as I said, these are things too long to bring in here, so neither can I make a promise of their coming out by themselves.

We cannot say, indeed, that this history is carried on quite to the end of the life of this famous Moll Flanders, for nobody can write their own life to the full end of it unless they can write it after they are dead. But her husband's life, being written by a third hand, gives a full account of them both, how long they lived together in that country, and how they came both to England again after about eight years, in which time they were grown very rich, and where she lived, it seems, to be very old, but was not so extraordinary a penitent as she was at first; it seems only that indeed she always spoke with abhorrence of her former life and every part of it.

In her last scene, at Maryland and Virginia, many pleasant things happened, which makes that part of her life very agreeable, but they are not told with the same elegancy as those accounted for by herself; so it is still to the more advantage that we break off here.

We cannot say, indeed, that this history is carried on quite to the end of the life of this famous Moll Flanders, for nobody can write their own life to the full end of it, unless they can write it after they are dead; but her husband's life, being written by a third hand, gives a full account of them both, how long they lived together in that country, and how they came both to England again, after about eight years, in which time they were grown very rich, and where she lived, it seems, to be very old, but was not so extraordinary a penitent as she was at first; it seems only that indeed she always spoke with abhorrence of her former life and of every part of it.

In her last scene, at Maryland and Virginia, many pleasant things happened, which makes that part of her life very agreeable, but they are not told with the same elegancy as those accounted for by herself; so it is still to the more advantage that we break off here.

My true name is so well known in the records, or registers, at Newgate and in the Old Bailey, and there are some things of such consequence still depending there relating to my particular conduct, that it is not to be expected I should set my name or the account of my family to this work; perhaps after my death it may be better known; at present it would not be proper, no, not though a general pardon should be issued, even without exceptions of persons or crimes.

It is enough to tell you that as some of my worst comrades, who are out of the way of doing me harm, having gone out of the world by the steps and the string, as I often expected to go, knew me by the name of Moll Flanders, so you may give me leave to go under that name till I dare own who I have been, as well as who I am.

I have been told that in one of our neighbour nations, whether it be in France or where else I know not, they have an order from the king that when any criminal is condemned, either to die, or to the galleys, or to be transported, if they leave any children, as such are generally unprovided for by the forfeiture of their parents, so they are immediately taken into the care of the government and put into an hospital called the House of Orphans, where they are bred up, clothed, fed, taught, and, when fit to go out, are placed to trades or to services, so as to be well able to provide for themselves by an honest, industrious behaviour.

Had this been the custom in our country, I had not been left a poor desolate girl without friends, without clothes, without help or helper, as was my fate; and by which I was not only exposed to very great distresses even before I was capable either of understanding my case or how to amend it, but brought into a course of life scandalous in itself and which in its ordinary course tended to the swift destruction both of soul and body.

But the case was otherwise here. My mother was convicted of felony for a petty theft scarce worth naming, *viz.*, borrowing three pieces of fine holland of a certain draper in Cheapside. The circumstances are too long to repeat, and I have heard them related so many ways that I can scarce tell which is the right account.

However it was, they all agree in this: that my mother pleaded her belly, and being found quick with child, she was respited for about seven months; after which she was called down, as they term it, to her former judgement, but obtained the favour afterward of being transported to the plantations, and left me about half a year old, and in bad hands, you may be sure.

This is too near the first hours of my life for me to relate anything of myself but by hearsay; 'tis enough to mention that as I was born in such an unhappy place, I had no parish to have recourse to for my nourishment in my infancy; nor can I give the least account how I was kept alive other than that, as I have been told, some relation of my mother took me away, but at whose expense or by whose direction I know nothing at all of it.

The first account that I can recollect or could ever learn of myself was that I had wandered among a crew of those people they call gipsies, or Egyptians; but I believe it was but a little while that I had been among them, for I had not had my skin discoloured, as they do to all children they carry about with them; nor can I tell how I came among them or how I got from them.

It was at Colchester, in Essex, that those people left me, and I have a notion in my head that I left them there (that is, that I hid myself and would not go any farther with them), but I am not able to be particular in that account; only this I remember: that being taken up by some of the parish officers of Colchester, I gave an account that I came into the town with the gipsies, but that I would not go any farther with them, and that so they had left me, but whither they were gone, that I knew not; for though they sent round the country to inquire after them, it seems they could not be found.

I was now in a way to be provided for; for though I was not a parish charge upon this or that part of the town by law, yet as my case came to be known, and that I was too young to do any work, being not above three years old, compassion moved the magistrates of the town to take care of me, and I became one of their own as much as if I had been born in the place.

In the provision they made for me, it was my good hap to be put to nurse, as they call it, to a woman who was indeed poor, but had been in better circumstances, and who got a little livelihood by taking such as I was supposed to be and keeping them with all necessaries till they were at a certain age, in which it might be supposed they might go to service or get their own bread.

This woman had also a little school, which she kept to teach children to read and to work; and having, I say, lived before that in good fashion, she bred up the children with a great deal of art, as well as with a great deal of care.

But, which was worth all the rest, she bred them up very religiously also, being herself a very sober, pious woman; secondly, very housewifely and clean; and thirdly, very mannerly and with good behaviour. So that excepting a plain diet, coarse lodging, and mean clothes, we were brought up as mannerly as if we had been at the dancing-school.

I was continued here till I was eight years old, when I was terrified with news that the magistrates (as I think they called them) had ordered that I should go to service. I was able to do but very little, wherever I was to go, except it was to run of errands and be a drudge to some cook-maid, and this they told me of often, which put me into a great fright; for I had a thorough aversion to going to service, as they called it, though I was so young;

and I told my nurse that I believed I could get my living without going to service if she pleased to let me; for she had taught me to work with my needle and spin worsted, which is the chief trade of that city, and I told her that if she would keep me, I would work for her, and I would work very hard.

I talked to her almost every day of working hard; and, in short, I did nothing but work and cry all day, which grieved the good, kind woman so much that at last she began to be concerned for me, for she loved me very well.

One day after this, as she came into the room where all the poor children were at work, she sat down just over against me, not in her usual place as mistress, but as if she had set herself on purpose to observe me and see me work. I was doing something she had set me to, as I remember it was marking some shirts which she had taken to make, and after a while she began to talk to me. "Thou foolish child," says she, "thou art always crying" (for I was crying then). "Prithee, what dost cry for?" "Because they will take me away," says I, "and put me to service, and I can't work house-work." "Well, child," says she, "but though you can't work house-work, you will learn it in time, and they won't put you to hard things at first." "Yes, they will," says I, "and if I can't do it they will beat me, and the maids will beat me to make me do great work, and I am but a little girl and I can't do it"; and then I cried again till I could not speak any more.

This moved my good motherly nurse, so that she resolved I should not go to service yet; so she bid me not cry, and she would speak to Mr. Mayor, and I should not go to service till I was bigger.

Well, this did not satisfy me, for to think of going to service at all was such a frightful thing to me that if she had assured me I should not have gone till I was twenty years old, it would have been the same to me; I should have cried all the time with the very apprehension of its being to be so at last.

When she saw that I was not pacified yet, she began to be angry with me. "And what would you have?" says she. "Don't I tell you that you shall not go to service till you are bigger?" "Aye," says I, "but then I must go at last." "Why, what," said she, "is the girl mad? What! Would you be a gentlewoman?" "Yes," says I, and cried heartily till I roared out again.

This set the old gentlewoman a-laughing at me, as you may be sure it would. "Well, madam, forsooth," says she, gibing at me, "you would be a gentlewoman; and how will you come to be a gentlewoman? What! Will you do it by your fingers' ends?"

"Yes," says I again, very innocently.

"Why, what can you earn?" says she. "What can you get a day at your work?"

"Threepence," said I, "when I spin, and fourpence when I work plain work."

"Alas! Poor gentlewoman," said she again, laughing, "what will that do for thee?"

"It will keep me," says I, "if you will let me live with you"; and this I said in such a poor petitioning tone that it made the poor woman's heart yearn to me, as she told me afterwards.

"But," says she, "that will not keep you and buy you clothes too; and who must buy the little gentlewoman clothes?" says she, and smiled all the while at me.

"I will work harder then," says I, "and you shall have it all."

"Poor child! It won't keep you," said she; "it will hardly find you in victuals."

"Then I would have no victuals," says I, again very innocently; "let me but live with you."

"Why, can you live without victuals?" says she. "Yes," again says I, very much like a child, you may be sure, and still I cried heartily.

I had no policy in all this; you may easily see it was all nature; but it was joined with so much innocence and so much passion that, in short, it set the good motherly creature a-weeping too, and at last she cried as fast as I did and then took me and led me out of the teaching-room. "Come," says she, "you shan't go to service; you shall live with me"; and this pacified me for the present.

After this, she going to wait on the Mayor, my story came up, and my good nurse told Mr. Mayor the whole tale; he was so pleased with it that he would call his lady and his two daughters to hear it, and it made mirth enough among them, you may be sure.

However, not a week had passed over but on a sudden comes Mrs. Mayoress and her two daughters to the house to see my old nurse and to see her school and the children. When they had looked about them a little, "Well, Mrs. ——," says the Mayoress to my nurse, "and pray which is the little lass that is to be a gentlewoman?" I heard her, and I was terrible frighted, though I did not know why neither; but Mrs. Mayoress comes up to me. "Well, miss," says she, "and what are you at work upon?" The word "miss" was a language that had hardly been heard of in our school, and I wondered what sad name it was she called me; however, I stood up, made a curtsy, and she took my work out of my hand, looked on it, and said it was very well; then she looked upon one of my hands. "Nay, she may come to be a gentlewoman," says she, "for aught I know; she has a lady's hand, I assure you." This pleased me mightily; but Mrs. Mayoress did not stop there, but put her hand in her pocket, gave me a shilling, and bid me mind my work and learn to work well, and I might be a gentlewoman for aught she knew.

All this while my good old nurse, Mrs. Mayoress, and all the rest of them did not understand me at all, for they meant one sort of thing by the word "gentlewoman" and I meant quite another; for, alas, all I understood by being a gentlewoman was to be able to work for myself and get enough to keep me without going to service, whereas they meant to live great and high, and I know not what.

Well, after Mrs. Mayoress was gone, her two daughters came in, and they called for the gentlewoman too and they talked a long while to me, and I answered them in my innocent way; but always if they asked me whether I resolved to be a gentlewoman, I answered, "Yes." At last they asked me what a gentlewoman was. That puzzled me much. However, I explained myself negatively: that it was one that did not go to service to do housework; they were mightily pleased and liked my little prattle to them, which, it seems, was agreeable enough to them, and they gave me money too.

As for my money, I gave it all to my Mistress Nurse, as I called her, and told her she should have all I got when I was a gentlewoman as well as now. By this and some other of my talk, my old tutoress began to understand what I meant by being a gentlewoman, and that it was no more than to be able to get my bread by my own work; and at last she asked me whether it was not so.

I told her yes and insisted on it, that to do so was to be a gentlewoman; "for," says I, "there is such a one," naming a woman that mended lace and washed the ladies' laced heads; "she," says I, "is a gentlewoman, and they call her madam."

"Poor child," says my good old nurse, "you may soon be such a gentlewoman as that, for she is a person of ill fame and has had two bastards."

I did not understand anything of that, but I answered, "I am sure they call her madam, and she does not go to service nor do house-work"; and therefore I insisted that she was a gentlewoman, and I would be such a gentlewoman as that.

The ladies were told all this again, and they made themselves merry with it, and every now and then Mr. Mayor's daughters would come and see me and ask where the little gentlewoman was, which made me not a little proud of myself besides. I was often visited by these young ladies, and sometimes they brought others with them; so that I was known by it almost all over the town.

I was now about ten years old and began to look a little womanish, for I was mighty grave, very mannerly, and as I had often heard the ladies say I was pretty and would be very handsome, you may be sure it made me not a little proud. However, that pride had no ill effect upon me yet; only, as they often gave me money, and I gave it my old nurse, she, honest woman, was so just as to lay it out again for me and gave me head-dresses and linen and gloves, and I went very neat, for if I had rags on, I would always be clean or else I would dabble them in water myself; but, I say, my good nurse, when I had money given me, very honestly laid it out for me and would always tell the ladies this or that was bought with their money; and this made them give me more, till at last I was indeed called upon by the magistrates to go out to service. But then I was become so good a workwoman myself, and the ladies were so kind to me, that I was past it; for I could earn as much for my nurse as was enough to keep me; so she told them that if they would give her leave, she would keep the gentlewoman, as she called me, to be her assistant and teach the children, which I was very well able to do; for I was very nimble at my work though I was yet very young.

But the kindness of the ladies did not end here, for when they understood that I was no more maintained by the town as before, they gave me money oftener; and as I grew up they brought me work to do for them, such as linen to make, laces to mend, and heads to dress up, and not only paid me for doing them but even taught me how to do them; so that I was a gentlewoman indeed, as I understood that word; for before I was twelve years old, I not only found myself clothes and paid my nurse for my keeping but got money in my pocket too.

The ladies also gave me clothes frequently of their own or their children's; some stockings, some petticoats, some gowns, some one thing, some another; and these my old woman managed for me like a mother and kept them for me, obliged me to mend them and turn them to the best advantage, for she was a rare housewife.

At last one of the ladies took such a fancy to me that she would have me home to her house, for a month, she said, to be among her daughters.

Now, though this was exceeding kind in her, yet, as my good woman said to her, unless she resolved to keep me for good and all, she would do the little gentlewoman more harm than good. "Well," says the lady, "that's true; I'll only take her home for a week, then, that I may see how my daughters and she agree and how I like her temper, and then I'll tell you more; and in the meantime, if anybody comes to see her as they used to do, you may only tell them you have sent her out to my house."

This was prudently managed enough, and I went to the lady's house; but I was so pleased there with the young ladies, and they so pleased with me, that I had enough to do to come away, and they were as unwilling to part with me.

However, I did come away and live almost a year more with my honest old woman, and began now to be very helpful to her; for I was almost fourteen years old, was tall of my age, and looked a little womanish; but I had such a taste of genteel living at the lady's house that I was not so easy in my old quarters as I used to be, and I thought it was fine to be a gentlewoman indeed, for I had quite other notions of a gentlewoman now than I had before; and as I thought that it was fine to be a gentlewoman, so I loved to be among gentlewomen, and therefore I longed to be there again.

When I was about fourteen years and a quarter old, my good old nurse—mother, I ought to call her—fell sick and died. I was then in a sad condition indeed, for as there is no great bustle in putting an end to a poor body's family when once they are carried to the grave, so the poor good woman being buried, the parish children were immediately removed by the churchwardens; the school was at an end, and the day-children of it had no more to do but just stay at home till they were sent somewhere else. As for what she left, a daughter, a married woman, came and swept it all away, and removing the goods, they had no more to say to me than to jest with me and tell me that the little gentlewoman might set up for herself if she pleased.

I was frighted out of my wits almost and knew not what to do; for I was, as it were, turned out-of-doors to the wide world, and that which was still worse, the old honest woman had two-and-twenty shillings of mine in her hand, which was all the estate the little gentlewoman had in the world; and when I asked the daughter for it, she huffed me and told me she had nothing to do with it.

It was true the good, poor woman had told her daughter of it, and that it lay in such a place, that it was the child's money, and had called once or twice for me to give it me, but I was unhappily out of the way, and when I came back she was past being in a condition to speak of it. However, the daughter was so honest afterwards as to give it me, though at first she used me cruelly about it.

Now was I a poor gentlewoman indeed, and I was just that very night to be turned into the wide world; for the daughter removed all the goods, and I had not so much as a lodging to go to or a bit of bread to eat. But it seems some of the neighbours took so much compassion of me as to acquaint the lady in whose family I had been; and immediately she sent her maid to fetch me, and away I went with them, bag and baggage, and with a glad heart, you may be sure. The fright of my condition had made such an impression upon me that I did not want now to be a gentlewoman, but was very willing to be a servant, and that any kind of servant they thought fit to have me be.

But my new generous mistress had better thoughts for me. I call her generous, for she exceeded the good woman I was with before in everything, as in estate; I say in everything except honesty; and for that, though this was a lady most exactly just, yet I must not forget to say on all occasions that the first, though poor, was as uprightly honest as it was possible.

I was no sooner carried away, as I have said, by this good gentlewoman, but the first lady, that is to say, the Mayoress that was, sent her daughters to take care of me; and another family which had taken notice of me when I was the little gentlewoman sent for me after her, so that I was mightily made of; nay, and they were not a little angry, especially the Mayoress, that her friend had taken me away from her; for, as she said, I was hers by right, she having been the first that took any notice of me. But they that had me would not part with me; and as for me, I could not be better than where I was.

Here I continued till I was between seventeen and eighteen years old, and here I had all the advantages for my education that could be imagined; the lady had masters home to teach her daughters to dance and to speak French and to write, and others to teach them music; and as I was always with them, I learnt as fast as they; and though the masters were not appointed to teach me, yet I learnt by imitation and inquiry all that they learnt by instruction and direction; so that, in short, I learnt to dance and speak French as well as any of them and to sing much better, for I had a better voice than any of them. I could not so readily come at playing the harpsichord or spinet, because I had no instrument of my own to practise on and could only come at theirs in the intervals when they left it; but yet I learnt tolerably well, and the young ladies at length got two instruments, that is to say, a harpsichord and a spinet too, and then they taught me themselves. But as to dancing, they could hardly help my learning country-dances, because they always wanted me to make up even number; and on the other hand, they were as heartily willing to learn me everything that they had been taught themselves as I could be to take the learning.

By this means I had, as I have said, all the advantages of education that I could have had if I had been as much a gentlewoman as they were with whom I lived; and in some things I had the advantage of my ladies though they were my superiors, *viz.*, that mine were all the gifts of nature and which all their fortunes could not furnish. First, I was apparently handsomer than any of them; secondly, I was better shaped; and thirdly, I sang better, by which I mean I had a better voice; in all which you will, I hope, allow me to say I do not speak my own conceit, but the opinion of all that knew the family.

I had with all these the common vanity of my sex, *viz.*, that being really taken for very handsome or, if you please, for a great beauty, I very well knew it, and had as good an opinion of myself as anybody else could have of me, and particularly I loved to hear anybody speak of it, which happened often and was a great satisfaction to me.

Thus far I have had a smooth story to tell of myself, and in all this part of my life I not only had the reputation of living in a very good family, and a family noted and respected everywhere for virtue and sobriety and for every valuable thing, but I had the character too of a very sober, modest, and virtuous young woman, and such I had always been; neither had I yet any occasion to think of anything else or to know what a temptation to wickedness meant.

But that which I was too vain of was my ruin, or rather my vanity was the cause of it. The lady in the house where I was had two sons, young gentlemen of extraordinary parts and behaviour, and it was my misfortune to be very well with them both, but they managed themselves with me in a quite different manner.

The eldest, a gay gentleman that knew the town as well as the country, and though he had levity enough to do an ill-natured thing, yet had too much judgement of things to pay too dear for his pleasures—he began with that unhappy snare to all women, *viz.*, taking notice upon all occasions how pretty I was, as he called it, how agreeable, how well carriaged, and the like; and this he contrived so subtly, as if he had known as well how to catch a woman in his net as a partridge when he went a-setting, for he would contrive to be talking this to his sisters when, though I was not by, yet when he knew I was not so far off but that I should be sure to hear him. His sisters would return softly to him, "Hush, brother, she will hear you; she is but in the next room." Then he would put it off and talk softlier, as if he had not known it, and begin to acknowledge he was wrong; and then, as if he had forgot himself, he would speak aloud again, and I, that was so well pleased to hear it, was sure to listen for it upon all occasions.

After he had thus baited his hook and found easily enough the method how to lay it in my way, he played an open game; and one day, going by his sister's chamber when I was there, he comes in with an air of gaiety. "Oh, Mrs. Betty," said he to me, "how do you do, Mrs. Betty? Don't your cheeks burn, Mrs. Betty?" I made a curtsy and blushed, but said nothing. "What makes you talk so, brother?" says the lady. "Why," says he, "we have been talking of her below-stairs this half-hour." "Well," says his sister, "you can say no harm of her, that I am sure, so 'tis no matter what you have been talking about." "Nay," says he, " 'tis so far from talking harm of her that we have been talking a great deal of good, and a great many fine things have been said of Mrs. Betty, I assure you; and particularly, that she is the handsomest young woman in Colchester, and in short, they begin to toast her health in the town."

"I wonder at you, brother," says the sister. "Betty wants but one thing, but she had as good want everything, for the market is against our sex just now; and if a young woman has beauty, birth, breeding, wit, sense, manners, modesty, and all to an extreme, yet if she has not money, she's nobody—she had as good want them all; nothing but money now recommends a woman; the men play the game all into their own hands."

Her younger brother, who was by, cried, "Hold, sister, you run too fast; I am an exception to your rule. I assure you, if I find a woman so accomplished as you talk of, I won't trouble myself about the money." "Oh," says the sister, "but you will take care not to fancy one then without the money."

"You don't know that neither," says the brother.

"But why, sister," says the elder brother, "why do you exclaim so about the fortune? You are none of them that want a fortune, whatever else you want."

"I understand you, brother," replies the lady very smartly; "you suppose I have the money and want the beauty; but as times go now, the first will do, so I have the better of my neighbours."

"Well," says the younger brother, "but your neighbours may be even with you, for beauty will steal a husband sometimes in spite of money, and when the maid chances to be handsomer than the mistress, she oftentimes makes as good a market and rides in a coach before her."

I thought it was time for me to withdraw, and I did so, but not so far but that I heard all their discourse, in which I heard abundance of fine things said of myself, which prompted my vanity, but, as I soon found, was not the way to increase my interest in the family, for the sister and the younger brother fell grievously out about it; and as he said some very disobliging things to her upon my account, so I could easily see that she resented them by her future conduct to me, which indeed was very unjust, for I had never had the least thought of what she suspected as to her younger brother; indeed, the elder brother, in his distant, remote way, had said a great many things as in jest, which I had the folly to believe were in earnest or to flatter myself with the hopes of what I ought to have supposed he never intended.

It happened one day that he came running upstairs, towards the room where his sisters used to sit and work, as he often used to do; and calling to them before he came in, as was his way too, I, being there alone, stepped to the door and said, "Sir, the ladies are not here; they are walked down the garden." As I stepped forward to say this he was just got to the door, and clasping me in his arms as if it had been by chance, "Oh, Mrs. Betty," says he, "are you here? That's better still; I want to speak with you more than I do with them"; and then, having me in his arms, he kissed me three or four times.

I struggled to get away, and yet did it but faintly neither, and he held me fast and still kissed me till he was out of breath, and sitting down, says he, "Dear Betty, I am in love with you."

His words, I must confess, fired my blood; all my spirits flew about my heart and put me into disorder enough. He repeated it afterwards several times, that he was in love with me, and my heart spoke as plain as a voice that I liked it; nay, whenever he said, "I am in love with you," my blushes plainly replied, "Would you were, sir." However, nothing else passed at that time; it was but a surprise and I soon recovered myself. He had stayed longer with me but he happened to look out at the window and see his sisters coming up the garden, so he took his leave, kissed me again, told me he was very serious, and I should hear more of him very quickly, and away he went infinitely pleased; and had there not been one misfortune in it, I had been in the right, but the mistake lay here, that Mrs. Betty was in earnest and the gentleman was not.

From this time my head run upon strange things, and I may truly say I was not myself, to have such a gentleman talk to me of being in love with me and of my being such a charming creature, as he told me I was. These were things I knew not how to bear; my vanity was elevated to the last degree. It is true I had my head full of pride, but knowing nothing of the wickedness of the times, I had not one thought of my virtue about me; and had my young master offered it at first sight, he might have taken any liberty he thought fit with me; but he did not see his advantage, which was my happiness for that time.

It was not long but he found an opportunity to catch me again, and almost in the same posture; indeed, it had more of design in it on his part though not on my part. It was thus: the young ladies were gone a-visiting with their mother; his brother was out of town; and as for his father, he had been at London for a week before. He had so well watched me that he knew where I was though I did not so much as know that he was in the house, and he briskly comes up the stairs and, seeing me at work, comes into the room to me directly, and began just as he did before, with taking me in his arms and kissing me for almost a quarter of an hour together.

It was his younger sister's chamber that I was in, and as there was nobody in the house but the maid below-stairs, he was, it may be, the ruder; in short, he began to be in earnest with me indeed. Perhaps he found me a little too easy, for I made no resistance to him while he only held me in his arms and kissed me; indeed, I was too well pleased with it to resist him much.

Well, tired with that kind of work, we sat down, and there he talked with me a great while; he said he was charmed with me and that he could not rest till he had told me how he was in love with me, and if I could love him again and would make him happy, I should be the saving of his life, and many such fine things. I said little to him again, but easily discovered that I was a fool and that I did not in the least perceive what he meant.

Then he walked about the room, and taking me by the hand, I walked with him; and by and by, taking his advantage, he threw me down upon the bed and kissed me there most violently, but, to give him his due, offered no manner of rudeness to me, only kissed me a great while. After this he thought he had heard somebody come upstairs, so he got off from the bed, lifted me up, professing a great deal of love for me, but told me it was all an honest affection and that he meant no ill to me, and with that put five guineas into my hand and went downstairs.

I was more confounded with the money than I was before with the love, and began to be so elevated that I scarce knew the ground I stood on. I am the more particular in this that if it comes to be read by any innocent young body, they may learn from it to guard themselves against the mischiefs which attend an early knowledge of their own beauty. If a young woman once thinks herself handsome, she never doubts the truth of any man that tells her he is in love with her; for if she believes herself charming enough to captivate him, 'tis natural to expect the effects of it.

This gentleman had now fired his inclination as much as he had my vanity, and as if he had found that he had an opportunity and was sorry he did not take hold of it, he comes up again in about half an hour, and falls to work with me again just as he did before, only with a little less introduction.

And first, when he entered the room, he turned about and shut the door. "Mrs. Betty," said he, "I fancied before somebody was coming upstairs, but it was not so; however," adds he, "if they find me in the room with you, they shan't catch me a-kissing of you." I told him I did not know who should be coming upstairs, for I believed there was nobody in the house but the cook and the other maid, and they never came up those stairs. "Well, my dear," says he, " 'tis good to be sure, however"; and so he sits down and we began to talk. And now, though I was still on fire with his first visit and said little, he did, as it were, put words in my mouth, telling me how passionately he loved me, and that though he could not till he came to his estate, yet he was resolved to make me happy then, and himself too; that is to say, to marry me, and abundance of such things, which I, poor fool, did not understand the drift of, but acted as if there was no kind of love but that which tended to matrimony; and if he had spoken of that, I had no room as well as no power to have said no; but we were not come to that length yet.

We had not sat long but he got up and, stopping my very breath with kisses, threw me upon the bed again; but then he went further with me than decency permits me to mention, nor had it been in my power to have denied him at that moment had he offered much more than he did.

However, though he took these freedoms with me, it did not go to that which they call the last favour, which, to do him justice, he did not attempt; and he made that self-denial of his a plea for all his freedoms with me upon other occasions after this. When this was over he stayed but a little while, but he put almost a handful of gold in my hand and left me a thousand protestations of his passion for me and of his loving me above all the women in the world.

It will not be strange if I now began to think; but, alas! it was but with very little solid reflections. I had a most unbounded stock of vanity and pride, and but a very little stock of virtue. I did indeed cast sometimes with myself what my young master aimed at, but thought of nothing but the fine words and the gold; whether he intended to marry me or not seemed a matter of no great consequence to me; nor did I so much as think of making any capitulation for myself till he made a kind of formal proposal to me, as you shall hear presently.

Thus I gave up myself to ruin without the least concern, and am a fair memento to all young women whose vanity prevails over their virtue. Nothing was ever so stupid on both sides. Had I acted as became me and resisted as virtue and honour required, he had either desisted his attacks, finding no room to expect the end of his design, or had made fair and honourable proposals of marriage; in which case, whoever blamed him, nobody could have blamed me. In short, if he had known me and how easy the trifle he aimed at was to be had, he would have troubled his head no farther, but have given me four or five guineas and have lain with me the next time he had come at me. On the other hand, if I had known his thoughts and how hard he supposed I would be to be gained, I might have made my own terms, and if I had not capitulated for an immediate marriage, I might for a maintenance till marriage and might have had what I would; for he was rich to excess, besides what he had in expectation; but I had wholly abandoned all such thoughts, and was taken up only with the pride of my beauty and of being beloved by such a gentleman. As for the gold, I spent whole hours in looking upon it; I told the guineas over a thousand times a day. Never poor vain creature was so wrapt up with every part of the story as I was, not considering what was before me and how near my ruin was at the door; and indeed I think I rather wished for that ruin than studied to avoid it.

In the meantime, however, I was cunning enough not to give the least room to any in the family to imagine that I had the least correspondence with him. I scarce ever looked towards him in public or answered if he spoke to me; when, but for all that, we had every now and then a little encounter, where we had room for a word or two and now and then a kiss, but no fair opportunity for the mischief intended; and especially considering that he made more circumlocution than he had occasion for; and the work appearing difficult to him, he really made it so.

But as the devil is an unwearied tempter, so he never fails to find an opportunity for the wickedness he invites to. It was one evening that I was in the garden with his two younger sisters and himself when he found means to convey a note into my hand, by which he told me that he would to-morrow desire me publicly to go of an errand for him and that I should see him somewhere by the way.

Accordingly after dinner he very gravely says to me, his sisters being all by, "Mrs. Betty, I must ask a favour of you." "What's that?" says the second sister. "Nay, sister," says he very gravely, "if you can't spare Mrs. Betty to-day, any other time will do." Yes, they said, they could spare her well enough; and the sister begged pardon for asking. "Well, but," says the eldest sister, "you must tell Mrs. Betty what it is; if it be any private business that we must not hear, you may call her out. There she is." "Why, sister," says the gentleman very gravely, "what do you mean? I only desire her to go into the High Street" (and then he pulls out a turn-over), "to such a shop"; and then he tells them a long story of two fine neckcloths he had bid money for, and he wanted to have me go and make an errand to buy a neck to that turn-over that he showed, and if they would not take my money for the neckcloths, to bid a shilling more and haggle with them; and then he made more errands and so continued to have such petty business to do that I should be sure to stay a good while.

When he had given me my errands, he told them a long story of a visit he was going to make to a family they all knew and where was to be such-and-such gentlemen, and very formally asked his sisters to go with him, and they as formally excused themselves because of company that they had notice was to come and visit them that afternoon; all which, by the way, he had contrived on purpose.

He had scarce done speaking but his man came up to tell him that Sir W—— H——'s coach stopped at the door; so he runs down and comes up again immediately. "Alas!" says he aloud. "There's all my mirth spoiled at once; Sir W—— has sent his coach for me and desires to speak with me." It seems this Sir W—— was a gentleman who lived about three miles off, to whom he had spoke on purpose to lend him his chariot for a particular occasion and had appointed it to call for him, as it did, about three o'clock.

Immediately he calls for his best wig, hat, and sword, and ordering his man to go to the other place to make his excuse—that was to say, he made an excuse to send his man away—he prepares to go into the coach. As he was going he stopped awhile and speaks mightily earnestly to me about his business and finds an opportunity to say very softly, "Come away, my dear, as soon as ever you can." I said nothing, but made a curtsy, as if I had done so to what he said in public. In about a quarter of an hour I went out too; I had no dress other than before, except that I had a hood, a mask, a fan, and a pair of gloves in my pocket; so that there was not the least suspicion in the house. He waited for me in a back-lane which he knew I must pass by, and the coachman knew whither to go, which was to a certain place, called Mile End, where lived a confidant of his, where we went in and where was all the convenience in the world to be as wicked as we pleased.

When we were together, he began to talk very gravely to me and to tell me he did not bring me there to betray me; that his passion for me would not suffer him to abuse me; that he resolved to marry me as soon as he came to his estate; that in the meantime, if I would grant his request, he would maintain me very honourably; and made me a thousand protestations of his sincerity and of his affection to me and that he would never abandon me and, as I may say, made a thousand more preambles than he need to have done.

However, as he pressed me to speak, I told him I had no reason to question the sincerity of his love to me after so many protestations, but— And there I stopped, as if I left him to guess the rest. "But what, my dear?" says he. "I guess what you mean: What if you should be with child? Is not that it? Why, then," says he, "I'll take care of you and provide for you and the child too; and that you may see I am not in jest," says he, "here's an earnest for you," and with that he pulls out a silk purse with an hundred guineas in it and gave it me; "and I'll give you such another," says he, "every year till I marry you."

My colour came and went at the sight of the purse and with the fire of his proposal together, so that I could not say a word, and he easily perceived it; so, putting the purse into my bosom, I made no more resistance to him, but let him do just what he pleased and as often as he pleased; and thus I finished my own destruction at once, for from this day, being forsaken of my virtue and my modesty, I had nothing of value left to recommend me, either to God's blessing or man's assistance.

But things did not end here. I went back to the town, did the business he directed me to, and was at home before anybody thought me long. As for my gentleman, he stayed out till late at night, and there was not the least suspicion in the family either on his account or on mine.

We had after this frequent opportunities to repeat our crime, and especially at home when his mother and the young ladies went abroad a-visiting, which he watched so narrowly as never to miss; knowing always beforehand when they went out, and then failed not to catch me all alone and securely enough; so that we took our fill of our wicked pleasures for near half a year; and yet, which was the most to my satisfaction, I was not with child.

But before this half-year was expired, his younger brother, of whom I have made some mention in the beginning of the story, falls to work with me; and he, finding me alone in the garden one evening, begins a story of the same kind to me, made good, honest professions of being in love with me, and in short, proposes fairly and honourably to marry me.

I was now confounded and driven to such an extremity as the like was never known to me. I resisted the proposal with obstinacy and began to arm myself with arguments. I laid before him the inequality of the match, the treatment I should meet with in the family, the ingratitude it would be to his good father and mother, who had taken me into their house upon such generous principles, and when I was in such a low condition; and in short, I said everything to dissuade him that I could imagine except telling him the truth, which would indeed have put an end to it all, but that I durst not think of mentioning.

But here happened a circumstance that I did not expect indeed, which put me to my shifts; for this young gentleman, as he was plain and honest, so he pretended to nothing but what was so too; and knowing his own innocence, he was not so careful to make his having a kindness for Mrs. Betty a secret in the house as his brother was. And though he did not let them know that he had talked to me about it, yet he said enough to let his sisters perceive he loved me, and his mother saw it too, which, though they took no notice of to me, yet they did to him, and immediately I found their carriage to me altered more than ever before.

I saw the cloud, though I did not foresee the storm. It was easy, I say, to see their carriage was altered and that it grew worse and worse every day, till at last I got information that I should in a very little while be desired to remove.

I was not alarmed at the news, having a full satisfaction that I should be provided for; and especially considering that I had reason every day to expect I should be with child and that then I should be obliged to remove without any pretences for it.

After some time the younger gentleman took an opportunity to tell me that the kindness he had for me had got vent in the family. He did not charge me with it, he said, for he knew well enough which way it came out. He told me his way of talking had been the occasion of it, for that he did not make his respect for me so much a secret as he might have done, and the reason was that he was at a point that if I would consent to have him, he would tell them all openly that he loved me and that he intended to marry me; that it was true his father and mother might resent it and be unkind, but he was now in a way to live, being bred to the law, and he did not fear maintaining me; and that, in short, as he believed I would not be ashamed of him, so he was resolved not to be ashamed of me, and that he scorned to be afraid to own me now, who he resolved to own after I was his wife, and therefore I had nothing to do but to give him my hand and he would answer for all the rest.

I was now in a dreadful condition indeed, and now I repented heartily my easiness with the eldest brother; not from any reflection of conscience, for I was a stranger to those things, but I could not think of being a whore to one brother and a wife to the other. It came also into my thoughts that the first brother had promised to make me his wife when he came to his estate; but I presently remembered what I had often thought of: that he had never spoken a word of having me for a wife after he had conquered me for a mistress; and indeed till now, though I said I thought of it often, yet it gave no disturbance at all, for as he did not seem in the least to lessen his affection to me, so neither did he lessen his bounty, though he had the discretion himself to desire me not to lay out a penny in clothes or to make the least show extraordinary, because it would necessarily give jealousy in the family since everybody knew I could come at such things no manner of ordinary way, but by some private friendship, which they would presently have suspected.

I was now in a great strait and knew not what to do; the main difficulty was this: The younger brother not only laid close siege to me, but suffered it to be seen. He would come into his sister's room and his mother's room, and sit down and talk a thousand kind things to me even before their faces; so that the whole house talked of it, and his mother reproved him for it, and their carriage to me appeared quite altered. In short, his mother had let fall some speeches as if she intended to put me out of the family; that is, in English, to turn me out-of-doors. Now I was sure this could not be a secret to his brother, only that he might think, as indeed nobody else yet did, that the youngest brother had made any proposal to me about it; but as I easily could see that it would go farther, so I saw likewise there was an absolute necessity to speak of it to him or that he would speak of it to me, but knew not whether I should break it to him or let it alone till he should break it to me.

Upon serious consideration, for indeed now I began to consider things very seriously, and never till now, I resolved to tell him of it first; and it was not long before I had an opportunity, for the very next day his brother went to London upon some business, and the family being out a-visiting, just as it happened before and as indeed was often the case, he came according to his custom to spend an hour or two with Mrs. Betty.

When he had sat down awhile, he easily perceived there was an alteration in my countenance, that I was not so free and pleasant with him as I used to be and, particularly, that I had been a-crying; he was not long before he took notice of it and asked me in very kind terms what was the matter and if anything troubled me. I would have put it off if I could, but it was not to be concealed; so after suffering many importunities to draw that out of me, which I longed as much as possible to disclose, I told him that it was true something did trouble me, and something of such a nature that I could hardly conceal from him, and yet that I could not tell how to tell him of it neither; that it was a thing that not only surprised me, but greatly perplexed me, and that I knew not what course to take unless he would direct me. He told me with great tenderness that, let it be what it would, I should not let it trouble me, for he would protect me from all the world.

I then began at a distance and told him I was afraid the ladies had got some secret information of our correspondence; for that it was easy to see that their conduct was very much changed towards me, and that now it was come to pass that they frequently found fault with me and sometimes fell quite out with me, though I never gave them the least occasion; that whereas I used always to lie with the eldest sister, I was lately put to lie by myself or with one of the maids; and that I had overheard them several times talking very unkindly about me; but that which confirmed it all was that one of the servants had told me that she had heard I was to be turned out, and that it was not safe for the family that I should be any longer in the house.

He smiled when he heard of this, and I asked him how he could make so light of it when he must needs know that if there was any discovery I was undone, and that it would hurt him, though not ruin him, as it would me. I upbraided him that he was like the rest of his sex; that when they had the character of a woman at their mercy, oftentimes made it their jest, and at least looked upon it as a trifle, and counted the ruin of those they had had their will of as a thing of no value.

He saw me warm and serious, and he changed his style immediately; he told me he was sorry I should have such a thought of him; that he had never given me the least occasion for it, but had been as tender of my reputation as he could be of his own; that he was sure our correspondence had been managed with so much address that not one creature in the family had so much as a suspicion of it; that if he smiled when I told him my thoughts, it was at the assurance he lately received that our understanding one another was not so much as guessed at, and that when he had told me how much reason he had to be easy, I should smile as he did, for he was very certain it would give me a full satisfaction.

"This is a mystery I cannot understand," says I, "or how it should be to my satisfaction that I am to be turned out-of-doors; for if our correspondence is not discovered, I know not what else I have done to change the faces of the whole family to me, who formerly used me with so much tenderness as if I had been one of their own children."

"Why, look you, child," says he, "that they are uneasy about you, that is true; but that they have the least suspicion of the case as it is, and as it respects you and I, is so far from being true that they suspect my brother, Robin; and in short, they are fully persuaded he makes love to you; nay, the fool has put it into their heads too himself, for he is continually bantering them about it and making a jest of himself. I confess I think he is wrong to do so, because he cannot but see it vexes them and makes them unkind to you; but 'tis a satisfaction to me because of the assurance it gives me that they do not suspect me in the least, and I hope this will be to your satisfaction too."

"So it is," says I, "one way; but this does not reach my case at all, nor is this the chief thing that troubles me, though I have been concerned about that too." "What is it, then?" says he. With which I fell into tears and could say nothing to him at all. He strove to pacify me all he could, but began at last to be very pressing upon me to tell what it was. At last I answered that I thought I ought to tell him too and that he had some right to know it; besides, that I wanted his direction in the case, for I was in such perplexity that I knew not what course to take, and then I related the whole affair to him. I told him how imprudently his brother had managed himself in making himself so public; for that if he had kept it a secret, I could but have denied him positively without giving any reason for it, and he would in time have ceased his solicitations; but that he had the vanity, first, to depend upon it that I would not deny him, and then had taken the freedom to tell his design to the whole house.

I told him how far I had resisted him and how sincere and honourable his offers were; "but," says I, "my case will be doubly hard; for as they carry it ill to me now because he desires to have me, they'll carry it worse when they shall find I have denied him; and they will presently say there's something else in it and that I am married already to somebody else, or that I would never refuse a match so much above me as this was."

This discourse surprised him indeed very much. He told me that it was a critical point indeed for me to manage, and he did not see which way I should get out of it; but he would consider of it and let me know next time we met what resolution he was come to about it; and in the meantime desired I would not give my consent to his brother nor yet give him a flat denial, but that I would hold him in suspense awhile.

I seemed to start at his saying I should not give him my consent. I told him he knew very well I had no consent to give; that he had engaged himself to marry me and that I was thereby engaged to him; that he had all along told me I was his wife, and I looked upon myself as effectually so as if the ceremony had passed; and that it was from his own mouth that I did so, he having all along persuaded me to call myself his wife.

"Well, my dear," says he, "don't be concerned at that now; if I am not your husband, I'll be as good as a husband to you; and do not let those things trouble you now, but let me look a little farther into this affair, and I shall be able to say more next time we meet."

He pacified me as well as he could with this, but I found he was very thoughtful, and that though he was very kind to me, and kissed me a thousand times and more I believe, and gave me money too, yet he offered no more all the while we were together, which was above two hours, and which I much wondered at, considering how it used to be and what opportunity we had.

His brother did not come from London for five or six days, and it was two days more before he got an opportunity to talk with him; but then, getting him by himself, he talked very close to him about it, and the same evening found means (for we had a long conference together) to repeat all their discourse to me, which as near as I can remember was to the purpose following. He told him he heard strange news of him since he went, *viz.*, that he made love to Mrs. Betty. "Well," says his brother a little angrily, "and what then? What has anybody to do with that?" "Nay," says his brother, "don't be angry, Robin; I don't pretend to have anything to do with it, but I find they do concern themselves about it and that they have used the poor girl ill about it, which I should take as done to myself." "Who do you mean by *they*?" says Robin. "I mean my mother and the girls," says the elder brother.

"But hark ye," says his brother, "are you in earnest? Do you really love the girl?" "Why, then," says Robin, "I will be free with you; I do love her above all the women in the world, and I will have her, let them say and do what they will. I believe the girl will not deny me."

It stuck me to the heart when he told me this, for though it was most rational to think I would not deny him, yet I knew in my own conscience I must, and I saw my ruin in my being obliged to do so; but I knew it was my business to talk otherwise then, so I interrupted him in his story thus: "Ay!" said I. "Does he think I cannot deny him? But he shall find I can deny him for all that." "Well, my dear," says he, "but let me give you the whole story as it went on between us, and then say what you will."

Then he went on and told me that he replied thus: "But, brother, you know she has nothing, and you may have several ladies with good fortunes." " 'Tis no matter for that," said Robin; "I love the girl, and I will never please my pocket in marrying and not please my fancy." "And so, my dear," adds he, "there is no opposing him."

"Yes, yes," says I, "I can oppose him; I have learnt to say no now though I had not learnt it before; if the best lord in the land offered me marriage now, I could very cheerfully say no to him."

"Well, but, my dear," says he, "what can you say to him? You know, as you said before, he will ask you many questions about it, and all the house will wonder what the meaning of it should be."

"Why," says I, smiling, "I can stop all their mouths at one clap by telling him and them too that I am married already to his elder brother."

He smiled a little too at the word, but I could see it startled him, and he could not hide the disorder it put him into. However, he returned, "Why, though that may be true in some sense, yet I suppose you are but in jest when you talk of giving such an answer as that; it may not be convenient on many accounts."

"No, no," says I pleasantly, "I am not so fond of letting that secret come out without your consent."

"But what, then, can you say to them," says he, "when they find you positive against a match which would be apparently so much to your advantage?" "Why," says I, "should I be at a loss? First, I am not obliged to give them any reason; on the other hand, I may tell them I am married already and stop there, and that will be a full stop too to him, for he can have no reason to ask one question after it."

"Aye," says he, "but the whole house will tease you about that, and if you deny them positively, they will be disobliged at you and suspicious besides."

"Why," says I, "what can I do? What would you have me do? I was in strait enough before, as I told you, and acquainted you with the circumstances that I might have your advice."

"My dear," says he, "I have been considering very much upon it, you may be sure, and though the advice has many mortifications in it to me and may at first seem strange to you, yet, all things considered, I see no better way for you than to let him go on, and if you find him hearty and in earnest, marry him."

I gave him a look full of horror at those words and, turning pale as death, was at the very point of sinking down out of the chair I sat in when, giving a start, "My dear," says he aloud, "what's the matter with you? Where are you a-going?" and a great many such things; and with jogging and calling to me, fetched me a little to myself, though it was a good while before I fully recovered my senses, and was not able to speak for several minutes.

When I was fully recovered he began again. "My dear," says he, "I would have you consider seriously of it. You may see plainly how the family stand in this case, and they would be stark mad if it was my case, as it is my brother's; and for aught I see, it would be my ruin and yours too."

"Ay!" says I, still speaking angrily. "Are all your protestations and vows to be shaken by the dislike of the family? Did I not always object that to you, and you made a light thing of it, as what you were above and would not value; and is it come to this now? Is this your faith and honour, your love, and the solidity of your promises?"

He continued perfectly calm, notwithstanding all my reproaches, and I was not sparing of them at all; but he replied at last, "My dear, I have not broken one promise with you yet; I did tell you I would marry you when I was come to my estate; but you see my father is a hale, healthy man, and may live these thirty years still and not be older than several are round us in the town; and you never proposed my marrying you sooner because you know it might be my ruin; and as to the rest, I have not failed you in anything."

I could not deny a word of this. "But why, then," says I, "can you persuade me to such a horrid step as leaving you since you have not left me? Will you allow no affection, no love, on my side, where there has been so much on your side? Have I made you no returns? Have I given no testimony of my sincerity and of my passion? Are the sacrifices I have made of honour and modesty to you no proof of my being tied to you in bonds too strong to be broken?"

"But here, my dear," says he, "you may come into a safe station and appear with honour, and the remembrance of what we have done may be wrapt up in an eternal silence, as if it had never happened; you shall always have my sincere affection; only then it shall be honest and perfectly just to my brother; you shall be my dear sister, as now you are my dear—" And there he stopped.

"Your dear whore," says I, "you would have said, and you might as well have said it; but I understand you. However, I desire you to remember the long discourses you have had with me, and the many hours' pain you have taken to persuade me to believe myself an honest woman; that I was your wife intentionally and that it was as effectual a marriage that had passed between us as if we had been publicly wedded by the parson of the parish. You know these have been your own words to me."

I found this was a little too close upon him, but I made

it up in what follows. He stood stock still for a while and said nothing, and I went on thus: "You cannot," says I, "without the highest injustice, believe that I yielded upon all these persuasions without a love not to be questioned, not to be shaken again by anything that could happen afterward. If you have such dishonourable thoughts of me, I must ask you what foundation have I given for such a suggestion.

"If, then, I have yielded to the importunities of my affection, and if I have been persuaded to believe that I am really your wife, shall I now give the lie to all those arguments and call myself your whore or mistress, which is the same thing? And will you transfer me to your brother? Can you transfer my affection? Can you bid me cease loving you and bid me love him? Is it in my power, think you, to make such a change at demand? No, sir," said I, "depend upon it, 'tis impossible, and whatever the change on your side may be, I will ever be true; and I had much rather, since it is come that unhappy length, be your whore than your brother's wife."

He appeared pleased and touched with the impression of this last discourse and told me that he stood where he did before; that he had not been unfaithful to me in any one promise he had ever made yet, but that there were so many terrible things presented themselves to his view in the affair before me that he had thought of the other as a remedy, only that he thought this would not be an entire parting us, but we might love as friends all our days and perhaps with more satisfaction than we should in the station we were now in; that he durst say I could not apprehend anything from him as to betraying a secret which could not but be the destruction of us both if it came out; that he had but one question to ask of me that could lie in the way of it, and if that question was answered, he could not but think still it was the only step I could take.

I guessed at his question presently, *viz.*, whether I was not with child. As to that, I told him he need not be concerned about it, for I was not with child. "Why, then, my dear," says he, "we have no time to talk farther now. Consider of it; I cannot but be of the opinion still that it will be the best course you can take." And with this he took his leave, and the more hastily too, his mother and sisters ringing at the gate just at the moment he had risen up to go.

He left me in the utmost confusion of thought; and he easily perceived it the next day and all of the rest of the week, but he had no opportunity to come at me all that week till the Sunday after, when I, being indisposed, did not go to church, and he, making some excuse, stayed at home.

And now he had me an hour and half again by myself, and we fell into the same arguments all over again; at last I asked him warmly what opinion he must have of my modesty that he could suppose I should so much as entertain a thought of lying with two brothers, and assured him it could never be. I added, if he was to tell me that he would never see me more, than which nothing but death could be more terrible, yet I could never entertain a thought so dishonourable to myself and so base to him; and therefore I entreated him if he had one grain of respect or affection left for me, that he would speak no more of it to me or that he would pull his sword out and kill me. He appeared surprised at my obstinacy, as he called it; told me I was unkind to myself and unkind to him in it; that it was a crisis unlooked for upon us both, but that he did not see any other way to save us both from ruin, and therefore he thought it the more unkind; but that if he must say no more of it to me, he added with an unusual coldness that he did not know anything else we had to talk of; and so he rose up to take his leave. I rose up too, as if with the same indifference; but when he came to give me, as it were, a parting kiss, I burst out into such a passion of crying that though I would have spoke, I could not, and only pressing his hand, seemed to give him the adieu, but cried vehemently.

He was sensibly moved with this; so he sat down again and said a great many kind things to me, but still urged the necessity of what he had proposed; all the while insisting that if I did refuse, he would notwithstanding provide for me; but letting me plainly see that he would decline me in the main point—nay, even as a mistress; making it a point of honour not to lie with the woman that, for aught he knew, might one time or other come to be his brother's wife.

The bare loss of him as a gallant was not so much my

affliction as the loss of his person, whom indeed I loved to distraction; and the loss of all the expectations I had, and which I always built my hopes upon, of having him one day for my husband. These things oppressed my mind so much that, in short, the agonies of my mind threw me into a high fever, and long it was that none of the family expected my life.

I was reduced very low indeed and was often delirious; but nothing lay so near me as the fear that when I was light-headed I should say something or other to his prejudice. I was distressed in my mind also to see him, and so he was to see me, for he really loved me most passionately; but it could not be; there was not the least room to desire it on one side or other.

It was near five weeks that I kept my bed; and though the violence of my fever abated in three weeks, yet it several times returned; and the physicians said two or three times they could do no more for me, but that they must leave nature and the distemper to fight it out. After the end of five weeks I grew better, but was so weak, so altered, and recovered so slowly that the physicians apprehended I should go into a consumption; and which vexed me most, they gave their opinion that my mind was oppressed, that something troubled me, and in short, that I was in love. Upon this, the whole house set upon me to press me to tell whether I was in love or not and with whom; but as I well might, I denied my being in love at all.

They had on this occasion a squabble one day about me at table that had like to put the whole family in an uproar. They happened to be all at table but the father; as for me, I was ill and in my chamber. At the beginning of the talk the old gentlewoman, who had sent me somewhat to eat, bid her maid go up and ask me if I would have any more; but the maid brought down word I had not eaten half what she had sent me already. "Alas," says the old lady, "that poor girl! I am afraid she will never be well." "Well!" says the elder brother. "How should Mrs. Betty be well? They say she is in love." "I believe nothing of it," says the old gentlewoman. "I don't know," says the eldest sister, 'what to say to it; they have made such a rout about her being so handsome, and so charming, and I know not what, and that in her hearing too, that has turned the creature's head, I believe, and who knows what possessions may follow such doings? For my part, I don't know what to make of it."

"Why, sister, you must acknowledge she is very handsome," says the elder brother. "Aye, and a great deal handsomer than you, sister," says Robin, "and that's your mortification." "Well, well, that is not the question," says his sister; "the girl is well enough, and she knows it; she need not be told of it to make her vain."

"We don't talk of her being vain," says the elder brother, "but of her being in love; maybe she is in love with herself; it seems my sisters think so."

"I would she was in love with me," says Robin; "I'd quickly put her out of her pain." "What d'ye mean by that, son?" says the old lady. "How can you talk so?" "Why, madam," says Robin again, very honestly, "do you think I'd let the poor girl die for love, and of me, too, that is so near at hand to be had?" "Fie, brother!" says the second sister. "How can you talk so? Would you take a creature that has not a groat in the world?" "Prithee, child," says Robin, "beauty's a portion, and good humour with it is a double portion; I wish thou hadst half her stock of both for thy portion." So there was her mouth stopped.

"I find," says the eldest sister, "if Betty is not in love, my brother is. I wonder he has not broke his mind to Betty; I warrant she won't say no." "They that yield when they are asked," says Robin, "are one step before them that were never asked to yield, and two steps before them that yield before they are asked; and that's an answer to you, sister."

This fired the sister, and she flew into a passion and said things were come to that pass that it was time the wench, meaning me, was out of the family; and but that she was not fit to be turned out, she hoped her father and mother would consider of it as soon as she could be removed.

Robin replied that was for the master and mistress of the family, who were not to be taught by one that had so little judgement as his eldest sister.

It run up a great deal farther; the sister scolded, Robin rallied and bantered, but poor Betty lost ground by it extremely in the family. I heard of it and cried heartily, and the old lady came up to me, somebody having told her that I was so much concerned about it. I complained to her that it was very hard the doctors should pass such a censure upon me, for which they had no ground; and that it was still harder, considering the circumstances I was under in the family; that I hoped I had done nothing to lessen her esteem for me or given any occasion for the bickering between her sons and daughters, and I had more need to think of a coffin than of being in love, and begged she would not let me suffer in her opinion for anybody's mistakes but my own.

She was sensible of the justice of what I said, but told me since there had been such a clamour among them, and that her younger son talked after such a rattling way as he did, she desired I would be so faithful to her as to answer her but one question sincerely. I told her I would, and with the utmost plainness and sincerity. Why, then, the question was, whether there was anything between her son Robert and me. I told her with all the protestations of sincerity that I was able to make, and as I might well do, that there was not nor ever had been; I told her that Mr. Robert had rattled and jested, as she knew it was his way, and that I took it always as I supposed he meant it, to be a wild, airy way of discourse that had no signification in it; and assured her that there was not the least tittle of what she understood by it between us; and that those who had suggested it had done me a great deal of wrong and Mr. Robert no service at all.

The old lady was fully satisfied, and kissed me, spoke cheerfully to me, and bid me take care of my health and want for nothing, and so took her leave. But when she came down she found the brother and all his sisters together by the ears; they were angry, even to passion, at his upbraiding them with their being homely, and having never had any sweethearts, never having been asked the question, their being so forward as almost to ask first, and the like. He rallied them with Mrs. Betty; how pretty, how good-humoured, how she sung better than they did, and danced better, and how much handsomer she was; and in doing this he omitted no ill-natured thing that could vex them. The old lady came down in the height of it and, to stop it, told them the discourse she had had with me, and how I answered that there was nothing between Mr. Robert and I.

"She's wrong there," says Robin, "for if there was not a great deal between us, we should be closer together than we are. I told her I loved her hugely," says he, "but I could never make the jade believe I was in earnest." "I do not know how you should," says his mother; "nobody in their senses could believe you were in earnest, to talk so to a poor girl whose circumstances you know so well."

"But prithee, son," adds she, "since you tell us you could not make her believe you were in earnest, what must we believe about it? For you ramble so in your discourse that nobody knows whether you are in earnest or in jest; but as I find the girl, by your own confession, has answered truly, I wish you would do so too, and tell me seriously so that I may depend upon it. Is there anything in it or no? Are you in earnest or no? Are you distracted, indeed, or are you not? 'Tis a weighty question; I wish you would make us easy about it."

"By my faith, madam," says Robin, " 'tis in vain to mince the matter or tell any more lies about it; I am in earnest, as much as a man is that's going to be hanged. If Mrs. Betty would say she loved me and that she would marry me, I'd have her to-morrow morning fasting, and say, 'To have and to hold,' instead of eating my breakfast."

"Well," says the mother, "then there's one son lost"; and she said it in a very mournful tone, as one greatly concerned at it. "I hope not, madam," says Robin; "no man is lost when a good wife has found him." "Why, but, child," says the old lady, "she is a beggar." "Why, then, madam, she has the more need of charity," says Robin; "I'll take her off the hands of the parish, and she and I'll beg together." "It's bad jesting with such things," says the mother. "I don't jest, madam," says Robin; "we'll come and beg your pardon, madam, and your blessing, madam, and my father's." "This is all out of the way, son," says the mother. "If you are in earnest you are undone." "I am afraid not," says he, "for I am really afraid she won't have me. After all my sister's huffing, I believe I shall never be able to persuade her to it."

"That's a fine tale, indeed. She is not so far gone neither. Mrs. Betty is no fool," says the youngest sister. "Do you think she has learnt to say no any more than other people?" "No, Mrs. Mirth-wit," says Robin, "Mrs. Betty's no fool, but Mrs. Betty may be engaged some other way, and what then?" "Nay," says the eldest sister, "we can say nothing to that. Who must it be to, then? She is never out of the doors; it must be between you." "I have nothing to say to that," says Robin. "I have been examined enough; there's my brother. If it must be between us, go to work with him."

This stung the elder brother to the quick, and he concluded that Robin had discovered something. However, he kept himself from appearing disturbed. "Prithee," says he, "don't go to sham your stories off upon me; I tell you I deal in no such ware; I have nothing to say to no Mrs. Bettys in the parish"; and with that he rose up and brushed off. "No," says the eldest sister, "I dare answer for my brother; he knows the world better."

Thus the discourse ended; but it left the eldest brother quite confounded. He concluded his brother had made a full discovery, and he began to doubt whether I had been concerned in it or not; but with all his management, he could not bring it about to get at me. At last he was so perplexed that he was quite desperate and resolved he would see me whatever came of it. In order to this, he contrived it so that one day, after dinner, watching his eldest sister till he could see her go upstairs, he runs after her. "Hark ye, sister," says he, "where is this sick woman? May not a body see her?" "Yes," says the sister, "I believe you may; but let me go in first a little and I'll tell you." So she run up to the door and gave me notice, and presently called to him again. "Brother," says she, "you may come in if you please." So in he came, just in the same kind of rant. "Well," says he at the door as he came in, "where's this sick body that's in love? How do ye do, Mrs. Betty?" I would have got up out of my chair, but was so weak I could not for a good while; and he saw it and his sister too; and she said, "Come, do not strive to stand up; my brother desires no ceremony, especially now you are so weak." "No, no, Mrs. Betty, pray sit still," says he, and so sits himself down in a chair over against me and appeared as if he was mighty merry.

He talked a deal of rambling stuff to his sister and to me; sometimes of one thing, sometimes another, on purpose to amuse her, and every now and then would turn it upon the old story. "Poor Mrs. Betty," says he, "it is a sad thing to be in love; why, it has reduced you sadly." At last

I spoke a little. "I am glad to see you so merry, sir," says I; "but I think the doctor might have found something better to do than to make his game of his patients. If I had been ill of no other distemper, I know the proverb too well to have let him come to me." "What proverb?" says he. "What—

'Where love is the case,
The doctor's an ass.'

Is not that it, Mrs. Betty?" I smiled and said nothing. "Nay," says he, "I think the effect has proved it to be love; for it seems the doctor has done you little service; you mend very slowly, they say. I doubt there's somewhat in it, Mrs. Betty; I doubt you are sick of the incurables." I smiled and said, "No, indeed, sir, that's none of my distemper."

We had a deal of such discourse, and sometimes others that signified as little. By and by he asked me to sing them a song, at which I smiled and said my singing days were over. At last he asked me if he should play upon his flute to me; his sister said she believed my head could not bear it. I bowed and said, "Pray, madam, do not hinder it; I love the flute very much." Then his sister said, "Well, do, then, brother." With that he pulled out the key of his closet. "Dear sister," says he, "I am very lazy; do step and fetch my flute; it lies in such a drawer," naming a place where he was sure it was not, that she might be a little while a-looking for it.

As soon as she was gone, he related the whole story to me of the discourse his brother had about me and his concern about it, which was the reason of his contriving this visit. I assured him I had never opened my mouth either to his brother or to anybody else. I told him the dreadful exigence I was in; that my love to him and his offering to have me forget that affection and remove it to another had thrown me down; and that I had a thousand times wished I might die rather than recover, and to have the same circumstances to struggle with as I had before. I added that I foresaw that as soon as I was well I must quit the family, and that as for marrying his brother, I abhorred the thoughts of it after what had been my case with him, and that he might depend upon it, I would never see his brother again upon that subject; that if he would break all his vows and oaths and engagements with me, be that between his conscience and himself; but he should never be able to say that I, who he had persuaded to call myself his wife and who had given him the liberty to use me as a wife, was not as faithful to him as a wife ought to be, whatever he might be to me.

He was going to reply, and had said that he was sorry I could not be persuaded, and was a-going to say more, but he heard his sister a-coming, and so did I; and yet I forced out these few words as a reply, that I could never be persuaded to love one brother and marry the other. He shook his head and said, "Then I am ruined," meaning himself; and that moment his sister entered the room and told him she could not find the flute. "Well," says he merrily, "this laziness won't do"; so he gets up and goes himself to look for it, but comes back without it too; not but that he could have found it, but he had no mind to play; and besides, the errand he sent his sister on was answered another way; for he only wanted to speak to me, which he had done, though not much to his satisfaction.

I had, however, a great deal of satisfaction in having spoken my mind to him in freedom and with such an honest plainness, as I have related; and though it did not at all work the way I desired, that is to say, to oblige the person to me the more, yet it took from him all possibility of quitting me but by a downright breach of honour, and giving up all the faith of a gentleman, which he had so often engaged by never to abandon me, but to make me his wife as soon as he came to his estate.

It was not many weeks after this before I was about the house again and began to grow well; but I continued melancholy and retired, which amazed the whole family except he that knew the reason of it; yet it was a great while before he took any notice of it, and I, as backward to speak as he, carried as respectfully to him, but never offered to speak a word that was particular of any kind whatsoever; and this continued for sixteen or seventeen weeks; so that, as I expected every day to be dismissed the family on account of what distaste they had taken another way, in which I had no guilt, I expected to hear no more of this gentleman after all his solemn vows but to be ruined and abandoned.

At last I broke the way myself in the family for my

removing; for being talking seriously with the old lady one day about my own circumstances and how my distemper had left a heaviness upon my spirits, the old lady said, "I am afraid, Betty, what I have said to you about my son has had some influence upon you and that you are melancholy on his account; pray, will you let me know how the matter stands with you both if it may not be improper? For, as for Robin, he does nothing but rally and banter when I speak of it to him." "Why, truly, madam," said I, "that matter stands as I wish it did not, and I shall be very sincere with you in it whatever befalls me. Mr. Robert has several times proposed marriage to me, which is what I had no reason to expect, my poor circumstances considered; but I have always resisted him, and that perhaps in terms more positive than became me, considering the regard that I ought to have for every branch of your family; but," said I, "madam, I could never so far forget my obligations to you and all your house to offer to consent to a thing which I knew must needs be disobliging to you, and have positively told him that I would never entertain a thought of that kind unless I had your consent and his father's also, to whom I was bound by so many invincible obligations."

"And is this possible, Mrs. Betty?" says the old lady. "Then you have been much juster to us than we have been to you; for we have all looked upon you as a kind of a snare to my son, and I had a proposal to make you for your removing, for fear of it; but I had not yet mentioned it to you because I was afraid of grieving you too much, lest it should throw you down again; for we have a respect for you still, though not so much as to have it be the ruin of my son; but if it be as you say, we have all wronged you very much."

"As to the truth of what I say, madam," said I, "I refer to your son himself; if he will do me any justice, he must tell you the story just as I have told it."

Away goes the old lady to her daughters and tells them the whole story, just as I had told it her; and they were surprised at it, you may be sure, as I believed they would be. One said she could never have thought it; another said Robin was a fool; a third said she would not believe a word of it, and she would warrant that Robin would tell the story another way. But the old lady, who was resolved to go to the bottom of it before I could have the least opportunity of acquainting her son with what had passed, resolved, too, that she would talk with her son immediately, and to that purpose sent for him, for he was gone but to a lawyer's house in the town, and upon her sending he returned immediately.

Upon his coming up to them, for they were all together, "Sit down, Robin," says the old lady; "I must have some talk with you." "With all my heart, madam," says Robin, looking very merry. "I hope it is about a good wife, for I am at a great loss in that affair." "How can that be?" says his mother. "Did you not say you resolved to have Mrs. Betty?" "Aye, madam," says Robin; "but there is one that has forbid the banns." "Forbid the banns! Who can that be?" "Even Mrs. Betty herself," says Robin. "How so?" says his mother. "Have you asked her the question, then?" "Yes, indeed, madam," says Robin; "I have attacked her in form five times since she was sick, and am beaten off; the jade is so stout she won't capitulate nor yield upon any terms except such as I can't effectually grant." "Explain yourself," says the mother, "for I am surprised; I do not understand you. I hope you are not in earnest."

"Why, madam," says he, "the case is plain enough upon me, it explains itself; she won't have me, she says; is not that plain enough? I think 'tis plain, and pretty rough too." "Well, but," says the mother, "you talk of conditions that you cannot grant; what does she want—a settlement? Her jointure ought to be according to her portion; what does she bring?" "Nay, as to fortune," says Robin, "she is rich enough; I am satisfied in that point; but 'tis I that am not able to come up to her terms, and she is positive she will not have me without."

Here the sisters put in. "Madam," says the second sister, " 'tis impossible to be serious with him; he will never give a direct answer to anything; you had better let him alone and talk no more of it; you know how to dispose of her out of his way." Robin was a little warmed with his sister's rudeness, but he was even with her presently. "There are two sorts of people, madam," says he, turning to his mother, "that there is no contending with; that is, a wise body and a fool; 'tis a little hard I should engage with both of them together."

The younger sister then put in. "We must be fools indeed," says she, "in my brother's opinion, that he should make us believe he has seriously asked Mrs. Betty to marry him and she has refused him."

"Answer, and answer not, says Solomon," replied her brother. "When your brother had said that he had asked her no less than five times, and that she positively denied him, methinks a younger sister need not question the truth of it when her mother did not." "My mother, you see, did not understand it," says the second sister. "There's some difference," says Robin, "between desiring me to explain it and telling me she did not believe it."

"Well, but, son," says the old lady, "if you are disposed to let us into the mystery of it, what were these hard conditions?" "Yes, madam," says Robin, "I had done it before now if the teasers here had not worried me by way of interruption. The conditions are that I bring my father and you to consent to it, and without that she protests she will never see me more upon that head; and the conditions, as I said, I suppose I shall never be able to grant. I hope my warm sisters will be answered now, and blush a little."

This answer was surprising to them all, though less to the mother because of what I had said to her. As to the daughters, they stood mute a great while; but the mother said with some passion, "Well, I heard this before, but I could not believe it; but if it is so, then we have all done Betty wrong, and she has behaved better than I expected." "Nay," says the eldest sister, "if it is so, she has acted handsomely indeed." "I confess," says the mother, "it was none of her fault if he was enough fool to take a fancy to her; but to give such an answer to him shows more respect to us than I can tell how to express; I shall value the girl the better for it as long as I know her." "But I shall not," says Robin, "unless you will give your consent." "I'll consider of that awhile," says the mother; "I assure you, if there were not some other objections, this conduct of hers would go a great way to bring me to consent." "I wish it would go quite through with it," says Robin; "if you had as much thought about making me easy as you have about making me rich, you would soon consent to it."

"Why, Robin," says the mother again, "are you really in earnest? Would you fain have her?" "Really, madam," says Robin, "I think 'tis hard you should question me again upon that head. I won't say that I will have her. How can I resolve that point when you see I cannot have her without your consent? But this I will say: I am earnest that I will never have anybody else if I can help it. Betty or nobody is the word, and the question which of the two shall be in your breast to decide, madam, provided only that my good-humoured sisters here may have no vote in it."

All this was dreadful to me, for the mother began to yield, and Robin pressed her home in it. On the other hand, she advised with the eldest son, and he used all the arguments in the world to persuade her to consent; alleging his brother's passionate love for me, and my generous regard to the family in refusing my own advantages upon such a nice point of honour, and a thousand such things. And as to the father, he was a man in a hurry of public affairs and getting money, seldom at home, thoughtful of the main chance, but left all those things to his wife.

You may easily believe that when the plot was thus, as they thought, broke out, it was not so difficult or so dangerous for the elder brother, who nobody suspected of anything, to have a freer access than before; nay, the mother, which was just as he wished, proposed it to him to talk with Mrs. Betty. "It may be, son," said she, "you may see farther into the thing than I, and see if she has been so positive as Robin says she has been, or no." This was as well as he could wish, and he, as it were, yielding to talk with me at his mother's request, she brought me to him into her own chamber, told me her son had some business with me at her request, and then she left us together and he shut the door after her.

He came back to me and took me in his arms and kissed me very tenderly, but told me it was now come to that crisis that I should make myself happy or miserable as long as I lived; that if I could not comply to his desire, we should both be ruined. Then he told me the whole story between Robin, as he called him, and his mother and his sisters and himself, as above. "And now, dear child," says he, "consider what it will be to marry a gentleman of a good family, in good circumstances, and with the consent of the whole house, and to enjoy all that the world can give you; and what, on the other hand, to be sunk into the dark circumstances of a woman that has lost her reputation; and that though I shall be a private friend to you while I live, yet as I shall be suspected always, so you will be afraid to see me and I shall be afraid to own you."

He gave me no time to reply, but went on with me thus: "What has happened between us, child, so long as we both agree to do so, may be buried and forgotten. I shall always be your sincere friend, without any inclination to nearer intimacy when you become my sister; and we shall have all the honest part of conversation without any reproaches between us of having done amiss. I beg of you to consider it, and do not stand in the way of your own safety and prosperity; and to satisfy you that I am sincere," added he, "I here offer you five hundred pounds to make you some amends for the freedoms I have taken with you, which we shall look upon as some of the follies of our lives, which 'tis hoped we may repent of."

He spoke this in so much more moving terms than it is possible for me to express that you may suppose as he held me above an hour and half in that discourse, so he answered all my objections and fortified his discourse with all the arguments that human wit and art could devise.

I cannot say, however, that anything he said made impression enough upon me so as to give me any thought of the matter till he told me at last, very plainly, that if I refused, he was sorry to add that he could never go on with me in that station as we stood before; that though he loved me as well as ever and that I was as agreeable to him, yet the sense of virtue had not so forsaken him as to suffer him to lie with a woman that his brother courted to make his wife; that if he took his leave of me with a denial from me in this affair, whatever he might do for me in the point of support, grounded on his first engagement of maintaining me, yet he would not have me be surprised that he was obliged to tell me he could not allow himself to see me any more; and that, indeed, I could not expect it of him.

I received this last part with some tokens of surprise and disorder and had much ado to avoid sinking down, for indeed I loved him to an extravagance not easy to imagine; but he perceived my disorder and entreated me to consider seriously of it; assured me that it was the only way to preserve our mutual affection; that in this station we might love as friends with the utmost passion, and with a love of relation untainted, free from our own just reproaches, and free from other people's suspicions; that he should ever acknowledge his happiness owing to me; that he would be debtor to me as long as he lived and would be paying that debt as long as he had breath. Thus he wrought me up, in short, to a kind of hesitation in the matter; having the dangers on one side represented in lively figures and, indeed, heightened by my imagination of being turned out to the wide world a mere cast-off whore, for it was no less, and perhaps exposed as such, with little to provide for myself, with no friend, no acquaintance in the whole world out of that town, and there I could not pretend to stay. All this terrified me to the last degree, and he took care upon all occasions to lay it home to me in the worst colours. On the other hand, he failed not to set forth the easy, prosperous life which I was going to live.

He answered all that I could object from affection and from former engagements with telling me the necessity that was before us of taking other measures now; and as to his promises of marriage, the nature of things, he said, had put an end to that by the probability of my being his brother's wife before the time to which his promises all referred.

Thus, in a word, I may say, he reasoned me out of my reason; he conquered all my arguments, and I began to see a danger that I was in, which I had not considered of before, and that was of being dropped by both of them and left alone in the world to shift for myself.

This and his persuasion at length prevailed with me to consent, though with so much reluctance that it was easy to see I should go to church like a bear to the stake. I had some little apprehensions about me, too, lest my new spouse, who, by the way, I had not the least affection for, should be skilful enough to challenge me on another account upon our first coming to bed together; but whether he did it with design or not I know not, but his elder brother took care to make him very much fuddled before he went to bed, so that I had the satisfaction of a drunken bedfellow the first night. How he did it I know not, but I concluded that he certainly contrived it, that his brother might be able to make no judgement of the difference between a maid and a married woman; nor did he ever entertain any notions of it or disturb his thoughts about it.

I should go back a little here to where I left off. The

elder brother having thus managed me, his next business was to manage his mother, and he never left till he had brought her to acquiesce and be passive, even without acquainting the father other than by post-letters; so that she consented to our marrying privately, leaving her to manage the father afterwards.

Then he cajoled with his brother and persuaded him what service he had done him and how he had brought his mother to consent, which, though true, was not indeed done to serve him, but to serve himself; but thus diligently did he cheat him, and had the thanks of a faithful friend for shifting off his whore into his brother's arms for a wife. So naturally do men give up honour and justice and even Christianity to secure themselves.

I must now come back to brother Robin, as we always called him, who, having got his mother's consent, as above, came big with the news to me, and told me the whole story of it with a sincerity so visible that I must confess it grieved me that I must be the instrument to abuse so honest a gentleman. But there was no remedy; he would have me, and I was not obliged to tell him that I was his brother's whore though I had no other way to put him off; so I came gradually into it, and behold we were married.

Modesty forbids me to reveal the secrets of the marriage-bed, but nothing could have happened more suitable to my circumstances than that, as above, my husband was so fuddled when he came to bed that he could not remember in the morning whether he had had any conversation with me or no, and I was obliged to tell him he had, though in reality he had not, that I might be sure he could make no inquiry about anything else.

It concerns the story in hand very little to enter into the farther particulars of the family or of myself for the five years that I lived with this husband, only to observe that I had two children by him, and that at the end of the five years he died. He had been really a very good husband to me, and we lived very agreeably together; but as he had not received much from them and had in the little time he lived acquired no great matters, so my circumstances were not great, nor was I much mended by the match. Indeed, I had preserved the elder brother's bonds to me to pay me £500, which he offered me for my consent to marry his brother; and this, with what I had saved of the money he formerly gave me and about as much more by my husband, left me a widow with about £1200 in my pocket.

My two children were, indeed, taken happily off of my hands by my husband's father and mother, and that was all they got by Mrs. Betty.

I confess I was not suitably affected with the loss of my husband; nor can I say that I ever loved him as I ought to have done or was suitable to the good usage I had from him, for he was a tender, kind, good-humoured man as any woman could desire; but his brother being so always in my sight, at least while we were in the country, was a continual snare to me; and I never was in bed with my husband but I wished myself in the arms of his brother. And though his brother never offered me the least kindness that way after our marriage, but carried it just as a brother ought to do, yet it was impossible for me to do so to him; in short, I committed adultery and incest with him every day in my desires, which, without doubt, was as effectually criminal.

Before my husband died, his elder brother was married, and we, being then removed to London, were written to by the old lady to come and be at the wedding. My husband went, but I pretended indisposition, so I stayed behind; for, in short, I could not bear the sight of his being given to another woman though I knew I was never to have him myself.

I was now, as above, left loose to the world, and being still young and handsome, as everybody said of me, and I assure you I thought myself so, and with a tolerable fortune in my pocket, I put no small value upon myself. I was courted by several very considerable tradesmen and particularly very warmly by one, a linen-draper, at whose house after my husband's death I took a lodging, his sister being my acquaintance. Here I had all the liberty and opportunity to be gay and appear in company that I could desire, my landlord's sister being one of the maddest, gayest things alive, and not so much mistress of her virtue as I thought at first she had been. She brought me into a world of wild company and even brought home several persons, such as she liked well enough to gratify, to see her pretty widow. Now, as fame and fools make an assembly, I was here wonderfully caressed, had abundance of admirers, and such as called themselves lovers; but I found not one fair proposal among them all. As for their common design, that I understood too well to be drawn into any more snares of that kind. The case was altered with me; I had money in my pocket and had nothing to say to them. I had been tricked once by that cheat called love, but the game was over; I was resolved now to be married or nothing, and to be well married or not at all.

I loved the company, indeed, of men of mirth and wit, and was often entertained with such, as I was also with others; but I found by just observation that the brightest men came upon the dullest errand, that is to say, the dullest as to what I aimed at. On the other hand, those who came with the best proposals were the dullest and most disagreeable part of the world. I was not averse to a tradesman; but then I would have a tradesman, forsooth, that was something of a gentleman too; that when my husband had a mind to carry me to the court or to the play, he might become a sword, and look as like a gentleman as another man, and not like one that had the mark of his apron-strings upon his coat or the mark of his hat upon his periwig; that should look as if he was set on to his sword when his sword was put on to him, and that carried his trade in his countenance.

Well, at last I found this amphibious creature, this land-water thing, called a gentleman-tradesman; and as a just plague upon my folly, I was catched in the very snare which, as I might say, I laid for myself.

This was a draper too, for though my comrade would have bargained for me with her brother, yet when they came to the point, it was, it seems, for a mistress, and I kept true to this notion that a woman should never be kept for a mistress that had money to make herself a wife.

Thus my pride, not my principle, my money, not my virtue, kept me honest; though, as it proved, I found I had much better have been sold by my she-comrade to her brother than have sold myself as I did to a tradesman that was rake, gentleman, shopkeeper, and beggar all together.

But I was hurried on (by my fancy to a gentleman) to ruin myself in the grossest manner that ever woman did; for my new husband, coming to a lump of money at once, fell into such a profusion of expense that all I had and all he had would not have held it out above one year.

He was very fond of me for about a quarter of a year, and what I got by that was that I had the pleasure of seeing a great deal of my money spent upon myself. "Come, my dear," says he to me one day, "shall we go and take a turn into the country for a week?" "Aye, my dear," says I. "Whither would you go?" "I care not whither," says he, "but I have a mind to look like quality for a week; we'll go to Oxford," says he. "How," says I, "shall we go? I am no horsewoman, and 'tis too far for a coach." "Too far!" says he. "No place is too far for a coach-and-six. If I carry you out, you shall travel like a duchess." "Hum," says I, "my dear, 'tis a frolic; but if you have a mind to it, I don't care." Well, the time was appointed; we had a rich coach, very good horses, a coachman, postilion, and two footmen in very good liveries; a gentleman on horse-back and a page with a feather in his hat upon another horse. The servants all called him my lord, and I was her honour the countess, and thus we travelled to Oxford, and a pleasant journey we had; for, give him his due, not a beggar alive knew better how to be a lord than my husband. We saw all the rarities at Oxford, talked with two or three fellows of colleges about putting a nephew that was left to his lordship's care to the university, and of their being his tutors. We diverted ourselves with bantering several other poor scholars with the hopes of being at least his lordship's chaplain and putting on a scarf; and thus having lived like quality indeed as to expense, we went away for Northampton and, in a word, in about twelve days' ramble came home again, to the tune of about £93 expense.

Vanity is the perfection of a fop. My husband had this excellence, that he valued nothing of expense. As his history, you may be sure, has very little weight in it, 'tis enough to tell you that in about two years and a quarter he broke, got into a sponging-house, being arrested in an action too heavy for him to give bail to, so he sent for me to come to him.

It was no surprise to me, for I had foreseen something before that all was going to wreck and had been taking care to reserve something, if I could, for myself; but when he sent for me, he behaved much better than I expected. He told me plainly he had played the fool and suffered himself to be surprised, which he might have prevented; that now he foresaw he could not stand it, and therefore he would have me go home and in the night take away everything I had in the house of any value and secure it; and after that, he told me that if I could get away £100 or £200 in goods out of the shop, I should do it; "only," says he, "let me know nothing of it, neither what you take or whither you carry it; for as for me," says he, "I am resolved to get out of this house and be gone; and if you never hear of me more, my dear," says he, "I wish you well; I am only sorry for the injury I have done you." He said some very handsome things to me indeed at parting; for I told you he was a gentleman, and that was all the benefit I had of his being so; that he used me very handsomely even to the last, only spent all I had and left me to rob the creditors for something to subsist on.

However, I did as he bade me, that you may be sure; and having thus taken my leave of him, I never saw him more, for he found means to break out of the bailiff's house that night or the next; how, I knew not, for I could come at no knowledge of anything more than this: that he came home about three o'clock in the morning, caused the rest of his goods to be removed into the Mint, and the shop to be shut up; and having raised what money he could, he got over to France, from whence I had one or two letters from him and no more.

I did not see him when he came home, for he having given me such instructions as above and I having made the best of my time, I had no more business back again at the house, not knowing but I might have been stopped there by the creditors; for a commission of bankrupt being soon after issued, they might have stopped me by orders from the commissioners. But my husband, having desperately got out from the bailiff's by letting himself down from almost the top of the house to the top of another building and leaping from thence, which was almost two stories and which was enough indeed to have broken his neck, he came home and got away his goods before the creditors could come to seize; that is to say, before they could get out the commission and be ready to send their officers to take possession.

My husband was so civil to me, for still I say he was much of a gentleman, that in the first letter he wrote me he let me know where he had pawned twenty pieces of fine holland for £30, which were worth above £90, and enclosed me the token for the taking them up, paying the money, which I did and made in time above £100 of them, having leisure to cut them and sell them to private families as opportunity offered.

However, with all this and all that I had secured before, I found, upon casting things up, my case was very much altered and my fortune much lessened; for, including the hollands and a parcel of fine muslins, which I carried off before, and some plate and other things, I found I could hardly muster up £500; and my condition was very odd, for though I had no child (I had had one by my gentleman-draper, but it was buried), yet I was a widow bewitched, I had a husband and no husband, and I could not pretend to marry again though I knew well enough my husband would never see England any more if he lived fifty years. Thus, I say, I was limited from marriage, what offer soever might be made me; and I had not one friend to advise with in the condition I was in, at least not one who I could trust the secret of my circumstances to; for if the commissioners were to have been informed where I was, I should have been fetched up and all I had saved be taken away.

Upon these apprehensions, the first thing I did was to go quite out of my knowledge and go by another name. This I did effectually, for I went into the Mint too, took lodgings in a very private place, dressed me up in the habit of a widow, and called myself Mrs. Flanders.

Here, however, I concealed myself, and though my new acquaintance knew nothing of me, yet I soon got a great deal of company about me; and whether it be that women are scarce among the people that generally are to be found there or that some consolations in the miseries of that place are more requisite than on other occasions, I soon found that an agreeable woman was exceedingly valuable among the sons of affliction there; and that those that could not pay half a crown in the pound to their creditors, and run in debt at the sign of the Bull for their dinners, would yet find money for a supper if they liked the woman.

However, I kept myself safe yet, though I began, like my Lord Rochester's mistress, that loved his company but would not admit him farther, to have the scandal of a whore without the joy; and upon this score, tired with the place and with the company too, I began to think of removing.

It was indeed a subject of strange reflection to me, to see men in the most perplexed circumstances, who were reduced some degrees below being ruined, whose families were objects of their own terror and other people's charity, yet while a penny lasted, nay, even beyond it, endeavouring to drown their sorrow in their wickedness; heaping up more guilt upon themselves, labouring to forget former things which now it was the proper time to remember, making more work for repentance, and sinning on as a remedy for sin past.

But it is none of my talent to preach; these men were too wicked even for me. There was something horrid and absurd in their way of sinning, for it was all a force even upon themselves; they did not only act against conscience, but against nature, and nothing was more easy than to see how sighs would interrupt their songs, and paleness and anguish sit upon their brows, in spite of the forced smiles they put on; nay, sometimes it would break out at their very mouths, when they had parted with their money for a lewd treat or a wicked embrace. I have heard them, turning about, fetch a deep sigh and cry, "What a dog am I! Well, Betty, my dear, I'll drink thy health, though," meaning the honest wife, that perhaps had not a half-crown for herself and three or four children. The next morning they were at their penitentials again, and perhaps the poor weeping wife comes over to him, either brings him some account of what his creditors are doing and how she and the children are turned out-of-doors, or some other dreadful news; and this adds to his self-reproaches; but when he has thought and pored on it till he is almost mad, having no principles to support him, nothing within him or above him to comfort him, but finding it all darkness on every side, he flies to the same relief again, *viz.*, to drink it away, debauch it away; and falling into company of men in just the same condition with himself, he repeats the crime and thus he goes every day one step onward of his way to destruction.

I was not wicked enough for such fellows as these. Yet, on the contrary, I began to consider here very seriously what I had to do, how things stood with me, and what course I ought to take. I knew I had no friends, no, not one friend or relation in the world; and that little I had left apparently wasted, which when it was gone, I saw nothing but misery and starving was before me. Upon these considerations, I say, and filled with horror at the place I was in, I resolved to be gone.

I had made an acquaintance with a sober, good sort of a woman, who was a widow, too, like me, but in better circumstances. Her husband had been a captain of a ship, and having had the misfortune to be cast away coming home from the West Indies, was so reduced by the loss that though he had saved his life then, it broke his heart and killed him afterwards; and his widow, being pursued by the creditors, was forced to take shelter in the Mint. She soon made things up with the help of friends and was at liberty again; and finding that I rather was there to be concealed than by any particular prosecutions, and finding also that I agreed with her, or rather she with me, in a just abhorrence of the place and of the company, she invited me to go home with her till I could put myself in some posture of settling in the world to my mind; withal telling me that it was ten to one but some good captain of a ship might take a fancy to me and court me in that part of the town where she lived.

I accepted of her offer and was with her half a year and should have been longer, but in that interval what she proposed to me happened to herself, and she married very much to her advantage. But whose fortune soever was upon the increase, mine seemed to be upon the wane, and I found nothing present except two or three boatswains or such fellows, but as for the commanders, they were generally of two sorts. 1. Such as, having good business, that is to say, a good ship, resolved not to marry but with advantage. 2. Such as, being out of employ, wanted a wife to help them to a ship; I mean (1) a wife, who, having some money, could enable them to hold a good part of a ship themselves, so to encourage owners to come in; or (2) a wife who if she had not money had friends who were concerned in shipping, and so could help to put the young man into a good ship; and neither of these was my case, so I looked like one that was to lie on hand.

This knowledge I soon learnt by experience, *viz.*, that the state of things was altered as to matrimony, that marriages were here the consequences of politic schemes, for forming interests, carrying on business, and that love had no share or but very little in the matter.

That as my sister-in-law at Colchester had said, beauty, wit, manners, sense, good humour, good behaviour, education, virtue, piety, or any other qualification, whether of body or mind, had no power to recommend; that money only made a woman agreeable; that men chose mistresses indeed by the gust of their affection, and it was requisite for a whore to be handsome, well shaped, have a good mien and a graceful behaviour; but that for a wife, no deformity would shock the fancy, no ill qualities the judgement; the money was the thing; the portion was neither crooked or monstrous, but the money was always agreeable, whatever the wife was.

On the other hand, as the market run all on the men's side, I found the women had lost the privilege of saying no; that it was a favour now for a woman to have the question asked, and if any young lady had so much arrogance as to counterfeit a negative, she never had the opportunity of denying twice, much less of recovering that false step and accepting what she had seemed to decline. The men had such choice everywhere that the case of the women was very unhappy; for they seemed to ply at every door, and if the man was by great chance refused at one house, he was sure to be received at the next.

Besides this, I observed that the men made no scruple to set themselves out and to go a-fortune-hunting, as they call it, when they had really no fortune themselves to demand it or merit to deserve it; and they carried it so high that a woman was scarce allowed to inquire after the character or estate of the person that pretended to her. This I had an example of in a young lady at the next house to me and with whom I had contracted an intimacy; she was courted by a young captain, and though she had near £2000 to her fortune, she did but inquire of some of his neighbours about his character, his morals, or substance, and he took occasion at the next visit to let her know, truly, that he took it very ill and that he should not give her the trouble of his visits any more. I heard of it, and I had begun my acquaintance with her. I went to see her upon it; she entered into a close conversation with me about it and unbosomed herself very freely. I perceived presently that though she thought herself very ill-used, yet she had no power to resent it; that she was exceedingly piqued she had lost him and particularly that another of less fortune had gained him.

I fortified her mind against such a meanness, as I called it; I told her that as low as I was in the world, I would have despised a man that should think I ought to take him upon his own recommendation only; also I told her that as she had a good fortune, she had no need to stoop to the disaster of the times; that it was enough that the men could insult us that had but little money, but if she suffered such an affront to pass upon her without resenting it, she would be rendered low-prized upon all occasions; that a woman can never want an opportunity to be revenged of a man that has used her ill, and that there were ways enough to humble such a fellow as that or else certainly women were the most unhappy creatures in the world.

She was very well pleased with the discourse and told me seriously that she would be very glad to make him sensible of her resentment, and either to bring him on again or have the satisfaction of her revenge being as public as possible.

I told her that if she would take my advice, I would tell her how she should obtain her wishes in both those things; and that I would engage I would bring the man to her door again and make him beg to be let in. She smiled at that and soon let me see that if he came to her door, her resentment was not so great to let him stand long there.

However, she listened very willingly to my offer of advice; so I told her that the first thing she ought to do was a piece of justice to herself, namely, that whereas he had reported among the ladies that he had left her, and pretended to give the advantage of the negative to himself, she should take care to have it well spread among the women, which she could not fail of an opportunity to do, that she had inquired into his circumstances and found he was not the man he pretended to be. "Let them be told, too, madam," said I, "that you found he was not the man you expected and that you thought it was not safe to meddle with him; that you heard he was of an ill temper, and that he boasted how he had used the women ill upon many occasions, and that particularly he was debauched in his morals," etc. The last of which, indeed, had some truth in it, but I did not find that she seemed to like him much the worse for that part.

She came most readily into all this, and immediately she went to work to find instruments. She had very little difficulty in the search, for telling her story in general to a couple of her gossips, it was the chat of the tea-table all over that part of the town, and I met with it wherever I visited; also as it was known that I was acquainted with the young lady herself, my opinion was asked very often, and I confirmed it with all the necessary aggravations and set out his character in the blackest colours; and as a piece of secret intelligence, I added what the gossips knew nothing of, *viz.*, that I had heard he was in very bad circumstances; that he was under a necessity of a fortune to support his interest with the owners of the ship he commanded; that his own part was not paid for, and if it was not paid quickly, his owners would put him out of the ship, and his chief mate was likely to command it, who offered to buy that part which the captain had promised to take.

I added, for I was heartily piqued at the rogue, as I called him, that I had heard a rumour too that he had a wife alive at Plymouth and another in the West Indies, a thing which they all knew was not very uncommon for such kind of gentlemen.

This worked as we both desired it, for presently the young lady at the next door, who had a father and mother that governed both her and her fortune, was shut up, and her father forbid him the house. Also in one place more the woman had the courage, however strange it was, to say no; and he could try nowhere but he was reproached with his pride, and that he pretended not to give the women leave to inquire into his character, and the like.

By this time he began to be sensible of his mistake, and seeing all the women on that side the water alarmed, he went over to Ratcliff and got access to some of the ladies there; but though the young women there too were, according to the fate of the day, pretty willing to be asked, yet such was his ill luck that his character followed him over the water; so that though he might have had wives enough, yet it did not happen among the women that had good fortunes, which was what he wanted.

But this was not all; she very ingeniously managed another thing herself, for she got a young gentleman who was a relation to come and visit her two or three times a week in a very fine chariot and good liveries, and her two agents and I also presently spread a report all over that this gentleman came to court her; that he was a gentleman of a thousand pounds a year, and that he was fallen in love with her, and that she was going to her aunt's in the city because it was inconvenient for the gentleman to come to her with his coach to Rotherhithe, the streets being so narrow and difficult.

This took immediately. The captain was laughed at in all companies, and was ready to hang himself; he tried all the ways possible to come at her again and wrote the most passionate letters to her in the world; and in short, by great application, obtained leave to wait on her again, as he said, only to clear his reputation.

At this meeting she had her full revenge of him; for she told him she wondered what he took her to be that she should admit any man to a treaty of so much consequence as that of marriage without inquiring into his circumstances; that if he thought she was to be huffed into wedlock and that she was in the same circumstances which her neighbours might be in, *viz.*, to take up the first good Christian that came, he was mistaken; that, in a word, his character was really bad or he was very ill beholden to his neighbours; and that unless he could clear up some points in which she had justly been prejudiced, she had no more to say to him but give him the satisfaction of knowing that she was not afraid to say no either to him or any man else.

With that she told him what she had heard, or rather

raised herself by my means, of his character; his not having paid for the part he pretended to own of the ship he commanded; of the resolution of his owners to put him out of the command and to put his mate in his stead; and of the scandal raised on his morals; his having been reproached with such-and-such women, and his having a wife at Plymouth and another in the West Indies, and the like; and she asked him whether she had not good reason, if these things were not cleared up, to refuse him and to insist upon having satisfaction in points so significant as they were.

He was so confounded at her discourse that he could not answer a word, and she began to believe that all was true, by his disorder, though she knew that she had been the raiser of these reports herself.

After some time he recovered a little, and from that time was the most humble, modest, and importunate man alive in his courtship.

She asked him if he thought she was so at her last shift that she could or ought to bear such treatment, and if he did not see that she did not want those who thought it worth their while to come farther to her than he did, meaning the gentleman whom she had brought to visit her by way of sham.

She brought him by these tricks to submit to all possible measures to satisfy her, as well of his circumstances as of his behaviour. He brought her undeniable evidence of his having paid for his part of the ship; he brought her certificates from his owners that the report of their intending to remove him from the command of the ship was false and groundless; in short, he was quite the reverse of what he was before.

Thus I convinced her that if the men made their advantage of our sex in the affair of marriage, upon the supposition of there being such a choice to be had and of the women being so easy, it was only owing to this: that the women wanted courage to maintain their ground and that according to my Lord Rochester:

> A woman's ne'er so ruined but she can
> Revenge herself on her undoer, man.

After these things this young lady played her part so

well that though she resolved to have him, and that indeed having him was the main bent of her design, yet she made his obtaining her to be to him the most difficult thing in the world; and this she did not by a haughty, reserved carriage, but by a just policy, playing back upon him his own game; for as he pretended by a kind of lofty carriage to place himself above the occasion of a character, she broke with him upon that subject, and at the same time that she made him submit to all possible inquiry after his affairs, she apparently shut the door against his looking into her own.

It was enough to him to obtain her for a wife. As to what she had, she told him plainly that as he knew her circumstances, it was but just she should know his; and though at the same time he had only known her circumstances by common fame, yet he had made so many protestations of his passion for her that he could ask no more but her hand to his grand request, and the like ramble according to the custom of lovers. In short, he left himself no room to ask any more questions about her estate, and she took the advantage of it, for she placed part of her fortune so in trustees, without letting him know anything of it, that it was quite out of his reach, and made him be very well contented with the rest.

It is true she was pretty well besides, that is to say, she had about £1400 in money, which she gave him; and the other after some time she brought to light as a perquisite to herself, which he was to accept as a mighty favour, seeing, though it was not to be his, it might ease him in the article of her particular expenses; and I must add that by this conduct, the gentleman himself became not only more humble in his applications to her to obtain her but also was much the more an obliging husband when he had her. I cannot but remind the ladies how much they place themselves below the common station of a wife, which, if I may be allowed not to be partial, is low enough already; I say, they place themselves below their common station and prepare their own mortifications by their submitting so to be insulted by the men beforehand, which I confess I see no necessity of.

This relation may serve, therefore, to let the ladies see that the advantage is not so much on the other side as the men think it is; and that though it may be true, the men have but too much choice among us, and that some women may be found who will dishonour themselves, be cheap, and too easy to come at, yet if they will have women worth having, they may find them as un-come-at-able as ever, and that those that are otherwise have often such deficiencies when had as rather recommend the ladies that are difficult than encourage the men to go on with their easy courtship and expect wives equally valuable that will come at first call.

Nothing is more certain than that the ladies always gain of the men by keeping their ground and letting their pretended lovers see they can resent being slighted, and that they are not afraid of saying no. They insult us mightily with telling us of the number of women; that the wars and the sea and trade and other incidents have carried the men so much away; that there is no proportion between the numbers of the sexes; but I am far from granting that the number of the women is so great or the number of the men so small; but if they will have me tell the truth, the disadvantage of the women is a terrible scandal upon the men, and it lies here only; namely, that the age is so wicked and the sex so debauched that, in short, the number of such men as an honest woman ought to meddle with is small indeed, and it is but here and there that a man is to be found who is fit for an honest woman to venture upon.

But the consequence even of that too amounts to no more than this: that women ought to be the more nice; for how do we know the just character of the man that makes the offer? To say that the woman should be the more easy on this occasion is to say we should be the forwarder to venture because of the greatness of the danger, which is very absurd.

On the contrary, the women have ten thousand times the more reason to be wary and backward, by how much the hazard of being betrayed is the greater; and would the ladies act the wary part, they would discover every cheat that offered; for, in short, the lives of very few men now-a-days will bear a character; and if the ladies do but make a little inquiry, they would soon be able to distinguish the men and deliver themselves. As for women that do not think their own safety worth their own thought, that, impatient of their present state, run into matrimony as a horse rushes into the battle, I can say nothing to them but this: that they are a sort of ladies that are to be prayed for among the rest of distempered people, and they look like people that venture their estates in a lottery where there is a hundred thousand blanks to one prize.

No man of common sense will value a woman the less for not giving up herself at the first attack or for not accepting his proposal without inquiring into his person or character; on the contrary, he must think her the weakest of all creatures, as the rate of men now goes; in short, he must have a very contemptible opinion of her capacities that, having but one cast for her life, shall cast that life away at once and make matrimony, like death, be a leap in the dark.

I would fain have the conduct of my sex a little regulated in this particular, which is the same thing in which, of all the parts of life, I think at this time we suffer most in; 'tis nothing but lack of courage, the fear of not being married at all and of that frightful state of life called an old maid. This, I say, is the woman's snare; but would the ladies once but get above that fear and manage rightly, they would more certainly avoid it by standing their ground in a case so absolutely necessary to their felicity than by exposing themselves as they do; and if they did not marry so soon, they would make themselves amends by marrying safer. She is always married too soon who gets a bad husband, and she is never married too late who gets a good one; in a word, there is no woman, deformity or lost reputation excepted, but if she manages well may be married safely one time or other; but if she precipitates herself, it is ten thousand to one but she is undone.

But I come now to my own case, in which there was at this time no little nicety. The circumstances I was in made the offer of a good husband the most necessary thing in the world to me, but I found soon that to be made cheap and easy was not the way. It soon began to be found that the widow had no fortune, and to say this was to say all that was ill of me, being well bred, handsome, witty, modest, and agreeable; all which I had allowed to my character, whether justly or no is not to the purpose; I say, all these would not do without the dross. In short, the widow, they said, had no money!

I resolved, therefore, that it was necessary to change my station and make a new appearance in some other place, and even to pass by another name if I found occasion.

I communicated my thoughts to my intimate friend, the captain's lady, who I had so faithfully served in her case with the captain and who was as ready to serve me in the same kind as I could desire. I made no scruple to lay my circumstances open to her; my stock was but low, for I had made but about £540 at the close of my last affair, and I had wasted some of that; however, I had about £460 left, a great many very rich clothes, a gold watch, and some jewels, though of no extraordinary value, and about £30 or £40 left in linen not disposed of.

My dear and faithful friend, the captain's wife, was so sensible of the service I had done her in the affair above that she was not only a steady friend to me but, knowing my circumstances, she frequently made me presents as money came into her hands, such as fully amounted to a maintenance, so that I spent none of my own; and at last she made this unhappy proposal to me, *viz.*, that as we had observed, as above, how the men made no scruple to set themselves out as persons meriting a woman of fortune of their own, it was but just to deal with them in their own way and, if it was possible, to deceive the deceiver.

The captain's lady, in short, put this project into my head and told me if I would be ruled by her, I should certainly get a husband of fortune without leaving him any room to reproach me with want of my own. I told her that I would give up myself wholly to her directions and that I would have neither tongue to speak or feet to step in that affair but as she should direct me, depending that she would extricate me out of every difficulty that she brought me into, which she said she would answer for.

The first step she put me upon was to call her cousin and go to a relation's house of hers in the country, where she directed me and where she brought her husband to visit me; and calling me cousin, she worked matters so about that her husband and she together invited me most passionately to come to town and live with them, for they now lived in a quite different place from where they were before. In the next place, she tells her husband that I had at last £1500 fortune and that I was like to have a great deal more.

It was enough to tell her husband this; there needed nothing on my side. I was but to sit still and wait the event, for it presently went all over the neighbourhood that the young widow at Captain ——'s was a fortune, that she had at least £1500 and perhaps a great deal more, and that the captain said so; and if the captain was asked at any time about me, he made no scruple to affirm it though he knew not one word of the matter other than that his wife had told him so; and in this he thought no harm, for he really believed it to be so. With the reputation of this fortune, I presently found myself blessed with admirers enough (and that I had my choice of men), as they said they were, which, by the way, confirms what I was saying before. This being my case, I, who had a subtle game to play, had nothing now to do but to single out from them all the properest man that might be for my purpose; that is to say, the man who was most likely to depend upon the hearsay of fortune and not inquire too far into the particulars; and unless I did this I did nothing, for my case would not bear much inquiry.

I picked out my man without much difficulty by the judgement I made of his way of courting me. I had let him run on with his protestations that he loved me above all the world; that if I would make him happy, that was enough; all which I knew was upon supposition that I was very rich, though I never told him a word of it myself.

This was my man; but I was to try him to the bottom; and indeed in that consisted my safety, for if he balked, I knew I was undone, as surely as he was undone if he took me; and if I did not make some scruple about his fortune, it was the way to lead him to raise some about mine; and first, therefore, I pretended on all occasions to doubt his sincerity and told him perhaps he only courted me for my fortune. He stopped my mouth in that part with the thunder of his protestations as above, but still I pretended to doubt.

One morning he pulls off his diamond ring and writes

upon the glass of the sash in my chamber this line:

You I love and you alone.

I read it and asked him to lend me the ring, with which I wrote under it thus:

And so in love says every one.

He takes his ring again and writes another line thus:

Virtue alone is an estate.

I borrowed it again, and I wrote under it:

But money's virtue, gold is fate.

He coloured as red as fire to see me turn so quick upon him, and in a kind of rage told me he would conquer me, and wrote again thus:

I scorn your gold, and yet I love.

I ventured all upon the last cast of poetry, as you'll see, for I wrote boldly under his last:

I'm poor; let's see how kind you'll prove.

This was a sad truth to me; whether he believed me or no I could not tell; I supposed then that he did not. However, he flew to me, took me in his arms, and kissing me very eagerly and with the greatest passion imaginable, he held me fast till he called for a pen and ink and told me he could not wait the tedious writing on a glass, but pulling out a piece of paper, he began and wrote again:

Be mine with all your poverty.

I took his pen and followed immediately thus:

Yet secretly you hope I lie.

He told me that was unkind because it was not just, and

that I put him upon contradicting me, which did not consist with good manners, and, therefore, since I had insensibly drawn him into this poetical scribble, he begged I would not oblige him to break it off. So he writes again:

Let love alone be our debate.

I wrote again:

She loves enough that does not hate.

This he took for a favour and so laid down the cudgels, that is to say, the pen; I say, he took it for a favour, and a mighty one it was if he had known all. However, he took it as I meant it, that is, to let him think I was inclined to go on with him, as indeed I had reason to do, for he was the best-humoured merry sort of a fellow that I ever met with; and I often reflected how doubly criminal it was to deceive such a man; but that necessity, which pressed me to a settlement suitable to my condition, was my authority for it; and certainly his affection to me and the goodness of his temper, however they might argue against using him ill, yet they strongly argued to me that he would better take the disappointment than some fiery-tempered wretch, who might have nothing to recommend him but those passions which would serve only to make a woman miserable.

Besides, though I had jested with him (as he supposed it) so often about my poverty, yet when he found it to be true, he had foreclosed all manner of objection, seeing, whether he was in jest or in earnest, he had declared he took me without any regard to my portion and, whether I was in jest or in earnest, I had declared myself to be very poor; so that, in a word, I had him fast both ways; and though he might say afterwards he was cheated, yet he could never say that I had cheated him.

He pursued me close after this, and as I saw there was no need to fear losing him, I played the indifferent part with him longer than prudence might otherwise have dictated to me; but I considered how much this caution and indifference would give me the advantage over him when I should come to own my circumstances to him; and I managed it the more warily because I found he inferred from thence that I had either the more money or the more judgement, and would not venture at all.

I took the freedom one day to tell him that it was true I had received the compliment of a lover from him, namely, that he would take me without inquiring into my fortune, and I would make him a suitable return in this, *viz.*, that I would make as little inquiry into his as consisted with reason, but I hoped he would allow me to ask some questions, which he should answer or not as he thought fit; one of these questions related to our manner of living and the place where, because I had heard he had a great plantation in Virginia, and I told him I did not care to be transported.

He began from this discourse to let me voluntarily into all his affairs and to tell me in a frank, open way all his circumstances, by which I found he was very well to pass in the world; but that great part of his estate consisted of three plantations, which he had in Virginia, which brought him in a very good income of about £300 a year, but that if he was to live upon them, would bring him in four times as much. "Very well," thought I; "you shall carry me thither, then, as soon as you please, though I won't tell you so beforehand."

I jested with him about the figure he would make in Virginia, but found he would do anything I desired, so I turned my tale. I told him I had good reason not to desire to go there to live; because if his plantations were worth so much there, I had not a fortune suitable to a gentleman of £1200 a year, as he said his estate would be.

He replied he did not ask what my fortune was; he had told me from the beginning he would not, and he would be as good as his word; but whatever it was, he assured me he would never desire me to go to Virginia with him or go thither himself without me unless I made it my choice.

All this, you may be sure, was as I wished, and indeed nothing could have happened more perfectly agreeable. I carried it on as far as this with a sort of indifferency that he often wondered at, and I mention it the rather to intimate again to the ladies that nothing but want of courage for such an indifferency makes our sex so cheap and prepares them to be ill-used as they are; would they venture the loss of a pretending fop now and then who carries it high upon the point of his own merit, they would certainly be slighted less and courted more. Had I discovered really what my great fortune was, and that in all I had not full £500 when he expected £1500, yet I hooked him so fast and played him so long that I was satisfied he would have had me in my worst circumstances; and indeed it was less a surprise to him when he learnt the truth than it would have been because, having not the least blame to lay on me, who had carried it with an air of indifference to the last, he could not say one word except that indeed he thought it had been more, but that if it had been less, he did not repent his bargain; only that he should not be able to maintain me so well as he intended.

In short, we were married, and very happily married on my side, I assure you, as to the man; for he was the best-humoured man that ever woman had, but his circumstances were not so good as I imagined, as, on the other hand, he had not bettered himself so much as he expected.

When we were married, I was shrewdly put to it to bring him that little stock I had and to let him see it was no more; but there was a necessity for it, so I took my opportunity one day when we were alone to enter into a short dialogue with him about it. "My dear," said I, "we have been married a fortnight; is it not time to let you know whether you have got a wife with something or with nothing?" "Your own time for that, my dear," says he; "I am satisfied I have got the wife I love; I have not troubled you much," says he, "with my inquiry after it."

"That's true," said I, "but I have a great difficulty about it, which I scarce know how to manage." "What's that, my dear?" says he. "Why," says I, " 'tis a little hard upon me, and 'tis harder upon you; I am told that Captain ——" (meaning my friend's husband) "has told you I had a great deal more than ever I pretended to have, and I am sure I never employed him so to do."

"Well," says he, "Captain —— may have told me so, but what then? If you have not so much, that may lie at his door, but you never told me what you had, so I have no reason to blame you if you have nothing at all."

"That is so just," said I, "and so generous that it makes my having but a little a double affliction to me."

"The less you have, my dear," says he, "the worse for us both; but I hope your affliction is not caused for fear I should be unkind to you for want of a portion. No, no, if you have nothing, tell me plainly; I may perhaps tell the captain he has cheated me, but I can never say you have, for did not you give it under your hand that you was poor? And so I ought to expect you to be."

"Well," said I, "my dear, I am glad I have not been concerned in deceiving you before marriage. If I deceive you since, 'tis ne'er the worse; that I am poor, 'tis too true, but not so poor as to have nothing neither"; so I pulled out some bank-bills and gave him about £160. "There is something, my dear," says I, "and not quite all neither."

I had brought him so near to expecting nothing by what I had said before that the money, though the sum was small in itself, was doubly welcome; he owned it was more than he looked for, and that he did not question by my discourse to him but that my fine clothes, gold watch, and a diamond ring or two had been all my fortune.

I let him please himself with that £160 two or three days, and then, having been abroad that day and as if I had been to fetch it, I brought him £100 more home in gold and told him there was a little more portion for him; and in short, in about a week more I brought him £180 more and about £60 in linen, which I made him believe I had been obliged to take with the £100 which I gave him in gold as a composition for a debt of £600, being little more than five shillings in the pound and overvalued too.

"And now, my dear," says I to him, "I am very sorry to tell you that I have given you my whole fortune." I added that if the person who had my £600 had not abused me, I had been worth £1000 to him, but that as it was, I had been faithful and reserved nothing to myself, but if it had been more he should have had it.

He was so obliged by the manner and so pleased with the sum, for he had been in a terrible fright lest it had been nothing at all, that he accepted it very thankfully. And thus I got over the fraud of passing for a fortune without money and cheating a man into marrying me on pretence of it, which, by the way, I take to be one of the most dangerous steps a woman can take, and in which she runs the most hazards of being ill-used afterwards.

My husband, to give him his due, was a man of infinite good nature, but he was no fool; and finding his income not suited to the manner of living which he had intended if I had brought him what he expected, and being under a disappointment in his return of his plantations in Virginia, he discovered many times his inclination of going over to Virginia to live upon his own, and often would be magnifying the way of living there, how cheap, how plentiful, how pleasant, and the like.

I began presently to understand his meaning, and I took him up very plainly one morning and told him that I did so; that I found his estate turned to no account at this distance, compared to what it would do if he lived upon the spot, and that I found he had a mind to go and live there; that I was sensible he had been disappointed in a wife, and that finding his expectations not answered that way, I could do no less to make him amends than tell him that I was very willing to go to Virginia with him and live there.

He said a thousand kind things to me upon the subject of my making such a proposal to him. He told me that though he was disappointed in his expectations of a fortune, he was not disappointed in a wife and that I was all to him that a wife could be, but that this offer was so kind that it was more than he could express.

To bring the story short, we agreed to go. He told me that he had a very good house there, well furnished; that his mother lived in it and one sister, which was all the relations he had; that as soon as he came there they would remove to another house, which was her own for life and his after her decease; so that I should have all the house to myself; and I found it all exactly as he said.

We put on board the ship which we went in a large quantity of good furniture for our house, with stores of linen and other necessaries, and a good cargo for sale, and away we went.

To give an account of the manner of our voyage, which was long and full of dangers, is out of my way; I kept no journal, neither did my husband. All that I can say is that after a terrible passage, frighted twice with dreadful storms and once with what was still more terrible, I mean a pirate, who came on board and took away almost all our provisions; and which would have been beyond all to me, they had once taken my husband, but by entreaties were prevailed with to leave him—I say, after all these terrible things, we arrived in York River in Virginia, and coming to our plantation, we were received with all the tenderness and affection, by my husband's mother, that could be expressed.

We lived here all together, my mother-in-law, at my entreaty, continuing in the house, for she was too kind a mother to be parted with; my husband likewise continued the same at first, and I thought myself the happiest creature alive when an odd and surprising event put an end to all that felicity in a moment and rendered my condition the most uncomfortable in the world.

My mother was a mighty cheerful, good-humoured old woman—I may call her so, for her son was above thirty; I say she was very pleasant, good company, and used to entertain me, in particular, with abundance of stories to divert me, as well of the country we were in as of the people.

Among the rest, she often told me how the greatest part of the inhabitants of that colony came thither in very indifferent circumstances from England; that, generally speaking, they were of two sorts; either, first, such as were brought over by masters of ships to be sold as servants; or, second, such as are transported after having been found guilty of crimes punishable with death.

"When they come here," says she, "we make no difference; the planters buy them, and they work together in the field till their time is out. When 'tis expired," said she, "they have encouragement given them to plant for themselves; for they have a certain number of acres of land allotted them by the country, and they go to work to clear and cure the land and then to plant it with tobacco and corn for their own use; and as the merchants will trust them with tools and necessaries upon the credit of their crop before it is grown, so they again plant every year a little more than the year before, and so buy whatever they want with the crop that is before them. Hence, child," says she, "many a Newgate-bird becomes a great man, and we have," continued she, "several justices of the peace, officers of the trained bands, and magistrates of the towns they live in that have been burnt in the hand."

She was going on with that part of the story when her own part in it interrupted her, and with a great deal of good-humoured confidence she told me she was one of the second sort of inhabitants herself; that she came away openly, having ventured too far in a particular case, so that she was become a criminal. "And here's the mark of it, child," says she, and showed me a very fine white arm and hand, but branded in the inside of the hand, as in such cases it must be.

This story was very moving to me, but my mother, smiling, said, "You need not think such a thing strange, daughter, for some of the best men in the country are burnt in the hand, and they are not ashamed to own it. There's Major ——," says she, "he was an eminent pickpocket; there's Justice Ba—r, was a shoplifter, and both of them were burnt in the hand; and I could name you several such as they are."

We had frequent discourses of this kind, and abundance of instances she gave me of the like. After some time, as she was telling some stories of one that was transported but a few weeks ago, I began in an intimate kind of way to ask her to tell me something of her own story, which she did with the utmost plainness and sincerity; how she had fallen into very ill company in London in her young days, occasioned by her mother sending her frequently to carry victuals to a kinswoman of hers who was a prisoner in Newgate in a miserable, starving condition, who was afterwards condemned to die, but having got respite by pleading her belly, perished afterwards in the prison.

Here my mother-in-law ran out in a long account of the wicked practices in that dreadful place. "And, child," says my mother, "perhaps you may know little of it or, it may be, have heard nothing about it; but depend upon it," says she, "we all know here that there are more thieves and rogues made by that one prison of Newgate than by all the clubs and societies of villains in the nation; 'tis that cursed place," says my mother, "that half peoples this colony."

Here she went on with her own story, so long and in so particular a manner that I began to be very uneasy; but coming to one particular that required telling her name, I thought I should have sunk down in the place. She perceived I was out of order and asked me if I was not well and what ailed me. I told her I was so affected with the melancholy story she had told that it had overcome me, and I begged of her to talk no more of it. "Why, my dear," says she very kindly, "what need these things trouble you? These passages were long before your time, and they give me no trouble at all now; nay, I look back on them with a particular satisfaction, as they have been a means to bring me to this place." Then she went on to tell me how she fell into a good family, where, behaving herself well and her mistress dying, her master married her, by whom she had my husband and his sister, and that by her diligence and good management after her husband's death, she had improved the plantations to such a degree as they then were, so that most of the estate was of her getting, not of her husband's, for she had been a widow upwards of sixteen years.

I heard this part of the story with very little attention because I wanted much to retire and give vent to my passions; and let any one judge what must be the anguish of my mind when I came to reflect that this was certainly no more or less than my own mother, and that I had now had two children, and was big with another, by my own brother, and lay with him still every night.

I was now the most unhappy of all women in the world. Oh! had the story never been told me, all had been well; it had been no crime to have lain with my husband if I had known nothing of it.

I had now such a load on my mind that it kept me perpetually waking; to reveal it I could not find would be to any purpose, and yet to conceal it would be next to impossible; nay, I did not doubt but I should talk in my sleep and tell my husband of it whether I would or no. If I discovered it, the least thing I could expect was to lose my husband, for he was too nice and too honest a man to have continued my husband after he had known I had been his sister; so that I was perplexed to the last degree.

I leave it to any man to judge what difficulties presented to my view. I was away from my native country, at a distance prodigious, and the return to me unpassable. I lived very well, but in a circumstance unsufferable in itself. If I had discovered myself to my mother, it might be difficult to convince her of the particulars, and I had no way to prove them. On the other hand, if she had questioned or doubted me, I had been undone, for the bare suggestion would have immediately separated me from my husband without gaining my mother or him; so that between the surprise on one hand and the uncertainty on the other, I had been sure to be undone.

In the meantime, as I was but too sure of the fact, I lived therefore in open avowed incest and whoredom, and all under the appearance of an honest wife; and though I was not much touched with the crime of it, yet the action had something in it shocking to nature and made my husband even nauseous to me. However, upon the most sedate consideration, I resolved that it was absolutely necessary to conceal it all and not make the least discovery of it either to mother or husband; and thus I lived with the greatest pressure imaginable for three years more.

During this time my mother used to be frequently telling me old stories of her former adventures, which, however, were no ways pleasant to me; for by it, though she did not tell it me in plain terms, yet I could understand, joined with what I heard myself of my first tutors, that in her younger days she had been whore and thief; but I verily believe she had lived to repent sincerely of both and that she was then a very pious, sober, and religious woman.

Well, let her life have been what it would then, it was certain that my life was very uneasy to me; for I lived, as I have said, but in the worst sort of whoredom, and as I could expect no good of it, so really no good issue came of it, and all my seeming prosperity wore off and ended in misery and destruction. It was some time, indeed, before it came to this, for everything went wrong with us afterwards, and that which was worse, my husband grew strangely altered, froward, jealous, and unkind, and I was as impatient of bearing his carriage as the carriage was unreasonable and unjust. These things proceeded so far, and we came at last to be in such ill terms with one another, that I claimed a promise of him, which he entered willingly into with me when I consented to come from England with him, *viz.,* that if I did not like to live there, I should come away to England again when I pleased, giving him a year's warning to settle his affairs.

I say, I now claimed this promise of him, and I must confess I did it not in the most obliging terms that could be, neither; but I insisted that he treated me ill, that I was remote from my friends and could do myself no justice, and that he was jealous without cause, my conversation having been unblameable, and he having no pretence for it, and that to remove to England would take away all occasion from him.

I insisted so peremptorily upon it that he could not avoid coming to a point, either to keep his word with me or to break it; and this, notwithstanding he used all the skill he was master of, and employed his mother and other agents to prevail with me to alter my resolutions; indeed, the bottom of the thing lay at my heart, and that made all his endeavours fruitless, for my heart was alienated from him. I loathed the thoughts of bedding with him and used a thousand pretences of illness and humour to prevent his touching me, fearing nothing more than to be with child again, which, to be sure, would have prevented or at least delayed my going over to England.

However, at last I put him so out of humour that he took up a rash and fatal resolution that, in short, I should not go to England; that though he had promised me, yet it was an unreasonable thing; that it would be ruinous to his affairs, would unhinge his whole family, and be next to an undoing him in the world; that therefore I ought not to desire it of him, and that no wife in the world that valued her family and her husband's prosperity would insist upon such a thing.

This plunged me again, for when I considered the thing calmly and took my husband as he really was, a diligent, careful man in the main, and that he knew nothing of the dreadful circumstances that he was in, I could not but confess to myself that my proposal was very unreasonable and what no wife that had the good of her family at heart would have desired.

But my discontents were of another nature; I looked upon him no longer as a husband, but as a near relation, the son of my own mother, and I resolved somehow or other to be clear of him, but which way I did not know.

It is said by the ill-natured world, of our sex, that if we are set on a thing, it is impossible to turn us from our resolutions; in short, I never ceased poring upon the means to bring to pass my voyage, and came that length with my husband at last as to propose going without him. This provoked him to the last degree, and he called me not only an unkind wife but an unnatural mother, and asked me how I could entertain such a thought without horror, as that of leaving my two children (for one was dead) without a mother and never to see them more. It was true, had things been right, I should not have done it, but now it was my real desire never to see them, or him either, any more; and as to the charge of unnatural, I could easily answer it to myself, while I knew that the whole relation was unnatural in the highest degree.

However, there was no bringing my husband to anything; he would neither go with me or let me go without him, and it was out of my power to stir without his consent, as any one that is acquainted with the constitution of that country knows very well.

We had many family quarrels about it, and they began to grow up to a dangerous height; for as I was quite estranged from him in affection, so I took no heed to my words, but sometimes gave him language that was provoking; in short, I strove all I could to bring him to a parting with me, which was what above all things I desired most.

He took my carriage very ill, and indeed he might well do so, for at last I refused to bed with him, and carrying on the breach upon all occasions to extremity, he told me once he thought I was mad, and if I did not alter my conduct, he would put me under cure; that is to say, into a madhouse. I told him he should find I was far enough from mad, and that it was not in his power or any other villain's to murder me. I confess at the same time I was heartily frighted at his thoughts of putting me into a madhouse, which would at once have destroyed all the possibility of bringing the truth out; for that then no one would have given credit to a word of it.

This therefore brought me to a resolution, whatever came of it, to lay open my whole case; but which way to do it, or to whom, was an inextricable difficulty, when another quarrel with my husband happened, which came up to such an extreme as almost pushed me on to tell it him all to his face; but though I kept it in so as not to come to the particulars, I spoke so much as put him into the utmost confusion, and in the end brought out the whole story.

He began with a calm expostulation upon my being so resolute to go to England; I defended it, and one hard word bringing on another, as is usual in all family strife, he told me I did not treat him as if he was my husband or talk of my chlidren as if I was a mother; and in short, that I did not deserve to be used as a wife; that he had used all the fair means possible with me; that he had argued with all the kindness and calmness that a husband or a Christian ought to do, and that I made him such a vile return, that I treated him rather like a dog than a man and rather like the most contemptible stranger than a husband; that he was very loath to use violence with me, but that, in short, he saw a necessity of it now, and that for the future he should be obliged to take such measures as should reduce me to my duty.

My blood was now fired to the utmost, and nothing could appear more provoked. I told him, for his fair means and his foul, they were equally contemned by me; that for my going to England, I was resolved on it, come what would; and that as to treating him not like a husband and not showing myself a mother to my children, there might be something more in it than he understood at present; but I thought fit to tell him thus much: that he neither was my lawful husband nor they lawful children, and that I had reason to regard neither of them more than I did.

I confess I was moved to pity him when I spoke it, for he turned pale as death and stood mute as one thunderstruck, and once or twice I thought he would have fainted; in short, it put him in a fit something like an apoplex; he trembled, a sweat or dew ran off his face, and yet he was cold as a clod, so that I was forced to fetch something to keep life in him. When he recovered of that, he grew sick and vomited, and in a little after was put to bed, and the next morning was in a violent fever.

However, it went off again and he recovered, though but slowly, and when he came to be a little better, he told me I had given him a mortal wound with my tongue and he had only one thing to ask before he desired an explanation. I interrupted him and told him I was sorry I had gone so far, since I saw what disorder it put him into, but I desired him not to talk to me of explanations, for that would but make things worse.

This heightened his impatience and, indeed, perplexed him beyond all bearing; for now he began to suspect that there was some mystery yet unfolded, but could not make the least guess at it; all that run in his brain was that I had another husband alive, but I assured him there was not the least of that in it; indeed, as to my other husband, he was effectually dead to me and had told me I should look on him as such, so I had not the least uneasiness on that score.

But now I found the thing too far gone to conceal it much longer, and my husband himself gave me an opportunity to ease myself of the secret, much to my satisfaction. He had laboured with me three or four weeks, but to no purpose, only to tell him whether I had spoken those words only to put him in a passion or whether there was anything of truth in the bottom of them. But I continued inflexible, and would explain nothing unless he would first consent to my going to England, which he would never do, he said, while he lived; on the other hand, I said it was in my power to make him willing when I pleased—nay, to make him entreat me to go; and this increased his curiosity and made him importunate to the highest degree.

At length he tells all this story to his mother and sets her upon me to get it out of me, and she used her utmost skill indeed; but I put her to a full stop at once by telling her that the mystery of the whole matter lay in herself; that it was my respect to her had made me conceal it; and that, in short, I could go no farther, and therefore conjured her not to insist upon it.

She was struck dumb at this suggestion and could not tell what to say or to think, but, laying aside the supposition as a policy of mine, continued her importunity on account of her son and, if possible, to make up the breach between us two. As to that, I told her that it was indeed a good design in her, but that it was impossible to be done; and that if I should reveal to her the truth of what she desired, she would grant it to be impossible and cease to desire it. At last I seemed to be prevailed on by her importunity, and told her I dare trust her with a secret of the greatest importance, and she would soon see that this was so, and that I would consent to lodge it in her breast if she would engage solemnly not to acquaint her son with it without my consent.

She was long in promising this part, but rather than not come at the main secret she agreed to that too, and after a great many other preliminaries, I began and told her the whole story. First I told her how much she was concerned in all the unhappy breach which had happened between her son and me by telling me her own story and her London name; and that the surprise she see I was in was upon that occasion. Then I told her my own story and my name, and assured her by such other tokens as she could not deny that I was no other, nor more or less, than her own child, her daughter, born of her body in Newgate; the same that had saved her from the gallows by being in her belly and that she left in such-and-such hands when she was transported.

It is impossible to express the astonishment she was in; she was not inclined to believe the story or to remember the particulars; for she immediately foresaw the confusion that must follow in the family upon it; but everything concurred so exactly with the stories she had told me of herself, and which if she had not told me she would perhaps have been content to have denied, that she had stopped her own mouth, and she had nothing to do but take me about the neck and kiss me and cry most vehemently over me, without speaking one word for a long time together. At last she broke out: "Unhappy child!" says she. "What miserable chance could bring thee hither? And in the arms of my son, too! Dreadful girl!" says she. "Why, we are all undone! Married to thy own brother! Three children, and two alive, all of the same flesh and blood! My son and my daughter lying together as husband and wife! All confusion and distraction! Miserable family! What will become of us? What is to be said? What is to be done?" And thus she run on a great while; nor had I any power to speak, or if I had, did I know what to say, for every word wounded me to the soul. With this kind of amazement we parted for the first time, though my mother was more surprised than I was because it was more news to her than to me. However, she promised again that she would say nothing of it to her son till we had talked of it again.

It was not long, you may be sure, before we had a second conference upon the same subject; when, as if she had been willing to forget the story she had told me of herself, or to suppose that I had forgot some of the particulars, she began to tell them with alterations and omissions; but I refreshed her memory in many things which

I supposed she had forgot, and then came in so opportunely with the whole history that it was impossible for her to go from it; and then she fell into her rhapsodies again and exclamations at the severity of her misfortunes. When these things were a little over with her, we fell into a close debate about what should be first done before we gave an account of the matter to my husband. But to what purpose could be all our consultations? We could neither of us see our way through it or how it could be safe to open such a scene to him. It was impossible to make any judgement, or give any guess at what temper he would receive it in, or what measures he would take upon it; and if he should have so little government of himself as to make it public, we easily foresaw that it would be the ruin of the whole family; and if at last he should take the advantage the law would give him, he might put me away with disdain, and leave me to sue for the little portion that I had, and perhaps waste it all in the suit, and then be a beggar; and thus I should see him, perhaps, in the arms of another wife in a few months, and be myself the most miserable creature alive.

My mother was as sensible of this as I; and upon the whole, we knew not what to do. After some time we came to more sober resolutions, but then it was with this misfortune too, that my mother's opinion and mine were quite different from one another, and indeed inconsistent with one another; for my mother's opinion was that I should bury the whole thing entirely and continue to live with him as my husband till some other event should make the discovery of it more convenient; and that in the meantime she would endeavour to reconcile us together again and restore our mutual comfort and family peace; that we might lie as we used to do together, and so let the whole matter remain a secret as close as death; "for, child," says she, "we are both undone if it comes out."

To encourage me to this, she promised to make me easy in my circumstances and to leave me what she could at her death, secured for me separately from my husband; so that if it should come out afterwards, I should be able to stand on my own feet and procure justice too from him.

This proposal did not agree with my judgement, though it was very fair and kind in my mother; but my thoughts run quite another way.

As to keeping the thing in our own breasts and letting it all remain as it was, I told her it was impossible; and I asked her how she could think I could bear the thoughts of lying with my own brother. In the next place I told her that her being alive was the only support of the discovery, and that while she owned me for her child and saw reason to be satisfied that I was so, nobody else would doubt it; but that if she should die before the discovery, I should be taken for an impudent creature that had forged such a thing to go away from my husband, or should be counted crazed and distracted. Then I told her how he had threatened already to put me into a madhouse, and what concern I had been in about it, and how that was the thing that drove me to the necessity of discovering it to her as I had done.

From all which I told her that I had, on the most serious reflections I was able to make in the case, come to this resolution, which I hoped she would like, as a medium between both, *viz.*, that she should use her endeavours with her son to give me leave to go for England, as I had desired, and to furnish me with a sufficient sum of money, either in goods along with me or in bills for my support there, all along suggesting that he might one time or other think it proper to come over to me.

That when I was gone, she should then in cold blood discover the case to him gradually and as her own discretion should guide; so that he might not be surprised with it and fly out into any passions and excesses; and that she should concern herself to prevent his slighting the children or marrying again unless he had a certain account of my being dead.

This was my scheme, and my reasons were good; I was really alienated from him in the consequence of these things; indeed I mortally hated him as a husband, and it was impossible to remove that riveted aversion I had to him; at the same time, it being an unlawful, incestuous living added to that aversion, and everything added to make cohabiting with him the most nauseous thing to me in the world; and I think verily it was come to such a height that I could almost as willingly have embraced a dog as have let him offer anything of that kind to me, for which reason I could not bear the thoughts of coming between the sheets with him. I cannot say that I was right in carrying it such a length while at the same time I did not resolve to discover the thing to him; but I am giving an account of what was, not of what ought or ought not to be.

In this directly opposite opinion to one another my mother and I continued a long time, and it was impossible to reconcile our judgements; many disputes we had about it, but we could never either of us yield our own or bring over the other.

I insisted on my aversion to lying with my own brother, and she insisted upon its being impossible to bring him to consent to my going to England; and in this uncertainty we continued, not differing so as to quarrel or anything like it, but so as not to be able to resolve what we should do to make up that terrible breach.

At last I resolved on a desperate course and told my mother my resolution, *viz.*, that, in short, I would tell him of it myself. My mother was frighted to the last degree at the very thoughts of it; but I bid her be easy, told her I would do it gradually and softly, and with all the art and good humour I was mistress of, and time it also as well as I could, taking him in good humour too. I told her I did not question but if I could be hypocrite enough to feign more affection to him than I really had, I should succeed in all my design, and we might part by consent and with a good agreement, for I might love him well enough for a brother though I could not for a husband.

All this while he lay at my mother to find out, if possible, what was the meaning of that dreadful expression of mine, as he called it, which I mentioned before; namely, that I was not his lawful wife nor my children his legal children. My mother put him off, told him she could bring me to no explanations, but found there was something that disturbed me very much, and she hoped she should get it out of me in time, and in the meantime recommended to him earnestly to use me more tenderly and win me with his usual good carriage; told him of his terrifying and affrighting me with his threats of sending me to a madhouse and the like, and advised him not to make a woman desperate on any account whatever.

He promised her to soften his behaviour, and bid her assure me that he loved me as well as ever, and that he had no such design as that of sending me to a madhouse whatever he might say in his passion; also he desired my mother to use the same persuasions to me too, and we might live together as we used to do.

I found the effects of this treaty presently. My husband's conduct was immediately altered, and he was quite another man to me; nothing could be kinder and more obliging than he was to me upon all occasions; and I could do no less than make some return to it, which I did as well as I could, but it was but in an awkward manner at best, for nothing was more frightful to me than his caresses, and the apprehensions of being with child again by him was ready to throw me into fits; and this made me see that there was an absolute necessity of breaking the case to him without any more delay, which, however, I did with all the caution and reserve imaginable.

He had continued his altered carriage to me near a month and we began to live a new kind of life with one another, and could I have satisfied myself to have gone on with it, I believe it might have continued as long as we had continued alive together. One evening, as we were sitting and talking together under a little awning, which served as an arbour at the entrance into the garden, he was in a very pleasant, agreeable humour and said abundance of kind things to me relating to the pleasure of our present good agreement and the disorders of our past breach, and what a satisfaction it was to him that we had room to hope we should never have any more of it.

I fetched a deep sigh and told him there was nobody in the world could be more delighted than I was in the good agreement we had always kept up or more afflicted with the breach of it; but I was sorry to tell him that there was an unhappy circumstance in our case, which lay too close to my heart and which I knew not how to break to him, that rendered my part of it very miserable and took from me all the comfort of the rest.

He importuned me to tell him what it was. I told him I could not tell how to do it; that while it was concealed from him, I alone was unhappy, but if he knew it also, we should be both so; and that, therefore, to keep him in the dark about it was the kindest thing that I could do, and it was on that account alone that I kept a secret from him, the very keeping of which, I thought, would first or last be my destruction.

It is impossible to express his surprise at this relation and the double importunity which he used with me to discover it to him. He told me I could not be called kind to him, nay, I could not be faithful to him, if I concealed it from him. I told him I thought so too, and yet I could not do it. He went back to what I had said before to him and told me he hoped it did not relate to what I said in my passion, and that he had resolved to forget all that as the effect of a rash, provoked spirit. I told him I wished I could forget it all too, but that it was not to be done, the impression was too deep, and it was impossible.

He then told me he was resolved not to differ with me in anything, and that therefore he would importune me no more about it, resolving to acquiesce in whatever I did or said; only begged I would then agree that whatever it was, it should no more interrupt our quiet and our mutual kindness.

This was the most provoking thing he could have said to me, for I really wanted his farther importunities, that I might be prevailed with to bring out that which indeed was like death to me to conceal. So I answered him plainly that I could not say I was glad not to be importuned though I could not tell how to comply. "But come, my dear," said I, "what conditions will you make with me upon the opening this affair to you?"

"Any conditions in the world," said he, "that you can in reason desire of me." "Well," said I, "come, give it me under your hand that if you do not find I am in any fault or that I am willingly concerned in the causes of the misfortunes that is to follow, you will not blame me, use me the worse, do me any injury, or make me be the sufferer for that which is not my fault."

"That," says he, "is the most reasonable demand in the world; not to blame you for that which is not your fault. Give me a pen and ink," says he; so I ran in and fetched pen, ink, and paper, and he wrote the condition down in the very words I had proposed it and signed it with his name. "Well," says he, "what is next, my dear?" "Why," says I, "the next is that you will not blame me for not discovering the secret to you before I knew it."

"Very just again," says he; "with all my heart"; so he wrote down that also and signed it.

"Well, my dear," says I, "then I have but one condition more to make with you, and that is that as there is nobody concerned in it but you and I, you shall not discover it to any person in the world except your own mother; and that in all the measures you shall take upon the discovery, as I am equally concerned in it with you, though as innocent as yourself, you shall do nothing in a passion, nothing to my prejudice or to your mother's prejudice, without my knowledge and consent."

This a little amazed him, and he wrote down the words distinctly, but read them over and over before he signed them, hesitating at them several times and repeating them: "My mother's prejudice! And your prejudice! What mysterious thing can this be?" However, at last he signed it.

"Well," says I, "my dear, I'll ask you no more under your hand; but as you are to hear the most unexpected and surprising thing that perhaps ever befell any family in the world, I beg you to promise me you will receive it with composure and a presence of mind suitable to a man of sense."

"I'll do my utmost," says he, "upon condition you will keep me no longer in suspense, for you terrify me with all these preliminaries."

"Well, then," says I, "it is this: As I told you before in a heat that I was not your lawful wife and that our children were not legal children, so I must let you know now in calmness and in kindness, but with affliction enough, that I am your own sister and you my own brother, and that we are both the children of our mother now alive and in the house, who is convinced of the truth of it in a manner not to be denied or contradicted."

I saw him turn pale and look wild; and I said, "Now remember your promise and receive it with presence of mind; for who could have said more to prepare you for it than I have done?" However, I called a servant and got him a little glass of rum (which is the usual dram of the country), for he was fainting away.

When he was a little recovered I said to him, "This story, you may be sure, requires a long explanation, and therefore have patience and compose your mind to hear it out, and I'll make it as short as I can"; and with this I told him what I thought was needful of the fact, and particularly how my mother came to discover it to me, as above. "And now, my dear," says I, "you will see reason for my capitulations, and that I neither have been the cause of this matter nor could be so, and that I could know nothing of it before now."

"I am fully satisfied of that," says he, "but 'tis a dreadful surprise to me; however, I know a remedy for it all, and a remedy that shall put an end to all your difficulties without your going to England." "That would be strange," said I, "as all the rest." "No, no," says he, "I'll make it easy; there's nobody in the way of it all but myself." He looked a little disordered when he said this, but I did not apprehend anything from it at that time, believing, as it used to be said, that they who do those things never talk of them or that they who talk of such things never do them.

But things were not come to their height with him, and I observed he became pensive and melancholy and, in a word, as I thought, a little distempered in his head. I endeavoured to talk him into temper and into a kind of scheme for our government in the affair, and sometimes he would be well and talk with some courage about it; but the weight of it lay too heavy upon his thoughts, and went so far that he made two attempts upon himself, and in one of them had actually strangled himself, and had not his mother come into the room in the very moment, he had died; but with the help of a Negro servant she cut him down and recovered him.

Things were now come to a lamentable height. My pity for him now began to revive that affection which at first I really had for him, and I endeavoured sincerely, by all the kind carriage I could, to make up the breach; but, in short, it had gotten too great a head, it preyed upon his spirits, and it threw him into a lingering consumption, though it happened not to be mortal. In this distress I did not know what to do, as his life was apparently declining, and I might perhaps have married again there very much to my advantage had it been my business to have stayed in the country; but my mind was restless too; I hankered after coming to England, and nothing would satisfy me without it.

In short, by an unwearied importunity, my husband, who was apparently decaying, as I observed, was at last prevailed with; and so my fate pushing me on, the way was made clear for me, and my mother concurring, I obtained a very good cargo for my coming to England.

When I parted with my brother (for such I am now to call him), we agreed that after I arrived, he should pretend to have an account that I was dead in England, and so might marry again when he would. He promised, and engaged to me to correspond with me as a sister, and to assist and support me as long as I lived; and that if he died before me, he would leave sufficient to his mother to take care of me still, in the name of a sister, and he was in some respects just to this; but it was so oddly managed that I felt the disappointments very sensibly afterwards, as you shall hear in its time.

I came away in the month of August, after I had been eight years in that country; and now a new scene of misfortunes attended me, which perhaps few women have gone through the like.

We had an indifferent good voyage till we came just upon the coast of England, and where we arrived in two-and-thirty days, but were then ruffled with two or three storms, one of which drove us away to the coast of Ireland, and we put in at Kinsale. We remained there about thirteen days, got some refreshment on shore, and put to sea again, though we met with very bad weather again in which the ship sprung her mainmast, as they called it. But we got at last into Milford Haven, in Wales, where, though it was remote from our port, yet having my foot safe upon the firm ground of the isle of Britain, I resolved to venture it no more upon the waters, which had been so terrible to me; so getting my clothes and money on shore, with my bills of loading and other papers, I resolved to come for London and leave the ship to get to her port as she could; the port whither she was bound was to Bristol, where my brother's chief correspondent lived.

I got to London in about three weeks, where I heard a little while after that the ship was arrived at Bristol, but at the same time had the misfortune to know that by the violent weather she had been in and the breaking of her mainmast, she had great damage on board and that a great part of her cargo was spoiled.

I had now a new scene of life upon my hands, and a dreadful appearance it had. I was come away with a kind of final farewell. What I brought with me was indeed considerable, had it come safe, and by the help of it I might have married again tolerably well; but as it was, I was reduced to between two or three hundred pounds in the whole, and this without any hope of recruit. I was entirely without friends, nay, even so much as without acquaintances, for I found it was absolutely necessary not to revive former acquaintance; and as for my subtle friend that set me up formerly for a fortune, she was dead and her husband also.

The looking after my cargo of goods soon after obliged me to take a journey to Bristol, and during my attendance upon that affair I took the diversion of going to the Bath, for as I was still far from being old, so my humour, which was always gay, continued so to an extreme; and being now, as it were, a woman of fortune, though I was a woman without a fortune, I expected something or other might happen in the way that might mend my circumstances, as had been my case before.

The Bath is a place of gallantry enough; expensive and full of snares. I went thither, indeed, in the view of taking what might offer; but I must do myself justice as to protest I meant nothing but in an honest way nor had any thoughts about me at first that looked the way which afterwards I suffered them to be guided.

Here I stayed the whole latter season, as it is called there, and contracted some unhappy acquaintance, which rather prompted the follies I fell afterwards into than fortified me against them. I lived pleasantly enough, kept good company, that is to say, gay, fine company; but had the discouragement to find this way of living sunk me exceedingly, and that as I had no settled income, so spending upon the main stock was but a certain kind of bleeding to death; and this gave me many sad reflections. However, I shook them off and still flattered myself that something or other might offer for my advantage.

But I was in the wrong place for it. I was not now at Redriff, where, if I had set myself tolerably up, some honest sea-captain or other might have talked with me upon the honourable terms of matrimony; but I was at the Bath, where men find a mistress sometimes, but very rarely look for a wife; and consequently all the particular acquaintances a woman can expect there must have some tendency that way.

I had spent the first season well enough; for though I had contracted some acquaintance with a gentleman who came to the Bath for his diversion, yet I had entered into no felonious treaty. I had resisted some casual offers of gallantry and had managed that way well enough. I was not wicked enough to come into the crime for the mere vice of it, and I had no extraordinary offers that tempted me with the main thing which I wanted.

However, I went this length the first season, *viz.*, I contracted an acquaintance with a woman in whose house I lodged, who, though she did not keep an ill house, yet had none of the best principles in herself. I had on all occasions behaved myself so well as not to get the least slur upon my reputation, and all the men that I had conversed with were of so good reputation that I had not gotten the least reflection by conversing with them; nor did any of them seem to think there was room for a wicked correspondence if they had offered it; yet there was one gentleman, as above, who always singled me out for the diversion of my company, as he called it, which, as he was pleased to say, was very agreeable to him, but at that time there was no more in it.

I had many melancholy hours at the Bath after all the company was gone; for though I went to Bristol sometimes for the disposing my effects and for recruits of money, yet I chose to come back to the Bath for my residence because, being on good terms with the woman in whose house I lodged in the summer, I found that during the winter I lived rather cheaper there than I could do anywhere else. Here, I say, I passed the winter as heavily as I had passed the autumn cheerfully; but having contracted a nearer intimacy with the said woman in whose house I lodged, I could not avoid communicating something of what lay hardest upon my mind, and particularly the narrowness of my circumstances. I told her also that I had a mother and a brother in Virginia in good circumstances; and as I had really written back to my mother in particular to represent my condition and the great loss I had received, so I did not fail to let my new friend know that I expected a supply from thence, and so indeed I did; and as the ships went from Bristol to York River, in Virginia, and back again generally in less time than from London, and that my brother corresponded chiefly at Bristol, I thought it was much better for me to wait here for my returns than to go to London.

My new friend appeared sensibly affected with my condition, and indeed was so very kind as to reduce the rate of my living with her to so low a price during the winter that she convinced me she got nothing by me; and as for lodging, during the winter I paid nothing at all.

When the spring season came on, she continued to be as kind to me as she could, and I lodged with her for a time till it was found necessary to do otherwise. She had some persons of character that frequently lodged in her house, and in particular the gentleman who, as I said, singled me out for his companion in the winter before; and he came down again with another gentleman in his company and two servants and lodged in the same house. I suspected that my landlady had invited him thither, letting him know that I was still with her; but she denied it.

In a word, this gentleman came down and continued to single me out for his peculiar confidence. He was a complete gentleman—that must be confessed—and his company was agreeable to me as mine, if I might believe him, was to him. He made no professions to me but of an extraordinary respect, and he had such an opinion of my virtue that, as he often professed, he believed if he should offer anything else, I should reject him with contempt. He soon understood from me that I was a widow; that I had arrived at Bristol from Virginia by the last ships; and that I waited at the Bath till the next Virginia fleet should arrive, by which I expected considerable effects. I understood by him that he had a wife, but that the lady was distempered in her head and was under the conduct of her own relations, which he consented to, to avoid any reflection that might be cast upon him for mismanaging her cure; and in the meantime he came to the Bath to divert his thoughts under such a melancholy circumstance.

My landlady, who of her own accord encouraged the

correspondence on all occasions, gave me an advantageous character of him, as a man of honour and of virtue, as well as of a great estate. And indeed I had reason to say so of him too; for though we lodged both on a floor, and he had frequently come into my chamber even when I was in bed, and I also into his, yet he never offered anything to me farther than a kiss or so much as solicited me to anything till long after, as you shall hear.

I frequently took notice to my landlady of his exceeding modesty, and she again used to tell me she believed it was so from the beginning; however, she used to tell me that she thought I ought to expect some gratifications from him for my company, for indeed he did, as it were, engross me. I told her I had not given him the least occasion to think I wanted it or that I would accept of it from him. She told me she would take that part upon her, and she managed it so dexterously that the first time we were together alone, after she had talked with him, he began to inquire a little into my circumstances, as how I had subsisted myself since I came on shore and whether I did not want money. I stood off very boldly. I told him that though my cargo of tobacco was damaged, yet that it was not quite lost; that the merchant that I had been consigned to had so honestly managed for me that I had not wanted, and that I hoped with frugal management I should make it hold out till more would come, which I expected by the next fleet; that in the meantime I had retrenched my expenses, and whereas I kept a maid last season, now I lived without; and whereas I had a chamber and a dining-room then on the first floor, I now had but one room two pair of stairs, and the like; "but I live," said I, "as well satisfied now as then"; adding that his company had made me live much more cheerfully than otherwise I should have done, for which I was much obliged to him; and so I put off all room for any offer at the present. It was not long before he attacked me again and told me he found that I was backward to trust him with the secret of my circumstances, which he was sorry for; assuring me that he inquired into it with no design to satisfy his own curiosity, but merely to assist me if there was any occasion; but since I would not own myself to stand in need of any assistance, he had but one thing more to desire of me, and that was that I would promise him that when I was any way straitened, I would frankly tell him of it, and that I would make use of him with the same freedom that he made the offer; adding that I should always find I had a true friend though perhaps I was afraid to trust him.

I omitted nothing that was fit to be said by one infinitely obliged, to let him know that I had a due sense of his kindness; and indeed from that time I did not appear so much reserved to him as I had done before, though still within the bounds of the strictest virtue on both sides; but how free soever our conversation was, I could not arrive to that freedom which he desired, *viz.*, to tell him I wanted money, though I was secretly very glad of his offer.

Some weeks passed after this, and still I never asked him for money, when my landlady, a cunning creature, who had often pressed me to it but found that I could not do it, makes a story of her own inventing and comes in bluntly to me when we were together. "Oh, widow!" says she, "I have bad news to tell you this morning." "What is that?" said I. "Is the Virginia ships taken by the French?"—for that was my fear. "No, no," says she, "but the man you sent to Bristol yesterday for money is come back and says he has brought none."

I could by no means like her project; I thought it looked too much like prompting him, which he did not want, and I saw that I should lose nothing by being backward, so took her up short. "I can't imagine why he should say so," said I, "for I assure you he brought me all the money I sent him for, and here it is," said I (pulling out my purse, with about twelve guineas in it); and added, "I intend you shall have most of it by and by."

He seemed distasted a little at her talking as she did, as well as I, taking it, as I fancied he would, as something forward of her; but when he saw me give such an answer, he came immediately to himself. The next morning we talked of it again, when I found he was fully satisfied and, smiling, said he hoped I would not want money and not tell him of it, and that I had promised him otherwise. I told him I had been very much dissatisfied at my landlady's talking so publicly the day before of what she had nothing to do with; but I supposed she wanted what I owed her, which was about eight guineas, which I had resolved to give her and had given it her the same night.

He was in a mighty good humour when he heard me say I had paid her, and it went off into some other discourse at that time. But the next morning, he having heard me up before him, he called to me and I answered. He asked me to come into his chamber; he was in bed when I came in, and he made me come and sit down on his bedside, for he said he had something to say to me. After some very kind expressions, he asked me if I would be very honest to him and give a sincere answer to one thing he would desire of me. After some little cavil with him at the word "sincere," and asking him if I had ever given him any answers which were not sincere, I promised him I would. Why, then, his request was, he said, to let him see my purse. I immediately put my hand into my pocket and, laughing at him, pulled it out, and there was in it three guineas and a half. Then he asked me if there was all the money I had. I told him no, laughing again, not by a great deal.

Well, then, he said, he would have me promise to go and fetch him all the money I had, every farthing. I told him I would, and I went into my chamber and fetched him a little private drawer, where I had about six guineas more and some silver, and threw it all down upon the bed and told him there was all my wealth, honestly to a shilling. He looked a little at it, but did not tell it, and huddled it all into the drawer again, and then, reaching his pocket, pulled out a key and bade me open a little walnut-tree box he had upon the table, and bring him such a drawer, which I did. In this drawer there was a great deal of money in gold, I believe near two hundred guineas, but I knew not how much. He took the drawer and, taking me by the hand, made me put it in and take a whole handful; I was backward at that, but he held my hand hard in his hand and put it into the drawer and made me take out as many guineas almost as I could well take up at once.

When I had done so, he made me put them into my lap, and took my little drawer and poured out all my own money among his, and bade me get me gone and carry it all into my own chamber.

I relate this story the more particularly because of the

good humour of it, and to show the temper with which we conversed. It was not long after this but he began every day to find fault with my clothes, with my laces, and head-dresses, and in a word pressed me to buy better, which, by the way, I was willing enough to do though I did not seem to be so. I loved nothing in the world better than fine clothes; but I told him I must housewife the money he had lent me or else I should not be able to pay him again. He then told me in a few words that as he had a sincere respect for me and knew my circumstances, he had not lent me that money, but given it me, and that he thought I had merited it from him by giving him my company so entirely as I had done. After this he made me take a maid and keep house, and his friend being gone, he obliged me to diet him, which I did very willingly, believing, as it appeared, that I should lose nothing by it, nor did the woman of the house fail to find her account in it too.

We had lived thus near three months when, the company beginning to wear away at the Bath, he talked of going away, and fain he would have me to go to London with him. I was not very easy in that proposal, not knowing what posture I was to live in there or how he might use me. But while this was in debate he fell very sick; he had gone out to a place in Somersetshire, called Shepton, and was there taken very ill, and so ill that he could not travel; so he sent his man back to the Bath to beg me that I would hire a coach and come over to him. Before he went, he had left his money and other things of value with me, and what to do with them I did not know, but I secured them as well as I could and locked up the lodgings and went to him, where I found him very ill indeed, so I persuaded him to be carried in a litter to Bath, where was more help and better advice to be had.

He consented, and I brought him to the Bath, which was about fifteen miles, as I remember. Here he continued very ill of a fever and kept his bed five weeks, all which time I nursed him and tended him as carefully as if I had been his wife; indeed, if I had been his wife I could not have done more. I sat up with him so much and so often that at last, indeed, he would not let me sit up any longer, and then I got a pallet-bed into his room and lay in it just at his bed's feet.

I was indeed sensibly affected with his condition, and with the apprehensions of losing such a friend as he was and was like to be to me, and I used to sit and cry by him many hours together. At last he grew better and gave hopes that he would recover, as indeed he did, though very slowly.

Were it otherwise than what I am going to say, I should not be backward to disclose it, as it is apparent I have done in other cases; but I affirm, through all this conversation, abating the coming into the chamber when I or he was in bed, and the necessary offices of attending him night and day when he was sick, there had not passed the least immodest word or action between us. Oh, that it had been so to the last!

After some time he gathered strength and grew well apace, and I would have removed my pallet-bed, but he would not let me till he was able to venture himself without anybody to sit up with him, when I removed to my own chamber.

He took many occasions to express his sense of my tenderness for him; and when he grew well he made me a present of fifty guineas for my care and, as he called it, hazarding my life to save his.

And now he made deep protestations of a sincere, inviolable affection for me, but with the utmost reserve for my virtue and his own. I told him I was fully satisfied of it. He carried it that length that he protested to me that if he was naked in bed with me, he would as sacredly preserve my virtue as he would defend it if I was assaulted by a ravisher. I believed him and told him I did so; but this did not satisfy him; he would, he said, wait for some opportunity to give me an undoubted testimony of it.

It was a great while after this that I had occasion on my business to go to Bristol, upon which he hired me a coach and would go with me; and now indeed our intimacy increased. From Bristol he carried me to Gloucester, which was merely a journey of pleasure, to take the air; and here it was our hap to have no lodgings in the inn, but in one large chamber with two beds in it. The master of the house, going with us to show his rooms and coming into that room, said very frankly to him, "Sir, it is none of my business to inquire whether the lady be your spouse or no, but if not, you may lie as honestly in these two beds as if you were in two chambers," and with that he pulls a great curtain which drew quite across the room and effectually divided the beds. "Well," says my friend very readily, "these beds will do; and as for the rest, we are too near akin to lie together though we may lodge near one another"; and this put an honest face on the thing too. When we came to go to bed, he decently went out of the room till I was in bed, and then went to bed in the other bed, but lay there talking to me a great while.

At last, repeating his usual saying, that he could lie naked in the bed with me and not offer me the least injury, he starts out of his bed. "And now, my dear," says he, "you shall see how just I will be to you, and that I can keep my word," and away he comes to my bed.

I resisted a little, but I must confess I should not have resisted him much if he had not made those promises at all; so after a little struggle I lay still and let him come to bed. When he was there he took me in his arms, and so I lay all night with him, but he had no more to do with me or offered anything to me other than embracing me, as I say, in his arms, no, not the whole night, but rose up and dressed him in the morning and left me as innocent for him as I was the day I was born.

This was a surprising thing to me, and perhaps may be so to others who know how the laws of nature work; for he was a vigorous, brisk person. Nor did he act thus on a principle of religion at all, but of mere affection; insisting on it that though I was to him the most agreeable woman in the world, yet because he loved me, he could not injure me.

I own it was a noble principle, but as it was what I never saw before, so it was perfectly amazing. We travelled the rest of the journey as we did before and came back to the Bath, where, as he had opportunity to come to me when he would, he often repeated the same moderation, and I frequently lay with him, and although all the familiarities of man and wife were common to us, yet he never once offered to go any farther, and he valued himself much upon it. I do not say that I was so wholly pleased with it as he thought I was, for I own I was much wickeder than he.

We lived thus near two years, only with this exception:

that he went three times to London in that time, and once he continued there four months; but, to do him justice, he always supplied me with money to subsist on very handsomely.

Had we continued thus, I confess we had had much to boast of; but, as wise men say, it is ill venturing too near the brink of a command. So we found it; and here again I must do him the justice to own that the first breach was not on his part. It was one night that we were in bed together, warm and merry, and having drank, I think, a little more both of us than usual, though not in the least to disorder us, when, after some other follies which I cannot name, and being clasped close in his arms, I told him (I repeat it with shame and horror of soul) that I could find in my heart to discharge him of his engagement for one night and no more.

He took me at my word immediately, and after that there was no resisting him; neither indeed had I any mind to resist him any more.

Thus the government of our virtue was broken, and I exchanged the place of friend for that unmusical, harsh-sounding title of whore. In the morning we were both at our penitentials; I cried very heartily, he expressed himself very sorry; but that was all either of us could do at that time, and the way being thus cleared and the bars of virtue and conscience thus removed, we had the less to struggle with.

It was but a dull kind of conversation that we had together for all the rest of that week; I looked on him with blushes and every now and then started that melancholy objection, "What if I should be with child now? What will become of me then?" He encouraged me by telling me that as long as I was true to him, he would be so to me; and since it was gone such a length (which indeed he never intended), yet if I was with child, he would take care of that and me too. This hardened us both. I assured him if I was with child, I would die for want of a midwife rather than name him as the father of it; and he assured me I should never want if I should be with child. These mutual assurances hardened us in the thing, and after this we repeated the crime as often as we pleased, till at length, as I feared, so it came to pass, and I was indeed with child.

After I was sure it was so and I had satisfied him of it too, we began to think of taking measures for the managing it, and I proposed trusting the secret to my landlady and asking her advice, which he agreed to. My landlady, a woman (as I found) used to such things, made light of it; she said she knew it would come to that at last and made us very merry about it. As I said above, we found her an experienced old lady at such work; she undertook everything, engaged to procure a midwife and a nurse, to satisfy all inquiries, and bring us off with reputation, and she did so very dexterously indeed.

When I grew near my time, she desired my gentleman to go away to London or make as if he did so. When he was gone, she acquainted the parish officers that there was a lady ready to lie in at her house, but that she knew her husband very well, and gave them, as she pretended, an account of his name, which she called Sir Walter Cleave, telling them he was a worthy gentleman, and that he would answer for all inquiries, and the like. This satisfied the parish officers presently, and I lay in, in as much credit as I could have done if I had really been my Lady Cleave, and was assisted in my travail by three or four of the best citizens' wives of Bath, which, however, made me a little the more expensive to him. I often expressed my concern to him about that part, but he bid me not be concerned at it.

As he had furnished me very sufficiently with money for the extraordinary expenses of my lying in, I had everything very handsome about me, but did not affect to be so gay or extravagant neither; besides, knowing the world as I had done, and that such kind of things do not often last long, I took care to lay up as much money as I could for a wet day, as I called it, making him believe it was all spent upon the extraordinary appearance of things in my lying in.

By this means, with what he had given me as above, I had at the end of my lying in two hundred guineas by me, including also what was left of my own.

I was brought to bed of a fine boy indeed, and a charming child it was; and when he heard of it, he wrote me a very kind, obliging letter about it and then told me he thought it would look better for me to come away for London as soon as I was up and well; that he had provided apartments for me at Hammersmith, as if I came only from London; and that after a while I should go back to the Bath and he would go with me.

I liked his offer very well and hired a coach on purpose, and taking my child and a wet-nurse to tend and suckle it, and a maidservant with me, away I went for London.

He met me at Reading in his own chariot and, taking me into that, left the servant and the child in the hired coach, and so he brought me to my new lodgings at Hammersmith, with which I had abundance of reason to be very well pleased, for they were very handsome rooms.

And now I was indeed in the height of what I might call prosperity, and I wanted nothing but to be a wife, which, however, could not be in this case, and therefore on all occasions I studied to save what I could, as I said above, against the time of scarcity, knowing well enough that such things as these do not always continue; that men that keep mistresses often change them, grow weary of them, or jealous of them, or something or other; and sometimes the ladies that are thus well used are not careful by a prudent conduct to preserve the esteem of their persons or the nice article of their fidelity, and then they are justly cast off with contempt.

But I was secured in this point, for as I had no inclination to change, so I had no manner of acquaintance, so no temptation to look any farther. I kept no company but in the family where I lodged, and with a clergyman's lady at next door; so that when he was absent I visited nobody, nor did he ever find me out of my chamber or parlour whenever he came down; if I went anywhere to take the air, it was always with him.

The living in this manner with him and his with me was certainly the most undesigned thing in the world; he often protested to me that when he became first acquainted with me, and even to the very night when we first broke in upon our rules, he never had the least design of lying with me; that he always had a sincere affection for me, but not the least real inclination to do what he had done. I assured him I never suspected him; that if I had I should not so easily have yielded to the freedoms which brought it on, but that it was all a surprise and was owing to our having yielded too far to our mutual inclinations that night; and indeed I have often observed since, and leave it as a caution to the readers of this story, that we ought to be cautious of gratifying our inclinations in loose and lewd freedoms lest we find our resolutions of virtue fail us in the juncture when their assistance should be most necessary.

It is true that from the first hour I began to converse with him I resolved to let him lie with me if he offered it; but it was because I wanted his help and knew of no other way of securing him. But when we were that night together and, as I have said, had gone such a length, I found my weakness; the inclination was not to be resisted, but I was obliged to yield up all even before he asked it.

However, he was so just to me that he never upbraided me with that; nor did he ever express the least dislike of my conduct on any other occasion, but always protested he was as much delighted with my company as he was the first hour we came together.

It is true that he had no wife, that is to say, she was no wife to him, but the reflections of conscience oftentimes snatch a man, especially a man of sense, from the arms of a mistress, as it did him at last, though on another occasion.

On the other hand, though I was not without secret reproaches of my own conscience for the life I led, and that even in the greatest height of the satisfaction I ever took, yet I had the terrible prospect of poverty and starving, which lay on me as a frightful spectre, so that there was no looking behind me; but as poverty brought me into it, so fear of poverty kept me in it, and I frequently resolved to leave it quite off if I could but come to lay up money enough to maintain me. But these were thoughts of no weight, and whenever he came to me they vanished; for his company was so delightful that there was no being melancholy when he was there; the reflections were all the subject of those hours when I was alone.

I lived six years in this happy but unhappy condition, in which time I brought him three children, but only the first of them lived; and though I removed twice in that six years, yet I came back the sixth year to my first lodgings at Hammersmith. Here it was that I was one morning surprised with a kind but melancholy letter from my gentleman, intimating that he was very ill and was afraid he should have another fit of sickness, but that his wife's relations being in the house with him, it would not be practicable to have me with him, which, however, he expressed his great dissatisfaction in, and that he wished I could be allowed to tend and nurse him as I did before.

I was very much concerned at this account and was very impatient to know how it was with him. I waited a fortnight or thereabouts and heard nothing, which surprised me, and I began to be very uneasy indeed. I think I may say that for the next fortnight I was near to distracted. It was my particular difficulty that I did not know directly where he was; for I understood at first he was in the lodgings of his wife's mother; but having removed myself to London, I soon found, by the help of the direction I had for writing my letters to him, how to inquire after him, and there I found that he was at a house in Bloomsbury, whither he had removed his whole family; and that his wife and wife's mother were in the same house, though the wife was not suffered to know that she was in the same house with her husband.

Here I also soon understood that he was at the last extremity, which made me almost at the last extremity too, to have a true account. One night I had the curiosity to disguise myself like a servant-maid, in a round cap and straw hat, and went to the door, as sent by a lady of his neighbourhood where he lived before, and giving master and mistress's service, I said I was sent to know how Mr. —— did and how he had rested that night. In delivering this message I got the opportunity I desired; for, speaking with one of the maids, I held a long gossip's tale with her and had all the particulars of his illness, which I found was a pleurisy, attended with a cough and fever. She told me also who was in the house and how his wife was, who, by her relation, they were in some hopes might recover her understanding; but as to the gentleman himself, the doctors said there was very little hopes of him, that in the morning they thought he had been dying, and that he was but little better then, for they did not expect that he could live over the next night.

This was heavy news for me, and I began now to see an end of my prosperity and to see that it was well I had played the good housewife and saved something while he was alive, for now I had no view of my own living before me.

It lay very heavy upon my mind, too, that I had a son, a fine, lovely boy, about five years old, and no provision made for it, at least that I knew of. With these considerations and a sad heart, I went home that evening and began to cast with myself how I should live and in what manner to bestow myself for the residue of my life.

You may be sure I could not rest without inquiring again very quickly what was become of him; and not venturing to go myself, I sent several sham messengers, till after a fortnight's waiting longer, I found that there was hopes of his life though he was still very ill; then I abated my sending to the house, and in some time after, I learnt in the neighbourhood that he was about house and then that he was abroad again.

I made no doubt then but that I should soon hear of him and began to comfort myself with my circumstances being, as I thought, recovered. I waited a week, and two weeks, and with much surprise near two months, and heard nothing but that, being recovered, he was gone into the country for the air after his distemper. After this it was yet two months more, and then I understood he was come to his city-house again, but still I heard nothing from him.

I had written several letters for him and directed them as usual, and found two or three of them had been called for, but not the rest. I wrote again in a more pressing manner than ever, and in one of them let him know that I must be forced to wait on him myself, representing my circumstances, the rent of lodgings to pay, and the provision for the child wanting, and my own deplorable condition, destitute of subsistence after his most solemn engagement to take care of and provide for me. I took a copy of this letter, and finding it lay at the house near a month and was not called for, I found means to have the copy of it put into his hands at a coffee-house where I found he had used to go.

This letter forced an answer from him, by which though I found I was to be abandoned, yet I found he had sent a letter to me some time before, desiring me to go down to the Bath again. Its contents I shall come to presently.

It is true that sick-beds are the times when such correspondences as this are looked on with different countenances and seen with other eyes than we saw them with before: my lover had been at the gates of death and at the very brink of eternity, and, it seems, struck with a due remorse and with sad reflections upon his past life of gallantry and levity; and among the rest, his criminal correspondence with me, which was indeed neither more or less than a long-continued life of adultery, had represented itself as it really was, not as it had been formerly thought by him to be, and he looked upon it now with a just abhorrence.

I cannot but observe also, and leave it for the direction of my sex in such cases of pleasure, that whenever sincere repentance succeeds such a crime as this, there never fails to attend a hatred of the object; and the more the affection might seem to be before, the hatred will be more in proportion. It will always be so; indeed it cannot be otherwise; for there cannot be a true and sincere abhorrence of the offence and the love to the cause of it remain; there will with an abhorrence of the sin be found a detestation of the fellow-sinner; you can expect no other.

I found it so here, though good manners and justice in this gentleman kept him from carrying it on to any extreme; but the short history of his part in this affair was thus; he perceived by my last letter and by the rest, which he went for after, that I was not gone to the Bath and that his first letter had not come to my hand, upon which he writes me this following:

Madam:

I am surprised that my letter, dated the 8th of last month, did not come to your hand; I give you my word it was delivered at your lodgings and to the hands of your maid.

I need not acquaint you with what has been my condition for some time past; and how, having been at the edge of the grave, I am, by the unexpected and undeserved mercy of Heaven, restored again. In the condition I have been in it cannot be strange to you that our unhappy correspondence has not been the least of the burthens which lay upon my conscience. I need say no more; those things that must be repented of must be also reformed.

I wish you would think of going back to the Bath. I enclose you here a bill for £50 for clearing yourself at your lodgings and carrying you down, and hope it will be no surprise to you to add that on this account only, and not for any offence given me on your side, I can *see you no more.* I will take due care of the child; leave him where he is or take him with you, as you please. I wish you the like reflections and that they may be to your advantage. I am, etc.

I was struck with this letter as with a thousand wounds; the reproaches of my own conscience were such as I cannot express, for I was not blind to my own crime; and I reflected that I might with less offence have continued with my brother, since there was no crime in our marriage on that score, neither of us knowing it.

But I never once reflected that I was all this while a married woman, a wife to Mr. ——, the linen-draper, who, though he had left me by the necessity of his circumstances, had no power to discharge me from the marriage contract which was between us or to give me a legal liberty to marry again; so that I had been no less than a whore and an adulteress all this while. I then reproached myself with the liberties I had taken, and how I had been a snare to this gentleman, and that indeed I was principal in the crime; that now he was mercifully snatched out of the gulf by a convincing work upon his mind, but that I was left as if I was abandoned by Heaven to a continuing in my wickedness.

Under these reflections I continued very pensive and sad for near a month and did not go down to the Bath, having no inclination to be with the woman who I was with before lest, as I thought, she should prompt me to some wicked course of life again, as she had done; and besides, I was loath she should know I was cast off as above.

And now I was greatly perplexed about my little boy. It was death to me to part with the child, and yet when I considered the danger of being one time or other left with him to keep without being able to support him, I then resolved to leave him; but then I concluded to be near him myself too, that I might have the satisfaction of seeing him without the care of providing for him. So I sent my gentleman a short letter that I had obeyed his orders in all things but that of going back to the Bath; that however parting from him was a wound to me that

I could never recover, yet that I was fully satisfied his reflections were just and would be very far from desiring to obstruct his reformation.

Then I represented my own circumstances to him in the most moving terms. I told him that those unhappy distresses which first moved him to a generous friendship for me would, I hope, move him to a little concern for me now, though the criminal part of our correspondence, which I believe neither of us intended to fall into at that time, was broken off; that I desired to repent as sincerely as he had done, but entreated him to put me in some condition that I might not be exposed to temptations from the frightful prospect of poverty and distress; and if he had the least apprehensions of my being troublesome to him, I begged he would put me in a posture to go back to my mother in Virginia, from whence he knew I came, and that would put an end to all his fears on that account. I concluded that if he would send me £50 more to facilitate my going away, I would send him back a general release and would promise never to disturb him more with any importunities unless it were to hear of the well-doing of the child, who, if I found my mother living and my circumstances able, I would send for and take him also off of his hands.

This was indeed all a cheat thus far, *viz.*, that I had no intention to go to Virginia, as the account of my former affairs there may convince anybody of; but the business was to get this last £50 of him if possible, knowing well enough it would be the last penny I was ever to expect.

However, the argument I used, namely, of giving him a general release and never troubling him any more, prevailed effectually, and he sent me a bill for the money by a person who brought with him a general release for me to sign and which I frankly signed; and thus, though full sore against my will, a final end was put to this affair.

And here I cannot but reflect upon the unhappy consequence of too great freedoms between persons stated as we were, upon the pretence of innocent intentions, love of friendship, and the like; for the flesh has generally so great a share in those friendships that it is great odds but inclination prevails at last over the most solemn resolutions and that vice breaks in at the breaches of decency, which really innocent friendship ought to preserve with the greatest strictness. But I leave the readers of these things to their own just reflections, which they will be more able to make effectual than I, who so soon forgot myself and am therefore but a very indifferent monitor.

I was now a single person again, as I may call myself; I was loosed from all the obligations either of wedlock or mistress-ship in the world, except my husband the linen-draper, who I having not now heard from in almost fifteen years nobody could blame me for thinking myself entirely freed from; seeing also he had at his going away told me that if I did not hear frequently from him, I should conclude he was dead, and I might freely marry again to whom I pleased.

I now began to cast up my accounts. I had by many letters and much importunity, and with the intercession of my mother too, had a second return of some goods from my brother, as I now call him, in Virginia, to make up the damage of the cargo I brought away with me, and this too was upon the condition of my sealing a general release to him, which, though I thought hard, but yet I was obliged to promise. I managed so well in this case that I got my goods away before the release was signed, and then I always found something or other to say to evade the thing and to put off the signing it at all; till at length I pretended I must write to my brother before I could do it.

Including this recruit and before I got the last £50, I found my strength to amount, put all together, to about £400, so that with that I had above £450. I had saved £100 more, but I met with a disaster with that, which was this—that a goldsmith in whose hands I had trusted it broke; so I lost £70 of my money, the man's composition not making above £30 out of his £100. I had a little plate, but not much, and was well enough stocked with clothes and linen.

With this stock I had the world to begin again; but you are to consider that I was not now the same woman as when I lived at Rotherhithe; for, first of all, I was near twenty years older, and did not look the better for my age nor for my rambles to Virginia and back again; and though I omitted nothing that might set me out to advantage except painting, for that I never stooped to, yet there would always be some difference seen between five-and-twenty and two-and-forty.

I cast about innumerable ways for my future state of life and began to consider very seriously what I should do, but nothing offered. I took care to make the world take me for something more than I was, and had it given out that I was a fortune, and that my estate was in my own hands; the last of which was very true, the first of it was as above. I had no acquaintance, which was one of my worst misfortunes, and the consequence of that was I had no adviser and, above all, I had nobody to whom I could in confidence commit the secret of my circumstances to; and I found by experience that to be friendless is the worst condition, next to being in want, that a woman can be reduced to; I say a woman because 'tis evident men can be their own advisers and their own directors, and know how to work themselves out of difficulties and into business better than women; but if a woman has no friend to communicate her affairs to and to advise and assist her, 'tis ten to one but she is undone; nay, and the more money she has, the more danger she is in of being wronged and deceived; and this was my case in the affair of the £100 which I left in the hand of the goldsmith, as above, whose credit, it seems, was upon the ebb before, but I, that had nobody to consult with, knew nothing of it and so lost my money.

When a woman is thus left desolate and void of counsel, she is just like a bag of money or a jewel dropped on the highway, which is a prey to the next comer; if a man of virtue and upright principles happens to find it, he will have it cried and the owner may come to hear of it again; but how many times shall such a thing fall into hands that will make no scruple of seizing it for their own, to once that it shall come into good hands?

This was evidently my case, for I was now a loose, unguided creature and had no help, no assistance, no guide for my conduct; I knew what I aimed at and what I wanted, but knew nothing how to pursue the end by direct means. I wanted to be placed in a settled state of living, and had I happened to meet with a sober, good husband, I should have been as true a wife to him as virtue itself could have formed. If I had been otherwise, the vice came in always at the door of necessity, not at the door of inclination; and I understood too well, by the want of it, what the value of a settled life was to do anything to forfeit the felicity of it; nay, I should have made the better wife for all the difficulties I had passed through by a great deal; nor did I in any of the times that I had been a wife give my husbands the least uneasiness on account of my behaviour.

But all this was nothing; I found no encouraging prospect. I waited; I lived regularly and with as much frugality as became my circumstances; but nothing offered, nothing presented, and the main stock wasted apace. What to do I knew not; the terror of approaching poverty lay hard upon my spirits. I had some money, but where to place it I knew not, nor would the interest of it maintain me, at least not in London.

At length a new scene opened. There was in the house where I lodged a north-country gentlewoman, and nothing was more frequent in her discourse than her account of the cheapness of provisions and the easy way of living in her country, how plentiful and how cheap everything was, what good company they kept, and the like; till at last I told her she almost tempted me to go and live in her country; for I that was a widow, though I had sufficient to live on, yet had no way of increasing it; and that London was an extravagant place; that I found I could not live here under £100 a year unless I kept no company, no servant, made no appearance, and buried myself in privacy, as if I was obliged to it by necessity.

I should have observed that she was always made to believe, as everybody else was, that I was a great fortune, or at least that I had three or four thousand pounds, if not more, and all in my own hands; and she was mighty sweet upon me when she thought me inclined in the least to go into her country. She said she had a sister lived near Liverpool; that her brother was a considerable gentleman there and had a great estate also in Ireland; that she would go down there in about two months, and if I would give her my company thither, I should be as welcome as herself for a month or more as I pleased, till I should see how I liked the country; and if I thought fit to live there, she would undertake they would take care; though they did not entertain lodgers themselves, they would recommend me to some agreeable family, where I should be placed to my content.

If this woman had known my real circumstances, she would never have laid so many snares and taken so many weary steps to catch a poor, desolate creature that was good for little when it was caught; and indeed I, whose case was almost desperate, and thought I could not be much worse, was not very anxious about what might befall me, provided they did me no personal injury; so I suffered myself, though not without a great deal of invitation and great professions of sincere friendship and real kindness—I say, I suffered myself to be prevailed upon to go with her, and accordingly I put myself in a posture for a journey, though I did not absolutely know whither I was to go.

And now I found myself in great distress; what little I had in the world was all in money except, as before, a little plate, some linen, and my clothes; as for household stuff, I had little or none, for I had lived always in lodgings; but I had not one friend in the world with whom to trust that little I had or to direct me how to dispose of it. I thought of the bank and of the other companies in London, but I had no friend to commit the management of it to; and to keep and carry about me bank-bills, tallies, orders, and such things, I looked upon as unsafe; that if they were lost, my money was lost, and then I was undone; and, on the other hand, I might be robbed and perhaps murdered in a strange place for them; and what to do I knew not.

It came into my thoughts one morning that I would go to the bank myself, where I had often been to receive the interest of some bills I had, and where I had found the clerk, to whom I applied myself, very honest to me, and particularly so fair one time that when I had mistold my money and taken less than my due and was coming away, he set me to rights and gave me the rest, which he might have put into his own pocket.

I went to him and asked if he would trouble himself to be my adviser, who was a poor, friendless widow and knew not what to do. He told me if I desired his opinion of anything within the reach of his business, he would do his endeavour that I should not be wronged, but that he would also help me to a good, sober person of his acquaintance, who was a clerk in such business too, though not in their house, whose judgement was good and whose honesty I might depend upon; "for," added he, "I will answer for him and for every step he takes; if he wrongs you, madam, of one farthing, it shall lie at my door; and he delights to assist people in such cases—he does it as an act of charity."

I was a little at a stand at this discourse; but after some pause I told him I had rather have depended upon him because I had found him honest, but if that could not be, I would take his recommendation sooner than any one's else. "I dare say, madam," says he, "that you will be as well satisfied with my friend as with me, and he is thoroughly able to assist you, which I am not." It seems he had his hands full of the business of the bank and had engaged to meddle with no other business than that of his office; he added that his friend should take nothing of me for his advice or assistance, and this indeed encouraged me.

He appointed the same evening, after the bank was shut, for me to meet him and his friend. As soon as I saw his friend and he began but to talk of the affair, I was fully satisfied I had a very honest man to deal with; his countenance spoke it, and his character, as I heard afterwards, was everywhere so good that I had no room for any more doubts upon me.

After the first meeting, in which I only said what I had said before, he appointed me to come the next day, telling me I might in the meantime satisfy myself of him by inquiry, which, however, I knew not how to do, having no acquaintance myself.

Accordingly I met him the next day, when I entered more freely with him into my case. I told him my circumstances at large; that I was a widow come over from America, perfectly desolate and friendless; that I had a little money, and but a little, and was almost distracted for fear of losing it, having no friend in the world to trust with the management of it; that I was going into the north of England to live cheap, that my stock might not waste; that I would willingly lodge my money in the bank, but that I durst not carry the bills about me; and how to correspond about it or with who I knew not.

He told me I might lodge the money in the bank as an

account, and its being entered in the books would entitle me to the money at any time; and if I was in the north, I might draw bills on the cashier and receive it when I would; but that then it would be esteemed as running cash and the bank would give no interest for it; that I might buy stock with it, and so it would lie in store for me, but that then if I wanted to dispose of it, I must come up to town to transfer it, and even it would be with some difficulty I should receive the half-yearly dividend unless I was here in person or had some friend I could trust with having the stock in his name to do it for me, and that would have the same difficulty in it as before; and with that he looked hard at me and smiled a little. At last says he, "Why do you not get a head-steward, madam, that may take you and your money together, and then you would have the trouble taken off of your hands?" "Aye, sir, and the money too, it may be," said I; "for truly I find the hazard that way is as much as 'tis t'other way"; but I remember I said secretly to myself, "I wish you would ask me the question fairly; I would consider very seriously on it before I said no."

He went on a good way with me, and I thought once or twice he was in earnest, but to my real affliction I found at last he had a wife; but when he owned he had a wife, he shook his head and said with some concern that indeed he had a wife, and no wife. I began to think he had been in the condition of my late lover, and that his wife had been lunatic or some such thing. However, we had not much more discourse at that time, but he told me he was in too much hurry of business then, but that if I would come home to his house after their business was over, he would consider what might be done for me to put my affairs in a posture of security. I told him I would come and desired to know where he lived. He gave me a direction in writing, and when he gave it me he read it to me and said, "There 'tis, madam, if you dare trust yourself with me." "Yes, sir," said I, "I believe I may venture to trust you with myself, for you have a wife, you say, and I don't want a husband; besides, I dare trust you with my money, which is all I have in the world, and if that were gone, I may trust myself anywhere."

He said some things in jest that were very handsome and mannerly and would have pleased me very well if they had been in earnest; but that passed over, I took the directions and appointed to be at this house at seven o'clock the same evening.

When I came he made several proposals for my placing my money in the bank, in order to my having interest for it; but still some difficulty or other came in the way, which he objected as not safe; and I found such a sincere, disinterested honesty in him that I began to think I had certainly found the honest man I wanted and that I could never put myself into better hands; so I told him with a great deal of frankness that I had never met with a man or woman yet that I could trust or in whom I could think myself safe, but that I saw he was so disinterestedly concerned for my safety that I would freely trust him with the management of that little I had if he would accept to be steward for a poor widow that could give him no salary.

He smiled and, standing up, with great respect saluted me. He told me he could not but take it very kindly that I had so good an opinion of him; that he would not deceive me; that he would do anything in his power to serve me, and expect no salary; but that he could not by any means accept of a trust that might bring him to be suspected of self-interest, and that if I should die he might have disputes with my executors, which he should be very loath to encumber himself with.

I told him if those were all his objections, I would soon remove them and convince him that there was not the least room for any difficulty; for that, first, as for suspecting him, if ever, now was the time to suspect him, and not to put the trust into his hands; and whenever I did suspect him, he could but throw it up then and refuse to go on. Then, as to executors, I assured him I had no heirs nor any relations in England, and I would have neither heirs or executors but himself unless I should alter my condition, and then his trust and trouble should cease together, which, however, I had no prospect of yet; but I told him if I died as I was, it should be all his own, and he would deserve it by being so faithful to me, as I was satisfied he would be.

He changed his countenance at this discourse and asked me how I came to have so much goodwill for him, and looking very much pleased, said he might very lawfully wish he was single for my sake. I smiled and told him that as he was not, my offer could have no design upon him, and to wish was not to be allowed, 'twas criminal to his wife.

He told me I was wrong; "for," says he, "as I said before, I have a wife and no wife, and 'twould be no sin to wish her hanged." "I know nothing of your circumstances that way, sir," said I; "but it cannot be innocent to wish your wife dead." "I tell you," says he again, "she is a wife and no wife; you don't know what I am or what she is."

"That's true," said I, "sir, I don't know what you are; but I believe you to be an honest man, and that's the cause of all my confidence in you."

"Well, well," says he, "and so I am; but I am something else too, madam; for," says he, "to be plain with you, I am a cuckold and she is a whore." He spoke it in a kind of jest, but it was with such an awkward smile that I perceived it stuck very close to him, and he looked dismally when he said it.

"That alters the case indeed, sir," said I, "as to that part you were speaking of; but a cuckold, you know, may be an honest man; it does not alter that case at all. Besides, I think," said I, "since your wife is so dishonest to you, you are too honest to her to own her for your wife; but that," said I, "is what I have nothing to do with." "Nay," says he, "I do think to clear my hands of her; for, to be plain with you, madam," added he, "I am no contented cuckold neither; on the other hand, I assure you it provokes me to the highest degree, but I can't help myself; she that will be a whore, will be a whore."

I waived the discourse and began to talk of my business; but I found he could not have done with it, so I let him alone, and he went on to tell me all the circumstances of his case, too long to relate here; particularly that having been out of England some time before he came to the post he was in, she had had two children in the meantime by an officer of the army; and that when he came to England and, upon her submission, took her again and maintained her very well, yet she run away from him with a linen-draper's apprentice, robbed him of what she could come at, and continued to live from him still; "so that, madam," says he, "she is a whore not by necessity, which is the common bait, but by inclination and for the sake of the vice."

Well, I pitied him and wished him well rid of her, and still would have talked of my business, but it would not do. At last he looked steadily at me. "Look you, madam," says he, "you came to ask advice of me, and I will serve you as faithfully as if you were my own sister; but I must turn the tables, since you oblige me to do it and are so friendly to me, and I think I must ask advice of you. Tell me, what must a poor abused fellow do with a whore? What can I do to do myself justice upon her?"

"Alas, sir," says I, " 'tis a case too nice for me to advise in, but it seems she has run away from you, so you are rid of her fairly; what can you desire more?" "Aye, she is gone indeed," said he, "but I am not clear of her for all that." "That's true," says I; "she may indeed run you into debt, but the law has furnished you with methods to prevent that also; you may cry her down, as they call it."

"No, no," says he, "that is not the case; I have taken care of all that; 'tis not that part that I speak of, but I would be rid of her that I might marry again."

"Well, sir," says I, "then you must divorce her; if you can prove what you say, you may certainly get that done, and then you are free."

"That's very tedious and expensive," says he.

"Why," says I, "if you can get any woman you like to take your word, I suppose your wife would not dispute the liberty with you that she takes herself."

"Aye," says he, "but 'twould be hard to bring an honest woman to do that; and for the other sort," says he, "I have had enough of her to meddle with any more whores."

It occurred to me presently: "I would have taken your word with all my heart if you had but asked me the question"; but that was to myself. To him I replied, "Why, you shut the door against any honest woman accepting you, for you condemn all that should venture upon you and conclude that a woman that takes you now can't be honest."

"Why," says he, "I wish you would satisfy me that an

honest woman would take me; I'd venture it." And then turns short upon me: "Will you take me, madam?"

"That's not a fair question," says I, "after what you have said; however, lest you should think I wait only a recantation of it, I shall answer you plainly—no, not I; my business is of another kind with you, and I did not expect you would have turned my serious application to you, in my distracted case, into a comedy."

"Why, madam," says he, "my case is as distracted as yours can be, and I stand in as much need of advice as you do, for I think if I have not relief somewhere, I shall be mad myself, and I know not what course to take, I protest to you."

"Why, sir," says I, " 'tis easier to give advice in your case than mine." "Speak, then," says he, "I beg of you, for now you encourage me."

"Why," says I, "if your case is so plain, you may be legally divorced, and then you may find honest women enough to ask the question of fairly; the sex is not so scarce that you can want a wife."

"Well, then," said he, "I am in earnest; I'll take your advice; but shall I ask you one question seriously beforehand?"

"Any question," said I, "but that you did before."

"No, that answer will not do," said he, "for, in short, that is the question I shall ask."

"You may ask what questions you please, but you have my answer to that already," said I; "besides, sir," said I, "can you think so ill of me as that I would give any answer to such a question beforehand? Can any woman alive believe you in earnest or think you design anything but to banter her?"

"Well, well," says he, "I do not banter you—I am in earnest; consider of it."

"But, sir," says I, a little gravely, "I came to you about my own business; I beg of you to let me know what you will advise me to do."

"I will be prepared," says he, "against you come again."

"Nay," says I, "you have forbid my coming any more."

"Why so?" said he, and looked a little surprised.

"Because," said I, "you can't expect I should visit you on the account you talk of."

"Well," says he, "you shall promise to come again,

however, and I will not say any more of it till I have the divorce. But I desire you'll prepare to be better conditioned when that's done, for you shall be the woman or I will not be divorced at all; I owe it to your unlooked-for kindness, if to nothing else, but I have other reasons too."

He could not have said anything in the world that pleased me better; however, I knew that the way to secure him was to stand off while the thing was so remote, as it appeared to be, and that it was time enough to accept of it when he was able to perform it. So I said very respectfully to him it was time enough to consider of these things when he was in a condition to talk of them; in the meantime, I told him, I was going a great way from him, and he would find objects enough to please him better. We broke off here for the present, and he made me promise him to come again the next day for my own business, which after some pressing I did; though had he seen farther into me, I wanted no pressing on that account.

I came the next evening accordingly and brought my maid with me to let him see that I kept a maid. He would have had me let the maid have stayed, but I would not, but ordered her aloud to come for me again about nine o'clock. But he forbid that and told me he would see me safe home, which I was not very well pleased with, supposing he might do that to know where I lived and inquire into my character and circumstances. However, I ventured that, for all the people there knew of me was to my advantage, and all the character he had of me was that I was a woman of fortune and that I was a very modest, sober body; which, whether true or not in the main, yet you may see how necessary it is for all women who expect anything in the world to preserve the character of their virtue even when perhaps they may have sacrificed the thing itself.

I found, and was not a little pleased with it, that he had provided a supper for me. I found also he lived very handsomely and had a house very handsomely furnished, and which I was rejoiced at indeed, for I looked upon it as all my own.

We had now a second conference upon the subject-matter of the last. He laid his business very home indeed; he protested his affection to me, and indeed I had no room to doubt it; he declared that it began from the first moment I talked with him and long before I had mentioned leaving my effects with him. " 'Tis no matter when it began," thought I; "if it will but hold, 'twill be well enough." He then told me how much the offer I had made of trusting him with my effects had engaged him. "So I intended it should," thought I, "but then I thought you had been a single man too." After we had supped I observed he pressed me very hard to drink two or three glasses of wine, which, however, I declined, but drank one glass or two. He then told me he had a proposal to make to me, which I should promise him I would not take ill if I should not grant it. I told him I hoped he would make no dishonourable proposal to me, especially in his own house, and that if it was such, I desired he would not mention it, that I might not be obliged to offer any resentment to him that did not become the respect I professed for him and the trust I had placed in him in coming to this house, and begged of him he would give me leave to go away, and accordingly began to put on my gloves and prepare to be gone, though at the same time I no more intended it than he intended to let me.

Well, he importuned me not to talk of going; he assured me he was very far from offering any such thing to me that was dishonourable, and if I thought so, he would choose to say no more of it.

That part I did not relish at all. I told him I was ready to hear anything that he had to say, depending that he would say nothing unworthy of himself or unfit for me to hear. Upon this, he told me his proposal was this: that I would marry him though he had not yet obtained the divorce from the whore his wife; and to satisfy me that he meant honourably, he would promise not to desire me to live with him or go to bed to him till the divorce was obtained. My heart said yes to this offer at first word, but it was necessary to play the hypocrite a little more with him; so I seemed to decline the motion with some warmth as unfair, told him that such a proposal could be of no signification but to entangle us both in great difficulties; for if he should not at last obtain the divorce, yet we could not dissolve the marriage, neither could we proceed in it; so that if he was disappointed in the divorce, I left him to consider what a condition we should both be in.

In short, I carried on the argument against this so far that I convinced him it was not a proposal that had any sense in it; then he went from it to another, *viz.*, that I would sign and seal a contract with him, conditioning to marry him as soon as the divorce was obtained and to be void if he could not get it.

I told him that was more rational than the other; but as this was the first time that ever I could imagine him weak enough to be in earnest, I did not use to say yes at first asking; I would consider of it. I played with this lover as an angler does with a trout: I found I had him fast on the hook, so I jested with his new proposal and put him off. I told him he knew little of me, and bade him inquire about me; I let him also go home with me to my lodging though I would not ask him to go in, for I told him it was not decent.

In short, I ventured to avoid signing a contract, and the reason why I did it was because the lady that had invited me to go with her into Lancashire insisted so positively upon it, and promised me such great fortunes and fine things there, that I was tempted to go and try. "Perhaps," said I, "I may mend myself very much"; and then I made no scruple of quitting my honest citizen, whom I was not so much in love with as not to leave him for a richer.

In a word, I avoided a contract, but told him I would go into the north; that he would know where to write to me by the business I had entrusted him with; that I would give him a sufficient pledge of my respect for him, for I would leave almost all I had in the world in his hands; and I would thus far give him my word that as soon as he had sued out the divorce, if he would send me an account of it, I would come up to London and that then we would talk seriously of the matter.

It was a base design I went with, that I must confess, though I was invited thither with a design much worse, as the sequel will discover. Well, I went with my friend, as I called her, into Lancashire. All the way we went she caressed me with the utmost appearance of a sincere, undissembled affection; treated me, except my coach-hire, all the way; and her brother brought a gentleman's coach to Warrington to receive us, and we were carried from thence to Liverpool with as much ceremony as I could desire.

We were also entertained at a merchant's house in Liverpool three or four days very handsomely; I forbear to tell his name because of what followed. Then she told me she would carry me to an uncle's house of hers where we should be nobly entertained; and her uncle, as she called him, sent a coach and four horses for us, and we were carried near forty miles I know not whither.

We came, however, to a gentleman's seat, where was a numerous family, a large park, extraordinary company indeed, and where she was called cousin. I told her if she had resolved to bring me into such company as this, she should have let me have furnished myself with better clothes. The ladies took notice of that and told me very genteelly they did not value people in their own country so much by their clothes as they did in London; that their cousin had fully informed them of my quality, and that I did not want clothes to set me off; in short, they entertained me not like what I was, but like what they thought I had been, namely, a widow lady of a great fortune.

The first discovery I made here was that the family were all Roman Catholics, and the cousin too; however, nobody in the world could behave better to me, and I had all the civility shown that I could have had if I had been of their opinion. The truth is, I had not so much principle of any kind as to be nice in point of religion; and I presently learnt to speak favourably of the Romish Church; particularly, I told them I saw little but the prejudice of education in all the differences that were among Christians about religion, and if it had so happened that my father had been a Roman Catholic, I doubted not but I should have been as well pleased with their religion as my own.

This obliged them in the highest degree, and as I was besieged day and night with good company and pleasant discourse, so I had two or three old ladies that lay at me upon the subject of religion too. I was so complaisant that I made no scruple to be present at their Mass and to conform to all their gestures as they showed me the pattern, but I would not come too cheap; so that I only in the main encouraged them to expect that I would turn Roman Catholic if I was instructed in the Catholic doctrine, as they called it; and so the matter rested.

I stayed here about six weeks, and then my conductor led me back to a country village, about six miles from Liverpool, where her brother, as she called him, came to visit me in his own chariot with two footmen in a good livery; and the next thing was to make love to me. As it happened to me, one would think I could not have been cheated, and indeed I thought so myself, having a safe card at home, which I resolved not to quit unless I could mend myself very much. However, in all appearance this brother was a match worth my listening to, and the least his estate was valued at was £1000 a year, but the sister said it was worth £1500 a year, and lay most of it in Ireland.

I, that was a great fortune and passed for such, was above being asked how much my estate was; and my false friend, taking it upon a foolish hearsay, had raised it from £500 to £5000, and by the time she came into the country she called it £15,000. The Irishman, for such I understood him to be, was stark mad at this bait; in short, he courted me, made me presents, and run in debt like a madman for the expenses of his courtship. He had, to give him his due, the appearance of an extraordinary fine gentleman; he was tall, well shaped, and had an extraordinary address; talked as naturally of his park and his stables, or his horses, his gamekeepers, his woods, his tenants, and his servants as if he had been in a mansion-house and I had seen them all about me.

He never so much as asked me about my fortune or estate, but assured me that when we came to Dublin he would jointure me in £600 a year in good land, and that he would enter into a deed of settlement, or contract, here for the performance of it.

This was such language indeed as I had not been used to, and I was here beaten out of all my measures; I had a she-devil in my bosom, every hour telling me how great her brother lived. One time she would come for my orders how I would have my coach painted and how lined, and another time what clothes my page should wear; in short, my eyes were dazzled. I had now lost my power of saying no, and, to cut the story short, I consented to be married; but to be more private, we were carried farther into the country and married by a priest, which I was assured would marry us as effectually as a Church of England parson.

I cannot say but I had some reflections in this affair upon the dishonourable forsaking my faithful citizen, who loved me sincerely and who was endeavouring to quit himself of a scandalous whore by whom he had been barbarously used, and promised himself infinite happiness in his new choice, which choice was now giving up herself to another in a manner almost as scandalous as hers could be.

But the glittering show of a great estate and of fine things which the deceived creature that was now my deceiver represented every hour to my imagination hurried me away and gave me no time to think of London or of anything there, much less of the obligation I had to a person of infinitely more real merit than what was now before me.

But the thing was done; I was now in the arms of my new spouse, who appeared still the same as before, great even to magnificence; and nothing less than a thousand pounds a year could support the ordinary equipage he appeared in.

After we had been married about a month he began to talk of my going to West Chester in order to embark for Ireland. However, he did not hurry me, for we stayed near three weeks longer, and then he sent to Chester for a coach to meet us at the Black Rock, as they call it, over against Liverpool. Thither we went in a fine boat they call a pinnace, with six oars; his servants and horses and baggage going in a ferry-boat. He made his excuse to me, that he had not acquaintance at Chester, but he would go before and get some handsome apartment for me at a private house. I asked him how long we should stay at Chester. He said not at all any longer than one night or two, but he would immediately hire a coach to go to Holyhead. Then I told him he should by no means give himself the trouble to get private lodgings for one night or two, for that Chester being a great place, I made no doubt but there would be very good inns and accommodation enough; so we lodged at an inn not far from the cathedral; I forget what sign it was at.

Here my spouse, talking of my going to Ireland, asked

me if I had no affairs to settle at London before we went off. I told him no, not of any great consequence but what might be done as well by letter from Dublin. "Madam," says he very respectfully, "I suppose the greatest part of your estate, which my sister tells me is most of it in money in the Bank of England, lies secure enough; but in case it required transferring or any way altering its property, it might be necessary to go up to London and settle those things before we went over."

I seemed to look strange at it and told him I knew not what he meant; that I had no effects in the Bank of England that I knew of, and I hoped he could not say that I had ever told him I had. No, he said, I had not told him so, but his sister had said the greatest part of my estate lay there; "and I only mentioned it, my dear," said he, "that if there was any occasion to settle it or order anything about it, we might not be obliged to the hazard and trouble of another voyage back again"; for he added that he did not care to venture me too much upon the sea.

I was surprised at this talk and began to consider what the meaning of it must be; and it presently occurred to me that my friend, who called him brother, had represented me in colours which were not my due; and I thought that I would know the bottom of it before I went out of England and before I should put myself into I knew not whose hands in a strange country.

Upon this I called his sister into my chamber the next morning, and letting her know the discourse her brother and I had been upon, I conjured her to tell me what she had said to him and upon what foot it was that she had made this marriage. She owned that she had told him that I was a great fortune and said that she was told so at London. "Told so?" says I warmly. "Did I ever tell you so?" No, she said, it was true I never did tell her so, but I had said several times that what I had was in my own disposal. "I did so," returned I very quick, "but I never told you I had anything called a fortune; no, that I had one hundred pounds or the value of an hundred pounds in the world. And how did it consist with my being a fortune," said I, "that I should come here into the north of England with you, only upon the account of living cheap?" At these words, which I spoke warm and high, my husband came into the room, and I desired him to come in and sit down, for I had something of moment to say before them both, which it was absolutely necessary he should hear.

He looked a little disturbed at the assurance with which I seemed to speak it and came and sat down by me, having first shut the door; upon which I began, for I was very much provoked, and turning myself to him, "I am afraid," says I, "my dear" (for I spoke with kindness on his side), "that you have a very great abuse put upon you and an injury done you never to be repaired in your marrying me, which, however, as I have had no hand in it, I desire I may be fairly acquitted of it and that the blame may lie where it ought and nowhere else, for I wash my hands of every part of it." "What injury can be done me, my dear," says he, "in marrying you? I hope it is to my honour and advantage every way." "I will soon explain it to you," says I, "and I fear there will be no reason to think yourself well used; but I will convince you, my dear," says I again, "that I have had no hand in it."

He looked now scared and wild, and began, I believed, to suspect what followed; however, looking towards me and saying only, "Go on," he sat silent, as if to hear what I had more to say; so I went on. "I asked you last night," said I, speaking to him, "if ever I made any boast to you of my estate or ever told you I had any estate in the Bank of England or anywhere else, and you owned I had not, as is most true; and I desire you will tell me here, before your sister, if ever I gave you any reason from me to think so or that ever we had any discourse about it"; and he owned again I had not, but said I had appeared always as a woman of fortune, and he depended on it that I was so and hoped he was not deceived. "I am not inquiring whether you have been deceived," said I; "I fear you have, and I too; but I am clearing myself from being concerned in deceiving you.

"I have been now asking your sister if ever I told her of any fortune or estate I had or gave her any particulars of it; and she owns I never did. And pray, madam," said I, "be so just to me to charge me, if you can, if ever I pretended to you that I had an estate; and why, if I had, should I ever come down into this country with you on purpose to spare that little I had and live cheap?" She could not deny one word, but said she had been told in London that I had a very great fortune and that it lay in the Bank of England.

"And now, dear sir," said I, turning myself to my new spouse again, "be so just to me as to tell me who has abused both you and me so much as to make you believe I was a fortune and prompt you to court me to this marriage?" He could not speak a word, but pointed to her, and after some more pause, flew out in the most furious passion that ever I saw a man in, in my life, cursing her and calling her all the whores and hard names he could think of, and that she had ruined him, declaring that she had told him I had £15,000 and that she was to have £500 of him for procuring this match for him. He then added, directing his speech to me, that she was none of his sister, but had been his whore for two years before; that she had had £100 of him in part of this bargain, and that he was utterly undone if things were as I said; and in his raving he swore he would let her heart's blood out immediately, which frightened her and me too. She cried, said she had been told so in the house where I lodged. But this aggravated him more than before, that she should put so far upon him and run things such a length upon no other authority than a hearsay, and then, turning to me again, said very honestly he was afraid we were both undone; "for, to be plain, my dear, I have no estate," says he; "what little I had, this devil has made me run out in putting me into this equipage." She took the opportunity of his being earnest in talking with me and got out of the room, and I never saw her more.

I was confounded now as much as he and knew not what to say. I thought many ways that I had the worst of it; but his saying he was undone, and that he had no estate neither, put me into a mere distraction. "Why," says I to him, "this has been a hellish juggle, for we are married here upon the foot of a double fraud: you are undone by the disappointment, it seems; and if I had had a fortune, I had been cheated too, for you say you have nothing."

"You would indeed have been cheated, my dear," says he, "but you would not have been undone, for fifteen thousand pounds would have maintained us both very handsomely in this country; and I had resolved to have dedicated every groat of it to you; I would not have wronged you of a shilling, and the rest I would have made up in my affection to you and tenderness of you as long as I lived."

This was very honest indeed, and I really believe he spoke as he intended and that he was a man that was as well qualified to make me happy, as to his temper and behaviour, as any man ever was; but his having no estate and being run into debt on this ridiculous account in the country made all the prospect dismal and dreadful, and I knew not what to say or what to think.

I told him it was very unhappy that so much love and so much good nature as I discovered in him should be thus precipitated into misery; that I saw nothing before us but ruin; for as to me, it was my unhappiness that what little I had was not able to relieve us a week, and with that I pulled out a bank-bill of £20 and eleven guineas, which I told him I had saved out of my little income, and that by the account that creature had given me of the way of living in that country, I expected it would maintain me three or four years; that if it was taken from me I was left destitute, and he knew what the condition of a woman must be if she had no money in her pocket; however, I told him if he would take it, there it was.

He told me with great concern, and I thought I saw tears in his eyes, that he would not touch it; that he abhorred the thoughts of stripping me and making me miserable; that he had fifty guineas left, which was all he had in the world, and he pulled it out and threw it down on the table, bidding me take it, though he were to starve for want of it.

I returned, with the same concern for him, that I could not bear to hear him talk so; that on the contrary, if he could propose any probable method of living, I would do anything that became me, and that I would live as narrow as he could desire.

He begged of me to talk no more at that rate, for it would make him distracted; he said he was bred a gentleman though he was reduced to a low fortune, and that there was but one way left which he could think of, and that would not do unless I could answer him one question, which, however, he said he would not press me to. I told him I would answer it honestly; whether it would be to his satisfaction or no, that I could not tell.

"Why, then, my dear, tell me plainly," says he, "will the little you have keep us together in any figure or in any station or place, or will it not?"

It was my happiness that I had not discovered myself or my circumstances at all—no, not so much as my name; and seeing there was nothing to be expected from him, however good-humoured and however honest he seemed to be but to live on what I knew would soon be wasted, I resolved to conceal everything but the bank-bill and eleven guineas; and I would have been very glad to have lost that and have been set down where he took me up. I had indeed another bank-roll about me of £30, which was the whole of what I brought with me, as well to subsist on in the country as not knowing what might offer; because this creature, the go-between that had thus betrayed us both, had made me believe strange things of marrying to my advantage, and I was not willing to be without money, whatever might happen. This bill I concealed, and that made me the freer of the rest, in consideration of his circumstances, for I really pitied him heartily.

But to return to this question, I told him I never willingly deceived him and I never would. I was very sorry to tell him that the little I had would not subsist us; that it was not sufficient to subsist me alone in the south country and that this was the reason that made me put myself into the hands of that woman who called him brother, she having assured me that I might board very handsomely at a town called Manchester, where I had not yet been, for about £6 a year; and my whole income not being above £15 a year, I thought I might live easy upon it and wait for better things.

He shook his head and remained silent, and a very melancholy evening we had; however, we supped together and lay together that night, and when we had almost supped, he looked a little better and more cheerful and called for a bottle of wine. "Come, my dear," says he, "though the case is bad, it is to no purpose to be dejected. Come, be as easy as you can; I will endeavour to find out some way or other to live; if you can but subsist yourself, that is better than nothing. I must try the world again; a man ought to think like a man; to be discouraged is to yield to the misfortune." With this he filled a glass and drank to me, holding my hand all the while the wine went down, and protesting his main concern was for me.

It was really a true, gallant spirit he was of, and it was the more grievous to me. 'Tis something of relief even to be undone by a man of honour, rather than by a scoundrel; but here the greatest disappointment was on his side, for he had really spent a great deal of money, and it was very remarkable on what poor terms she proceeded. First, the baseness of the creature herself is to be observed, who, for the getting £100 herself, could be content to let him spend three or four more, though perhaps it was all he had in the world and more than all; when she had not the least ground more than a little tea-table chat to say that I had any estate, or was a fortune, or the like. It is true the design of deluding a woman of fortune, if I had been so, was base enough; the putting the face of great things upon poor circumstances was a fraud and bad enough; but the case a little differed too, and that in his favour, for he was not a rake that made a trade to delude women and, as some have done, get six or seven fortunes after one another and then rifle and run away from them; but he was already a gentleman, unfortunate and low, but had lived well; and though if I had had a fortune I should have been enraged at the slut for betraying me, yet really for the man, a fortune would not have been ill-bestowed on him, for he was a lovely person indeed, of generous principles, good sense, and of abundance of good humour.

We had a great deal of close conversation that night, for we neither of us slept much; he was as penitent for having put all those cheats upon me as if it had been felony and that he was going to execution; he offered me again every shilling of the money he had about him and said he would go into the army and seek for more.

I asked him why he would be so unkind to carry me into Ireland when I might suppose he could not have subsisted me there. He took me in his arms. "My dear," said he, "I never designed to go to Ireland at all, much less to have carried you thither, but came hither to be out of the observation of the people who had heard what

I pretended to, and that nobody might ask me for money before I was furnished to supply them."

"But where, then," said I, "were we to have gone next?"

"Why, my dear," said he, "I'll confess the whole scheme to you as I had laid it: I purposed here to ask you something about your estate, as you see I did, and when you, as I expected you would, had entered into some account of the particulars, I would have made an excuse to have put off our voyage to Ireland for some time, and so have gone for London. Then, my dear," says he, "I resolved to have confessed all the circumstances of my own affairs to you and let you know I had indeed made use of these artifices to obtain your consent to marry me, but had now nothing to do but to ask your pardon and to tell you how abundantly I would endeavour to make you forget what was past by the felicity of the days to come."

"Truly," said I to him, "I find you would soon have conquered me; and it is my affliction now that I am not in a condition to let you see how easily I should have been reconciled to you, and have passed by all the tricks you had put upon me, in recompense of so much good humour. But, my dear," said I, "what can we do now? We are both undone; and what better are we for our being reconciled, seeing we have nothing to live on?"

We proposed a great many things, but nothing could offer where there was nothing to begin with. He begged me at last to talk no more of it, for, he said, I would break his heart; so we talked of other things a little, till at last he took a husband's leave of me and so went to sleep.

He rose before me in the morning; and indeed having lain awake almost all night, I was very sleepy and lay till near eleven o'clock. In this time he took his horses and three servants and all his linen and baggage, and away he went, leaving a short but moving letter for me on the table, as follows:

My dear:

I am a dog; I have abused you; but I have been drawn in to do it by a base creature contrary to my principle and the general practice of my life. Forgive me, my dear! I ask your pardon with the greatest sincerity; I am the most miserable of men in having deluded you. I have been so happy to possess you and am now so wretched as to be forced to fly from you. Forgive me, my dear; once more I say, forgive me! I am not able to see you ruined by me and myself unable to support you. Our marriage is nothing; I shall never be able to see you again; I here discharge you from it; if you can marry to your advantage, do not decline it on my account. I here swear to you on my faith, and on the word of a man of honour, I will never disturb your repose if I should know of it, which, however, is not likely. On the other hand, if you should not marry and if good fortune should befall me, it shall be all yours wherever you are.

I have put some of the stock of money I have left into your pocket; take places for yourself and your maid in the stage-coach and go for London. I hope it will bear your charges thither without breaking into your own. Again I sincerely ask your pardon, and will do so as often as I shall ever think of you. Adieu, my dear, forever! I am yours most affectionately,

J. E.

Nothing that ever befell me in my life sunk so deep into my heart as this farewell. I reproached him a thousand times in my thoughts for leaving me, for I would have gone with him through the world if I had begged my bread. I felt in my pocket, and there I found ten guineas, his gold watch, and two little rings, one a small diamond ring worth only about £6 and the other a plain gold ring.

I sat down and looked upon these things two hours together and scarce spoke a word till my maid interrupted me by telling me my dinner was ready. I eat but little, and after dinner I fell into a violent fit of crying, every now and then calling him by his name, which was James. "Oh, Jemmy!" said I. "Come back, come back. I'll give you all I have; I'll beg, I'll starve with you." And thus I run raving about the room several times, and then sat down between whiles, and then walking about again, called upon him to come back, and then cried again; and thus I passed the afternoon till about seven o'clock, when it was near dusk in the evening, being August, when to my unspeakable surprise he comes back into the inn and comes directly up into my chamber.

I was in the greatest confusion imaginable, and so

was he too. I could not imagine what should be the occasion of it, and began to be at odds with myself whether to be glad or sorry; but my affection biased all the rest, and it was impossible to conceal my joy, which was too great for smiles, for it burst out into tears. He was no sooner entered the room but he run to me and took me in his arms, holding me fast and almost stopping my breath with his kisses, but spoke not a word. At length I began: "My dear," said I, "how could you go away from me?"—to which he gave no answer, for it was impossible for him to speak.

When our ecstasies were a little over, he told me he was gone above fifteen miles, but it was not in his power to go any farther without coming back to see me again and to take his leave of me once more.

I told him how I had passed my time and how loud I had called him to come back again. He told me he heard me very plain upon Delamere Forest, at a place about twelve miles off. I smiled. "Nay," says he, "do not think I am in jest, for if ever I heard your voice in my life, I heard you call me aloud, and sometimes I thought I saw you running after me." "Why," said I, "what did I say?"—for I had not named the words to him. "You called aloud," says he, "and said, Oh, Jemmy! Oh, Jemmy! Come back, come back."

I laughed at him. "My dear," says he, "do not laugh, for, depend upon it, I heard your voice as plain as you hear mine now; if you please, I'll go before a magistrate and make oath of it." I then began to be amazed and surprised and indeed frighted, and told him what I had really done and how I had called after him, as above. When we had amused ourselves a while about this, I said to him, "Well, you shall go away from me no more; I'll go all over the world with you rather." He told me it would be a very difficult thing for him to leave me, but since it must be, he hoped I would make it as easy to me as I could; but as for him, it would be his destruction—that he foresaw.

However, he told me that he had considered he had left me to travel to London alone, which was a long journey; and that as he might as well go that way as any way else, he was resolved to see me thither or near it; and if he did go away then without taking his leave, I should not take it ill of him; and this he made me promise.

He told me how he had dismissed his three servants, sold their horses, and sent the fellows away to seek their fortunes, and all in a little time at a town on the road, I know not where; "and," says he, "it cost me some tears all alone by myself to think how much happier they were than their master, for they could go to the next gentleman's house to see for a service, whereas," said he, "I knew not whither to go or what to do with myself."

I told him I was so completely miserable in parting with him that I could not be worse; and that now he was come again, I would not go from him if he would take me with him, let him go whither he would. And in the meantime I agreed that we would go together to London; but I could not be brought to consent he should go away at last and not take his leave of me, but told him, jesting, that if he did, I would call him back again as loud as I did before. Then I pulled out his watch and gave it him back, and his two rings, and his ten guineas; but he would not take them, which made me very much suspect that he resolved to go off upon the road and leave me.

The truth is, the circumstances he was in, the passionate expressions of his letter, the kind, gentlemanly treatment I had from him in all the affair, with the concern he showed for me in it, his manner of parting with that large share which he gave me of his little stock left—all these had joined to make such impressions on me that I could not bear the thoughts of parting with him.

Two days after this we quitted Chester, I in the stage-coach and he on horse-back. I dismissed my maid at Chester. He was very much against my being without a maid, but she being hired in the country (keeping no servant at London), I told him it would have been barbarous to have taken the poor wench and have turned her away as soon as I came to town, and it would also have been a needless charge on the road; so I satisfied him and he was easy on that score.

He came with me as far as Dunstable, within thirty miles of London, and then he told me fate and his own misfortunes obliged him to leave me and that it was not convenient for him to go to London, for reasons which it was of no value to me to know, and I saw him preparing to go. The stage-coach we were in did not usually stop at Dunstable, but I desiring it for a quarter of an hour, they were content to stand at an inn-door awhile, and we went into the house.

Being in the inn, I told him I had but one favour more to ask him, and that was that since he could not go any farther, he would give me leave to stay a week or two in the town with him, that we might in that time think of something to prevent such a ruinous thing to us both as a final separation would be, and that I had something of moment to offer to him, which perhaps he might find practicable to our advantage.

This was too reasonable a proposal to be denied, so he called the landlady of the house and told her his wife was taken ill, and so ill that she could not think of going any farther in the stage-coach, which had tired her almost to death, and asked if she could not get us a lodging for two or three days in a private house where I might rest me a little, for the journey had been too much for me. The landlady, a good sort of a woman, well bred and very obliging, came immediately to see me, told me she had two or three very good rooms in a part of the house quite out of the noise, and if I saw them she did not doubt but I would like them, and I should have one of her maids, that should do nothing else but wait on me. This was so very kind that I could not but accept of it; so I went to look on the rooms and liked them very well, and indeed they were extraordinarily furnished and very pleasant lodgings; so we paid the stage-coach, took out our baggage, and resolved to stay here awhile.

Here I told him I would live with him now till all my money was spent, but would not let him spend a shilling of his own. We had some kind squabble about that, but I told him it was the last time I was like to enjoy his company, and I desired he would let me be master in that thing only and he should govern in everything else; so he acquiesced.

Here one evening, taking a walk into the fields, I told him I would now make the proposal to him I had told him of; accordingly I related to him how I had lived in Virginia, that I had a mother I believed was alive there still, though my husband was dead some years. I told him that had not my effects miscarried, which, by the way, I magnified pretty much, I might have been fortune good enough to him to have kept us from being parted in this manner. Then I entered into the manner of people's settling in those countries, how they had a quantity of land given them by the constitution of the place, and if not, that it might be purchased at so easy a rate that it was not worth naming.

I then gave him a full and distinct account of the nature of planting, how with carrying over but two or three hundred pounds' value in English goods, with some servants and tools, a man of application would presently lay a foundation for a family and in a few years would raise an estate.

I let him into the nature of the product of the earth, how the ground was cured and prepared, and what the usual increase of it was, and demonstrated to him that in a very few years, with such a beginning, we should be as certain of being rich as we were now certain of being poor.

He was surprised at my discourse, for we made it the whole subject of our conversation for near a week together, in which time I laid it down in black and white, as we say, that it was morally impossible, with a supposition of any reasonable good conduct, but that we must thrive there and do very well.

Then I told him what measures I would take to raise such a sum as £300 or thereabouts; and I argued with him how good a method it would be to put an end to our misfortunes and restore our circumstances in the world to what we had both expected; and I added that after seven years we might be in a posture to leave our plantation in good hands and come over again and receive the income of it and live here and enjoy it; and I gave him examples of some that had done so and lived now in very good figure in London.

In short, I pressed him so to it that he almost agreed to it, but still something or other broke it off; till at last he turned the tables and began to talk almost to the same purpose of Ireland.

He told me that a man that could confine himself to a country life, and that could but find stock to enter upon any land, should have farms there for £50 a year as good as were let here for £200 a year; that the produce was such, and so rich the land, that if much was not laid up, we were sure to live as handsomely upon it as a gentleman of £3000 a year could do in England; and that he had laid a scheme to leave me in London and go over and try; and if he found he could lay a handsome foundation of living suitable to the respect he had for me, as he doubted not he should do, he would come over and fetch me.

I was dreadfully afraid that upon such a proposal he would have taken me at my word, *viz.*, to turn my little income into money and let him carry it over into Ireland and try his experiment with it; but he was too just to desire it or to have accepted it if I had offered it; and he anticipated me in that, for he added that he would go and try his fortune that way, and if he found he could do anything at it to live, then by adding mine to it when I went over we should live like ourselves; but that he would not hazard a shilling of mine till he had made the experiment with a little, and he assured me that if he found nothing to be done in Ireland, he would then come to me and join in my project for Virginia.

He was so earnest upon his project being to be tried first that I could not withstand him; however, he promised to let me hear from him in a very little time after his arriving there to let me know whether his prospect answered his design; that if there was not a probability of success, I might take the occasion to prepare for our other voyage, and then, he assured me, he would go with me to America with all his heart.

I could bring him to nothing farther than this, and which entertained us near a month, during which I enjoyed his company, which was the most entertaining that ever I met with in my life before. In this time he let me into part of the story of his own life, which was indeed surprising and full of an infinite variety, sufficient to fill up a much brighter history for its adventures and incidents than any I ever saw in print; but I shall have occasion to say more of him hereafter.

We parted at last, though with the utmost reluctance on my side; and indeed he took his leave very unwillingly too, but necessity obliged him, for his reasons were very good why he would not come to London, as I understood more fully afterwards.

I gave him a direction how to write to me, though still I reserved the grand secret, which was not to let him ever know my true name, who I was, or where to be found; he likewise let me know how to write a letter to him so that, he said, he would be sure to receive it.

I came to London the next day after we parted, but did not go directly to my old lodgings, but for another nameless reason took a private lodging in St. John's Street, or as it is vulgarly called, St. Jones's, near Clerkenwell; and here, being perfectly alone, I had leisure to sit down and reflect seriously upon the last seven months' ramble I had made, for I had been abroad no less. The pleasant hours I had with my last husband I looked back on with an infinite deal of pleasure; but that pleasure was very much lessened when I found, some time after, that I was really with child.

This was a perplexing thing because of the difficulty which was before me where I should get leave to lie in, it being one of the nicest things in the world at that time of day for a woman that was a stranger and had no friends to be entertained in that circumstance without security, which I had not; neither could I procure any.

I had taken care all this while to preserve a correspondence with my friend at the bank, or rather he took care to correspond with me, for he wrote to me once a week; and though I had not spent my money so fast as to want any from him, yet I often wrote also to let him know I was alive. I had left directions in Lancashire, so that I had these letters conveyed to me; and during my recess at St. Jones's I received a very obliging letter from him, assuring me that his process for a divorce went on with success, though he met with some difficulties in it that he did not expect.

I was not displeased with the news that his process was more tedious than he expected; for though I was in no condition to have had him yet, not being so foolish to marry him when I knew myself to be with child by another man, as some I know have ventured to do, yet I was not willing to lose him and, in a word, resolved to have him if he continued in the same mind as soon as I was up again; for I saw apparently I should hear no more from my other husband; and as he had all along pressed me to marry and had assured me he would not be at all disgusted at it or ever offer to claim me again, so I made no scruple to resolve to do it if I could and if my other friend stood to his bargain; and I had a great deal of reason to be assured that he would by the letters he wrote to me, which were the kindest and most obliging that could be.

I now grew big, and the people where I lodged perceived it and began to take notice of it to me, and as far as civility would allow, intimated that I must think of removing. This put me to extreme perplexity and I grew very melancholy, for indeed I knew not what course to take; I had money, but no friends, and was like now to have a child upon my hands to keep, which was a difficulty I had never had upon me yet, as my story hitherto makes appear.

In the course of this affair I fell very ill, and my melancholy really increased my distemper. My illness proved at length to be only an ague, but my apprehensions were really that I should miscarry. I should not say apprehensions, for indeed I would have been glad to miscarry, but I could never entertain so much as a thought of taking anything to make me miscarry; I abhorred, I say, so much as the thought of it.

However, speaking of it, the gentlewoman who kept the house proposed to me to send for a midwife. I scrupled it at first, but after some time consented, but told her I had no acquaintance with any midwife and so left it to her.

It seems the mistress of the house was not so great a stranger to such cases as mine was as I thought at first she had been, as will appear presently; and she sent for a midwife of the right sort—that is to say, the right sort for me.

The woman appeared to be an experienced woman in her business, I mean as a midwife; but she had another calling too, in which she was as expert as most women if not more. My landlady had told her I was very melancholy and that she believed that had done me harm; and once, before me, said to her, "Mrs. B——, I believe this lady's trouble is of a kind that is pretty much in your way, and therefore if you can do anything for her, pray do, for she is a very civil gentlewoman"; and so she went out of the room.

I really did not understand her, but my Mother Midnight began very seriously to explain what she meant as soon as she was gone. "Madam," says she, "you seem not to understand what your landlady means; and when you do, you need not let her know at all that you do so.

"She means that you are under some circumstances that may render your lying in difficult to you, and that you are not willing to be exposed. I need say no more but to tell you that if you think fit to communicate so much of your case to me as is necessary, for I do not desire to pry into those things, I perhaps may be in a condition to assist you, and to make you easy, and remove all your dull thoughts upon that subject."

Every word this creature said was a cordial to me and put new life and new spirit into my very heart; my blood began to circulate immediately, and I was quite another body; I eat my victuals again and grew better presently after it. She said a great deal more to the same purpose, and then, having pressed me to be free with her and promised in the solemnest manner to be secret, she stopped a little, as if waiting to see what impression it made on me and what I would say.

I was too sensible of the want I was in of such a woman not to accept her offer; I told her my case was partly as she guessed and partly not, for I was really married and had a husband, though he was so remote at that time as that he could not appear publicly.

She took me short and told me that was none of her business; all the ladies that came under her care were married women to her. "Every woman," says she, "that is with child has a father for it," and whether that father was a husband or no husband was no business of hers; her business was to assist me in my present circumstances, whether I had a husband or no; "for, madam," says she, "to have a husband that cannot appear is to have no husband, and therefore whether you are a wife or a mistress is all one to me."

I found presently that whether I was a whore or a wife, I was to pass for a whore here, so I let that go. I told her it was true, as she said, but that, however, if I must tell her my case, I must tell it her as it was; so I related it as short as I could and I concluded it to her: "I trouble you with this, madam," said I, "not that, as you said before, it is much to the purpose in your affair; but this is to the purpose, namely, that I am not in any pain about being seen or being concealed, for 'tis perfectly indifferent to me; but my difficulty is that I have no acquaintance in this part of the nation."

"I understand you, madam," says she; "you have no security to bring to prevent the parish impertinences usual in such cases, and perhaps," says she, "do not know very well how to dispose of the child when it comes." "The last," says I, "is not so much my concern as the first." "Well, madam," answers the midwife, "dare you put yourself into my hands? I live in such a place; though I do not inquire after you, you may inquire after me. My name is B——; I live in such a street"—naming the street—"at the sign of the Cradle. My profession is a midwife, and I have many ladies that come to my house to lie in. I have given security to the parish in general to secure them from any charge from what shall come into the world under my roof. I have but one question to ask in the whole affair, madam," says she, "and if that be answered, you shall be entirely easy of the rest."

I presently understood what she meant and told her, "Madam, I believe I understand you. I thank God, though I want friends in this part of the world I do not want money, so far as may be necessary, though I do not abound in that neither." This I added because I would not make her expect great things. "Well, madam," says she, "that is the thing, indeed, without which nothing can be done in these cases; and yet," says she, "you shall see that I will not impose upon you or offer anything that is unkind to you, and you shall know everything beforehand, that you may suit yourself to the occasion and be either costly or sparing as you see fit."

I told her she seemed to be so perfectly sensible of my condition that I had nothing to ask of her but this: that as I had money sufficient, but not a great quantity, she would order it so that I might be at as little superfluous charge as possible.

She replied that she should bring in an account of the expenses of it in two or three shapes; I should choose as I pleased; and I desired her to do so.

The next day she brought it, and the copy of her three bills was as follows:

	£	s.	d.
1. For three months' lodging in her house, including my diet, at 10*s.* a week	6	0	0
2. For a nurse for the month and use of childbed-linen	1	10	0
3. For a minister to christen the child, and to the godfathers and clerk	1	10	0
4. For a supper at the christening if I had five friends at it	1	0	0
For her fees as a midwife and the taking off the trouble of the parish	3	3	0
To her maidservant attending	0	10	0
	£13	13	0

This was the first bill; the second was in the same terms:

	£	s.	d.
1. For three months' lodging and diet, etc., at 20*s.* per week	12	0	0
2. For a nurse for the month and the use of linen and lace	2	10	0
3. For the minister to christen the child, etc., as above	2	0	0
4. For a supper and for sweetmeats	3	3	0
For her fees, as above	5	5	0
For a servant-maid	1	0	0
	£25	18	0

This was the second-rate bill; the third, she said, was for a degree higher and when the father or friends appeared:

	£	s.	d.
1. For three months' lodging and diet, having two rooms and a garret for a servant	30	0	0
2. For a nurse for the month and the finest suit of childbed-linen	4	4	0
3. For the minister to christen the child, etc. ..	2	10	0
4. For a supper, the gentleman to send in the wine	6	0	0
For my fees, etc.	10	10	0
The maid, besides their own maid, only	0	10	0
	£53	14	0

I looked upon all the three bills and smiled, and told her I did not see but that she was very reasonable in her demands, and things considered, and I did not doubt but her accommodations were good.

She told me I should be a judge of that when I saw them. I told her I was sorry to tell her that I feared I must be her lowest-rated customer; "and perhaps, madam," said I, "you will make me the less welcome upon that account." "No, not at all," said she; "for where I have one of the third sort, I have two of the second and four of the first, and I get as much by them in proportion as by any; but if you doubt my care of you, I will allow any friend you have to see if you are well waited on or no."

Then she explained the particulars of her bill. "In the first place, madam," said she, "I would have you observe that here is three months keeping you at but ten shillings a week; I undertake to say you will not complain of my table. I suppose," says she, "you do not live cheaper where you are now?" "No, indeed," said I, "nor so cheap, for I give six shillings per week for my chamber and find my own diet, which costs me a great deal more."

"Then, madam," says she, "if the child should not live, as it sometimes happens, there is the minister's article saved; and if you have no friends to come, you may save the expense of a supper; so that take those articles out, madam," says she, "your lying in will not cost you above five pounds three shillings more than your ordinary charge of living."

This was the most reasonable thing that I ever heard of; so I smiled and told her I would come and be a customer; but I told her also that as I had two months and more to go, I might perhaps be obliged to stay longer with her than three months, and desired to know if she would not be obliged to remove me before it was proper. No, she said; her house was large, and besides, she never put anybody to remove that had lain in till they were willing to go; and if she had more ladies offered, she was not so ill-beloved among her neighbours but she could provide accommodation for twenty if there was occasion.

I found she was an eminent lady in her way, and in short, I agreed to put myself into her hands. She then talked of other things, looked about into my accommodations where I was, found fault with my wanting attendance and conveniences, and that I should not be used so at her house. I told her I was shy of speaking, for the woman of the house looked stranger, or at least I thought so, since I had been ill, because I was with child; and I was afraid she would put some affront or other upon me, supposing that I had been able to give but a slight account of myself.

"Oh, dear," says she, "her ladyship is no stranger to these things; she has tried to entertain ladies in your condition, but could not secure the parish; and besides, such a nice lady, as you take her to be. However, since you are a-going, you shall not meddle with her, but I'll see you are a little better looked after while you are here, and it shall not cost you the more neither."

I did not understand her; however, I thanked her, so we parted. The next morning she sent me a chicken roasted and hot, and a bottle of sherry, and ordered the maid to tell me that she was to wait on me every day as long as I stayed there.

This was surprisingly good and kind, and I accepted it very willingly. At night she sent to me again, to know if I wanted anything and to order the maid to come to her in the morning for dinner. The maid had orders to make me some chocolate in the morning before she came away, and at noon she brought me the sweetbread of a breast of veal, whole, and a dish of soup for my dinner; and after this manner she nursed me up at a distance, so that I was mightily well pleased and quickly well, for indeed my dejections before were the principal part of my illness.

I expected, as is usually the case among such people, that the servant she sent me would have been some impudent brazen wench of Drury Lane breeding, and I was very uneasy upon that account; so I would not let her lie in the house the first night, but had my eyes about me as narrowly as if she had been a public thief.

My gentlewoman guessed presently what was the matter and sent her back with a short note that I might depend upon the honesty of her maid; that she would be answerable for her upon all accounts; and that she took no servants without very good security. I was then perfectly easy, and indeed the maid's behaviour spoke for itself, for a modester, quieter, soberer girl never came into anybody's family, and I found her so afterwards.

As soon as I was well enough to go abroad, I went with

the maid to see the house and to see the apartment I was to have; and everything was so handsome and so clean that, in short, I had nothing to say, but was wonderfully pleased with what I had met with, which, considering the melancholy circumstances I was in, was beyond what I looked for.

It might be expected that I should give some account of the nature of the wicked practices of this woman in whose hands I was now fallen; but it would be but too much encouragement to the vice to let the world see what easy measures were here taken to rid the women's burthen of a child clandestinely gotten. This grave matron had several sorts of practice, and this was one: that if a child was born, though not in her house (for she had the occasion to be called to many private labours), she had people always ready who for a piece of money would take the child off their hands and off from the hands of the parish too; and those children, as she said, were honestly taken care of. What should become of them all, considering so many as by her account she was concerned with, I cannot conceive.

I had many times discourses upon that subject with her; but she was full of this argument: that she saved the life of many an innocent lamb, as she called them, which would perhaps have been murdered; and of many a woman who, made desperate by the misfortune, would otherwise be tempted to destroy their children. I granted her that this was true and a very commendable thing, provided the poor children fell into good hands afterwards and were not abused and neglected by the nurses. She answered that she always took care of that, and had no nurses in her business but what were very good people and such as might be depended upon.

I could say nothing to the contrary, and so was obliged to say, "Madam, I do not question but you do your part, but what those people do is the main question"; and she stopped my mouth again with saying she took the utmost care about it.

The only thing I found in all her conversation on these subjects that gave me any distaste was that one time in discoursing about my being so far gone with child, she said something that looked as if she could help me off with my burthen sooner if I was willing; or, in English, that she could give me something to make me miscarry if I had a desire to put an end to my troubles that way; but I soon let her see that I abhorred the thoughts of it; and to do her justice, she put it off so cleverly that I could not say she really intended it or whether she only mentioned the practice as a horrible thing; for she couched her words so well and took my meaning so quickly that she gave her negative before I could explain myself.

To bring this part into as narrow a compass as possible, I quitted my lodging at St. Jones's and went to my new governess, for so they called her in the house, and there I was indeed treated with so much courtesy, so carefully looked to, and everything so well that I was surprised at it and could not at first see what advantage my governess made of it; but I found afterwards that she professed to make no profit of the lodgers' diet, nor indeed could she get much by it, but that her profit lay in the other articles of her management, and she made enough that way, I assure you; for 'tis scarce credible what practice she had, as well abroad as at home, and yet all upon the private account, or, in plain English, the whoring account.

While I was in her house, which was near four months, she had no less than twelve ladies of pleasure brought to bed within doors, and I think she had two-and-thirty or thereabouts under her conduct without doors; whereof one, as nice as she was with me, was lodged with my old landlady at St. Jones's.

This was a strange testimony of the growing vice of the age, and as bad as I had been myself, it shocked my very senses; I began to nauseate the place I was in and, above all, the practice; and yet I must say that I never saw, or do I believe there was to be seen, the least indecency in the house the whole time I was there.

Not a man was ever seen to come upstairs except to visit the lying-in ladies within their month, nor then without the old lady with them, who made it a piece of the honour of her management that no man should touch a woman, no, not his own wife, within the month; nor would she permit any man to lie in the house upon any pretence whatever, no, not though it was with his own wife; and her saying for it was that she cared not how many children were born in her house, but she would have none got there if she could help it.

It might perhaps be carried farther than was needful, but it was an error of the right hand if it was an error, for by this she kept up the reputation, such as it was, of her business and obtained this character: that though she did take care of the women when they were debauched, yet she was not instrumental to their being debauched at all; and yet it was a wicked trade she drove too.

While I was here, and before I was brought to bed, I received a letter from my trustee at the bank, full of kind, obliging things and earnestly pressing me to return to London; it was near a fortnight old when it came to me because it had first been sent into Lancashire and then returned to me. He concludes with telling me that he had obtained a decree against his wife and that he would be ready to make good his engagement to me if I would accept of him, adding a great many protestations of kindness and affection, such as he would have been far from offering if he had known the circumstances I had been in, and which, as it was, I had been very far from deserving.

I returned an answer to this letter and dated it at Liverpool, but sent it by a messenger, alleging that it came in cover to a friend in town. I gave him joy of his deliverance, but raised some scruples at the lawfulness of his marrying again, and told him I supposed he would consider very seriously upon that point before he resolved on it, the consequence being too great for a man of his judgement to venture rashly upon; so concluded wishing him very well in whatever he resolved without letting him into anything of my own mind or giving any answer to his proposal of my coming to London to him, but mentioned at a distance my intention to return the latter end of the year, this being dated in April.

I was brought to bed about the middle of May, and had another brave boy, and myself in as good condition as usual on such occasions. My governess did her part as a midwife with the greatest art and dexterity imaginable, and far beyond all that ever I had had any experience of before.

Her care of me in my travail, and after in my lying in, was such that if she had been my own mother, it could not have been better. Let none be encouraged in their loose practices from this dexterous lady's management, for she is gone to her place and I dare say has left nothing behind her that can or will come up to it.

I think I had been brought to bed about twenty days when I received another letter from my friend at the bank, with the surprising news that he had obtained a final sentence of divorce against his wife and had served her with it on such a day, and that he had such an answer to give to all my scruples about his marrying again as I could not expect and as he had no desire of; for that his wife, who had been under some remorse before for her usage of him, as soon as she heard that he had gained his point, had very unhappily destroyed herself that same evening.

He expressed himself very handsomely as to his being concerned at her disaster, but cleared himself of having any hand in it and that he had only done himself justice in a case in which he was notoriously injured and abused. However, he said that he was extremely afflicted at it and had no view of any satisfaction left in this world but only in the hope that I would come and relieve him by my company; and then he pressed me violently indeed to give him some hopes that I would at least come up to town and let him see me, when he would farther enter into discourse about it.

I was exceedingly surprised at the news and began now seriously to reflect on my circumstances and the inexpressible misfortune it was to have a child upon my hands; and what to do in it I knew not. At last I opened my case at a distance to my governess; I appeared melancholy for several days, and she lay at me continually to know what troubled me. I could not for my life tell her that I had an offer of marriage after I had so often told her that I had a husband, so that I really knew not what to say to her. I owned I had something which very much troubled me, but at the same time told her I could not speak of it to any one alive.

She continued importuning me several days, but it was impossible, I told her, for me to commit the secret to anybody. This, instead of being an answer to her, increased her importunities; she urged her having been trusted with the greatest secrets of this nature, that it was her business to conceal everything, and that to discover things of that nature would be her ruin. She asked me if ever I had found her tattling of other people's affairs, and how could I suspect her? She told me to unfold myself to her was telling it to nobody; that she was silent as death; that it must be a very strange case indeed that she could not help me out of; but to conceal it was to deprive myself of all possible help or means of help, and to deprive her of the opportunity of serving me. In short, she had such a bewitching eloquence and so great a power of persuasion that there was no concealing anything from her.

So I resolved to unbosom myself to her. I told her the history of my Lancashire marriage and how both of us had been disappointed; how we came together and how we parted; how he discharged me, as far as lay in him, and gave me free liberty to marry again, protesting that if he knew it he would never claim me or disturb or expose me; that I thought I was free, but was dreadfully afraid to venture for fear of the consequences that might follow in case of a discovery.

Then I told her what a good offer I had, showed her my friend's letters inviting me to London, and with what affection they were written, but blotted out the name and also the story about the disaster of his wife, only that she was dead.

She fell a-laughing at my scruples about marrying and told me the other was no marriage but a cheat on both sides, and that as we were parted by mutual consent, the nature of the contract was destroyed and the obligation was mutually discharged. She had arguments for this at the tip of her tongue and, in short, reasoned me out of my reason; not but that it was too by the help of my own inclination.

But then came the great and main difficulty, and that was the child; this, she told me, must be removed, and that so as that it should never be possible for any one to discover it. I knew there was no marrying without concealing that I had had a child, for he would soon have discovered by the age of it that it was born, nay, and gotten too, since my parley with him, and that would have destroyed all the affair.

But it touched my heart so forcibly to think of parting entirely with the child and, for aught I knew, of having it murdered or starved by neglect and ill usage, which was much the same, that I could not think of it without horror. I wish all those women who consent to the disposing their children out of the way, as it is called for decency sake, would consider that 'tis only a contrived method for murder, that is to say, killing their children with safety.

It is manifest to all that understand anything of children that we are born into the world helpless and uncapable either to supply our own wants or so much as make them known, and that without help we must perish; and this help requires not only an assisting hand, whether of the mother or somebody else, but there are two things necessary in that assisting hand, that is, care and skill; without both which, half the children that are born would die, nay, though they were not to be denied food, and one-half more of those that remained would be cripples or fools, lose their limbs and perhaps their sense. I question not but that these are partly the reasons why affection was placed by nature in the hearts of mothers to their children; without which they would never be able to give themselves up, as 'tis necessary they should, to the care and waking pains needful to the support of children.

Since this care is needful to the life of children, to neglect them is to murder them; again, to give them up to be managed by those people who have none of that needful affection placed by nature in them is to neglect them in the highest degree; nay, in some it goes farther, and is in order to their being lost; so that 'tis an intentional murder, whether the child lives or dies.

All those things represented themselves to my view, and that in the blackest and most frightful form; and as I was very free with my governess, who I had now learnt to call mother, I represented to her all the dark thoughts which I had about it and told her what distress I was in. She seemed graver by much at this part than at the other; but as she was hardened in these things beyond all possibility of being touched with the religious part and the scruples about the murder, so she was equally impenetrable in that part which related to affection. She asked me if she had not been careful and tender of me in my lying in as if I had been her own child. I told her I owned she had. "Well, my dear," says she, "and when you are gone, what are you to me? And what would it be to me if you were to be hanged? Do you think there are not women who, as it is their trade and they get their bread by it, value themselves upon their being as careful of children as their own mothers? Yes, yes, child," says she, "fear it not. How were we nursed ourselves? Are you sure you was nursed up by your own mother? And yet you look fat and fair, child," says the old beldam; and with that she stroked me over the face. "Never be concerned, child," says she, going on in her drolling way; "I have no murderers about me; I employ the best nurses that can be had, and have as few children miscarry under their hands as there would if they were all nursed by mothers; we want neither care nor skill."

She touched me to the quick when she asked if I was sure that I was nursed by my own mother; on the contrary, I was sure I was not; and I trembled and looked pale at the very expression. "Sure," said I to myself, "this creature cannot be a witch or have any conversation with a spirit that can inform her what I was before I was able to know it myself"; and I looked at her as if I had been frighted; but reflecting that it could not be possible for her to know anything about me, that went off and I began to be easy, but it was not presently.

She perceived the disorder I was in, but did not know the meaning of it; so she run on in her wild talk upon the weakness of my supposing that children were murdered because they were not all nursed by the mother, and to persuade me that the children she disposed of were as well used as if the mothers had the nursing of them themselves.

"It may be true, Mother," says I, "for aught I know, but my doubts are very strongly grounded." "Come, then," says she, "let's hear some of them." "Why, first," says I, "you give a piece of money to these people to take the child off the parent's hands and to take care of it as long as it lives. Now we know, Mother," said I, "that those are poor people, and their gain consists in being quit of the charge as soon as they can; how can I doubt but that as it is best for them to have the child die, they are not over-solicitous about its life?"

"This is all vapours and fancy," says she; "I tell you their credit depends upon the child's life, and they are as careful as any mother of you all."

"Oh, Mother," says I, "if I was but sure my little baby would be carefully looked to and have justice done it, I should be happy; but it is impossible I can be satisfied in that point unless I saw it, and to see it would be ruin and destruction as my case now stands; so what to do I know not."

"A fine story!" says the governess. "You would see the child and you would not see the child; you would be concealed and discovered both together. These are things impossible, my dear, and so you must e'en do as other conscientious mothers have done before you and be contented with things as they must be though not as you wish them to be."

I understood what she meant by conscientious mothers; she would have said conscientious whores, but she was not willing to disoblige me, for really in this case I was not a whore because legally married, the force of my former marriage excepted.

However, let me be what I would, I was not come up to that pitch of hardness common to the profession; I mean, to be unnatural and regardless of the safety of my child; and I preserved this honest affection so long that I was upon the point of giving up my friend at the bank, who lay so hard at me to come to him and marry him that there was hardly any room to deny him.

At last my old governess came to me with her usual assurance. "Come, my dear," says she, "I have found out a way how you shall be at a certainty that your child shall be used well, and yet the people that take care of it shall never know you."

"Oh, Mother," says I, "if you can do so, you will engage me to you forever." "Well," says she, "are you willing to be at some small annual expense, more than what we usually give to the people we contract with?" "Aye," says I, "with all my heart, provided I may be concealed." "As to that," says she, "you shall be secure, for the nurse shall never dare to inquire about you; and you shall once or twice a year go with me and see your child and see how 'tis used, and be satisfied that it is in good hands, nobody knowing who you are."

"Why," said I, "do you think that when I come to see my child I shall be able to conceal my being the mother of it? Do you think that possible?"

"Well," says she, "if you discover it, the nurse shall be never the wiser; she shall be forbid to take any notice. If she offers it, she shall lose the money which you are to be supposed to give her, and the child be taken from her too."

I was very well pleased with this. So the next week a countrywoman was brought from Hertford or thereabouts, who was to take the child off our hands entirely for £10 in money. But if I would allow £5 a year more to her, she would be obliged to bring the child to my governess' house as often as we desired, or we should come down and look at it and see how well she used it.

The woman was a very wholesome-looked, likely woman, a cottager's wife, but she had very good clothes and linen and everything well about her; and with a heavy heart and many a tear I let her have my child. I had been down at Hertford and looked at her and at her dwelling, which I liked well enough; and I promised her great things if she would be kind to the child, so she knew at first word that I was the child's mother. But she seemed to be so much out of the way and to have no room to inquire after me that I thought I was safe enough. So, in short, I consented to let her have the child and I gave her £10; that is to say, I gave it to my governess, who gave it the poor woman before my face, she agreeing never to return the child back to me or to claim anything more for its keeping or bringing up; only that I promised if she took a great deal of care of it, I would give her something more as often as I came to see it; so that I was not bound to pay the £5, only that I promised my governess I would do it. And thus my great care was over, after a manner, which, though it did not at all satisfy my mind, yet was the most convenient for me, as my affairs then stood, of any that could be thought of at that time.

I then began to write to my friend at the bank in a more kindly style, and particularly about the beginning of July I sent him a letter that I purposed to be in town some time in August. He returned me an answer in the most passionate terms imaginable, and desired me to let him have timely notice and he would come and meet me two days' journey. This puzzled me scurvily, and I did not know what answer to make to it. Once I was resolved to take the stage-coach to West Chester, on purpose only to have the satisfaction of coming back, that he might see me really come in the same coach; for I had a jealous thought, though I had no ground for it at all, lest he should think I was not really in the country.

I endeavoured to reason myself out of it, but it was in vain; the impression lay so strong on my mind that it was not to be resisted. At last it came as an addition to my new design of going into the country that it would be an excellent blind to my old governess and would cover entirely all my other affairs, for she did not know in the least whether my new lover lived in London or in Lancashire; and when I told her my resolution, she was fully persuaded it was in Lancashire.

Having taken my measures for this journey, I let her know it and sent the maid that tended me from the beginning to take a place for me in the coach. She would have had me let the maid have waited on me down to the last stage and come up again in the waggon, but I convinced her it would not be convenient. When I went away, she told me she would enter into no measures for correspondence, for she saw evidently that my affection to my child would cause me to write to her and to visit her too when I came to town again. I assured her it would and so took my leave, well satisfied to have been freed from such a house, however good my accommodations there had been.

I took the place in the coach not to its full extent, but to a place called Stone, in Cheshire, where I not only had no manner of business but not the least acquaintance with any person in the town. But I knew that with money in the pocket one is at home anywhere; so I lodged there two or three days till, watching my opportunity, I found room in another stage-coach and took passage back again for London, sending a letter to my gentleman that I should be such a certain day at Stony-Stratford, where the coachman told me he was to lodge.

It happened to be a chance coach that I had taken up, which, having been hired on purpose to carry some gentlemen to West Chester who were going for Ireland, was now returning, and did not tie itself up to exact times or places, as the stages did; so that having been obliged to lie still on Sunday, he had time to get himself ready to come out, which otherwise he could not have done.

His warning was so short that he could not reach Stony-Stratford time enough to be with me at night, but he met me at a place called Brickhill the next morning, just as we were coming into the town.

I confess I was very glad to see him, for I thought myself a little disappointed overnight. He pleased me doubly too by the figure he came in, for he brought a very handsome (gentleman's) coach and four horses, with a servant to attend him.

He took me out of the stage-coach immediately, which stopped at an inn in Brickhill; and putting into the same inn, he set up his own coach and bespoke his dinner. I asked him what he meant by that, for I was for going forward with the journey. He said no, I had need of a little rest upon the road, and that was a very good sort of a house, though it was but a little town; so we would go no farther that night, whatever came of it.

I did not press him much, for since he had come so far to meet me and put himself to so much expense, it was but reasonable I should oblige him a little too; so I was easy as to that point.

After dinner we walked to see the town, to see the church, and to view the fields and the country, as is usual for strangers to do; and our landlord was our guide in going to see the church. I observed my gentleman inquired pretty much about the parson, and I took the hint immediately that he certainly would propose to be married; and it followed presently that, in short, I would not refuse him; for to be plain, with my circumstances I was in no condition now to say no; I had no reason now to run any more such hazards.

But while these thoughts run round in my head, which was the work but of a few moments, I observed my landlord took him aside and whispered to him, though not very softly neither, for so much I overheard: "Sir, if you shall have occasion—" The rest I could not hear, but it seems it was to this purpose: "Sir, if you shall have occasion for a minister, I have a friend a little way off that will serve you and be as private as you please." My gentleman answered loud enough for me to hear, "Very well, I believe I shall."

I was no sooner come back to the inn but he fell upon me with irresistible words, that since he had had the good fortune to meet me, and everything concurred, it would be hastening his felicity if I would put an end to the matter just there. "What do you mean?" says I, colouring a little. "What, in an inn, and on the road! Bless us all," said I, "how can you talk so?" "Oh, I can talk so very well," says he; "I came on purpose to talk so, and I'll show you that I did"; and with that he pulls out a great bundle of papers. "You fright me," said I. "What are all these?" "Don't be frighted, my dear," said he, and kissed me. This was the first time that he had been so free to call me my dear; then he repeated it: "Don't be frighted; you shall see what it is all"; then he laid them all abroad. There was first the deed, or sentence, of divorce from his wife and the full evidence of her playing the whore; then there was the certificates of the minister and churchwardens of the parish where she lived, proving that she was buried, and intimating the manner of her death; the copy of the coroner's warrant for a jury to sit upon her; and the verdict of the jury, who brought it in *non compos mentis*. All this was to give me satisfaction, though, by the way, I was not so scrupulous, had he known all, but that I might have taken him without it; however, I looked them all over as well as I could and told him that this was all very clear indeed, but that he need not have brought them out with him, for it was time enough. Well, he said, it might be time enough for me, but no time but the present time was time enough for him.

There were other papers rolled up, and I asked him what they were. "Why, aye," says he, "that's the question I wanted to have you ask me"; so he takes out a little shagreen case and gives me out of it a very fine diamond ring. I could not refuse it, if I had a mind to do so, for he put it upon my finger; so I only made him a curtsy. Then he takes out another ring. "And this," says he, "is for another occasion," and puts that into his pocket. "Well, but let me see it, though," says I, and smiled. "I guess what it is; I think you are mad." "I should have been mad if I had done less," says he; and still he did not show it me, and I had a great mind to see it. So I says, "Well, but let me see it." "Hold," says he, "first look here." Then he took up the roll again and read it, and behold! It was a licence for us to be married. "Why," says I, "are you distracted? You were fully satisfied, sure, that I would yield at first word, or resolved to take no denial." "The last is certainly the case," said he. "But you may be mistaken," said I. "No, no," says he, "I must not be denied, I can't be denied"; and with that he fell to kissing me so violently I could not get rid of him.

There was a bed in the room, and we were walking to and again, eager in the discourse; at last, he takes me by surprise in his arms and threw me on the bed, and himself with me, and holding me still fast in his arms, but without the least offer of any undecency, courted me to consent with such repeated entreaties and arguments, protesting his affection and vowing he would not let me go till I had promised him, that at last I said, "Why, you resolve not to be denied indeed, I think." "No, no," says he, "I must not be denied, I won't be denied, I can't be denied." "Well, well," said I, and giving him a slight kiss, "then you shan't be denied; let me get up."

He was so transported with my consent and the kind manner of it that I began to think once he took it for a marriage, and would not stay for the form; but I wronged him, for he took me by the hand, pulled me up again, and then, giving me two or three kisses, thanked me for my kind yielding to him, and was so overcome with the satisfaction of it that I saw tears stand in his eyes.

I turned from him, for it filled my eyes with tears too, and asked him leave to retire a little to my chamber. If I had a grain of true repentance for an abominable life of twenty-four years past, it was then. "Oh, what a felicity is it to mankind," said I to myself, "that they cannot see into the hearts of one another! How happy had it been if I had been wife to a man of so much honesty and so much affection from the beginning!"

Then it occurred to me: "What an abominable creature am I! And how is this innocent gentleman going to be abused by me! How little does he think that having divorced a whore, he is throwing himself into the arms of another! That he is going to marry one that has lain with two brothers and has had three children by her own brother! One that was born in Newgate, whose mother was a whore, and is now a transported thief! One that has lain with thirteen men and has had a child since he saw me! Poor gentleman!" said I. "What is he going to do?" After this reproaching myself was over, it followed thus: "Well, if I must be his wife, if it please God to give me grace, I'll be a true wife to him and love him suitably to the strange excess of his passion for me; I will make him amends, by what he shall see, for the abuses I put upon him, which he does not see."

He was impatient for my coming out of my chamber, but finding me long, he went downstairs and talked with my landlord about the parson.

My landlord, an officious though well-meaning fellow, had sent away for the clergyman; and when my gentleman began to speak to him of sending for him, "Sir," says he to him, "my friend is in the house"; so without any more words he brought them together. When he came to the minister, he asked him if he would venture to marry a couple of strangers that were both willing. The parson said that Mr. —— had said something to him of it; that he hoped it was no clandestine business; that he seemed to be a grave gentleman, and he supposed madam was not a girl, so that the consent of friends should be wanted. "To put you out of doubt of that," says my gentleman, "read this paper"; and out he pulls the licence. "I am satisfied," says the minister. "Where is the lady?" "You shall see her presently," says my gentleman.

When he had said thus he comes upstairs, and I was by that time come out of my room; so he tells me the minister was below, and that upon showing him the licence, he was free to marry us with all his heart. "But he asks to see you"; so he asked if I would let him come up.

" 'Tis time enough," said I, "in the morning, is it not?" "Why," said he, "my dear, he seemed to scruple whether it was not some young girl stolen from her parents, and I assured him we were both of age to command our own consent; and that made him ask to see you." "Well," said I, "do as you please"; so up they brings the parson, and a merry, good sort of gentleman he was. He had been told, it seems, that we had met there by accident; that I came in a Chester coach and my gentleman in his own coach to meet me; that we were to have met last night at Stony-Stratford, but that he could not reach so far. "Well, sir," says the parson, "every ill turn has some good in it. The disappointment, sir," says he to my gentleman, "was yours, and the good turn is mine, for if you had met at Stony-Stratford I had not had the honour to marry you. Landlord, have you a Common Prayer Book?"

I started as if I had been frighted. "Sir," says I, "what do you mean? What, to marry in an inn, and at night too!" "Madam," says the minister, "if you will have it be in the church, you shall; but I assure you your marriage will be as firm here as in the church; we are not tied by the canons to marry nowhere but in the church; and as for the time of day, it does not at all weigh in this case; our princes are married in their chambers, and at eight or ten o'clock at night."

I was a great while before I could be persuaded, and pretended not to be willing at all to be married but in the church. But it was all grimace; so I seemed at last to be prevailed on, and my landlord and his wife and daughter were called up. My landlord was father and clerk and all together, and we were married, and very merry we were; though I confess the self-reproaches which I had upon me before lay close to me and extorted every now and then a deep sigh from me, which my bridegroom took notice of and endeavoured to encourage me, thinking, poor man, that I had some little hesitations at the step I had taken so hastily.

We enjoyed ourselves that evening completely, and yet all was kept so private in the inn that not a servant in the house knew of it, for my landlady and her daughter waited on me and would not let any of the maids come upstairs. My landlady's daughter I called my bridemaid; and sending for a shopkeeper the next morning, I gave the young woman a good suit of knots, as good as the town would afford, and finding it was a lace-making town, I gave her mother a piece of bone-lace for a head.

One reason that my landlord was so close was that he was unwilling the minister of the parish should hear of it; but for all that, somebody heard of it, so as that we had the bells set a-ringing the next morning early, and the music, such as the town would afford, under our window. But my landlord brazened it out that we were married before we came thither, only that, being his former guests, we would have our wedding-supper at his house.

We could not find in our hearts to stir the next day; for, in short, having been disturbed by the bells in the morning and having perhaps not slept overmuch before, we were so sleepy afterwards that we lay in bed till almost twelve o'clock.

I begged my landlady that we might have no more music in the town nor ringing of bells, and she managed it so well that we were very quiet; but an odd passage interrupted all my mirth for a good while. The great room of the house looked into the street, and I had walked to the end of the room, and it being a pleasant, warm day, I had opened the window and was standing at it for some air when I saw three gentlemen ride by and go into an inn just against us.

It was not to be concealed, nor did it leave me any room to question it, but the second of the three was my Lancashire husband. I was frighted to death; I never was in such a consternation in my life; I thought I should have sunk into the ground; my blood run chill in my veins, and I trembled as if I had been in a cold fit of an ague. I say, there was no room to question the truth of it; I knew his clothes, I knew his horse, and I knew his face.

The first reflection I made was that my husband was not by to see my disorder, and that I was very glad of. The gentlemen had not been long in the house but they came to the window of their room, as is usual; but my window was shut, you may be sure. However, I could not keep from peeping at them, and there I saw him again, heard him call to one of the servants for something he wanted, and received all the terrifying confirmations of its being the same person that were possible to be had.

My next concern was to know what was his business there; but that was impossible. Sometimes my imagination formed an idea of one frightful thing, sometimes of another; sometimes I thought he had discovered me and was come to upbraid me with ingratitude and breach of honour; then I fancied he was coming upstairs to insult me; and innumerable thoughts came into my head of what was never in his head, nor ever could be, unless the devil had revealed it to him.

I remained in the fright near two hours and scarce ever kept my eye from the window or door of the inn where they were. At last, hearing a great clutter in the passage of their inn, I run to the window, and to my great satisfaction I saw them all three go out again and travel on westward. Had they gone towards London, I should have been still in a fright lest I should meet him again and that he should know me; but he went the contrary way, and so I was eased of that disorder.

We resolved to be going the next day, but about six o'clock at night we were alarmed with a great uproar in the street and people riding as if they had been out of their wits; and what was it but a hue and cry after three highwaymen that had robbed two coaches and some travellers near Dunstable Hill, and notice had, it seems, been given that they had been seen at Brickhill at such a house, meaning the house where those gentlemen had been.

The house was immediately beset and searched, but there were witnesses enough that the gentlemen had been gone above three hours. The crowd having gathered about, we had the news presently; and I was heartily concerned now another way. I presently told the people of the house that I durst say those were honest persons, for that I knew one of the gentlemen to be a very honest person and of a good estate in Lancashire.

The constable who came with the hue and cry was immediately informed of this, and came over to me to be satisfied from my own mouth; and I assured him that I saw the three gentlemen as I was at the window; that I saw them afterwards at the windows of the room they dined in; that I saw them take horse, and I would assure him I knew one of them to be such a man, that he was a gentleman of a very good estate and an undoubted character in Lancashire, from whence I was just now upon my journey.

The assurance with which I delivered this gave the mob gentry a check and gave the constable such satisfaction that he immediately sounded a retreat, told his people these were not the men, but that he had an account they were very honest gentlemen; and so they went all back again. What the truth of the matter was I knew not, but certain it was that the coaches were robbed at Dunstable Hill and £560 in money taken; besides, some of the lace-merchants that always travel that way had been visited too. As to the three gentlemen, that remains to be explained hereafter.

Well, this alarm stopped us another day, though my

spouse told me it was always safest travelling after a robbery, for that the thieves were sure to be gone far enough off when they had alarmed the country; but I was uneasy, and indeed principally lest my old acquaintance should be upon the road still and should chance to see me.

I never lived four pleasanter days together in my life. I was a mere bride all this while, and my new spouse strove to make me easy in everything. Oh, could this state of life have continued, how had all my past troubles been forgot and my future sorrows been avoided! But I had a past life of a most wretched kind to account for, some of it in this world as well as in another.

We came away the fifth day; and my landlord, because he saw me uneasy, mounted himself, his son, and three honest country-fellows with good fire-arms and, without telling us of it, followed the coach and would see us safe into Dunstable.

We could do no less than treat them very handsomely at Dunstable, which cost my spouse about ten or twelve shillings, and something he gave the men for their time too, but my landlord would take nothing for himself.

This was the most happy contrivance for me that could have fallen out; for had I come to London unmarried, I must either have come to him for the first night's entertainment, or have discovered to him that I had not one acquaintance in the whole city of London that could receive a poor bride for the first night's lodging with her spouse. But now I made no scruple of going directly home with him, and there I took possession at once of a house well furnished and a husband in very good circumstances, so that I had a prospect of a very happy life if I knew how to manage it; and I had leisure to consider of the real value of the life I was likely to live. How different it was to be from the loose part I had acted before, and how much happier a life of virtue and sobriety is than that which we call a life of pleasure!

Oh, had this particular scene of life lasted, or had I learnt from that time I enjoyed it to have tasted the true sweetness of it, and had I not fallen into that poverty which is the sure bane of virtue, how happy had I been, not only here but perhaps forever! For while I lived thus I was really a penitent for all my life past. I looked back on it with abhorrence, and might truly be said to hate myself for it. I often reflected how my lover at Bath, struck by the hand of God, repented and abandoned me and refused to see me any more, though he loved me to an extreme; but I, prompted by that worst of devils, poverty, returned to the vile practice and made the advantage of what they call a handsome face be the relief to my necessities, and beauty be a pimp to vice.

Now I seemed landed in a safe harbour after the stormy voyage of life past was at an end, and I began to be thankful for my deliverance. I sat many an hour by myself and wept over the remembrance of past follies and the dreadful extravagances of a wicked life, and sometimes I flattered myself that I had sincerely repented.

But there are temptations which it is not in the power of human nature to resist, and few know what would be their case if driven to the same exigences. As covetousness is the root of all evil, so poverty is the worst of all snares. But I waive that discourse till I come to the experiment.

I lived with this husband in the utmost tranquillity; he was a quiet, sensible, sober man; virtuous, modest, sincere, and in his business diligent and just. His business was in a narrow compass, and his income sufficient to a plentiful way of living in the ordinary way. I do not say to keep an equipage and make a figure, as the world calls it, nor did I expect it or desire it; for as I abhorred the levity and extravagance of my former life, so I chose now to live retired, frugal, and within ourselves. I kept no company, made no visits, minded my family, and obliged my husband; and this kind of life became a pleasure to me.

We lived in an uninterrupted course of ease and content for five years, when a sudden blow from an almost invisible hand blasted all my happiness and turned me out into the world in a condition the reverse of all that had been before it.

My husband having trusted one of his fellow-clerks with a sum of money, too much for our fortunes to bear the loss of, the clerk failed and the loss fell very heavy on my husband; yet it was not so great but that if he had had courage to have looked his misfortunes in the face, his credit was so good that, as I told him, he would easily recover it; for to sink under trouble is to double the weight, and he that will die in it shall die in it.

It was in vain to speak comfortably to him; the wound had sunk too deep; it was a stab that touched the vitals; he grew melancholy and disconsolate, and from thence lethargic, and died. I foresaw the blow and was extremely oppressed in my mind, for I saw evidently that if he died I was undone.

I had had two children by him and no more, for it began to be time for me to leave bearing children, for I was now eight-and-forty, and I suppose if he had lived I should have had no more.

I was now left in a dismal and disconsolate case indeed, and in several things worse than ever. First, it was past the flourishing time with me when I might expect to be courted for a mistress; that agreeable part had declined some time, and the ruins only appeared of what had been; and that which was worse than all was this: that I was the most dejected, disconsolate creature alive. I that had encouraged my husband and endeavoured to support his spirits under his trouble could not support my own; I wanted that spirit in trouble which I told him was so necessary for bearing the burthen.

But my case was indeed deplorable, for I was left perfectly friendless and helpless, and the loss my husband had sustained had reduced his circumstances so low that though indeed I was not in debt, yet I could easily foresee that what was left would not support me long; that it wasted daily for subsistence so that it would be soon all spent, and then I saw nothing before me but the utmost distress; and this represented itself so lively to my thoughts that it seemed as if it was come before it was really very near; also my very apprehensions doubled the misery, for I fancied every sixpence that I paid for a loaf of bread was the last I had in the world, and that tomorrow I was to fast and be starved to death.

In this distress I had no assistant, no friend to comfort or advise me; I sat and cried and tormented myself night and day, wringing my hands and sometimes raving like a distracted woman; and indeed I have often wondered it had not affected my reason, for I had the vapours to such a degree that my understanding was sometimes quite lost in fancies and imaginations.

I lived two years in this dismal condition, wasting that little I had, weeping continually over my dismal circumstances, and, as it were, only bleeding to death, without the least hope or prospect of help; and now I had cried so long and so often that tears were exhausted, and I began to be desperate, for I grew poor apace.

For a little relief I had put off my house and took lodgings; and as I was reducing my living, so I sold off most of my goods, which put a little money in my pocket, and I lived near a year upon that, spending very sparingly and eking things out to the utmost; but still when I looked before me, my heart would sink within me at the inevitable approach of misery and want. Oh, let none read this part without seriously reflecting on the circumstances of a desolate state and how they would grapple with want of friends and want of bread; it will certainly make them think not of sparing what they have only, but of looking up to Heaven for support, and of the wise man's prayer, "Give me not poverty, lest I steal."

Let 'em remember that a time of distress is a time of dreadful temptation, and all the strength to resist is taken away; poverty presses, the soul is made desperate by distress, and what can be done? It was one evening, when being brought, as I may say, to the last gasp, I think I may truly say I was distracted and raving, when prompted by I know not what spirit and, as it were, doing I did not know what or why, I dressed me (for I had still pretty good clothes) and went out. I am very sure I had no manner of design in my head when I went out; I neither knew or considered where to go or on what business; but as the devil carried me out and laid his bait for me, so he brought me, to be sure, to the place, for I knew not whither I was going or what I did.

Wandering thus about, I knew not whither, I passed by an apothecary's shop in Leadenhall Street, where I saw lie on a stool just before the counter a little bundle wrapt in a white cloth; beyond it stood a maidservant with her back to it, looking up towards the top of the shop, where the apothecary's apprentice, as I suppose, was standing upon the counter with his back also to the door and a candle in his hand, looking and reaching up to the upper shelf for something he wanted, so that both were engaged and nobody else in the shop.

This was the bait; and the devil, who laid the snare, prompted me as if he had spoke, for I remember, and shall never forget it, 'twas like a voice spoken over my shoulder: "Take the bundle; be quick; do it this moment." It was no sooner said but I stepped into the shop, and with my back to the wench, as if I had stood up for a cart that was going by, I put my hand behind me and took the bundle and went off with it, the maid or fellow not perceiving me, or any one else.

It is impossible to express the horror of my soul all the while I did it. When I went away I had no heart to run or scarce to mend my pace. I crossed the street indeed, and went down the first turning I came to, and I think it was a street that went through into Fenchurch Street; from thence I crossed and turned through so many ways and turnings that I could never tell which way it was nor where I went; I felt not the ground I stepped on, and the farther I was out of danger, the faster I went, till, tired and out of breath, I was forced to sit down on a little bench at a door, and then found I was got into Thames Street, near Billingsgate. I rested me a little and went on; my blood was all in a fire; my heart beat as if I was in a sudden fright. In short, I was under such a surprise that I knew not whither I was a-going or what to do.

After I had tired myself thus with walking a long way about, and so eagerly, I began to consider and make home to my lodging, where I came about nine o'clock at night.

What the bundle was made up for or on what occasion laid where I found it I knew not, but when I came to open it, I found there was a suit of childbed-linen in it, very good and almost new, the lace very fine; there was a silver porringer of a pint, a small silver mug and six spoons, with some other linen, a good smock, and three silk handkerchiefs, and in the mug, in a paper, 18*s.* 6*d.* in money.

All the while I was opening these things I was under such dreadful impressions of fear and in such terror of mind, though I was perfectly safe, that I cannot express the manner of it. I sat me down and cried most vehemently. "Lord," said I, "what am I now? A thief! Why, I shall be taken next time, and be carried to Newgate, and be tried for my life!" And with that I cried again a long time, and I am sure, as poor as I was, if I had durst for fear, I would certainly have carried the things back again; but that went off after a while. Well, I went to bed for that night, but slept little; the horror of the fact was upon my mind, and I knew not what I said or did all night and all the next day. Then I was impatient to hear some news of the loss, and would fain know how it was, whether they were a poor body's goods or a rich. "Perhaps," said I, "it may be some poor widow like me, that had packed up these goods to go and sell them for a little bread for herself and a poor child, and are now starving and breaking their hearts for want of that little they would have fetched." And this thought tormented me worse than all the rest for three or four days.

But my own distresses silenced all these reflections, and the prospect of my own starving, which grew every day more frightful to me, hardened my heart by degrees. It was then particularly heavy upon my mind that I had been reformed and had, as I hoped, repented of all my past wickedness; that I had lived a sober, grave, retired life for several years, but now I should be driven by the dreadful necessity of my circumstances to the gates of destruction, soul and body; and two or three times I fell upon my knees, praying to God, as well as I could, for deliverance; but I cannot but say my prayers had no hope in them. I knew not what to do; it was all fear without and dark within; and I reflected on my past life as not repented of, that Heaven was now beginning to punish me and would make me as miserable as I had been wicked.

Had I gone on here, I had perhaps been a true penitent; but I had an evil counsellor within, and he was continually prompting me to relieve myself by the worst means; so one evening he tempted me again by the same wicked impulse that had said, "Take that bundle," to go out again and seek for what might happen.

I went out now by daylight, and wandered about I knew not whither and in search of I knew not what, when the devil put a snare in my way of a dreadful nature indeed, and such a one as I have never had before or since. Going through Aldersgate Street, there was a pretty little child had been at a dancing-school and was a-going home all alone; and my prompter, like a true devil, set me upon this innocent creature. I talked to it, and it prattled to me again, and I took it by the hand and led it along till I came to a paved alley that goes into Bartholomew Close, and I led it in there. The child said that was not its way home. I said, "Yes, my dear, it is; I'll show you the way home." The child had a little necklace on of gold beads, and I had my eye upon that, and in the dark of the alley I stooped, pretending to mend the child's clog that was loose, and took off her necklace, and the child never felt it, and so led the child on again. Here, I say, the devil put me upon killing the child in the dark alley, that it might not cry, but the very thought frighted me so that I was ready to drop down; but I turned the child about and bade it go back again, for that was not its way home; the child said, so she would; and I went through into Bartholomew Close, and then turned around to another passage that goes into Long Lane, so away into Charterhouse Yard and out into St. John's Street; then, crossing into Smithfield, went down Chick Lane and into Field Lane to Holborn Bridge, when, mixing with the crowd of people usually passing there, it was not possible to have been found out; and thus I made my second sally into the world.

The thoughts of this booty put out all the thoughts of the first, and the reflections I had made wore quickly off; poverty hardened my heart, and my own necessities made me regardless of anything. The last affair left no great concern upon me, for as I did the poor child no harm, I only thought I had given the parents a just reproof for their negligence in leaving the poor lamb to come home by itself, and it would teach them to take more care another time.

This string of beads was worth about twelve or fourteen pounds. I suppose it might have been formerly the mother's, for it was too big for the child's wear, but that, perhaps, the vanity of the mother to have her child look fine at the dancing-school had made her let the child wear it; and no doubt the child had a maid sent to take care of it, but she, like a careless jade, was taken up perhaps with some fellow that had met her, and so the poor baby wandered till it fell into my hands.

However, I did the child no harm; I did not so much as fright it, for I had a great many tender thoughts about me yet and did nothing but what, as I may say, mere necessity drove me to.

I had a great many adventures after this, but I was young in the business and did not know how to manage otherwise than as the devil put things into my head; and, indeed, he was seldom backward to me. One adventure I had which was very lucky to me. I was going through Lombard Street in the dusk of the evening, just by the end of Three King Court, when on a sudden comes a fellow running by me as swift as lightning, and throws a bundle that was in his hand just behind me, as I stood up against the corner of the house at the turning into the alley. Just as he threw it in, he said, "God bless you, mistress, let it lie there a little," and away he runs. After him comes two more, and immediately a young fellow without his hat, crying, "Stop, thief!" They pursued the two last fellows so close that they were forced to drop what they had got, and one of them was taken, into the bargain; the other got off free.

I stood stock still all this while, till they came back dragging the poor fellow they had taken and lugging the things they had found, extremely well satisfied that they had recovered the booty and taken the thief; and thus they passed by me, for I looked only like one who stood up while the crowd was gone.

Once or twice I asked what was the matter, but the people neglected answering me, and I was not very importunate; but after the crowd was wholly passed I took my opportunity to turn about and take up what was behind me and walk away. This, indeed, I did with less disturbance than I had done formerly, for these things I did not steal, but they were stolen to my hand. I got safe to my lodgings with this cargo, which was a piece of fine black lustring silk and a piece of velvet; the latter was but part of a piece of about eleven yards; the former was a whole piece of near fifty yards. It seems it was a mercer's shop that they had rifled. I say rifled because the goods were so considerable that they had lost; for the the goods that they recovered were pretty many, and I believe came to about six or seven several pieces of silk. How they came to get so many I could not tell; but as I had only robbed the thief, I made no scruple at taking these goods and being very glad of them too.

I had pretty good luck thus far, and I made several adventures more, though with but small purchase yet with good success; but I went in daily dread that some mischief would befall me and that I should certainly come to be hanged at last. The impression this made on me was too strong to be slighted, and it kept me from making attempts that for aught I knew might have been very safely performed; but one thing I cannot omit, which was a bait to me many a day. I walked frequently out into the villages round the town to see if nothing would fall in my way there; and going by a house near Stepney, I saw on the window-board two rings, one a small diamond ring and the other a plain gold ring, to be sure laid there by some thoughtless lady that had more money than forecast, perhaps only till she washed her hands.

I walked several times by the window to observe if I could see whether there was anybody in the room or no, and I could see nobody, but still I was not sure. It came presently into my thoughts to rap at the glass, as if I wanted to speak with somebody, and if anybody was there they would be sure to come to the window, and then I would tell them to remove those rings, for that I had seen two suspicious fellows take notice of them. This was a ready thought. I rapped once or twice and nobody came, when I thrust hard against the square of glass and broke it with little noise and took out the two rings and walked away; the diamond ring was worth about £3 and the other about 9*s*.

I was now at a loss for a market for my goods, and especially for my two pieces of silk. I was very loath to dispose of them for a trifle, as the poor unhappy thieves in general do, who, after they have ventured their lives for perhaps a thing of value, are forced to sell it for a song when they have done; but I was resolved I would not do thus, whatever shift I made; however, I did not well know what course to take. At last I resolved to go to my old governess and acquaint myself with her again. I had punctually supplied the £5 a year to her for my little boy as long as I was able, but at last was obliged to put a stop to it. However, I had written a letter to her wherein I had told her that my circumstances were reduced, that I had lost my husband, and that I was not able to do it any longer, and begged the poor child might not suffer too much for its mother's misfortunes.

I now made her a visit, and I found that she drove something of the old trade still, but that she was not in such flourishing circumstances as before; for she had been sued by a certain gentleman who had had his daughter stolen from him, and who, it seems, she had helped to convey away; and it was very narrowly that she escaped the gallows. The expense also had ravaged her, so that her house was but meanly furnished and she was not in such repute for her practice as before; however, she stood upon her legs, as they say, and as she was a bustling woman and had some stock left, she was turned pawnbroker and lived pretty well.

She received me very civilly and with her usual obliging manner told me she would not have the less respect for me for my being reduced; that she had taken care my boy was very well looked after though I could not pay for him, and that the woman that had him was easy, so that I needed not to trouble myself about him till I might be better able to do it effectually.

I told her I had not much money left, but that I had some things that were money's worth if she could tell me how I might turn them into money. She asked what it was I had. I pulled out the string of gold beads and told her it was one of my husband's presents to me; then I showed her the two parcels of silk, which I told her I had from Ireland and brought up to town with me, and the little diamond ring. As to the small parcel of plate and spoons, I had found means to dispose of them myself before; and as for the childbed-linen I had, she offered me to take it herself, believing it to have been my own. She told me that she was turned pawnbroker and that she would sell those things for me as pawned to her; and so she sent presently for proper agents that bought them, being in her hands, without any scruple, and gave good prices too.

I now began to think this necessary woman might help me a little in my low condition to some business, for I would gladly have turned my hand to any honest employment if I could have got it; but honest business did not come within her reach. If I had been younger, perhaps she might have helped me, but my thoughts were off of that kind of livelihood, as being quite out of the way after fifty, which was my case, and so I told her.

She invited me at last to come and be at her house till I could find something to do, and it should cost me very little, and this I gladly accepted of; and now living a little easier, I entered into some measures to have my little son by my last husband taken off; and this she made easy too, reserving a payment only of £5 a year if I could pay it. This was such a help to me that for a good while I left off the wicked trade that I had so newly taken up; and gladly I would have got work, but that was very hard to do for one that had no acquaintance.

However, at last I got some quilting work for ladies' beds, petticoats, and the like; and this I liked very well and worked very hard, and with this I began to live; but the diligent devil, who resolved I should continue in his service, continually prompted me to go out and take a walk, that is to say, to see if anything would offer in the old way.

One evening I blindly obeyed his summons and fetched a long circuit through the streets, but met with no purchase; but not content with that, I went out the next evening too, when, going by an ale-house, I saw the door of a little room open, next the very street, and on the table a silver tankard, things much in use in public-houses at that time. It seems some company had been drinking there, and the careless boys had forgot to take it away. I went into the box frankly, and setting the silver tankard on the corner of the bench, I sat down before it and knocked with my foot; a boy came presently, and I bade him fetch me a pint of warm ale, for it was cold weather; the boy run and I heard him go down the cellar to draw the ale. While the boy was gone another boy come and cried, "D'ye call?" I spoke with a melancholy air and said, "No, the boy is gone for a pint of ale for me."

While I sat here I heard the woman in the bar say, "Are they all gone in the five?" which was the box I sat in, and the boy said, "Yes." "Who fetched the tankard away?" says the woman. "I did," says another boy; "that's it," pointing, it seems, to another tankard, which he had fetched from another box by mistake; or else it must be that the rogue forgot that he had not brought it in, which certainly he had not.

I heard all this much to my satisfaction, for I found plainly that the tankard was not missed and yet they concluded it was fetched away; so I drank my ale, called to pay, and as I went away I said, "Take care of your plate, child," meaning a silver pint mug which he brought me to drink in. The boy said, "Yes, madam, very welcome." And away I came.

I came home to my governess, and now I thought it was a time to try her, that if I might be put to the necessity of being exposed, she might offer me some assistance. When I had been at home some time and had an opportunity of talking to her, I told her I had a secret of the greatest consequence in the world to commit to her if she had respect enough for me to keep it a secret. She told me she had kept one of my secrets faithfully; why should I doubt her keeping another? I told her the strangest thing in the world had befallen me, even without any design, and so told her the whole story of the tankard. "And have you brought it away with you, my dear?" says she. "To be sure I have," says I, and showed it her. "But what shall I do now?" says I. "Must not I carry it again?"

"Carry it again!" says she. "Aye, if you want to go to Newgate." "Why," says I, "they can't be so base to stop me when I carry it to them again?" "You don't know those sort of people, child," says she; "they'll not only carry you to Newgate but hang you too, without any regard to the honesty of returning it; or bring in an account of all the other tankards as they have lost, for you to pay for." "What must I do, then?" says I. "Nay," says she, "as you have played the cunning part and stole it, you must e'en keep it; there's no going back now. Besides, child," says she, "don't you want it more than they do? I wish you could light of such a bargain once a week."

This gave me a new notion of my governess, and that since she was turned pawnbroker, she had a sort of people about her that were none of the honest ones that I had met with there before.

I had not been long there but I discovered it more plainly than before, for every now and then I saw hilts of swords, spoons, forks, tankards, and all such kind of ware brought in, not to be pawned but to be sold downright; and she bought them all without asking any questions, but had good bargains, as I found by her discourse.

I found also that in following this trade she always melted down the plate she bought, that it might not be challenged; and she came to me and told me one morning that she was going to melt, and if I would, she would put my tankard in, that it might not be seen by anybody. I told her, with all my heart; so she weighed it and allowed me the full value in silver again; but I found she did not do so to the rest of her customers.

Some time after this, as I was at work and very melancholy, she begins to ask me what the matter was. I told her my heart was very heavy; I had little work and nothing to live on and knew not what course to take. She laughed and told me I must go out again and try my fortune; it might be that I might meet with another piece of plate. "Oh, Mother!" says I. "That is a trade that I have no skill in, and if I should be taken I am undone at once." Says she, "I could help you to a schoolmistress that shall make you as dexterous as herself." I trembled at that proposal, for hitherto I had had no confederates nor any acquaintance among that tribe. But she conquered all my modesty and all my fears; and in a little time, by the help of this confederate, I grew as impudent a thief and as dexterous as ever Moll Cutpurse was, though, if fame does not belie her, not half so handsome.

The comrade she helped me to dealt in three sorts of craft, *viz.*, shoplifting, stealing of shop-books and pocket-books, and taking off gold watches from the ladies' sides; and this last she did so dexterously that no woman ever arrived to the perfection of that art like her. I liked the first and the last of these things very well, and I attended her some time in the practice, just as a deputy attends a midwife, without any pay.

At length she put me to practice. She had shown me her art, and I had several times unhooked a watch from her own side with great dexterity. At last she showed me a prize, and this was a young lady with child who had a charming watch. The thing was to be done as she came out of the church. She goes on one side of the lady and pretends, just as she came to the steps, to fall, and fell against the lady with so much violence as put her into a great fright, and both cried out terribly. In the very moment that she jostled the lady, I had hold of the watch, and holding it the right way, the start she gave drew the hook out, and she never felt it. I made off immediately and left my schoolmistress to come out of her fright gradually, and the lady too; and presently the watch was missed. "Aye," says my comrade, "then it was those rogues that thrust me down, I warrant ye; I wonder the gentlewoman did not miss her watch before, then we might have taken them."

She humoured the thing so well that nobody suspected her, and I was got home a full hour before her. This was my first adventure in company. The watch was indeed a very fine one and had many trinkets about it, and my governess allowed us £20 for it, of which I had half. And thus I was entered a complete thief, hardened to a pitch above all the reflections of conscience or modesty, and to a degree which I never thought possible in me.

Thus the devil, who began by the help of an irresistible poverty to push me into this wickedness, brought me on to a height beyond the common rate, even when my necessities were not so terrifying; for I had now got into a little vein of work, and as I was not at a loss to handle my needle, it was very probable I might have got my bread honestly enough.

I must say that if such a prospect of work had presented itself at first, when I began to feel the approach of my miserable circumstances—I say, had such a prospect of getting bread by working presented itself then, I had never fallen into this wicked trade or into such a wicked gang as I was now embarked with; but practice had hardened me, and I grew audacious to the last degree; and the more so because I had carried it on so long and had never been taken; for, in a word, my new partner in wickedness and I went on together so long without being ever detected that we not only grew bold but we grew rich, and we had at one time one-and-twenty gold watches in our hands.

I remember that one day, being a little more serious than ordinary and finding I had so good a stock beforehand as I had, for I had near £200 in money for my share, it came strongly into my mind, no doubt from some kind spirit, if such there be, that as at first poverty excited me and my distresses drove me to these dreadful shifts, so seeing those distresses were now relieved and I could also get something towards a maintenance by working and had so good a bank to support me, why should I not now leave off while I was well? That I could not expect to go always free; and if I was once surprised, I was undone.

This was doubtless the happy minute when, if I had hearkened to the blessed hint, from whatsoever hand it came, I had still a cast for an easy life. But my fate was otherwise determined; the busy devil that drew me in had too fast hold of me to let me go back; but as poverty brought me in, so avarice kept me in, till there was no going back. As to the arguments which my reason dictated for persuading me to lay down, avarice stepped in and said, "Go on; you have had very good luck; go on till you have gotten four or five hundred pound, and then you shall leave off, and then you may live easy without working at all."

Thus I, that was once in the devil's clutches, was held fast there as with a charm, and had no power to go without the circle till I was engulfed in labyrinths of trouble too great to get out at all.

However, these thoughts left some impression upon me and made me act with some more caution than before, and more than my directors used for themselves. My comrade, as I called her (she should have been called my teacher), with another of her scholars, was the first in the misfortune; for, happening to be upon the hunt for purchase, they made an attempt upon a linen-draper in Cheapside, but were snapped by a hawk's-eyed journeyman and seized with two pieces of cambric, which were taken also upon them.

This was enough to lodge them both in Newgate, where they had the misfortune to have some of their former sins brought to remembrance. Two other indictments being brought against them and the facts being proved upon them, they were both condemned to die. They both pleaded their bellies, and were both voted quick with child; though my tutoress was no more with child than I was.

I went frequently to see them and condole with them,

expecting that it would be my turn next; but the place gave me so much horror, reflecting that it was the place of my unhappy birth and of my mother's misfortunes, that I could not bear it, so I left off going to see them.

And oh! could I but have taken warning by their disasters, I had been happy still, for I was yet free and had nothing brought against me; but it could not be, my measure was not yet filled up.

My comrade, having the brand of an old offender, was executed; the young offender was spared, having obtained a reprieve, but lay starving a long while in prison till at last she got her name into what they call a circuit pardon and so came off.

This terrible example of my comrade frighted me heartily, and for a good while I made no excursions; but one night, in the neighbourhood of my governess' house, they cried, "Fire." My governess looked out, for we were all up, and cried immediately that such a gentlewoman's house was all of a light fire atop, and so indeed it was. Here she gives me a jog. "Now, child," says she, "there is a rare opportunity, the fire being so near that you may go to it before the street is blocked up with the crowd." She presently gave me my cue. "Go, child," says she, "to the house and run in and tell the lady or anybody you see that you come to help them and that you came from such a gentlewoman"; that is, one of her acquaintance farther up the street.

Away I went, and coming to the house, I found them all in confusion, you may be sure. I run in, and finding one of the maids, "Alas! Sweetheart," said I, "how came this dismal accident? Where is your mistress? Is she safe? And where are the children? I come from Madam —— to help you." Away runs the maid. "Madam, madam," says she, screaming as loud as she could yell, "here is a gentlewoman come from Madam —— to help us." The poor woman, half out of her wits, with a bundle under her arm and two little children, comes towards me. "Madam," says I, "let me carry the poor children to Madam ——; she desires you to send them; she'll take care of the poor lambs"; and so I takes one of them out of her hand and she lifts the other up into my arms. "Aye, do, for God's sake," says she, "carry them. Oh, thank her for her kindness." "Have you anything else to secure, madam?" says I. "She will take care of it." "Oh, dear!" says she. "God bless her; take this bundle of plate and carry it to her too. Oh, she is a good woman! Oh, we are utterly ruined, undone!" And away she runs from me out of her wits, and the maids after her, and away comes I with the two children and the bundle.

I was no sooner got into the street but I saw another woman come to me. "Oh!" says she, "mistress," in a piteous tone, "you will let fall the child. Come, come, this is a sad time; let me help you," and immediately lays hold of my bundle to carry it for me. "No," says I, "if you will help me, take the child by the hand and lead it for me but to the upper end of the street; I'll go with you and satisfy you for your pains."

She could not avoid going, after what I said; but the creature, in short, was one of the same business with me and wanted nothing but the bundle; however, she went with me to the door, for she could not help it. When we were come there I whispered her, "Go, child," said I, "I understand your trade; you may meet with purchase enough."

She understood me and walked off. I thundered at the door with the children, and as the people were raised before by the noise of the fire, I was soon let in, and I said, "Is madam awake? Pray tell her Mrs. —— desires the favour of her to take the two children in; poor lady, she will be undone, their house is all of a flame." They took the children in very civilly, pitied the family in distress, and away came I with my bundle. One of the maids asked me if I was not to leave the bundle too. I said, "No, sweetheart, 'tis to go to another place; it does not belong to them."

I was a great way out of the hurry now, and so I went on and brought the bundle of plate, which was very considerable, straight home to my old governess. She told me she would not look into it, but bade me go again and look for more.

She gave me the like cue to the gentlewoman of the next house to that which was on fire, and I did my endeavour to go, but by this time the alarm of fire was so great, and so many engines playing, and the street so thronged with people that I could not get near the house whatever I could do; so I came back again to my governess', and taking the bundle up into my chamber, I began to examine it. It is with horror that I tell what a treasure I found there; 'tis enough to say that besides most of the family plate, which was considerable, I found a gold chain, an old-fashioned thing, the locket of which was broken, so that I suppose it had not been used some years, but the gold was not the worse for that; also a little box of burying-rings, the lady's wedding-ring, and some broken bits of old lockets of gold, a gold watch, and a purse with about £24 value in old pieces of gold coin, and several other things of value.

This was the greatest and the worst prize that ever I was concerned in; for indeed, though, as I have said above, I was hardened now beyond the power of all reflection in other cases, yet it really touched me to the very soul when I looked into this treasure to think of the poor, disconsolate gentlewoman who had lost so much besides, and who would think, to be sure, that she had saved her plate and best things; how she would be surprised when she should find that she had been deceived, and that the person that took her children and her goods had not come, as was pretended, from the gentlewoman in the next street, but that the children had been put upon her without her own knowledge.

I say, I confess the inhumanity of this action moved me very much and made me relent exceedingly, and tears stood in my eyes upon that subject; but with all my sense of its being cruel and inhuman, I could never find in my heart to make any restitution. The reflection wore off, and I quickly forgot the circumstances that attended it.

Nor was this all; for though by this job I was become considerably richer than before, yet the resolution I had formerly taken of leaving off this horrid trade when I had gotten a little more did not return, but I must still get more; and the avarice had such success that I had no more thoughts of coming to a timely alteration of life, though without it I could expect no safety, no tranquillity in the possession of what I had gained; a little more, and a little more, was the case still.

At length, yielding to the importunities of my crime, I cast off all remorse, and all the reflections on that head turned to no more than this: that I might perhaps come to have one booty more that might complete all; but though I certainly had that one booty, yet every hit looked towards another and was so encouraging to me to go on with the trade that I had no gust to the laying it down.

In this condition, hardened by success and resolving to go on, I fell into the snare in which I was appointed to meet with my last reward for this kind of life. But even this was not yet, for I met with several successful adventures more in this way.

My governess was for a while really concerned for this misfortune of my comrade that had been hanged, for she knew enough of my governess to have sent her the same way, and which made her very uneasy; indeed she was in a very great fright.

It is true that when she was gone and had not told what she knew, my governess was easy as to that point and perhaps glad she was hanged, for it was in her power to have obtained a pardon at the expense of her friends; but the loss of her and the sense of her kindness in not making her market of what she knew moved my governess to mourn very sincerely for her. I comforted her as well as I could, and she in return hardened me to merit more completely the same fate.

However, as I had said, it made me the more wary, and particularly I was very shy of shoplifting, especially among the mercers and drapers, who are a set of fellows that have their eyes very much about them. I made a venture or two among the lace-folks and the milliners, and particularly at one shop where two young women were newly set up and had not been bred to trade. There I carried off a piece of bone-lace worth six or seven pound, and a paper of thread. But this was but once; it was a trick that would not serve again.

It was always reckoned a safe job when we heard of a new shop, and especially when the people were such as were not bred to shops. Such may depend upon it that they will be visited once or twice at their beginning, and they must be very sharp indeed if they can prevent it.

I made another adventure or two after this, but they were but trifles. Nothing considerable offering for a good while, I began to think that I must give over trade in earnest; but my governess, who was not willing to lose me and expected great things of me, brought me one day into company with a young woman and a fellow that went for her husband, though, as it appeared afterwards, she was not his wife, but they were partners in the trade they carried on and in something else too. In short, they robbed together, lay together, were taken together, and at last were hanged together.

I came into a kind of league with these two by the help of my governess, and they carried me out into three or four adventures, where I rather saw them commit some coarse and unhandy robberies, in which nothing but a great stock of impudence on their side and gross negligence on the people's side who were robbed could have made them successful. So I resolved from that time forward to be very cautious how I adventured with them; and, indeed, when two or three unlucky projects were proposed by them, I declined the offer and persuaded them against it. One time they particularly proposed robbing a watchmaker of three gold watches, which they had eyed in the day-time and found the place where he laid them. One of them had so many keys of all kinds that he made no question to open the place where the watchmaker had laid them; and so we made a kind of an appointment; but when I came to look narrowly into the thing, I found they proposed breaking open the house, and this I would not embark in, so they went without me. They did get into the house by main force and broke up the locked place where the watches were, but found but one of the gold watches and a silver one, which they took, and got out of the house again very clear. But the family, being alarmed, cried out, "Thieves," and the man was pursued and taken; the young woman had got off too, but unhappily was stopped at a distance and the watches found upon her. And thus I had a second escape, for they were convicted and both hanged, being old offenders, though but young people; and as I said before that they robbed together, so now they hanged together, and there ended my new partnership.

I began now to be very wary, having so narrowly escaped a scouring and having such an example before me; but I had a new tempter, who prompted me every day—I mean my governess; and now a prize presented, which as it came by her management, so she expected a good share of the booty. There was a good quantity of Flanders lace lodged in a private house where she had heard of it, and Flanders lace being prohibited, it was a good booty to any custom-house officer that could come at it. I had a full account from my governess, as well of the quantity as of the very place where it was concealed; so I went to a custom-house officer and told him I had a discovery to make to him if he would assure me that I should have my due share of the reward. This was so just an offer that nothing could be fairer; so he agreed, and taking a constable and me with him, we beset the house. As I told him I could go directly to the place, he left it to me; and the hole being very dark, I squeezed myself into it with a candle in my hand, and so reached the pieces out to him, taking care as I gave him some so to secure as much about myself as I could conveniently dispose of. There was near £300 worth of lace in the whole, and I secured about £50 worth of it myself. The people of the house were not owners of the lace, but a merchant who had entrusted them with it; so that they were not so surprised as I thought they would be.

I left the officer overjoyed with his prize and fully satisfied with what he had got, and appointed to meet him at a house of his own directing, where I came after I had disposed of the cargo I had about me, of which he had not the least suspicion. When I came he began to capitulate, believing I did not understand the right I had in the prize, and would fain have put me off with £20; but I let him know that I was not so ignorant as he supposed I was; and yet I was glad, too, that he offered to bring me to a certainty. I asked £100, and he rose up to £30; I fell to £80, and he rose again to £40; in a word, he offered £50 and I consented, only demanding a piece of lace which I thought came to about £8 or £9, as if it had been for my own wear, and he agreed to it. So I got £50 in money paid me that same night and made an end of the bargain; nor did he ever know who I was or where to inquire for me, so that if it had been discovered that part of the goods were embezzled, he could have made no challenge upon me for it.

I very punctually divided this spoil with my governess, and I passed with her from this time for a very dexterous manager in the nicest cases. I found that this last was the best and easiest sort of work that was in my way, and I made it my business to inquire out prohibited goods, and after buying some, usually betrayed them; but none of these discoveries amounted to anything considerable, not like that I related just now; but I was cautious of running the great risks which I found others did, and in which they miscarried every day.

The next thing of moment was an attempt at a gentlewoman's gold watch. It happened in a crowd, at a meeting-house, where I was in very great danger of being taken. I had full hold of her watch, but giving a great jostle as if somebody had thrust me against her, and in the juncture giving the watch a fair pull, I found it would not come, so I let it go that moment and cried, as if I had been killed, that somebody had trod upon my foot and that there was certainly pickpockets there, for somebody or other had given a pull at my watch; for you are to observe that on these adventures we always went very well dressed, and I had very good clothes on and a gold watch by my side, as like a lady as other folks.

I had no sooner said so but the other gentlewoman cried out, "A pickpocket," too, for somebody, she said, had tried to pull her watch away.

When I touched her watch I was close to her, but when I cried out I stopped, as it were, short, and the crowd bearing her forward a little, she made a noise too, but it was at some distance from me, so that she did not in the least suspect me; but when she cried out, "A pickpocket," somebody cried out, "Aye, and here has been another; this gentlewoman has been attempted too."

At that very instant, a little farther in the crowd, and very luckily too, they cried out, "A pickpocket," again, and really seized a young fellow in the very fact. This, though unhappy for the wretch, was very opportunely for my case, though I had carried it handsomely enough before; but now it was out of doubt, and all the loose part of the crowd ran that way, and the poor boy was delivered up to the rage of the street, which is a cruelty I need not describe, and which, however, they are always glad of, rather than be sent to Newgate, where they lie often a long time, and sometimes they are hanged, and the best they can look for if they are convicted is to be transported.

This was a narrow escape to me, and I was so frighted that I ventured no more at gold watches a great while.

There were indeed many circumstances in this adventure which assisted to my escape; but the chief was that the woman whose watch I had pulled at was a fool; that is to say, she was ignorant of the nature of the attempt, which one would have thought she should not have been, seeing she was wise enough to fasten her watch so that it could not be slipped up; but she was in such a fright that she had no thought about her; for she, when she felt the pull, screamed out and pushed herself forward, and put all the people about her into disorder, but said not a word of her watch or of a pickpocket for at least two minutes, which was time enough for me, and to spare; for as I had cried out behind her, as I have said, and bore myself back in the crowd as she bore forward, there were several people, at least seven or eight, the throng being still moving on, that were got between me and her in that time, and then I crying out "A pickpocket" rather sooner than she, she might as well be the person suspected as I, and the people were confused in their inquiry; whereas had she, with a presence of mind needful on such an occasion, as soon as she felt the pull, not screamed out as she did but turned immediately round and seized the next body that was behind her, she had infallibly taken me.

This is a direction not of the kindest sort to the fraternity, but 'tis certainly a key to the clue of a pickpocket's motions; and whoever can follow it will as certainly catch the thief as he will be sure to miss if he does not.

I had another adventure, which puts this matter out of doubt and which may be an instruction for posterity in the case of a pickpocket. My good old governess, to give a short touch at her history, though she had left off the trade, was, as I may say, born a pickpocket and, as I understood afterward, had run through all the several degrees of that art, and yet had been taken but once, when she was so grossly detected that she was convicted, and ordered to be transported; but being a woman of a rare tongue, and withal having money in her pocket, she found means, the ship putting into Ireland for provisions, to get on shore there, where she practised her old trade some years; when, falling into another sort of company, she turned midwife and procuress and played a hundred pranks, which she gave me a little history of, in confidence between us as we grew more intimate; and it was to this wicked creature that I owed all the dexterity I arrived to, in which there were few that ever went beyond me or that practised so long without any misfortune.

It was after those adventures in Ireland, and when she was pretty well known in that country, that she left Dublin and came over to England, where, the time of her transportation being not expired, she left her former trade for fear of falling into bad hands again, for then she was sure to have gone to wreck. Here she set up the same trade she had followed in Ireland, in which she soon, by her admirable management and a good tongue, arrived to the height which I have already described, and indeed began to be rich, though her trade fell again afterwards.

I mention thus much of the history of this woman here, the better to account for the concern she had in the wicked life I was now leading, into all the particulars of which she led me, as it were, by the hand, and gave me such directions, and I so well followed them, that I grew the greatest artist of my time, and worked myself out of every danger with such dexterity that when several more of my comrades run themselves into Newgate, by that time they had been half a year at the trade, I had now practised upwards of five years, and the people at Newgate did not so much as know me; they had heard much of me indeed, and often expected me there, but I always got off, though many times in the extremest danger.

One of the greatest dangers I was now in was that I was too well known among the trade, and some of them, whose hatred was owing rather to envy than any injury I had done them, began to be angry that I should always escape when they were always catched and hurried to Newgate. These were they that gave me the name of Moll Flanders; for it was no more of affinity with my real name or with any of the names I had ever gone by than black is of kin to white, except that once, as before, I called myself Mrs. Flanders when I sheltered myself in the Mint; but that these rogues never knew, nor could I ever learn how they came to give me the name or what the occasion of it was.

I was soon informed that some of these who were gotten fast into Newgate had vowed to impeach me; and as I knew that two or three of them were but too able to do it, I was under a great concern and kept within doors for a good while. But my governess, who was partner in my success and who now played a sure game, for she had no share in the hazard—I say, my governess was something impatient of my leading such a useless, unprofitable life, as she called it; and she laid a new contrivance for my going abroad, and this was to dress me up in men's clothes and so put me into a new kind of practice.

I was tall and personable, but a little too smooth-faced for a man; however, as I seldom went abroad but in the night, it did well enough; but it was long before I could behave in my new clothes. It was impossible to be so nimble, so ready, so dexterous at these things in a dress contrary to nature; and as I did everything clumsily, so I had neither the success or easiness of escape that I had before, and I resolved to leave it off; but that resolution was confirmed soon after by the following accident.

As my governess had disguised me like a man, so she joined me with a man, a young fellow that was nimble enough at his business, and for about three weeks we did very well together. Our principal trade was watching shopkeepers' counters and slipping off any kinds of goods we could see carelessly laid anywhere, and we made several good bargains, as we called them, at this work. And as we kept always together, so we grew very intimate, yet he never knew that I was not a man, nay, though I several times went home with him to his lodgings, according as our business directed, and four or five times lay with him all night. But our design lay another way, and it was absolutely necessary to me to conceal my sex from him, as appeared afterwards. The circumstances of our living, coming in late and having such business to do as required that nobody should be trusted with coming into our lodgings, were such as made it impossible to me to refuse lying with him, unless I would have owned my sex; and as it was, I effectually concealed myself.

But his ill and my good fortune soon put an end to this life, which I must own I was sick of too. We had made several prizes in this new way of business, but the last would have been extraordinary. There was a shop in a certain street which had a warehouse behind it that looked into another street, the house making the corner.

Through the window of the warehouse we saw lying on the counter, or showboard, which was just before it, five pieces of silks, besides other stuffs, and though it was almost dark, yet the people, being busy in the fore-shop, had not had time to shut up those windows or else had forgot it.

This the young fellow was so overjoyed with that he could not restrain himself. It lay within his reach, he said, and he swore violently to me that he would have it if he broke down the house for it. I dissuaded him a little, but saw there was no remedy; so he run rashly upon it, slipped out a square out of the sash-window dexterously enough, and got four pieces of the silks and came with them towards me, but was immediately pursued with a terrible clutter and noise. We were standing together indeed, but I had not taken any of the goods out of his hand when I said to him hastily, "You are undone!" He run like lightning, and I too, but the pursuit was hotter after him because he had the goods. He dropped two of the pieces, which stopped them a little, but the crowd increased and pursued us both. They took him soon after with the other two pieces, and then the rest followed me. I run for it and got into my governess' house, whither some quick-eyed people followed me so warmly as to fix me there. They did not immediately knock at the door, by which I got time to throw off my disguise and dress me in my own clothes; besides, when they came there, my governess, who had her tale ready, kept her door shut and called out to them and told them there was no man came in there. The people affirmed there did a man come in there, and swore they would break open the door.

My governess, not at all surprised, spoke calmly to them, told them they should very freely come and search her house if they would bring a constable and let in none but such as the constable would admit, for it was unreasonable to let in a whole crowd. This they could not refuse, though they were a crowd. So a constable was fetched immediately, and she very freely opened the door; the constable kept the door, and the men he appointed searched the house, my governess going with them from room to room. When she came to my room she called to me and said aloud, "Cousin, pray open the door; here's some gentlemen that must come and look into your room."

I had a little girl with me, which was my governess' grandchild, as she called her; and I bade her open the door, and there sat I at work with a great litter of things about me, as if I had been at work all day, being undressed, with only night-clothes on my head and a loose morning-gown about me. My governess made a kind of excuse for their disturbing me, telling partly the occasion of it, and that she had no remedy but to open the doors to them and let them satisfy themselves, for all she could say would not satisfy them. I sat still and bid them search if they pleased, for if there was anybody in the house, I was sure they was not in my room; and for the rest of the house, I had nothing to say to that, I did not understand what they looked for.

Everything looked so innocent and so honest about me that they treated me civiller than I expected; but it was not till they had searched the room to a nicety, even under the bed and in the bed and everywhere else where it was possible anything could be hid. When they had done and could find nothing, they asked my pardon and went down.

When they had thus searched the house from bottom to top and then from top to bottom and could find nothing, they appeased the mob pretty well; but they carried my governess before the justice. Two men swore that they see the man who they pursued go into her house. My governess rattled and made a great noise that her house should be insulted and that she should be used thus for nothing; that if a man did come in, he might go out again presently for aught she knew, for she was ready to make oath that no man had been within her doors all that day as she knew of, which was very true; that it might be that as she was above-stairs, any fellow in a fright might find the door open and run in for shelter when he was pursued, but that she knew nothing of it; and if it had been so, he certainly went out again, perhaps at the other door, for she had another door into an alley, and so had made his escape.

This was indeed probable enough, and the justice satisfied himself with giving her an oath that she had not received or admitted any man into her house to conceal him or protect or hide him from justice. This oath she might justly take, and did so, and so she was dismissed.

It is easy to judge what a fright I was in upon this occasion, and it was impossible for my governess ever to bring me to dress in that disguise again; for, as I told her, I should certainly betray myself.

My poor partner in this mischief was now in a bad case, for he was carried away before my lord mayor, and by his worship committed to Newgate, and the people that took him were so willing, as well as able, to prosecute him that they offered themselves to enter into recognizances to appear at the sessions and pursue the charge against him.

However, he got his indictment deferred upon promise to discover his accomplices, and particularly the man that was concerned with him in this robbery; and he failed not to do his endeavour, for he gave in my name, who he called Gabriel Spencer, which was the name I went by to him; and here appeared the wisdom of my concealing myself from him, without which I had been undone.

He did all he could to discover this Gabriel Spencer; he described me; he discovered the place where he said I lodged; and, in a word, all the particulars that he could of my dwelling; but having concealed the main circumstances of my sex from him, I had a vast advantage, and he could never hear of me. He brought two or three families into trouble by his endeavouring to find me out, but they knew nothing of me any more than that he had a fellow with him that they had seen, but knew nothing of. And as to my governess, though she was the means of his coming to me, yet it was done at second hand, and he knew nothing of her neither.

This turned to his disadvantage; for having promised discoveries but not being able to make it good, it was looked upon as trifling, and he was the more fiercely pursued by the shopkeeper.

I was, however, terribly uneasy all this while, and that I might be quite out of the way, I went away from my governess for a while; but not knowing whither to wander, I took a maidservant with me and took the stage-coach to Dunstable, to my old landlord and landlady, where I lived so handsomely with my Lancashire husband. Here I told her a formal story: that I expected my husband every day from Ireland, and that I had sent a letter to him that I would meet him at Dunstable at her house, and that he would certainly land, if the wind was fair, in a few days; so that I was come to spend a few days with them till he could come, for he would either come post or in the West Chester coach, I knew not which; but whichsoever it was, he would be sure to come to that house to meet me.

My landlady was mighty glad to see me, and my landlord made such a stir with me that if I had been a princess I could not have been better used, and here I might have been welcome a month or two if I had thought fit.

But my business was of another nature. I was very uneasy (though so well disguised that it was scarce possible to detect me) lest this fellow should find me out; and though he could not charge me with the robbery, having persuaded him not to venture and having done nothing of it myself, yet he might have charged me with other things and have bought his own life at the expense of mine.

This filled me with horrible apprehensions. I had no recourse, no friend, no confidant but my old governess, and I knew no remedy but to put my life into her hands; and so I did, for I let her know where to send to me and had several letters from her while I stayed here. Some of them almost scared me out of my wits; but at last she sent me the joyful news that he was hanged, which was the best news to me that I had heard a great while.

I had stayed here five weeks and lived very comfortably indeed, the secret anxiety of my mind excepted. But when I received this letter, I looked pleasantly again and told my landlady that I had received a letter from my spouse in Ireland, that I had the good news of his being very well but had the bad news that his business would not permit him to come away so soon as he expected, and so I was like to go back again without him.

My landlady complimented me upon the good news, however, that I had heard he was well. "For I have observed, madam," says she, "you han't been so pleasant as you used to be; you have been over head and ears in care for him, I dare say," says the good woman; " 'tis easy to be seen there's an alteration in you for the better," says she. "Well, I am sorry the squire can't come yet," says my landlord; "I should have been heartily glad to have seen him. When you have certain news of his coming, you'll take a step hither again, madam," says he; "you shall be very welcome whenever you please to come."

With all these fine compliments we parted, and I came merry enough to London and found my governess as well pleased as I was. And now she told me she would never recommend any partner to me again, for she always found, she said, that I had the best luck when I ventured by myself. And so indeed I had, for I was seldom in any danger when I was by myself, or if I was, I got out of it with more dexterity than when I was entangled with the dull measures of other people, who had perhaps less forecast and were more impatient than I; for though I had as much courage to venture as any of them, yet I used more caution before I undertook a thing and had more presence of mind to bring myself off.

I have often wondered even at my own hardiness another way, that when all my companions were surprised and fell so suddenly into the hand of justice, yet I could not all this while enter into one serious resolution to leave off this trade, and especially considering that I was now very far from being poor; that the temptation of necessity, which is the general introduction of all such wickedness, was now removed; that I had near £500 by me in ready money, on which I might have lived very well if I had thought fit to have retired; but, I say, I had not so much as the least inclination to leave off; no, not so much as I had before when I had but £200 beforehand and when I had no such frightful examples before my eyes as these were. From hence 'tis evident that when once we are hardened in crime, no fear can affect us, no example give us any warning.

I had indeed one comrade whose fate went very near me for a good while, though I wore it off too in time. That case was indeed very unhappy. I had made a prize of a piece of very good damask in a mercer's shop and went clear off myself, but had conveyed the piece to this companion of mine when we went out of the shop, and she went one way, I went another. We had not been long out of the shop but the mercer missed the piece of stuff and sent his messengers, one one way and one another, and they presently seized her that had the piece with the damask upon her; as for me, I had very luckily stepped into a house where there was a lace-chamber, up one pair of stairs, and had the satisfaction or the terror, indeed, of looking out of the window and seeing the poor creature dragged away to the justice, who immediately committed her to Newgate.

I was careful to attempt nothing in the lace-chamber, but tumbled their goods pretty much to spend time; then bought a few yards of edging and paid for it, and came away very sad-hearted indeed for the poor woman who was in tribulation for what I only had stolen.

Here again my old caution stood me in good stead; though I often robbed with these people, yet I never let them know who I was, nor could they ever find out my lodging though they often endeavoured to watch me to it. They all knew me by the name of Moll Flanders, though even some of them rather believed I was she than knew me to be so. My name was public among them indeed, but how to find me out they knew not, nor so much as how to guess at my quarters, whether they were at the east end of the town or the west; and this wariness was my safety upon all these occasions.

I kept close a great while upon the occasion of this woman's disaster. I knew that if I should do anything that should miscarry, and should be carried to prison, she would be there and ready to witness against me, and perhaps save her life at my expense. I considered that I began to be very well known by name at the Old Bailey, though they did not know my face, and that if I should fall into their hands, I should be treated as an old offender; and for this reason I was resolved to see what this poor creature's fate should be before I stirred, though several times in her distress I conveyed money to her for her relief.

At length she came to her trial. She pleaded she did not steal the things, but that one Mrs. Flanders, as she heard her called (for she did not know her), gave the bundle to her after they came out of the shop and bade her carry it home. They asked her where this Mrs. Flanders was, but she could not produce her, neither could she give the least account of me; and the mercer's men swearing positively that she was in the shop when the goods were stolen, that they immediately missed them and pursued her and found them upon her, thereupon the jury brought her in guilty; but the court, considering that she really was not the person that stole the goods, and that it was very possible she could not find out this Mrs. Flanders, meaning me, though it would save her life, which indeed was true, they allowed her to be transported, which was the utmost favour she could obtain, only that the court told her if she could in the meantime produce the said Mrs. Flanders, they would intercede for her pardon; that is to say, if she could find me out and hang me, she should not be transported. This I took care to make impossible to her, and so she was shipped off in pursuance of her sentence a little while after.

I must repeat it again, that the fate of this poor woman troubled me exceedingly, and I began to be very pensive, knowing that I was really the instrument of her disaster; but my own life, which was so evidently in danger, took off my tenderness; and seeing she was not put to death, I was easy at her transportation, because she was then out of the way of doing me any mischief, whatever should happen.

The disaster of this woman was some months before that of the last-recited story, and was indeed partly the occasion of my governess proposing to dress me up in men's clothes, that I might go about unobserved; but I was soon tired of that disguise, as I have said, for it exposed me to too many difficulties.

I was now easy as to all fear of witnesses against me, for all those that had either been concerned with me or that knew me by the name of Moll Flanders were either hanged or transported; and if I should have had the misfortune to be taken, I might call myself anything else, as well as Moll Flanders, and no old sins could be placed to my account; so I began to run a-tick again with the more freedom, and several successful adventures I made, though not such as I had made before.

We had at that time another fire happened not a great way off from the place where my governess lived, and I made an attempt there as before; but as I was not soon enough before the crowd of people came in and could not get to the house I aimed at, instead of a prize, I got a mischief, which had almost put a period to my life and all my wicked doings together; for the fire being very furious, and the people in a great fright in removing their goods and throwing them out of window, a wench from out of a window threw a feather-bed just upon me. It is true, the bed being soft, it broke no bones; but as the weight was great and made greater by the fall, it beat me down and laid me dead for a while; nor did the people concern themselves much to deliver me from it or to recover me at all; but I lay like one dead and neglected a good while till somebody going to remove the bed out of the way helped me up. It was indeed a wonder the people in the house had not thrown other goods out after it, and which might have fallen upon it, and then I had been inevitably killed; but I was reserved for further afflictions.

This accident, however, spoiled my market for that time, and I came home to my governess very much hurt and frighted, and it was a good while before she could set me upon my feet again.

It was now a merry time of the year, and Bartholomew Fair was begun. I had never made any walks that way, nor was the fair of much advantage to me; but I took a turn this year into the cloisters, and there I fell into one of the raffling shops. It was a thing of no great consequence to me, but there came a gentleman extremely well dressed and very rich, and as 'tis frequent to talk to everybody in those shops, he singled me out and was very particular with me. First he told me he would put in for me to raffle, and did so; and some small matter coming to his lot, he presented it to me—I think it was a feather muff; then he continued to keep talking to me with a more than common appearance of respect, but still very civil and much like a gentleman.

He held me in talk so long, till at last he drew me out of the raffling place to the shop-door, and then to take a walk in the cloister, still talking of a thousand things cursorily without anything to the purpose. At last he told me that he was charmed with my company, and asked me if I durst trust myself in a coach with him; he told me he was a man of honour and would not offer anything to me unbecoming him. I seemed to decline it awhile, but suffered myself to be importuned a little, and then yielded.

I was at a loss in my thoughts to conclude at first what this gentleman designed; but I found afterward he had had some drink in his head and that he was not very unwilling to have some more. He carried me to the Spring Garden, at Knightsbridge, where we walked in the gardens, and he treated me very handsomely; but I found he drank freely. He pressed me also to drink, but I declined it.

Hitherto he kept his word with me and offered me nothing amiss. We came away in the coach again, and he brought me into the streets, and by this time it was near ten o'clock at night, when he stopped the coach at a house where, it seems, he was acquainted, and where they made no scruple to show us upstairs into a room with a bed in it. At first I seemed to be unwilling to go up, but after a few words I yielded to that too, being indeed willing to see the end of it and in hopes to make something of it at last. As for the bed, etc., I was not much concerned about that part.

Here he began to be a little freer with me than he had promised; and I by little and little yielded to everything, so that, in a word, he did what he pleased with me; I need say no more. All this while he drank freely too, and about one in the morning we went into the coach again. The air and the shaking of the coach made the drink get more up in his head, and he grew uneasy, and was for acting over again what he had been doing before; but as I thought my game now secure, I resisted and brought him to be a little still, which had not lasted five minutes but he fell fast asleep.

I took this opportunity to search him to a nicety. I took a gold watch, with a silk purse of gold, his fine full-bottom periwig and silver-fringed gloves, his sword and fine snuff-box, and gently opening the coach-door, stood ready to jump out while the coach was going on; but the coach stopping in the narrow street beyond Temple Bar to let another coach pass, I got softly out, fastened the door again, and gave my gentleman and the coach the slip together.

This was an adventure indeed unlooked for and perfectly undesigned by me, though I was not so past the merry part of life as to forget how to behave when a fop so blinded by his appetite should not know an old woman from a young. I did not indeed look so old as I was by ten or twelve years; yet I was not a young wench of seventeen, and it was easy enough to be distinguished. There is nothing so absurd, so surfeiting, so ridiculous, as a man heated by wine in his head and a wicked gust in his inclination together; he is in the possession of two devils at once, and can no more govern himself by his reason than a mill can grind without water; vice tramples upon all that was in him that had any good in it; nay, his very sense is blinded by its own rage, and he acts absurdities even in his view; such as drinking more when he is drunk already; picking up a common woman without any regard to what she is or who she is, whether sound or rotten, clean or unclean, whether ugly or handsome, old or young, and so blinded as not really to distinguish. Such a man is worse than lunatic; prompted by his vicious head, he no more knows what he is doing than this wretch of mine knew when I picked his pocket of his watch and his purse of gold.

These are the men of whom Solomon says, "They go like an ox to the slaughter, till a dart strikes through their liver"; an admirable description, by the way, of the foul disease, which is a poisonous, deadly contagion mingling with the blood, whose centre or fountain is in the liver; from whence, by the swift circulation of the whole mass, that dreadful, nauseous plague strikes immediately through his liver, and his spirits are infected, his vitals stabbed through as with a dart.

It is true this poor unguarded wretch was in no danger from me, though I was greatly apprehensive at first what danger I might be in from him; but he was really to be pitied in one respect: that he seemed to be a good sort of a man in himself—a gentleman that had no harm in his design, a man of sense and of a fine behaviour, a comely handsome person, a sober and solid countenance, a charming beautiful face, and everything that could be agreeable; only had unhappily had some drink the night before, had not been in bed, as he told me when we were together; was hot, and his blood fired with wine, and in that condition his reason, as it were asleep, had given him up.

As for me, my business was his money and what I could make of him; and after that, if I could have found out any way to have done it, I would have sent him safe home to his house and to his family, for 'twas ten to one but he had an honest, virtuous wife and innocent children that were anxious for his safety, and would have been glad to have gotten him home and taken care of him till he was restored to himself. And then with what shame and regret would he look back upon himself! How would he reproach himself with associating himself with a whore picked up in the worst of all holes, the cloister, among the dirt and filth of the town! How would he be trembling for fear he had got the pox, for fear a dart had struck through his liver, and hate himself every time he looked back upon the madness and brutality of his debauch! How would he, if he had any principles of honour, abhor the thought of giving any ill distemper, if he had it, as for aught he knew he might, to his modest and virtuous wife, and thereby sowing the contagion in the life-blood of his posterity!

Would such gentlemen but consider the contemptible thoughts which the very women they are concerned with in such cases as these have of them, it would be a surfeit to them. As I said above, they value not the pleasure, they are raised by no inclination to the man; the passive jade thinks of no pleasure but the money; and when he is, as it were, drunk in the ecstasies of his wicked pleasure, her hands are in his pockets for what she can find there, and of which he can no more be sensible in the moment of his folly than he can forethink of it when he goes about it.

I knew a woman that was so dexterous with a fellow who indeed deserved no better usage that while he was busy with her another way, conveyed his purse with twenty guineas in it out of his fob-pocket, where he had put it for fear of her, and put another purse with gilded counters in it into the room of it. After he had done, he says to her, "Now, han't you picked my pocket?" She jested with him and told him she supposed he had not much to lose; he put his hand to his fob and with his fingers felt that his purse was there, which fully satisfied him, and so she brought off his money. And this was a trade with her; she kept a sham gold watch and a purse of counters in her pocket to be ready on all such occasions, and I doubt not practised it with success.

I came home with this last booty to my governess, and really when I told her the story, it so affected her that she was hardly able to forbear tears to think how such a gentleman run a daily risk of being undone every time a glass of wine got into his head.

But as to the purchase I got and how entirely I stripped him, she told me it pleased her wonderfully. "Nay, child," says she, "the usage may, for aught I know, do more to reform him than all the sermons that ever he will hear in his life." And if the remainder of the story be true, so it did.

I found the next day she was wonderful inquisitive about this gentleman; the description I gave her of him—his dress, his person, his face—all concurred to make her think of a gentleman whose character she knew. She mused awhile, and I going on in the particulars, says she, "I lay a hundred pound I know the man."

"I am sorry if you do," says I, "for I would not have him exposed on any account in the world; he has had injury enough already, and I would not be instrumental to do him any more." "No, no," says she, "I will do him no injury, but you may let me satisfy my curiosity a little, for if it is he, I warrant you I find it out." I was a little startled at that, and I told her, with an apparent concern in my face, that by the same rule he might find me out, and then I was undone. She returned warmly, "Why, do you think I will betray you, child? No, no," says she, "not for all he is worth in the world. I have kept your counsel in worse things than these; sure you may trust me in this." So I said no more.

She laid her scheme another way, and without acquainting me with it, but she was resolved to find it out. So she goes to a certain friend of hers who was acquainted in the family that she guessed at and told her she had some extraordinary business with such a gentleman (who, by the way, was no less than a baronet and of a very good family), and that she knew not how to come at him without somebody to introduce her. Her friend promised her readily to do it, and accordingly goes to the house to see if the gentleman was in town.

The next day she comes to my governess and tells her that Sir —— was at home, but that he had met with a disaster and was very ill, and there was no speaking to him. "What disaster?" says my governess hastily, as if she was surprised at it. "Why," says her friend, "he had been at Hampstead to visit a gentleman of his acquaintance, and as he came back again he was set upon and robbed; and having got a little drink too, as they suppose, the rogues abused him, and he is very ill." "Robbed!" says my governess. "And what did they take from him?" "Why," says her friend, "they took his gold watch and his gold snuff-box, his fine periwig, and what money he had in his pocket, which was considerable, to be sure, for Sir —— never goes without a purse of guineas about him."

"Pshaw!" says my old governess, jeering. "I warrant you he has got drunk now and got a whore, and she has picked his pocket, and so he comes home to his wife and tells her he has been robbed; that's an old sham; a thousand such tricks are put upon the poor women every day."

"Fie!" says her friend. "I find you don't know Sir ——; why, he is as civil a gentleman, there is not a finer man, nor a soberer, modester person in the whole city; he abhors such things; there's nobody that knows him will think such a thing of him." "Well, well," says my governess, "that's none of my business; if it was, I warrant I should find there was something of that in it; your modest men in common opinion are sometimes no better than other people, only they keep a better character or, if you please, are the better hypocrites."

"No, no," says her friend, "I can assure you Sir —— is no hypocrite; he is really an honest, sober gentleman, and he has certainly been robbed." "Nay," says my governess, "it may be he has; it is no business of mine, I tell you; I only want to speak with him; my business is of another nature." "But," says her friend, "let your business be of what nature it will, you cannot see him yet, for he is not fit to be seen, for he is very ill and bruised very much." "Ay," says my governess, "nay, then he has fallen into bad hands, to be sure." And then she asked gravely, "Pray, where is he bruised?" "Why, in his head," says her friend, "and one of his hands, and his face, for they used him barbarously." "Poor gentleman," says my governess. "I must wait, then, till he recovers"; and adds, "I hope it will not be long."

Away she comes to me and tells me this story. "I have found out your fine gentleman, and a fine gentleman he was," says she; "but, mercy on him, he is in a sad pickle now. I wonder what the d—l you have done to him; why, you have almost killed him." I looked at her with disorder enough. "I killed him!" says I. "You must mistake the person; I am sure I did nothing to him; he was very well when I left him," said I, "only drunk and fast asleep." "I know nothing of that," says she, "but he is in a sad pickle now"; and so she told me all that her friend had said. "Well, then," says I, "he fell into bad hands after I left him, for I left him safe enough."

About ten days after, my governess goes again to her friend to introduce her to this gentleman; she had inquired other ways in the meantime and found that he was about again, so she got leave to speak with him.

She was a woman of an admirable address and wanted nobody to introduce her; she told her tale much better than I shall be able to tell it for her, for she was mistress of her tongue, as I said already. She told him that she came, though a stranger, with a single design of doing him a service, and he should find she had no other end in it; that as she came purely on so friendly an account, she begged a promise from him, that if he did not accept what she should officiously propose, he would not take it ill that she meddled with what was not her business; she assured him that as what she had to say was a secret that belonged to him only, so whether he accepted her offer or not, it should remain a secret to all the world unless he exposed it himself; nor should his refusing her service in it make her so little show her respect as to do him the least injury, so that he should be entirely at liberty to act as he thought fit.

He looked very shy at first and said he knew nothing that related to him that required much secrecy; that he had never done any man any wrong and cared not what anybody might say of him; that it was no part of his character to be unjust to anybody, nor could he imagine in what any man could render him any service; but that if it was as she said, he could not take it ill from any one that should endeavour to serve him; and so, as it were, left her at liberty either to tell him or not to tell him, as she thought fit.

She found him so perfectly indifferent that she was almost afraid to enter into the point with him; but, however, after some other circumlocutions, she told him that by a strange and unaccountable accident she came to have a particular knowledge of the late unhappy adventure he had fallen into, and that in such a manner that there was nobody in the world but herself and him that were acquainted with it, no, not the very person that was with him.

He looked a little angrily at first. "What adventure?" said he. "Why, sir," said she, "of your being robbed coming from Knightsbr—, Hampstead, sir, I should say," says she. "Be not surprised, sir," says she, "that I am able to tell you every step you took that day from the cloister in Smithfield to the Spring Garden at Knightsbridge, and thence to the —— in the Strand, and how you were left asleep in the coach afterwards. I say, let not this surprise you, for, sir, I do not come to make a booty of you, I ask nothing of you, and I assure you the woman that was with you knows nothing who you are and never shall; and yet perhaps I may serve you farther still, for I did not come barely to let you know that I was informed of these things, as if I wanted a bribe to conceal them; assure yourself, sir," said she, "that whatever you think fit to do or say to me, it shall be all a secret, as it is, as much as if I were in my grave."

He was astonished at her discourse and said gravely to her, "Madam, you are a stranger to me, but it is very unfortunate that you should be let into the secret of the worst action of my life and a thing that I am justly ashamed of, in which the only satisfaction I had was that I thought it was known only to God and my own conscience." "Pray, sir," says she, "do not reckon the discovery of it to me to be any part of your misfortune. It was a thing, I believe, you were surprised into, and perhaps the woman used some art to prompt you to it. However, you will never find any just cause," said she, "to repent that I came to hear of it; nor can your mouth be more silent in it than I have been and ever shall be."

"Well," says he, "but let me do some justice to the woman too; whoever she is, I do assure you she prompted me to nothing, she rather declined me. It was my own folly and madness that brought me into it all; aye, and brought her into it too; I must give her her due so far. As to what she took from me, I could expect no less from her in the condition I was in, and to this hour I know not whether she robbed me or the coachman; if she did it, I forgive her. I think all gentlemen that do so should be used in the same manner; but I am more concerned for some other things than I am for all that she took from me."

My governess now began to come into the whole matter, and he opened himself freely to her. First she said to him in answer to what he had said about me, "I am glad, sir, you are so just to the person that you were with. I assure you she is a gentlewoman, and no woman of the town; and however you prevailed with her as you did, I am sure 'tis not her practice. You run a great venture indeed, sir; but if that be part of your care, you may be perfectly easy, for I do assure you no man has touched her before you since her husband, and he has been dead now almost eight years."

It appeared that this was his grievance and that he was in a very great fright about it; however, when my governess said this to him, he appeared very well pleased and said, "Well, madam, to be plain with you, if I was satisfied of that, I should not so much value what I lost; for as to that, the temptation was great, and perhaps she was poor and wanted it." "If she had not been poor, sir," says she, "I assure you she would never have yielded to you; and as her poverty first prevailed with her to let you do as you did, so the same poverty prevailed with her to pay herself at last when she saw you was in such a condition that if she had not done it, perhaps the next coachman or chairman might have done it more to your hurt."

"Well," says he, "much good may it do her. I say again, all the gentlemen that do so ought to be used in the same manner, and then they would be cautious of themselves. I have no more concern about it but on the score which you hinted at before." Here he entered into some freedoms with her on the subject of what passed between us, which are not so proper for a woman to write, and the great terror that was upon his mind with relation to his wife for fear she should have received any injury from me and should communicate it farther; and asked her at last if she could not procure him an opportunity to speak with me. My governess gave him farther assurances of my being a woman clear from any such thing, and that he was as entirely safe in that respect as he was with his own lady; but as for seeing me, she said it might be of dangerous consequence; but, however, that she would talk with me and let him know, endeavouring at the same time to persuade him not to desire it and that it could be of no service to him, seeing she hoped he had no desire to renew the correspondence and that on my account it was a kind of putting my life in his hands.

He told her he had a great desire to see me, that he would give her any assurances that were in his power not to take any advantages of me, and that in the first place he would give me a general release from all demands of any kind. She insisted how it might tend to farther divulging the secret and might be injurious to him, entreating him not to press for it; so at length he desisted.

They had some discourse upon the subject of the things he had lost, and he seemed to be very desirous of his gold watch, and told her if she could procure that for him, he would willingly give as much for it as it was worth. She told him she would endeavour to procure it for him and leave the valuing it to himself.

Accordingly the next day she carried the watch, and he gave her thirty guineas for it, which was more than I should have been able to make of it, though it seems it cost much more. He spoke something of his periwig, which it seems cost him threescore guineas, and his snuff-box; and in a few days more she carried them too, which obliged him very much, and he gave her thirty more. The next day I sent him his fine sword and cane gratis, and demanded nothing of him, but had no mind to see him unless he might be satisfied I knew who he was, which he was not willing to.

Then he entered into a long talk with her of the manner how she came to know all this matter. She formed a long tale of that part; how she had it from one that I had told the whole story to and that was to help me dispose of the goods; and this confidante brought things to her, she being by profession a pawnbroker; and she, hearing of his worship's disaster, guessed at the thing in general; that having gotten the things into her hands, she had resolved to come and try as she had done. She then gave him repeated assurances that it should never go out of her mouth, and though she knew the woman very well, yet she had not let her know, meaning me, anything of who the person was, which, by the way, was false; but, however, it was not to his damage, for I never opened my mouth of it to anybody.

I had a great many thoughts in my head about my seeing him again and was often sorry that I had refused it. I was persuaded that if I had seen him and let him know that I knew him, I should have made some advantage of him and perhaps have had some maintenance from him; and though it was a life wicked enough, yet it was not so full of danger as this I was engaged in. However, those thoughts wore off, and I declined seeing him again for that time; but my governess saw him often, and he was very kind to her, giving her something almost every time he saw her. One time in particular she found him very merry, and as she thought he had some wine in his head then, and he pressed her again to let him see that woman that, as he said, had bewitched him so that night, my governess, who was from the beginning for my seeing him, told him he was so desirous of it that she could almost yield to it if she could prevail upon me; adding that if he would please to come to her house in the evening, she would endeavour it upon his repeated assurances of forgetting what was past.

Accordingly she came to me and told me all the discourse; in short, she soon biased me to consent in a case which I had some regret in my mind for declining before; so I prepared to see him. I dressed me to all the advantage possible, I assure you, and for the first time used a little art; I say for the first time, for I had never yielded to the baseness of paint before, having always had vanity enough to believe I had no need of it.

At the hour appointed he came; and as she observed before, so it was plain still that he had been drinking, though very far from what we call being in drink. He appeared exceeding pleased to see me and entered into a long discourse with me upon the old affair. I begged his pardon very often for my share of it, protested I had not any such design when first I met him, that I had not gone out with him but that I took him for a very civil gentleman, and that he made me so many promises of offering no incivility to me.

He alleged the wine he drank, and that he scarce knew

what he did, and that if it had not been so, he should never have taken the freedom with me he had done. He protested to me that he never touched any woman but me since he was married to his wife, and it was a surprise upon him; complimented me upon being so particularly agreeable to him, and the like; and talked so much of that kind till I found he had talked himself almost into a temper to do the thing again. But I took him up short. I protested I had never suffered any man to touch me since my husband died, which was near eight years. He said he believed it and added that madam had intimated as much to him, and that it was his opinion of that part which made him desire to see me again; and since he had once broken in upon his virtue with me and found no ill consequences, he could be safe in venturing again; and so, in short, he went on to what I expected and to what will not bear relating.

My old governess had foreseen it, as well as I, and therefore led him into a room which had not a bed in it, and yet had a chamber within it which had a bed, whither we withdrew for the rest of the night; and in short, after some time being together, he went to bed and lay there all night. I withdrew, but came again undressed before it was day and lay with him the rest of the time.

Thus, you see, having committed a crime once is a sad handle to the committing of it again; all the reflections wear off when the temptation renews itself. Had I not yielded to see him again, the corrupt desire in him had worn off, and 'tis very probable he had never fallen into it with anybody else, as I really believe he had not done before.

When he went away, I told him I hoped he was satisfied he had not been robbed again. He told me he was fully satisfied in that point and, putting his hand in his pocket, gave me five guineas, which was the first money I had gained that way for many years.

I had several visits of the like kind from him, but he never came into a settled way of maintenance, which was what I would have been best pleased with. Once, indeed, he asked me how I did to live. I answered him pretty quick that I assured him I had never taken that course that I took with him, but that indeed I worked at my needle and could just maintain myself; that sometimes it was as much as I was able to do, and I shifted hard enough.

He seemed to reflect upon himself that he should be the first person to lead me into that which he assured me he never intended to do himself; and it touched him a little, he said, that he should be the cause of his own sin and mine too. He would often make just reflections also upon the crime itself and upon the particular circumstances of it, with respect to himself; how wine introduced the inclinations, how the devil led him to the place and found out an object to tempt him, and he made the moral always himself.

When these thoughts were upon him, he would go away and perhaps not come again in a month's time or longer; but then as the serious part wore off the lewd part would wear in, and then he came prepared for the wicked part. Thus we lived for some time; though he did not keep, as they call it, yet he never failed doing things that were handsome, and sufficient to maintain me without working, and, which was better, without following my old trade.

But this affair had its end too; for after about a year, I found that he did not come so often as usual, and at last he left it off altogether without any dislike or bidding adieu; and so there was an end of that short scene of life, which added no great store to me, only to make more work for repentance.

During this interval I confined myself pretty much at home; at least, being thus provided for, I made no adventures, no, not for a quarter of a year after; but then, finding the fund fail and being loath to spend upon the main stock, I began to think of my old trade and to look abroad into the street; and my first step was lucky enough.

I had dressed myself up in a very mean habit, for as I had several shapes to appear in, I was now in an ordinary stuff gown, a blue apron, and a straw hat; and I placed myself at the door of the Three Cups Inn in St. John's Street. There were several carriers used the inn, and the stage-coaches for Barnet, for Totteridge, and other towns that way stood always in the street in the evening, when they prepared to set out, so that I was ready for anything that offered. The meaning was this:

people come frequently with bundles and small parcels to those inns, and call for such carriers or coaches as they want to carry them into the country; and there generally attends women, porters' wives or daughters, ready to take in such things for the people that employ them.

It happened very oddly that I was standing at the inn-gate, and a woman that stood there before, and which was the porter's wife belonging to the Barnet stage-coach, having observed me, asked if I waited for any of the coaches. I told her yes, I waited for my mistress, that was coming to go to Barnet. She asked me who was my mistress, and I told her any madam's name that came next me; but it seemed I happened upon a name a family of which name lived at Hadley, near Barnet.

I said no more to her or she to me a good while; but by and by, somebody calling her at a door a little way off, she desired me that if anybody called for the Barnet coach, I would step and call her at the house, which it seems was an ale-house. I said yes very readily, and away she went.

She was no sooner gone but comes a wench and a child, puffing and sweating, and asks for the Barnet coach. I answered presently, "Here." "Do you belong to the Barnet coach?" says she. "Yes, sweetheart," said I. "What do you want?" "I want room for two passengers," says she. "Where are they, sweetheart?" said I. "Here's this girl; pray let her go into the coach," says she, "and I'll go and fetch my mistress." "Make haste, then, sweetheart," says I, "for we may be full else." The maid had a great bundle under her arm; so she put the child into the coach, and I said, "You had best put your bundle into the coach too." "No," said she, "I am afraid somebody should slip it away from the child." "Give it me, then," said I. "Take it, then," says she, "and be sure you take care of it." "I'll answer for it," said I, "if it were twenty-pound value." "There, take it, then," says she, and away she goes.

As soon as I got the bundle and the maid was out of sight, I goes on towards the ale-house where the porter's wife was, so that if I met her, I had then only been going to give her the bundle and to call her to her business, as if I was going away and could stay no longer; but as I did not meet her, I walked away, and turning into

Charterhouse Lane, made off through Charterhouse Yard into Long Lane, then into Bartholomew Close, so into Little Britain, and through the Bluecoat Hospital to Newgate Street.

To prevent being known, I pulled off my blue apron and wrapt the bundle in it, which was made up in a piece of painted calico; I also wrapt up my straw hat in it, and so put the bundle upon my head; and it was very well that I did thus, for, coming through the Bluecoat Hospital, who should I meet but the wench that had given me the bundle to hold. It seems she was going with her mistress, who she had been to fetch, to the Barnet coaches.

I saw she was in haste, and I had no business to stop her; so away she went, and I brought my bundle safe to my governess. There was no money, plate, or jewels in it, but a very good suit of Indian damask, a gown and petticoat, a laced head and ruffles of very good Flanders lace, and some other things, such as I knew very well the value of.

This was not indeed my own invention, but was given me by one that had practised it with success, and my governess liked it extremely; and indeed I tried it again several times, though never twice near the same place; for the next time I tried in Whitechapel, just by the corner of Petticoat Lane, where the coaches stand that go out to Stratford and Bow and that side of the country; and another time at the Flying Horse, without Bishopsgate, where the Cheston coaches then lay; and I had always the good luck to come off with some booty.

Another time I placed myself at a warehouse by the waterside, where the coasting vessels from the north come, such as Newcastle-upon-Tyne, Sunderland, and other places. Here, the warehouse being shut, comes a young fellow with a letter; and he wanted a box and a hamper that was come from Newcastle-upon-Tyne. I asked him if he had the marks of it; so he shows me the letter by virtue of which he was to ask for it and which gave an account of the contents, the box being full of linen and the hamper full of glass-ware. I read the letter and took care to see the name, and the marks, the name of the person that sent the goods, and the name of the person they were sent to; then I bade the messenger come in the morning, for that the warehouse-keeper would not be there any more that night.

Away went I and wrote a letter from Mr. John Richardson of Newcastle to his dear cousin, Jemmy Cole, in London, with an account that he had sent by such a vessel (for I remembered all the particulars to a tittle) so many pieces of huckaback linen, and so many ells of Dutch holland, and the like, in a box, and a hamper of flint-glasses from Mr. Henzill's glass-house; and that the box was marked I. C. No. 1, and the hamper was directed by a label on the cording.

About an hour after, I came to the warehouse, found the warehouse-keeper, and had the goods delivered me without any scruple, the value of the linen being about £22.

I could fill up this whole discourse with the variety of such adventures which daily invention directed to, and which I managed with the utmost dexterity, and always with success.

At length—as when does the pitcher come safe home that goes so often to the well?—I fell into some broils, which though they could not affect me fatally, yet made me known, which was the worst thing next to being found guilty that could befall me.

I had taken up the disguise of a widow's dress; it was without any real design in view, but only waiting for anything that might offer, as I often did. It happened that while I was going along a street in Covent Garden there was a great cry of "Stop, thief! Stop, thief!" Some artists had, it seems, put a trick upon a shopkeeper, and being pursued, some of them fled one way and some another; and one of them was, they said, dressed up in widow's weeds, upon which the mob gathered about me, and some said I was the person, others said no. Immediately came the mercer's journeyman, and he swore aloud I was the person, and so seized on me. However, when I was brought back by the mob to the mercer's shop, the master of the house said freely that I was not the woman, and would have let me go immediately, but another fellow said gravely, "Pray stay till Mr. ——," meaning the journeyman, "comes back, for he knows her"; so they kept me near half an hour. They had called a constable, and he stood in the shop as my jailer. In talking with the constable I inquired where he lived and what trade he was; the man, not apprehending in the least what happened afterwards, readily told me his name and where he lived, and told me as a jest that I might be sure to hear of his name when I came to the Old Bailey.

The servants likewise used me saucily, and had much ado to keep their hands off me; the master indeed was civiller to me than they, but he would not let me go though he owned I was not in his shop before.

I began to be a little surly with him and told him I hoped he would not take it ill if I made myself amends upon him another time, and desired I might send for friends to see me have right done. No, he said, he could give no such liberty; I might ask it when I came before the justice of peace; and seeing I threatened him, he would take care of me in the meantime and would lodge me safe in Newgate. I told him it was his time now, but it would be mine by and by, and governed my passion as well as I was able. However, I spoke to the constable to call me a porter, which he did, and then I called for pen, ink, and paper, but they would let me have none. I asked the porter his name and where he lived, and the poor man told it me very willingly. I bade him observe and remember how I was treated there; that he saw I was detained there by force. I told him I should want him in another place, and it should not be the worse for him to speak. The porter said he would serve me with all his heart. "But, madam," says he, "let me hear them refuse to let you go, then I may be able to speak the plainer."

With that, I spoke aloud to the master of the shop and said, "Sir, you know in your own conscience that I am not the person you look for and that I was not in your shop before; therefore I demand that you detain me here no longer or tell me the reason of your stopping me." The fellow grew surlier upon this than before and said he would do neither till he thought fit. "Very well," said I to the constable and to the porter, "you will be pleased to remember this, gentlemen, another time." The porter said, "Yes, madam"; and the constable began not to like it, and would have persuaded the mercer to dismiss him and let me go, since, as he said, he owned I was not the person. "Good sir," says the mercer to him tauntingly, "are you a justice of peace or a constable? I charged you with her; pray do your duty." The constable told him, a little moved, but very handsomely, "I know my duty and what I am, sir; I doubt you know hardly what you are doing." They had some other hard words, and in the meantime the journeymen, impudent and unmanly to the last degree, used me barbarously, and one of them, the same that first seized upon me, pretended he would search me and began to lay hands on me. I spit in his face, called out to the constable, and bade him take notice of my usage. "And pray, Mr. Constable," said I, "ask that villain's name," pointing to the man. The constable reproved him decently, told him that he did not know what he did, for he knew that his master acknowledged I was not the person; "and," says the constable, "I am afraid your master is bringing himself and me, too, into trouble if this gentlewoman comes to prove who she is, and where she was, and it appears that she is not the woman you pretend to." "Damn her," says the fellow again, with an impudent, hardened face. "She is the lady, you may depend upon it; I'll swear she is the same body that was in the shop and that I gave the pieces of satin that is lost into her own hand. You shall hear more of it when Mr. William and Mr. Anthony"—those were other journeymen—"come back; they will know her again as well as I."

Just as the insolent rogue was talking thus to the constable, comes back Mr. William and Mr. Anthony, as he called them, and a great rabble with them, bringing along with them the true widow that I was pretended to be; and they came sweating and blowing into the shop, and with a great deal of triumph dragging the poor creature in a most butcherly manner up towards their master, who was in the back shop; and they cried out aloud, "Here's the widow, sir; we have catched her at last." "What do you mean by that?" says the master. "Why, we have her already; there she sits, and Mr. —— says he can swear this is she." The other man, who they called Mr. Anthony, replied, "Mr. —— may say what he will and swear what he will, but this is the woman, and there's the remnant of satin she stole; I took it out of her clothes with my own hand."

I now began to take a better heart, but smiled and said nothing; the master looked pale; the constable turned about and looked at me. "Let 'em alone, Mr. Constable," said I; "let 'em go on." The case was plain and could not be denied, so the constable was charged with the right thief, and the mercer told me very civilly he was sorry for the mistake and hoped I would not take it ill; that they had so many things of this nature put upon them every day that they could not be blamed for being very sharp in doing themselves justice. "Not take it ill, sir!" said I. "How can I take it well? If you had dismissed me when your insolent fellow seized on me in the street and brought me to you, and when you yourself acknowledged I was not the person, I would have put it by and not have taken it ill because of the many ill things I believe you have put upon you daily; but your treatment of me since has been insufferable, and especially that of your servant; I must and will have reparation for that."

Then he began to parley with me, said he would make me any reasonable satisfaction, and would fain have had me told him what it was I expected. I told him I should not be my own judge; the law should decide it for me; and as I was to be carried before a magistrate, I should let him hear there what I had to say. He told me there was no occasion to go before the justice now; I was at liberty to go where I pleased; and calling to the constable, told him he might let me go, for I was discharged. The constable said calmly to him, "Sir, you asked me just now if I knew whether I was a constable or a justice, and bade me do my duty, and charged me with this gentlewoman as a prisoner. Now, sir, I find you do not understand what is my duty, for you would make me a justice indeed; but I must tell you it is not in my power; I may keep a prisoner when I am charged with him, but 'tis the law and the magistrate alone that can discharge that prisoner; therefore 'tis a mistake, sir; I must carry her before a justice now, whether you think well of it or not." The mercer was very high with the constable at first, but the constable, happening to be not a hired officer, but a good, substantial kind of man (I think he was a corn-chandler) and a man of good sense, stood to his business, would not discharge me without going to a justice of the peace; and I insisted upon it too. When the mercer see that, "Well," says he to the constable, "you may carry her where you please; I have nothing to say to her." "But, sir," says the constable, "you will go with us, I hope, for 'tis you that charged me with her." "No, not I," says the mercer; "I tell you I have nothing to say to her." "But pray, sir, do," says the constable; "I desire it of you for your own sake, for the justice can do nothing without you." "Prithee, fellow," says the mercer, "go about your business; I tell you I have nothing to say to the gentlewoman. I charge you in the king's name to dismiss her." "Sir," says the constable, "I find you don't know what it is to be a constable; I beg of you, don't oblige me to be rude to you." "I think I need not; you are rude enough already," says the mercer. "No, sir," says the constable, "I am not rude; you have broken the peace in bringing an honest woman out of the street when she was about her lawful occasions, confining her in your shop, and ill-using her here by your servants. And now can you say I am rude to you? I think I am civil to you in not commanding you in the king's name to go with me, and charging every man I see that passes your door to aid and assist me in carrying you by force; this you know I have power to do, and yet I forbear it and once more entreat you to go with me." Well, he would not for all this, and gave the constable ill language. However, the constable kept his temper and would not be provoked; and then I put in and said, "Come, Mr. Constable, let him alone; I shall find ways enough to fetch him before a magistrate—I don't fear that; but there's that fellow," says I, "he was the man that seized on me as I was innocently going along the street, and you are a witness of his violence with me since; give me leave to charge you with him, and carry him before a justice." "Yes, madam," says the constable. And turning to the fellow, "Come, young gentleman," says he to the journeyman, "you must go along with us; I hope you are not above the constable's power, though your master is."

The fellow looked like a condemned thief and hung back, then looked at his master as if he could help him; and he, like a fool, encouraged the fellow to be rude, and he truly resisted the constable and pushed him back with a good force when he went to lay hold on him, at which the constable knocked him down and called out for help. Immediately the shop was filled with people, and the constable seized the master and man and all his servants.

The first ill consequence of this fray was that the woman who was really the thief made off and got clear away in the crowd, and two others that they had stopped also; whether they were really guilty or not, that I can say nothing to.

By this time some of his neighbours, having come in and seeing how things went, had endeavoured to bring the mercer to his senses, and he began to be convinced that he was in the wrong; and so at length we went all very quietly before the justice, with a mob of about five hundred people at our heels; and all the way we went I could hear the people ask what was the matter, and others reply and say a mercer had stopped a gentlewoman instead of a thief, and had afterwards taken the thief, and now the gentlewoman had taken the mercer and was carrying him before the justice. This pleased the people strangely and made the crowd increase, and they cried out as they went, "Which is the rogue? Which is the mercer?" and especially the women. Then, when they saw him they cried out, "That's he, that's he"; and every now and then came a good dab of dirt at him; and thus we marched a good while till the mercer thought fit to desire the constable to call a coach to protect himself from the rabble; so we rode the rest of the way, the constable and I, and the mercer and his man.

When we came to the justice, which was an ancient gentleman in Bloomsbury, the constable giving first a summary account of the matter, the justice bade me speak and tell what I had to say. And first he asked my name, which I was very loath to give, but there was no remedy; so I told him my name was Mary Flanders, that I was a widow, my husband, being a sea-captain, died on a voyage to Virginia; and some other circumstances I told which he could never contradict, and that I lodged at present in town with such a person, naming my governess; but that I was preparing to go over to America, where my husband's effects lay, and that I was going that day to buy some clothes to put myself into second mourning, but had not yet been in any shop when that fellow, pointing to the mercer's journeyman, came rushing upon me with such fury as very much frighted me, and carried me back to his master's shop, where, though his master acknowledged I was not the person, yet he would not dismiss me, but charged a constable with me.

Then I proceeded to tell how the journeymen treated me; how they would not suffer me to send for any of my friends; how afterwards they found the real thief and took the goods they had lost upon her, and all the particulars as before.

Then the constable related his case: his dialogue with the mercer about discharging me, and at last his servant's refusing to go with him when I had charged him with him, and his master encouraging him to do so, and at last his striking the constable, and the like, all as I have told it already.

The justice then heard the mercer and his man. The mercer indeed made a long harangue of the great loss they have daily by the lifters and thieves; that it was easy for them to mistake, and that when he found it, he would have dismissed me, etc., as above. As to the journeyman, he had very little to say but that he pretended other of the servants told him that I was really the person.

Upon the whole, the justice first of all told me very courteously I was discharged; that he was very sorry that the mercer's man should in his eager pursuit have so little discretion as to take up an innocent person for a guilty; that if he had not been so unjust as to detain me afterwards, he believed I would have forgiven the first affront; that, however, it was not in his power to award me any reparation other than by openly reproving them, which he should do; but he supposed I would apply to such methods as the law directed; in the meantime he would bind him over.

But as to the breach of the peace committed by the journeyman, he told me he should give me some satisfaction for that, for he should commit him to Newgate for assaulting the constable and for assaulting of me also.

Accordingly he sent the fellow to Newgate for that assault, and his master gave bail, and so we came away; but I had the satisfaction of seeing the mob wait upon them both as they came out, hallooing and throwing stones and dirt at the coaches they rode in; and so I came home.

After this hustle, coming home and telling my governess the story, she falls a-laughing at me. "Why are you so merry?" says I. "The story has not so much laughing-room in it as you imagine. I am sure I have had a great deal of hurry and fright too, with a pack of ugly rogues." "Laugh!" says my governess. "I laugh, child, to see what a lucky creature you are; why, this job will be the best bargain to you that ever you made in your life if you manage it well. I warrant you, you shall make the mercer pay five hundred pounds for damages, besides what you shall get of the journeyman."

I had other thoughts of the matter than she had; and especially because I had given in my name to the justice of peace; and I knew that my name was so well known among the people at Hicks's Hall, the Old Bailey, and such places that if this cause came to be tried openly and my name came to be inquired into, no court would give much damages for the reputation of a person of such a character. However, I was obliged to begin a prosecution in form, and accordingly my governess found me out a very creditable sort of a man to manage it, being an attorney of very good business and of good reputation, and she was certainly in the right of this; for had she employed a pettifogging hedge solicitor or a man not known, I should have brought it to but little.

I met this attorney and gave him all the particulars at large, as they are recited above; and he assured me it was a case, as he said, that he did not question but that a jury would give very considerable damages; so taking his full instructions, he began the prosecution, and the mercer, being arrested, gave bail. A few days after his giving bail, he comes with his attorney to my attorney to let him know that he desired to accommodate the matter; that it was all carried on in the heat of an unhappy passion; that his client, meaning me, had a sharp, provoking tongue and that I used them ill, gibing at them and jeering them even while they believed me to be the very person, and that I had provoked them, and the like.

My attorney managed as well on my side; made them believe I was a widow of fortune, that I was able to do myself justice and had great friends to stand by me too, who had all made me promise to sue to the utmost if it cost me £1000, for that the affronts I had received were insufferable.

However, they brought my attorney to this: that he promised he would not blow the coals; that if I inclined to an accommodation, he would not hinder me, and that he would rather persuade me to peace than to war, for which they told him he should be no loser; all which he told me very honestly, and told me that if they offered him any bribe, I should certainly know it; but upon the whole, he told me very honestly that if I would take his opinion, he would advise me to make it up with them, for that as they were in a great fright and were desirous above all things to make it up, and knew that, let it be what it would, they must bear all the costs, he believed they would give me freely more than any jury would give upon a trial. I asked him what he thought they would be brought to; he told me he could not tell as to that, but he would tell me more when I saw him again.

Some time after this they came again to know if he had talked with me. He told them he had; that he found me not so averse to an accommodation as some of my friends were, who resented the disgrace offered me and set me on; that they blowed the coals in secret, prompting me to revenge or to do myself justice, as they called it; so that he could not tell what to say to it; he told them he would do his endeavour to persuade me, but he ought to be able to tell me what proposal they made. They pretended they could not make any proposal because it might be made use of against them; and he told them that by the same rule he could not make any offers, for that might be pleaded in abatement of what damages a jury might be inclined to give. However, after some discourse and mutual promises that no advantage should be taken on either side by what was transacted then or at any other of those meetings, they came to a kind of a treaty, but so remote and so wide from one another that nothing could be expected from it; for my attorney demanded £500 and charges, and they offered £50 without charges; so they broke off, and the mercer proposed to have a meeting with me myself; and my attorney agreed to that very readily.

My attorney gave me notice to come to this meeting in good clothes and with some state, that the mercer might see I was something more than I seemed to be that time they had me. Accordingly I came in a new suit of second mourning, according to what I had said at the justice's. I set myself out, too, as well as a widow's dress would admit; my governess also furnished me with a good pearl necklace that shut in behind with a locket of diamonds, which she had in pawn; and I had a very good gold watch by my side; so that I made a very good figure; and as I stayed till I was sure they were come, I came in a coach to the door with my maid with me.

When I came into the room, the mercer was surprised. He stood up and made his bow, which I took a little notice of, and but a little, and went and sat down where my own attorney had appointed me to sit, for it was his house. After a while the mercer said he did not know me again, and began to make some compliments. I told him I believed he did not know me at first, and that if he had, he would have not treated me as he did.

He told me he was very sorry for what had happened, and that it was to testify the willingness he had to make all possible reparation that he had appointed this meeting; that he hoped I would not carry things to extremity, which might be not only too great a loss to him, but might be the ruin of his business and shop, in which case I might have the satisfaction of repaying an injury with an injury ten times greater but that I would then get nothing, whereas he was willing to do me any justice that was in his power without putting himself or me to the trouble or charge of a suit of law.

I told him I was glad to hear him talk so much more like a man of sense than he did before; that it was true, acknowledgement in most cases of affronts was counted reparation sufficient, but this had gone too far to be made up so; that I was not revengeful, nor did I seek his ruin or any man's else, but that all my friends were unanimous not to let me so far neglect my character as to adjust a thing of this kind without reparation; that to be taken up for a thief was such an indignity as could not be put up; that my character was above being treated so by any that knew me, but because in my condition of a widow I had been careless of myself, I might be taken for such a creature; but that for the particular usage I had from him afterward—and then I repeated all as before; it was so provoking, I had scarce patience to repeat it.

He acknowledged all and was mighty humble indeed; he came up to £100 and to pay all the law charges, and added that he would make me a present of a very good suit of clothes. I came down to £300 and demanded that I should publish an advertisement of the particulars in the common newspapers.

This was a clause he never could comply with. However, at last he came up, by good management of my attorney, to £150 and a suit of black silk clothes; and there, as it were, at my attorney's request, I complied, he paying my attorney's bill and charges, and gave us a good supper into the bargain.

When I came to receive the money, I brought my governess with me, dressed like an old duchess, and a gentleman very well dressed, who we pretended courted me, but I called him cousin, and the lawyer was only to hint privately to them that this gentleman courted the widow.

He treated us handsomely indeed, and paid the money cheerfully enough; so that it cost him £200 in all or rather more. At our last meeting, when all was agreed, the case of the journeyman came up, and the mercer begged very hard for him; told me he was a man that had kept a shop of his own and been in good business, had a wife and several children and was very poor; that he had nothing to make satisfaction with, but should beg my pardon on his knees. I had no spleen at the saucy rogue, nor were his submissions anything to me, since there was nothing to be got by him, so I thought it was as good to throw that in generously as not; so I told him I did not desire the ruin of any man, and therefore at his request I would forgive the wretch; it was below me to seek any revenge.

When we were at supper, he brought the poor fellow in to make his acknowledgement, which he would have done with as much mean humility as his offence was with insulting pride; in which he was an instance of a complete baseness of spirit, imperious, cruel, and relentless when uppermost, abject and low-spirited when down. However, I abated his cringes, told him I forgave him, and desired he might withdraw, as if I did not care for the sight of him, though I had forgiven him.

I was now in good circumstances indeed, if I could

have known my time for leaving off, and my governess often said I was the richest of the trade in England; and so I believe I was, for I had £700 by me in money, besides clothes, rings, some plate, and two gold watches, and all of them stolen; for I had innumerable jobs besides these I have mentioned. Oh! had I even now had the grace of repentance, I had still leisure to have looked back upon my follies and have made some reparation; but the satisfaction I was to make for the public mischiefs I had done was yet left behind; and I could not forbear going abroad again, as I called it now, any more than I could when my extremity really drove me out for bread.

It was not long after the affair with the mercer was made up that I went out in an equipage quite different from any I had ever appeared in before. I dressed myself like a beggar-woman, in the coarsest and most despicable rags I could get, and I walked about peering and peeping into every door and window I came near; and, indeed, I was in such a plight now that I knew as ill how to behave in as ever I did in any. I naturally abhorred dirt and rags; I had been bred up tight and cleanly, and could be no other, whatever condition I was in, so that this was the most uneasy disguise to me that ever I put on. I said presently to myself that this would not do, for this was a dress that everybody was shy and afraid of; and I thought everybody looked at me as if they were afraid I should come near them lest I should take something from them, or afraid to come near me lest they should get something from me. I wandered about all the evening the first time I went out and made nothing of it, and came home again wet, draggled, and tired. However, I went out again the next night, and then I met with a little adventure which had like to have cost me dear. As I was standing near a tavern door there comes a gentleman on horse-back and lights at the door, and wanting to go into the tavern, he calls one of the drawers to hold his horse. He stayed pretty long in the tavern, and the drawer heard his master call, and thought he would be angry with him. Seeing me stand by him, he called to me. "Here, woman," says he, "hold this horse awhile till I go in; if the gentleman comes, he'll give you something." "Yes," says I, and takes the horse, and walks off with him soberly, and carried him to my governess.

This had been a booty to those that had understood it; but never was poor thief more at a loss to know what to do with anything that was stolen; for when I came home, my governess was quite confounded, and what to do with the creature we neither of us knew. To send him to a stable was doing nothing, for it was certain that notice would be given in the gazette, and the horse described, so that we durst not go to fetch it again.

All the remedy we had for this unlucky adventure was to go and set up the horse at an inn, and send a note by a porter to the tavern that the gentleman's horse that was lost at such a time was left at such an inn, and that he might be had there; that the poor woman that held him, having led him about the street, not being able to lead him back again, had left him there. We might have waited till the owner had published and offered a reward, but we did not care to venture the receiving the reward.

So this was a robbery and no robbery, for little was lost by it and nothing was got by it, and I was quite sick of going out in a beggar's dress; it did not answer at all, and besides, I thought it ominous and threatening.

While I was in this disguise I fell in with a parcel of folks of a worse kind than any I ever sorted with, and I saw a little into their ways too. These were coiners of money, and they made some very good offers to me as to profit; but the part they would have had me embarked in was the most dangerous. I mean that of the very working of the die, as they call it, which, had I been taken, had been certain death, and that at a stake; I say, to be burnt to death at a stake; so that though I was to appearance but a beggar, and they promised mountains of gold and silver to me to engage, yet it would not do. 'Tis true, if I had been really a beggar or had been desperate as when I began, I might, perhaps, have closed with it; for what care they to die that cannot tell how to live? But at present that was not my condition; at least I was for no such terrible risks as those; besides, the very thoughts of being burnt at a stake struck terror to my very soul, chilled my blood, and gave me the vapours to such a degree as I could not think of it without trembling.

This put an end to my disguise too, for though I did not like the proposal, yet I did not tell them so, but seemed to relish it, and promised to meet again. But I durst see them no more; for if I had seen them and not complied, though I had declined it with the greatest assurances of secrecy in the world, they would have gone near to have murdered me, to make sure work and make themselves easy, as they call it. What kind of easiness that is, they may best judge that understand how easy men are that can murder people to prevent danger.

This and horse-stealing were things quite out of my way, and I might easily resolve I would have no more to say to them. My business seemed to lie another way, and though it had hazard enough in it too, yet it was more suitable to me, and what had more of art in it and more chances for a coming off if a surprise should happen.

I had several proposals made also to me about that time to come into a gang of housebreakers; but that was a thing I had no mind to venture at neither, any more than I had at the coining trade. I offered to go along with two men and a woman that made it their business to get into houses by stratagem. I was willing enough to venture, but there were three of them already, and they did not care to part nor I to have too many in a gang; so I did not close with them, and they paid dear for their next attempt.

But at length I met with a woman that had often told me what adventures she had made, and with success, at the waterside, and I closed with her, and we drove on our business pretty well. One day we came among some Dutch people at St. Catherine's, where we went on pretence to buy goods that were privately got on shore. I was two or three times in a house where we saw a good quantity of prohibited goods, and my companion once brought away three pieces of Dutch black silk that turned to good account, and I had my share of it; but in all the journeys I made by myself, I could not get an opportunity to do anything, so I laid it aside, for I had been there so often that they began to suspect something.

This balked me a little, and I resolved to push at something or other, for I was not used to come back so often without purchase; so the next day I dressed myself up fine and took a walk to the other end of the town. I passed through the Exchange in the Strand, but had no notion of finding anything to do there, when on a sudden

I saw a great clutter in the place, and all the people, shopkeepers as well as others, standing up and staring; and what should it be but some great duchess come into the Exchange, and they said the queen was coming. I set myself close up to a shop-side with my back to the counter, as if to let the crowd pass by, when, keeping my eye upon a parcel of lace which the shopkeeper was showing to some ladies that stood by me, the shopkeeper and her maid were so taken up with looking to see who was a-coming and what shop they would go to that I found means to slip a paper of lace into my pocket and come clear off with it; so the lady-milliner paid dear enough for her gaping after the queen.

I went off from the shop, as if driven along by the throng, and mingling myself with the crowd, went out at the other door of the Exchange and so got away before they missed their lace; and because I would not be followed, I called a coach and shut myself up in it. I had scarce shut the coach doors but I saw the milliner's maid and five or six more come running out into the street and crying out as if they were frighted. They did not cry "Stop, thief!" because nobody ran away, but I could hear the word "robbed," and "lace," two or three times, and saw the wench wringing her hands, and run staring to and again, like one scared. The coachman that had taken me up was getting up into the box, but was not quite up, and the horses had not begun to move, so that I was terrible uneasy, and I took the packet of lace and laid it ready to have dropped it out at the flap of the coach, which opens before, just behind the coachman; but to my great satisfaction, in less than a minute the coach began to move, that is to say, as soon as the coachman had got up and spoken to his horses; so he drove away, and I brought off my purchase, which was worth near £20.

The next day I dressed me up again, but in quite different clothes, and walked the same way again, but nothing offered till I came into St. James's Park. I saw abundance of fine ladies in the park, walking in the Mall, and among the rest there was a little miss, a young lady of about twelve or thirteen years old, and she had a sister, as I supposed, with her, that might be about nine. I observed the biggest had a fine gold watch on and a good necklace of pearl, and they had a footman in livery with them; but as it is not usual for the footmen to go behind the ladies in the Mall, so I observed the footman stopped at their going into the Mall, and the biggest of the sisters spoke to him to bid him be just there when they came back.

When I heard her dismiss the footman, I stepped up to him and asked him what little lady that was, and held a little chat with him about what a pretty child it was with her, and how genteel and well carriaged the eldest would be, how womanish and how grave; and the fool of a fellow told me presently who she was; that she was Sir Thomas ——'s eldest daughter, of Essex, and that she was a great fortune; that her mother was not come to town yet; but she was with Sir William ——'s lady at her lodgings in Suffolk Street, and a great deal more; that they had a maid and a woman to wait on them, besides Sir Thomas' coach, the coachman, and himself; and that young lady was governess to the whole family, as well here as at home; and told me abundance of things, enough for my business.

I was well dressed and had my gold watch as well as she; so I left the footman, and I puts myself in a rank with this lady, having stayed till she had taken one turn in the Mall and was going forward again; by and by I saluted her by her name, with the title of Lady Betty. I asked her when she heard from her father, when my lady her mother would be in town, and how she did.

I talked so familiarly to her of her whole family that she could not suspect but that I knew them all intimately. I asked her why she would come abroad without Mrs. Chime with her (that was the name of her woman) to take care of Mrs. Judith (that was her sister). Then I entered into a long chat with her about her sister, what a fine little lady she was, and asked her if she had learnt French, and a thousand such little things, when on a sudden the guards came, and the crowd run to see the king go by to the Parliament House.

The ladies run all to the side of the Mall, and I helped my lady to stand upon the edge of the boards on the side of the Mall, that she might be high enough to see; and took the little one and lifted her quite up; during which I took care to convey her gold watch so clean away from the Lady Betty that she never missed it till the crowd was gone and she was gotten into the middle of the Mall.

I took my leave in the very crowd and said, as if in haste, "Dear Lady Betty, take care of your little sister." And so the crowd did, as it were, thrust me away, and that I was unwilling to take my leave.

The hurry in such cases is immediately over and the place clear as soon as the king is gone by; but as there is always a great running and clutter just as the king passes, so having dropped the two little ladies and done my business with them without any miscarriage, I kept hurrying on among the crowd, as if I run to see the king, and so I kept before the crowd till I came to the end of the Mall, when, the king going on toward the Horse Guards, I went forward to the passage, which went then through against the end of the Haymarket, and there I bestowed a coach upon myself and made off; and I confess I have not yet been so good as my word, *viz.*, to go and visit my Lady Betty.

I was once in the mind to venture staying with Lady Betty till she missed the watch, and so have made a great outcry about it with her, and have got her into her coach and put myself in the coach with her, and have gone home with her; for she appeared so fond of me, and so perfectly deceived by my so readily talking to her of all her relations and family, that I thought it was very easy to push the thing farther and to have got at least the necklace of pearl; but when I considered that though the child would not perhaps have suspected me, other people might, and that if I was searched I should be discovered, I thought it was best to go off with what I had got.

I came accidentally afterwards to hear that when the young lady missed her watch, she made a great outcry in the park and sent her footman up and down to see if he could find me, she having described me so perfectly that he knew it was the same person that had stood and talked so long with him and asked him so many questions about them; but I was gone far enough out of their reach before she could come at her footman to tell him the story.

I made another adventure after this, of a nature different from all I had been concerned in yet, and this was at a gaming-house near Covent Garden.

I saw several people go in and out; and I stood in the

passage a good while with another woman with me, and seeing a gentleman go up that seemed to be of more than ordinary fashion, I said to him, "Sir, pray, don't they give women leave to go up?" "Yes, madam," says he, "and to play too, if they please." "I mean so, sir," said I. And with that he said he would introduce me if I had a mind; so I followed him to the door, and he looking in, "There, madam," says he, "are the gamesters, if you have a mind to venture." I looked in and said to my comrade aloud, "Here's nothing but men; I won't venture." At which one of the gentlemen cried out, "You need not be afraid, madam, here's none but fair gamesters; you are very welcome to come and set what you please." So I went a little nearer and looked on, and some of them brought me a chair, and I sat down and see the box and dice go round apace; then I said to my comrade, "The gentlemen play too high for us; come, let us go."

The people were all very civil, and one gentleman encouraged me and said, "Come, madam, if you please to venture, if you dare trust me, I'll answer for it you shall have nothing put upon you here." "No, sir," said I, smiling, "I hope the gentlemen would not cheat a woman." But still I declined venturing, though I pulled out a purse with money in it, that they might see I did not want money.

After I had sat awhile, one gentleman said to me, jeering, "Come, madam, I see you are afraid to venture for yourself; I always had good luck with the ladies; you shall set for me if you won't set for yourself." I told him, "Sir, I should be very loath to lose your money," though I added, "I am pretty lucky too; but the gentlemen play so high that I dare not venture my own."

"Well, well," says he, "there's ten guineas, madam; set them for me"; so I took the money and set, himself looking on. I run out the guineas by one and two at a time, and then the box coming to the next man to me, my gentleman gave me ten guineas more and made me set five of them at once, and the gentleman who had the box threw out, so there was five guineas of his money again. He was encouraged at this and made me take the box, which was a bold venture; however, I held the box so long that I gained him his whole money and had a handful of guineas in my lap; and which was the better luck, when I threw out, I threw but at one or two of those that had set me, and so went off easy.

When I was come this length, I offered the gentleman all the gold, for it was his own; and so would have had him play for himself, pretending that I did not understand the game well enough. He laughed and said if I had but good luck, it was no matter whether I understood the game or no; but I should not leave off. However, he took out the fifteen guineas that he had put in first and bade me play with the rest. I would have him to have seen how much I had got, but he said, "No, no, don't tell them; I believe you are very honest, and 'tis bad luck to tell them"; so I played on.

I understood the game well enough, though I pretended I did not, and played cautiously, which was to keep a good stock in my lap, out of which I every now and then conveyed some into my pocket, but in such a manner as I was sure he could not see it.

I played a great while and had very good luck for him; but the last time I held the box they set me high, and I threw boldly at all, and held the box till I had gained near fourscore guineas, but lost above half of it back at the last throw; so I got up, for I was afraid I should lose it all back again, and said to him, "Pray come, sir, now, and take it and play for yourself; I think I have done pretty well for you." He would have had me play on, but it grew late, and I desired to be excused. When I gave it up to him, I told him I hoped he would give me leave to tell it now, that I might see what he had gained and how lucky I had been for him; when I told them, there were threescore and three guineas. "Ay," says I, "if it had not been for that unlucky throw, I had got you a hundred guineas." So I gave him all the money, but he would not take it till I had put my hand into it and taken some for myself, and bid me please myself. I refused it, and was positive I would not take it myself; if he had a mind to do anything of that kind, it should be all his own doings.

The rest of the gentlemen, seeing us striving, cried, "Give it her all"; but I absolutely refused that. Then one of them said, "D—n ye, Jack, half it with her; don't you know you should be always upon even terms with the ladies?" So, in short, he divided it with me, and I brought away thirty guineas besides about forty-three which I had stole privately, which I was sorry for because he was so generous.

Thus I brought home seventy-three guineas and let my old governess see what good luck I had at play. However, it was her advice that I should not venture again, and I took her counsel, for I never went there any more; for I knew as well as she, if the itch of play came in, I might soon lose that and all the rest of what I had got.

Fortune had smiled upon me to that degree, and I had thriven so much, and my governess too, for she always had a share with me, that really the old gentlewoman began to talk of leaving off while we were well and being satisfied with what we had got; but, I know not what fate guided me, I was as backward to it now as she was when I proposed it to her before, and so in an ill hour we gave over the thoughts of it for the present, and in a word, I grew more hardened and audacious than ever, and the success I had, made my name as famous as any thief of my sort ever had been.

I had sometimes taken the liberty to play the same game over again, which is not according to practice, which however succeeded not amiss; but generally I took up new figures and contrived to appear in new shapes every time I went abroad.

It was now a rumbling time of the year, and the gentlemen being most of them gone out of town, Tunbridge and Epsom and such places were full of people. But the city was thin, and I thought our trade felt it a little, as well as others; so that at the latter end of the year I joined myself with a gang who usually go every year to Stourbridge Fair, and from thence to Bury Fair, in Suffolk. We promised ourselves great things here, but when I came to see how things were, I was weary of it presently; for except mere picking of pockets, there was little worth meddling with; neither if a booty had been made was it so easy carrying it off, nor was there such a variety of occasion for business in our way as in London; all that I made of the whole journey was a gold watch at Bury Fair and a small parcel of linen at Cambridge, which gave me occasion to take leave of the place. It was an old bite, and I thought might do with a country shopkeeper, though in London it would not.

I bought at a linen-draper's shop, not in the fair, but in the town of Cambridge, as much fine holland and other things as came to about £7; when I had done, I bade them be sent to such an inn, where I had taken up my being the same morning, as if I was to lodge there that night.

I ordered the draper to send them home to me, about such an hour, to the inn where I lay, and I would pay him his money. At the time appointed the draper sends the goods, and I placed one of our gang at the chamber-door, and when the innkeeper's maid brought the messenger to the door, who was a young fellow, an apprentice, almost a man, she tells him her mistress was asleep, but if he would leave the things and call in about an hour, I should be awake and he might have the money. He left the parcel very readily and goes his way, and in about half an hour my maid and I walked off, and that very evening I hired a horse and a man to ride before me and went to Newmarket, and from thence got my passage in a coach that was not quite full to St. Edmund's Bury, where, as I told you, I could make but little of my trade; only at a little country opera-house I got a gold watch from a lady's side, who was not only intolerably merry but a little fuddled, which made my work much easier.

I made off with this little booty to Ipswich, and from thence to Harwich, where I went into an inn as if I had newly arrived from Holland, not doubting but I should make some purchase among the foreigners that came on shore there; but I found them generally empty of things of value except what was in their portmanteaus and Dutch hampers, which were always guarded by footmen; however, I fairly got one of their portmanteaus one evening out of the chamber where the gentleman lay, the footman being fast asleep on the bed and, I suppose, very drunk.

The room in which I lodged lay next to the Dutchman's, and having dragged the heavy thing with much ado out of the chamber into mine, I went out into the street to see if I could find any possibility of carrying it off. I walked about a great while, but could see no probability either of getting out the thing or of conveying away the goods that was in it, the town being so small, and I a perfect stranger in it; so I was returning with a resolution to carry it back again and leave it where I found it. Just in that very moment I heard a man make a noise to some people to make haste, for the boat was going to put off and the tide would be spent. I called the fellow: "What boat is it, friend," said I, "that you belong to?" "The Ipswich wherry, madam," says he. "When do you go off?" says I. "This moment, madam," says he. "Do you want to go thither?" "Yes," said I, "if you can stay till I fetch my things." "Where are your things, madam?" says he. "At such an inn," said I. "Well, I'll go with you, madam," says he very civilly, "and bring them for you." "Come away, then," says I, and takes him with me.

The people of the inn were in a great hurry, the packet-boat from Holland being just come in and two coaches just come also with passengers from London for another packet-boat that was going off for Holland, which coaches were to go back next day with the passengers that were just landed. In this hurry it was that I came to the bar and paid my reckoning, telling my landlady I had gotten my passage by sea in a wherry.

These wherries are large vessels with good accommodation for carrying passengers from Harwich to London; and though they are called wherries, which is a word used in the Thames for a small boat rowed with one or two men, yet these are vessels able to carry twenty passengers and ten or fifteen tons of goods, and fitted to bear the sea. All this I had found out by inquiring the night before into the several ways of going to London.

My landlady was very courteous, took my money for the reckoning, but was called away, all the house being in a hurry. So I left her, took the fellow up into my chamber, gave him the trunk, or portmanteau, for it was like a trunk, and wrapt it about with an old apron, and he went directly to his boat with it and I after him, nobody asking us the least question about it. As for the drunken Dutch footman, he was still asleep, and his master with other foreign gentlemen at supper, and very merry below; so I went clean off with it to Ipswich, and going in the night, the people of the house knew nothing but that I was gone to London by the Harwich wherry, as I had told my landlady.

I was plagued at Ipswich with the custom-house officers, who stopped my trunk, as I called it, and would open and search it. I was willing, I told them, that they should search it, but my husband had the key, and that he was not yet come from Harwich; this I said: that if upon searching it they should find all the things be such as properly belonged to a man rather than a woman, it should not seem strange to them. However, they being positive to open the trunk, I consented to have it broken open, that is to say, to have the lock taken off, which was not difficult.

They found nothing for their turn, for the trunk had been searched before; but they discovered several things much to my satisfaction, as particularly a parcel of money in French pistoles, and some Dutch ducatoons, or rix-dollars; and the rest was chiefly two periwigs, wearing-linen, razors, wash-balls, perfumes, and other useful things necessary for a gentleman, which all passed for my husband's, and so I was quit of them.

It was now very early in the morning, and not light, and I knew not well what course to take; for I made no doubt but I should be pursued in the morning and perhaps be taken with the things about me; so I resolved upon taking new measures. I went publicly to an inn in the town with my trunk, as I called it, and having taken the substance out, I did not think the lumber of it worth my concern; however, I gave it the landlady of the house with a charge to take care of it and lay it up safe till I should come again, and away I walked into the street.

When I was got into the town a great way from the inn, I met with an ancient woman who had just opened her door, and I fell into chat with her and asked her a great many wild questions of things all remote to my purpose and design; but in my discourse I found by her how the town was situated, that I was in a street which went out towards Hadley, but that such a street went towards the waterside, such a street went into the heart of the town, and at last, such a street went towards Colchester, and so the London road lay there.

I had soon my ends of this old woman, for I only wanted to know which was the London road, and away I walked as fast as I could; not that I intended to go on foot either to London or to Colchester, but I wanted to get quietly away from Ipswich.

I walked about two or three miles, and then I met a plain countryman, who was busy about some husbandry work, I did not know what, and I asked him a great many questions, first not much to the purpose, but at last told him I was going for London, and the coach was full, and I could not get a passage, and asked him if he could not tell me where to hire a horse that would carry double and an honest man to ride before me to Colchester, so that I might get a place there in the coaches. The honest clown looked earnestly at me and said nothing for above half a minute, when, scratching his poll, "A horse, say you, and to Colchester, to carry double? Why, yes, mistress, alack-a-day, you may have horses enough for money." "Well, friend," says I, "that I take for granted; I don't expect it without money." "Why, but, mistress," says he, "how much are you willing to give?" "Nay," says I again, "friend, I don't know what your rates are in the country here, for I am a stranger; but if you can get one for me, get it as cheap as you can, and I'll give you somewhat for your pains."

"Why, that's honestly said, too," says the countryman. "Not so honest, neither," said I to myself, "if thou knewest all." "Why, mistress," says he, "I have a horse that will carry double, and I don't much care if I go myself with you, an' you like." "Will you?" says I. "Well, I believe you are an honest man; if you will, I shall be glad of it; I'll pay you in reason." "Why, look ye, mistress," says he, "I won't be out of reason with you; then if I carry you to Colchester, it will be worth five shillings for myself and my horse, for I shall hardly come back to-night."

In short, I hired the honest man and his horse; but when we came to a town upon the road (I do not remember the name of it, but it stands upon a river), I pretended myself very ill, and I could go no farther that night, but if he would stay there with me, because I was a stranger, I would pay him for himself and his horse with all my heart.

This I did because I knew the Dutch gentlemen and their servants would be upon the road that day, either in the stage-coaches or riding post, and I did not know but the drunken fellow or somebody else that might have seen me at Harwich might see me again, and I thought that in one day's stop they would be all gone by.

We lay all that night there, and the next morning it was not very early when I set out, so that it was near ten o'clock by the time I got to Colchester. It was no little pleasure that I saw the town where I had so many pleasant days, and I made many inquiries after the good old friends I had once had there, but could make little out; they were all dead or removed. The young ladies had been all married or gone to London; the old gentleman and the old lady that had been my early benefactress all dead; and which troubled me most, the young gentleman my first lover, and afterwards my brother-in law, was dead; but two sons, men grown, were left of him, but they too were transplanted to London.

I dismissed my old man here, and stayed incognito for three or four days in Colchester, and then took a passage in a waggon because I would not venture being seen in the Harwich coaches. But I needed not have used so much caution, for there was nobody in Harwich but the woman of the house could have known me; nor was it rational to think that she, considering the hurry she was in, and that she never saw me but once and that by candlelight, should have ever discovered me.

I was now returned to London, and though by the accident of the last adventure I got something considerable, yet I was not fond of any more country rambles; nor should I have ventured abroad again if I had carried the trade on to the end of my days. I gave my governess a history of my travels; she liked the Harwich journey well enough, and in discoursing of these things between ourselves she observed that a thief being a creature that watches the advantages of other people's mistakes, 'tis impossible but that to one that is vigilant and industrious many opportunities must happen, and therefore she thought that one so exquisitely keen in the trade as I was would scarce fail of something wherever I went.

On the other hand, every branch of my story, if duly considered, may be useful to honest people and afford a due caution to people of some sort or other to guard against the like surprises and to have their eyes about them when they have to do with strangers of any kind, for 'tis very seldom that some snare or other is not in their way. The moral, indeed, of all my history is left to be gathered by the senses and judgement of the reader; I am not qualified to preach to them. Let the experience of one creature completely wicked and completely miserable be a storehouse of useful warning to those that read.

I am drawing now towards a new variety of life. Upon my return, being hardened by a long race of crime and success unparalleled, I had, as I have said, no thoughts of laying down a trade which, if I was to judge by the example of others, must, however, end at last in misery and sorrow.

It was on the Christmas Day following, in the evening, that, to finish a long train of wickedness, I went abroad to see what might offer in my way; when, going by a working silversmith's in Foster Lane, I saw a tempting bait indeed, and not to be resisted by one of my occupation, for the shop had nobody in it, and a great deal of loose plate lay in the window and at the seat of the man, who, I suppose, worked at one side of the shop.

I went boldly in and was just going to lay my hand upon a piece of plate, and might have done it and carried it clear off, for any care that the men who belonged to the shop had taken of it; but an officious fellow in a house on the other side of the way, seeing me go in and that there was nobody in the shop, comes running over the street and, without asking me what I was or who, seizes upon me and cries out for the people of the house.

I had not touched anything in the shop, and seeing a glimpse of somebody running over, I had so much presence of mind as to knock very hard with my foot on the floor of the house, and was just calling out too when the fellow laid hands on me.

However, as I had always most courage when I was in most danger, so when he laid hands on me I stood very high upon it, that I came in to buy half a dozen of silver spoons; and to my good fortune, it was a silversmith's that sold plate as well as worked plate for other shops. The fellow laughed at that part, and put such a value upon the service that he had done his neighbour that he would have it be that I came not to buy, but to steal; and raising a great crowd, I said to the master of the shop, who by this time was fetched home from some neighbouring place, that it was in vain to make a noise and enter into talk there of the case; the fellow had insisted that I came to steal, and he must prove it, and I desired we might go before a magistrate without any more words; for I began to see I should be too hard for the man that had seized me.

The master and mistress of the shop were really not so violent as the man from t'other side of the way; and the man said, "Mistress, you might come into the shop with a good design for aught I know, but it seemed a dangerous thing for you to come into such a shop as mine is when you see nobody there; and I cannot do so little justice to my neighbour, who was so kind, as not to acknowledge he had reason on his side; though, upon the whole, I do not find you attempted to take anything, and I really know not what to do in it." I pressed him to go before a magistrate with me, and if anything could be proved on me that was like a design, I should willingly submit, but if not, I expected reparation.

Just while we were in this debate, and a crowd of people gathered about the door, came by Sir T. B., an alderman of the city and justice of the peace, and the goldsmith, hearing of it, entreated his worship to come in and decide the case.

Give the goldsmith his due, he told his story with a great deal of justice and moderation, and the fellow that had come over and seized upon me told his with as much heat and foolish passion, which did me good still. It came then to my turn to speak, and I told his worship that I was a stranger in London, being newly come out of the north; that I lodged in such a place, that I was passing this street, and went into a goldsmith's shop to buy half a dozen of spoons. By great good luck I had an old silver spoon in my pocket, which I pulled out, and told him I had carried that spoon to match it with half a dozen of new ones, that it might match some I had in the country; that seeing nobody in the shop, I knocked with my foot very hard to make the people hear and had also called aloud with my voice; 'tis true there was loose plate in the shop, but that nobody could say I had touched any of it; that a fellow came running into the shop out of the street, and laid hands on me in a furious manner in the very moment while I was calling for the people of the house; that if he had really had a mind to have done his neighbour any service, he should have stood at a distance and silently watched to see whether I had touched anything or no, and then have taken me in the fact. "That is very true," says Mr. Alderman, and turning to the fellow that stopped me, he asked him if it was true that I knocked with my foot. He said yes, I had knocked, but that might be because of his coming. "Nay," says the alderman, taking him short, "now you contradict yourself, for just now you said she was in the shop with her back to you, and did not see you till you came upon her." Now it was true that my back was partly to the street, but yet as my business was of a kind that required me to have eyes every way, so I really had a glance of him running over, as I said before, though he did not perceive it.

After a full hearing, the alderman gave it as his opinion that his neighbour was under a mistake, and that I was innocent, and the goldsmith acquiesced in it too and his wife, and so I was dismissed; but as I was going to depart, Mr. Alderman said, "But hold, madam, if you were designing to buy spoons, I hope you will not let my friend here lose his customer by the mistake." I readily answered, "No, sir, I'll buy the spoons still if he can match my odd spoon, which I brought for a pattern"; and the goldsmith showed me some of the very same fashion. So he weighed the spoons, and they came to five-and-thirty shillings; so I pulls out my purse to pay him, in which I had near twenty guineas, for I never went without such a sum about me, whatever might happen, and I found it of use at other times as well as now.

When Mr. Alderman saw my money, he said, "Well, madam, now I am satisfied you were wronged, and it was for this reason that I moved you should buy the spoons and stayed till you had bought them, for if you had not had money to pay for them, I should have suspected that you did not come into the shop to buy, for the sort of people who come upon those designs that you have been charged with are seldom troubled with much gold in their pockets, as I see you are."

I smiled and told his worship that then I owed something of his favour to my money, but I hoped he saw reason also in the justice he had done me before. He said yes, he had, but this had confirmed his opinion, and he was fully satisfied now of my having been injured. So I came well off from an affair in which I was at the very brink of destruction.

It was but three days after this that, not at all made cautious by my former danger, as I used to be, and still pursuing the art which I had so long been employed in, I ventured into a house where I saw the doors open, and furnished myself, as I thought verily without being perceived, with two pieces of flowered silks, such as they call brocaded silk, very rich. It was not a mercer's shop nor a warehouse of a mercer, but looked like a private dwelling-house, and was, it seems, inhabited by a man that sold goods for a weaver to the mercers, like a broker, or factor.

That I may make short of the black part of this story, I was attacked by two wenches that came open-mouthed at me just as I was going out at the door, and one of them pulled me back into the room while the other shut the door upon me. I would have given them good words, but there was no room for it—two fiery dragons could not have been more furious; they tore my clothes, bullied and roared as if they would have murdered me; the mistress of the house came next, and then the master, and all outrageous.

I gave the master very good words, told him the door was open and things were a temptation to me, that I was poor and distressed, and poverty was what many could not resist, and begged him with tears to have pity on me. The mistress of the house was moved with compassion and inclined to have let me go, and had almost persuaded her husband to it also but the saucy wenches were run even before they were sent and had fetched a constable, and then the master said he could not go back, I must go before a justice, and answered his wife that he might come into trouble himself if he should let me go.

The sight of a constable, indeed, struck me, and I thought I should have sunk into the ground. I fell into faintings, and indeed the people themselves thought I would have died, when the woman argued again for me and entreated her husband, seeing they had lost nothing, to let me go. I offered him to pay for the two pieces, whatever the value was, though I had not got them, and argued that as he had his goods and had really lost nothing, it would be cruel to pursue me to death and have my blood for the bare attempt of taking them. I put the constable in mind, too, that I had broke no doors nor carried anything away; and when I came to the justice and pleaded there that I had neither broken anything to get in nor carried anything out, the justice was inclined to have released me; but the first saucy jade that stopped me, affirming that I was going out with the goods but that she stopped me and pulled me back, the justice upon that point committed me, and I was carried to Newgate, that horrid place! My very blood chills at the mention of its name; the place where so many of my comrades had been locked up and from whence they went to the fatal tree; the place where my mother suffered so deeply, where I was brought into the world and from whence I expected no redemption but by an infamous death—to conclude, the place that had so long expected me, and which with so much art and success I had so long avoided.

I was now fixed indeed; 'tis impossible to describe the terror of my mind when I was first brought in and when I looked round upon all the horrors of that dismal place. I looked on myself as lost, and that I had nothing to think of but of going out of the world, and that with the utmost infamy: the hellish noise, the roaring, swearing, and clamour, the stench and nastiness, and all the dreadful afflicting things that I saw there joined to make the place seem an emblem of hell itself, and a kind of an entrance into it.

Now I reproached myself with the many hints I had had, as I have mentioned above, from my own reason, from the sense of my good circumstances, and of the many dangers I had escaped, to leave off while I was well, and how I had withstood them all and hardened my thoughts against all fear. It seemed to me that I was hurried on by an inevitable fate to this day of misery, and that now I was to expiate all my offences at the gallows; that I was now to give satisfaction to justice with my blood, and that I was to come to the last hour of my life and of my wickedness together. These things poured themselves in upon my thoughts in a confused manner and left me overwhelmed with melancholy and despair.

Then I repented heartily of all my life past, but that repentance yielded me no satisfaction, no peace, no, not in the least, because, as I said to myself, it was repenting after the power of farther sinning was taken away. I seemed not to mourn that I had committed such crimes, and for the fact as it was an offence against God and my neighbour, but that I was to be punished for it. I was a penitent, as I thought, not that I had sinned, but that I was to suffer, and this took away all the comfort of my repentance in my own thoughts.

I got no sleep for several nights or days after I came into that wretched place, and glad I would have been for some time to have died there, though I did not consider dying as it ought to be considered neither; indeed, nothing could be filled with more horror to my imagination than the very place, nothing was more odious to me than the company that was there. Oh! if I had but been sent to any place in the world and not to Newgate, I should have thought myself happy.

In the next place, how did the hardened wretches that were there before me triumph over me! What! Mrs. Flanders come to Newgate at last? What! Mrs. Mary, Mrs. Molly, and after that plain Moll Flanders! They thought the devil had helped me, they said, that I had reigned so long; they expected me there many years ago, they said, and was I come at last? Then they flouted me with dejections, welcomed me to the place, wished me joy, bid me have a good heart, not be cast down, things might not be so bad as I feared, and the like; then called for brandy and drank to me, but put it all up to my score, for they told me I was but just come to the college, as they called it, and sure I had money in my pocket, though they had none.

I asked one of this crew how long she had been there. She said four months. I asked her how the place looked to her when she first came into it. Just as it did now to me, says she, dreadful and frightful; that she thought she was in hell; "and I believe so still," adds she, "but it is natural to me now; I don't disturb myself about it." "I suppose," says I, "you are in no danger of what is to follow?" "Nay," says she, "you are mistaken there, I am sure, for I am under sentence, only I pleaded my belly, but am no more with child than the judge that tried me, and I expect to be called down next session." This "calling down" is calling down to their former judgement, when a woman has been respited for her belly but proves not to be with child, or if she has been with child and has been brought to bed. "Well," says I, "and are you thus easy?" "Aye," says she, "I can't help myself. What signifies being sad? If I am hanged, there's an end of me." And away she turned, dancing, and sings as she goes, the following piece of Newgate wit:

"If I swing by the string,
I shall hear the bell ring,[1]
And then there's an end of poor Jenny."

I mention this because it would be worth the observation of any prisoner who shall hereafter fall into the same misfortune and come to that dreadful place of Newgate—how time, necessity, and conversing with the wretches that are there familiarizes the place to them, how at last they become reconciled to that which at first was the greatest dread upon their spirits in the world, and are as impudently cheerful and merry in their misery as they were when out of it.

I cannot say, as some do, this devil is not so black as he is painted; for indeed no colours can represent that place to the life nor any soul conceive aright of it but those who have been sufferers there. But how hell should become by degrees so natural, and not only tolerable but even agreeable, is a thing unintelligible but by those who have experienced it, as I have.

The same night that I was sent to Newgate I sent the news of it to my old governess, who was surprised at it, you may be sure, and spent the night almost as ill out of Newgate as I did in it.

The next morning she came to see me; she did what she could to comfort me, but she saw that was to no purpose; however, as she said, to sink under the weight was but to increase the weight; she immediately applied herself to all the proper methods to prevent the effects of it, which we feared, and first she found out the two fiery jades that had surprised me. She tampered with them, persuaded them, offered them money, and, in a word, tried all imaginable ways to prevent a prosecution; she offered one of the wenches £100 to go away from her

[1] The bell of St. Sepulchre's, which tolls upon execution-day.

mistress and not to appear against me, but she was so resolute that though she was but a servant-maid at £3 a year wages or thereabouts, she refused it, and would have refused, as my governess said she believed, if she had offered her £500. Then she attacked the other maid; she was not so hard-hearted as the other, and sometimes seemed inclined to be merciful; but the first wench kept her up and would not so much as let my governess talk with her, but threatened to have her up for tampering with the evidence.

Then she applied to the master, that is to say, the man whose goods had been stolen, and particularly to his wife, who was inclined at first to have some compassion for me; she found the woman the same still, but the man alleged he was bound to prosecute, and that he should forfeit his recognizance.

My governess offered to find friends that should get his recognizances off of the file, as they call it, and that he should not suffer; but it was not possible to convince him that he could be safe any way in the world but by appearing against me; so I was to have three witnesses of fact against me, the master and his two maids; that is to say, I was as certain to be cast for my life as I was that I was alive, and I had nothing to do but to think of dying. I had but a sad foundation to build upon for that, as I said before, for all my repentance appeared to me to be only the effect of my fear of death, not a sincere regret for the wicked life that I had lived, and which had brought this misery upon me, or for the offending my Creator, who was now suddenly to be my judge.

I lived many days here under the utmost horror; I had death, as it were, in view, and thought of nothing night or day but of gibbets and halters, evil spirits and devils; it is not to be expressed how I was harassed between the dreadful apprehensions of death and the terror of my conscience reproaching me with my past horrible life.

The ordinary of Newgate came to me and talked a little in his way, but all his divinity run upon confessing my crime, as he called it (though he knew not what I was in for), making a full discovery, and the like, without which he told me God would never forgive me; and he said so little to the purpose that I had no manner of consolation from him; and then to observe the poor creature preaching confession and repentance to me in the morning and find him drunk with brandy by noon—this had something in it so shocking that I began to nauseate the man and his work too by degrees for the sake of the man; so that I desired him to trouble me no more.

I know not how it was, but by the indefatigable application of my diligent governess I had no bill preferred against me the first sessions, I mean to the grand jury, at Guildhall; so I had another month or five weeks before me, and without doubt this ought to have been accepted by me as so much time given me for reflection upon what was past and preparation for what was to come. I ought to have esteemed it as a space given me for repentance and have employed it as such, but it was not in me. I was sorry, as before, for being in Newgate, but had few signs of repentance about me.

On the contrary, like the water in the hollows of mountains, which petrifies and turns into stone whatever they are suffered to drop upon, so the continual conversing with such a crew of hell-hounds had the same common operation upon me as upon other people. I degenerated into stone; I turned first stupid and senseless, and then brutish and thoughtless, and at last raving mad as any of them were; in short, I became as naturally pleased and easy with the place as if indeed I had been born there.

It is scarce possible to imagine that our natures should be capable of so much degeneracy as to make that pleasant and agreeable that in itself is the most complete misery. Here was a circumstance that I think it is scarce possible to mention a worse: I was as exquisitely miserable as it was possible for any one to be that had life and health and money to help them, as I had.

I had a weight of guilt upon me, enough to sink any creature who had the least power of reflection left and had any sense upon them of the happiness of this life or the misery of another. I had at first some remorse indeed, but no repentance; I had now neither remorse or repentance. I had a crime charged on me, the punishment of which was death; the proof so evident that there was no room for me so much as to plead not guilty. I had the name of an old offender, so that I had nothing to expect but death, neither had I myself any thoughts of escaping; and yet a certain strange lethargy of soul possessed me. I had no trouble, no apprehensions, no sorrow about me; the first surprise was gone; I was, I may well say, I know not how; my senses, my reason, nay, my conscience, were all asleep; my course of life for forty years had been a horrid complication of wickedness, whoredom, adultery, incest, lying, theft; and in a word, everything but murder and treason had been my practice from the age of eighteen or thereabouts to threescore; and now I was engulfed in the misery of punishment and had an infamous death at the door; and yet I had no sense of my condition, no thought of heaven or hell, at least that went any farther than a bare flying touch, like the stitch or pain that gives a hint and goes off. I neither had a heart to ask God's mercy or indeed to think of it. And in this, I think, I have given a brief description of the completest misery on earth.

All my terrifying thoughts were past, the horrors of the place were become familiar, and I felt no more uneasiness at the noise and clamours of the prison than they did who made that noise; in a word, I was become a mere Newgate-bird, as wicked and as outrageous as any of them; nay, I scarce retained the habit and custom of good breeding and manners, which all along till now run through my conversation; so thorough a degeneracy had possessed me that I was no more the same thing that I had been than if I had never been otherwise than what I was now.

In the middle of this hardened part of my life I had another sudden surprise, which called me back a little to that thing called sorrow, which, indeed, I began to be past the sense of before. They told me one night that there was brought into the prison late the night before three highwaymen, who had committed a robbery somewhere on Hounslow Heath, I think it was, and were pursued to Uxbridge by the country, and there taken after a gallant resistance, in which many of the country-people were wounded and some killed.

It is not to be wondered that we prisoners were all desirous enough to see these brave, topping gentlemen, that were talked up to be such as their fellows had not been known, and especially because it was said they would in the morning be removed into the press-yard, having given money to the head master of the prison to be allowed the liberty of that better place. So we that were women placed ourselves in the way, that we would be sure to see them; but nothing could express the amazement and surprise I was in when the first man that came out I knew to be my Lancashire husband, the same with whom I lived so well at Dunstable, and the same who I afterwards saw at Brickhill when I was married to my last husband, as has been related.

I was struck dumb at the sight, and knew neither what to say or what to do; he did not know me, and that was all the present relief I had. I quitted my company and retired as much as that dreadful place suffers anybody to retire, and cried vehemently for a great while. "Dreadful creature that I am," said I, "how many poor people have I made miserable! How many desperate wretches have I sent to the devil!" This gentleman's misfortunes I placed all to my own account. He had told me at Chester he was ruined by that match, and that his fortunes were made desperate on my account; for that thinking I had been a fortune, he was run into debt more than he was able to pay; that he would go into the army and carry a musket or buy a horse and take a tour, as he called it; and though I never told him that I was a fortune, and so did not actually deceive him myself, yet I did encourage its having it thought so, and so I was the occasion originally of his mischief.

The surprise of this thing only struck deeper in my thoughts and gave me stronger reflections than all that had befallen me before. I grieved day and night, and the more for that they told me he was the captain of the gang and that he had committed so many robberies that Hind or Whitney or the Golden Farmer were fools to him; that he would surely be hanged if there were no more men left in the country; and that there would be abundance of people come in against him.

I was overwhelmed with grief for him; my own case gave me no disturbance compared to this, and I loaded myself with reproaches on his account. I bewailed my misfortunes and the ruin he was now come to at such a rate that I relished nothing now as I did before, and the first reflections I made upon the horrid life I had lived began to return upon me; and as these things returned, my abhorrence of the place and of the way of living in it returned also; in a word, I was perfectly changed and become another body.

While I was under these influences of sorrow for him came notice to me that the next sessions there would be a bill preferred to the grand jury against me, and that I should be tried for my life. My temper was touched before, the wretched boldness of spirit which I had acquired abated, and conscious guilt began to flow in my mind. In short, I began to think, and to think indeed is one real advance from hell to heaven. All that hardened state and temper of soul, which I said so much of before, is but a deprivation of thought; he that is restored to his thinking is restored to himself.

As soon as I began, I say, to think, the first thing that occurred to me broke out thus: "Lord! what will become of me? I shall be cast, to be sure, and there is nothing beyond that but death! I have no friends; what shall I do? I shall be certainly cast! Lord, have mercy upon me! What will become of me?" This was a sad thought, you will say, to be the first, after so long time, that had started in my soul of that kind, and yet even this was nothing but fright at what was to come; there was not a word of sincere repentance in it all. However, I was dreadfully dejected, and disconsolate to the last degree; and as I had no friend to communicate my distressed thoughts to, it lay so heavy upon me that it threw me into fits and swoonings several times a day. I sent for my old governess, and she, give her her due, acted the part of a true friend. She left no stone unturned to prevent the grand jury finding the bill. She went to several of the jurymen, talked with them, and endeavoured to possess them with favourable dispositions on account that nothing was taken away and no house broken, etc.; but all would not do; the two wenches swore home to the fact, and the jury found the bill for robbery and housebreaking, that is, for felony and burglary.

I sunk down when they brought the news of it, and after I came to myself I thought I should have died with the weight of it. My governess acted a true mother to me; she pitied me, she cried with me and for me, but she could not help me; and, to add to the terror of it, 'twas the discourse all over the house that I should die for it.

I could hear them talk it among themselves very often, and see them shake their heads and say they were sorry for it and the like, as is usual in the place. But still nobody came to tell me their thoughts till at last one of the keepers came to me privately and said with a sigh, "Well, Mrs. Flanders, you will be tried a Friday" (this was but a Wednesday). "What do you intend to do?" I turned as white as a clout and said, "God knows what I shall do; for my part, I know not what to do." "Why," says he, "I won't flatter you; I would have you prepare for death, for I doubt you will be cast; and as you are an old offender, I doubt you will find but little mercy. They say," added he, "your case is very plain, and that the witnesses swear so home against you there will be no standing it."

This was a stab into the very vitals of one under such a burthen, and I could not speak a word, good or bad, for a great while. At last I burst out into tears and said to him, "Oh, sir, what must I do?" "Do!" says he. "Send for a minister and talk with him; for, indeed, Mrs. Flanders, unless you have very good friends, you are no woman for this world."

This was plain dealing indeed, but it was very harsh to me; at least I thought it so. He left me in the greatest confusion imaginable, and all that night I lay awake. And now I began to say my prayers, which I had scarce done before since my last husband's death or from a little while after. And truly I may well call it saying my prayers, for I was in such a confusion and had such horror upon my mind that though I cried, and repeated several times the ordinary expression of "Lord, have mercy upon me!" I never brought myself to any sense of being a miserable sinner, as indeed I was, and of confessing my sins to God and begging pardon for the sake of Jesus Christ. I was overwhelmed with the sense of my condition, being tried for my life and being sure to be executed, and on this account I cried out all night, "Lord! what will become of me? Lord! what shall I do? Lord, have mercy upon me!" and the like.

My poor afflicted governess was now as much concerned as I, and a great deal more truly penitent, though she had no prospect of being brought to a sentence. Not but that she deserved it as much as I, and so she said herself; but she had not done anything for many years other than receiving what I and others had stolen and encouraging us to steal it. But she cried and took on like a distracted body, wringing her hands and crying out that she was undone, that she believed there was a curse from Heaven upon her, that she should be damned, that she had been the destruction of all her friends, that she brought such a one, and such a one, and such a one to the gallows; and there she reckoned up ten or eleven people, some of which I have given an account of, that came to untimely ends; and that now she was the occasion of my ruin, for she had persuaded me to go on when I would have left off. I interrupted her there. "No, Mother, no," said I, "don't speak of that, for you would have had me left off when I got the mercer's money again and when I came home from Harwich, and I would not hearken to you; therefore you have not been to blame; it is I only have ruined myself; I have brought myself to this misery"; and thus we spent many hours together.

Well, there was no remedy; the prosecution went on, and on the Thursday I was carried down to the sessions-house, where I was arraigned, as they called it, and the next day I was appointed to be tried. At the arraignment I pleaded not guilty, and well I might, for I was indicted for felony and burglary; that is, for feloniously stealing two pieces of brocaded silk, value £46, the goods of Anthony Johnson, and for breaking open the doors; whereas I knew very well they could not pretend I had broken up the doors or so much as lifted up a latch.

On the Friday I was brought to my trial, I had exhausted my spirits with crying for two or three days before, that I slept better the Thursday night than I expected, and had more courage for my trial than I thought possible for me to have.

When the trial began and the indictment was read, I would have spoke, but they told me the witnesses must be heard first and then I should have time to be heard. The witnesses were the two wenches, a couple of hard-mouthed jades indeed, for though the thing was truth in the main, yet they aggravated it to the utmost extremity and swore I had the goods wholly in my possession, that I had hid them among my clothes, that I was going off with them, that I had one foot over the threshold when they discovered themselves, and then I put t'other over, so that

I was quite out of the house in the street with the goods before they took me, and then they seized me and took the goods upon me. The fact in general was true, but I insisted upon it that they stopped me before I had set my foot clear of the threshold. But that did not argue much, for I had taken the goods and was bringing them away if I had not been taken.

I pleaded that I had stole nothing, they had lost nothing, that the door was open, and I went in with design to buy. If, seeing nobody in the house, I had taken any of them up in my hand, it could not be concluded that I intended to steal them, for that I never carried them farther than the door to look on them with the better light.

The court would not allow that by any means and made a kind of jest of my intending to buy the goods, that being no shop for the selling of anything; and as to carrying them to the door to look at them, the maids made their impudent mocks upon that and spent their wit upon it very much; told the court I had looked at them sufficiently and approved them very well, for I had packed them up and was a-going with them.

In short, I was found guilty of felony, but acquitted of the burglary, which was but small comfort to me, the first bringing me to a sentence of death, and the last would have done no more. The next day I was carried down to receive the dreadful sentence, and when they came to ask me what I had to say why sentence should not pass, I stood mute awhile, but somebody prompted me aloud to speak to the judges, for that they could represent things favourably for me. This encouraged me, and I told them I had nothing to say to stop the sentence, but that I had much to say to bespeak the mercy of the court; that I hoped they would allow something in such a case for the circumstances of it; that I had broken no doors, had carried nothing off; that nobody had lost anything; that the person whose goods they were was pleased to say he desired mercy might be shown (which indeed he very honestly did); that, at the worst, it was the first offence, and that I had never been before any court of justice before; and, in a word, I spoke with more courage than I thought I could have done, and in such a moving tone, and though with tears yet not so many tears as to obstruct my speech, that I could see it moved others to tears that heard me.

The judges sat grave and mute, gave me an easy hearing and time to say all that I would, but, saying neither yes or no to it, pronounced the sentence of death upon me, a sentence to me like death itself, which confounded me. I had no more spirit left in me. I had no tongue to speak or eyes to look up either to God or man.

My poor governess was utterly disconsolate; and she that was my comforter before wanted comfort now herself, and sometimes mourning, sometimes raging, was as much out of herself as any madwoman in Bedlam. Nor was she only disconsolate as to me, but she was struck with horror at the sense of her own wicked life, and began to look back upon it with a taste quite different from mine, for she was penitent to the highest degree for her sins, as well as sorrowful for the misfortune. She sent for a minister, too, a serious, pious, good man, and applied herself with such earnestness, by his assistance, to the work of a sincere repentance that I believe, and so did the minister too, that she was a true penitent; and, which is still more, she was not only so for the occasion and at that juncture but she continued so, as I was informed, to the day of her death.

It is rather to be thought of than expressed what was now my condition. I had nothing before me but death; and as I had no friends to assist me, I expected nothing but to find my name in the dead warrant, which was to come for the execution, next Friday, of five more and myself.

In the meantime my poor distressed governess sent me a minister, who at her request came to visit me. He exhorted me seriously to repent of all my sins and to dally no longer with my soul; not flattering myself with hopes of life, which, he said, he was informed there was no room to expect, but unfeignedly to look up to God with my whole soul and to cry for pardon in the name of Jesus Christ. He backed his discourses with proper quotations of Scripture encouraging the greatest sinner to repent and turn from their evil way; and when he had done, he kneeled down and prayed with me.

It was now that for the first time I felt any real signs of repentance. I now began to look back upon my past life with abhorrence, and having a kind of view into the other side of time, the things of life, as I believe they do with everybody at such a time, began to look with a different aspect and quite another shape than they did before. The views of felicity, the joy, the griefs of life, were quite other things; and I had nothing in my thoughts but was so infinitely superior to what I had known in life that it appeared to be the greatest stupidity to lay a weight upon anything though the most valuable in this world.

The word "eternity" represented itself with all its incomprehensible additions, and I had such extended notions of it that I know not how to express them. Among the rest, how absurd did every pleasant thing look—I mean, that we had counted pleasant before—when I reflected that these sordid trifles were the things for which we forfeited eternal felicity.

With these reflections came in of mere course severe reproaches for my wretched behaviour in my past life; that I had forfeited all hope of happiness in the eternity that I was just going to enter into; and, on the contrary, was entitled to all that was miserable; and all this with the frightful addition of its being also eternal.

I am not capable of reading lectures of instruction to anybody, but I relate this in the very manner in which things then appeared to me as far as I am able, but infinitely short of the lively impressions which they made on my soul at that time; indeed, those impressions are not to be explained by words, or if they are, I am not mistress of words to express them. It must be the work of every sober reader to make just reflections as their own circumstances may direct; and this is what every one at some time or other may feel something of; I mean, a clearer sight into things to come than they had here, and a dark view of their own concern in them.

But I go back to my own case. The minister pressed me to tell him as far as I thought convenient in what state I found myself as to the sight I had of things beyond life. He told me he did not come as ordinary of the place, whose business it is to extort confessions from prisoners for the farther detecting of other offenders; that his business was to move me to such freedom of discourse as might serve to disburthen my own mind and furnish him to administer comfort to me as far as was in his power; assured me that whatever I said to him should remain with him and be as much a secret as if it was known only to God and myself; and that he desired to know nothing of me but to qualify him to give proper advice to me and to pray to God for me.

This honest, friendly way of treating me unlocked all the sluices of my passions. He broke into my very soul by it, and I unravelled all the wickedness of my life to him. In a word, I gave him an abridgement of this whole history; I gave him the picture of my conduct for fifty years in miniature.

I hid nothing from him, and he in return exhorted me to a sincere repentance, explained to me what he meant by repentance, and then drew out such a scheme of infinite mercy, proclaimed from Heaven to sinners of the greatest magnitude, that he left me nothing to say that looked like despair or doubting of being accepted; and in this condition he left me the first night.

He visited me again the next morning and went on with his method of explaining the terms of divine mercy, which according to him consisted of nothing more difficult than that of being sincerely desirous of it and willing to accept it; only a sincere regret for and hatred of those things which rendered me so just an object of divine vengeance. I am not able to repeat the excellent discourses of this extraordinary man; all that I am able to do is to say that he revived my heart and brought me into such a condition that I never knew anything of in my life before. I was covered with shame and tears for things past, and yet had at the same time a secret, surprising joy at the prospect of being a true penitent and obtaining the comfort of a penitent—I mean the hope of being forgiven; and so swift did thoughts circulate, and so high did the impressions they had made upon me run, that I thought I could freely have gone out that minute to execution without any uneasiness at all, casting my soul entirely into the arms of infinite mercy as a penitent.

The good gentleman was so moved with a view of the influence which he saw these things had on me that he blessed God he had come to visit me, and resolved not to leave me till the last moment.

It was no less than twelve days after our receiving

sentence before any were ordered for execution, and then the dead warrant, as they call it, came down, and I found my name was among them. A terrible blow this was to my new resolutions; indeed my heart sunk within me, and I swooned away twice, one after another, but spoke not a word. The good minister was sorely afflicted for me and did what he could to comfort me with the same arguments and the same moving eloquence that he did before, and left me not that evening so long as the prison-keepers would suffer him to stay in the prison, unless he would be locked up with me all night, which he was not willing to be.

I wondered much that I did not see him all the next day, it being but the day before the time appointed for execution; and I was greatly discouraged and dejected, and indeed almost sunk for want of that comfort which he had so often and with such success yielded me in his former visits. I waited with great impatience and under the greatest oppressions of spirits imaginable till about four o'clock, when he came to my apartment; for I had obtained the favour, by the help of money, nothing being to be done in that place without it, not to be kept in the condemned hole among the rest of the prisoners who were to die, but to have a little dirty chamber to myself.

My heart leaped within me for joy when I heard his voice at the door, even before I saw him; but let any one judge what kind of motion I found in my soul when, after having made a short excuse for his not coming, he showed me that his time had been employed on my account, that he had obtained a favourable report from the recorder in my case, and, in short, that he had brought me a reprieve.

He used all the caution that he was able in letting me know what it would have been double cruelty to have concealed; for as grief had overset me before, so joy overset me now, and I fell into a more dangerous swooning than at first, and it was not without difficulty that I was recovered at all.

The good man having made a very Christian exhortation to me not to let the joy of my reprieve put the remembrance of my past sorrow out of my mind, and told me that he must leave me to go and enter the reprieve in the books and show it to the sheriffs, he stood up just before his going away, and in a very earnest manner prayed to God for me that my repentance might be made unfeigned and sincere; and that my coming back, as it were, into life again might not be a returning to the follies of life, which I had made such solemn resolutions to forsake. I joined heartily in that petition, and must needs say I had deeper impressions upon my mind all that night of the mercy of God in sparing my life, and a greater detestation of my sins from a sense of that goodness, than I had in all my sorrow before.

This may be thought inconsistent in itself and wide from the business of this book; particularly, I reflect that many of those who may be pleased and diverted with the relation of the wicked part of my story may not relish this, which is really the best part of my life, the most advantageous to myself, and the most instructive to others. Such, however, will, I hope, allow me liberty to make my story complete. It would be a severe satire on such to say they do not relish the repentance as much as they do the crime, and they had rather the history were a complete tragedy, as it was very likely to have been.

But I go on with my relation. The next morning there was a sad scene indeed in the prison. The first thing I was saluted with in the morning was the tolling of the great bell at St. Sepulchre's, which ushered in the day. As soon as it began to toll, a dismal groaning and crying was heard from the condemned hole, where there lay six poor souls who were to be executed that day, some for one crime, some for another, and two for murder.

This was followed by a confused clamour in the house among the several prisoners, expressing their awkward sorrows for the poor creatures that were to die, but in a manner extremely differing one from another. Some cried for them; some brutishly huzzaed and wished them a good journey; some damned and cursed those that had brought them to it, many pitying them, and some few, but very few, praying for them.

There was hardly room for so much composure of mind as was required for me to bless the merciful Providence that had, as it were, snatched me out of the jaws of this destruction. I remained, as it were, dumb and silent, overcome with the sense of it and not able to express what I had in my heart; for the passions on such occasions as these are certainly so agitated as not to be able presently to regulate their own motions.

All the while the poor condemned creatures were preparing for death, and the ordinary, as they call him, was busy with them, disposing them to submit to their sentence—I say, all this while I was seized with a fit of trembling, as much as I could have been if I had been in the same condition as I was the day before; I was so violently agitated by this surprising fit that I shook as if it had been an ague, so that I could not speak or look but like one distracted. As soon as they were all put into the carts and gone, which, however, I had not courage enough to see—I say, as soon as they were gone, I fell into a fit of crying involuntarily, as a mere distemper, and yet so violent and it held me so long that I knew not what course to take; nor could I stop or put a check to it, no, not with all the strength and courage I had.

This fit of crying held me near two hours and, as I believe, held me till they were all out of the world, and then a most humble, penitent, serious kind of joy succeeded; a real transport it was or passion of thankfulness, and in this I continued most part of the day.

In the evening the good minister visited me again and fell to his usual good discourses. He congratulated my having a space yet allowed me for repentance, whereas the state of those six poor creatures was determined, and they were now past the offers of salvation; he pressed me to retain the same sentiments of the things of life that I had when I had a view of eternity, and at the end of all, told me that I should not conclude that all was over, that a reprieve was not a pardon, that he could not answer for the effects of it; however, I had this mercy: that I had more time given me, and it was my business to improve that time.

This discourse left a kind of sadness on my heart, as if I might expect the affair would have a tragical issue still, which, however, he had no certainty of; yet I did not at that time question him about it, he having said he would do his utmost to bring it to a good end, and that he hoped he might, but he would not have me be secure; and the consequence showed that he had reason for what he said.

It was about a fortnight after this that I had some just

apprehensions that I should be included in the dead warrant at the ensuing sessions; and it was not without great difficulty, and at last an humble petition for transportation, that I avoided it, so ill was I beholding to fame and so prevailing was the report of being an old offender; though in that they did not do me strict justice, for I was not in the sense of the law an old offender, whatever I was in the eye of the judge, for I had never been before them in a judicial way before; so the judges could not charge me with being an old offender, but the recorder was pleased to represent my case as he thought fit.

I had now a certainty of life indeed, but with the hard conditions of being ordered for transportation, which was, I say, a hard condition in itself, but not when comparatively considered; and therefore I shall make no comments upon the sentence nor upon the choice I was put to. We all shall choose anything rather than death, especially when 'tis attended with an uncomfortable prospect beyond it, which was my case.

The good minister, whose interest, though a stranger to me, had obtained me the reprieve, mourned sincerely for his part. He was in hopes, he said, that I should have ended my days under the influence of good instruction, that I might not have forgot my former distresses, and that I should not have been turned loose again among such a wretched crew as are thus sent abroad, where, he said, I must have more than ordinary secret assistance from the grace of God if I did not turn as wicked again as ever.

I have not for a good while mentioned my governess, who had been dangerously sick, and being in as near a view of death by her disease as I was by my sentence, was a very great penitent; I say, I have not mentioned her, nor indeed did I see her in all this time; but being now recovering and just able to come abroad, she came to see me.

I told her my condition and what a different flux and reflux of fears and hopes I had been agitated with; I told her what I had escaped and upon what terms; and she was present when the minister expressed his fears of my relapsing again into wickedness upon my falling into the wretched company that are generally transported. Indeed I had a melancholy reflection upon it in my own mind, for I knew what a dreadful gang was always sent away together, and said to my governess that the good minister's fears were not without cause. "Well, well," says she, "but I hope you will not be tempted with such a horrid example as that." And as soon as the minister was gone, she told me she would not have me discouraged, for perhaps ways and means might be found to dispose of me in a particular way, by myself, of which she would talk farther with me afterward.

I looked earnestly at her and thought she looked more cheerful than she usually had done, and I entertained immediately a thousand notions of being delivered, but could not for my life imagine the methods or think of one that was feasible; but I was too much concerned in it to let her go from me without explaining herself, which though she was very loath to do, yet as I was still pressing, she answered me in a few words, thus: "Why, you have money, have you not? Did you ever know one in your life that was transported and had a hundred pound in his pocket? I'll warrant ye, child," says she.

I understood her presently, but told her I saw no room to hope for anything but a strict execution of the order, and as it was a severity that was esteemed a mercy, there was no doubt but it would be strictly observed. She said no more but this: "We will try what can be done"; and so we parted.

I lay in the prison near fifteen weeks after this. What the reason of it was I know not, but at the end of this time I was put on board of a ship in the Thames, and with me a gang of thirteen as hardened, vile creatures as ever Newgate produced in my time; and it would really well take up a history longer than mine to describe the degrees of impudence and audacious villainy that those thirteen were arrived to and the manner of their behaviour in the voyage, of which I have a very diverting account by me, which the captain of the ship who carried them over gave me and which he caused his mate to write down at large.

It may perhaps be thought trifling to enter here into a relation of all the little incidents which attended me in this interval of my circumstances; I mean, between the final order for my transportation and the time of going on board the ship; and I am too near the end of my story to allow room for it; but something relating to me and my Lancashire husband I must not omit.

He had, as I have observed already, been carried from the master's side of the ordinary prison into the press-yard with three of his comrades, for they found another to add to them after some time; here, for what reason I knew not, they were kept without being brought to a trial almost three months. It seems they found means to bribe or buy off some who were to come in against them, and they wanted evidence to convict them. After some puzzle on this account they made shift to get proof enough against two of them to carry them off; but the other two, of which my Lancashire husband was one, lay still in suspense. They had, I think, one positive evidence against each of them, but the law obliging them to have two witnesses, they could make nothing of it. Yet they were resolved not to part with the men neither, not doubting but evidence would at last come in; and in order to this, I think publication was made that such prisoners were taken and any one might come to the prison and see them.

I took this opportunity to satisfy my curiosity, pretending I had been robbed in the Dunstable coach, and that I would go to see the two highwaymen. But when I came into the press-yard, I so disguised myself and muffled my face up so that he could see little of me and knew nothing of who I was; but when I came back, I said publicly that I knew them very well.

Immediately it was all over the prison that Moll Flanders would turn evidence against one of the highwaymen, and that I was to come off by it from the sentence of transportation.

They heard of it, and immediately my husband desired to see this Mrs. Flanders that knew him so well and was to be an evidence against him; and accordingly I had leave to go to him. I dressed myself up as well as the best clothes that I suffered myself ever to appear in there would allow me, and went to the press-yard, but had a hood over my face. He said little to me at first, but asked me if I knew him. I told him, "Yes, very well"; but as I concealed my face, so I counterfeited my voice too, that he had no guess at who I was. He asked me where I had seen him. I told him between Dunstable and Brickhill;

but, turning to the keeper that stood by, I asked if I might not be admitted to talk with him alone. He said, "Yes, yes," and so very civilly withdrew.

As soon as he was gone and I had shut the door, I threw off my hood and, bursting out into tears, "My dear," said I, "do you not know me?" He turned pale and stood speechless, like one thunderstruck, and not able to conquer the surprise, said no more but this: "Let me sit down"; and sitting down by the table, leaning his head on his hand, fixed his eyes on the ground as one stupid. I cried so vehemently, on the other hand, that it was a good while ere I could speak any more; but after I had given vent to my passion I repeated the same words: "My dear, do you not know me?" At which he answered, "Yes," and said no more a good while.

After some time continuing in the surprise, as above, he cast up his eyes towards me and said, "How could you be so cruel?" I did not really understand what he meant, and I answered, "How can you call me cruel?" "To come to me," says he, "in such a place as this—is it not to insult me? I have not robbed you, at least not on the highway."

I perceived by this that he knew nothing of the miserable circumstances I was in and thought that having got intelligence of his being there, I had come to upbraid him with his leaving me. But I had too much to say to him to be affronted, and told him in a few words that I was far from coming to insult him, but at best I came to condole mutually; that he would be easily satisfied that I had no such view when I should tell him that my condition was worse than his, and that many ways. He looked a little concerned at the expression of my condition being worse than his, but with a kind of a smile said, "How can that be? When you see me fettered, and in Newgate, and two of my companions executed already, can you say your condition is worse than mine?"

"Come, my dear," says I, "we have a long piece of work to do if I should be to relate or you to hear my unfortunate history; but if you will hear it, you will soon conclude with me that my condition is worse than yours." "How is that possible," says he, "when I expect to be cast for my life the very next sessions?" "Yes," says I, "'tis very possible when I shall tell you that I have been cast for my life three sessions ago, and am now under sentence of death. Is not my case worse than yours?"

Then, indeed, he stood silent again, like one struck dumb, and after a little while he starts up. "Unhappy couple!" says he. "How can this be possible?" I took him by the hand. "Come, my dear," said I, "sit down and let us compare our sorrows. I am a prisoner in this very house and in a much worse circumstance than you, and you will be satisfied I do not come to insult you when I tell you the particulars." And with this we sat down together, and I told him so much of my story as I thought convenient, bringing it at last to my being reduced to great poverty, and representing myself as fallen into some company that led me to relieve my distresses by a way that I had been utterly unacquainted with, and that they making an attempt on a tradesman's house, I was seized upon for having been but just at the door, the maidservant pulling me in; that I neither had broke any lock or taken anything away, and that notwithstanding that, I was brought in guilty and sentenced to die; but that the judges, having been made sensible of the hardship of my circumstances, had obtained leave for me to be transported.

I told him I fared the worse for being taken in the prison for one Moll Flanders, who was a famous, successful thief that all of them had heard of but none of them had ever seen; but that, as he knew, was none of my name. But I placed all to the account of my ill fortune, and that under this name I was dealt with as an old offender though this was the first thing they had ever known of me. I gave him a long account of what had befallen me since I saw him, but told him I had seen him since he might think I had; then gave him an account how I had seen him at Brickhill, how he was pursued, and how, by giving an account that I knew him and that he was a very honest gentleman, the hue and cry was stopped and the high constable went back again.

He listened most attentively to all my story and smiled at the particulars, being all of them infinitely below what he had been at the head of; but when I came to the story of Little Brickhill, he was surprised. "And was it you, my dear," said he, "that gave the check to the mob at Brickhill?" "Yes," said I, "it was I indeed." Then I told him the particulars which I had observed of him there. "Why, then," said he, "it was you that saved my life at that time, and I am glad I owe my life to you, for I will pay the debt to you now, and I'll deliver you from the present condition you are in or I will die in the attempt."

I told him by no means; it was a risk too great, not worth his running the hazard of and for a life not worth his saving. 'Twas no matter for that, he said; it was a life worth all the world to him, a life that had given him a new life; "for," says he, "I was never in real danger but that time till the last minute when I was taken." Indeed, his danger then lay in his believing he had not been pursued that way; for they had gone off from Hockley quite another way, and had come over the enclosed country into Brickhill, and were sure they had not been seen by anybody.

Here he gave a long history of his life, which indeed would make a very strange history and be infinitely diverting. He told me that he took the road about twelve years before he married me; that the woman which called him brother was not any kin to him, but one that belonged to their gang and who, keeping correspondence with them, lived always in town, having great acquaintance; that she gave them perfect intelligence of persons going out of town, and that they had made several good booties by her correspondence; that she thought she had fixed a fortune for him when she brought me to him, but happened to be disappointed, which he really could not blame her for; that if I had had an estate, which she was informed I had, he had resolved to leave off the road and live a new life, but never to appear in public till some general pardon had been passed or till he could for money have got his name into some particular pardon, so that he might have been perfectly easy; but that as it had proved otherwise, he was obliged to take up the old trade again.

He gave a long account of some of his adventures and particularly one where he robbed the West Chester coaches near Lichfield, when he got a very great booty; and after that, how he robbed five graziers in the west, going to Burford Fair, in Wiltshire, to buy sheep. He told me he got so much money on those two occasions that if he had known where to have found me, he would certainly have embraced my proposal of going with me to

Virginia, or to have settled in a plantation, or some other of the English colonies in America.

He told me he wrote three letters to me, directed according to my order, but heard nothing from me. This indeed I knew to be true, but the letters coming to my hand in the time of my latter husband, I could do nothing in it and therefore gave no answer, that so he might believe they had miscarried.

Being thus disappointed, he said he carried on the old trade ever since, though when he had gotten so much money, he said, he did not run such desperate risks as he did before. Then he gave me some account of several hard and desperate encounters which he had with gentlemen on the road, who parted too hardly with their money, and showed me some wounds he had received; and he had one or two very terrible wounds indeed, particularly one by a pistol-bullet which broke his arm, and another with a sword which run him quite through the body, but that missing his vitals, he was cured again; one of his comrades having kept with him so faithfully and so friendly as that he assisted him in riding near eighty miles before his arm was set, and then got a surgeon in a considerable city remote from the place where it was done, pretending they were gentlemen travelling towards Carlisle, that they had been attacked on the road by highwaymen, and that one of them had shot him into the arm.

This, he said, his friend managed so well that they were not suspected, but lay still till he was cured. He gave me also so many distinct accounts of his adventures that it is with great reluctance that I decline the relating them; but this is my own story, not his.

I then inquired into the circumstances of his present case and what it was he expected when he came to be tried. He told me that they had no evidence against him; for that of the three robberies which they were all charged with, it was his good fortune that he was but in one of them, and that there was but one witness to be had to that fact, which was not sufficient; but that it was expected some others would come in, and that he thought when he first see me I had been one that came of that errand; but that if nobody came in against him, he hoped he should be cleared; that he had some intimation that if he would submit to transport himself, he might be admitted to it without a trial; but that he could not think of it with any temper and thought he could much easier submit to be hanged.

I blamed him for that; first, because if he was transported, there might be an hundred ways for him that was a gentleman and a bold enterprising man to find his way back again, and perhaps some ways and means to come back before he went. He smiled at that part and said he should like the last the best of the two, for he had a kind of horror upon his mind at his being sent to the plantations as the Romans sent slaves to work in the mines; that he thought the passage into another state much more tolerable at the gallows, and that this was the general notion of all the gentlemen who were driven by the exigence of their fortunes to take the road; that at the place of execution there was at least an end of all the miseries of the present state; and as for what was to follow, a man was, in his opinion, as likely to repent sincerely in the last fortnight of his life under the agonies of a jail and the condemned hole as he would ever be in the woods and wildernesses of America; that servitude and hard labour were things gentlemen could never stoop to; that it was but the way to force them to be their own executioners, which was much worse; and that he could not have any patience when he did but think of it.

I used the utmost of my endeavour to persuade him, and joined that known woman's rhetoric to it—I mean that of tears. I told him the infamy of a public execution was certainly a greater pressure upon the spirits of a gentleman than any mortifications that he could meet with abroad; that he had at least in the other a chance for his life, whereas here he had none at all; that it was the easiest thing in the world for him to manage the captain of a ship, who were, generally speaking, men of good humour; and a small matter of conduct, especially if there was any money to be had, would make way for him to buy himself off when he came to Virginia.

He looked wishfully at me, and I guessed he meant that he had no money; but I was mistaken, his meaning was another way. "You hinted just now, my dear," said he, "that there might be a way of coming back before I went, by which I understood you that it might be possible to buy it off here. I had rather give £200 to prevent going than £100 to be set at liberty when I came there." "That is, my dear," said I, "because you do not know the place so well as I do." "That may be," said he, "and yet I believe, as well as you know it, you would do the same, unless it is because, as you told me, you have a mother there."

I told him, as to my mother, she must be dead many years before; and as for any other relations that I might have there, I knew them not; that since my misfortunes had reduced me to the condition I had been in for some years, I had not kept up any correspondence with them, and that he would easily believe I should find but a cold reception from them if I should be put to make my first visit in the condition of a transported felon; that therefore, if I went thither, I resolved not to see them; but that I had many views in going there, which took off all the uneasy part of it; and if he found himself obliged to go also, I should easily instruct him how to manage himself so as never to go a servant at all, especially since I found he was not destitute of money, which was the only friend in such a condition.

He smiled and said he did not tell me he had money. I took him up short and told him I hoped he did not understand by my speaking that I should expect any supply from him if he had money; that on the other hand, though I had not a great deal, yet I did not want, and while I had any I would rather add to him than weaken him, seeing, whatever he had, I knew in the case of transportation he would have occasion of it all.

He expressed himself in a most tender manner upon that head. He told me what money he had was not a great deal, but that he would never hide any of it from me if I wanted it, and assured me he did not speak with any such apprehensions; that he was only intent upon what I had hinted to him; that here he knew what to do, but there he should be the most helpless wretch alive.

I told him he frighted himself with that which had no terror in it; that if he had money, as I was glad to hear he had, he might not only avoid the servitude supposed to be the consequence of transportation but begin the world upon such a new foundation as he could not fail of success in, with but the common application usual in such cases; that he could not but call to mind I had recommended it to him many years before and proposed it for restoring our fortunes in the world; and I would tell him now that to convince him both of the certainty of it and of my being fully acquainted with the method, and also fully satisfied in the probability of success, he should first see me deliver myself from the necessity of going over at all, and then that I would go with him freely and of my own choice, and perhaps carry enough with me to satisfy him; that I did not offer it for want of being able to live without assistance from him, but that I thought our mutual misfortunes had been such as were sufficient to reconcile us both to quitting this part of the world and living where nobody could upbraid us with what was past, and without the agonies of a condemned hole to drive us to it; where we should look back on all our past disasters with infinite satisfaction when we should consider that our enemies should entirely forget us and that we should live as new people in a new world, nobody having anything to say to us or we to them.

I pressed this home to him with so many arguments, and answered all his own passionate objections so effectually, that he embraced me and told me I treated him with such a sincerity as overcame him; that he would take my advice and would strive to submit to his fate in hope of having the comfort of so faithful a counsellor and such a companion in his misery. But still he put me in mind of what I had mentioned before, namely, that there might be some way to get off before he went and that it might be possible to avoid going at all, which he said would be much better. I told him he should see and be fully satisfied that I would do my utmost in that part too, and if it did not succeed, yet that I would make good the rest.

We parted after this long conference with such testimonies of kindness and affection as I thought were equal, if not superior, to that at our parting at Dunstable; and now I saw more plainly the reason why he then declined coming with me toward London, and why, when we parted there, he told me it was not convenient to come to London with me, as he would otherwise have done. I have observed that the account of his life would have made a much more pleasing history than this of mine; and, indeed, nothing in it was more strange than this part, *viz.*, that he carried on that desperate trade full five-and-twenty years and had never been taken; the success he had met with had been so very uncommon, and such that sometimes he had lived handsomely and retired in one place for a year or two at a time, keeping himself and a manservant to wait on him, and has often sat in the coffee-houses and heard the very people who he had robbed give accounts of their being robbed, and of the places and circumstances, so that he could easily remember that it was the same.

In this manner, it seems, he lived near Liverpool at the time he unluckily married me for a fortune. Had I been the fortune he expected, I verily believe he would have taken up and lived honestly.

He had with the rest of his misfortunes the good luck not to be actually upon the spot when the robbery was done which they were committed for, and so none of the persons robbed could swear to him. But, it seems, as he was taken with the gang, one hard-mouthed countryman swore home to him; and according to the publication they had made, they expected more evidence against him, and for that reason he was kept in hold.

However, the offer which was made to him of transportation was made, as I understood, upon the intercession of some great person who pressed him hard to accept of it; and as he knew there were several that might come in against him, I thought his friend was in the right, and I lay at him night and day to delay it no longer.

At last, with much difficulty, he gave his consent; and as he was not therefore admitted to transportation in court, and on his petition, as I was, so he found himself under a difficulty to avoid embarking himself, as I had said he might have done, his friend having given security for him that he should transport himself and not return within the term.

This hardship broke all my measures, for the steps I took afterwards for my own deliverance were hereby rendered wholly ineffectual unless I would abandon him and leave him to go to America by himself, than which he protested he would much rather go directly to the gallows.

I must now return to my own case. The time of my being transported was near at hand; my governess, who continued my fast friend, had tried to obtain a pardon, but it could not be done unless with an expense too heavy for my purse, considering that to be left empty, unless I had resolved to return to my old trade, had been worse than transportation, because there I could live, here I could not. The good minister stood very hard on another account to prevent my being transported also; but he was answered that my life had been given me at his first solicitations, and therefore he ought to ask no more. He was sensibly grieved at my going because, as he said, he feared I should lose the good impressions which a prospect of death had at first made on me and which were since increased by his instructions; and the pious gentleman was exceedingly concerned on that account.

On the other hand, I was not so solicitous about it now, but I concealed my reasons for it from the minister, and to the last he did not know but that I went with the utmost reluctance and affliction.

It was in the month of February that I was, with thirteen other convicts, delivered to a merchant that traded to Virginia, on board a ship riding in Deptford Reach. The officer of the prison delivered us on board, and the master of the vessel gave a discharge for us.

We were for that night clapped under hatches and kept so close that I thought I should have been suffocated for want of air; and the next morning the ship weighed, and fell down the river to a place called Bugby's Hole, which was done, as they told us, by the agreement of the merchant, that all opportunity of escape should be taken from us. However, when the ship came thither and cast anchor, we were permitted to come upon the deck, but not upon the quarter-deck, that being kept particularly for the captain and for passengers.

When by the noise of the men over my head and the motion of the ship I perceived they were under sail, I was at first greatly surprised, fearing we should go away and that our friends would not be admitted to see us; but I was easy soon after, when I found they had come to an anchor, and that we had notice given by some of the men that the next morning we should have the liberty to come upon deck and to have our friends come to see us.

All that night I lay upon the hard deck as the other prisoners did, but we had afterwards little cabins allowed for such as had any bedding to lay in them, and room to stow any box or trunk for clothes, and linen if we had it (which might well be put in), for some of them had neither shirt or shift, linen or woollen, but what was on their backs, or one farthing of money to help themselves; yet I did not find but they fared well enough in the ship, especially the women, who got money of the seamen for washing their clothes, etc., sufficient to purchase anything they wanted.

When the next morning we had the liberty to come upon deck, I asked one of the officers whether I might not be allowed to send a letter on shore to let my friends know where we lay and to get some necessary things sent to me. This was the boatswain, a very civil, courteous man, who told me I should have any liberty that I desired that he could allow me with safety. I told him I desired no other; and he answered, the ship's boat would go up to London next tide, and he would order my letter to be carried.

Accordingly, when the boat went off, the boatswain came and told me the boat was going off, that he went in it himself, and if my letter was ready, he would take care of it. I had prepared pen, ink, and paper beforehand, and had gotten a letter ready directed to my governess and enclosed another to my fellow-prisoner, which, however, I did not let her know was my husband, not to the last. In that to my governess, I let her know where the ship lay and pressed her to send me what things she had got ready for me for my voyage.

When I gave the boatswain the letter, I gave him a shilling with it, which I told him was for the charge of a porter, which I had entreated him to send with the letter as soon as he came on shore, that if possible I might have an answer brought back by the same hand, that I might know what was become of my things; "for, sir," says I, "if the ship should go away before I have them, I am undone."

I took care, when I gave him the shilling, to let him see I had a little better furniture about me than the ordinary prisoners; that I had a purse and in it a pretty deal of money; and I found that the very sight of it immediately furnished me with very different treatment from what I should otherwise have met with; for though he was courteous indeed before, in a kind of natural compassion to me as a woman in distress, yet he was more than ordinarily so afterwards, and procured me to be better treated in the ship than, I say, I might otherwise have been; as shall appear in its place.

He very honestly delivered my letter to my governess' own hands and brought me back her answer; and when he gave it me, gave me the shilling again. "There," says he, "there's your shilling again too, for I delivered the letter myself." I could not tell what to say, I was so surprised at the thing; but after some pause I said, "Sir, you are too kind; it had been but reasonable that you had paid yourself coach-hire, then."

"No, no," says he, "I am overpaid. What is that gentlewoman? Is she your sister?"

"No, sir," said I, "she is no relation to me, but she is a dear friend, and all the friends I have in the world." "Well," says he, "there are few such friends. Why, she cries after you like a child." "Aye," says I again, "she would give a hundred pound, I believe, to deliver me from this dreadful condition."

"Would she so?" says he. "For half the money I believe I could put you in a way how to deliver yourself." But this he spoke softly, that nobody could hear.

"Alas! sir," said I, "but then that must be such a deliverance as if I should be taken again would cost me my life." "Nay," said he, "if you were once out of the ship, you must look to yourself afterwards; that I can say nothing to." So we dropped the discourse for that time.

In the meantime, my governess, faithful to the last moment, conveyed my letter to the prison to my husband, and got an answer to it, and the next day came down herself, bringing me, in the first place, a sea-bed, as they call it, and all its ordinary furniture. She brought me also a sea-chest—that is, a chest such as are made for seamen, with all the conveniences in it and filled with everything almost that I could want; and in one of the corners of the chest, where there was a private drawer, was my bank of money—that is to say, so much of it as I had resolved to carry with me; for I ordered part of my stock to be left behind to be sent afterwards in such goods as I should want when I came to settle; for money in that country is not of much use where all things are bought for tobacco; much more is it a great loss to carry it from hence.

But my case was particular; it was by no means proper for me to go without money or goods, and for a poor convict that was to be sold as soon as I came on shore, to carry a cargo of goods would be to have notice taken of it, and perhaps to have them seized; so I took part of my stock with me thus, and left the rest with my governess.

My governess brought me a great many other things, but it was not proper for me to appear too well, at least till I knew what kind of a captain we should have. When she came into the ship, I thought she would have died indeed; her heart sunk at the sight of me and at the thoughts of parting with me in that condition; and she cried so intolerably I could not for a long time have any talk with her.

I took that time to read my fellow-prisoner's letter, which greatly perplexed me. He told me it would be impossible for him to be discharged time enough for going in the same ship, and which was more than all, he began to question whether they would give him leave to go in what ship he pleased, though he did voluntarily transport himself; but that they would see him put on board such a ship as they should direct, and that he would be charged upon the captain as other convict prisoners were; so that he began to be in despair of seeing me till he came to Virginia, which made him almost desperate, seeing that, on the other hand, if I should not be there, if any accident of the sea or of mortality should take me away, he should be the most undone creature in the world.

This was very perplexing, and I knew not what course to take. I told my governess the story of the boatswain, and she was mighty eager with me to treat with him; but I had no mind to it till I heard whether my husband, or fellow-prisoner, so she called him, could be at liberty to go with me or no. At last I was forced to let her into the whole matter, except only that of his being my husband. I told her that I had made a positive agreement with him to go if he could get the liberty of going in the same ship and I found he had money.

Then I told her what I proposed to do when we came there, how we could plant, settle, and, in short, grow rich without any more adventures; and as a great secret I told her we were to marry as soon as he came on board.

She soon agreed cheerfully to my going when she heard this, and she made it her business from that time to get him delivered in time so that he might go in the same ship with me, which at last was brought to pass, though with great difficulty and not without all the forms of a transported convict, which he really was not, for he had not been tried, and which was a great mortification to him. As our fate was now determined, and we were both on board, actually bound to Virginia, in the despicable quality of transported convicts destined to be sold for slaves, I for five years and he under bonds and security not to return to England any more as long as he lived, he was very much dejected and cast down; the mortification of being brought on board as he was, like a prisoner, piqued him very much, since it was first told him he should transport himself, so that he might go as a gentleman at liberty. It is true he was not ordered to be sold when he came there, as we were, and for that reason he was obliged to pay for his passage to the captain, which we were not; as to the rest, he was as much at a loss as a child what to do with himself but by directions.

However, I lay in an uncertain condition full three weeks, not knowing whether I should have my husband with me or no, and therefore not resolved how or in what manner to receive the honest boatswain's proposal, which indeed he thought a little strange.

At the end of this time, behold my husband came on board. He looked with a dejected, angry countenance; his great heart was swelled with rage and disdain to be dragged along with three keepers of Newgate and put on board like a convict when he had not so much as been brought to a trial. He made loud complaints of it by his friends, for it seems he had some interest; but they got some check in their application, and were told he had had favour enough and that they had received such an account of him since the last grant of his transportation that he ought to think himself very well treated that he was not prosecuted anew. This answer quieted him, for he knew too much what might have happened and what he had room to expect; and now he saw the goodness of that advice to him which prevailed with him to accept of the offer of transportation. And after his chagrin at these hell-hounds, as he called them, was a little over, he looked more composed, began to be cheerful, and as I was telling him how glad I was to have him once more out of their hands he took me in his arms and acknowledged with great tenderness that I had given him the best advice possible. "My dear," says he, "thou hast twice saved my life; from henceforward it shall be employed for you, and I'll always take your advice."

Our first business was to compare our stock. He was very honest to me and told me his stock was pretty good when he came into the prison, but that living there as he did like a gentleman and, which was much more, the making of friends and soliciting his case had been very expensive; and, in a word, all his stock left was £108, which he had about him in gold.

I gave him an account of my stock as faithfully, that is to say, what I had taken with me; for I was resolved, whatever should happen, to keep what I had left in reserve; that in case I should die, what I had was enough to give him, and what was left in my governess' hands would be her own, which she had well deserved of me indeed.

My stock which I had with me was £246, some odd shillings; so that we had £354 between us, but a worse-gotten estate was never put together to begin the world with.

Our greatest misfortune as to our stock was that it was in money, an unprofitable cargo to be carried to the plantations. I believe his was really all he had left in the world, as he told me it was; but I, who had between £700 and £800 in bank when this disaster befell me, and who had one of the faithfullest friends in the world to manage it for me, considering she was a woman of no principles, had still £300 left in her hand, which I had reserved, as above; besides, I had some very valuable things with me, as particularly two gold watches, some small pieces of plate, and some rings—all stolen goods. With this fortune, and in the sixty-first year of my age, I launched out into a new world, as I may call it, in the condition only of a poor convict ordered to be transported in respite from the gallows. My clothes were poor and mean, but not ragged or dirty, and none knew in the whole ship that I had anything of value about me.

However, as I had a great many very good clothes and

linen in abundance, which I had ordered to be packed up in two great boxes, I had them shipped on board, not as my goods but as consigned to my real name in Virginia; and had the bills of loading in my pocket; and in these boxes was my plate and watches and everything of value except my money, which I kept by itself in a private drawer in my chest, and which could not be found or opened if found without splitting the chest to pieces.

The ship began now to fill; several passengers came on board who were embarked on no criminal account, and these had accommodations assigned them in the great cabin and other parts of the ship, whereas we, as convicts, were thrust down below, I know not where. But when my husband came on board, I spoke to the boatswain, who had so early given me hints of his friendship. I told him he had befriended me in many things and I had not made any suitable return to him, and with that I put a guinea into his hand. I told him that my husband was now come on board; that though we were under the present misfortunes, yet we had been persons of a differing character from the wretched crew that we came with, and desired to know whether the captain might not be moved to admit us to some conveniences in the ship, for which we would make him what satisfaction he pleased, and that we would gratify him for his pains in procuring this for us. He took the guinea, as I could see, with great satisfaction, and assured me of his assistance.

Then he told us he did not doubt but that the captain, who was one of the best-humoured gentlemen in the world, would be easily brought to accommodate us as well as we could desire; and to make me easy, told me he would go up the next tide on purpose to speak to him about it. The next morning, happening to sleep a little longer than ordinary, when I got up and began to look abroad, I saw the boatswain among the men in his ordinary business. I was a little melancholy at seeing him there, and going forwards to speak to him, he saw me and came towards me, but not giving him time to speak first, I said, smiling, "I doubt, sir, you have forgot us, for I see you are very busy." He returned presently, "Come along with me and you shall see." So he took me into the great cabin, and there sat a good sort of a gentlemanly man writing, and a great many papers before him.

"Here," says the boatswain to him that was a-writing, "is the gentlewoman that the captain spoke to you of." And turning to me, he said, "I have been so far from forgetting your business that I have been up at the captain's house and have represented faithfully what you said, of your being furnished with conveniences for yourself and your husband; and the captain has sent this gentleman, who is mate of the ship, down on purpose to show you everything and to accommodate you to your content, and bid me assure you that you shall not be treated like what you were expected to be, but with the same respect as other passengers are treated."

The mate then spoke to me and, not giving me time to thank the boatswain for his kindness, confirmed what the boatswain had said, and added that it was the captain's delight to show himself kind and charitable, especially to those that were under any misfortunes; and with that he showed me several cabins built up, some in the great cabin and some partitioned off, out of the steerage but opening into the great cabin, on purpose for passengers, and gave me leave to choose where I would. I chose a cabin in the steerage, in which were very good conveniences to set our chest and boxes, and a table to eat on.

The mate then told me that the boatswain had given so good a character of me and of my husband that he had orders to tell me we should eat with him, if we thought fit, during the whole voyage, on the common terms of passengers; that we might lay in some fresh provisions if we pleased; or if not, he should lay in his usual store, and that we should have share with him. This was very reviving news to me after so many hardships and afflictions. I thanked him and told him the captain should make his own terms with us, and asked him leave to go and tell my husband of it, who was not very well and was not yet out of his cabin. Accordingly I went, and my husband, whose spirits were still so much sunk with the indignity (as he understood it) offered him that he was scarce yet himself, was so revived with the account I gave him of the reception we were like to have in the ship that he was quite another man, and new vigour and courage appeared in his very countenance. So true is it that the greatest spirits when overwhelmed by their afflictions are subject to the greatest dejections.

After some little pause to recover himself, my husband came up with me and gave the mate thanks for the kindness which he had expressed to us, and sent suitable acknowledgements by him to the captain, offering to pay him by advance whatever he demanded for our passage and for the conveniences he had helped us to. The mate told him that the captain would be on board in the afternoon, and that he would leave all that to him. Accordingly in the afternoon the captain came, and we found him the same courteous, obliging man that the boatswain had represented him; and he was so well pleased with my husband's conversation that, in short, he would not let us keep the cabin we had chosen, but gave us one that, as I said before, opened into the great cabin.

Nor were his conditions exorbitant or the man craving and eager to make a prey of us, but for fifteen guineas we had our whole passage and provisions, eat at the captain's table, and were very handsomely entertained.

The captain lay himself in the other part of the great cabin, having let his round-house, as they call it, to a rich planter who went over with his wife and three children, who eat by themselves. He had some other ordinary passengers, who quartered in the steerage; and as for our old fraternity, they were kept under the hatches, and came very little on the deck.

I could not refrain acquainting my governess with what had happened; it was but just that she, who was really concerned for me, should have part in my good fortune. Besides, I wanted her assistance to supply me with several necessaries which before I was shy of letting anybody see me have; but now I had a cabin and room to set things in, I ordered abundance of good things for our comfort in the voyage, as brandy, sugar, lemons, etc., to make punch and treat our benefactor, the captain; and abundance of things for eating and drinking; also a larger bed and bedding proportioned to it; so that, in a word, we resolved to want for nothing.

All this while I had provided nothing for our assistance when we should come to the place and begin to call ourselves planters; and I was far from being ignorant of what was needful on that occasion; particularly all sorts of tools for the planter's work and for building, and all kinds of house furniture, which, if to be bought in the country, must necessarily cost double the price.

I discoursed that point with my governess, and she went and waited upon the captain and told him that she hoped ways might be found out for her two unfortunate cousins, as she called us, to obtain our freedom when we came into the country, and so entered into a discourse with him about the means and terms also, of which I shall say more in its place; and after thus sounding the captain, she let him know, though we were unhappy in the circumstance that occasioned our going, yet that we were not unfurnished to set ourselves to work in the country, and were resolved to settle and live there as planters. The captain readily offered his assistance, told her the method of entering upon such business, and how easy, nay, how certain it was for industrious people to recover their fortunes in such a manner. "Madam," says he, " 'tis no reproach to any man in that country to have been sent over in worse circumstances than I perceive your cousins are in, provided they do but apply with good judgement to the business of the place when they come there."

She then inquired of him what things it was necessary we should carry over with us, and he, like a knowing man, told her thus: "Madam, your cousins first must procure somebody to buy them as servants, in conformity to the conditions of their transportation, and then, in the name of that person, they may go about what they will; they may either purchase some plantations already begun or they may purchase land of the government of the country and begin where they please, and both will be done reasonably." She bespoke his favour in the first article, which he promised to her to take upon himself, and indeed faithfully performed it. And as to the rest, he promised to recommend us to such as should give us the best advice and not to impose upon us, which was as much as could be desired.

She then asked him if it would not be necessary to furnish us with a stock of tools and materials for the business of planting; and he said, "Yes, by all means." Then she begged his assistance in that and told him she would furnish us with everything that was convenient, whatever it cost her. He accordingly gave her a list of things necessary for a planter, which, by his account, came to about fourscore or £100. And, in short, she went about as dexterously to buy them as if she had been an old Virginia merchant; only that she bought by my direction above twice as much of everything as he had given her a list of.

These she put on board in her own name, took his bills of loading for them, and endorsed those bills of loading to my husband, insuring the cargo afterwards in her own name; so that we were provided for all events and for all disasters.

I should have told you that my husband gave her all his own stock of £108, which, as I have said, he had about him in gold, to lay out thus, and I gave her a good sum besides; so that I did not break into the stock which I had left in her hands at all, but after all we had near £200 in money, which was more than enough for our purpose.

In this condition, very cheerful and indeed joyful at being so happily accommodated, we set sail from Bugby's Hole to Gravesend, where the ship lay about ten days more and where the captain came on board for good and all. Here the captain offered us a civility which indeed we had no reason to expect, namely, to let us go on shore and refresh ourselves upon giving our words that we would not go from him and that we would return peaceably on board again. This was such an evidence of his confidence in us that it overcome my husband, who in a mere principle of gratitude told him as he could not be in any capacity to make a suitable return for such a favour, so he could not think of accepting it, nor could he be easy that the captain should run such a risk. After some mutual civilities I gave my husband a purse, in which was eighty guineas, and he put it into the captain's hand. "There, Captain," says he, "there's part of a pledge for our fidelity; if we deal dishonestly with you on any account, 'tis your own." And on this we went on shore.

Indeed, the captain had assurance enough of our resolutions to go, for that having made such provision to settle there, it did not seem rational that we would choose to remain here at the peril of life, for such it must have been. In a word, we went all on shore with the captain and supped together in Gravesend, where we were very merry, stayed all night, lay at the house where we supped, and came all very honestly on board again with him in the morning. Here we bought ten dozen of bottles of good beer, some wine, some fowls, and such things as we thought might be acceptable on board.

My governess was with us all this while and went round with us into the Downs, as did also the captain's wife, with whom she went back. I was never so sorrowful at parting with my own mother as I was at parting with her, and I never saw her more. We had a fair easterly wind the third day after we came to the Downs, and we sailed from thence the 10th of April. Nor did we touch any more at any place till, being driven on the coast of Ireland by a very hard gale of wind, the ship came to an anchor in a little bay near a river whose name I remember not, but they said the river came down from Limerick and that it was the largest river in Ireland.

Here, being detained by bad weather for some time, the captain, who continued the same kind, good-humoured man as at first, took us two on shore with him again. He did it now in kindness to my husband indeed, who bore the sea very ill, especially when it blew so hard. Here we bought again store of fresh provisions, beef, pork, mutton, and fowls, and the captain stayed to pickle up five or six barrels of beef to lengthen out the ship's store. We were here not above five days when, the weather turning mild, and a fair wind, we set sail again and in two-and-forty days came safe to the coast of Virginia.

When we drew near to the shore, the captain called me to him and told me that he found by my discourse I had some relations in the place and that I had been there before, and so he supposed I understood the custom in their disposing the convict prisoners when they arrived. I told him I did not; and that as to what relations I had in the place, he might be sure I would make myself known to none of them while in the circumstances of a prisoner, and that as to the rest, we left ourselves entirely to him to assist us, as he was pleased to promise us he would do. He told me I must get somebody in the place to come and buy me as a servant, and who must answer for me to the governor of the country if he demanded me. I told him we should do as he should direct; so he brought a planter to treat with him, as it were, for the purchase of me for a servant, my husband not being ordered to be sold, and there I was formally sold to him, and went ashore with him. The captain went with us and carried us to a certain house, whether it was to be called a tavern or not I know not, but we had a bowl of punch there made of rum, etc., and were very merry. After some time the planter gave us a certificate of discharge and an acknowledgement of having served him faithfully, and I was free from him the next morning to go whither I would.

For this piece of service the captain demanded of me 6000 weight of tobacco, which he said he was accountable for to his freighter, and we bought for him, and made him a present of twenty guineas besides, which he was abundantly satisfied with.

It is not proper to enter here into the particulars of what part of the colony of Virginia we settled in for divers reasons; it may suffice to mention that we went into the great river of Potomac, the ship being bound thither; and there we intended to have settled at first, though afterwards we altered our minds.

The first thing I did of moment after having gotten all our goods on shore and placed them in a storehouse, which with a lodging we hired at the small place or village where we landed; I say, the first thing was to inquire after my mother and after my brother (that fatal person who I married as a husband, as I have related at large). A little inquiry furnished me with information that Mrs. ——, that is, my mother, was dead; that my brother, or husband, was alive, and which was worse, I found he was removed from the plantation where I lived, and lived with one of his sons in a plantation just by the place where we landed and had hired a warehouse.

I was a little surprised at first, but as I ventured to satisfy myself that he could not know me, I was not only perfectly easy but had a great mind to see him if it was possible without his seeing me. In order to that, I found out by inquiry the plantation where he lived, and with a woman of the place who I got to help me, like what we call a charwoman, I rambled about towards the place as if I had only a mind to see the country and look about me. At last I came so near that I saw the dwelling-house. I asked the woman whose plantation that was; she said it belonged to such a man, and looking out a little to our right hands, "There," says she, "is the gentleman that owns the plantation, and his father with him." "What are their Christian names?" said I. "I know not," said she, "what the old gentleman's name is, but his son's name is Humphry; and I believe," says she, "the father's is so too." You may guess, if you can, what a confused mixture of joy and fright possessed my thoughts upon this occasion, for I immediately knew that this was nobody else but my own son by that father she showed me, who was my own brother. I had no mask, but I ruffled my hoods so about my face that I depended upon it that after above twenty years' absence, and withal not expecting anything of me in that part of the world, he would not be able to know me. But I need not have used all that caution, for he was grown dim-sighted by some distemper which had fallen upon his eyes, and could but just see well enough to walk about and not run against a tree or into a ditch. As they drew near to us I said, "Does he know you, Mrs. Owen?" (So they called the woman.) "Yes," she said, "if he hears me speak, he will know me; but he can't see well enough to know me or anybody else"; and so she told me the story of his sight, as I have related. This made me secure, and so I threw open my hoods again and let them pass by me. It was a wretched thing for a mother thus to see her own son, a handsome, comely young gentleman in flourishing circumstances, and durst not make herself known to him and durst not take any notice of him. Let any mother of children that reads this consider it and but think with what anguish of mind I restrained myself; what yearnings of soul I had in me to embrace him and weep over him; and how I thought all my entrails turned within me, that my very bowels moved, and I knew not what to do, as I now know not how to express those agonies! When he went from me, I stood gazing and trembling and looking after him as long as I could see him; then, sitting down on the grass just at a place I had marked, I made as if I lay down to rest me, but turned from her and, lying on my face, wept and kissed the ground that he had set his foot on.

I could not conceal my disorder so much from the woman but that she perceived it and thought I was not well, which I was obliged to pretend was true; upon which she pressed me to rise, the ground being damp and dangerous, which I did, and walked away.

As I was going back again, and still talking of this gentleman and his son, a new occasion of melancholy offered itself thus. The woman began, as if she would tell me a story to divert me: "There goes," says she, "a very odd tale among the neighbours where this gentleman formerly lived." "What was that?" said I. "Why," says she, "that old gentleman, going to England when he was a young man, fell in love with a young lady there, one of the finest women that ever was seen here, and married her and brought her over hither to his mother, who was then living. He lived here several years with her," continued she, "and had several children by her, of which the young gentleman that was with him now was one; but after some time the old gentlewoman, his mother, talking to her of something relating to herself and of her circumstances in England, which were bad enough, the daughter-in-law began to be very much surprised and uneasy; and in short, in examining further into things, it appeared past all contradiction that she, the old gentlewoman, was her own mother and that consequently that son was her own brother, which struck the family with horror and put them into such confusion that it had almost ruined them all. The young woman would not live with him, he for a time went distracted, and at last the young woman went away for England and has never been heard of since."

It is easy to believe that I was strangely affected with this story, but 'tis impossible to describe the nature of my disturbance. I seemed astonished at the story and asked her a thousand questions about the particulars, which I found she was thoroughly acquainted with. At last I began to inquire into the circumstances of the family, how the old gentlewoman, I mean my mother, died, and how she left what she had; for my mother had promised me very solemnly that when she died, she would do something for me and leave it so as that if I was living, I should, one way or other, come at it without its being in the power of her son, my brother and husband, to prevent it. She told me she did not know exactly how it was ordered, but she had been told that my mother had left a sum of money, and had tied her plantation for the payment of it, to be made good to the daughter if ever she could be heard of, either in England or elsewhere; and that the trust was left with this son, who we saw with his father.

This was news too good for me to make light of, and you may be sure filled my heart with a thousand thoughts, what course I should take, and in what manner I should make myself known, or whether I should ever make myself known or no.

Here was a perplexity that I had not indeed skill to manage myself in, neither knew I what course to take. It lay heavy upon my mind night and day. I could neither sleep or converse, so that my husband perceived it, wondered what ailed me, and strove to divert me, but it was all to no purpose. He pressed me to tell him what it was troubled me, but I put it off till at last, importuning me continually, I was forced to form a story which yet had a plain truth to lay it upon too. I told him I was troubled because I found we must shift our quarters and alter our scheme of settling, for that I found I should be known if I stayed in that part of the country; for that my mother being dead, several of my relations were come into that part where we then was, and that I must either discover myself to them, which in our present circumstances was not proper on many accounts, or remove; and which to do I knew not, and that this it was that made me melancholy.

He joined with me in this, that it was by no means proper for me to make myself known to anybody in the circumstances in which we then were; and therefore he told me he would be willing to remove to any part of the country or even to any other country if I thought fit. But now I had another difficulty, which was that if I removed to another colony, I put myself out of the way of ever making a due search after those things which my mother had left; again, I could never so much as think of breaking the secret of my former marriage to my new husband; it was not a story would bear telling, nor could

I tell what might be the consequences of it; it was impossible, too, without making it public all over the country as well who I was as what I now was also.

This perplexity continued a great while and made my spouse very uneasy; for he thought I was not open with him and did not let him into every part of my grievance; and he would often say he wondered what he had done that I would not trust him, whatever it was, especially if it was grievous and afflicting. The truth is, he ought to have been trusted with everything, for no man could deserve better of a wife; but this was a thing I knew not how to open to him, and yet having nobody to disclose any part of it to, the burthen was too heavy for my mind; for, let them say what they please of our sex not being able to keep a secret, my life is a plain conviction to me of the contrary; but be it our sex or the men's sex, a secret of moment should always have a confidant, a bosom friend to whom we may communicate the joy of it, or the grief of it, be it which it will, or it will be a double weight upon the spirits and perhaps become even insupportable in itself; and this I appeal to human testimony for the truth of.

And this is the cause why many times men as well as women, and men of the greatest and best qualities other ways, yet have found themselves weak in this part, and have not been able to bear the weight of a secret joy or of a secret sorrow, but have been obliged to disclose it, even for the mere giving vent to themselves and to unbend the mind oppressed with the weights which attended it. Nor was this any token of folly at all, but a natural consequence of the thing; and such people, had they struggled longer with the oppression, would certainly have told it in their sleep and disclosed the secret, let it have been of what fatal nature soever, without regard to the person to whom it might be exposed. This necessity of nature is a thing which works sometimes with such vehemency in the minds of those who are guilty of any atrocious villainy, such as a secret murder in particular, that they have been obliged to discover it though the consequence has been their own destruction. Now, though it may be true that the divine justice ought to have the glory of all those discoveries and confessions, yet 'tis as certain that Providence, which ordinarily works by the hands of nature, makes use here of the same natural causes to produce those extraordinary effects.

I could give several remarkable instances of this in my long conversation with crime and with criminals. I knew one fellow that, while I was a prisoner in Newgate, was one of those they called then night-fliers. I know not what word they may have understood it by since, but he was one who by connivance was admitted to go abroad every evening, when he played his pranks, and furnished those honest people they call thief-catchers with business to find out the next day, and restore for a reward what they had stolen the evening before. This fellow was as sure to tell in his sleep all that he had done, and every step he had taken, what he had stolen, and where, as sure as if he had engaged to tell it waking, and therefore he was obliged, after he had been out, to lock himself up, or be locked up by some of the keepers that had him in fee, that nobody should hear him; but on the other hand, if he had told all the particulars and given a full account of his rambles and success to any comrade, any brother thief, or to his employers, as I may justly call them, then all was well and he slept as quietly as other people.

As the publishing this account of my life is for the sake of the just moral of every part of it, and for instruction, caution, warning, and improvement to every reader, so this will not pass, I hope, for an unnecessary digression, concerning some people being obliged to disclose the greatest secrets either of their own or other people's affairs.

Under the oppression of this weight, I laboured in the case I have been naming; and the only relief I found for it was to let my husband into so much of it as I thought would convince him of the necessity there was for us to think of settling in some other part of the world; and the next consideration before us was which part of the English settlements we should go to. My husband was a perfect stranger to the country and had not yet so much as a geographical knowledge of the situation of the several places; and I, that till I wrote this did not know what the word "geographical" signified, had only a general knowledge from long conversation with people that came from or went to several places; but this I knew: that Maryland, Pennsylvania, East and West Jersey, New York, and New England lay all north of Virginia, and that they were consequently all colder climates, to which for that very reason I had an aversion. For that as I naturally loved warm weather, so now I grew into years, I had a stronger inclination to shun a cold climate. I therefore considered of going to Carolina, which is the most southern colony of the English on the continent; and hither I proposed to go, the rather because I might with ease come from thence at any time when it might be proper to inquire after my mother's effects and to demand them.

With this resolution, I proposed to my husband our going away from where we was and carrying our effects with us to Carolina, where we resolved to settle; for my husband readily agreed to the first part, *viz.*, that it was not at all proper to stay where we was since I had assured him we should be known there; and the rest I concealed from him.

But now I found a new difficulty upon me. The main affair grew heavy upon my mind still, and I could not think of going out of the country without somehow or other making inquiry into the grand affair of what my mother had done for me; nor could I with any patience bear the thought of going away, and not make myself known to my old husband (brother) or to my child, his son; only I would fain have had it done without my new husband having any knowledge of it or they having any knowledge of him.

I cast about innumerable ways in my thoughts how this might be done. I would gladly have sent my husband away to Carolina and have come after myself, but this was impracticable; he would not stir without me, being himself unacquainted with the country and with the methods of settling anywhere. Then I thought we would both go first, and that when we were settled I should come back to Virginia; but even then I knew he would never part with me and be left there alone. The case was plain: he was bred a gentleman, and was not only unacquainted but indolent, and when we did settle, would much rather go into the woods with his gun, which they call there hunting and which is the ordinary work of the Indians; I say, he would much rather do that than attend to the natural business of the plantation.

These were, therefore, difficulties unsurmountable and such as I knew not what to do in. I had such strong impressions on my mind about discovering myself to my old husband that I could not withstand them; and the rather because it run in my thoughts that if I did not while he lived, I might in vain endeavour to convince my son afterward that I was really the same person and that I was his mother, and so might both lose the assistance and comfort of the relation and lose whatever it was my mother had left me; and yet, on the other hand, I could never think it proper to discover the circumstances I was in, as well relating to the having a husband with me as to my being brought over as a criminal; on both which accounts it was absolutely necessary to me to remove from the place where I was, and come again to him as from another place and in another figure.

Upon those considerations I went on with telling my husband the absolute necessity there was of our not settling in Potomac River, that we should presently be made public there; whereas if we went to any other place in the world, we could come in with as much reputation as any family that came to plant; that as it was always agreeable to the inhabitants to have families come among them to plant who brought substance with them, so we should be sure of agreeable reception, and without any possibility of a discovery of our circumstances.

I told him too that as I had several relations in the place where we was, and that I durst not now let myself be known to them because they would soon come to know the occasion of my coming over, which would be to expose myself to the last degree, so I had reason to believe that my mother, who died here, had left me something, and perhaps considerable, which it might be very well worth my while to inquire after; but that this too could not be done without exposing us publicly unless we went from hence; and then, wherever we settled, I might come, as it were, to visit and to see my brother and nephews, make myself known, inquire after what was my due, be received with respect, and at the same time have justice done me; whereas if I did it now, I could expect nothing but with trouble, such as exacting it by force, receiving it with curses and reluctance and with all kinds of affronts, which he would not perhaps bear to see; that in case of being obliged to legal proofs of being really her daughter, I might be at a loss, be obliged to have recourse to England, and, it may be, to fail at last and so lose it. With these arguments, and having thus acquainted my husband with the whole secret so far as was needful to him, we resolved to go and seek a settlement in some other colony, and at first Carolina was the place pitched upon.

In order to this we began to make inquiry for vessels going to Carolina, and in a very little while got information that on the other side of the bay, as they call it, namely, in Maryland, there was a ship which came from Carolina, loaden with rice and other goods, and was going back again thither. On this news we hired a sloop to take in our goods, and taking, as it were, a final farewell of Potomac River, we went with all our cargo over to Maryland.

This was a long and unpleasant voyage, and my spouse said it was worse to him than all the voyage from England, because the weather was bad, the water rough, and the vessel small and inconvenient. In the next place we were full a hundred miles up Potomac River, in a part they call Westmoreland County; and as that river is by far the greatest in Virginia, and I have heard say it is the greatest river in the world that falls into another river and not directly into the sea, so we had base weather in it and were frequently in great danger; for though they call it but a river, 'tis frequently so broad that when we were in the middle we could not see land on either side for many leagues together. Then we had the great bay of Chesapeake to cross, which is, where the river Potomac falls into it, near thirty miles broad, so that our voyage was full two hundred miles, in a poor, sorry sloop, with all our treasure, and if any accident had happened to us we might at last have been very miserable; supposing we had lost our goods and saved our lives only, and had then been left naked and destitute and in a wild, strange place, not having one friend or acquaintance in all that part of the world. The very thoughts of it gives me some horror, even since the danger is past.

Well, we came to the place in five days' sailing; I think they call it Philip's Point; and behold, when we came thither, the ship bound to Carolina was loaded and gone away but three days before. This was a disappointment; but, however, I, that was to be discouraged with nothing, told my husband that since we could not get passage to Carolina, and that the country we was in was very fertile and good, we would see if we could find out anything for our turn where we was, and that if he liked things we would settle here.

We immediately went on shore, but found no conveniences just at that place either for our being on shore or preserving our goods on shore, but was directed by a very honest Quaker who we found there to go to a place about sixty miles east; that is to say, nearer the mouth of the bay, where he said he lived and where we should be accommodated either to plant or to wait for any other place to plant in that might be more convenient; and he invited us with so much kindness that we agreed to go, and the Quaker himself went with us.

Here we bought us two servants, *viz.*, an English woman-servant just come on shore from a ship of Liverpool and a Negro man-servant, things absolutely necessary for all people that pretended to settle in that country. This honest Quaker was very helpful to us and, when we came to the place that he proposed, found us out a convenient storehouse for our goods, and lodging for ourselves and servants; and about two months or thereabout afterwards, by his direction we took up a large piece of land from the government of that country in order to form our plantation, and so we laid the thoughts of going to Carolina wholly aside, having been very well received here and accommodated with a convenient lodging till we could prepare things, and have land enough cured, and materials provided for building us a house, all which we managed by the direction of the Quaker; so that in one year's time we had near fifty acres of land cleared, part of it enclosed, and some of it planted with tobacco, though not much; besides, we had garden-ground and corn sufficient to supply our servants with roots and herbs and bread.

And now I persuaded my husband to let me go over the bay again and inquire after my friends. He was the willinger to consent to it now because he had business upon his hands sufficient to employ him besides his gun to divert him, which they call hunting there and which he greatly delighted in; and indeed we used to look at one another, sometimes with a great deal of pleasure, reflecting how much better that was, not than Newgate only but than the most prosperous of our circumstances in the wicked trade we had been both carrying on.

Our affair was now in a very good posture; we purchased of the proprietors of the colony as much land for £35, paid in ready money, as would make a sufficient plantation to us as long as we could either of us live; and as for children, I was past anything of that kind.

But our good fortune did not end here. I went, as I have said, over the bay to the place where my brother, once a husband, lived; but I did not go to the same village where I was before, but went up another great river, on the east side of the river Potomac, called Rappahannock River, and by this means came on the back of his plantation, which was large, and by the help of a navigable creek that run into the Rappahannock, I came very near it.

I was now fully resolved to go up point-blank to my brother (husband) and to tell him who I was; but not knowing what temper I might find him in, or how much out of temper, rather, I might make him by such a rash visit, I resolved to write a letter to him first to let him know who I was and that I was come not to give him any trouble upon the old relation, which I hoped was entirely forgot, but that I applied to him as a sister to a brother, desiring his assistance in the case of that provision which our mother, at her decease, had left for my support and which I did not doubt but he would do me justice in, especially considering that I was come thus far to look after it.

I said some very tender, kind things in the letter about his son, which I told him he knew to be my own child, and that as I was guilty of nothing in marrying him any more than he was in marrying me, neither of us having then known our being at all related to one another, so I hoped he would allow me the most passionate desire of once seeing my own and only child, and of showing something of the infirmities of a mother in preserving a violent affection for him, who had never been able to retain any thought of me one way or other.

I did believe that having received this letter, he would immediately give it to his son to read, his eyes being, I knew, so dim that he could not see to read it; but it fell out better than so, for as his sight was dim, so he had allowed his son to open all letters that came to his hand for him, and the old gentleman being from home or out of the way when my messenger came, my letter came directly to my son's hand, and he opened and read it.

He called the messenger in, after some little stay, and asked him where the person was who gave him that letter. The messenger told him the place, which was about seven miles off; so he bid him stay, and ordering a horse to be got ready, and two servants, away he came to me with the messenger. Let any one judge the consternation I was in when my messenger came back and told me the old gentleman was not at home, but his son was come along with him and was just coming up to me. I was perfectly confounded, for I knew not whether it was peace or war, nor could I tell how to behave; however, I had but a very few moments to think, for my son was at the heels of the messenger, and coming up into my lodgings, asked the fellow at the door something. I suppose it was, for I did not hear it, which was the gentlewoman that sent him? For the messenger said, "There she is, sir"; at which he comes directly up to me, kisses me, took me in his arms, embraced me with so much passion that he could not speak, but I could feel his breast heave and throb like a child that cries, but sobs, and cannot cry it out.

I can neither express or describe the joy that touched my very soul when I found, for it was easy to discover that part, that he came not as a stranger, but as a son to a mother, and indeed a son who had never before known what a mother of his own was; in short, we cried over one another a considerable while, when at last he broke out first. "My dear mother," says he, "are you still alive? I never expected to have seen your face." As for me, I could say nothing a great while.

After we had both recovered ourselves a little and were able to talk, he told me how things stood. He told me he had not showed my letter to his father or told him anything about it; that what his grandmother left me was in his hands, and that he would do me justice to my full satisfaction; that as to his father, he was old and infirm both in body and mind; that he was very fretful and passionate, almost blind, and capable of nothing; and he questioned whether he would know how to act in an affair which was of so nice a nature as this; and that therefore he had come himself, as well to satisfy himself in seeing me, which he could not restrain himself from, as also to put it into my power to make a judgement, after I had seen how things were, whether I would discover myself to his father or no.

This was really so prudently and wisely managed that I found my son was a man of sense and needed no direction from me. I told him I did not wonder that his father was as he had described him, for that his head was a little touched before I went away; and principally his disturbance was because I could not be persuaded to live with him as my husband after I knew that he was my brother; that as he knew better than I what his father's present condition was, I should readily join with him in such measures as he would direct; that I was indifferent as to seeing his father since I had seen him first, and he could not have told me better news than to tell me that what his grandmother had left me was entrusted in his hands, who, I doubted not, now he knew who I was, would, as he said, do me justice. I inquired then how long my mother had been dead and where she died, and told so many particulars of the family that I left him no room to doubt the truth of my being really and truly his mother.

My son then inquired where I was and how I had disposed myself. I told him I was on the Maryland side of the bay at the plantation of a particular friend, who came from England in the same ship with me; that as for that side of the bay where he was, I had no habitation. He told me I should go home with him and live with him, if I pleased, as long as I lived; that as to his father, he knew nobody and would never so much as guess at me. I considered of that a little and told him that though it was really no little concern to me to live at a distance from him, yet I could not say it would be the most comfortable thing in the world to me to live in the house with him, and to have that unhappy object always before me which had been such a blow to my peace before; that though I should be glad to have his company (my son) or to be as near him as possible, yet I could not think of being in the house where I should be also under constant restraint for fear of betraying myself in my discourse, nor should I be able to refrain some expressions in my conversing with him as my son that might discover the whole affair, which would by no means be convenient.

He acknowledged that I was right in all this. "But then, dear mother," says he, "you shall be as near me as you can." So he took me with him on horse-back to a plantation next to his own, and where I was as well entertained as I could have been in his own. Having left me there, he went away home, telling me he would talk of the main business the next day; and having first called me his aunt and given a charge to the people, who it seems were his tenants, to treat me with all possible respect, about two hours after he was gone, he sent me a maidservant and a Negro boy to wait on me, and provisions ready dressed for my supper; and thus I was as if I had been in a new world, and began almost to wish that I had not brought my Lancashire husband from England at all.

However, that wish was not hearty neither, for I loved my Lancashire husband entirely, as I had ever done from the beginning; and he merited it as much as it was possible for a man to do; but that by the way.

The next morning my son came to visit me again, almost as soon as I was up. After a little discourse, he first of all pulled out a deerskin bag and gave it me, with five-and-fifty Spanish pistoles in it, and told me that was to supply my expenses from England, for though it was not his business to inquire, yet he ought to think I did not bring a great deal of money out with me, it not being usual to bring much money into that country. Then he pulled out his grandmother's will and read it over to me, whereby it appeared that she left a plantation on York River to me, with the stock of servants and cattle upon it, and had given it in trust to this son of mine for my use whenever he should hear of me, and to my heirs if I had any children, and in default of heirs to whomsoever I should by will dispose of it; but gave the income of it, till I should be heard of, to my said son; and if I should not be living, then it was to him and his heirs.

This plantation, though remote from him, he said he did not let out, but managed it by a head clerk, as he did another that was his father's, that lay hard by it, and went over himself three or four times a year to look after it. I asked him what he thought the plantation might be worth. He said if I would let it out, he would give me about £60 a year for it; but if I would live on it, then it would be worth much more, and he believed would bring me in about £150 a year. But seeing I was likely either to settle on the other side the bay or might perhaps have a mind to go back to England, if I would let him be my steward he would manage it for me as he had done for himself, and that he believed he should be able to send me as much tobacco from it as would yield me about £100 a year, sometimes more.

This was all strange news to me, and things I had not been used to; and really my heart began to look up more seriously than I think it ever did before and to look with great thankfulness to the hand of Providence, which had done such wonders for me, who had been myself the greatest wonder of wickedness perhaps that had been suffered to live in the world. And I must again observe that not on this occasion only, but even on all other occasions of thankfulness, my past wickedness and abominable life never looked so monstrous to me, and I never so completely abhorred it and reproached myself with it as when I had a sense upon me of Providence doing good to me while I had been making those vile returns on my part.

But I leave the reader to improve these thoughts, as no doubt they will see cause, and I go on to the fact. My son's tender carriage and kind offers fetched tears from me almost all the while he talked with me. Indeed, I could scarce discourse with him but in the intervals of my passion; however, at length I began, and expressing myself with wonder at my being so happy to have the trust of what I had left put into the hands of my own child, I told him that as to the inheritance of it, I had no child but him in the world, and was now past having any if I should marry, and therefore would desire him to get a writing drawn, which I was ready to execute, by which I would, after me, give it wholly to him and to his heirs. And in the meantime, smiling, I asked him what made him continue a bachelor so long. His answer was kind and ready, that Virginia did not yield any great plenty of wives, and that since I talked of going back to England, I should send him a wife from London.

This was the substance of our first day's conversation, the pleasantest day that ever passed over my head in my life and which gave me the truest satisfaction. He came every day after this and spent great part of his time with me, and carried me about to several of his friends' houses, where I was entertained with great respect. Also I dined several times at his own house, when he took care always to see his half-dead father so out of the way that I never saw him or he me. I made him one present, and it was all I had of value, and that was one of the gold watches of which I said I had two in my chest, and this I happened to have with me and gave it him at his third visit. I told him I had nothing of any value to bestow but that, and I desired he would now and then kiss it for my sake. I did not, indeed, tell him that I stole it from a gentlewoman's side at a meeting-house in London. That's by the way.

He stood a little while hesitating, as if doubtful whether to take it or no. But I pressed it on him and made him accept it, and it was not much less worth than his leather pouch full of Spanish gold, no, though it were to be reckoned as if at London, whereas it was worth twice as much there. At length he took it, kissed it, told me the watch should be a debt upon him that he would be paying as long as I lived.

A few days after, he brought the writings of gift and the scrivener with him, and I signed them very freely and delivered them to him with a hundred kisses; for sure nothing ever passed between a mother and a tender, dutiful child with more affection. The next day he brings me an obligation under his hand and seal, whereby he engaged himself to manage the plantation for my account and to remit the produce to my order wherever I should be; and withal, obliged himself to make up the produce £100 a year to me. When he had done so, he told me that as I came to demand before the crop was off, I had a right to the produce of the current year; and so he paid £100 in Spanish pieces of eight, and desired me to give him a receipt for it as in full for that year, ending at Christmas following, this being about the latter end of August.

I stayed here above five weeks and indeed had much ado to get away then. Nay, he would have come over the bay with me, but I would by no means allow it. However, he would send me over in a sloop of his own, which was built like a yacht and served him as well for pleasure as business. This I accepted of, and so, after the utmost expressions both of duty and affection, he let me come away, and I arrived safe in two days at my friend's the Quaker's.

I brought over with me for the use of our plantation three horses with harness and saddles, some hogs, two cows, and a thousand other things, the gift of the kindest and tenderest child that ever woman had. I related to my husband all the particulars of this voyage, except that I called my son my cousin; and first I told him that I had lost my watch, which he seemed to take as a misfortune; but then I told him how kind my cousin had been, that my mother had left me such a plantation, and that he had preserved it for me in hopes some time or other he should hear from me; then I told him that I had left it to his management, that he would render me a faithful account of its produce; and then I pulled him out the £100 in silver as the first year's produce; and then, pulling out the deerskin purse with the pistoles, "And here, my dear," says I, "is the gold watch." Says my husband, "So is Heaven's goodness sure to work the same effects in all sensible minds where mercies touch the heart"; lifted up both his hands, and with an ecstasy of joy, "what is God a-doing," says he, "for such an ungrateful dog as I am!" Then I let him know what I had brought over in the sloop besides all this; I mean the horses, hogs, and cows, and other stores for our plantation; all which added to his surprise and filled his heart with thankfulness; and from this time forward I believe he was as sincere a penitent and as thoroughly a reformed man as ever God's goodness brought back from a profligate, a highwayman, and a robber. I could fill a larger history than this with the evidences of this truth, and but that I doubt that part of the story will not be equally diverting as the wicked part.

But this is to be my own story, not my husband's. I return therefore to my own part. We went on with our own plantation and managed it with the help and direction of such friends as we got there, and especially the honest Quaker, who proved a faithful, generous, and steady friend to us; and we had very good success, for having a flourishing stock to begin with, as I have said, and this being now increased by the addition of £150 sterling in money, we enlarged our number of servants, built us a very good house, and cured every year a great deal of land. The second year I wrote to my old governess, giving her part with us of the joy of our success, and ordered her how to lay out the money I had left with her, which was £250, as above, and to send it to us in goods, which she performed with her usual kindness and fidelity, and all this arrived safe to us.

Here we had a supply of all sorts of clothes, as well for my husband as for myself; and I took especial care to buy for him all those things that I knew he delighted to have, as two good long wigs, two silver-hilted swords, three or four fine fowling-pieces, a fine saddle with holsters and pistols very handsome, with a scarlet cloak, and in a word, everything I could think of to oblige him and to make him appear as he really was, a very fine gentleman. I ordered a good quantity of such household stuff as we wanted, with linen for us both. As for myself, I wanted very little of clothes or linen, being very well furnished before. The rest of my cargo consisted in ironwork of all sorts, harness for horses, tools, clothes for servants, and woollen cloth, stuffs, serges, stockings, shoes, hats, and the like, such as servants wear; and whole pieces also to make up for servants, all by direction of the Quaker; and all this cargo arrived safe and in good condition, with three women-servants, lusty wenches which my old governess had picked up for me, suitable enough to the place and to the work we had for them to do, one of which happened to come double, having been got with child by one of the seamen in the ship, as she owned afterwards, before the ship got so far as Gravesend; so she brought us a stout boy about seven months after our landing.

My husband, you may suppose, was a little surprised at the arriving of this cargo from England; and talking with me one day after he saw the particulars, "My dear," says he, "what is the meaning of all this? I fear you will run us too deep in debt. When shall we be able to make returns for it all?" I smiled and told him that it was all paid for; and then I told him that not knowing what might befall us in the voyage, and considering what our circumstances might expose us to, I had not taken my whole stock with me, that I had reserved so much in my friend's hands, which, now we were come over safe and settled in a way to live, I had sent for, as he might see.

He was amazed and stood awhile telling upon his fingers, but said nothing. At last he began thus: "Hold, let's see," says he, telling upon his fingers still and first on his thumb; "there's £246 in money at first, then two gold watches, diamond rings, and plate," says he, upon the forefinger. Then upon the next finger, "Here's a plantation on York River, £100 a year, then £150 in money, then a sloop-load of horses, cows, hogs, and stores"; and so on to the thumb again. "And now," says he, "a cargo cost £250 in England, and worth here twice the money." "Well," says I, "what do you make of all that?" "Make of it?" says he. "Why, who says I was deceived when I married a wife in Lancashire? I think I have married a fortune, and a very good fortune too," says he.

In a word, we were now in very considerable circumstances, and every year increasing; for our new plantation grew upon our hands insensibly, and in eight years which we lived upon it, we brought it to such a pitch that the produce was at least £300 sterling a year—I mean, worth so much in England.

After I had been a year at home again, I went over the bay to see my son and to receive another year's income of my plantation; and I was surprised to hear, just at my landing there, that my old husband was dead and had not been buried above a fortnight. This, I confess, was not disagreeable news, because now I could appear as I was, in a married condition; so I told my son before I came from him that I believed I should marry a gentleman who had a plantation near mine; and though I was legally free to marry, as to any obligation that was on me before, yet that I was shy of it lest the blot should some time or other be revived, and it might make a husband uneasy. My son, the same kind, dutiful, and obliging creature as ever, treated me now at his own house, paid me my hundred pound, and sent me home again loaded with presents.

Some time after this, I let my son know I was married

and invited him over to see us, and my husband wrote a very obliging letter to him also, inviting him to come and see him; and he came accordingly some months after and happened to be there just when my cargo from England came in, which I let him believe belonged all to my husband's estate and not to me.

It must be observed that when the old wretch, my brother (husband), was dead, I then freely gave my husband an account of all that affair, and of this cousin, as I called him before, being my own son by that mistaken match. He was perfectly easy in the account and told me he should have been easy if the old man, as we called him, had been alive; "for," said he, "it was no fault of yours nor of his; it was a mistake impossible to be prevented." He only reproached him with desiring me to conceal it, and to live with him as a wife after I knew that he was my brother; that, he said, was a vile part. Thus all these little difficulties were made easy, and we lived together with the greatest kindness and comfort imaginable. We are now grown old; I am come back to England, being almost seventy years of age, my husband sixty-eight, having performed much more than the limited terms of my transportation; and now, notwithstanding all the fatigues and all the miseries we have both gone through, we are both in good heart and health. My husband remained there some time after me to settle our affairs, and at first I had intended to go back to him, but at his desire I altered that resolution, and he is come over to England also, where we resolve to spend the remainder of our years in sincere penitence for the wicked lives we have lived.

Written in the year 1683.

FINIS

A NOTE ON THE TEXT

The text of this edition, which is based on the third edition of *Moll Flanders,* published in December 1722 by Chetwood, contains the corrections made by Defoe subsequent to the first edition (January 1722). The spelling and punctuation have largely been brought into conformity with modern British usage.

THE HISTORY OF THE ADVENTURES OF

JOSEPH ANDREWS

AND HIS FRIEND MR. ABRAHAM ADAMS

Written in imitation of the manner of Cervantes
by
HENRY FIELDING

PREFACE

As it is possible the mere English reader may have a different idea of romance from the author of these little[1] volumes, and may consequently expect a kind of entertainment not to be found, nor which was even intended, in the following pages, it may not be improper to premise a few words concerning this kind of writing, which I do not remember to have seen hitherto attempted in our language.

The Epic, as well as the Drama, is divided into tragedy and comedy. Homer, who was the father of this species of poetry, gave us a pattern of both these, though that of the latter kind is entirely lost, which, Aristotle tells us, bore the same relation to comedy which his *Iliad* bears to tragedy. And, perhaps, that we have no more instances of it among the writers of antiquity is owing to the loss of this great pattern, which, had it survived, would have found its imitators equally with the other poems of this great original.

And farther, as this poetry may be tragic or comic, I will not scruple to say it may be likewise either in verse or prose: for though it wants one particular which the critic enumerates in the constituent parts of an epic poem, namely, metre, yet, when any kind of writing contains all its other parts, such as fable, action, characters, sentiments, and diction, and is deficient in metre only, it seems, I think, reasonable to refer it to the epic; at least, as no critic hath thought proper to range it under any other head or to assign it a particular name to itself.

Thus the *Telemachus* of the archbishop of Cambray appears to me of the epic kind, as well as the *Odyssey* of Homer; indeed, it is much fairer and more reasonable to give it a name common with that species from which it differs only in a single instance than to confound it with those which it resembles in no other. Such are those voluminous works commonly called Romances, namely, *Clelia, Cleopatra, Astraea, Cassandra,* the *Grand Cyrus,* and innumerable others, which contain, as I apprehend, very little instruction or entertainment.

Now, a comic romance is a comic epic poem in prose, differing from comedy as the serious epic from tragedy, its action being more extended and comprehensive, containing a much larger circle of incidents, and introducing a greater variety of characters. It differs from the serious romance in its fable and action in this, that as in the one these are grave and solemn, so in the other they are light and ridiculous; it differs in its characters by introducing persons of inferior rank, and consequently of inferior manners, whereas the grave romance sets the highest before us; lastly, in its sentiments and diction, by preserving the ludicrous instead of the sublime. In the diction, I think, burlesque itself may be sometimes admitted, of which many instances will occur in this work, as in the description of the battles, and some other places, not necessary to be pointed out to the classical reader, for whose entertainment those parodies or burlesque imitations are chiefly calculated.

But though we have sometimes admitted this in our diction, we have carefully excluded it from our sentiments and characters, for there it is never properly introduced, unless in writings of the burlesque kind, which this is not intended to be. Indeed, no two species of writing can differ more widely than the comic and the burlesque, for as the latter is ever the exhibition of what is monstrous and unnatural, and where our delight, if we examine it, arises from the surprising absurdity, as in appropriating the manners of the highest to the lowest, or *è converso;* so in the former we should ever confine ourselves strictly to nature, from the just imitation of which will flow all the pleasure we can this way convey to a sensible reader. And perhaps there is one reason why a comic writer should of all others be the least excused for deviating from nature, since it may not be always so easy for a serious poet to meet with the great and the admirable, but life everywhere furnishes an accurate observer with the ridiculous.

I have hinted this little concerning burlesque: because I have often heard that name given to performances which have been truly of the comic kind from the author's having sometimes admitted it in his diction only, which, as it is the dress of poetry, doth, like the dress of men, establish characters (the one of the whole poem, and the other of the whole man), in vulgar opinion, beyond any of their greater excellences; but surely, a certain drollery in style, where the characters and sentiments are perfectly natural, no more constitutes the burlesque than an empty pomp and dignity of words, where everything else is mean and low, can entitle any performance to the appellation of the true sublime.

And I apprehend my Lord Shaftesbury's opinion of mere burlesque agrees with mine when he asserts, There is no such thing to be found in the writings of the ancients. But perhaps I have less abhorrence than he professes for it, and that, not because I have had some little success on the stage this way, but rather as it contributes more to exquisite mirth and laughter than any other; and these are probably more wholesome physic for the mind, and conduce better to purge away spleen, melancholy, and ill affections, than is generally imagined. Nay, I will appeal to common observation whether the same companies are not found more full of good humour and benevolence after they have been sweetened for two or three hours with entertainments of this kind than when soured by a tragedy or a grave lecture.

But to illustrate all this by another science, in which, perhaps, we shall see the distinction more clearly and plainly, let us examine the works of a comic history-painter, with those performances which the Italians call *caricatura*, where we shall find the true excellence of the former to consist in the exactest copying of nature; insomuch that a judicious eye instantly rejects anything *outré*, any liberty which the painter hath taken with the features of that *alma mater*. Whereas in the *caricatura* we allow all licence: Its aim is to exhibit monsters, not men; and all distortions and exaggerations whatever are within its proper province.

Now, what *caricatura* is in painting, burlesque is in writing, and in the same manner the comic writer and painter correlate to each other. And here I shall observe that, as in the former the painter seems to have the advantage; so it is in the latter infinitely on the side of the writer; for the Monstrous is much easier to paint than describe, and the Ridiculous to describe than paint.

And though perhaps this latter species doth not in either science so strongly affect and agitate the muscles as the other, yet it will be owned, I believe, that a more rational and useful pleasure arises to us from it. He who should call the ingenious Hogarth a burlesque painter would, in my opinion, do him very little honour; for sure it is much easier, much less the subject of admiration, to paint a man with a nose, or any other feature, of a preposterous size, or to expose him in some absurd or monstrous attitude, than to express the affections of men on canvas. It hath been thought a vast commendation of a painter to say his figures seem to breathe, but surely it is a much greater and nobler applause that they appear to think.

But to return: the ridiculous only, as I have before said, falls within my province in the present work. Nor will some explanation of this word be thought impertinent by the reader, if he considers how wonderfully it hath been mistaken, even by writers who have professed it; for to what but such a mistake can we attribute the many attempts to ridicule the blackest villainies, and, what is yet worse, the most dreadful calamities? What could exceed the absurdity of an author who should write the comedy of Nero, with the merry incident of ripping up his mother's belly; or what would give a greater shock to humanity than an attempt to expose the miseries of poverty and distress to ridicule? And yet the reader will not want much learning to suggest such instances to himself.

Besides, it may seem remarkable that Aristotle, who is so fond and free of definitions, hath not thought proper to define the ridiculous. Indeed, where he tells us it is proper to comedy, he hath remarked that villainy is not its object, but he hath not, as I remember, positively asserted what is. Nor doth the Abbé Bellegarde, who hath written a treatise on this subject, though he shows us many species of it, once trace it to its fountain.

The only source of the true ridiculous (as it appears to me) is affectation. But though it arises from one spring only, when we consider the infinite streams into which this one branches, we shall presently cease to admire at the copious field it affords to an observer. Now, affectation proceeds from one of these two causes: vanity or hypocrisy; for as vanity puts us on affecting false characters, in order to purchase applause, so hypocrisy sets us on an endeavour to avoid censure, by concealing our vices under an appearance of their opposite virtues. And though these two causes are often confounded (for there is some difficulty in distinguishing them), yet, as they proceed from very different motives, so they are as clearly distinct in their operations; for, indeed, the affectation which arises from vanity is nearer to truth than the other, as it hath not that violent repugnancy of nature to struggle with which that of the hypocrite hath. It may be likewise noted that affectation doth not imply an absolute negation of those qualities which are affected, and therefore, though, when it proceeds from hypocrisy, it be nearly allied to deceit, yet when it comes from vanity only, it partakes of the nature of ostentation; for instance, the affectation of liberality in a vain man differs visibly from the same affectation in the avaricious; for though the vain man is not what he would appear, or hath not the virtue he affects, to the degree he would be thought to have it, yet it sits less awkwardly on him than on the avaricious man, who is the very reverse of what he would seem to be.

From the discovery of this affectation arises the ridiculous —which always strikes the reader with surprise and pleasure; and that in a higher and stronger degree when the affectation arises from hypocrisy than when from vanity; for to discover anyone to be the exact reverse of what he affects is more surprising, and consequently more ridiculous, than to find him a little deficient in the quality he desires the reputation of. I might observe that our Ben Jonson, who of all men understood the ridiculous the best, hath chiefly used the hypocritical affectation.

Now from affectation only, the misfortunes and calamities of life, or the imperfections of nature, may become the objects of ridicule. Surely he hath a very ill-framed mind who can look on ugliness, infirmity, or poverty as ridiculous in themselves, nor do I believe any man living who meets a dirty fellow riding through the streets in a cart is struck with an idea of the ridiculous from it; but if he should see the same figure descend from his coach and six, or bolt from his chair with his hat under his arm, he would then begin to laugh, and with justice. In the same manner, were we to enter a poor house and behold a wretched family shivering with cold and languishing with hunger, it would not incline us to laughter (at least we must have very diabolical natures if it would); but should we discover there a grate, instead of coals, adorned with flowers, empty plate, or china dishes on the sideboard, or any other affectation of riches and finery, either on their persons or in their furniture, we might then indeed be excused for ridiculing so fantastical an appearance. Much less are natural imperfections the object of derision; but when ugliness aims at the applause of beauty, or lameness endeavours to display agility, it is then that these unfortunate circumstances, which at first moved our compassion, tend only to raise our mirth.

The poet [1] carries this very far:

> None are for being what they are in fault,
> But for not being what they would be thought

—where if the metre would suffer the word "ridiculous" to close the first line, the thought would be rather more proper. Great vices are the proper objects of our detestation, smaller faults, of our pity; but affectation appears to me the only true source of the ridiculous.

But perhaps it may be objected to me that I have against my own rules introduced vices, and of a very black kind, into this work. To which I shall answer: First, that it is very difficult to pursue a series of human actions and keep clear from them. Secondly, that the vices to be found here are rather the accidental consequences of some human frailty or foible than causes habitually existing in the mind. Thirdly, that they are never set forth as the objects of ridicule, but detestation. Fourthly, that they are never the principal figure at that time on the scene; and lastly, they never produce the intended evil.

Having thus distinguished *Joseph Andrews* from the productions of romance writers on the one hand and burlesque writers on the other, and given some few very short hints (for I intended no more) of this species of writing, which I have affirmed to be hitherto unattempted in our language, I shall leave to my good-natured reader to apply my piece to my observations, and will detain him no longer than with a word concerning the characters in this work.

And here I solemnly protest I have no intention to vilify or asperse anyone; for though everything is copied from the book of nature, and scarce a character or action produced which I have not taken from my own observations and experience, yet I have used the utmost care to obscure the persons by such different circumstances, degrees, and colours, that it will be impossible to guess at them with any degree of certainty; and if it ever happens otherwise, it is only where the failure characterized is so minute that it is a foible only which the party himself may laugh at as well as any other.

As to the character of Adams, as it is the most glaring in the whole, so I conceive it is not to be found in any book now extant. It is designed a character of perfect simplicity, and as the goodness of his heart will recommend him to the good-natured, so I hope it will excuse me to the gentlemen of his cloth, for whom, while they are worthy of their sacred order, no man can possibly have a greater respect. They will therefore excuse me, notwithstanding the low adventures in which he is engaged, that I have made him a clergyman, since no other office could have given him so many opportunities of displaying his worthy inclinations.

[illegible]; so I hope it will excuse me to the gentlemen of [illegible] cloth, for whom, while they are worthy of their [illegible] order, no man can possibly have a greater respect. They will therefore excuse me, notwithstanding the low adventures in which he is engaged, that I have made him a clergyman; since no other office could have given him so many opportunities of displaying his worthy inclinations.

CONTENTS

CHAPTER PAGE

BOOK II

BOOK IV

BOOK ONE

CHAPTER I: *Of writing lives in general, and particularly of* Pamela; *with a word by the bye of Colley Cibber and others.*

It is a trite but true observation that examples work more forcibly on the mind than precepts, and if this be just in what is odious and blameable, it is more strongly so in what is amiable and praiseworthy. Here emulation most effectually operates upon us, and inspires our imitation in an irresistible manner. A good man, therefore, is a standing lesson to all his acquaintance, and of far greater use in that narrow circle than a good book.

But, as it often happens that the best men are but little known, and consequently cannot extend the usefulness of their examples a great way, the writer may be called in aid to spread their history farther, and to present the amiable pictures to those who have not the happiness of knowing the originals; and so, by communicating such valuable patterns to the world, he may perhaps do a more extensive service to mankind than the person whose life originally afforded the pattern.

In this light I have always regarded those biographers who have recorded the actions of great and worthy persons of both sexes. Not to mention those ancient writers which of late days are little read, being written in obsolete, and, as they are generally thought, unintelligible languages, such as Plutarch, Nepos, and others which I heard of in my youth; our own language affords many of excellent use and instruction, finely calculated to sow the seeds of virtue in youth, and very easy to be comprehended by persons of moderate capacity. Such as the history of John the Great, who, by his brave and heroic actions against men of large and athletic bodies, obtained the glorious appellation of the Giant-Killer; that of an Earl of Warwick, whose Christian name was Guy; the lives of Argalus and Parthenia; and, above all, the history of those seven worthy personages, the Champions of

Christendom. In all these delight is mixed with instruction, and the reader is almost as much improved as entertained.

But I pass by these and many others to mention two books, lately published, which represent an admirable pattern of the amiable in either sex. The former of these, which deals in male virtue, was written by the great person himself, who lived the life he hath recorded, and is by many thought to have lived such a life only in order to write it; the other, communicated to us by an historian who borrows his lights, as the common method is, from authentic papers and records. The reader, I believe, already conjectures I mean the lives of Mr. Colley Cibber and of Mrs. Pamela Andrews. How artfully doth the former, by insinuating that he escaped being promoted to the highest stations in church and state, teach us a contempt of worldly grandeur! how strongly doth he inculcate an absolute submission to our superiors! Lastly, how completely doth he arm us against so uneasy, so wretched, a passion as the fear of shame! how clearly doth he expose the emptiness and vanity of that phantom, reputation!

What the female readers are taught by the memoirs of Mrs. Andrews is so well set forth in the excellent essays or letters prefixed to the second and subsequent editions of that work that it would be here a needless repetition. The authentic history with which I now present the public is an instance of the great good that book is likely to do, and of the prevalence of example which I have just observed, since it will appear that it was by keeping the excellent pattern of his sister's virtues before his eyes that Mr. Joseph Andrews was chiefly enabled to preserve his purity in the midst of such great temptations. I shall only add that this character of male chastity, though doubtless as desirable and becoming in one part of the human species as in the other, is almost the only virtue which the great apologist hath not given himself for the sake of giving the example to his readers.

CHAPTER II: *Of Mr. Joseph Andrews, his birth, parentage, education, and great endowments, with a word or two concerning ancestors.*

MR. JOSEPH ANDREWS, the hero of our ensuing history, was esteemed to be the only son of Gaffer and Gammer Andrews, and brother to the illustrious Pamela, whose virtue is at present so famous. As to his ancestors, we have searched with great diligence but little success, being unable to trace them farther than his great-grandfather, who, as an elderly person in the parish remembers to have heard his father say, was an excellent cudgel-player. Whether he had any ancestors before this, we must leave to the opinion of our curious reader, finding nothing of sufficient certainty to rely on. However, we cannot omit inserting an epitaph which an ingenious friend of ours hath communicated:

Stay, traveller, for underneath this pew
Lies fast asleep that merry man Andrew:
When the last day's great sun shall gild the skies,
Then he shall from his tomb get up and rise.
Be merry while thou canst, for surely thou
Shalt shortly be as sad as he is now.

The words are almost out of the stone with antiquity. But it is needless to observe that Andrew here is writ without an *s*, and is, besides, a Christian name. My friend moreover conjectures this to have been the founder of that sect of laughing philosophers since called Merry-Andrews.

To waive, therefore, a circumstance, which, though mentioned in conformity to the exact rules of biography, is not greatly material, I proceed to things of more consequence. Indeed, it is sufficiently certain that he had as many ancestors as the best man living, and perhaps, if we look five or six hundred years backwards, might be related to some persons of very great figure at present, whose ancestors within half the last century are buried in as great obscurity. But suppose, for argument's sake, we should admit that he had no ancestors at all, but had sprung up, according to the modern phrase, out of a dunghill, as the Athenians pretended they themselves did from the earth, would not this *autokopros* * have been justly entitled to all the praise arising from his own virtues? Would it not be hard that a man who hath no ancestors should therefore be rendered incapable of acquiring honour, when we see so many who have no virtues enjoying the honour of their forefathers? At ten years old (by which time his education was advanced to writing and reading) he was bound an apprentice, according to the statute, to Sir Thomas Booby, an uncle of Mr. Booby's by the father's side. Sir Thomas having then an estate in his own hands, the young Andrews was at first employed in what in the country they call keeping birds. His office was to perform the part the ancients assigned to the god Priapus, which deity the moderns call by the name of Jack-o'-Lent; but, his voice being so extremely musical that it rather allured the birds than terrified them, he was soon transplanted from the fields into the dog-kennel, where he was placed under the huntsman, and made what sportsmen term Whipper-in. For this place likewise the sweetness of his voice disqualified him, the dogs preferring the melody of his chiding to all the alluring notes of the huntsman, who soon became so incensed at it that he desired Sir Thomas to provide otherwise for him, and constantly laid every fault the dogs were at to the account of the poor boy, who was now transplanted to the stable. Here he soon gave proofs of his strength and agility beyond his years, and constantly rode the most spirited and vicious horses to water with an intrepidity which surprised everyone. While he was in this station, he rode several races for Sir Thomas, and this with such expertness and success that the neighbouring gentlemen frequently solicited the knight to permit little Joey (for so he was called) to ride their matches. The best gamesters, before they laid their money, always inquired which horse little Joey was to ride; and the bets were rather proportioned by the rider than by the horse himself, especially after he had scornfully refused a considerable bribe to play booty on such an occasion. This extremely raised his character, and so pleased the Lady Booby that she desired to have him (being now seventeen years of age) for her own foot-boy. Joey was now preferred from the stable to attend on his lady, to go on her errands, stand behind her chair, wait at her tea-table, and carry her prayer-book to church, at which place his voice gave him an opportunity of distinguishing himself by singing psalms; he behaved likewise in every other respect so well at divine service that it recommended him to the notice of Mr. Abraham Adams, the curate, who took an opportunity one day, as he was drinking a cup of ale in Sir Thomas's kitchen, to ask the young man several questions concerning religion, with his answers to which he was wonderfully pleased.

CHAPTER III: *Of Mr. Abraham Adams the curate, Mrs. Slipslop the chambermaid, and others.*

MR. ABRAHAM ADAMS was an excellent scholar. He was a perfect master of the Greek and Latin languages, to which he added a great share of knowledge in the Oriental tongues, and could read and translate French, Italian, and Spanish. He had applied many years to the most severe study, and had treasured up a fund of learning rarely to be met with in a university. He was, besides, a man of good sense, good parts, and good nature, but was at the same time as entirely ignorant of the ways of this world as an infant just entered into it could possibly be. As he had never any intention to deceive, so he never suspected such a design in others. He was generous, friendly, and brave, to an excess, but simplicity was his characteristic: he did no more than Mr. Colley Cibber apprehend any such passions as malice and envy to exist in mankind; which was indeed less remarkable in a country parson than in a gentleman who hath passed his life behind the scenes, a place which hath been seldom thought the school of innocence, and where a very little observation would have convinced the great apologist that those passions have a real existence in the human mind.

His virtue and his other qualifications, as they rendered him equal to his office, so they made him an agreeable and valuable companion, and had so much endeared and well recommended him to a bishop that at the age of fifty he was provided with a handsome income of twenty-three pounds a year; which, however, he could not make any great figure with because he lived in a dear country and was a little incumbered with a wife and six children.

It was this gentleman who, having, as I have said, observed the singular devotion of young Andrews, had found means to question him concerning several particulars, as, how many books there were in the New Testament? which were they? how many chapters they contained? and such like; to all which, Mr. Adams privately said, he answered much better than Sir Thomas or two other neighbouring justices of the peace could probably have done.

Mr. Adams was wonderfully solicitous to know at what time, and by what opportunity, the youth became acquainted with these matters. Joey told him that he had very early learnt to read and write by the goodness of his father, who, though he had not interest enough to get him into a charity-school, because a cousin of his father's landlord did not vote on the right side for a church-warden in a borough-town, yet had been himself at the expense of sixpence a week for his learning. He told him likewise that ever since he was in Sir Thomas's family he had employed all his hours of leisure in reading good books; that he had read the Bible, the *Whole Duty of Man*, and Thomas à Kempis, and that, as often as he could without being perceived, he had studied a great good book which lay open in the hall window, where he had read, "as how the devil carried away half a church in sermon-time, without hurting one of the congregation; and as how a field of corn ran away down a hill with all the trees upon it, and covered another man's meadow." This sufficiently assured Mr. Adams that the good book meant could be no other than Baker's *Chronicle.*

The curate, surprised to find such instances of industry and application in a young man who had never met with the least encouragement, asked him if he did not extremely regret the want of a liberal education, and the not having been born of parents who might have indulged his talents and desire of knowledge? To which he answered, he hoped he had profited somewhat better from the books he had read than to lament his condition in this world. That, for his part, he was perfectly content with the state to which he was called, that he should endeavour to improve his talent, which was all required of him, but not repine at his own lot, nor envy those of his betters. "Well said, my lad," replied the curate, "and I wish some who have read many more good books, nay, and some who have written good books themselves, had profited so much by them."

Adams had no nearer access to Sir Thomas or my lady than through the waiting-gentlewoman, for Sir Thomas was too apt to estimate men merely by their dress, or fortune; and my lady was a woman of gaiety, who had been blessed with a town education, and never spoke of any of her country neighbours by any other appellation than that of the Brutes. They both regarded the curate as a kind of domestic only, belonging to the parson of the parish, who was at this time at variance with the knight; for the parson had for many years lived in a constant state of civil war, or, which is perhaps as bad, of civil law, with Sir Thomas himself and the tenants of his manor. The foundation of this quarrel was a modus,[1] by setting which aside an advantage of several shillings per annum would have accrued to the rector; but he had not yet been able to accomplish his purpose, and had reaped hitherto nothing better from the suits than the pleasure (which he used indeed frequently to say was no small one) of reflecting that he had utterly undone many of the poor tenants, though he had at the same time greatly impoverished himself.

Mrs. Slipslop, the waiting-gentlewoman, being herself the daughter of a curate, preserved some respect for Adams;

she professed great regard for his learning and would frequently dispute with him on points of theology, but always insisted on a deference to be paid to her understanding, as she had been frequently at London and knew more of the world than a country parson could pretend to.

She had in these disputes a particular advantage over Adams, for she was a mighty affecter of hard words, which she used in such a manner that the parson, who durst not offend her by calling her words in question, was frequently at some loss to guess her meaning, and would have been much less puzzled by an Arabian manuscript.

Adams therefore took an opportunity one day, after a pretty long discourse with her on the essence (or, as she pleased to term it, the incense) of matter, to mention the case of young Andrews, desiring her to recommend him to her lady as a youth very susceptible of learning and one whose instruction in Latin he would himself undertake, by which means he might be qualified for a higher station than that of a footman; and added, she knew it was in his master's power easily to provide for him in a better manner. He therefore desired that the boy might be left behind under his care.

"La, Mr. Adams," said Mrs. Slipslop, "do you think my lady will suffer any preambles about any such matter? She is going to London very concisely, and I am confidous would not leave Joey behind her on any account, for he is one of the genteelest young fellows you may see in a summer's day, and I am confidous she would as soon think of parting with a pair of her grey mares, for she values herself as much on the one as the other." Adams would have interrupted, but she proceeded: "And why is Latin more necessitous for a footman than a gentleman? It is very proper that you clergymen must learn it, because you can't preach without it, but I have heard gentlemen say in London that it is fit for nobody else. I am confidous my lady would be angry with me for mentioning it, and I shall draw myself into no such delemy." At which words her lady's bell rung, and Mr. Adams was forced to retire, nor could he gain a second opportunity with her before their London journey, which happened a few days afterwards. However, Andrews behaved very thankfully and gratefully to him for his intended kindness, which he told him he never would forget, and at the same time received from the good man many admonitions concerning the regulation of his future conduct and his perseverance in innocence and industry.

CHAPTER IV: *What happened after their journey to London.*

No sooner was young Andrews arrived at London than he began to scrape an acquaintance with his party-coloured brethren, who endeavoured to make him despise his former course of life. His hair was cut after the newest fashion and became his chief care; he went abroad with it all the morning in papers, and dressed it out in the afternoon. They could not, however, teach him to game, swear, drink, nor any other genteel vice the town abounded with. He applied most of his leisure hours to music, in which he greatly improved himself and became so perfect a connoisseur in that art that he led the opinion of all the other footmen at an opera and they never condemned or applauded a single song contrary to his approbation or dislike. He was a little too forward in riots, at the play-houses and assemblies, and when he attended his lady at church (which was but seldom) he behaved with less seeming devotion than formerly; however, if he was outwardly a pretty fellow, his morals remained entirely uncorrupted, though he was at the same time smarter and genteeler than any of the beaux in town, either in or out of livery.

His lady, who had often said of him that Joey was the handsomest and genteelest footman in the kingdom, but that it was a pity he wanted spirit, began now to find that fault no longer; on the contrary, she was frequently heard to cry out, "Aye, there is some life in this fellow." She plainly saw the effects which the town air hath on the soberest constitutions. She would now walk out with him into Hyde Park in a morning, and when tired, which happened almost every minute, would lean on his arm, and converse with him in great familiarity. Whenever she stepped out of her coach she would take him by the hand and sometimes, for fear of stumbling, press it very hard; she admitted him to deliver messages at her bed-side in a morning, leered at him at table, and indulged him in all those innocent freedoms which women of figure may permit without the least sully of their virtue.

But though their virtue remains unsullied, yet now and then some small arrows will glance on the shadow of it, their reputation; and so it fell out to Lady Booby, who happened to be walking arm-in-arm with Joey one morning in Hyde Park when Lady Tittle and Lady Tattle came accidentally by in their coach. "Bless me," says Lady Tittle, "can I believe my eyes? Is that Lady Booby?" "Surely," says Tattle. "But what makes you surprised?" "Why, is not that her footman?" replied Tittle. At which Tattle laughed, and cried, "An old business, I assure you; is it possible you should not have heard it? The whole town hath known it this half year." The consequence of this interview was a whisper through a hundred visits, which were separately performed by the two ladies * the same afternoon, and might have had a mischievous effect had it not been stopped by two fresh reputations which were published the day afterwards and engrossed the whole talk of the town.

But whatever opinion or suspicion the scandalous inclination of defamers might entertain of Lady Booby's innocent freedoms, it is certain they made no impression on young Andrews, who never offered to encroach beyond the liberties which his lady allowed him.—A behaviour which she imputed to the violent respect he preserved for her, and which served only to heighten a something she began to conceive, and which the next chapter will open a little farther.

CHAPTER V: *The death of Sir Thomas Booby, with the affectionate and mournful behaviour of his widow, and the great purity of Joseph Andrews.*

AT THIS time an accident happened which put a stop to those agreeable walks, which probably would have soon puffed up the cheeks of Fame, and caused her to blow her brazen trumpet through the town, and this was no other than the death of Sir Thomas Booby, who, departing this life, left his disconsolate lady confined to her house as closely as if she herself had been attacked by some violent disease. During the first six days the poor lady admitted none but Mrs. Slipslop and three female friends, who made a party at cards; but on the seventh she ordered Joey, whom, for a good reason, we shall hereafter call Joseph, to bring up her teakettle. The lady, being in bed, called Joseph to her, bade him sit down, and, having accidentally laid her hand on his, she asked him if he had ever been in love. Joseph answered, with some confusion, it was time enough for one so young as himself to think on such things. "As young as you are," replied the lady, "I am convinced you are no stranger to that passion. Come, Joey," says she, "tell me truly, who is the happy girl whose eyes have made a conquest of you?" Joseph returned that all the women he had ever seen were equally indifferent to him. "Oh then," said the lady, "you are a general lover. Indeed, you handsome fellows, like handsome women, are very long and difficult in fixing: but yet you shall never persuade me that your heart is so insusceptible of affection. I rather impute what you say to your secrecy, a very commendable quality, and what I am far from being angry with you for. Nothing can be more unworthy in a young man than to betray any intimacies with the ladies." "Ladies! madam," said Joseph, "I am sure I never had the impudence to think of any that deserve that name." "Don't pretend to too much modesty," said she, "for that sometimes may be impertinent, but pray answer me this question. Suppose a lady should happen to like you, suppose she should prefer you to all your sex, and admit you to the same familiarities as you might have hoped for if you had been born her equal—are you certain that no vanity could tempt you to discover her? Answer me honestly, Joseph; have you so much more sense, and so much more virtue, than you handsome young fellows generally have, who make no scruple of sacrificing our dear reputation to your pride without considering the great obligation we lay on you by our condescension and confidence? Can you keep a secret, my Joey?" "Madam," says he, "I hope your ladyship can't tax me with ever betraying the secrets of the family; and I hope, if you was to turn me away, I might have that character of you." "I don't intend to turn you away, Joey," said she, and sighed; "I am afraid it is not in my power." She then raised herself a little in her bed and discovered one of the whitest necks that ever was seen, at which Joseph blushed. "La!" says she, in an affected surprise, "what am I doing? I have trusted myself with a man alone, naked in bed; suppose you should have any wicked intentions upon my honour, how should I defend myself?" Joseph protested that he never had the least evil design against her. "No," says she, "perhaps you may not call your designs wicked; and perhaps they are not so." He swore they were not. "You misunderstand me," says she. "I mean, if they were against my honour, they may not be wicked; but the world calls them so. But then, say you, the world will never know anything of the matter; yet would not that be trusting to your secrecy? Must not my reputation be then in your power? Would you not then be my master?" Joseph begged her ladyship to be comforted, for that he would never imagine the least wicked thing against her, and that he had rather die a thousand deaths than give her any reason to suspect him. "Yes," said she, "I must have reason to suspect you. Are you not a man? And without vanity I may pretend to some charms. But perhaps you may fear I should prosecute you—indeed I hope you do—and yet heaven knows I should never have the confidence to appear before a court of justice, and you know, Joey, I am of a forgiving temper. Tell me, Joey, don't you think I should forgive you?" "Indeed, madam," says Joseph, "I will never do anything to disoblige your ladyship." "How," says she, "do you think it would not disoblige me then? Do you think I would willingly suffer you?" "I don't understand you, madam," says Joseph. "Don't you?" said she. "Then you are either a fool or pretend to be so; I find I was mistaken in you. So get you downstairs and never let me see your face again; your pretended innocence cannot impose on me." "Madam," said Joseph, "I would not have your ladyship think any evil of me. I have always endeavoured to be a dutiful servant both to you and my master." "O thou villain!" answered my lady; "why didst thou mention the name of that dear man unless to torment me, to bring his precious memory to my mind" (and then she burst into a fit of tears). "Get thee from my sight! I shall never endure thee more." At which words she turned away from him, and Joseph retreated from the room in a most disconsolate condition and writ that letter which the reader will find in the next chapter.

CHAPTER VI: *How Joseph Andrews writ a letter to his sister Pamela.*

"To Mrs. Pamela Andrews, living with Squire Booby.

"Dear Sister—Since I received your letter of your good lady's death, we have had a misfortune of the same kind in our family. My worthy master Sir Thomas died about four days ago, and, what is worse, my poor lady is certainly gone distracted. None of the servants expected her to take it so to heart, because they quarrelled almost every day of their lives—but no more of that, because you know, Pamela, I never loved to tell the secrets of my master's family, but to be sure you must have known they never loved one another, and I have heard her ladyship wish His Honour dead above a thousand times, but nobody knows what it is to lose a friend till they have lost him.

"Don't tell anybody what I write, because I should not care to have folks say I discover what passes in our family, but if it had not been so great a lady I should have thought she had had a mind to me. Dear Pamela, don't tell anybody, but she ordered me to sit down by her bed-side, when she was naked in bed, and she held my hand, and talked exactly as a lady does to her sweet-heart in a stage-play, which I have seen in Covent Garden, while she wanted him to be no better than he should be.

"If Madam be mad, I shall not care for staying long in the family, so I heartily wish you could get me a place, either at the Squire's or some other neighbouring gentleman's, unless it be true that you are going to be married to Parson Williams, as folks talk, and then I should be very willing to be his clerk, for which you know I am qualified, being able to read and to set a psalm.

"I fancy I shall be discharged very soon; and the moment I am, unless I hear from you, I shall return to my old master's country-seat, if it be only to see Parson Adams, who is the best man in the world. London is a bad place, and there is so little good fellowship that the next-door neighbours don't know one another. Pray give my service to all friends that inquire for me; so I rest

"Your loving brother,
"JOSEPH ANDREWS."

As soon as Joseph had sealed and directed this letter he walked downstairs, where he met Mrs. Slipslop, with whom we shall take this opportunity to bring the reader a little better acquainted. She was a maiden gentlewoman of about forty-five years of age who, having made a small slip in her youth, had continued a good maid ever since. She was not at this time remarkably handsome, being very short and rather too corpulent in body and somewhat red, with the addition of pimples in the face. Her nose was likewise rather too large and her eyes too little, nor did she resemble a cow so much in her breath as in two brown globes which she carried before her; one of her legs was also a little shorter than the other, which occasioned her to limp as she walked. This fair creature had long cast the eyes of affection on Joseph, in which she had not met with quite so good success as she probably wished, though, besides the allurements of her native charms, she had given him tea, sweetmeats, wine, and many other delicacies, of which, by keeping the keys, she had the absolute command. Joseph, however, had not returned the least gratitude to all these favours, not even so much as a kiss; though I would not insinuate she was so easily to be satisfied, for surely then he would have been highly blameable. The truth is, she was arrived at an age when she thought she might indulge herself in any liberties with a man without the danger of bringing a third person into the world to betray them. She imagined that by so long a self-denial she had not only made amends for the small slip of her youth above hinted at, but had likewise laid up a quantity of merit to excuse any future failings. In a word, she resolved to give a loose to her amorous inclinations, and to pay off the debt of pleasure which she found she owed herself as fast as possible.

With these charms of person, and in this disposition of mind, she encountered poor Joseph at the bottom of the stairs, and asked him if he would drink a glass of something good this morning. Joseph, whose spirits were not a little cast down, very readily and thankfully accepted the offer, and together they went into a closet, where, having delivered him a full glass of ratifia and desired him to sit down, Mrs. Slipslop thus began:

"Sure nothing can be a more simple contract in a woman, than to place her affections on a boy. If I had ever thought it would have been my fate I should have wished to die a thousand deaths rather than live to see that day. If we like a man, the lightest hint sophisticates. Whereas a boy proposes upon us to break through all the regulations of modesty before we can make any oppression upon him." Joseph, who did not understand a word she said, answered, "Yes, madam." "Yes, madam!" replied Mrs. Slipslop with some warmth, "Do you intend to result my passion? Is it not enough, ungrateful as you are, to make no return to all the favours I have done you, but you must treat me with ironing? Barbarous monster! how have I deserved that my passion should be resulted and treated with ironing?" "Madam," answered Joseph, "I don't understand your hard words, but I am certain you have no occasion to call me ungrateful, for, so far from intending you any wrong, I have always loved you as well as if you had been my own mother." "How, sirrah," says Mrs. Slipslop in a rage. "Your own mother? Do you assinuate that I am old enough to be your mother? I don't know what a stripling may think, but I believe a man would refer me to any green-sickness silly girl whatsomdever. But I ought to despise you rather than be angry with you for referring the conversation of girls to that of a woman of sense." "Madam," says Joseph, "I am sure I have always valued the honour you did me by your conversation, for I know you are a woman of learning." "Yes, but, Joseph," said she, a little softened by the compliment to her learning, "if you had a value for me, you certainly would have found some method of showing it me; for I am convicted you must see the value I have for you. Yes, Joseph, my eyes, whether I would or no, must have declared a passion I cannot conquer.——Oh! Joseph!"

As when a hungry tigress who long has traversed the woods in fruitless search sees within the reach of her claws a lamb, she prepares to leap on her prey; or as a voracious pike, of immense size, surveys through the liquid element a roach or gudgeon which cannot escape her jaws, opens them wide to swallow the little fish; so did Mrs. Slipslop prepare to lay her violent amorous hands on the poor Joseph, when luckily her mistress's bell rung and delivered the intended martyr from her clutches. She was obliged to leave him abruptly and to defer the execution of her purpose till some other time. We shall therefore return to the Lady Booby and give our reader some account of her behaviour after she was left by Joseph in a temper of mind not greatly different from that of the inflamed Slipslop.

CHAPTER VII: *Sayings of wise men. A dialogue between the lady and her maid, and a panegyric, or rather satire, on the passion of love, in the sublime style.*

It is the observation of some ancient sage, whose name I have forgot, that passions operate differently on the human mind, as diseases on the body, in proportion to the strength or weakness, soundness or rottenness, of the one and the other.

We hope, therefore, a judicious reader will give himself some pains to observe, what we have so greatly laboured to describe, the different operations of this passion of love in the gentle and cultivated mind of the Lady Booby from those which it effected in the less polished and coarser disposition of Mrs. Slipslop.

Another philosopher, whose name also at present escapes my memory, hath somewhere said that resolutions taken in the absence of the beloved object are very apt to vanish in its presence, on both which wise sayings the following chapter may serve as a comment.

No sooner had Joseph left the room in the manner we have before related than the lady, enraged at her disappointment, began to reflect with severity on her conduct. Her love was now changed to disdain, which pride assisted to torment her. She despised herself for the meanness of her passion, and Joseph for its ill success. However, she had now got the better of it in her own opinion, and determined immediately to dismiss the object. After much tossing and turning in her bed, and many soliloquies, which if we had no better matter for our reader we would give him, she at last rung the bell as above-mentioned and was presently attended by Mrs. Slipslop, who was not much better pleased with Joseph than the lady herself.

"Slipslop," said Lady Booby, "when did you see Joseph?" The poor woman was so surprised at the unexpected sound of his name at so critical a time that she had the greatest difficulty to conceal the confusion she was under from her mistress, whom she answered, nevertheless, with pretty good confidence, though not entirely void of fear of suspicion, that she had not seen him that morning. "I am afraid," said Lady Booby, "he is a wild young fellow." "That he is," said Slipslop, "and a wicked one too. To my knowledge he games, drinks, swears, and fights eternally; besides, he is horribly indicted to wenching." "Aye!" said the lady, "I never heard that of him." "Oh, madam!" answered the other, "he is so lewd a rascal that if your ladyship keeps him much longer you will not have one virgin in your house except myself. And yet I can't conceive what the wenches see in him, to be so foolishly fond as they are; in my eyes, he is as ugly a scarecrow as I ever upheld." "Nay," said the lady, "the boy is well enough." "La, ma'am," cries Slipslop, "I think him the ragmaticallest fellow in the family." "Sure, Slipslop," says she, "you are mistaken. But which of the women do you most suspect?" "Madam," says Slipslop, "there is Betty the chamber-maid, I am almost convicted, is with child by him." "Aye!" says the lady, "then pray pay her her wages instantly. I will keep no such sluts in my family. And as for Joseph, you may discard him too." "Would your ladyship have him paid off immediately?" cries Slipslop, "for perhaps, when Betty is gone, he may mend; and really the boy is a good servant, and a strong healthy luscious boy enough." "This morning," answered the lady, with some vehemence. "I wish, madam," cries Slipslop, "your ladyship would be so good as to try him a little longer." "I will not have my commands disputed," said the lady; "sure you are not fond of him yourself." "I, madam!" cries Slipslop, reddening, if not blushing. "I should be sorry to think your ladyship had any reason to respect me of fondness for a fellow; and if it be your pleasure, I shall fulfill it with as much reluctance as possible." "As little, I suppose you mean," said the lady; "and so about it instantly." Mrs. Slipslop went out, and the lady had scarce taken two turns before she fell to knocking and ringing with great violence. Slipslop, who did not travel post-haste, soon returned, and was countermanded as to Joseph, but ordered to send Betty about her business without delay. She went out a second time with much greater alacrity than before, when the lady began immediately to accuse herself of want of resolution, and to apprehend the return of her affection, with its pernicious consequences; she therefore applied herself again to the bell and resummoned Mrs. Slipslop into her presence, who again returned, and was told by her mistress that she had considered better of the matter and was absolutely resolved to turn away Joseph, which she ordered her to do immediately. Slipslop, who knew the violence of her lady's temper, and would not venture her place for any Adonis or Hercules in the universe, left her a third time; which she had no sooner done, than the little god Cupid, fearing he had not yet done the lady's business, took a fresh arrow with the sharpest point out of his quiver and shot it directly into her heart; in other and plainer language, the lady's passion got the better of her reason. She called back Slipslop once more, and told her she had resolved to see the boy and examine him herself, therefore bid her send him up. This wavering in her mistress's temper probably put something into the waiting-gentlewoman's head not necessary to mention to the sagacious reader.

Lady Booby was going to call her back again, but could not prevail with herself. The next consideration therefore was how she should behave to Joseph when he came in. She resolved to preserve all the dignity of the woman of fashion to her servant, and to indulge herself in this last view of Joseph (for that she was most certainly resolved it should be) at his own expense, by first insulting and then discarding him.

O Love, what monstrous tricks dost thou play with thy votaries of both sexes! How dost thou deceive them, and make them deceive themselves! Their follies are thy delight!

Their sighs make thee laugh, and their pangs are thy merriment!

Not the great Rich,[1] who turns men into monkeys, wheelbarrows, and whatever else best humours his fancy, hath so strangely metamorphosed the human shape, nor the great Cibber, who confounds all number, gender, and breaks through every rule of grammar at his will, hath so distorted the English language as thou dost metamorphose and distort the human senses.

Thou puttest out our eyes, stoppest up our ears, and takest away the power of our nostrils so that we can neither see the largest objects, hear the loudest noise, nor smell the most poignant perfume. Again, when thou pleasest, thou canst make a mole-hill appear as a mountain, a Jew's-harp sound like a trumpet, and a daisy smell like a violet. Thou canst make cowardice brave, avarice generous, pride humble, and cruelty tender-hearted. In short, thou turnest the heart of man inside out as a juggler doth a petticoat, and bringest whatsoever pleasest thee out from it. If there be anyone who doubts all this, let him read the next chapter.

CHAPTER VIII: *In which, after some very fine writing, the history goes on, and relates an interview between the lady and Joseph, where the latter hath set an example which we despair of seeing followed by his sex in this vicious age.*

Now the rake Hesperus had called for his breeches, and having well rubbed his drowsy eyes, prepared to dress himself for all night; by whose example his brother rakes on earth likewise leave those beds in which they had slept away the day. Now Thetis, the good housewife, began to put on the pot, in order to regale the good man Phoebus after his daily labours were over. In vulgar language, it was in the evening when Joseph attended his lady's orders.

But as it becomes us to preserve the character of this lady, who is the heroine of our tale; and as we have naturally a wonderful tenderness for that beautiful part of the human species called the fair sex, before we discover too much of her frailty to our reader it will be proper to give him a lively idea of the vast temptation which overcame all the efforts of a modest and virtuous mind, and then we humbly hope his good nature will rather pity than condemn the imperfection of human virtue.

Nay, the ladies themselves will, we hope, be induced, by

considering the uncommon variety of charms which united in this young man's person, to bridle their rampant passion for chastity and be at least as mild as their violent modesty and virtue will permit them in censuring the conduct of a woman who, perhaps, was in her own disposition as chaste as those pure and sanctified virgins who, after a life innocently spent in the gaieties of the town, begin about fifty to attend twice *per diem* at the polite churches and chapels, to return thanks for the grace which preserved them formerly amongst beaux from temptations perhaps less powerful than what now attacked the Lady Booby.

Mr. Joseph Andrews was now in the one-and-twentieth year of his age. He was of the highest degree of middle stature. His limbs were put together with great elegance and no less strength. His legs and thighs were formed in the exactest proportion. His shoulders were broad and brawny, but yet his arms hung so easily that he had all the symptoms of strength without the least clumsiness. His hair was of a nut-brown colour and was displayed in wanton ringlets down his back. His forehead was high, his eyes dark and as full of sweetness as of fire. His nose a little inclined to the Roman. His teeth white and even. His lips full, red, and soft. His beard was only rough on his chin and upper lip, but his cheeks, in which his blood glowed, were overspread with a thick down. His countenance had a tenderness joined with a sensibility inexpressible. Add to this the most perfect neatness in his dress and an air which, to those who have not seen many noblemen, would give an idea of nobility.

Such was the person who now appeared before the lady. She viewed him some time in silence, and twice or thrice before she spake changed her mind as to the manner in which she should begin. At length she said to him, "Joseph, I am sorry to hear such complaints against you. I am told you behave so rudely to the maids that they cannot do their business in quiet—I mean those who are not wicked enough to hearken to your solicitations. As to others, they may, perhaps, not call you rude, for there are wicked sluts, who make one ashamed of one's own sex and are as ready to admit any nauseous familiarity as fellows to offer it; nay, there are such in my family but they shall not stay in it; that impudent trollop who is with child by you is discharged by this time."

As a person who is struck through the heart with a thunderbolt looks extremely surprised, nay, and perhaps is so too, thus the poor Joseph received the false accusation of his mistress; he blushed and looked confounded, which she misinterpreted to be symptoms of his guilt, and thus went on: "Come hither, Joseph; another mistress might discard you for these offences, but I have a compassion for your youth, and if I could be certain you would be no more guilty—consider, child" (laying her hand carelessly upon his), "you are a handsome young fellow and might do better; you might make your fortune." "Madam," said Joseph, "I do assure your ladyship I don't know whether any maid in the house is man or woman." "Oh fie! Joseph," answered the lady, "don't commit another crime in denying the truth. I could pardon the first; but I hate a liar." "Madam," cries Joseph, "I hope your ladyship will not be offended at my asserting my innocence, for by all that is sacred, I have never offered more than kissing." "Kissing!" said the lady with great discomposure of countenance, and more redness in her cheeks than anger in her eyes; "do you call that no crime? Kissing, Joseph, is as a prologue to a play. Can I believe a young fellow of your age and complexion will be content with kissing? No, Joseph, there is no woman who grants that but will grant more, and I am deceived greatly in you if you would not put her closely to it. What would you think, Joseph, if I admitted you to kiss me?" Joseph replied he would sooner die than have any such thought. "And yet, Joseph," returned she, "ladies have admitted their footmen to such familiarities; and footmen, I confess to you, much less deserving them, fellows without half your charms, for such might almost excuse the crime. Tell me, therefore, Joseph, if I should admit you to such freedom, what would you think of me?—tell me freely." "Madam," said Joseph, "I should think your ladyship condescended a great deal below yourself." "Pugh!" said she, "that I am to answer to myself. But would not you insist on more? Would you be contented with a kiss? Would not your inclinations be all on fire rather by such a favour?" "Madam," said Joseph, "if they were, I hope I should be able to control them without suffering them to get the better of my virtue."—You have heard, reader, poets talk of the statue of Surprise; you have heard likewise, or else you have heard very little, how surprise made one of the sons of Croesus speak, though he was dumb. You have seen the faces, in the eighteen-penny gallery, when, through the trap-door, to soft or no music, Mr. Bridgwater, Mr. William Mills,[1] or some other of ghostly appearance, hath ascended, with a face all pale with powder and a shirt all bloody with ribbons; but from none of these, nor from

Phidias or Praxiteles if they should return to life, no, not from the inimitable pencil of my friend Hogarth, could you receive such an idea of surprise as would have entered in at your eyes had they beheld the Lady Booby when those last words issued out from the lips of Joseph.—"Your virtue!" (said the lady, recovering after a silence of two minutes) "I shall never survive it. Your virtue!—intolerable confidence! Have you the assurance to pretend that when a lady demeans herself to throw aside the rules of decency in order to honour you with the highest favour in her power your virtue should resist her inclination? that when she had conquered her own virtue she should find an obstruction in yours?" "Madam," said Joseph, "I can't see why her having no virtue should be a reason against my having any, or why, because I am a man, or because I am poor, my virtue must be subservient to her pleasures." "I am out of patience," cries the lady. "Did ever mortal hear of a man's virtue! Did ever the greatest, or the gravest, men pretend to any of this kind! Will magistrates who punish lewdness, or parsons who preach against it, make any scruple of committing it? And can a boy, a stripling, have the confidence to talk of his virtue?" "Madam," says Joseph, "that boy is the brother of Pamela, and would be ashamed that the chastity of his family, which is preserved in her, should be stained in him. If there are such men as your ladyship mentions, I am sorry for it, and I wish they had an opportunity of reading over those letters which my father hath sent me of my sister Pamela's; nor do I doubt but such an example would amend them." "You impudent villain!" cries the lady in a rage, "do you insult me with the follies of my relation, who hath exposed himself all over the country upon your sister's account? a little vixen whom I have always wondered my late Lady Booby ever kept in her house. Sirrah! get out of my sight, and prepare to set out this night; for I will order you your wages immediately and you shall be stripped and turned away." "Madam," says Joseph, "I am sorry I have offended your ladyship, I am sure I never intended it." "Yes, sirrah," cries she, "you have had the vanity to misconstrue the little innocent freedom I took in order to try whether what I had heard was true. O' my conscience, you have had the assurance to imagine I was fond of you myself." Joseph answered he had only spoke out of tenderness for his virtue; at which words she flew into a violent passion, and, refusing to hear more, ordered him instantly to leave the room.

He was no sooner gone than she burst forth into the

following exclamation: "Whither doth this violent passion hurry us? What meannesses do we submit to from its impulse? Wisely we resist its first and least approaches, for it is then only we can assure ourselves the victory. No woman could ever safely say, so far only will I go. Have I not exposed myself to the refusal of my footman? I cannot bear the reflection." Upon which she applied herself to the bell and rung it with infinite more violence than was necessary, the faithful Slipslop attending near at hand—to say the truth, she had conceived a suspicion at her last interview with her mistress and had waited ever since in the antechamber, having carefully applied her ears to the key-hole during the whole time that the preceding conversation passed between Joseph and the lady.

CHAPTER IX: *What passed between the lady and Mrs. Slipslop, in which we prophesy there are some strokes which everyone will not truly comprehend at the first reading.*

"SLIPSLOP," said the lady, "I find too much reason to believe all thou hast told me of this wicked Joseph. I have determined to part with him instantly, so go you to the steward and bid him pay him his wages." Slipslop, who had preserved hitherto a distance to her lady, rather out of necessity than inclination, and who thought the knowledge of this secret had thrown down all distinction between them, answered her mistress very pertly, She wished she knew her own mind, and that she was certain she would call her back again before she was got half-way downstairs. The lady replied, She had taken a resolution, and was resolved to keep it. "I am sorry for it," cries Slipslop, "and if I had known you would have punished the poor lad so severely you should never have heard a particle of the matter. Here's a fuss indeed about nothing." "Nothing!" returned my lady. "Do you think I will countenance lewdness in my house?" "If you will turn away every footman," said Slipslop, "that is a lover of the sport, you must soon open the coach door yourself, or get a set of mophrodites to wait upon you, and I am sure I hated the sight of them even singing in an opera." "Do as I bid you," says my lady, "and don't shock my ears with your beastly language." "Marry-come-up," cries Slipslop, "people's ears are sometimes the nicest part about them."

The lady, who began to admire the new style in which her waiting-gentlewoman delivered herself, and by the conclusion of her speech suspected somewhat of the truth, called her back and desired to know what she meant by the extraordinary degree of freedom in which she thought proper to indulge her tongue. "Freedom!" says Slipslop, "I don't know what you call freedom, madam; servants have tongues as well as their mistresses." "Yes, and saucy ones too," answered the lady, "but I assure you I shall bear no such impertinence." "Impertinence! I don't know that I am impertinent," says Slipslop. "Yes, indeed you are," cries my lady, "and unless you mend your manners, this house is no place for you." "Manners!" cries Slipslop, "I never was thought to want manners, nor modesty neither; and for places, there are more places than one; and I know what I know." "What do you know, mistress?" answered the lady. "I am not obliged to tell everybody," says Slipslop, "any more than I am obliged to keep it a secret." "I desire you would provide yourself," answered the lady. "With all my heart," replied the waiting-gentlewoman, and so departed in a passion, and slapped the door after her.

The lady too plainly perceived that her waiting-gentlewoman knew more than she would willingly have had her acquainted with; and this she imputed to Joseph's having discovered to her what passed at the first interview. This therefore blew up her rage against him and confirmed her in a resolution of parting with him.

But the dismissing Mrs. Slipslop was a point not so easily to be resolved upon. She had the utmost tenderness for her reputation, as she knew on that depended many of the most valuable blessings of life; particularly cards, making curtseys in public places, and, above all, the pleasure of demolishing the reputations of others, in which innocent amusement she had an extraordinary delight. She therefore determined to submit to any insult from a servant rather than run a risk of losing the title to so many great privileges.

She therefore sent for her steward, Mr. Peter Pounce, and ordered him to pay Joseph his wages, to strip off his livery, and turn him out of the house that evening.

She then called Slipslop up, and, after refreshing her spirits with a small cordial, which she kept in her closet, she began in the following manner:

"Slipslop, why will you, who know my passionate temper, attempt to provoke me by your answers? I am convinced you are an honest servant, and should be very unwilling to part with you. I believe, likewise, you have found me an indulgent mistress on many occasions, and have as little reason on your side to desire a change. I can't help being surprised, therefore, that you will take the surest method to offend me. I mean, repeating my words, which you know I have always detested."

The prudent waiting-gentlewoman had duly weighed the whole matter and found, on mature deliberation, that a good place in possession was better than one in expectation. As she found her mistress, therefore, inclined to relent, she thought proper also to put on some small condescension, which was as readily accepted, and so the affair was reconciled, all offences forgiven, and a present of a gown and petticoat made her, as an instance of her lady's future favour.

She offered once or twice to speak in favour of Joseph, but found her lady's heart so obdurate that she prudently dropped all such efforts. She considered there were more footmen in the house, and some as stout fellows, though not quite so handsome as Joseph; besides, the reader hath already seen her tender advances had not met with the encouragement she might have reasonably expected. She thought she had thrown away a great deal of sack and sweetmeats on an ungrateful rascal, and, being a little inclined to the opinion of that female sect who hold one lusty young fellow to be near as good as another lusty young fellow, she at last gave up Joseph and his cause, and, with a triumph over her passion highly commendable, walked off with her present, and with great tranquility paid a visit to a stone-bottle, which is of sovereign use to a philosophical temper.

She left not her mistress so easy. The poor lady could not reflect without agony that her dear reputation was in the power of her servants. All her comfort, as to Joseph, was that she hoped he did not understand her meaning; at least she could say for herself, she had not plainly expressed anything to him, and as to Mrs. Slipslop, she imagined she could bribe her to secrecy.

But what hurt her most was that in reality she had not so entirely conquered her passion; the little god lay lurking in her heart, though anger and disdain so hoodwinked her that she could not see him. She was a thousand times on the very brink of revoking the sentence she had passed against the poor youth. Love became his advocate, and whispered many things in his favour. Honour likewise endeavoured to vindicate his crime, and Pity to mitigate his punishment. On the other side, Pride and Revenge spoke as loudly against him; and thus the poor lady was tortured with perplexity, opposite passions distracting and tearing her mind different ways.

So have I seen, in the hall of Westminster, where Serjeant Bramble hath been retained on the right side and Serjeant Puzzle on the left, the balance of opinion (so equal were their fees) alternately incline to either scale. Now Bramble throws in an argument and Puzzle's scale strikes the beam; again, Bramble shares the like fate, overpowered by the weight of Puzzle. Here Bramble hits, there Puzzle strikes; here one has you, there t'other has you, till at last all becomes one scene of confusion in the tortured minds of the hearers; equal wagers are laid on the success, and neither judge nor jury can possibly make anything of the matter, all things are so enveloped by the careful serjeants in doubt and obscurity.

Or, as it happens in the conscience, where honour and honesty pull one way, and a bribe and necessity another.—— If it was our present business only to make similes, we could produce many more to this purpose; but a simile (as well as a word) to the wise.—We shall therefore see a little after our hero, for whom the reader is doubtless in some pain.

CHAPTER X: *Joseph writes another letter. His transactions with Mr. Peter Pounce, etc., with his departure from Lady Booby.*

THE disconsolate Joseph would not have had an understanding sufficient for the principal subject of such a book as this if he had any longer misunderstood the drift of his mistress, and, indeed, that he did not discern it sooner, the reader will be pleased to apply to an unwillingness in him to discover what he must condemn in her as a fault. Having therefore quitted her presence, he retired into his own garret and entered himself into an ejaculation on the numberless calamities which attended beauty and the misfortune it was to be handsomer than one's neighbours.

He then sat down and addressed himself to his sister Pamela, in the following words:

"DEAR SISTER PAMELA—Hoping you are well, what news have I to tell you! O Pamela, my mistress is fallen in love with me—that is, what great folks call falling in love—she has a mind to ruin me; but I hope I shall have more resolution and more grace than to part with my virtue to any lady upon earth.

"Mr. Adams hath often told me that chastity is as great a virtue in a man as in a woman. He says he never knew any more than his wife, and I shall endeavour to follow his example. Indeed, it is owing entirely to his excellent sermons and advice, together with your letters, that I have been able to resist a temptation which, he says, no man complies with but he repents in this world or is damned for it in the next; and why should I trust to repentance on my death-bed since I may die in my sleep? What fine things are good advice and good examples! But I am glad she turned me out of the chamber as she did, for I had once almost forgotten every word Parson Adams had ever said to me.

"I don't doubt, dear sister, but you will have grace to preserve your virtue against all trials; and I beg you earnestly to pray I may be enabled to preserve mine, for truly it is very severely attacked by more than one; but I hope I shall copy your example, and that of Joseph my namesake, and maintain my virtue against all temptations."

Joseph had not finished his letter when he was summoned downstairs by Mr. Peter Pounce to receive his wages; for, besides that out of eight pounds a year he allowed his father and mother four, he had been obliged, in order to furnish himself with musical instruments, to apply to the generosity of the afore-said Peter, who, on urgent occasions, used to advance the servants their wages—not before they were due, but before they were payable, that is, perhaps half a year after they were due; and this at the moderate premium of fifty per cent. or a little more; by which charitable methods, together with lending money to other people, and even to his own master and mistress, the honest man had, from nothing, in a few years amassed a small sum of twenty thousand pounds or thereabouts.

Joseph, having received his little remainder of wages, and having stripped off his livery, was forced to borrow a frock and breeches of one of the servants (for he was so beloved in the family, that they would all have lent him anything), and, being told by Peter that he must not stay a moment longer in the house than was necessary to pack up his linen, which he easily did in a very narrow compass, he took a melancholy leave of his fellow-servants and set out at seven in the evening.

He had proceeded the length of two or three streets before

he absolutely determined with himself whether he should leave the town that night, or, procuring a lodging, wait till the morning. At last, the moon shining very bright helped him to come to a resolution of beginning his journey immediately, to which likewise he had some other inducements, which the reader, without being a conjurer, cannot possibly guess till we have given him those hints which it may be now proper to open.

CHAPTER XI: *Of several new matters not expected.*

IT IS an observation sometimes made that, to indicate our idea of a simple fellow, we say he is easily to be seen through. Nor do I believe it a more improper denotation of a simple book. Instead of applying this to any particular performance, we choose rather to remark the contrary in this history, where the scene opens itself by small degrees, and he is a sagacious reader who can see two chapters before him.

For this reason, we have not hitherto hinted a matter which now seems necessary to be explained, since it may be wondered at, first, that Joseph made such extraordinary haste out of town, which hath been already shown; and secondly, which will be now shown, that, instead of proceeding to the habitation of his father and mother, or to his beloved sister Pamela, he chose rather to set out full speed to the Lady Booby's country-seat, which he had left on his journey to London.

Be it known then, that in the same parish where this seat stood there lived a young girl whom Joseph (though the best of sons and brothers) longed more impatiently to see than his parents or his sister. She was a poor girl who had formerly been bred up in Sir John's family, whence, a little before the journey to London, she had been discarded by Mrs. Slipslop on account of her extraordinary beauty—for I never could find any other reason.

This young creature (who now lived with a farmer in the parish) had been always beloved by Joseph, and returned his affection. She was two years only younger than our hero. They had been acquainted from their infancy, and had conceived a very early liking for each other, which had grown to such a degree of affection that Mr. Adams had with much ado prevented them from marrying and persuaded them to wait till a few years' service and thrift had a little improved their experience and enabled them to live comfortably together.

They followed this good man's advice, as indeed his word was little less than a law in his parish; for as he had shown his parishioners, by an uniform behaviour of thirty-five years' duration, that he had their good entirely at heart, so they consulted him on every occasion and very seldom acted contrary to his opinion.

Nothing can be imagined more tender than was the parting between these two lovers. A thousand sighs heaved the bosom of Joseph, a thousand tears distilled from the lovely eyes of Fanny (for that was her name). Though her modesty would only suffer her to admit his eager kisses, her violent love made her more than passive in his embrace, and she often pulled him to her breast with a soft pressure which, though perhaps it would not have squeezed an insect to death, caused more emotion in the heart of Joseph than the closest Cornish hug could have done.

The reader may perhaps wonder that so fond a pair should, during a twelvemonth's absence, never converse with one another; indeed, there was but one reason which did, or could, have prevented them, and this was that poor Fanny could neither write nor read, nor could she be prevailed upon to transmit the delicacies of her tender and chaste passion by the hands of an amanuensis.

They contented themselves, therefore, with frequent inquiries after each other's health, with a mutual confidence in each other's fidelity, and the prospect of their future happiness.

Having explained these matters to our reader, and, as far as possible, satisfied all his doubts, we return to honest Joseph, whom we left just set out on his travels by the light of the moon.

Those who have read any romance or poetry, ancient or modern, must have been informed that Love hath wings—by which they are not to understand, as some young ladies by mistake have done, that a lover can fly, the writers, by this ingenious allegory, intending to insinuate no more than that lovers do not march like horse-guards; in short, that they put the best leg foremost, which our lusty youth, who could walk with any man, did so heartily on this occasion that within four hours he reached a famous house of hospitality well known to the western traveller. It presents you a lion on the sign-post, and the master, who was christened

Timotheus, is commonly called plain Tim. Some have conceived that he hath particularly chosen the lion for his sign as he doth in countenance greatly resemble that magnanimous beast, though his disposition savours more of the sweetness of the lamb. He is a person well received among all sorts of men, being qualified to render himself agreeable to any, as he is well versed in history and politics, hath a smattering in law and divinity, cracks a good jest, and plays wonderfully well on the French horn.

A violent storm of hail forced Joseph to take shelter in this inn, where he remembered Sir Thomas had dined in his way to town. Joseph had no sooner seated himself by the kitchen fire than Timotheus, observing his livery, began to condole the loss of his late master, who was, he said, his very particular and intimate acquaintance, with whom he had cracked many a merry bottle, aye many a dozen in his time. He then remarked that all those things were over now, all past, and just as if they had never been, and concluded with an excellent observation on the certainty of death, which his wife said was indeed very true. A fellow now arrived at the same inn with two horses, one of which he was leading farther down into the country to meet his master; these he put into the stable, and came and took his place by Joseph's side, who immediately knew him to be the servant of a neighbouring gentleman who used to visit at their house.

This fellow was likewise forced in by the storm, for he had orders to go twenty miles farther that evening, and luckily on the same road which Joseph himself intended to take. He therefore embraced this opportunity of complimenting his friend with his master's horse (notwithstanding he had received express commands to the contrary), which was readily accepted; and so after they had drank a loving pot, and the storm was over, they set out together.

CHAPTER XII: *Containing many surprising adventures which Joseph Andrews met with on the road, scarce credible to those who have never travelled in a stage-coach.*

Nothing remarkable happened on the road till their arrival at the inn to which the horses were ordered, whither they came about two in the morning. The moon then shone very bright; and Joseph, making his friend a present of a pint of wine, and thanking him for the favour of his horse, notwithstanding all entreaties to the contrary proceeded on his journey on foot.

He had not gone above two miles, charmed with the hopes of shortly seeing his beloved Fanny, when he was met by two fellows in a narrow lane and ordered to stand and deliver. He readily gave them all the money he had, which was somewhat less than two pounds, and told them he hoped they would be so generous as to return him a few shillings to defray his charges on his way home.

One of the ruffians answered with an oath, "Yes, we'll give you something, presently—but first strip and be d—ned to you." "Strip," cried the other, "or I'll blow your brains to the devil." Joseph, remembering that he had borrowed his coat and breeches of a friend, and that he should be ashamed of making any excuse for not returning them, replied he hoped they would not insist on his clothes, which were not worth much, but consider the coldness of the night. "You are cold, are you, you rascal!" says one of the robbers, "I'll warm you with a vengeance," and, damning his eyes, snapped a pistol at his head; which he had no sooner done than the other levelled a blow at him with his stick, which Joseph, who was expert at cudgel-playing, caught with his, and returned the favour so successfully on his adversary that he laid him sprawling at his feet, and at the same instant received a blow from behind with the butt end of a pistol from the other villain which felled him to the ground and totally deprived him of his senses.

The thief who had been knocked down had now recovered himself, and both together fell to belabouring poor Joseph with their sticks till they were convinced they had put an end to his miserable being. They then stripped him entirely naked, threw him into a ditch, and departed with their booty.

The poor wretch, who lay motionless a long time, just began to recover his senses as a stage-coach came by. The postilion, hearing a man's groans, stopped his horses, and told the coachman he was certain there was a dead man lying in the ditch, for he heard him groan. "Go on, sirrah," says the coachman, "we are confounded late, and have no time to look after dead men." A lady, who heard what the postilion said, and likewise heard the groan, called eagerly to the coachman to stop and see what was the matter. Upon which he bid the postilion alight and look into the ditch. He did so, and returned, "That there was a man sitting upright, as naked as ever he was born."—"O J—sus!"

cried the lady. "A naked man! Dear coachman, drive on and leave him." Upon this the gentlemen got out of the coach; and Joseph begged them to have mercy upon him, for that he had been robbed, and almost beaten to death. "Robbed," cries an old gentleman. "Let us make all the haste imaginable, or we shall be robbed too." A young man who belonged to the law answered he wished they had passed by without taking any notice, but that now they might be proved to have been last in his company; if he should die they might be called to some account for his murder. He therefore thought it advisable to save the poor creature's life, for their own sakes, if possible; at least, if he died, to prevent the jury's finding that they fled for it. He was therefore of opinion to take the man into the coach, and carry him to the next inn. The lady insisted that he should not come into the coach. That if they lifted him in, she would herself alight; for she had rather stay in that place to all eternity than ride with a naked man. The coachman objected that he could not suffer him to be taken in, unless somebody would pay a shilling for his carriage the four miles. Which the two gentlemen refused to do. But the lawyer, who was afraid of some mischief happening to himself if the wretch was left behind in that condition, saying, no man could be too cautious in these matters, and that he remembered very extraordinary cases in the books, threatened the coachman, and bid him deny taking him up at his peril; for that if he died, he should be indicted for his murder; and if he lived, and brought an action against him, he would willingly take a brief in it.—These words had a sensible effect on the coachman, who was well acquainted with the person who spoke them; and the old gentleman above mentioned, thinking the naked man would afford him frequent opportunities of showing his wit to the lady, offered to join with the company in giving a mug of beer for his fare; till, partly alarmed by the threats of the one, and partly by the promises of the other, and being perhaps a little moved with compassion at the poor creature's condition, who stood bleeding and shivering with the cold, he at length agreed; and Joseph was now advancing to the coach, where, seeing the lady, who held the sticks of her fan before her eyes, he absolutely refused, miserable as he was, to enter, unless he was furnished with sufficient covering to prevent giving the least offence to decency—so perfectly modest was this young man; such mighty effects had the spotless example of the amiable Pamela, and the excellent sermons of Mr. Adams, wrought upon him.

Though there were several great-coats about the coach, it was not easy to get over this difficulty which Joseph had started. The two gentlemen complained they were cold, and could not spare a rag, the man of wit saying with a laugh, that charity began at home; and the coachman, who had two great-coats spread under him, refused to lend either, lest they should be made bloody; the lady's footman desired to be excused for the same reason, which the lady herself, notwithstanding her abhorrence of a naked man, approved; and it is more than probable poor Joseph, who obstinately adhered to his modest resolution, must have perished unless the postilion (a lad who hath since been transported for robbing a henroost) had voluntarily stripped off a great-coat, his only garment, at the same time swearing a great oath (for which he was rebuked by the passengers) that he would rather ride in his shirt all his life than suffer a fellow-creature to lie in so miserable a condition.

Joseph, having put on the great-coat, was lifted into the coach, which now proceeded on its journey. He declared himself almost dead with the cold, which gave the man of wit an occasion to ask the lady if she could not accommodate him with a dram. She answered, with some resentment, she wondered at his asking her such a question; but assured him she never tasted any such thing.

The lawyer was inquiring into the circumstances of the robbery when the coach stopped and one of the ruffians, putting a pistol in, demanded their money of the passengers, who readily gave it them; and the lady, in her fright, delivered up a little silver bottle, of about a half-pint size, which the rogue, clapping it to his mouth, and drinking her health, declared held some of the best Nantes he had ever tasted—this the lady afterwards assured the company was the mistake of her maid, for that she had ordered her to fill the bottle with Hungary-water.

As soon as the fellows were departed, the lawyer, who had, it seems, a case of pistols in the seat of the coach, informed the company that if it had been daylight, and he could have come at his pistols, he would not have submitted to the robbery; he likewise set forth that he had often met highwaymen when he travelled on horseback, but none ever durst attack him, concluding that, if he had not been more afraid for the lady than for himself, he should not have now parted with his money so easily.

As wit is generally observed to love to reside in empty pockets, so the gentleman whose ingenuity we have above remarked, as soon as he had parted with his money, began to grow wonderfully facetious. He made frequent allusions to Adam and Eve, and said many excellent things on figs and fig-leaves; which perhaps gave more offence to Joseph than to any other in the company.

The lawyer likewise made several very pretty jests, without departing from his profession. He said if Joseph and the lady were alone, he would be more capable of making a conveyance to her, as his affairs were not fettered with any incumbrance; he'd warrant he soon suffered a recovery by a writ of entry, which was the proper way to create heirs in tail; that, for his own part, he would engage to make so firm a settlement in a coach that there should be no danger of an ejectment, with an inundation of the like gibberish, which he continued to vent till the coach arrived at an inn, where one servant-maid only was up, in readiness to attend the coachman, and furnish him with cold meat and a dram. Joseph desired to alight, and that he might have a bed prepared for him, which the maid readily promised to perform; and, being a good-natured wench, and not so squeamish as the lady had been, she clapped a large faggot on the fire, and, furnishing Joseph with a great-coat belonging to one of the hostlers, desired him to sit down and warm himself while she made his bed. The coachman, in the meantime, took an opportunity to call up a surgeon who lived within a few doors; after which he reminded his passengers how late they were, and, after they had taken leave of Joseph, hurried them off as fast as he could.

The wench soon got Joseph to bed and promised to use her interest to borrow him a shirt, but imagined, as she afterwards said, by his being so bloody, that he must be a dead man; she ran with all speed to hasten the surgeon, who was more than half dressed, apprehending that the coach had been overturned and some gentleman or lady hurt. As soon as the wench had informed him at his window that it was a poor foot-passenger who had been stripped of all he had, and almost murdered, he chid her for disturbing him so early, slipped off his clothes again, and very quietly returned to bed and to sleep.

Aurora now began to show her blooming cheeks over the hills, whilst ten millions of feathered songsters, in jocund chorus, repeated odes a thousand times sweeter than those of our laureate, and sung both the day and the song; when the master of the inn, Mr. Tow-wouse, arose, and, learning from his maid an account of the robbery, and the situation of his poor naked guest, he shook his head and cried, "good-lack-a-day!" and then ordered the girl to carry him one of his own shirts.

Mrs. Tow-wouse was just awake, and had stretched out her arms in vain to fold her departed husband, when the maid entered the room. "Who's there? Betty?" "Yes, madam." "Where's your master?" "He's without, madam; he hath sent me for a shirt to lend a poor naked man, who hath been robbed and murdered." "Touch one, if you dare, you slut," said Mrs. Tow-wouse. "Your master is a pretty sort of a man, to take in naked vagabonds, and clothe them with his own clothes. I shall have no such doings. If you offer to touch anything, I'll throw the chamber-pot at your head. Go, send your master to me." "Yes, madam," answered Betty. As soon as he came in, she thus began: "What the devil do you mean by this, Mr. Tow-wouse? Am I to buy shirts to lend to a set of scabby rascals?" "My dear," said Mr. Tow-wouse, "this is a poor wretch." "Yes," says she, "I know it is a poor wretch; but what the devil have we to do with poor wretches? The law makes us provide for too many already. We shall have thirty or forty poor wretches in red coats shortly." "My dear," cries Tow-wouse, "this man hath been robbed of all he hath." "Well then," says she, "where's his money to pay his reckoning? Why doth not such a fellow go to an ale-house? I shall send him packing as soon as I am up, I assure you." "My dear," said he, "common charity won't suffer you to do that." "Common charity, a f—t!" says she. "Common charity teaches us to provide for ourselves, and our families; and I and mine won't be ruined by your charity, I assure you." "Well," says he, "my dear, do as you will, when you are up; you know I never contradict you." "No," says she, "if the devil was to contradict me, I would make the house too hot to hold him."

With such-like discourses they consumed near half an hour, whilst Betty provided a shirt from the hostler, who was one of her sweet-hearts, and put it on poor Joseph. The surgeon had likewise at last visited him, and washed and dressed his wounds, and was now come to acquaint Mr. Tow-wouse that his guest was in such extreme danger of his life that he scarce saw any hopes of his recovery. "Here's a pretty kettle of fish," cries Mrs. Tow-wouse, "you have brought upon us! We are like to have a funeral at our own expense." Tow-wouse (who, notwithstanding his charity, would have given his vote as freely as ever he did at an election that any other house in the kingdom should have quiet possession of his guest) answered, "My dear, I am not to blame: he was brought hither by the stage-coach, and Betty had put him to bed before I was stirring." "I'll Betty her," says she. At which, with half her garments on, the other half under her arm, she sallied out in quest of the unfortunate Betty, whilst Tow-wouse and the surgeon went to pay a visit to poor Joseph, and inquire into the circumstances of this melancholy affair.

CHAPTER XIII: *What happened to Joseph during his sickness at the inn, with the curious discourse between him and Mr. Barnabas, the parson of the parish.*

As SOON as Joseph had communicated a particular history of the robbery, together with a short account of himself and his intended journey, he asked the surgeon if he apprehended him to be in any danger. To which the surgeon very honestly answered he feared he was, for that his pulse was very exalted and feverish, and if his fever should prove more than symptomatic, it would be impossible to save him. Joseph, fetching a deep sigh, cried, "Poor Fanny, I would I could have lived to see thee! but God's will be done."

The surgeon then advised him if he had any worldly affairs to settle that he would do it as soon as possible, for though he hoped he might recover, yet he thought himself obliged to acquaint him he was in great danger, and if the malign concoction of his humours should cause a suscitation of his fever, he might soon grow delirious and incapable to make his will. Joseph answered that it was impossible for any creature in the universe to be in a poorer condition than himself, for, since the robbery, he had not one thing of any kind whatever which he could call his own. "I had," said he, "a poor little piece of gold, which they took away, that would have been a comfort to me in all my afflictions, but surely, Fanny, I want nothing to remind me of thee. I have thy dear image in my heart, and no villain can ever tear it thence."

Joseph desired paper and pens to write a letter, but they were refused him, and he was advised to use all his endeavours to compose himself. They then left him, and Mr. Tow-wouse sent to a clergyman to come and administer his good offices to the soul of poor Joseph, since the surgeon despaired of making any successful applications to his body.

Mr. Barnabas (for that was the clergyman's name) came as soon as sent for, and, having first drank a dish of tea with the landlady, and afterwards a bowl of punch with the landlord, he walked up to the room where Joseph lay; but, finding him asleep, returned to take the other sneaker, which when he had finished, he again crept softly up to the chamber-door, and, having opened it, heard the sick man talking to himself in the following manner:

"O most adorable Pamela! most virtuous sister! whose example could alone enable me to withstand all the temptations of riches and beauty, and to preserve my virtue pure and chaste, for the arms of my dear Fanny, if it had pleased Heaven that I should ever have come unto them. What riches, or honours, or pleasures, can make us amends for the loss of innocence? Doth not that alone afford us more consolation than all worldly acquisitions? What but innocence and virtue could give any comfort to such a miserable wretch as I am? Yet these can make me prefer this sick and painful bed to all the pleasures I should have found in my lady's. These can make me face death without fear, and, though I love my Fanny more than ever man loved a woman, these can teach me to resign myself to the divine will without repining. O, thou delightful charming creature! if Heaven had indulged thee to my arms, the poorest, humblest state would have been a paradise; I could have lived with thee in the lowest cottage without envying the palaces, the dainties, or the riches of any man breathing. But I must leave thee, leave thee forever, my dearest angel! I must think of another world; and I heartily pray thou mayst meet comfort in this."—Barnabas thought he had heard enough, so downstairs he went and told Tow-wouse he could do his guest no service, for that he was very light-headed and had uttered nothing but a rhapsody of nonsense all the time he stayed in the room.

The surgeon returned in the afternoon, and found his patient in a higher fever, as he said, than when he left him, though not delirious, for, notwithstanding Mr. Barnabas's opinion, he had not been once out of his senses since his arrival at the inn.

Mr. Barnabas was again sent for and with much difficulty prevailed on to make another visit. As soon as he entered the room he told Joseph he was come to pray by him, and to prepare him for another world. In the first place, therefore, he hoped he had repented of all his sins. Joseph answered he hoped he had, but there was one thing which he knew not whether he should call a sin; if it was, he feared he should die in the commission of it; and that was the regret of parting with a young woman whom he loved as tenderly as he did his heart-strings. Barnabas bade him be assured, that any repining at the divine will was one of the greatest sins he could commit; that he ought to forget all carnal affections, and think of better things. Joseph said that neither in this world nor the next could he forget his Fanny; and that the thought, however grievous, of parting from her forever was not half so tormenting as the fear of what she would suffer when she knew his misfortune. Barnabas said that such fears argued a diffidence and despondence very criminal; that he must divest himself of all human passions and fix his heart above. Joseph answered that was what he desired to do and should be obliged to him if he would enable him to accomplish it. Barnabas replied, "That must be done by grace." Joseph besought him to discover how he might attain it. Barnabas answered, "By prayer and faith." He then questioned him concerning his forgiveness of the thieves. Joseph answered he feared that was more than he could do, for nothing would give him more pleasure than to hear they were taken. "That," cries Barnabas, "is for the sake of justice." "Yes," said Joseph, "but if I was to meet them again, I am afraid I should attack them, and kill them too, if I could." "Doubtless," answered Barnabas, "it is lawful to kill a thief; but can you say you forgive them as a Christian ought?" Joseph desired to know what that forgiveness was. "That is," answered Barnabas, "to forgive them as—as—it is to forgive them as—in short, it is to forgive them as a Christian." Joseph replied he forgave them as much as he could. "Well, well," said Barnabas, "that will do." He then demanded of him if he remembered any more sins unrepented of, and if he did, he desired him to make haste and repent of them as fast as he could, that they might repeat over a few prayers together. Joseph answered he could not recollect any great crimes he had been guilty of, and that those he had committed he was sincerely sorry for. Barnabas said that was enough, and then proceeded to prayer with all the expedition he was master of, some company then waiting for him below in the parlour, where the ingredients for punch were all in readiness but no one would squeeze the oranges till he came.

Joseph complained he was dry, and desired a little tea,

which Barnabas reported to Mrs. Tow-wouse, who answered she had just done drinking it, and could not be slopping all day, but ordered Betty to carry him up some small beer.

Betty obeyed her mistress's command; but Joseph, as soon as he had tasted it, said he feared it would increase his fever, and that he longed very much for tea. To which the good-natured Betty answered he should have tea, if there was any in the land. She accordingly went and bought him some herself and attended him with it, where we will leave her and Joseph together for some time, to entertain the reader with other matters.

CHAPTER XIV: *Being very full of adventures, which succeeded each other at the inn.*

IT WAS now the dusk of the evening, when a grave person rode into the inn, and, committing his horse to the hostler, went directly into the kitchen, and, having called for a pipe of tobacco, took his place by the fire-side, where several other persons were likewise assembled.

The discourse ran altogether on the robbery which was committed the night before, and on the poor wretch who lay above in the dreadful condition in which we have already seen him. Mrs. Tow-wouse said she wondered what the devil Tom Whipwell meant by bringing such guests to her house, when there were so many ale-houses on the road proper for their reception. But she assured him, if he died, the parish should be at the expense of the funeral. She added, Nothing would serve the fellow's turn but tea, she would assure him. Betty, who was just returned from her charitable office, answered she believed he was a gentleman, for she never saw a finer skin in her life. "Pox on his skin!" replied Mrs. Tow-wouse, "I suppose that is all we are like to have for the reckoning. I desire no such gentleman should ever call at the Dragon" (which it seems was the sign of the inn).

The gentleman lately arrived discovered a great deal of emotion at the distress of this poor creature, whom he observed to be fallen not into the most compassionate hands. And indeed, if Mrs. Tow-wouse had given no utterance to the sweetness of her temper, nature had taken such pains in her countenance that Hogarth himself never gave more expression to a picture.

Her person was short, thin, and crooked. Her forehead

projected in the middle, and thence descended in a declivity to the top of her nose, which was sharp and red, and would have hung over her lips, had not nature turned up the end of it. Her lips were two bits of skin which, whenever she spoke, she drew together in a purse. Her chin was peaked, and at the upper end of that skin which composed her cheeks stood two bones that almost hid a pair of small, red eyes. Add to this a voice most wonderfully adapted to the sentiments it was to convey, being both loud and hoarse.

It is not easy to say whether the gentleman had conceived a greater dislike for his landlady or compassion for her unhappy guest. He inquired very earnestly of the surgeon, who was now come into the kitchen, whether he had any hopes of his recovery? He begged him to use all possible means towards it, telling him it was the duty of men of all professions, to apply their skill gratis for the relief of the poor and necessitous. The surgeon answered he should take proper care, but he defied all the surgeons in London to do him any good. "Pray, sir," said the gentleman, "what are his wounds?" "Why, do you know anything of wounds?" says the surgeon (winking upon Mrs. Tow-wouse). "Sir, I have a small smattering in surgery," answered the gentleman. "A smattering—ho, ho, ho!" said the surgeon, "I believe it is a smattering indeed."

The company were all attentive, expecting to hear the doctor, who was what they call a dry fellow, expose the gentleman.

He began therefore with an air of triumph: "I suppose, sir, you have travelled." "Not really, sir," said the gentleman. "Ho! then you have practised in the hospitals perhaps." "No, sir." "Hum! not that neither? Whence, sir, then, if I may be so bold to inquire, have you got your knowledge in surgery?" "Sir," answered the gentleman, "I do not pretend to much, but the little I know I have from books." "Books!" cries the doctor; "what, I suppose you have—you have read Galen and Hippocrates!" "No, sir," said the gentleman. "How! you understand surgery," answers the doctor, "and not read Galen and Hippocrates?" "Sir," cries the other, "I believe there are many surgeons who have never read these authors." "I believe so too," says the doctor, "more shame for them; but, thanks to my education, I have them by heart, and very seldom go without them both in my pocket." "They are pretty large books," said the gentleman. "Aye," said the doctor, "I believe I know how large they are better than you."

At which he fell a-winking, and the whole company burst into a laugh.

The doctor, pursuing his triumph, asked the gentleman if he did not understand physic as well as surgery. "Rather better," answered the gentleman. "Aye, like enough," cries the doctor, with a wink; "why, I know a little of physic too." "I wish I knew half so much," said Tow-wouse, "I'd never wear an apron again." "Why, I believe, landlord," cries the doctor, "there are few men, though I say it, within twelve miles of the place that handle a fever better.—*Veniente accurrite morbo:*[1] that is my method.—I suppose, brother, you understand *Latin?*" "A little," says the gentleman. "Aye, and Greek, now, I'll warrant you: *Ton dapomibominos poluflosboio thalasses.*[2] But I have almost forgot these things; I could have repeated Homer by heart once."—"Ifags! the gentleman has caught a traitor," says Mrs. Tow-wouse; at which they all fell a-laughing.

The gentleman, who had not the least affection for joking, very contentedly suffered the doctor to enjoy his victory, which he did with no small satisfaction, and, having sufficiently sounded his depth, told him he was thoroughly convinced of his great learning and abilities, and that he would be obliged to him if he would let him know his opinion of his patient's case above-stairs. "Sir," says the doctor, "his case is that of a dead man. The contusion on his head has perforated the internal membrane of the occiput, and divellicated that radical small minute invisible nerve which coheres to the pericranium; and this was attended with a fever at first symptomatic, then pneumatic; and he is at length grown deliriuus, or delirious, as the vulgar express it."

He was proceeding in this learned manner when a mighty noise interrupted him. Some young fellows in the neighbourhood had taken one of the thieves, and were bringing him into the inn. Betty ran upstairs with this news to Joseph, who begged they might search for a little piece of broken gold which had a ribband tied to it, and which he could swear to amongst all the hoards of the richest men in the universe.

Notwithstanding the fellow's persisting in his innocence, the mob were very busy in searching him, and presently, among other things, pulled out the piece of gold just mentioned, which Betty no sooner saw, than she laid violent hands on it and conveyed it up to Joseph, who received it with raptures of joy, and, hugging it in his bosom, declared he could now die contented.

Within a few minutes afterwards, came in some other fellows, with a bundle which they had found in a ditch, and which was indeed the clothes which had been stripped off from Joseph and the other things they had taken from him. The gentleman no sooner saw the coat than he declared he knew the livery, and, if it had been taken from the poor creature above-stairs, desired he might see him, for that he was very well acquainted with the family to whom that livery belonged.

He was accordingly conducted up by Betty—but what, reader, was the surprise on both sides, when he saw Joseph was the person in bed, and when Joseph discovered the face of his good friend Mr. Abraham Adams!

It would be impertinent to insert a discourse which chiefly turned on the relation of matters already well known to the reader, for as soon as the curate had satisfied Joseph concerning the perfect health of his Fanny, he was on his side very inquisitive into all the particulars which had produced this unfortunate accident.

To return therefore to the kitchen, where a great variety of company were now assembled from all the rooms of the house, as well as the neighbourhood—so much delight do men take in contemplating the countenance of a thief.

Mr. Tow-wouse began to rub his hands with pleasure at seeing so large an assembly, who would, he hoped, shortly adjourn into several apartments in order to discourse over the robbery and drink a health to all honest men. But Mrs. Tow-wouse, whose misfortune it was commonly to see things a little perversely, began to rail at those who brought the fellow into her house, telling her husband, "They were very likely to thrive, who kept a house of entertainment for beggars and thieves."

The mob had now finished their search, and could find nothing about the captive likely to prove any evidence; for as to the clothes, though the mob were very well satisfied with that proof, yet, as the surgeon observed, they could not convict him, because they were not found in his custody; to which Barnabas agreed, and added that these were *bona waviata,* and belonged to the lord of the manor.

"How," says the surgeon, "do you say these goods belong to the lord of the manor?" "I do," cried Barnabas. "Then I deny it," says the surgeon: "what can the lord of the manor have to do in the case? Will anyone attempt to persuade me that what a man finds is not his own?" "I have heard," says an old fellow in the corner, "Justice Wiseone say that if every man had his right, whatever is found belongs to the king of London." "That may be true," says Barnabas, "in some sense, for the law makes a difference between things stolen and things found, for a thing may be stolen that never is found; and a thing may be found that never was stolen. Now goods that are both stolen and found are *waviata,* and they belong to the lord of the manor." "So the lord of the manor is the receiver of stolen goods?" says the doctor, at which there was a universal laugh, being first begun by himself.

While the prisoner, by persisting in his innocence, had almost (as there was no evidence against him) brought over Barnabas, the surgeon, Tow-wouse, and several others to his side, Betty informed them that they had overlooked a little piece of gold, which she had carried up to the man in bed, and which he offered to swear to amongst a million, aye, amongst ten thousand. This immediately turned the scale against the prisoner, and everyone now concluded him guilty. It was resolved, therefore, to keep him secured that night, and early in the morning to carry him before a justice.

CHAPTER XV: *Showing how Mrs. Tow-wouse was a little mollified; and how officious Mr. Barnabas and the surgeon were to prosecute the thief; with a dissertation accounting for their zeal, and that of many other persons not mentioned in this history.*

BETTY told her mistress she believed the man in bed was a greater man than they took him for, for, besides the extreme whiteness of his skin, and the softness of his hands, she observed a very great familiarity between the gentleman and him, and added she was certain they were intimate acquaintance, if not relations.

This somewhat abated the severity of Mrs. Tow-wouse's countenance. She said God forbid she should not discharge the duty of a Christian, since the poor gentleman was brought to her house. She had a natural antipathy to vagabonds, but could pity the misfortunes of a Christian as soon as another. Tow-wouse said, "If the traveller be a gentleman, though he hath no money about him now, we shall most likely be paid hereafter, so you may begin to score whenever you will." Mrs. Tow-wouse answered, "Hold your simple tongue, and don't instruct me in my business. I am sure I am sorry for the gentleman's misfortune with all my heart, and I hope the villain who hath used him so barbarously will be hanged. Betty, go see what he wants. God forbid he should want anything in my house."

Barnabas and the surgeon went up to Joseph to satisfy themselves concerning the piece of gold. Joseph was with difficulty prevailed upon to show it them, but would by no entreaties be brought to deliver it out of his own possession. He however attested this to be the same which had been taken from him, and Betty was ready to swear to the finding it on the thief.

The only difficulty that remained was, how to produce this gold before the justice, for as to carrying Joseph himself it seemed impossible, nor was there any great likelihood of obtaining it from him, for he had fastened it with a ribband to his arm and solemnly vowed that nothing but irresistible force should ever separate them; in which resolution, Mr. Adams, clenching a fist rather less than the knuckle of an ox, declared he would support him.

A dispute arose on this occasion concerning evidence not very necessary to be related here, after which the surgeon dressed Mr. Joseph's head, still persisting in the imminent danger in which his patient lay, but concluding, with a very important look, that he began to have some hopes, that he should send him a sanative soporiferous draught and would see him in the morning. After which Barnabas and he departed and left Mr. Joseph and Mr. Adams together.

Adams informed Joseph of the occasion of this journey which he was making to London, namely, to publish three volumes of sermons, being encouraged, as he said, by an advertisement lately set forth by the society of book-sellers, who proposed to purchase any copies offered to them at a price to be settled by two persons; but though he imagined he should get a considerable sum of money on this occasion, which his family were in urgent need of, he protested he would not leave Joseph in his present condition; finally, he told him, he had nine shillings and threepence half-penny in his pocket, which he was welcome to use as he pleased.

This goodness of Parson Adams brought tears into Joseph's eyes: he declared he had now a second reason to desire life, that he might show his gratitude to such a friend. Adams bade him be cheerful, for that he plainly saw the surgeon, besides his ignorance, desired to make a merit of curing him, though the wounds in his head, he perceived, were by no means dangerous; that he was convinced he had no fever and doubted not but he would be able to travel in a day or two.

These words infused a spirit into Joseph; he said he found himself very sore from the bruises but had no reason to think any of his bones injured, or that he had received any harm in his inside, unless that he felt something very odd in his stomach, but he knew not whether that might not arise from not having eaten one morsel for above twenty-four hours. Being then asked if he had any inclination to eat, he answered in the affirmative. Then Parson Adams desired him to name what he had the greatest fancy for, whether a poached egg or chicken broth; he answered he could eat both very well, but that he seemed to have the greatest appetite for a piece of boiled beef and cabbage.

Adams was pleased with so perfect a confirmation that he had not the least fever, but advised him to a lighter diet for that evening. He accordingly ate either a rabbit or a fowl, I never could with any tolerable certainty discover which; after this he was, by Mrs. Tow-wouse's order, conveyed into a better bed, and equipped with one of her husband's shirts.

In the morning early, Barnabas and the surgeon came to the inn in order to see the thief conveyed before the justice. They had consumed the whole night in debating what measures they should take to produce the piece of gold in evidence against him, for they were both extremely zealous in the business, though neither of them were in the least interested in the prosecution; neither of them had ever received any private injury from the fellow, nor had either of them ever been suspected of loving the public well enough to give them a sermon or a dose of physic for nothing.

To help our reader, therefore, as much as possible to account for this zeal, we must inform him that, as this parish was so unfortunate as to have no lawyer in it, there had been a constant contention between the two doctors, spiritual and physical, concerning their abilities in a science in which, as neither of them professed it, they had equal pretensions to dispute each other's opinions. These disputes were carried on with great contempt on both sides, and had almost divided the parish, Mr. Tow-wouse and one half of the neighbours inclining to the surgeon, and Mrs. Tow-wouse with the other half to the parson. The surgeon drew his knowledge from those inestimable fountains called *The Attorney's Pocket-Companion* and Mr. Jacob's *Law-Tables;* Barnabas trusted entirely to Wood's *Institutes.* It happened on this occasion, as was pretty frequently the case, that these two learned men differed about the sufficiency of evidence, the doctor being of opinion that the maid's oath would convict the prisoner without producing the gold, the parson, *è contra, totis viribus.*[1] To display their parts therefore before the justice and the parish was the sole motive which we can discover to this zeal, which both of them pretended to have for public justice.

O Vanity! how little is thy force acknowledged, or thy operations discerned! How wantonly dost thou deceive mankind under different disguises! Sometimes thou dost wear the face of pity, sometimes of generosity; nay, thou hast the assurance even to put on those glorious ornaments which belong only to heroic virtue. Thou odious, deformed monster! whom priests have railed at, philosophers despised, and poets ridiculed; is there a wretch so abandoned as to own thee for an acquaintance in public?—yet how few will refuse to enjoy thee in private? nay, thou art the pursuit of most men through their lives. The greatest villainies are daily practised to please thee, nor is the meanest thief below, or the greatest hero above, thy notice. Thy embraces are often the sole aim and sole reward of the private robbery and the plundered province. It is to pamper up thee, thou harlot, that we attempt to withdraw from others what we do not want, or to withhold from them what they do. All our passions are thy slaves. Avarice itself is often no more than thy handmaid, and even Lust thy pimp. The bully Fear like a coward flies before thee, and Joy and Grief hide their heads in thy presence.

I know thou wilt think that whilst I abuse thee I court thee, and that thy love hath inspired me to write this sarcastical panegyric on thee, but thou art deceived: I value thee not of a farthing, nor will it give me any pain if thou shouldst prevail on the reader to censure this digression as arrant nonsense, for know, to thy confusion, that I have introduced thee for no other purpose than to lengthen out a short chapter; and so I return to my history.

CHAPTER XVI: *The escape of the thief. Mr. Adams's disappointment. The arrival of two very extraordinary personages, and the introduction of Parson Adams to Parson Barnabas.*

BARNABAS and the surgeon being returned, as we have said, to the inn, in order to convey the thief before the justice, were greatly concerned to find a small accident had happened which somewhat disconcerted them, and this was no other than the thief's escape, who had modestly withdrawn himself by night, declining all ostentation, and not choosing, in imitation of some great men, to distinguish himself at the expense of being pointed at.

When the company had retired the evening before, the thief was detained in a room where the constable and one of the young fellows who took him were planted as his guard. About the second watch, a general complaint of drought was made both by the prisoner and his keepers, among whom it was at last agreed that the constable should remain on duty and the young fellow call up the tapster, in which disposition the latter apprehended not the least danger, as the constable was well armed and could besides easily summon him back to his assistance if the prisoner made the least attempt to gain his liberty.

The young fellow had not long left the room before it came into the constable's head that the prisoner might leap on him by surprise, and, thereby preventing him of the use of his weapons, especially the long staff in which he chiefly confided, might reduce the success of a struggle to an equal chance. He wisely, therefore, to prevent this inconvenience, slipped out of the room himself, and locked the door, waiting without with his staff in his hand, ready lifted to fell the unhappy prisoner, if by ill fortune he should attempt to break out.

But human life, as hath been discovered by some great man or other (for I would by no means be understood to affect the honour of making any such discovery), very much resembles a game at chess, for as in the latter, while a gamester is too attentive to secure himself very strongly on one side of the board, he is apt to leave an unguarded opening on the other, so doth it often happen in life; and so did it happen on this occasion, for, whilst the cautious constable with such wonderful sagacity had possessed himself of the door, he most unhappily forgot the window.

The thief who played on the other side no sooner perceived this opening, than he began to move that way, and, finding the passage easy, he took with him the young fellow's hat, and without any ceremony stepped into the street and made the best of his way.

The young fellow returning with a double mug of strong beer was a little surprised to find the constable at the door but much more so when, the door being opened, he perceived the prisoner had made his escape, and which way. He threw down the beer, and, without uttering anything to the constable except a hearty curse or two, he nimbly leapt out of the window and went again in pursuit of his prey, being very unwilling to lose the reward which he had assured himself of.

The constable hath not been discharged of suspicion on this account; it hath been said that, not being concerned in the taking of the thief, he could not have been entitled to any part of the reward if he had been convicted; that the thief had several guineas in his pocket; that it was very unlikely he should have been guilty of such an oversight; that his pretence for leaving the room was absurd; that it was his constant maxim that a wise man never refused money on any conditions; that at every election he always had sold his vote to both parties, etc.

But, notwithstanding these and many other such allegations, I am sufficiently convinced of his innocence, having been positively assured of it by those who received their informations from his own mouth; which, in the opinion of some moderns, is the best and indeed only evidence.

All the family were now up, and with many others assembled in the kitchen, where Mr. Tow-wouse was in some tribulation, the surgeon having declared that by law he was liable to be indicted for the thief's escape, as it was out of his house; he was a little comforted, however, by Mr. Barnabas's opinion that, as the escape was by night, the indictment would not lie.

Mrs. Tow-wouse delivered herself in the following words: "Sure never was such a fool as my husband! Would any other person living have left a man in the custody of such a drunken drowsy blockhead as Tom Suckbribe" (which was the constable's name), "and if he could be indicted without any harm to his wife and children, I should be glad of it." Then the bell rung in Joseph's room. "Why, Betty, John, chamberlain, where the devil are you all? Have you no ears, or no conscience, not to tend the sick better? See what the gentleman wants. Why don't you go yourself, Mr. Tow-wouse? But anyone may die for you; you have no more feeling than a deal-board. If a man lived a fortnight in your house without spending a penny, you would never put him in mind of it. See whether he drinks tea or coffee for breakfast." "Yes, my dear," cried Tow-wouse. She then asked the doctor and Mr. Barnabas what morning's draught they chose, who answered they had a pot of cider-and at the fire; which we will leave them merry over, and return to Joseph.

He had rose pretty early this morning, but though his wounds were far from threatening any danger, he was so sore with the bruises that it was impossible for him to think of undertaking a journey yet; Mr. Adams, therefore, whose stock was visibly decreased with the expenses of supper and breakfast, and which could not survive that day's scoring, began to consider how it was possible to recruit it. At last he cried he had luckily hit on a sure method, and, though it would oblige him to return himself home together with Joseph, it mattered not much. He then sent for Tow-wouse, and, taking him into another room, told him he wanted to borrow three guineas, for which he would put ample security into his hands. Tow-wouse, who expected a watch, or ring, or something of double the value, answered he believed he could furnish him. Upon which Adams, pointing to his saddle-bag, told him with a face and voice full of solemnity, that there were in that bag no less than nine volumes of manuscript sermons, as well worth a hundred pounds as a shilling was worth twelve pence, and that he would deposit one of the volumes in his hands by way of pledge, not doubting but that he would have the honesty to return it on his repayment of the money, for otherwise he must be a very great loser, seeing that every volume would at least bring him ten pounds, as he had been informed by a neighbouring clergyman in the country; "for," said he, "as to my own part, having never yet dealt in printing, I do not pretend to ascertain the exact value of such things."

Tow-wouse, who was a little surprised at the pawn, said (and not without some truth), that he was no judge of the price of such kind of goods, and as for money, he really was very short. Adams answered, certainly he would not scruple to lend him three guineas on what was undoubtedly worth at least ten. The landlord replied he did not believe he had so much money in the house, and, besides, he was to make up a sum.[1] He was very confident the books were of much higher value, and heartily sorry it did not suit him. He then cried out, "Coming, sir!" though nobody called, and ran downstairs without any fear of breaking his neck.

Poor Adams was extremely dejected at this disappointment, nor knew he what farther stratagem to try. He immediately applied to his pipe, his constant friend and comfort in his afflictions, and, leaning over the rails, he devoted himself to meditation, assisted by the inspiring fumes of tobacco.

He had on a nightcap drawn over his wig and a short great-coat which half covered his cassock—a dress which, added to something comical enough in his countenance, composed a figure likely to attract the eyes of those who were not overgiven to observation.

Whilst he was smoking his pipe in this posture, a coach and six, with a numerous attendance, drove into the inn. There alighted from the coach a young fellow and a brace of pointers, after which another young fellow leapt from the box and shook the former by the hand, and both together, with the dogs, were instantly conducted by Mr. Tow-wouse into an apartment, whither as they passed they entertained themselves with the following short facetious dialogue.

"You are a pretty fellow for a coachman, Jack!" says he from the coach; "you had almost overturned us just now." "Pox take you!" says the coachman. "If I had only broke your neck, it would have been saving somebody else the trouble, but I should have been sorry for the pointers." "Why, you son of a b—," answered the other, "if nobody could shoot better than you, the pointers would be of no use." "D—n me," says the coachman, "I will shoot with you, five guineas a shot." "You be hanged," says the other; "for five guineas you shall shoot at my a—." "Done," says the coachman. "I'll pepper you better than ever you was peppered by Jenny Bouncer." "Pepper your grandmother," says the other; "here's Tow-wouse will let you shoot at him for a shilling a time." "I know his honour better," cries Tow-wouse; "I never saw a surer shot at a partridge. Every man misses now and then, but if I could shoot half as well as his honour, I would desire no better livelihood than I could get by my gun." "Pox on you," said the coachman, "you demolish more game now than your head's worth. There's a bitch. Tow-wouse: by G—d she never blinked * a bird in her life." "I have a puppy not a year old shall hunt with her for a hundred," cries the other gentleman. "Done," says the coachman, "but you will be poxed before you make the bet." "If you have a mind for a bet," cries the coachman, "I'll match my spotted dog with your white bitch for a hundred play or pay." "Done," says the other, "and I'll run Baldface against Slouch with you for another." "No," cries he from the box, "but I'll venture Miss Jenny against Baldface, or Hannibal either." "Go to the devil," cries he from the coach. "I will make every bet your own way, to be sure! I will match Hannibal with Slouch for a thousand, if you dare, and I say done first."

They were now arrived, and the reader will be very contented to leave them and repair to the kitchen, where Barnabas, the surgeon, and an exciseman were smoking their pipes, over some cider-and; and where the servants who attended the two noble gentlemen we have just seen alight were now arrived.

"Tom," cries one of the footmen, "there's Parson Adams smoking his pipe in the gallery." "Yes," says Tom, "I pulled off my hat to him, and the parson spoke to me."

"Is the gentleman a clergyman, then?" says Barnabas (for his cassock had been tied up when he first arrived). "Yes, sir," answered the footman, "and one there be but few like." "Aye," said Barnabas, "if I had known it sooner, I should have desired his company; I would always show a proper respect for the cloth. But what say you, Doctor, shall we adjourn into a room, and invite him to take part of a bowl of punch?"

This proposal was immediately agreed to and executed, and Parson Adams accepting the invitation, much civility passed between the two clergymen, who both declared the great honour they had for the cloth. They had not been long together before they entered into a discourse on small tithes, which continued a full hour without the doctor or exciseman's having one opportunity to offer a word.

It was then proposed to begin a general conversation, and the exciseman opened on foreign affairs, but a word unluckily dropping from one of them introduced a dissertation on the hardships suffered by the inferior clergy, which, after a long duration, concluded with bringing the nine volumes of sermons on the carpet.

Barnabas greatly discouraged poor Adams; he said the age was so wicked that nobody read sermons. "Would you think it, Mr. Adams," said he, "I once intended to print a volume of sermons myself, and they had the approbation of two or three bishops, but what do you think a book-seller offered me?" "Twelve guineas perhaps," cried Adams. "Not twelve pence, I assure you," answered Barnabas, "nay, the dog refused me a concordance in exchange. At last I offered to give him the printing them for the sake of dedicating them to that very gentleman who just now drove his own coach into the inn, and, I assure you, he had the impudence to refuse my offer; by which means I lost a good living, that was afterwards given away in exchange for a pointer, to one who—but I will not say anything against the cloth. So you may guess, Mr. Adams, what you are to expect, for if sermons would have gone down, I believe—I will not be vain, but, to be concise with you, three bishops said they were the best that ever were writ: but indeed there are a pretty moderate number printed already, and not all sold yet." "Pray, sir," said Adams, "to what do you think the numbers may amount?" "Sir," answered Barnabas, "a book-seller told me he believed five thousand volumes at least." "Five thousand!" quoth the surgeon. "What can they be writ upon? I remember, when I was a boy, I used to read one Tillotson's sermons, and I am sure if a man practised half so much as is in one of those sermons, he will go to heaven." "Doctor," cried Barnabas, "you have a profane way of talking, for which I must reprove you. A man can never have his duty too frequently inculcated into him. And as for Tillotson, to be sure he was a good writer, and said things very well, but comparisons are odious; another man may write as well as he—I believe there are some of my sermons——" and then he applied the candle to his pipe. "And I believe there are some of my discourses," cries Adams, "which the bishops would not think totally unworthy of being printed, and I have been informed I might procure a very large sum (indeed an immense one) on them." "I doubt that," answered Barnabas. "However, if you desire to make some money of them, perhaps you may sell them by advertising the manuscript sermons of a clergyman lately deceased, all warranted originals, and never printed. And now I think of it, I should be obliged to you, if there be ever a funeral one among them, to lend it me, for I am this very day to preach a funeral sermon for which I have not penned a line, though I am to have a double price." Adams answered he had but one, which he feared would not serve his purpose, being sacred to the memory of a magistrate who had exerted himself very singularly in the preservation of the morality of his neighbours, insomuch that he had neither ale-house nor lewd woman in the parish where he lived. "No," replied

Barnabas, "that will not do quite so well, for the deceased upon whose virtues I am to harangue was a little too much addicted to liquor, and publicly kept a mistress. I believe I must take a common sermon, and trust to my memory to introduce something handsome on him." "To your invention rather," said the doctor; "your memory will be apter to put you out, for no man living remembers anything good of him."

With such kind of spiritual discourse they emptied the bowl of punch, paid their reckoning, and separated: Adams and the doctor went up to Joseph, Parson Barnabas departed to celebrate the afore-said deceased, and the exciseman descended into the cellar to gauge the vessels.

Joseph was now ready to sit down to a loin of mutton, and waited for Mr. Adams when he and the doctor came in. The doctor, having felt his pulse and examined his wounds, declared him much better, which he imputed to that sanative soporiferous draught, a medicine whose virtues, he said, were never to be sufficiently extolled. And great indeed they must be, if Joseph was so much indebted to them as the doctor imagined, since nothing more than those effluvia which escaped the cork could have contributed to his recovery, for the medicine had stood untouched in the window ever since its arrival.

Joseph passed that day, and the three following, with his friend Adams, in which nothing so remarkable happened as the swift progress of his recovery. As he had an excellent habit of body, his wounds were now almost healed, and his bruises gave him so little uneasiness that he pressed Mr. Adams to let him depart, told him he should never be able to return sufficient thanks for all his favours, but begged that he might no longer delay his journey to London.

Adams, notwithstanding the ignorance, as he conceived it, of Mr. Tow-wouse, and the envy (for such he thought it) of Mr. Barnabas, had great expectations from his sermons; seeing therefore Joseph in so good a way, he told him he would agree to his setting out the next morning in the stage-coach, that he believed he should have sufficient, after the reckoning paid, to procure him one day's conveyance in it, and afterwards he would be able to get on on foot or might be favoured with a lift in some neighbour's waggon, especially as there was then to be a fair in the town whither the coach would carry him to which numbers from his parish resorted —and as to himself, he agreed to proceed to the great city.

They were now walking in the inn-yard, when a fat, fair,

short person rode in, and, alighting from his horse, went directly up to Barnabas, who was smoking his pipe on a bench. The parson and the stranger shook one another very lovingly by the hand, and went into a room together.

The evening now coming on, Joseph retired to his chamber, whither the good Adams accompanied him and took this opportunity to expatiate on the great mercies God had lately shown him, of which he ought not only to have the deepest inward sense but likewise to express outward thankfulness for them. They therefore fell both on their knees and spent a considerable time in prayer and thanksgiving.

They had just finished when Betty came in and told Mr. Adams Mr. Barnabas desired to speak to him on some business of consequence below-stairs. Joseph desired, if it was likely to detain him long, he would let him know it, that he might go to bed, which Adams promised, and in that case they wished one another good night.

CHAPTER XVII: *A pleasant discourse between the two parsons and the book-seller, which was broke off by an unlucky accident happening in the inn, which produced a dialogue between Mrs. Tow-wouse and her maid of no gentle kind.*

As SOON as Adams came into the room, Mr. Barnabas introduced him to the stranger, who was, he told him, a bookseller, and would be as likely to deal with him for his sermons as any man whatever. Adams, saluting the stranger, answered Barnabas that he was very much obliged to him; that nothing could be more convenient, for he had no other business to the great city and was heartily desirous of returning with the young man, who was just recovered of his misfortune. He then snapped his fingers (as was usual with him) and took two or three turns about the room in an ecstasy. And to induce the book-seller to be as expeditious as possible, as likewise to offer him a better price for his commodity, he assured them their meeting was extremely lucky to himself, for that he had the most pressing occasion for money at that time, his own being almost spent, and having a friend then in the same inn who was just recovered from some wounds he had received from robbers and was in a most indigent condition. "So that nothing," says he, "could be so opportune for the supplying both our necessities as my making an immediate bargain with you."

As soon as he had seated himself, the stranger began in these words: "Sir, I do not care absolutely to deny engaging in what my friend Mr. Barnabas recommends, but sermons are mere drugs. The trade is so vastly stocked with them that, really, unless they come out with the name of Whitefield or Wesley, or some other such great man, as a bishop or those sort of people, I don't care to touch, unless now it was a sermon preached on the 30th of January,[1] or we could say in the title-page 'published at the earnest request of the congregation, or the inhabitants'; but, truly, for a dry piece of sermons I had rather be excused, especially as my hands are so full at present. However, sir, as Mr. Barnabas mentioned them to me, I will, if you please, take the manuscript with me to town and send you my opinion of it in a very short time."

"Oh!" said Adams, "if you desire it, I will read two or three discourses as a specimen." This, Barnabas, who loved sermons no better than a grocer doth figs, immediately objected to, and advised Adams to let the book-seller have his sermons, telling him, if he gave him a direction, he might be certain of a speedy answer, adding he need not scruple trusting them in his possession. "No," said the book-seller, "if it was a play that had been acted twenty nights together, I believe it would be safe."

Adams did not at all relish the last expression; he said he was sorry to hear sermons compared to plays. "Not by me, I assure you," cried the book-seller, "though I don't know whether the licencing act may not shortly bring them to the same footing, but I have formerly known a hundred guineas given for a play." "More shame for those who gave it," cried Barnabas. "Why so?" said the book-seller, "for they got hundreds by it." "But is there no difference between conveying good or ill instructions to mankind?" said Adams. "Would not an honest mind rather lose money by the one than gain it by the other?" "If you can find any such, I will not be their hindrance," answered the book-seller, "but I think those persons who get by preaching sermons are the properest to lose by printing them: for my part, the copy that sells best will be always the best copy in my opinion; I am no enemy to sermons but because they don't sell, for I would as soon print one of Whitefield's as any farce whatever."

"Whoever prints such heterodox stuff ought to be hanged," says Barnabas. "Sir," said he, turning to Adams, "this fellow's writings (I know not whether you have seen them) are levelled at the clergy. He would reduce us to the example of the primitive ages, forsooth, and would insinuate to the people that a clergyman ought to be always preaching and praying. He pretends to understand the Scripture literally, and would make mankind believe that the poverty and low estate which was recommended to the Church in its infancy, and was only temporary doctrine adapted to her under persecution, was to be preserved in her flourishing and established state. Sir, the principles of Toland, Woolston, and all the free-thinkers, are not calculated to do half the mischief as those professed by this fellow and his followers."

"Sir," answered Adams, "if Mr. Whitefield had carried his doctrine no farther than you mention, I should have remained, as I once was, his well-wisher. I am, myself, as great an enemy to the luxury and splendour of the clergy as he can be. I do not more than he, by the flourishing estate of the Church, understand the palaces, equipages, dress, furniture, rich dainties, and vast fortunes of her ministers. Surely those things, which savour so strongly of this world, become not the servants of one who professed his kingdom was not of it; but when he began to call nonsense and enthusiasm to his aid, and set up the detestable doctrine of faith against good works, I was his friend no longer; for surely that doctrine was coined in hell, and one would think none but the devil himself could have the confidence to preach it. For can anything be more derogatory to the honour of God than for men to imagine that the all-wise Being will hereafter say to the good and virtuous, 'Notwithstanding the purity of thy life, notwithstanding that constant rule of virtue and goodness in which thou walkedst upon earth, still, as thou didst not believe everything in the true orthodox manner, thy want of faith shall condemn thee?' Or, on the other side, can any doctrine have a more pernicious influence on society than a persuasion that it will be a good plea for the villain, at the last day: 'Lord, it is true, I never obeyed one of thy commandments, yet punish me not, for I believe them all?' " "I suppose, sir," said the book-seller, "your sermons are of a different kind." "Aye, sir," said Adams; "the contrary, I thank Heaven, is inculcated in almost every page, or I should belie my own opinion, which hath always been that a virtuous and good Turk, or heathen, are more acceptable in the sight of their Creator than a vicious and wicked Christian, though his faith was as perfectly orthodox as St. Paul himself." "I wish you success," says the book-seller, "but must beg to be excused, as my hands are so very full at present, and, indeed, I am afraid you will find a backwardness in the trade to engage in a book which the clergy would be certain to cry down." "God forbid," says Adams, "any books should be propagated which the clergy would cry down; but if you mean by the clergy some few designing factious men, who have it at heart to establish some favourite schemes at the price of the liberty of mankind and the very essence of religion, it is not in the power of such persons to decry any book they please, witness that excellent book called *A Plain Account of the Nature and End of the Sacrament*, a book written (if I may venture on the expression) with the pen of an angel, and calculated to restore the true use of Christianity and of that sacred institution; for what could tend more to the noble purposes of religion than frequent cheerful meetings among the members of a society, in which they should, in the presence of one another and in the service of the supreme Being, make promises of being good, friendly, and benevolent to each other? Now, this excellent book was attacked by a party, but unsuccessfully." At these words Barnabas fell a-ringing with all the violence imaginable; upon which a servant attending, he bid him "bring a bill immediately, for that he was in company, for aught he knew, with the devil himself, and he expected to hear the Alcoran, the Leviathan, or Woolston commended if he stayed a few minutes longer." Adams desired, As he was so much moved at his mentioning a book, which he did without apprehending any possibility of offence, that he would be so kind to propose any objections he had to it, which he would endeavour to answer. "I propose objections!" said Barnabas. "I never read a syllable in any such wicked book; I never saw it in my life, I assure you." Adams was going to answer, when a most hideous uproar began in the inn, Mrs. Tow-wouse, Mr. Tow-wouse, and Betty, all lifting up their voices together; but Mrs. Tow-wouse's voice, like a bass viol in a concert, was clearly and distinctly distinguished among the rest, and was heard to articulate the following sounds: "O you damned villain! is this the return to all the care I have taken of your family? This is the reward of my virtue? Is this the manner in which you behave to one who brought you a fortune, and preferred you to so many matches, all your betters? To abuse my bed, my own bed, with my own servant! but I'll maul the slut, I'll tear her nasty eyes out; was ever such a pitiful dog, to take up with such a mean trollop? If she had been a gentlewoman, like myself, it had been some excuse; but a beggarly, saucy, dirty servant maid.—Get you out of my house, you whore." To which she added another name, which we do not care to stain our paper with. It was a monosyllable beginning with a b—, and indeed was the same as if she had pronounced the words "she dog." Which term we shall, to avoid offence, use on this occasion, though indeed both the mistress and the maid uttered the above-mentioned b—, a word extremely disgustful to females of the lower sort. Betty had borne all hitherto with patience, and had uttered only lamentations, but the last appellation stung her to the quick. "I am a woman as well as yourself," she roared out, "and no she dog, and if I have been a little naughty, I am not the first; if I have been no better than I should be," cries she, sobbing, "that's no reason you should call me out of my name: my be-betters are wo-rse than me." "Hussy, hussy," says Mrs. Tow-wouse, "have you the impudence to answer me? Did I not catch you, you saucy"—and then again repeated the terrible word so odious to female ears. "I can't bear that name," answered Betty. "If I have been wicked, I am to answer for it myself in the other world, but I have done nothing that's unnatural, and I will go out of your house this moment, for I will never be called 'she dog' by any mistress in England." Mrs. Tow-wouse then armed herself with the spit, but was prevented from executing any dreadful purpose by Mr. Adams, who confined her arms with the strength of a wrist which Hercules would not have been ashamed of. Mr. Tow-wouse being caught, as our lawyers express it, with the manner, and having no defence to make, very prudently withdrew himself; and Betty committed herself to the protection of the hostler, who, though she could not conceive him pleased with what had happened, was, in her opinion, rather a gentler beast than her mistress.

Mrs. Tow-wouse, at the intercession of Mr. Adams, and finding the enemy vanished, began to compose herself, and at length recovered the usual serenity of her temper; in which we will leave her, to open to the reader the steps which led to a catastrophe, common enough, and comical enough too perhaps, in modern history, yet often fatal to the repose and well-being of families, and the subject of many tragedies, both in life and on the stage.

CHAPTER XVIII: *The history of Betty the chambermaid, and an account of what occasioned the violent scene in the preceding chapter.*

BETTY, who was the occasion of all this hurry, had some good qualities. She had good nature, generosity, and compassion, but unfortunately her constitution was composed of those warm ingredients which, though the purity of courts or nunneries might have happily controlled them, were by no means able to endure the ticklish situation of a chamber-maid at an inn, who is daily liable to the solicitations of lovers of all complexions; to the dangerous addresses of fine gentlemen of the army, who sometimes are obliged to reside with them a whole year together; and, above all, are exposed to the caresses of footmen, stage-coachmen, and drawers, all of whom employ the whole artillery of kissing, flattering, bribing, and every other weapon which is to be found in the whole armoury of love against them.

Betty, who was but one-and-twenty, had now lived three years in this dangerous situation, during which she had escaped pretty well. An ensign of foot was the first person who made an impression on her heart; he did indeed raise a flame in her which required the care of a surgeon to cool.

While she burnt for him, several others burnt for her. Officers of the army, young gentlemen travelling the western circuit, inoffensive squires, and some of graver character, were set afire by her charms!

At length, having perfectly recovered the effects of her first unhappy passion, she seemed to have vowed a state of perpetual chastity. She was long deaf to all the sufferings of her lovers till one day, at a neighbouring fair, the rhetoric of John the hostler, with a new straw hat and a pint of wine, made a second conquest over her.

She did not, however, feel any of those flames on this occasion which had been the consequence of her former amour, nor indeed those other ill effects which prudent young women very justly apprehend from too absolute an indulgence to the pressing endearments of their lovers. This latter, perhaps, was a little owing to her not being entirely constant to John, with whom she permitted Tom Whipwell the stage-coachman, and now and then a handsome young traveller, to share her favours.

Mr. Tow-wouse had for some time cast the languishing eyes of affection on this young maiden. He had laid hold on every opportunity of saying tender things to her, squeezing her by the hand, and sometimes kissing her lips, for as the violence of his passion had considerably abated to Mrs. Tow-wouse, so, like water which is stopped from its usual current in one place, it naturally sought a vent in another. Mrs. Tow-wouse is thought to have perceived this abatement, and probably it added very little to the natural sweetness of her temper, for, though she was as true to her husband as the dial to the sun, she was rather more desirous of being shone on, as being more capable of feeling his warmth.

Ever since Joseph's arrival, Betty had conceived an extraordinary liking to him, which discovered itself more and more as he grew better and better, till that fatal evening, when, as she was warming his bed, her passion grew to such a height, and so perfectly mastered both her modesty and her reason, that, after many fruitless hints and sly insinuations, she at last threw down the warming-pan, and, embracing him with great eagerness, swore he was the handsomest creature she had ever seen.

Joseph, in great confusion, leapt from her, and told her he was sorry to see a young woman cast off all regard to modesty; but she had gone too far to recede and grew so very indecent that Joseph was obliged, contrary to his inclination, to use some violence to her, and, taking her in his arms, he shut her out of the room and locked the door.

How ought man to rejoice that his chastity is always in his own power; that if he hath sufficient strength of mind, he hath always a competent strength of body to defend himself, and cannot, like a poor weak woman, be ravished against his will!

Betty was in the most violent agitation at this disappointment. Rage and lust pulled her heart, as with two strings, two different ways; one moment she thought of stabbing Joseph, the next, of taking him in her arms and devouring him with kisses, but the latter passion was far more prevalent. Then she thought of revenging his refusal on herself; but whilst she was engaged in this meditation, happily death presented himself to her in so many shapes of drowning, hanging, poisoning, etc., that her distracted mind could resolve on none. In this perturbation of spirit, it accidentally occurred to her memory that her master's bed was not made; she therefore went directly to his room, where he happened at that time to be engaged at his bureau. As soon as she saw him, she attempted to retire, but he called her back, and, taking her by the hand, squeezed her so tenderly, at the same time whispering so many soft things into her ears, and then pressed her so closely with his kisses, that the vanquished fair one, whose passions were already raised, and which were not so whimsically capricious that one man only could lay them, though, perhaps, she would have rather preferred that one—the vanquished fair one quietly submitted, I say, to her master's will, who had just attained the accomplishment of his bliss when Mrs. Towwouse unexpectedly entered the room and caused all that confusion which we have before seen and which it is not necessary at present to take any farther notice of, since, without the assistance of a single hint from us, every reader of any speculation or experience, though not married himself, may easily conjecture that it concluded with the discharge of Betty, the submission of Mr. Tow-wouse, with some things to be performed on his side by way of gratitude for his wife's goodness in being reconciled to him, with many hearty promises never to offend any more in the like manner, and, lastly, his quietly and contentedly bearing to be reminded of his transgressions, as a kind of penance, once or twice a day during the residue of his life.

BOOK TWO

CHAPTER I: *Of divisions in authors.*

THERE are certain mysteries or secrets in all trades, from the highest to the lowest, from that of prime-ministering to this of authoring, which are seldom discovered, unless to members of the same calling. Among those used by us gentlemen of the latter occupation, I take this of dividing our works into books and chapters to be none of the least considerable. Now, for want of being truly acquainted with this secret, common readers imagine that by this art of dividing we mean only to swell our works to a much larger bulk than they would otherwise be extended to. These several places, therefore, in our paper which are filled with our books and chapters are understood as so much buckram, stays, and stay-tape in a tailor's bill, serving only to make up the sum total commonly found at the bottom of our first page, and of his last.

But in reality the case is otherwise, and in this, as well as all other instances, we consult the advantage of our reader, not our own; and indeed many notable uses arise to him from this method, for, first, those little spaces between our chapters may be looked upon as an inn or resting-place where he may stop and take a glass, or any other refreshment, as it pleases him. Nay, our fine readers will, perhaps, be scarce able to travel farther than through one of them in a day. As to those vacant pages which are placed between our books, they are to be regarded as those stages where, in long journeys, the traveller stays some time to repose himself, and consider of what he hath seen in the parts he hath already passed through; a consideration which I take the liberty to recommend a little to the reader, for, however swift his capacity may be, I would not advise him to travel through these pages too fast, for if he doth, he may probably miss the seeing some curious productions of nature which will be observed by the slower and more accurate reader. A volume without any such places of rest resembles the opening of wilds or seas, which tires the eye and fatigues the spirit when entered upon.

Secondly, what are the contents prefixed to every chapter but so many inscriptions over the gates or inns (to continue the same metaphor) informing the reader what entertainment he is to expect, which if he like not, he may travel on to the next; for, in biography, as we are not tied down to an exact concatenation equally with other historians, so a chapter or two (for instance this I am now writing) may be often passed over without any injury to the whole. And in these inscriptions I have been as faithful as possible, not imitating the celebrated Montaigne, who promises you one thing and gives you another, nor some title-page authors, who promise a great deal and produce nothing at all.

There are, besides these more obvious benefits, several others which our readers enjoy from this art of dividing, though perhaps most of them too mysterious to be presently understood by any who are not initiated into the science of authoring. To mention, therefore, but one which is most obvious, it prevents spoiling the beauty of a book by turning down its leaves, a method otherwise necessary to those readers who, though they read with great improvement and advantage, are apt, when they return to their study after half an hour's absence, to forget where they left off.

These divisions have the sanction of great antiquity. Homer not only divided his great work into twenty-four books (in compliment perhaps to the twenty-four letters to which he had very particular obligations), but, according to the opinion of some very sagacious critics, hawked them all separately, delivering only one book at a time (probably by subscription). He was the first inventor of the art, which hath so long lain dormant, of publishing by numbers,[1] an art now brought to such perfection that even dictionaries are divided and exhibited piecemeal to the public; nay one book-seller hath (to encourage learning and ease the public) contrived to give them a dictionary in this divided manner for only fifteen shillings more than it would have cost entire.

Vergil hath given us his poem in twelve books, an argument of his modesty, for by that, doubtless, he would insinuate that he pretends to no more than half the merit of the Greek; for the same reason, our Milton went originally no farther than ten, till, being puffed up by the praise of his friends, he put himself on the same footing with the Roman poet.

I shall not, however, enter so deep into this matter as some very learned critics have done who have, with infinite labour and acute discernment, discovered what books are proper for embellishment, and what require simplicity only, particularly with regard to similes, which I think are now generally agreed to become any book but the first.

I will dismiss this chapter with the following observation: that it becomes an author generally to divide a book as it does a butcher to joint his meat, for such assistance is of great help to both the reader and the carver. And now, having indulged myself a little, I will endeavour to indulge the curiosity of my reader, who is no doubt impatient to know what he will find in the subsequent chapters of this book.

CHAPTER II: *A surprising instance of Mr. Adams's short memory, with the unfortunate consequences which it brought on Joseph.*

MR. ADAMS and Joseph were now ready to depart different ways when an accident determined the former to return with his friend, which Tow-wouse, Barnabas, and the book-seller had not been able to do. This accident was that those sermons which the parson was travelling to London to publish were, O my good reader, left behind, what he had mistaken for them in the saddle-bags being no other than three shirts, a pair of shoes, and some other necessaries, which Mrs. Adams, who thought her husband would want shirts more than sermons on his journey, had carefully provided him.

This discovery was now luckily owing to the presence of Joseph at the opening the saddle-bags, who, having heard his friend say he carried with him nine volumes of sermons, and not being of that sect of philosophers who can reduce all the matter of the world into a nutshell, seeing there was no room for them in the bags where the parson had said they were deposited, had the curiosity to cry out, "Bless me, sir, where are your sermons?" The parson answered, "There, there, child; there they are, under my shirts." Now it happened that he had taken forth his last shirt, and the vehicle remained visibly empty. "Sure, sir," says Joseph, "there is nothing in the bags." Upon which Adams, starting and testifying some surprise, cried, "Hey! fie, fie upon it; they are not here sure enough. Aye, they are certainly left behind."

Joseph was greatly concerned at the uneasiness which he apprehended his friend must feel from his disappointment; he begged him to pursue his journey, and promised he would himself return with the books to him with the utmost expedition. "No, thank you, child," answered Adams; "it shall not be so. What would it avail me to tarry in the great city unless I had my discourses with me, which are *ut ita dicam*,[1] the sole cause, the *aitia monotate*[2] of my peregrination? No, child, as this accident hath happened, I am resolved to return back to my cure, together with you, which indeed my inclination sufficiently leads me to. This disappointment may perhaps be intended for my good." He concluded with a verse out of Theocritus, which signifies no more than that sometimes it rains, and sometimes the sun shines.

Joseph bowed with obedience and thankfulness for the inclination which the parson expressed of returning with him; and now the bill was called for, which, on examination amounted within a shilling to the sum Mr. Adams had in his pocket. Perhaps the reader may wonder how he was able to produce a sufficient sum for so many days: that he may not be surprised, therefore, it cannot be unnecessary to acquaint him that he had borrowed a guinea of a servant belonging to the coach and six, who had been formerly one of his parishioners, and whose master, the owner of the coach, then lived within three miles of him; for so good was the credit of Mr. Adams that even Mr. Peter, the Lady Booby's steward, would have lent him a guinea with very little security.

Mr. Adams discharged the bill, and they were both setting out, having agreed to ride and tie—a method of travelling much used by persons who have but one horse between them, and is thus performed. The two travellers set out together, one on horseback, the other on foot: now as it generally happens that he on horseback outgoes him on foot, the custom is that, when he arrives at the distance agreed on, he is to dismount, tie the horse to some gate, tree, post, or other thing, and then proceed on foot; when the other comes up to the horse, he unties him, mounts, and gallops on till, having passed by his fellow-traveller, he likewise arrives at the place of tying. And this is that method of travelling so much in use among our prudent ancestors, who knew that horses had mouths as well as legs, and that they could not use the latter without being at the expense of suffering the beasts themselves to use the former. This was the method in use in those days when, instead of a coach and six, a Member of Parliament's lady used to mount a pillion behind her husband, and a grave serjeant-at-law condescended to amble to Westminster on an easy pad with his clerk kicking his heels behind him.

Adams was now gone some minutes, having insisted on Joseph's beginning the journey on horseback, and Joseph had his foot in the stirrup, when the hostler presented him a bill for the horse's board during his residence at the inn. Joseph said Mr. Adams had paid all, but this matter being referred to Mr. Tow-wouse, was by him decided in favour of the hostler, and indeed with truth and justice, for this was a fresh instance of that shortness of memory, which did not arise from want of part, but that continual hurry in which Parson Adams was always involved.

Joseph was now reduced to a dilemma which extremely puzzled him. The sum due for horse-meat was twelve shillings, for Adams, who had borrowed the beast of his clerk, had ordered him to be fed as well as they could feed him, and the cash in his pocket amounted to sixpence, for Adams had divided the last shilling with him. Now, though there have been some ingenious persons who have contrived to pay twelve shillings with sixpence, Joseph was not one of them. He had never contracted a debt in his life, and was consequently the less ready at an expedient to extricate himself. Tow-wouse was willing to give him credit till next time, to which Mrs. Tow-wouse would probably have consented (for such was Joseph's beauty that it had made some impression even on that piece of flint which that good woman wore in her bosom by way of heart). Joseph would have found, therefore, very likely, the passage free, had he not, when he honestly discovered the nakedness of his pockets, pulled out that little piece of gold which we have mentioned before. This caused Mrs. Tow-wouse's eyes to water; she told Joseph she did not conceive a man could want money whilst he had gold in his pocket. Joseph answered he had such a value for that little piece of gold that he would not part with it for a hundred times the riches which the greatest esquire in the county was worth. "A pretty way, indeed," said Mrs. Tow-wouse, "to run in debt and then refuse to part with your money because you have a value for it. I never knew any piece of gold of more value than as many shillings as it would change for." "Not to preserve my life from starving, nor to redeem it from a robber, would I part with this dear piece," answered Joseph. "What," says Mrs. Tow-wouse, "I suppose it was given you by some vile trollop, some miss or other; if it had been the present of a virtuous woman you would not have had such a value for it. My husband is a fool if he parts with the horse without being paid for him." "No, no, I can't part with the horse, indeed, till I have the money," cried Tow-wouse—a resolution highly commended by a lawyer then in the yard, who declared Mr. Tow-wouse might justify the detainer.

As we cannot, therefore, at present get Mr. Joseph out of the inn, we shall leave him in it, and carry our reader on after Parson Adams, who, his mind being perfectly at ease, fell into a contemplation on a passage in Aeschylus which entertained him for three miles together without suffering him once to reflect on his fellow-traveller.

At length, having spun out his thread, and being now at the summit of a hill, he cast his eyes backwards and wondered that he could not see any sign of Joseph. As he left him ready to mount the horse, he could not apprehend any mischief had happened, neither could he suspect that he missed his way, it being so broad and plain; the only reason which presented itself to him was that he had met with an acquaintance who had prevailed with him to delay some time in discourse.

He therefore resolved to proceed slowly forwards, not doubting but that he should be shortly overtaken, and soon came to a large water, which, filling the whole road, he saw no method of passing unless by wading through, which he accordingly did up to his middle, but was no sooner got to the other side than he perceived if he had looked over the hedge he would have found a footpath capable of conducting him without wetting his shoes.

His surprise at Joseph's not coming up grew now very troublesome: he began to fear he knew not what; and as he determined to move no farther, and, if he did not shortly overtake him, to return back, he wished to find a house of public entertainment where he might dry his clothes and refresh himself with a pint; but seeing no such (for no other reason than because he did not cast his eyes a hundred yards forward), he sat himself down on a stile and pulled out his Aeschylus.

A fellow passing presently by, Adams asked him if he could direct him to an ale-house. The fellow, who had just left it, and perceived the house and sign to be within sight, thinking he had jeered him, and being of a morose temper, bade him follow his nose and be d—ned. Adams told him he was a saucy jackanapes, upon which the fellow turned about angrily, but, perceiving Adams clench his fist, he thought proper to go on without taking any farther notice.

A horseman following immediately after and being asked the same question, answered, "Friend, there is one within a stone's throw; I believe you may see it before you." Adams, lifting up his eyes, cried, "I protest, and so there is," and, thanking his informer, proceeded directly to it.

CHAPTER III: *The opinion of two lawyers concerning the same gentleman, with Mr. Adams's inquiry into the religion of his host.*

HE HAD just entered the house, had called for his pint, and seated himself, when two horsemen came to the door, and, fastening their horses to the rails, alighted. They said there was a violent shower of rain coming on which they intended to weather there, and went into a little room by themselves, not perceiving Mr. Adams.

One of these immediately asked the other if he had seen a more comical adventure in a great while. Upon which the other said he doubted whether, by law, the landlord could justify detaining the horse for his corn and hay. But the former answered, "Undoubtedly he can; it is an adjudged case, and I have known it tried."

Adams, who, though he was, as the reader may suspect, a little inclined to forgetfulness, never wanted more than a hint to remind him, overhearing their discourse, immediately suggested to himself that this was his own horse, and that he had forgot to pay for him, which, upon inquiry, he was certified of by the gentlemen, who added that the horse was likely to have more rest than food unless he was paid for.

The poor parson resolved to return presently to the inn, though he knew no more than Joseph how to procure his horse his liberty; he was, however, prevailed on to stay under covert till the shower, which was now very violent, was over.

The three travellers then sat down together over a mug of good beer, when Adams, who had observed a gentleman's house as he passed along the road, inquired to whom it belonged; one of the horsemen had no sooner mentioned the owner's name than the other began to revile him in the most opprobrious terms. The English language scarce affords a single reproachful word which he did not vent on this occasion. He charged him likewise with many particular facts. He said he no more regarded a field of wheat when he was hunting than he did the highway; that he had injured several poor farmers by trampling their corn under his horse's heels, and if any of them begged him with the utmost submission to refrain his horsewhip was always ready to do them justice. He said that he was the greatest tyrant to the neighbours in every other instance, and would not suffer a farmer to keep a gun, though he might justify it by law, and in his own family so cruel a master that he never kept a servant a twelvemonth. "In his capacity as a justice," continued he, "he behaves so partially that he commits or acquits just as he is in the humour, without any regard to truth or evidence; the devil may carry anyone before him for me; I would rather be tried before some judges than be a prosecutor before him: if I had an estate in the neighbourhood, I would sell it for half the value, rather than live near him."

Adams shook his head and said he was sorry such men were suffered to proceed with impunity, and that riches could set any man above the law. The reviler a little after retiring into the yard, the gentleman who had first mentioned his name to Adams began to assure him that his companion was a prejudiced person. "It is true," says he, "perhaps, that he may have sometimes pursued his game over a field of corn, but he hath always made the party ample satisfaction," that so far from tyrannizing over his neighbours or taking away their guns, he himself knew several farmers not qualified who not only kept guns, but killed game with them; that he was the best of masters to his servants, and several of them had grown old in his service; that he was the best justice of peace in the kingdom, and, to his certain knowledge, had decided many difficult points which were referred to him with the greatest equity and the highest wisdom; and he verily believed several persons would give a year's purchase more for an estate near him than under the wings of any other great man. He had just finished his encomium, when his companion returned and acquainted him the storm was over, upon which they presently mounted their horses and departed.

Adams, who was in the utmost anxiety at those different characters of the same person, asked his host if he knew the gentleman, for he began to imagine they had by mistake been speaking of two several gentlemen. "No, no, master," answered the host (a shrewd cunning fellow); "I know the gentleman very well of whom they have been speaking, as I do the gentlemen who spoke of him. As for riding over other men's corn, to my knowledge he hath not been on horseback these two years. I never heard he did any injury of that kind, and as to making reparation, he is not so free of his money as that comes to neither. Nor did I ever hear of his taking away any man's gun—nay, I know several who have guns in their houses; but as for killing game with them, no man is stricter, and I believe he would ruin any who did. You heard one of the gentlemen say he was the worst master in the world, and the other that he is the best; but, for my own part, I know all his servants and never heard from any of them that he was either one or the other." "Aye! aye!" says Adams; "and how doth he behave as a justice, pray?" "Faith, friend," answered the host, "I question whether he is in the commission; the only cause I have heard he hath decided a great while was one between those very two persons who just went out of this house, and I am sure he determined that justly, for I heard the whole matter." "Which did he decide it in favour of?" quoth Adams. "I think I need not answer that question," cried the host, "after the different characters you have heard of him. It is not my business to contradict gentlemen while they are drinking in my house, but I knew neither of them spoke a syllable of truth." "God forbid!" said Adams, "that men should arrive at such a pitch of wickedness to belie the character of their neighbour from a little private affection, or, what is infinitely worse, a private spite. I rather believe we have mistaken them, and they mean two other persons, for there are many houses on the road." "Why, pr'ythee, friend," cries the host, "dost thou pretend never to have told a lie in thy life?" "Never a malicious one, I am certain," answered Adams, "nor with a design to injure the reputation of any man living." "Pugh! malicious; no, no," replied the host, "not malicious with a design to hang a man, or bring him into trouble; but surely, out of love to one's self, one must speak better of a friend than an enemy." "Out of love to yourself, you should confine yourself to truth," says Adams, "for by doing otherwise you injure the noblest part of yourself, your immortal soul. I can hardly believe any man such an idiot to risk the loss of that by any trifling gain, and the greatest gain in this world is but dirt in comparison of what shall be revealed hereafter." Upon which the host, taking up the cup with a smile, drank a health to Hereafter, adding he was for something present. "Why," says Adams very gravely, "do not you believe in another world?" To which the host answered, yes; he was no atheist. "And you believe you have an immortal soul?" cries Adams. He answered, God forbid he should not. "And heaven and hell?" said the parson. The host then bid him not to profane, for those were things not to be mentioned nor thought of but in church. Adams asked him why he went to church if what he learned there had no influence on his conduct in life? "I go to church," answered the host, "to say my prayers and behave godly." "And dost not thou," cried Adams, "believe what thou hearest at church?" "Most part of it, master," returned the host. "And dost not thou then tremble," cried Adams, "at the thought of eternal punishment?" "As for that, master," said he, "I never once thought about it; but what signifies talking about matters so far off? The mug is out, shall I draw another?"

Whilst he was going for that purpose, a stage-coach drove up to the door. The coachman coming into the house, was asked by the mistress what passengers he had in his coach? "A parcel of squinny-gut b—s," says he. "I have a good mind to overturn them; you won't prevail upon them to drink anything, I assure you." Adams asked him if he had not seen a young man on horseback on the road (describing Joseph). "Aye," said the coachman, "a gentlewoman in my coach that is his acquaintance redeemed him and his horse; he would have been here before this time, had not the storm driven him to shelter." "God bless her," said Adams in a rapture, nor could he delay walking out to satisfy himself who this charitable woman was, but what was his surprise when he saw his old acquaintance Madam Slipslop? Hers indeed was not so great, because she had been informed by Joseph that he was on the road. Very civil were the salutations on both sides, and Mrs. Slipslop rebuked the hostess for denying the gentleman to be there when she asked for him; but indeed the poor woman had not erred designedly, for Mrs. Slipslop asked for a clergyman and she had unhappily mistaken Adams for a person travelling to a neighbouring fair with the thimble and button, or some other such operation, for he marched in a swingeing great but short white coat with black buttons, a short wig, and a hat which, so far from having a black hat-band, had nothing black about it.

Joseph was now come up, and Mrs. Slipslop would have had him quit his horse to the parson and come himself into the coach, but he absolutely refused, saying he thanked heaven he was well enough recovered to be able to ride and added he hoped he knew his duty better than to ride in a coach while Mr. Adams was on horseback.

Mrs. Slipslop would have persisted longer had not a lady in the coach put a short end to the dispute by refusing to suffer a fellow in a livery to ride in the same coach with herself, so it was at length agreed that Adams should fill the vacant place in the coach and Joseph should proceed on horseback.

They had not proceeded far before Mrs. Slipslop, addressing herself to the parson, spoke thus: "There hath been a strange alteration in our family, Mr. Adams, since Sir Thomas's death." "A strange alteration indeed!" says Adams, "as I gather from some hints which have dropped from Joseph." "Aye," says she, "I could never have believed it; but the longer one lives in the world, the more one sees. So Joseph hath given you hints." "But of what nature will always remain a perfect secret with me," cries the parson; "he forced me to promise before he would communicate anything. I am indeed concerned to find her ladyship behave in so unbecoming a manner. I always thought her in the main a good lady, and should never have suspected her of thoughts so unworthy a Christian, and with a young lad her own servant." "These things are no secrets to me, I assure you," cries Slipslop, "and I believe they will be none anywhere shortly; for ever since the boy's departure she hath behaved more like a mad-woman than anything else." "Truly, I am heartily concerned," said Adams, "for she was a good sort of a lady. Indeed, I have often wished she had attended a little more constantly at the service, but she hath done a great deal of good in the parish." "O Mr. Adams," says Slipslop, "people that don't see all often know nothing. Many things have been given away in our family, I do assure you, without her knowledge. I have heard you say in the pulpit we ought not to brag, but indeed I can't avoid saying if she had kept the keys herself, the poor would have wanted many a cordial which I have let them have. As for my late master, he was as worthy a man as ever lived, and would have done infinite good if he had not been controlled, but he loved a quiet life, heavens rest his soul! I am confidous he is there, and enjoys a quiet life, which some folks would not allow him here." Adams answered he had never heard this before, and was mistaken if she herself (for he remembered she used to commend her mistress and blame her master) had not formerly been of another opinion. "I don't know," replied she, "what I might once think, but now I am confidous matters are as I tell you; the world will shortly see who hath been deceived; for my part I say nothing but that it is wondersome how some people can carry all things with a grave face."

Thus Mr. Adams and she discoursed, till they came opposite to a great house which stood at some distance from the road; a lady in the coach spying it, cried, "Yonder lives the unfortunate Leonora, if one can justly call a woman unfortunate whom we must own at the same time guilty, and the author of her own calamity." This was abundantly sufficient to awaken the curiosity of Mr. Adams, as indeed it did that of the whole company, who jointly solicited the lady to acquaint them with Leonora's history, since it seemed by what she had said to contain something remarkable.

The lady, who was perfectly well bred, did not require many entreaties, and having only wished their entertainment might make amends for the company's attention, she began in the following manner.

CHAPTER IV: *The history of Leonora, or the unfortunate jilt.*

"LEONORA was the daughter of a gentleman of fortune; she was tall and well shaped, with a sprightliness in her countenance which often attracts beyond more regular features joined with an insipid air; nor is this kind of beauty less apt to deceive than allure, the good-humour which it indicates being often mistaken for good nature, and the vivacity for true understanding.

"Leonora, who was now at the age of eighteen, lived with an aunt of hers in a town in the north of England. She was an extreme lover of gaiety, and very rarely missed a ball or any other public assembly, where she had frequent opportunities of satisfying a greedy appetite of vanity, with the preference which was given her by the men to almost every other woman present.

"Among many young fellows who were particular in their gallantries towards her, Horatio soon distinguished himself in her eyes beyond all his competitors; she danced with more than ordinary gaiety when he happened to be her partner; neither the fairness of the evening, nor the music of the nightingale, could lengthen her walk like his company. She affected no longer to understand the civilities of others, whilst she inclined so attentive an ear to every compliment of Horatio that she often smiled even when it was too delicate for her comprehension."

"Pray, madam," says Adams, "who was this Squire Horatio?"

"Horatio," says the lady, "was a young gentleman of a good family, bred to the law, and had been some few years called to the degree of a barrister. His face and person were such as the generality allowed handsome, but he had a dignity in his air very rarely to be seen. His temper was of the saturnine complexion, and without the least taint of moroseness. He had wit and humour, with an inclination to satire, which he indulged rather too much.

"This gentleman, who had contracted the most violent passion for Leonora, was the last person who perceived the probability of its success. The whole town had made the match for him before he himself had drawn a confidence from her actions sufficient to mention his passion to her; for it was his opinion (and perhaps he was there in the right), that it is highly impolitic to talk seriously of love to a woman before you have made such a progress in her affections that she herself expects and desires to hear it.

"But whatever diffidence the fears of a lover may create, which are apt to magnify every favour conferred on a rival, and to see the little advances towards themselves through the other end of the perspective, it was impossible that Horatio's passion should so blind his discernments as to prevent his conceiving hopes from the behaviour of Leonora, whose fondness for him was now as visible to an indifferent person in their company as his for her."

"I never knew any of these forward sluts come to good," says the lady who refused Joseph's entrance into the coach, "nor shall I wonder at anything she doth in the sequel."

The lady proceeded in her story thus: "It was in the midst of a gay conversation in the walks one evening when Horatio whispered Leonora that he was desirous to take a turn or two with her in private, for that he had something to communicate to her of great consequence. 'Are you sure it is of consequence?' said she smiling. 'I hope,' answered he, 'you will think so too, since the whole future happiness of my life must depend on the event.'

"Leonora, who very much suspected what was coming, would have deferred it till another time, but Horatio, who had more than half conquered the difficulty of speaking by the first motion, was so very importunate that she at last yielded, and, leaving the rest of the company, they turned aside into an unfrequented walk.

"They had retired far out of the sight of the company, both maintaining a strict silence. At last Horatio made a full stop, and taking Leonora, who stood pale and trembling, gently by the hand he fetched a deep sigh and then, looking on her eyes with all the tenderness imaginable, he cried out in a faltering accent: 'O Leonora! is it necessary for me to declare to you on what the future happiness of my life must be founded! Must I say there is something belonging to you which is a bar to my happiness, and which unless you will part with, I must be miserable!' 'What can that be?' replied Leonora. 'No wonder,' said he, 'you are surprised that I should make an objection to anything which is yours, yet sure you may guess, since it is the only one which the riches of the world, if they were mine, should purchase of me. Oh, it is that which you must part with to bestow all the rest! Can Leonora, or rather will she, doubt longer? Let me then whisper it in her ears—It is your name, madam. It is by parting with that, by your condescension to be forever mine, which must at once prevent me from being the most miserable, and will render me the happiest, of mankind.'

"Leonora, covered with blushes, and with as angry a look as she could possibly put on, told him that had she suspected what his declaration would have been he should not have decoyed her from her company, that he had so surprised and frighted her that she begged him to convey her back as quick as possible; which he, trembling very near as much as herself, did."

"More fool he," cried Slipslop; "it is a sign he knew very little of our sect." "Truly, madam," said Adams, "I think you are in the right. I should have insisted to know a piece of her mind, when I had carried matters so far." But Mrs. Graveairs desired the lady to omit all such fulsome stuff in her story, for that it made her sick.

"Well then, madam, to be as concise as possible," said the lady, "many weeks had not passed after this interview, before Horatio and Leonora were what they call on a good footing together. All ceremonies except the last were now over; the writings were now drawn and everything was in the utmost forwardness preparative to the putting Horatio in possession of all his wishes. I will, if you please, repeat you a letter from each of them, which I have got by heart, and which will give you no small idea of their passion on both sides."

Mrs. Graveairs objected to hearing these letters, but being put to the vote, it was carried against her by all the rest in the coach, Parson Adams contending for it with the utmost vehemence.

HORATIO TO LEONORA

" 'How vain, most adorable creature, is the pursuit of pleasure in the absence of an object to which the mind is entirely devoted, unless it have some relation to that object! I was last night condemned to the society of men of wit and learning, which, however agreeable it might have formerly been to me, now only gave me a suspicion that they imputed my absence in conversation to the true cause. For which reason, when your engagements forbid me the ecstatic happiness of seeing you, I am always desirous to be alone; since my sentiments for Leonora are so delicate that I cannot bear the apprehension of another's prying into those delightful endearments with which the warm imagination of a lover will sometimes indulge him, and which I suspect my eyes then betray. To fear this discovery of our thoughts may perhaps appear too ridiculous a nicety to minds not susceptible of all the tenderness of this delicate passion. And surely we shall suspect there are few such, when we consider that it requires every human virtue to exert itself in its full extent; since the beloved, whose happiness it ultimately respects, may give us charming opportunities of being brave in her defence, generous to her wants, compassionate to her afflictions, grateful to her kindness; and in the same manner of exercising every other virtue which he, who would not do to any degree, and that with the utmost rapture, can never deserve the name of a lover. It is therefore with a view to the delicate modesty of your mind that I cultivate it so purely in my own; and it is that which will sufficiently suggest to you the uneasiness I bear from those liberties which men to whom the world allow politeness will sometimes give themselves on these occasions.

" 'Can I tell you with what eagerness I expect the arrival of that blest day when I shall experience the falsehood of a common assertion, that the greatest human happiness consists in hope? A doctrine which no person had ever stronger reasons to believe than myself at present, since none ever tasted such bliss as fires my bosom with the thoughts of spending my future days with such a companion, and that every action of my life will have the glorious satisfaction of conducing to your happiness.'

LEONORA TO HORATIO *

" 'The refinement of your mind has been so evidently proved by every word and action ever since I had the first pleasure of knowing you, that I thought it impossible my good opinion of Horatio could have been heightened to any additional proof of merit. This very thought was my amusement when I received your last letter, which when I opened, I confess I was surprised to find the delicate sentiments expressed there so far exceeded what I thought could come even from you (although I know all the generous principles human nature is capable of are centred in your breast), that words cannot paint what I feel on the reflection that my happiness shall be the ultimate end of all your actions.

" 'Oh, Horatio! what a life must that be where the meanest domestic cares are sweetened by the pleasing consideration that the man on earth who best deserves, and to whom you are most inclined to give, your affections is to reap either profit or pleasure from all you do! In such a case, toils must be turned into diversions, and nothing but the unavoidable inconveniencies of life can make us remember that we are mortal.

" 'If the solitary turn of your thoughts, and the desire of keeping them undiscovered, makes even the conversation of men of wit and learning tedious to you, what anxious hours must I spend who am condemned by custom to the conversation of women, whose natural curiosity leads them to pry into all my thoughts and whose envy can never suffer Horatio's heart to be possessed by anyone without forcing them into malicious designs against the person who is so happy as to possess it? But, indeed, if every envy can possibly have any excuse, or even alleviation, it is in this case, where the good is so great, and, it must be equally natural to all who wish it for themselves; nor am I ashamed to own it—and to your merit, Horatio, I am obliged—that prevents my being in that most uneasy of all the situations I can figure in my imagination, of being led by inclination to love the person whom my own judgement forces me to condemn.'

"Matters were in so great forwardness between this fond couple that the day was fixed for their marriage, and was now within a fortnight, when the sessions chanced to be held for that county in a town about twenty miles' distance from that which is the scene of our story. It seems it is usual for the young gentlemen of the bar to repair to these sessions, not so much for the sake of profit, as to show their parts and learn the law of the justices of peace; for which purpose one of the wisest and gravest of all the justices is appointed speaker, or chairman as they modestly call it, and he reads them a lecture and instructs them in the true knowledge of the law."

"You are here guilty of a little mistake," says Adams, "which, if you please, I will correct: I have attended at one of these quarter-sessions, where I observed the counsel taught the justices, instead of learning anything of them."

"It is not very material," said the lady. "Hither repaired

Horatio, who, as he hoped by his profession to advance his fortune, which was not at present very large, for the sake of his dear Leonora, he resolved to spare no pains nor lose any opportunity of improving or advancing himself in it.

"The same afternoon in which he left the town, as Leonora stood at her window a coach and six passed by, which she declared to be the completest, genteelest, prettiest equipage she ever saw, adding these remarkable words, 'Oh, I am in love with that equipage!' which, though her friend Florella at that time did not greatly regard, she hath since remembered.

"In the evening an assembly was held, which Leonora honoured with her company, but intended to pay her dear Horatio the compliment of refusing to dance in his absence.

"Oh, why have not women as good resolution to maintain their vows as they have often good inclinations in making them!

"The gentleman who owned the coach and six came to the assembly. His clothes were as remarkably fine as his equipage could be. He soon attracted the eyes of the company; all the smarts, all the silk waistcoats with silver and gold edgings, were eclipsed in an instant."

"Madam," says Adams, "if it be not impertinent, I should be glad to know how this gentleman was dressed."

"Sir," answered the lady, "I have been told he had on a cut-velvet coat of a cinnamon colour, lined with a pink satin, embroidered all over with gold; his waistcoat, which was cloth of silver, was embroidered with gold likewise. I cannot be particular as to the rest of his dress, but it was all in the French fashion, for Bellarmine (that was his name) was just arrived from Paris.

"This fine figure did not more entirely engage the eyes of every lady in the assembly than Leonora did his. He had scarce beheld her but he stood motionless and fixed as a statue, or at least would have done so if good breeding had permitted him. However, he carried it so far before he had power to correct himself that every person in the room easily discovered where his admiration was settled. The other ladies began to single out their former partners, all perceiving who would be Bellarmine's choice, which they however endeavoured, by all possible means, to prevent, many of them saying to Leonora, 'O madam! I suppose we sha'n't have the pleasure of seeing you dance tonight,' and then crying out, in Bellarmine's hearing, 'Oh! Leonora will not dance, I assure you: her partner is not here.' One maliciously attempted to prevent her by sending a disagreeable fellow to ask her, that so she might be obliged either to dance with him or sit down; but this scheme proved abortive.

"Leonora saw herself admired by the fine stranger, and envied by every woman present. Her little heart began to flutter within her, and her head was agitated with a convulsive motion; she seemed as if she would speak to several of her acquaintance, but had nothing to say, for as she would not mention her present triumph, so she could not disengage her thoughts one moment from the contemplation of it—she had never tasted anything like this happiness. She had before known what it was to torment a single woman, but to be hated and secretly cursed by a whole assembly was a joy reserved for this blessed moment. As this vast profusion of ecstasy had confounded her understanding, so there was nothing so foolish as her behaviour: she played a thousand childish tricks, distorted her person into several shapes, and her face into several laughs, without any reason. In a word, her carriage was as absurd as her desires, which were to affect an insensibility of the stranger's admiration and at the same time a triumph, from that admiration, over every woman in the room.

"In this temper of mind, Bellarmine, having inquired who she was, advanced to her and with a low bow begged the honour of dancing with her, which she, with as low a curtsey, immediately granted. She danced with him all night, and enjoyed perhaps the highest pleasure that she was capable of feeling."

At these words, Adams fetched a deep groan, which frighted the ladies, who told him they hoped he was not ill. He answered he groaned only for the folly of Leonora.

"Leonora retired," continued the lady, "about six in the morning, but not to rest. She tumbled and tossed in her bed, with very short intervals of sleep, and those entirely filled with dreams of the equipage and fine clothes she had seen, and the balls, operas, and ridottos which had been the subject of their conversation.

"In the afternoon, Bellarmine, in the dear coach and six, came to wait on her. He was indeed charmed with her person, and was, on inquiry, so well pleased with the circumstances of her father (for he himself, notwithstanding all his finery, was not quite so rich as a Croesus or an Attălus)." "Attălus," says Mr. Adams; "but pray how came you acquainted with these names?" The lady smiled at the question, and proceeded. "He was so pleased, I say, that he resolved to make his addresses to her directly. He did so accordingly, and that with so much warmth and briskness that he quickly baffled her weak repulses, and obliged the lady to refer him to her father, who, she knew, would quickly declare in favour of a coach and six.

"Thus, what Horatio had by sighs and tears, love and tenderness, been so long obtaining, the French-English Bellarmine with gaiety and gallantry possessed himself of in an instant. In other words, what modesty had employed a full year in raising, impudence demolished in twenty-four hours."

Here Adams groaned a second time, but the ladies, who began to smoke him, took no notice.

"From the opening of the assembly till the end of Bellarmine's visit, Leonora had scarce once thought of Horatio, but he now began, though an unwelcome guest, to enter into her mind. She wished she had seen the charming Bellarmine and his charming equipage before matters had gone so far. 'Yet why,' said she, 'should I wish to have seen him before, or what signifies it that I have seen him now? Is not Horatio my lover —almost my husband? Is he not as handsome, nay handsomer, than Bellarmine? Aye, but Bellarmine is the genteeler and the finer man; yes, that he must be allowed. Yes, yes, he is that certainly. But did not I, no longer ago than yesterday, love Horatio more than all the world? Aye, but yesterday I had not seen Bellarmine. But doth not Horatio dote on me, and may he not in despair break his heart if I abandon him? Well, and hath not Bellarmine a heart to break too? Yes, but I promised Horatio first; but that was poor Bellarmine's misfortune: if I had seen him first, I should certainly have preferred him. Did not the dear creature prefer me to every woman in the assembly, when every she was laying out for him? When was it in Horatio's power to give me such an instance of affection? Can he give me an equipage, or any of those things which Bellarmine will make me mistress of? How vast is the difference between being the wife of a poor counsellor and the wife of one of Bellarmine's fortune! If I marry Horatio, I shall triumph over no more than one rival, but by marrying Bellarmine, I shall be the envy of all my acquaintance. What happiness! But can I suffer Horatio to die? for he hath sworn he cannot survive my loss. But perhaps he may not die; if he should, can I prevent it? Must I sacrifice myself to him? Besides, Bellarmine may be as miserable for me too.' She was thus arguing with herself when some young ladies called her to the walk, and a little relieved her anxiety for the present.

"The next morning Bellarmine breakfasted with her in presence of her aunt, whom he sufficiently informed of his passion for Leonora. He was no sooner withdrawn than the old lady began to advise her niece on this occasion. 'You see, child,' says she, 'what fortune hath thrown in your way, and I hope you will not withstand your own preferment.' Leonora, sighing, begged her not to mention any such thing, when she knew her engagements to Horatio. 'Engagements to a fig,' cried the aunt; 'you should thank heaven on your knees that you have it yet in your power to break them. Will any woman hesitate a moment whether she shall ride in a coach or walk on foot all the days of her life? But Bellarmine drives six, and Horatio not even a pair.' 'Yes, but, madam, what will the world say?' answered Leonora; 'will not they condemn me?' 'The world is always on the side of prudence,' cries the aunt, 'and would surely condemn you if you sacrificed your interest to any motive whatever. Oh, I know the world very well, and you show your ignorance, my dear, by your objection. O' my conscience! the world is wiser. I have lived longer in it than you, and I assure you there is not anything worth our regard besides money, nor did I ever know one person who married from other considerations who did not afterwards heartily repent it. Besides, if we examine the two men, can you prefer a sneaking fellow, who hath been bred at the university, to a fine gentleman just come from his travels? All the world must allow Bellarmine to be a fine gentleman, positively a fine gentleman, and a handsome man.' 'Perhaps, madam, I should not doubt, if I knew how to be handsomely off with the other' 'Oh, leave that to me,' says the aunt. 'You know your father hath not been acquainted with the affair. Indeed, for my part I thought it might do well enough, not dreaming of such an offer; but I'll disengage you: leave me to give the fellow an answer. I warrant you shall have no farther trouble.'

"Leonora was at length satisfied with her aunt's reasoning, and, Bellarmine supping with her that evening, it was agreed he should the next morning go to her father and propose the match, which she consented should be consummated at his return.

"The aunt retired soon after supper, and, the lovers being left together, Bellarmine began in the following manner: 'Yes, madam, this coat, I assure you, was made at Paris, and I defy the best English tailor even to imitate it. There is not one of them can cut, madam; they can't cut. If you observe how this skirt is turned, and this sleeve: a clumsy English rascal can do nothing like it. Pray, how do you like my liveries?' Leonora answered she thought them very pretty. 'All French,' says he, "I assure you, except the great-coats; I never trust anything more than a great-coat to an Englishman. You know, one must encourage our own people what one can, especially as, before I had a place, I was in the country interest, hee, hee, hee! But for myself, I would see the dirty island at the bottom of the sea rather than wear a single rag of English work about me, and I am sure, after you have made one tour to Paris, you will be of the same opinion with regard to your own clothes. You can't conceive what an addition a French dress would be to your beauty; I positively assure you, at the first opera I saw since I came over, I mistook the English ladies for chambermaids, hee, hee, hee!'

"With such sort of polite discourse did the gay Bellarmine entertain his beloved Leonora, when the door opened on a sudden and Horatio entered the room. Here 'tis impossible to express the surprise of Leonora."

"Poor woman," says Mrs. Slipslop, "what a terrible quandary she must be in!" "Not at all," says Graveairs; "such sluts can never be confounded." "She must have then more than Corinthian assurance," said Adams, "aye, more than Lais herself."

"A long silence," continued the lady, "prevailed in the whole company. If the familiar entrance of Horatio struck the greatest astonishment into Bellarmine, the unexpected presence of Bellarmine no less surprised Horatio. At length Leonora, collecting all the spirit she was mistress of, addressed herself to the latter, and pretended to wonder at the reason of so late a visit. 'I should, indeed,' answered he, 'have made some apology for disturbing you at this hour, had not my finding you in company assured me I do not break in upon your repose.' Bellarmine rose from his chair, traversed the room in a minuet step, and hummed an opera tune, while Horatio, advancing to Leonora, asked her in a whisper if that gentleman was not a relation of hers; to which she answered with a smile, or rather sneer. 'No, he is no relation of mine yet.' adding she could not guess the meaning of his question. Horatio told her softly it did not arise from jealousy. 'Jealousy! I assure you, it would be very strange in a common acquaintance to give himself any of those airs.' These words a little surprised Horatio, but before he had time to answer Bellarmine danced up to the lady and told her he feared he interrupted some business between her and the gentleman.— 'I can have no business,' said she, 'with the gentleman, nor any other, which need be any secret to you.'

" 'You'll pardon me,' said Horatio, 'if I desire to know who this gentleman is who is to be intrusted with all our secrets.'

'You'll know soon enough,' cries Leonora, 'but I can't guess what secrets can ever pass between us of such mighty consequence.' 'No, madam!' cries Horatio, 'I'm sure you would not have me understand you in earnest.' ' 'Tis indifferent to me,' says she, 'how you understand me, but I think so unseasonable a visit is difficult to be understood at all, at least when people find one engaged: though one's servants do not deny one, one may expect a well-bred person should soon take the hint.' 'Madam,' said Horatio, 'I did not imagine any engagement with a stranger, as it seems this gentleman is, would have made my visit impertinent, or that any such ceremonies were to be preserved between persons in our situation.' 'Sure you are in a dream,' says she, 'or would persuade me that I am in one. I know no pretensions a common acquaintance can have to lay aside the ceremonies of good breeding.' 'Sure,' says he, 'I am in a dream, for it is impossible I should be really esteemed a common acquaintance by Leonora, after what has passed between us!' 'Passed between us! Do you intend to affront me before this gentleman?' 'D—n me, affront the lady,' says Bellarmine, cocking his hat, and strutting up to Horatio. 'Does any man dare affront this lady before me, d—n me?' 'Hearkee, sir,' says Horatio, 'I would advise you to lay aside that fierce air, for I am mightily deceived if this lady has not a violent desire to get your worship a good drubbing.' 'Sir,' said Bellarmine, 'I have the honour to be her protector, and d—n me, if I understand your meaning.' 'Sir,' answered Horatio, 'she is rather your protectress; but give yourself no more airs for you see I am prepared for you' (shaking his whip at him). 'Oh! *serviteur très humble,'* says Bellarmine, *'je vous entends parfaitement bien.'* [1] At which time the aunt, who had heard of Horatio's visit, entered the room and soon satisfied all his doubts. She convinced him that he was never more awake in his life, and that nothing more extraordinary had happened in his three days' absence than a small alteration in the affections of Leonora; who now burst into tears and wondered what reason she had given him to use her in so barbarous a manner. Horatio desired Bellarmine to withdraw with him, but the ladies prevented it by laying violent hands on the latter; upon which the former took his leave without any great ceremony and departed, leaving the lady with his rival to consult for his safety, which Leonora feared her indiscretion might have endangered; but the aunt comforted her with assurances that Horatio would not venture his person against so accomplished a cavalier as Bellarmine, and that, being a lawyer, he would seek revenge in his own way, and the most they had to apprehend from him was an action.

"They at length therefore agreed to permit Bellarmine to retire to his lodgings, having first settled all matters relating to the journey which he was to undertake in the morning, and their preparations for the nuptials at his return.

"But alas! as wise men have observed, the seat of valour is not the countenance, and many a grave and plain man will, on a just provocation, betake himself to that mischievous metal, cold iron, while men of a fiercer brow, and sometimes with that emblem of courage, a cockade, will more prudently decline it.

"Leonora was awakened in the morning, from a visionary coach and six, with a dismal account that Bellarmine was run through the body by Horatio, that he lay languishing at an inn, and the surgeons had declared the wound mortal. She immediately leapt out of the bed and danced about the room in a frantic manner, tore her hair and beat her breast in all the agonies of despair; in which sad condition her aunt, who likewise arose at the news, found her. The good old lady applied her utmost art to comfort her niece. She told her while there was life there was hope, but that if he should die her affliction would be of no service to Bellarmine, and would only expose herself, which might probably keep her some time without any future offer; that as matters had happened her wisest way would be to think no more of Bellarmine but to endeavour to regain the affections of Horatio. 'Speak not to me,' cried the disconsolate Leonora: 'is it not owing to me that poor Bellarmine has lost his life? Have not these cursed charms' (at which words she looked steadfastly in the glass) 'been the ruin of the most charming man of this age? Can I ever bear to contemplate my own face again?' (with her eyes still fixed on the glass.) 'Am I not the murderess of the finest gentleman? No other woman in the town could have made any impression on him.' 'Never think of things past,' cries the aunt; 'think of regaining the affections of Horatio.' 'What reason,' said the niece, 'have I to hope he would forgive me? No, I have lost him as well as the other, and it was your wicked advice which was the occasion of all; you seduced me, contrary to my inclinations, to abandon poor Horatio' at which words she burst into tears. 'You prevailed upon me, whether I would or no, to give up my affections for him: had it not been for you, Bellarmine never would have entered into my thoughts; had not his addresses been backed by your persuasions, they never would have made any impression on me; I should have defied all the fortune and equipage in the world—but it was you, it was you, who got the better of my youth and simplicity, and forced me to lose my dear Horatio forever.'

"The aunt was almost borne down with this torrent of words; she however rallied all the strength she could, and, drawing her mouth up in a purse, began: 'I am not surprised, niece, at this ingratitude. Those who advise young women for their interest must always expect such a return; I am convinced my brother will thank me for breaking off your match with Horatio at any rate.' 'That may not be in your power yet,' answered Leonora, 'though it is very ungrateful in you to desire or attempt it, after the presents you have received from him.' (For indeed true it is that many presents, and some pretty valuable ones, had passed from Horatio to the old lady; but as true it is that Bellarmine, when he breakfasted with her and her niece, had complimented her with a brilliant from his finger of much greater value than all she had touched of the other.)

"The aunt's gall was on float to reply when a servant brought a letter into the room, which Leonora, hearing it came from Bellarmine, with great eagerness opened, and read as follows:

" 'MOST DIVINE CREATURE—The wound which I fear you have heard I received from my rival is not like to be so fatal as those shot into my heart which have been fired from your eyes, *tout-brilliant*.[2] Those are the only cannons by which I am to fall, for my surgeon gives me hopes of being soon able to attend your *ruelle;* till when, unless you would do me an honour which I have scarce the *hardiesse* to think of, your absence will be the greatest anguish which can be felt by,

" 'Madam,

" '*Avec tout le respecte* in the world,

" 'Your most obedient, most absolute *dévoté,*

" 'BELLARMINE.'

"As soon as Leonora perceived such hopes of Bellarmine's recovery, and that the gossip Fame hád, according to custom, so enlarged his danger, she presently abandoned all further thoughts of Horatio, and was soon reconciled to her aunt, who received her again into favour with a more Christian forgiveness than we generally meet with. Indeed, it is possible she might be a little alarmed at the hints which her niece had given her concerning the presents. She might apprehend such rumours, should they get abroad, might injure a reputation which, by frequenting church twice a day, and preserving the utmost rigour and strictness in her countenance and behaviour for many years, she had established.

"Leonora's passion returned now for Bellarmine with greater force, after its small relaxation, than ever. She proposed to her aunt to make him a visit in his confinement, which the old lady, with great and commendable prudence, advised her to decline: 'For,' says she, 'should any accident intervene to prevent your intended match, too forward a behaviour with this lover may injure you in the eyes of others. Every woman, till she is married, ought to consider of, and provide against, the possibility of the affair's breaking off.' Leonora said she should be indifferent to whatever might happen in such a case, for she had now so absolutely placed her affections on this dear man (so she called him), that if it was her misfortune to lose him she should forever abandon all thoughts of mankind. She therefore resolved to visit him notwithstanding all the prudent advice of her aunt to the contrary, and that very afternoon executed her resolution."

The lady was proceeding in her story when the coach drove into the inn where the company were to dine, sorely to the dissatisfaction of Mr. Adams, whose ears were the most hungry part about him, he being, as the reader may perhaps guess, of an insatiable curiosity, and heartily desirous of hearing the end of this amour, though he professed he could scarce wish success to a lady of so inconstant a disposition.

CHAPTER V: *A dreadful quarrel which happened at the inn where the company dined, with its bloody consequences to Mr. Adams.*

As soon as the passengers had alighted from the coach, Mr. Adams, as was his custom, made directly to the kitchen, where he found Joseph sitting by the fire and the hostess anointing his leg; for the horse which Mr. Adams had borrowed of his clerk had so violent a propensity to kneeling that one would have thought it had been his trade, as well as his master's, nor would he always give any notice of such his intention: he was often found on his knees when the rider least expected it. This foible, however, was of no great inconvenience to the parson, who was accustomed to it, and, as his legs almost touched the ground when he bestrode the beast, had but a little way to fall and threw himself forward on such occasions with so much dexterity that he never received any mischief, the horse and he frequently rolling many paces' distance and afterwards both getting up and meeting as good friends as ever.

Poor Joseph, who had not been used to such kind of cattle, though an excellent horseman did not so happily disengage himself, but, falling with his leg under the beast, received a violent contusion, to which the good woman was, as we have said, applying a warm hand, with some camphorated spirits, just at the time when the parson entered the kitchen.

He had scarce expressed his concern for Joseph's misfortune before the host likewise entered. He was by no means of Mr. Tow-wouse's gentle disposition, and was, indeed, perfect master of his house, and everything in it but his guests.

This surly fellow, who always proportioned his respect to the appearance of a traveller, from "God bless your honour," down to plain "coming presently," observing his wife on her knees to a footman, cried out, without considering his circumstances, "What a pox is the woman about? Why don't you mind the company in the coach? Go and ask them what they will have for dinner." "My dear," says she, "you know they can have nothing but what is at the fire, which will be ready presently; and really the poor young man's leg is very much bruised." At which words she fell to chafing more violently than before; the bell then happening to ring, he damned his wife and bid her go in to the company and not stand rubbing there all day, for he did not believe the young fellow's leg was so bad as he pretended, and if it was, within twenty miles he would find a surgeon to cut it off. Upon these words, Adams fetched two strides across the room, and, snapping his fingers over his head, muttered aloud he would excommunicate such a wretch for a farthing, for he believed the devil had more humanity. These words occasioned a dialogue between Adams and the host in which there were two or three sharp replies, till Joseph bade the latter know how to behave himself to his betters. At which the host, having first strictly surveyed Adams, scornfully repeating the words "betters," flew into a rage, and telling Joseph he was as able to walk out of his house as he had been to walk into it, offered to lay violent hands on him; which perceiving, Adams dealt him so sound a compliment over his face with his fist, that the blood immediately gushed out of his nose in a stream. The host being unwilling to be outdone in courtesy, especially by a person of Adams's figure, returned the favour with so much gratitude that the parson's nostrils began to look a little redder than usual. Upon which he again assailed his antagonist, and with another stroke laid him sprawling on the floor.

The hostess, who was a better wife than so surly a husband deserved, seeing her husband all bloody and stretched along, hastened presently to his assistance, or rather to revenge the blow, which, to all appearance, was the last he would ever receive, when, lo! a pan full of hog's blood, which unluckily stood on the dresser, presented itself first to her hands. She seized it in her fury, and, without any reflection, discharged it into the parson's face, and with so good an aim that much the greater part first saluted his countenance and trickled thence in so large a current down to his beard and all over his garments that a more horrible spectacle was hardly to be seen, or even imagined. All which was perceived by Mrs. Slipslop, who entered the kitchen at that instant. This good gentlewoman, not being of a temper so extremely cool and patient as perhaps was required to ask many questions on this occasion, flew with great impetuosity at the hostess's cap, which, together with some of her hair, she plucked from her head in a moment, giving her, at the same time, several hearty cuffs in the face, which, by frequent practise on the inferior servants, she had learned an excellent knack of delivering with a good grace. Poor Joseph could hardly rise from his chair; the parson was employed in wiping the blood from his eyes, which had entirely blinded him; and the landlord was but just beginning to stir; whilst Mrs. Slipslop, holding down the landlady's face with her left hand, made so dexterous a use of her right that the poor woman began to roar in a key which alarmed all the company in the inn.

There happened to be in the inn at this time, besides the ladies who arrived in the stage-coach, the two gentlemen who were present at Mr. Tow-wouse's when Joseph was detained for his horse's meat, and whom we have before mentioned to have stopped at the ale-house with Adams. There was likewise a gentleman just returned from his travels to Italy; all whom the horrid outcry of murder presently brought into the kitchen, where the several combatants were found in the postures already described.

It was now no difficulty to put an end to the fray, the conquerors being satisfied with the vengeance they had taken, and the conquered having no appetite to renew the fight. The principal figure, and which engaged the eyes of all, was Adams, who was all over covered with blood, which the whole company concluded to be his own, and consequently imagined him no longer for this world. But the host, who had now recovered from his blow and was risen from the ground, soon delivered them from this apprehension, by damning his wife for wasting the hog's puddings and telling her all would have been very well if she had not intermeddled, like a b— as she was, adding he was very glad the gentlewoman had paid her, though not half what she deserved. The poor woman had indeed fared much the worst, having, besides the unmerciful cuffs received, lost a quantity of hair, which Mrs. Slipslop in triumph held in her left hand.

The traveller, addressing himself to Mrs. Graveairs, desired her not to be frightened, for here had been only a little boxing, which, he said, to their *disgracia*[1] the English were *accustomata* to, adding it must be, however, a sight somewhat strange to him, who was just come from Italy, the Italians not being addicted to the *cuffardo,* but *bastonza,* says he. He then went up to Adams, and, telling him he looked like the ghost of Othello, bid him not shake his gory locks at him, for he could not say he did it. Adams very innocently answered, "Sir, I am far from accusing you." He then returned to the lady, and cried, "I find the bloody gentleman is *uno insipido del nullo senso. Damnata di me,* if I have seen such a *spectaculo* in my way from Viterbo."

One of the gentlemen, having learned from the host the occasion of this bustle, and being assured by him that Adams had struck the first blow, whispered in his ear he'd warrant he would recover. "Recover! master," said the host smiling; "yes, yes, I am not afraid of dying with a blow or two neither; I am not such a chicken as that." "Pugh!" said the gentleman, "I mean you will recover damages in that action which, undoubtedly, you intend to bring, as soon as a writ can be returned from London, for you look like a man of too much spirit and courage to suffer anyone to beat you without bringing your action against him: he must be a scandalous fellow indeed who would put up with a drubbing whilst the law is open to revenge it; besides, he hath drawn blood from you, and spoiled your coat, and the jury will give damages for that too. An excellent new coat, upon my word, and now not worth a shilling! I don't care," continued he, "to intermeddle in these cases, but you have a right to my evidence, and, if I am sworn, I must speak the truth. I saw you sprawling on the floor, and blood gushing from your nostrils. You may take your own opinion, but was I in your circumstances every drop of my blood should convey an ounce of gold into my pocket: remember I don't advise you to go to law, but if your jury were Christians, they must give swingeing damages. That's all." "Master," cried the host, scratching his head, "I have no stomach to law, I thank you. I have seen enough of that in the parish, where two of my neighbours have been at law about a house till they have both lawed themselves into a gaol." At which word he turned about, and began to inquire again after his hog's puddings, nor would it probably have been a sufficient excuse for his wife that she spilt them in his defence, had not some awe of the company, especially of the Italian traveller, who was a person of great dignity, withheld his rage.

Whilst one of the above-mentioned gentlemen was employed, as we have seen him, on the behalf of the landlord, the other was no less hearty on the side of Mr. Adams, whom he advised to bring his action immediately. He said the assault of the wife was in law the assault of the husband, for they were but one person, and he was liable to pay damages, which he said must be considerable where so bloody a disposition appeared. Adams answered, if it was true that they were but one person, he had assaulted the wife, for he was sorry to own he had struck the husband the first blow. "I am sorry you own it too," cries the gentleman, "for it could not possibly appear to the court, for here was no evidence present but the lame man in the chair, whom I suppose to be your friend and would consequently say nothing but what made for you." "How, sir," says Adams; "do you take me for a villain who would prosecute revenge in cold blood and use unjustifiable means to obtain it? If you knew me, and my order, I should think you affronted both." At the word order, the gentleman stared (for he was too bloody to be of any modern order of knights), and, turning hastily about, said, "Every man knew his own business."

Matters being now composed, the company retired to their several apartments, the two gentlemen congratulating each other on the success of their good offices in procuring a perfect reconciliation between the contending parties, and the traveller went to his repast, crying, "as the Italian poet says,

> " '*Je voi* very well, *que tuta e pace,* [2]
> So send dinner up, good Boniface.' "

The coachman began now to grow importunate with his passengers, whose entrance into the coach was retarded by

Miss Graveairs insisting, against the remonstrance of all the rest, that she would not admit a footman into the coach, for poor Joseph was too lame to mount a horse. A young lady who was, as it seems, an earl's grand-daughter, begged it, with almost tears in her eyes. Mr. Adams prayed, and Mrs. Slipslop scolded, but all to no purpose. She said she would not demean herself to ride with a footman: that there were waggons on the road; that if the master of the coach desired it, she would pay for two places, but would suffer no such fellow to come in. "Madam," says Slipslop, "I am sure no one can refuse another coming into a stage-coach." "I don't know, madam," says the lady; "I am not much used to stage-coaches; I seldom travel in them." "That may be, madam," replied Slipslop; "very good people do; and some people's betters for aught I know." Miss Graveairs said some folks might sometimes give their tongues a liberty to some people that were their betters, which did not become them; for her part, she was not used to converse with servants. Slipslop returned, some people kept no servants to converse with; for her part, she thanked heaven she lived in a family where there were a great many, and had more under her own command than any paltry little gentlewoman in the kingdom. Miss Graveairs cried, she believed her mistress would not encourage such sauciness to her betters. "My betters," says Slipslop; "who is my betters, pray?" "I am your betters," answered Miss Graveairs, "and I'll acquaint your mistress." At which Mrs. Slipslop laughed aloud and told her her lady was one of the great gentry, and such little paltry gentlewomen as some folks who travelled in stage-coaches would not easily come at her.

This smart dialogue between some people and some folks was going on at the coach-door when a solemn person riding into the inn, and seeing Miss Graveairs, immediately accosted her with "Dear child, how do you?" She presently answered, "Oh! Papa, I am glad you have overtaken me." "So am I," answered he, "for one of our coaches is just at hand, and there being room for you in it, you shall go no farther in the stage, unless you desire it." "How can you imagine I should desire it?" says she; so, bidding Slipslop ride with her fellow, if she pleased, she took her father by the hand, who was just alighted, and walked with him into a room.

Adams instantly asked the coachman, in a whisper, if he knew who the gentleman was? The coachman answered, he was now a gentleman, and kept his horse and man, "but times are altered, master," said he; "I remember when he was no better born than myself." "Aye! aye!" says Adams. "My father drove the squire's coach," answered me, "when that very man rode postilion, but he is now his steward and a great gentleman." Adams then snapped his fingers and cried he thought she was some such trollop.

Adams made haste to acquaint Mrs. Slipslop with this good news, as he imagined it, but it found a reception different from what he expected. The prudent gentlewoman, who despised the anger of Miss Graveairs whilst she conceived her the daughter of a gentleman of small fortune, now she heard her alliance with the upper servants of a great family in her neighbourhood began to fear her interest with the mistress. She wished she had not carried the dispute so far, and began to think of endeavouring to reconcile herself to the young lady before she left the inn, when luckily the scene at London, which the reader can scarce have forgotten, presented itself to her mind, and comforted her with such assurance that she no longer apprehended any enemy with her mistress.

Everything being now adjusted, the company entered the coach, which was just on its departure when one lady recollected she had left her fan, a second her gloves, a third a snuff-box, and a fourth a smelling-bottle behind her; to find all which occasioned some delay, and much swearing to the coachman.

As soon as the coach had left the inn, the women all together fell to the character of Miss Graveairs; whom one of them declared she had suspected to be some low creature, from the beginning of their journey; and another affirmed had not even the looks of a gentlewoman; a third warranted she was no better than she should be, and turning to the lady who had related the story in the coach, said, "Did you ever hear, madam, anything so prudish as her remarks? Well, deliver me from the censoriousness of such a prude." The fourth added, "Oh, madam! all these creatures are censorious, but for my part I wonder where the wretch was bred; indeed, I must own I have seldom conversed with these mean kind of people, so that it may appear stranger to me, but to refuse the general desire of a whole company had something in it so astonishing that, for my part, I own I should hardly believe it if my own ears had not been witnesses to it." "Yes, and so handsome a young fellow," cries Slipslop; "the woman must have no compulsion in her: I believe she is more of a Turk than a Christian; I am certain, if she had any Christian woman's blood in her veins the sight of such a young fellow must have warmed it. Indeed, there are some wretched, miserable old objects that turn one's stomach; I should not wonder if she had refused such a one. I am as nice as herself, and should have cared no more than herself for the company of stinking old fellows, but hold up thy head, Joseph, thou art none of those, and she who hath not compulsion for thee is a Myhummetman, and I will maintain it." This conversation made Joseph uneasy, as well as the ladies, who, perceiving the spirits which Mrs. Slipslop was in (for indeed she was not a cup too low), began to fear the consequence; one of them therefore desired the lady to conclude the story. "Aye, madam," said Slipslop, "I beg your ladyship to give us that story you commensated in the morning," which request that well-bred woman immediately complied with.

CHAPTER VI: *Conclusion of the unfortunate jilt.*

"Leonora, having once broke through the bounds which custom and modesty impose on her sex, soon gave an unbridled indulgence to her passion. Her visits to Bellarmine were more constant, as well as longer, than his surgeon's, in a word, she became absolutely his nurse, made his water-gruel, administered him his medicines, and, notwithstanding the prudent advice of her aunt to the contrary, almost entirely resided in her wounded lover's apartment.

"The ladies of the town began to take her conduct under consideration; it was the chief topic of discourse at their tea-tables, and was very severely censured by the most part, especially by Lindamira, a lady whose discreet and starch carriage, together with a constant attendance at church three times a day, had utterly defeated many malicious attacks on her own reputation, for such was the envy that Lindamira's virtue had attracted that, notwithstanding her own strict behaviour, and strict inquiry into the lives of others, she had not been able to escape being the mark of some arrows herself, which, however, did her no injury; a blessing, perhaps, owed by her to the clergy, who were her chief male companions, and with two or three of whom she had been barbarously and unjustly calumniated."

"Not so unjustly neither perhaps," says Slipslop, "for the clergy are men, as well as other folks."

"The extreme delicacy of Lindamira's virtue was cruelly

hurt by those freedoms which Leonora allowed herself; she said it was an affront to her sex, that she did not imagine it consistent with any woman's honour to speak to the creature or to be seen in her company, and that, for her part, she should always refuse to dance at an assembly with her for fear of contamination by taking her by the hand.

"But to return to my story: as soon as Bellarmine was recovered, which was somewhat within a month from his receiving the wound, he set out, according to agreement, for Leonora's father's, in order to propose the match and settle all matters with him touching settlements, and the like.

"A little before his arrival, the old gentleman had received an intimation of the affair by the following letter, which I can repeat *verbatim,* and which, they say, was written neither by Leonora nor her aunt, though it was in a woman's hand. The letter was in these words:

" 'Sir—I am sorry to acquaint you that your daughter Leonora hath acted one of the basest as well as most simple parts with a young gentleman to whom she had engaged herself, and whom she hath (pardon the word) jilted for another of inferior fortune, notwithstanding his superior figure. You may take what measures you please on this occasion; I have performed what I thought my duty, as I have, though unknown to you, a very great respect for your family.'

"The old gentleman did not give himself the trouble to answer this kind epistle, nor did he take any notice of it after he had read it till he saw Bellarmine. He was, to say the truth, one of those fathers who look on children as an unhappy consequence of their youthful pleasures, which as he would have been delighted not to have had attended them, so was he no less pleased with any opportunity to rid himself of the incumbrance. He passed, in the world's language, as an exceeding good father, being not only so rapacious as to rob and plunder all mankind to the utmost of his power, but even to deny himself the conveniencies, and almost necessaries of life, which his neighbours attributed to a desire of raising immense fortunes for his children; but in fact it was not so: he heaped up money for its own sake only, and looked on his children as his rivals, who were to enjoy his beloved mistress when he was incapable of possessing her, and which he would have been much more charmed with the power of carrying along with him; nor had his children any other security of being his heirs than that the law would constitute them such without a will and that he had not affection enough for anyone living to take the trouble of writing one.

"To this gentleman came Bellarmine, on the errand I have mentioned. His person, his equipage, his family, and his estate seemed to the father to make him an advantageous match for his daughter; he therefore very readily accepted his proposals, but when Bellarmine imagined the principal affair concluded, and began to open the incidental matters of fortune, the old gentleman presently changed his countenance, saying he resolved never to marry his daughter on a Smithfield match; that whoever had love for her to take her would, when he died, find her share of his fortune in his coffers, but he had seen such examples of undutifulness happen from the too early generosity of parents that he had made a vow never to part with a shilling whilst he lived. He commended the saying of Solomon, He that spareth the rod spoileth the child, but added he might have likewise asserted that he that spareth the purse, saveth the child. He then ran into a discourse on the extravagance of the youth of the age; whence he launched into a dissertation on horses; and came at length to commend those Bellarmine drove. That fine gentleman, who at another season would have been well enough pleased to dwell a little on that subject, was now very eager to resume the circumstance of fortune. He said he had a very high value for the young lady, and would receive her with less than he would any other whatever, but that even his love to her made some regard to worldly matters necessary, for it would be a most distracting sight for him to see her, when he had the honour to be her husband, in less than a coach and six. The old gentleman answered, 'Four will do, four will do,' and then took a turn from horses to extravagance, and from extravagance to horses, till he came round to the equipage again, whither he was no sooner arrived, than Bellarmine brought him back to the point; but all to no purpose: he made his escape from that subject in a minute, till at last the lover declared that in the present situation of his affairs it was impossible for him, though he loved Leonora more than *tout le monde,*[1] to marry her without any fortune. To which the father answered he was sorry then his daughter must lose so valuable a match; that if he had an inclination, at present it was not in his power to advance a shilling; that he had had great losses, and been at great expenses on projects, which, though he had great expectation from them, had yet produced him nothing; that he did not know what might happen hereafter, as on the birth of a son, or such accidents, but he would make no promise, nor enter into any article, for he would not break his vow for all the daughters in the world.

"In short, ladies, to keep you no longer in suspense, Bellarmine having tried every argument and persuasion which he could invent, and finding them all ineffectual, at length took his leave, but not in order to return to Leonora; he proceeded directly to his own seat, whence, after a few days' stay, he returned to Paris, to the great delight of the French and the honour of the English nation.

"But as soon as he arrived at his home, he presently dispatched a messenger with the following epistle to Leonora.

" 'Adorable and Charmante[2]—I am sorry to have the honour to tell you I am not the *heureux* person destined for your divine arms. Your papa hath told me so with a *politesse* not often seen on this side Paris. You may perhaps guess his manner of refusing me. *Ah, mon Dieu!* You will certainly believe me, madam, incapable myself of delivering this *triste* message, which I intend to try the French air to cure the consequences of. *A jamais! Coeur! Ange! Au diable!* If your papa obliges you to a marriage, I hope we shall see you at Paris; till when, the wind that flows from thence will be the warmest *dans le monde,* for it will consist almost entirely of my sighs. *Adieu, ma princesse! Ah, l'amour!*

" 'BELLARMINE.'

"I shall not attempt, ladies, to describe Leonora's condition when she received this letter. It is a picture of horror which I should have as little pleasure in drawing as you in beholding. She immediately left the place, where she was the subject of conversation and ridicule, and retired to that house I showed you when I began the story; where she hath ever since led a disconsolate life, and deserves, perhaps, pity for her misfortunes, more than our censure for a behaviour to which the artifices of her aunt very probably contributed, and to which very young women are often rendered too liable by that blameable levity in the education of our sex."

"If I was inclined to pity her," said a young lady in the coach, "it would be for the loss of Horatio, for I cannot discern any misfortune in her missing such a husband as Bellarmine."

"Why, I must own," said Slipslop, "the gentleman was a little false-hearted; but, howsumever, it was hard to have two lovers and get never a husband at all. But pray, madam, what became of *Ourasho?*"

"He remains," said the lady, "still unmarried, and hath applied himself so strictly to his business that he hath raised, I hear, a very considerable fortune. And, what is remarkable, they say he never hears the name of Leonora without a sigh, nor hath ever uttered one syllable to charge her with her ill conduct towards him."

CHAPTER VII: *A very short chapter, in which Parson Adams went a great way.*

THE lady, having finished her story, received the thanks of the company; and now Joseph, putting his head out of the coach, cried out, "Never believe me, if yonder be not our Parson Adams walking along without his horse." "Oh my word, and so he is," says Slipslop, "and as sure as twopence he hath left him behind at the inn." Indeed, true it is the parson had exhibited a fresh instance of his absence of mind, for he was so pleased with having got Joseph into the coach that he never once thought of the beast in the stable, and, finding his legs as nimble as he desired, he sallied out, brandishing a crab-stick, and had kept on before the coach, mending and slackening his pace occasionally, so that he had never been much more or less than a quarter of a mile distant from it.

Mrs. Slipslop desired the coachman to overtake him, which he attempted, but in vain; for the faster he drove, the faster ran the parson, often crying out, "Aye, aye, catch me if you can," till at length the coachman swore he would as soon attempt to drive after a greyhound, and giving the parson two or three hearty curses he cried, "softly, softly, boys," to his horses, which the civil beasts immediately obeyed.

But we will be more courteous to our reader than he was to Mrs. Slipslop, and, leaving the coach and its company to pursue their journey, we will carry our reader on after Parson Adams, who stretched forwards without once looking behind him, till, having left the coach full three miles in his rear, he came to a place where, by keeping the extremest track to the right, it was just barely possible for a human creature to miss his way. This track, however, did he keep, as indeed he had a wonderful capacity at these kinds of bare possibilities, and traveling in it about three miles over the plain he arrived at the summit of a hill, whence, looking a great way backwards, and perceiving no coach in sight, he sat himself down on the turf, and, pulling out his Aeschylus, determined to wait here for its arrival.

He had not sat long here before a gun going off very near a little startled him; he looked up, and saw a gentleman within a hundred paces taking up a partridge which he had just shot.

Adams stood up and presented a figure to the gentleman which would have moved laughter in many, for his cassock had just again fallen down below his great-coat—that is to say, it reached his knees, whereas the skirts of his great-coat descended no lower than halfway down his thighs—but the gentleman's mirth gave way to his surprise at beholding such a personage in such a place.

Adams, advancing to the gentleman, told him he hoped he had good sport, to which the other answered, "Very little." "I see, sir," says Adams, "you have smote one partridge"; to which the sportsman made no reply, but proceeded to charge his piece.

Whilst the gun was charging, Adams remained in silence, which he at last broke by observing that it was a delightful evening. The gentleman, who had at first sight conceived a very distasteful opinion of the parson, began, on perceiving a book in his hand and smoking likewise the information of the cassock, to change his thoughts, and made a small advance to conversation on his side, by saying, "Sir, I suppose you are not one of these parts?"

Adams immediately told him, No, that he was a traveller, and invited by the beauty of the evening and the place to repose a little, and amuse himself with reading. "I may as well repose myself too," said the sportsman, "for I have been out this whole afternoon, and the devil a bird have I seen till I came hither."

"Perhaps then the game is not very plenty hereabouts," cries Adams. "No, sir," said the gentleman: "the soldiers, who are quartered in the neighbourhood, have killed it all." "It is very probable," cries Adams, "for shooting is their profession." "Aye, shooting the game," answered the other, "but I don't see they are so forward to shoot our enemies. I don't like that affair of Carthagena: if I had been there, I believe I should have done other-guess things, d—n me. What's a man's life when his country demands it? A man who won't sacrifice his life for his country deserves to be hanged, d—n me." Which words he spoke with so violent a gesture, so loud a voice, so strong an accent, and so fierce a countenance, that he might have frightened a captain of trained-bands at the head of his company; but Mr. Adams was not greatly subject to fear: he told him intrepidly that he very much approved his virtue but disliked his swearing, and begged him not to addict himself to so bad a custom, without which he said he might fight as bravely as Achilles did. Indeed, he was charmed with this discourse: he told the gentleman he would willingly have gone many miles to have met a man of his generous way of thinking; that if he pleased to sit down, he should be greatly delighted to commune with him, for though he was clergyman he would himself be ready, if thereto called, to lay down his life for his country.

The gentleman sat down and Adams by him, and then the latter began, as in the following chapter, a discourse which we have placed by itself, as it is not only the most curious in this but perhaps in any other book.

CHAPTER VIII: *A notable dissertation by Mr. Abraham Adams, wherein that gentleman appears in a political light.*

"I DO assure you, sir," says he, taking the gentleman by the hand, "I am heartily glad to meet with a man of your kidney, for though I am a poor parson, I will be bold to say I am an honest man and would not do an ill thing to be made a bishop; nay, though it hath not fallen in my way to offer so noble a sacrifice, I have not been without opportunities of suffering for the sake of my conscience, I thank heaven for them; for I have had relations, though I say it, who made some figure in the world, particularly a nephew, who was a shopkeeper, and an alderman of a corporation. He was a good lad, and was under my care when a boy, and I believe would do what I bade him to his dying day. Indeed, it looks like extreme vanity in me to affect being a man of such consequence as to have so great an interest in an alderman; but others have thought so too, as manifestly appeared by the rector, whose curate I formerly was, sending for me on the approach of an election and telling me, if I expected to continue in his cure, that I must bring my nephew to vote for one Colonel Courtly, a gentleman whom I had never heard tidings of till that instant. I told the rector I had no power over my nephew's vote (God forgive me for such prevarication!); that I supposed he would give it according to his conscience; that I would by no means endeavour to influence him to give it otherwise. He told me it was in vain to equivocate; that he knew I had already spoke to him in favour of esquire Fickle, my neighbour; and, indeed, it was true I had, for it was at a season when the church was in danger and when all good men expected they knew not what would happen to us all. I then answered boldly, if he thought I had given my promise, he affronted me in proposing any breach of it. Not to be too prolix, I persevered, and so did my nephew, in the esquire's interest, who was chose chiefly through his means; and so I lost my curacy. Well, sir, but do you think the esquire ever mentioned a word of the church? *Ne verbum quidem, ut ita dicam*: [1] within two years he got a place, and hath ever since lived in London, where, I have been informed (but God forbid I should believe that), that he never so much as goeth to church. I remained, sir, a considerable time without any cure, and lived a full month on one funeral sermon, which I preached on the indisposition of a clergyman: but this by the bye. At last, when Mr. Fickle got his place, Colonel Courtly stood again, and who should make interest for him but Mr. Fickle himself. That very identical Mr. Fickle who had formerly told me the Colonel was an enemy to both the church and state had the confidence to solicit my nephew for him; and the Colonel himself offered me to make me chaplain to his regiment, which I refused in favour of Sir Oliver Hearty, who told us he would sacrifice everything to his country; and I believe he would, except his hunting, which he stuck so close to that in five years together he went but twice up to Parliament, and one of those times, I have been told, never was within sight of the House. However, he was a worthy man, and the best friend I ever had, for, by his interest with a bishop, he got me replaced into my curacy, and gave me eight pounds out of his own pocket to buy me a gown and cassock and furnish my house. He had our interest while he lived, which was not many years. On his death I had fresh applications made to me, for all the world knew the interest I had with my good nephew, who was now a leading man in the corporation; and Sir Thomas Booby, buying the estate which had been Sir Oliver's, proposed himself a candidate. He was then a young gentleman just come from his travels, and it did me good to hear him discourse on affairs which, for my part, I knew nothing of. If I had been master of a thousand votes he should have had them all. I engaged my nephew in his interest, and he was elected, and a very fine Parliament man he was. They tell me he made speeches of an hour long, and, I have been told, very fine ones; but he could never persuade the Parliament to be of his opinion. *Non omnia possumus omnes.*[2] He promised me a living, poor man, and I believe I should have had it, but an accident happened, which was that my lady had promised it before, unknown to him. This, indeed, I never heard till afterwards, for my nephew, who died about a month before the incumbent, always told me I might be assured of it. Since that time, Sir Thomas, poor man, had always so much business that he never could find leisure to see me. I believe it was partly my lady's fault too, who did not think my dress good enough for the gentry at her table. However, I must do him the justice to say he never was ungrateful, and I have always found his kitchen, and his cellar too, open to me: many a time, after service on a Sunday—for I preach at four churches—have I recruited my spirits with a glass of his ale. Since my nephew's death, the corporation is in other hands, and I am not a man of that consequence I was formerly. I have now no longer any talents to lay out in the service of my country; and to whom nothing is given, of him can nothing be required. However, on all proper seasons, such as the approach of an election, I throw a suitable dash or two into my sermons, which I have the pleasure to hear is not disagreeable to Sir Thomas and the other honest gentlemen my neighbours, who have all promised me these five years to procure an ordination for a son of mine, who is now near thirty, hath an infinite stock of learning, and is, I thank heaven, of an unexceptionable life, though, as he was never at an university, the bishop refuses to ordain him. Too much care cannot indeed be taken in admitting any to the sacred office, though I hope he will never act so as to be a disgrace to any order but will serve his God and his country to the utmost of his power, as I have endeavoured to do before him, nay, and will lay down his life whenever called to that purpose. I am sure I have educated him in those principles, so that I have acquitted my duty and shall have nothing to answer for on that account. But I do not distrust him, for he is a good boy, and if Providence should throw it in his way to be of as much consequence in a public light as his father once was, I can answer for him he will use his talents as honestly as I have done."

CHAPTER IX: *In which the gentleman descants on bravery and heroic virtue, till an unlucky accident puts an end to the discourse.*

THE gentleman highly commended Mr. Adams for his good resolutions, and told him he hoped his son would tread in his steps, adding that if he would not die for his country, he would not be worthy to live in it. "I'd make no more of shooting a man that would not die for his country, than——

"Sir," said he, "I have disinherited a nephew, who is in the army, because he would not exchange his commission and go to the West Indies. I believe the rascal is a coward, though he pretends to be in love, forsooth. I would have all such fellows hanged, sir; I would have them hanged." Adams answered, that would be too severe: that men did not make themselves, and, if fear had too much ascendance in the mind, the man was rather to be pitied than abhorred; that reason and time might teach him to subdue it. He said a man might be a coward at one time, and brave at another. "Homer," says he, "who so well understood and copied nature, hath taught us this lesson, for Paris fights and Hector runs away. Nay, we have a mighty instance of this in the history of later ages, no longer ago than the 705th year of Rome, when the great Pompey, who had won so many battles and been honoured with so many triumphs, and of whose valour several authors, especially Cicero and Paterculus, have formed such eulogiums—this very Pompey left the battle of Pharsalia before he had lost it, and retreated to his tent, where he sat like the most pusillanimous rascal in a fit of despair, and yielded a victory which was to determine the empire of the world, to Caesar. I am not much travelled in the history of modern times, that is to say, these last thousand years, but those who are, can, I make no question, furnish you with parallel instances." He concluded, therefore, that had he taken any such hasty resolutions against his nephew, he hoped he would consider better, and retract them. The gentleman answered with great warmth, and talked much of courage and his country, till, perceiving it grew late, he asked Adams what place he intended for that night? He told him he waited there for the stage-coach. "The stage-coach! Sir," said the gentleman, "they are all past by long ago. You may see the last yourself almost three miles before us." "I protest and so they are," cries Adams; "then I must make haste and follow them." The gentleman told him he would hardly be able to overtake them, and that if he did not know his way he would be in danger of losing himself on the downs, for it would be presently dark and he might ramble about all night, and perhaps find himself farther from his journey's end in the morning than he was now. He advised him, therefore, to accompany him to his house, which was very little out of his way, assuring him that he would find some country fellow in his parish who would conduct him for sixpence to the city where he was going. Adams accepted this proposal, and on they travelled, the gentleman renewing his discourse on courage, and the infamy of not being ready at all times to sacrifice our lives to our country. Night overtook them much about the same time as they arrived near some bushes, whence, on a sudden, they heard the most violent shrieks imaginable in a female voice. Adams offered to snatch the gun out of his companion's hand. "What are you doing?" said he. "Doing!" says Adams; "I am hastening to the assistance of the poor creature whom some villains are murdering." "You are not mad enough, I hope," says the gentleman trembling. "Do you consider this gun is only charged with shot, and that the robbers are most probably furnished with pistols loaded with bullets? This is no business of ours; let us make as much haste as possible out of the way, or we may fall into their hands ourselves." The shrieks now increasing, Adams made no answer, but snapped his fingers, and, brandishing his crab-stick, made directly to the place whence the voice issued; and the man of courage made as much expedition towards his own home, whither he escaped in a very short time without once looking behind him; where we will leave him, to contemplate his own bravery, and to censure the want of it in others, and return to the good Adams, who, on coming up to the place whence the noise proceeded, found a woman struggling with a man who had thrown her on the ground and had almost overpowered her. The great abilities of Mr. Adams were not necessary to have formed a right judgement of this affair on the first sight. He did not therefore want the entreaties of the poor wretch to assist her, but, lifting up his crab-stick, he immediately levelled a blow at that part of the ravisher's head where, according to the opinion of the ancients, the brains of some persons are deposited, and which he had undoubtedly let forth, had not Nature (who, as wise men have observed, equips all creatures with what is most expedient for them) taken a provident care (as she always doth with those she intends for encounters) to make this part of the head three times as thick as those of ordinary men, who are designed to exercise talents which are vulgarly called rational, and for whom, as brains are necessary, she is obliged to leave some room for them in the cavity of the skull, whereas, those ingredients being entirely useless to persons of the heroic calling, she hath an opportunity of thickening the bone so as to make it less subject to any impression, or liable to be cracked or broken; and indeed, in some who are predestined to the command of armies and empires, she is supposed sometimes to make that part perfectly solid.

As a game-cock, when engaged in amorous toying with a hen, if perchance he espies another cock at hand immediately quits his female and opposes himself to his rival, so did the ravisher, on the information of the crab-stick, immediately leap from the woman and hasten to assail the man. He had no weapons but what nature had furnished him with. However, he clenched his fist, and presently darted it at that part of Adams's breast where the heart is lodged. Adams staggered at the violence of the blow, when, throwing away his staff, he likewise clenched that fist which we have before commemorated and would have discharged it full in the breast of his antagonist had he not dexterously caught it with his left hand, at the same time darting his head (which some modern heroes of the lower class use, like the battering-ram of the ancients, for a weapon of offence; another reason to admire the cunningness of Nature in composing it of those impenetrable materials); dashing his head, I say, into the stomach of Adams, he tumbled him on his back, and, not having any regard to the laws of heroism, which would have restrained him from any farther attack on his enemy till he was again on his legs, he threw himself upon him, and, laying hold on the ground with his left hand, he with his right belaboured the body of Adams till he was weary, and indeed till he concluded (to use the language of fighting) that he had done his business, or, in the language of poetry, "that he had sent him to the shades below"—in plain English, "that he was dead."

But Adams, who was no chicken, and could bear a drubbing as well as any boxing champion in the universe, lay still only to watch his opportunity, and now perceiving his antagonist to pant with his labours, he exerted his utmost force at once, and with such success that he overturned him and became his superior, when, fixing one of his knees in his breast, he cried out in an exulting voice, "It is my turn now," and after a few minutes' constant application, he gave him so dexterous a blow just under his chin that the fellow no longer retained any motion and Adams began to fear he had struck him once too often, for he often asserted he should be concerned to have the blood of even the wicked upon him.

Adams got up and called aloud to the young woman. "Be of good cheer, damsel," said he; "you are no longer in danger of your ravisher, who, I am terribly afraid, lies dead at my feet; but God forgive me what I have done in defence of innocence." The poor wretch, who had been some time in recovering strength enough to rise, and had afterwards, during the engagement, stood trembling, being disabled by fear even from running away, hearing her champion was victorious, came up to him, but not without apprehensions even of her deliverer; which, however, she was soon relieved from, by his courteous behaviour and gentle words. They were both standing by the body, which lay motionless on the ground, and which Adams wished to see stir much more than the woman did, when he earnestly begged her to tell him by what misfortune she came, at such a time of night, into so lonely a place. She acquainted him. She was travelling towards London and had accidentally met with the person from whom he had delivered her, who told her he was likewise on his journey to the same place and would keep her company, an offer which, suspecting no harm, she had accepted; that he told her they were at a small distance from an inn where she might take up her lodging that evening, and he would show her a nearer way to it than by following the road; that if she had suspected him (which she did not, he spoke so kindly to her), being alone on these downs in the dark, she had no human means to avoid him; that therefore she put her whole trust in Providence and walked on, expecting every moment to arrive at the inn, when on a sudden, being come to those bushes, he desired her to stop, and, after some rude kisses, which she resisted, and some entreaties, which she rejected, he laid violent hands on her and was attempting to execute his wicked will, when, she thanked G—, he timely came up and prevented him. Adams encouraged her for saying she had put her whole trust in Providence, and told her he doubted not but Providence had sent him to her deliverance, as a reward for that trust. He wished indeed he had not deprived the wicked wretch of life, but G—'s will be done. He said he hoped the goodness of his intention would excuse him in the next world, and he trusted in her evidence to acquit him in this. He was then silent, and began to consider with himself whether it would be properer to make his escape or to deliver himself into the hands of justice; which meditation ended as the reader will see in the next chapter.

CHAPTER X: *Giving an account of the strange catastrophe of the preceding adventure, which drew poor Adams into fresh calamities, and who the woman was who owed the preservation of her chastity to his victorious arm.*

THE silence of Adams, added to the darkness of the night and loneliness of the place, struck dreadful apprehensions into the poor woman's mind; she began to fear as great an enemy in her deliverer as he had delivered her from; and, as she had not light enough to discover the age of Adams, and the benevolence visible in his countenance, she suspected he had used her as some very honest men have used their country and had rescued her out of the hands of one rifler in order to rifle her himself. Such were the suspicions she drew from his silence; but indeed they were ill grounded. He stood over his vanquished enemy, wisely weighing in his mind the objections which might be made to either of the two methods of proceeding mentioned in the last chapter, his judgement sometimes inclining to the one, and sometimes to the other, for both seemed to him so equally advisable, and so equally dangerous, that probably he would have ended his days, at least two or three of them, on that very spot before he had taken any resolution; at length he lifted up his eyes and spied a light at a distance, to which he instantly addressed himself with *Heus tu,*[1] *Traveller, heus tu!* He presently heard several voices and perceived the light approaching toward him. The persons who attended the light began some to laugh, others to sing, and others to hallo, at which the woman testified some fear (for she had concealed her suspicions of the parson himself); but Adams said, "Be of good cheer, damsel, and repose thy trust in the same Providence which hath hitherto protected thee, and never will forsake the innocent." These people, who now approached, were no other, reader, than a set of young fellows who came to these bushes in pursuit of a diversion which they call bird-batting. This, if thou art ignorant of it (as perhaps if thou hast never travelled beyond Kensington, Islington,

Hackney, or the Borough, thou mayst be), I will inform thee, is performed by holding a large clap-net before a lantern and at the same time beating the bushes; for the birds, when they are disturbed from their places of rest or roost, immediately make to the light, and so are inticed within the net. Adams immediately told them what had happened and desired them to hold the lantern to the face of the man on the ground, for he feared he had smote him fatally. But indeed his fears were frivolous, for the fellow, though he had been stunned by the last blow he received, had long since recovered his senses, and, finding himself quit of Adams, had listened attentively to the discourse between him and the young woman, for whose departure he had patiently waited that he might likewise withdraw himself, having no longer hopes of succeeding in his desires, which were moreover almost as well cooled by Mr. Adams as they could have been by the young woman herself had he obtained his utmost wish. This fellow, who had a readiness at improving any accident, thought he might now play a better part than that of a dead man, and accordingly, the moment the candle was held to his face, he leapt up, and, laying hold on Adams, cried out, "No, villain, I am not dead, though you and your wicked whore might well think me so, after the barbarous cruelties you have exercised on me. Gentlemen," said he, "you are luckily come to the assistance of a poor traveller who would otherwise have been robbed and murdered by this vile man and woman, who led me hither out of my way from the high-road, and both falling on me have used me as you see." Adams was going to answer, when one of the young fellows cried, "D—n them, let's carry them both before the justice." The poor woman began to tremble, and Adams lifted up his voice, but in vain. Three or four of them laid hands on him, and, one holding the lantern to his face, they all agreed he had the most villainous countenance they ever beheld, and an attorney's clerk who was of the company declared he was sure he had remembered him at the bar. As to the woman, her hair was dishevelled in the struggle and her nose had bled, so that they could not perceive whether she was handsome or ugly, but they said her fright plainly discovered her guilt. And searching her pockets, as they did those of Adams, for money, which the fellow said he had lost, they found in her pocket a purse with some gold in it, which abundantly convinced them, especially as the fellow offered to swear to it. Mr. Adams was found to have no more than one halfpenny about him. This the clerk said was a great presumption that he was an old offender, by cunningly giving all the booty to the woman. To which all the rest readily assented.

This accident promising them better sport than what they had proposed, they quitted their intention of catching birds, and unanimously resolved to proceed to the justice with the offenders. Being informed what a desperate fellow Adams was, they tied his hands behind him, and having hid their nets among the bushes, and the lantern being carried before them, they placed the two prisoners in their front and then began their march, Adams not only submitting patiently to his own fate but comforting and encouraging his companion under her sufferings.

Whilst they were on their way the clerk informed the rest that this adventure would prove a very beneficial one, for that they would be all entitled to their proportions of £80 for apprehending the robbers. This occasioned a contention concerning the parts which they had severally borne in taking them, one insisting he ought to have the greatest share, for he had first laid his hands on Adams; another claiming a superior part for having first held the lantern to the man's face on the ground, by which, he said, "the whole was discovered"; the clerk claiming four-fifths of the reward for having proposed to search the prisoners, and likewise the carrying them before the justice—he said, indeed, in strict justice, he ought to have the whole. These claims, however, they at last consented to refer to a future decision, but seemed all to agree that the clerk was entitled to a moiety. They then debated what money should be allotted to the young fellow who had been employed only in holding the nets. He very modestly said that he did not apprehend any large proportion would fall to his share, but hoped they would allow him something; he desired them to consider that they had assigned their nets to his care, which prevented him from being as forward as any in laying hold of the robbers (for so these innocent people were called); that if he had not occupied the nets, some other must; concluding however, that he should be contented with the smallest share imaginable, and should think that rather their bounty than his merit. But they were all unanimous in excluding him from any part whatever, the clerk particularly swearing, if they gave him a shilling, they might do what they pleased with the rest for he would not concern himself with the affair. This contention was so hot, and so totally engaged the attention of all the parties, that a dexterous nimble thief, had he been in Mr. Adams's situation, would have taken care to have given the justice no trouble that evening. Indeed, it required not the art of Sheppard[2] to escape, especially as the darkness of the night would have so much befriended him, but Adams trusted rather to his innocence than his heels, and without thinking of flight, which was easy, or resistance, which was impossible, as there were six lusty young fellows, besides the villain himself, present, he walked with perfect resignation the way they thought proper to conduct him.

Adams frequently vented himself in ejaculations during their journey; at last poor Joseph Andrews occurring to his mind, he could not refrain sighing forth his name, which being heard by his companion in affliction, she cried with some vehemence, "Sure, I should know that voice; you cannot certainly, sir, be Mr. Abraham Adams?" "Indeed, damsel," says he, "that is my name; there is something also in your voice which persuades me I have heard it before." "La, sir," says she, "don't you remember poor Fanny?" "How, Fanny!" answered Adams; "indeed, I very well remember you; what can have brought you hither?" "I have told you, sir," replied she, "I was travelling towards London; but I thought you mentioned Joseph Andrews, pray what is become of him?" "I left him, child, this afternoon," said Adams, "in the stage-coach, in his way towards our parish, whither he is going to see you." "To see me! La, sir," answered Fanny, "sure you jeer me: what should he be going to see me for?" "Can you ask that?" replied Adams. "I hope, Fanny, you are not inconstant; I assure you he deserves much better of you." "La, Mr. Adams," said she, "what is Mr. Joseph to me? I am sure I never had anything to say to him but as one fellow-servant might to another." "I am sorry to hear this," said Adams; "a virtuous passion for a young man is what no woman need be ashamed of. You either do not tell me truth, or you are false to a very worthy man." Adams then told her what had happened at the inn, to which she listened very attentively, and a sigh often escaped from her, notwithstanding her utmost endeavours to the contrary, nor could she prevent herself from asking a thousand questions, which would have assured anyone but Adams, who never saw farther into people than they desired to let him, of the truth of a passion she endeavoured to conceal. Indeed, the fact was that this poor girl having heard of Joseph's misfortune by some of the servants belonging to the coach which we have formerly mentioned to have stopped at the inn while the poor youth was confined to his bed, that instant abandoned the cow she was milking, and, taking with her a little bundle of clothes under her arm and all the money she was worth in her own purse, without consulting anyone immediately set forward in pursuit of one whom, notwithstanding her shyness to the parson, she loved with inexpressible violence, though with the purest and most delicate passion. This shyness, therefore, as we trust it will recommend her character to all our female readers, and not greatly surprise such of our males as are well acquainted with the younger part of the other sex, we shall not give ourselves any trouble to vindicate.

CHAPTER XI: *What happened to them while before the justice. A chapter very full of learning.*

THEIR fellow-travellers were so engaged in the hot dispute concerning the division of the reward for apprehending these innocent people that they attended very little to their discourse. They were now arrived at the justice's house, and had sent one of his servants in to acquaint his worship that they had taken two robbers and brought them before him. The justice, who was just returned from a fox-chase and had not yet finished his dinner, ordered them to carry the prisoners into the stable, whither they were attended by all the servants in the house and all the people in the neighbourhood, who flocked together to see them with as much curiosity as if there was something uncommon to be seen, or that a rogue did not look like other people.

The justice now, being in the height of his mirth and his cups, bethought himself of the prisoners, and telling his company he believed they should have good sport in their examination, he ordered them into his presence. They had no sooner entered the room than he began to revile them, saying that robberies on the highway were now grown so frequent that people could not sleep safely in their beds, and assured them they both should be made examples of at the ensuing assizes. After he had gone on some time in this manner, he was reminded by his clerk that it would be proper to take the depositions of the witnesses against them. Which he bid him do, and he would light his pipe in the meantime. Whilst the clerk was employed in writing down the deposition of the fellow who had pretended to be robbed, the justice employed himself in cracking jests on poor Fanny, in which he was seconded by all the company at table. One asked whether she was to be indicted for a highwayman? Another whispered in her ear if she had not provided herself a great belly, he was at her service. A third said he warranted she was a relation of Turpin. To which one of the company, a great wit, shaking his head and then his sides, answered, he believed she was nearer related to Turpis,[1] at which there was an universal laugh. They were proceeding thus with the poor girl when somebody, smoking the cassock peeping forth from under the great-coat of Adams, cried out, "What have we here, a parson?" "How, sirrah," says the justice, "do you go robbing in the dress of a clergyman? Let me tell you, your habit will not entitle you to the benefit of the clergy." "Yes," said the witty fellow, "he will have one benefit of clergy, he will be exalted above the heads of the people," at which there was a second laugh. And now the witty spark, seeing his jokes take, began to rise in spirits, and, turning to Adams, challenged him to cap verses,[2] and, provoking him by giving the first blow, he repeated,

"Molle meum levibus cord est vilebile telis."

Upon which Adams, with a look full of ineffable contempt, told him he deserved scourging for his pronunciation. The witty fellow answered, "What do you deserve, doctor, for not being able to answer the first time? Why, I'll give one, you blockhead, with an S.

"Si licet, ut fulvum spectatur in ignibus haurum.

"What, canst not with an M neither? Thou art a pretty fellow for a parson. Why didst not steal some of the parson's Latin as well as his gown?" Another at the table then answered, "If he had, you would have been too hard for him; I remember you at the college a very devil at this sport; I have seen you catch a fresh man, for nobody that knew you would engage with you." "I have forgot those things now," cried the wit. "I believe I could have done pretty well formerly.—Let's see, what did I end with—an M again—aye——

"Mars, Bacchus, Apollo, virorum.

I could have done it once." "Ah! evil betide you, and so you can now," said the other; "nobody in this country will undertake you." Adams could hold no longer. "Friend," said he, "I have a boy not above eight years old who would instruct thee that the last verse runs thus:

"Ut sunt Divorum, Mars, Bacchus, Apollo, virorum."

"I'll hold thee a guinea of that," said the wit, throwing the money on the table. "And I'll go your halves," cries the other. "Done," answered Adams, but upon applying to his pocket he was forced to retract and own he had no money about him, which set them all a-laughing and confirmed the triumph of his adversary, which was not moderate, any more than the approbation he met with from the whole company, who told Adams he must go a little longer to school before he attempted to attack that gentleman in Latin.

The clerk having finished the depositions, as well of the fellow himself as of those who apprehended the prisoners, delivered them to the justice, who, having sworn the several witnesses without reading a syllable, ordered his clerk to make the mittimus.

Adams then said he hoped he should not be condemned unheard. "No, no," cries the justice, "you will be asked what you have to say for yourself, when you come on your trial: we are not trying you now; I shall only commit you to gaol: if you can prove your innocence at 'size, you will be found ignoramus, and so no harm done." "Is it no punishment, sir, for an innocent man to lie several months in gaol?" cries Adams. "I beg you would at least hear me before you sign the mittimus." "What signifies all you can say?" says the justice. "Is it not here in black and white against you? I must tell you you are a very impertinent fellow to take up so much of my time.—So make haste with his mittimus."

The clerk now acquainted the justice that among other suspicious things, as a penknife, etc., found in Adams's pocket, they had discovered a book written, as he apprehended, in ciphers, for no one could read a word in it. "Aye," says the justice, "the fellow may be more than a common robber, he may be in a plot against the government.—Produce the book." Upon which the poor manuscript of Aeschylus, which Adams had transcribed with his own hand, was brought forth, and the justice looking at it shook his head, and, turning to the prisoner, asked the meaning of those ciphers. "Ciphers!" answered Adams; "it is a manuscript of Aeschylus." "Who? who?" said the justice. Adams repeated, "Aeschylus." "That is an outlandish name," cried the clerk. "A fictitious name rather, I believe," said the justice. One of the company declared it looked very much like Greek. "Greek?" said the justice; "why, 'tis all writing." "No," says the other, "I don't positively say it is so; for it is a very long time since I have seen any Greek." "There's one," says he, turning to the parson of the parish, who was present, "will tell us immediately." The parson, taking up the book and putting on his spectacles and gravity together, muttered some words to himself, and then pronounced aloud: "Aye, indeed, it is a Greek manuscript; a very fine piece of antiquity. I make no doubt but it was stolen from the same clergyman from whom the rogue took the cassock." "What did the rascal mean by his Aeschylus?" says the justice. "Pooh!" answered the doctor, with a contemptuous grin, "do you think that fellow knows anything of this book? Aeschylus! ho! ho! I see now what it is—a manuscript of one of the fathers.[3] I know a nobleman who would give a great deal of money for such a piece of antiquity. Aye, aye, question and answer. The beginning is the catechism in Greek. Aye, aye, *Pollaki toi:* What's your name?" "Aye, what's your name?" says the justice to Adams, who answered, "It is Aeschylus, and I will maintain it." "Oh! it is," says the justice: "make Mr. Aeschylus his mittimus. I will teach you to banter me with a false name."

One of the company having looked steadfastly at Adams, asked him if he did not know Lady Booby? Upon which Adams, presently calling him to mind, answered in a rapture, "O Squire! are you there? I believe you will inform his worship I am innocent." "I can indeed say," replied the Squire, "that I am very much surprised to see you in this situation," and then addressing himself to the justice, he said, "Sir, I assure you Mr. Adams is a clergyman, as he appears, and a gentleman of a very good character. I wish you would inquire a little farther into this affair, for I am convinced of his innocence." "Nay," says the justice, "if he is a gentleman, and you are sure he is innocent, I don't desire to commit him, not I; I will commit the woman by herself, and take your bail for the gentleman: look into the book, clerk, and see how it is to take bail—come, and make the mittimus for the woman as fast as you can." "Sir," cries Adams, "I assure you she is as innocent as myself." "Perhaps," said the Squire, "there may be some mistake; pray let us hear Mr. Adams's relation." "With all my heart," answered the justice; "and give the gentleman a glass to whet his whistle before he begins. I know how to behave myself to gentlemen as well as another. Nobody can say I have committed a gentleman since I have been in the commission." Adams then began the narrative, in which, though he was very prolix, he was uninterrupted, unless by several hums and hahs of the justice, and his desire to repeat those parts which seemed to him most material. When he had finished, the justice, who, on what the Squire had said, believed every syllable of his story on his bare affirmation, notwithstanding the depositions on oath to the contrary, began to let loose several "rogues" and "rascals" against the witness, whom he ordered to stand forth, but in vain—the said witness, long since finding what turn matters were like to take, had privily withdrawn, without attending the issue. The justice now flew into a violent passion and was hardly prevailed with not to commit the innocent fellows who had been imposed on as well as himself. He swore they had best find out the fellow who was guilty of perjury and bring him before him within two days, or he would bind them all over to their good behaviour. They all promised to use their best endeavours to that purpose, and were dismissed. Then the justice insisted that Mr. Adams should sit down and take a glass with him, and the parson of the parish delivered him back the manuscript without saying a word; nor would Adams, who plainly discerned his ignorance, expose it. As for Fanny, she was, at her own request, recommended to the care of a maid-servant of the house, who helped her to new dress and clean herself.

The company in the parlour had not been long seated before they were alarmed with a horrible uproar from without, where the persons who had apprehended Adams and Fanny had been regaling, according to the custom of the house, with the justice's strong beer. These were all fallen together by the ears and were cuffing each other without any mercy. The justice himself sallied out, and with the dignity of his presence soon put an end to the fray. On his returning into the parlour, he reported that the occasion of the quarrel was no other than a dispute to whom, if Adams had been convicted, the greater share of the reward for apprehending him had belonged. All the company laughed at this except Adams, who, taking his pipe from his mouth, fetched a deep groan and said he was concerned to see so litigious a temper in men. That he remembered a story something like it in one of the parishes where his cure lay: "There was," continued he, "a competition between three young fellows for the place of the clerk, which I disposed of to the best of my abilities, according to merit; that is, I gave it to him who had the happiest knack at setting a psalm. The clerk was no sooner established in his place than a contention began between the two disappointed candidates concerning their excellence, each contending on whom, had they two been the only competitors, my election would have fallen. This dispute frequently disturbed the congregation and introduced a discord into the psalmody, till I was forced to silence them both. But, alas, the litigious spirit could not be stifled, and being no longer able to vent itself in singing, it now broke forth in fighting. It produced many battles (for they were very near a match), and I believe would have ended fatally had not the death of the clerk given me an opportunity to promote one of them to his place, which presently put an end to the dispute and entirely reconciled the contending parties." Adams then proceeded to make some philosophical observations on the folly of growing warm in disputes in which neither party is interested. He then applied himself vigorously to smoking and a long silence ensued, which was at length broke by the justice, who began to sing forth his own praises and to value himself exceedingly on his nice discernment in the cause which had lately been before him. He was quickly interrupted by Mr. Adams, between whom and his worship a dispute now arose whether he ought not, in strictness of law, to have committed him, the said Adams; in which the latter maintained he ought to have been committed, and the justice as vehemently held he ought not. This had most probably produced a quarrel (for both were very violent and positive in their opinions), had not Fanny accidentally heard that a young fellow was going from the justice's house to the very inn where the stage-coach in which Joseph was, put up. Upon this news, she immediately sent for the parson out of the parlour. Adams, when he found her resolute to go (though she would not own the reason, but pretended she could not bear to see the faces of those who had suspected her of such a crime), was as fully determined to go with her; he accordingly took leave of the justice and company, and so ended a dispute in which the law seemed shamefully to intend to set a magistrate and a divine together by the ears.

CHAPTER XII: *A very delightful adventure, as well to the persons concerned as to the good-natured reader.*

ADAMS, Fanny, and the guide set out together about one in the morning, the moon being then just risen. They had not gone above a mile before a most violent storm of rain obliged them to take shelter in an inn, or rather ale-house, where Adams immediately procured himself a good fire, a toast and ale, and a pipe, and began to smoke with great content, utterly forgetting everything that had happened.

Fanny sat likewise down by the fire, but was much more impatient at the storm. She presently engaged the eyes of the host, his wife, the maid of the house, and the young fellow who was their guide; they all conceived they had never seen anything half so handsome; and indeed, reader, if thou art of an amorous hue, I advise you to skip over the next paragraph; which, to render our history perfect, we are obliged to set down, humbly hoping that we may escape the fate of Pygmalion; for if it should happen to us, or to thee, to be struck with this picture, we should be perhaps in as helpless a condition as Narcissus, and might say to ourselves, *quod petis est nusquam.*[1] Or, if the finest features in it should set Lady ——'s image before our eyes, we should be still in as bad a situation, and might say to our desires, *Coelum ipsum petimus stultitia.*[2]

Fanny was now in the nineteenth year of her age; she was tall and delicately shaped, but not one of those slender young women who seem rather intended to hang up in the hall of an anatomist than for any other purpose. On the contrary, she was so plump that she seemed bursting through her tight stays, especially in the part which confined her swelling breasts. Nor did her hips want the assistance of a hoop to extend them. The exact shape of her arms denoted the form of those limbs which she concealed, and though they were a little reddened by her labour, yet if her sleeve slipped above her elbow or her handkerchief discovered any part of her neck, a whiteness appeared which the finest Italian paint would be unable to reach. Her hair was of a chestnut brown, and nature had been extremely lavish to her of it, which she had cut, and on Sundays used to curl down her neck in the modern fashion. Her forehead was high, her eyebrows arched, and rather full than otherwise. Her eyes black and sparkling; her nose just inclining to the Roman; her lips red and moist, and her underlip, according to the opinion of the ladies, too pouting. Her teeth were white, but not exactly even. The small-pox had left one only mark on her chin, which was so large, it might have been mistaken for a dimple, had not her left cheek produced one so near a neighbour to it, that the former served only for a foil to the latter. Her complexion was fair, a little injured by the sun, but overspread with such a bloom that the finest ladies would have exchanged all their white for it; add to these, a countenance in which, though she was extremely bashful, a sensibility appeared almost incredible, and a sweetness, whenever she smiled, beyond either imitation or description. To conclude all, she had a natural gentility superior to the acquisition of art, and which surprised all who beheld her.

This lovely creature was sitting by the fire with Adams when her attention was suddenly engaged by a voice from an inner room which sung the following song:

THE SONG

Say, Chloe, where must the swain stray
    Who is by thy beauties undone?
To wash their remembrance away
    To what distant Lethe must run?
The wretch who is sentenced to die
    May escape, and leave justice behind;
From his country perhaps he may fly,
    But, oh, can he fly from his mind!

O rapture unthought of before!
    To be thus of Chloe possessed;
Nor she, nor no tyrant's hard power,
    Her image can tear from my breast.
But felt not Narcissus more joy,
    With his eyes he beheld his loved charms?
Yet what he beheld the fond boy
    More eagerly wished in his arms.

How can it thy dear image be,
    Which fills thus my bosom with woe?
Can aught bear resemblance to thee
    Which grief and not joy can bestow?
This counterfeit snatch from my heart,
    Ye Powers, though with torment I rave,
Though mortal will prove the fell smart,
    I then shall find rest in my grave.

Ah! see the dear nymph o'er the plain
    Come smiling and tripping along,
A thousand Loves dance in her train;
    The Graces around her all throng.
To meet her soft Zephyrus flies,
    And wafts all the sweets from the flowers,
Ah rogue! whilst he kisses her eyes,
    More sweets from her breath he devours.

My soul, whilst I gaze, is on fire,
    But her looks were so tender and kind,
My hope almost reached my desire,
    And left lame Despair far behind.
Transported with madness, I flew,
    And eagerly seized on my bliss;
Her bosom but half she withdrew,
    But half she refused my fond kiss.

Advances like these made me bold,
  I whispered her—Love, we're alone.—
The rest let immortals unfold:
  No language can tell but their own.
Ah, Chloe, expiring, I cried,
  How long I thy cruelty bore!
Ah! Strephon, she blushing replied,
  You ne'er was so pressing before.

Adams had been ruminating all this time on a passage in Aeschylus, without attending in the least to the voice, though one of the most melodious that ever was heard, when, casting his eyes on Fanny, he cried out, "Bless you, you look extremely pale." "Pale! Mr. Adams," says she; "O Jesus!" and fell backwards in her chair. Adams jumped up, flung his Aeschylus into the fire, and fell a-roaring to the people of the house for help. He soon summoned everyone into the room, and the songster among the rest; but, O reader! when this nightingale, who was no other than Joseph Andrews himself, saw his beloved Fanny in the situation we have described her, canst thou conceive the agitations of his mind? If thou canst not, waive that meditation to behold his happiness when, clasping her in his arms, he found life and blood returning into her cheeks; when he saw her open her beloved eyes, and heard her with the softest accent whisper, "Are you Joseph Andrews?"—"Art thou my Fanny?" he answered eagerly, and, pulling her to his heart, he imprinted numberless kisses on her lips, without considering who were present.

If prudes are offended at the lusciousness of this picture, they may take their eyes off from it and survey Parson Adams dancing about the room in a rapture of joy. Some philosophers may perhaps doubt whether he was not the happiest of the three, for the goodness of his heart enjoyed the blessings which were exulting in the breasts of both the other two, together with his own. But we shall leave such disquisitions, as too deep for us, to those who are building some favourite hypothesis, which they will refuse no metaphysical rubbish to erect and support; for our part, we give it clearly on the side of Joseph, whose happiness was not only greater than the parson's but of longer duration; for, as soon as the first tumults of Adams's rapture were over, he cast his eyes towards the fire, where Aeschylus lay expiring, and immediately rescued the poor remains, to wit, the sheepskin covering, of his dear friend, which was the work of his own hands and had been his inseparable companion for upwards of thirty years.

Fanny had no sooner perfectly recovered herself than she began to restrain the impetuosity of her transports, and, reflecting on what she had done and suffered in the presence of so many, she was immediately covered with confusion, and pushing Joseph gently from her, she begged him to be quiet, nor would admit of either kiss or embrace any longer. Then, seeing Mrs. Slipslop, she curtseyed and offered to advance to her, but that high woman would not return her curtseys, but, casting her eyes another way, immediately withdrew into another room, muttering as she went, she wondered who the creature was.

CHAPTER XIII: *A dissertation concerning high people and low people, with Mrs. Slipslop's departure in no very good temper of mind, and the evil plight in which she left Adams and his company.*

IT WILL doubtless seem extremely odd to many readers that Mrs. Slipslop, who had lived several years in the same house with Fanny, should, in a short separation, utterly forget her. And indeed the truth is, that she remembered her very well. As we would not willingly, therefore, that anything should appear unnatural in this our history, we will endeavour to explain the reasons of her conduct, nor do we doubt being able to satisfy the most curious reader that Mrs. Slipslop did not in the least deviate from the common road in this behaviour; and, indeed, had she done otherwise, she must have descended below herself, and would have very justly been liable to censure.

Be it known then, that the human species are divided into two sorts of people, to wit, High people and Low people. As by high people I would not be understood to mean persons literally born higher in their dimensions than the rest of the species, nor metaphorically those of exalted characters or abilities; so by low people I cannot be construed to intend the reverse. High people signify no other than people of fashion, and low people those of no fashion. Now this word of "fashion" hath by long use lost its original meaning, from which at present it gives us a very different idea, for I am deceived if by persons of fashion we do not generally include a conception of birth and accomplishments superior to the herd of mankind; whereas, in reality, nothing more was originally meant by a person of fashion than a person who dressed himself in the fashion of the times, and the word really and truly signifies no more at this day. Now the world being thus divided into people of fashion and people of no fashion, a fierce contention arose between them; nor would those of one party, to avoid suspicion, be seen publicly to speak to those of the other, though they often held a very good correspondence in private. In this contention it is difficult to say which party succeeded, for whilst the people of fashion seized several places to their own use, such as courts, assemblies, operas, balls, etc.; the people of no fashion, besides one royal place, called His Majesty's bear-garden, have been in constant possession of all hops, fairs, revels, etc. Two places have been agreed to be divided between them, namely, the church and the play-house, where they segregate themselves from each other in a remarkable manner: for as the people of fashion exalt themselves at church over the heads of the people of no fashion, so in the play-house they abase themselves in the same degree under their feet. This distinction I have never met with anyone able to account for it: it is sufficient, that, so far from looking on each other as brethren in the Christian language, they seem scarce to regard each other as of the same species. This the terms "strange persons, people one does not know, the creature, wretches, beasts, brutes," and many other appellations, evidently demonstrate, which Mrs. Slipslop having often heard her mistress use, thought she had also a right to use in her turn; and perhaps she was not mistaken, for these two parties, especially those bordering nearly on each other, to wit, the lowest of the high and the highest of the low, often change their parties according to place and time, for those who are people of fashion in one place, are often people of no fashion in another. And with regard to time, it may not be unpleasant to survey the picture of dependence like a kind of ladder, as for instance; early in the morning arises the postilion, or some other boy, which great families no more than great ships, are without, and falls to brushing the clothes and cleaning the shoes of John the footman; who being dressed himself, applies his hands to the same labours for Mr. Second-hand, the squire's gentleman; the gentleman in the like manner, a little later in the day, attends the squire; the squire is no sooner equipped than he attends the levee of my lord; which is no sooner over, than my lord himself is seen at the levee of the favourite, who, after the hour of homage is at an end, appears himself to pay homage to the levee of his sovereign. Nor is there, perhaps, in this whole ladder of dependence, any one step at a greater distance from the other than the first from the second, so that to a philosopher the question might only seem whether you would choose to be a great man at six in the morning or at two in the afternoon. And yet there are scarce two of these who do not think the least familiarity with the persons below them a condescension, and, if they were to go one step farther, a degradation.

And now, reader, I hope thou wilt pardon this long digression, which seemed to me necessary to vindicate the great character of Mrs. Slipslop from what low people, who have never seen high people, might think an absurdity, but we, who know them, must have daily found very high persons know us in one place and not in another, today and not tomorrow, all which it is difficult to account for otherwise than I have here endeavoured; and, perhaps, if the gods, according to the opinion of some, made men only to laugh at them, there is no part of our behaviour which answers the end of our creation better than this.

But to return to our history: Adams, who knew no more of this than the cat which sat on the table, imagining Mrs. Slipslop's memory had been much worse than it really was, followed her into the next room, crying out, "Madam Slipslop, here is one of your old acquaintance; do but see what a fine woman she is grown since she left Lady Booby's service." "I think I reflect something of her," answered she, with great dignity, "but I can't remember all the inferior servants in our family." She then proceeded to satisfy Adams's curiosity by telling him when she arrived at the inn she found a chaise ready for her; that, her lady being expected very shortly in the country, she was obliged to make the utmost haste, and, in commensuration of Joseph's lameness, she had taken him with her; and lastly, that the excessive virulence of the storm had driven them into the house where he found them. After which, she acquainted Adams with his having left his horse, and expressed some wonder at his having strayed so far out of his way, and at meeting him, as she said, in the company of that wench, who she feared was no better than she should be.

The horse was no sooner put into Adams's head but he was immediately driven out by this reflection on the character of Fanny. He protested. He believed there was not a chaster damsel in the universe. "I heartily wish, I heartily wish," cried he, snapping his fingers, "that all her betters were as good." He then proceeded to inform her of the accident of their meeting, but when he came to mention the circumstance of delivering her from the rape, she said she thought him properer for the army than the clergy; that it did not become a clergyman to lay violent hands on anyone; that he should have rather prayed that she might be strengthened. Adams said he was very far from being ashamed of what he had done; she replied want of shame was not the currycuristic of a clergyman. This dialogue might have probably grown warmer had not Joseph opportunely entered the room to ask leave of Madam Slipslop to introduce Fanny, but she positively refused to admit any such trollops, and told him she would have been burnt before she would have suffered him to get into a chaise with her if she had once respected him of having his sluts way-laid on the road for him, adding that Mr. Adams acted a very pretty part, and she did not doubt but to see him a bishop. He made the best bow he could and cried out, "I thank you, madam, for that right-reverend appellation, which I shall take all honest means to deserve." "Very honest means," returned she with a sneer, "to bring people together." At these words Adams took two or three strides across the room, when the coachman came to inform Mrs. Slipslop that the storm was over and the moon shone very bright. She then sent for Joseph, who was sitting without with his Fanny, and would have had him gone with her, but he peremptorily refused to leave Fanny behind, which threw the good woman into a violent rage. She said she would inform her lady what doings were carrying on, and did not doubt but she would rid the parish of all such people, and concluded a long speech full of bitterness and very hard words with some reflections on the clergy, not decent to repeat; at last, finding Joseph unmovable, she flung herself into the chaise, casting a look at Fanny as she went not unlike that which Cleopatra gives Octavia in the play. To say the truth, she was most disagreeably disappointed by the presence of Fanny: she had, from her first seeing Joseph at the inn, conceived hopes of something which might have been accomplished at an ale-house as well as a palace. Indeed, it is probable Mr. Adams had rescued more than Fanny from the danger of a rape that evening.

When the chaise had carried off the enraged Slipslop, Adams, Joseph, and Fanny assembled over the fire, where they had a great deal of innocent chat, pretty enough, but as, possibly, it would not be very entertaining to the reader, we shall hasten to the morning, only observing that none of them went to bed that night. Adams, when he had smoked three pipes, took a comfortable nap in a great chair and left the lovers, whose eyes were too well employed to permit any desire of shutting them, to enjoy by themselves, during some hours, an happiness of which none of my readers who have never been in love are capable of the least conception of, though we had as many tongues as Homer desired to describe it with, and which all true lovers will represent to their own minds without the least assistance from us.

Let it suffice then to say that Fanny, after a thousand entreaties, at last gave up her whole soul to Joseph, and, almost fainting in his arms, with a sigh infinitely softer and sweeter too than any Arabian breeze, she whispered to his lips, which were then close to hers, "O Joseph, you have won me; I will be yours forever." Joseph having thanked her on his knees, and embraced her with an eagerness which she now almost returned, leapt up in a rapture and awakened the parson, earnestly begging him that he would that instant join their hands together. Adams rebuked him for his request, and told him he would by no means consent to anything contrary to the forms of the Church; that he had no licence, nor indeed would he advise him to obtain one; that the Church had prescribed a form, namely, the publication of banns, with which all good Christians ought to comply, and to the omission of which he attributed the many miseries which befell great folks in marriage, concluding, "As many as are joined together otherwise than G—'s word doth allow, are not joined together by G—, neither is their matrimony lawful." Fanny agreed with the parson, saying to Joseph, with a blush, she assured him she would not consent to any such thing, and that she wondered at his offering it. In which resolution she was comforted and commended by Adams, and Joseph was obliged to wait patiently till after the third publication of the banns, which, however, he obtained the consent of Fanny, in the presence of Adams, to put in at their arrival.

The sun had been now risen some hours, when Joseph, finding his leg surprisingly recovered, proposed to walk forwards, but when they were all ready to set out, an accident a little retarded them. This was no other than the reckoning, which amounted to seven shillings—no great sum, if we consider the immense quantity of ale which Mr. Adams poured in. Indeed, they had no objection to the reasonableness of the bill, but many to the probability of paying it, for the fellow who had taken poor Fanny's purse had unluckily forgot to return it. So that the account stood thus:

Mr. Adams and company, Dr. . . .	0 7 0
In Mr. Adams's Pocket	0 0 6½
In Mr. Joseph's	0 0 0
In Mrs. Fanny's	0 0 0
Balance	0 6 5½

They stood silent some few minutes, staring at each other, when Adams whipped out on his toes and asked the hostess if there was no clergyman in that parish? She answered, there was. "Is he wealthy?" replied he, to which she likewise answered in the affirmative. Adams then, snapping his fingers, returned overjoyed to his companions, crying out, "Heureka, Heureka," which not being understood, he told them in plain English they need give themselves no trouble, for he had a brother in the parish who would defray the reckoning, and that he would just step to his house and fetch the money and return to them instantly.

CHAPTER XIV: *An interview between Parson Adams and Parson Trulliber.*

PARSON ADAMS came to the house of Parson Trulliber, whom he found stripped into his waistcoat, with an apron on and a pail in his hand, just come from serving his hogs, for Mr. Trulliber was a parson on Sundays but all the other six days might more properly be called a farmer. He occupied a small piece of land of his own, besides which he rented a considerable deal more. His wife milked his cows, managed his dairy, and followed the markets with butter and eggs. The hogs fell chiefly to his care, which he carefully waited on at home, and attended to fairs, on which occasion he was liable to many jokes, his own size being with much ale rendered little inferior to that of the beasts he sold. He was indeed one of the largest men you should see, and could have acted the part of Sir John Falstaff without stuffing. Add to this that the rotundity of his belly was considerably increased by the shortness of his stature, his shadow ascending very near as far in height when he lay on his back, as when he stood on his legs. His voice was loud and hoarse, and his accents extremely broad. To complete the whole, he had a stateliness in his gait, when he walked, not unlike that of a goose, only he stalked slower.

Mr. Trulliber, being informed that somebody wanted to speak with him, immediately slipped off his apron and clothed himself in an old night-gown, being the dress in which he always saw his company at home. His wife, who informed him of Mr. Adams's arrival, had made a small mistake, for she had told her husband she believed here was a man come for some of his hogs. This supposition made Mr. Trulliber hasten with the utmost expedition to attend his guest. He no sooner saw Adams than, not in the least doubting the cause of his errand to be what his wife had imagined, he told him he was come in very good time, that he expected a dealer that very afternoon, and added they were all pure and fat, and upwards of twenty score apiece. Adams answered he believed he did not know him. "Yes, yes," cried Trulliber, "I have seen you often at fair; why we have dealt before now, mun, I warrant you. Yes, yes," cries he, "I remember thy face very well, but won't mention a word more till you have seen them, though I have never sold thee a flitch of such bacon as is now in the stye." Upon which he laid violent hands on Adams and dragged him into the hog-stye, which was indeed but two steps from his parlour window. They were no sooner arrived there than he cried out, "Do but handle them; step in, friend; art welcome to handle them, whether dost buy or no." At which words, opening the gate, he pushed Adams into the pig-stye, insisting on it that he should handle them before he would talk one word with him.

Adams, whose natural complacence was beyond any artificial, was obliged to comply before he was suffered to explain himself; and, laying hold on one of their tails, the unruly beast gave such a sudden spring, that he threw poor Adams all along in the mire. Trulliber, instead of assisting him to get up, burst into a laughter, and, entering the stye, said to Adams with some contempt, "Why, dost not know how to handle a hog?" and was going to lay hold of one himself; but Adams, who thought he had carried his complacence far enough, was no sooner on his legs than he escaped out of the reach of the animals and cried out, "*Nil habeo cum porcis:* [1] I am a clergyman, sir, and am not come to buy hogs." Trulliber answered he was sorry for the mistake, but that he must blame his wife, adding she was a fool and always committed blunders. He then desired him to walk in and clean himself, that he would only fasten up the stye and follow him. Adams desired leave to dry his great-coat, wig, and hat by the fire, which Trulliber granted. Mrs. Trulliber would have brought him a basin of water to wash his face, but her husband bid her be quiet like a fool as she was or she would commit more blunders, and then directed Adams to the pump. While Adams was thus employed, Trulliber, conceiving no great respect for the appearance of his guest, fastened the parlour-door and now conducted him into the kitchen, telling him he believed a cup of drink would do him no harm, and whispered his wife to draw a little of the worst ale. After a short silence, Adams said, "I fancy, sir, you already perceive me to be a clergyman." "Aye, aye," cries Trulliber, grinning, "I perceive you have some cassock; I will not venture to caale it a whole one." Adams answered it was indeed none of the best, but he had the misfortune to tear it about ten years ago in passing over a stile. Mrs. Trulliber, returning with the drink, told her husband she fancied the gentleman was a traveller, and that he would be glad to eat a bit. Trulliber bid her hold her impertinent tongue and asked her if parsons used to travel without horses, adding he supposed the gentleman had none by his having no boots on. "Yes, sir, yes," says Adams; "I have a horse, but I have left him behind me." "I am glad to hear you have one," says Trulliber, "for I assure you I don't love to see clergymen on foot; it is not seemly, nor suiting the dignity of the cloth." Here Trulliber made a long oration on the dignity of the cloth (or rather gown) not much worth relating, till his wife had spread the table and set a mess of porridge on it for his breakfast. He then said to Adams, "I don't know, friend, how you came to caale on me; however, as you are here, if you think proper to eat a morsel, you may." Adams accepted the invitation, and the two parsons sat down together, Mrs. Trulliber waiting behind her husband's chair, as was, it seems, her custom. Trulliber ate heartily, but scarce put anything in his mouth without finding fault with his wife's cookery. All which the poor woman bore patiently. Indeed, she was so absolute an admirer of her husband's greatness and importance, of which she had frequent hints from his own mouth, that she almost carried her adoration to an opinion of his infallibility. To say the truth, the parson had exercised her more ways than one; and the pious woman had so well edified by her husband's sermons that she had resolved to receive the bad things of this world together with the good. She had indeed been at first a little contentious, but he had long since got the better, partly by her love for this; partly by her fear of that; partly by her religion; partly by the respect he paid himself; and partly by that which he received from the parish: She had, in short, absolutely submitted, and now worshipped her husband as Sarah did Abraham, calling him (not lord, but) master. Whilst they were at table, her husband gave her a fresh example of his greatness, for as she had just delivered a cup of ale to Adams, he snatched it out of his hand, and, crying out, "I caaled vurst," swallowed down the ale. Adams denied it; it was referred to the wife, who, though her conscience was on the side of Adams, durst not give it against her husband. Upon which he said, "No, sir, no; I should not have been so rude to have taken it from you, if you had caaled vurst; but I'd have you know I'm a better man than to suffer the best he in the kingdom to drink before me in my own house when I caale vurst."

As soon as their breakfast was ended, Adams began in the following manner: "I think, sir, it is high time to inform you of the business of my embassy. I am a traveller, and am passing this way in company with two young people, a lad and a damsel, my parishioners, towards my own cure; we stopped at a house of hospitality in the parish, where they directed me to you, as having the cure."—"Though I am but a curate," says Trulliber, "I believe I am as warm as the vicar himself, or perhaps the rector of the next parish too; I believe I could buy them both." "Sir," cries Adams, "I rejoice thereat. Now, sir, my business is that we are by various accidents stripped of our money, and are not able to pay our reckoning, being seven shillings. I therefore request you to assist me with the loan of those seven shillings, and also seven shillings more, which, peradventure, I shall return to you, but if not, I am convinced you will joyfully embrace such an opportunity of laying up a treasure in a better place than any this world affords."

Suppose a stranger who entered the chambers of a lawyer, being imagined a client, when the lawyer was preparing his palm for the fee, should pull out a writ against him. Suppose an apothecary at the door of a chariot containing some great doctor of eminent skill, should, instead of directions to a patient, present him with a potion for himself. Suppose a minister should, instead of a good round sum, treat my lord ——, or Sir ——, or Esq. ——, with a good broomstick. Suppose a civil companion, or a led captain, should, instead of virtue, and honour, and beauty, and parts, and admiration, thunder vice, and infamy, and ugliness, and folly, and contempt in his patron's ears. Suppose when a tradesman first carries in his bill the man of fashion should pay it; or suppose, if he did so, the tradesman should abate what he had overcharged, on the supposition of waiting. In short—suppose what you will, you never can nor will suppose anything equal to the astonishment which seized on Trulliber as soon as Adams had ended his speech. A while he rolled his eyes in silence, sometimes surveying Adams, then his wife, then casting them on the ground, then lifting them up to heaven. At last he burst forth in the following accents: "Sir, I believe I know where to lay up my little treasure as well as another. I thank G— if I am not so warm as some I am content; that is a blessing greater than riches, and he to whom that is given need ask no more. To be content with a little is greater than to possess the world, which a man may possess without being so. Lay up my treasure! What matters where a man's treasure is, whose heart is in the Scriptures; there is the treasure of a Christian." At these words the water ran from Adams's eyes, and, catching Trulliber by the hand in a rapture, "Brother," says he, "heavens bless the accident by which I came to see you; I would have walked many a mile to have communed with you, and believe me I will shortly pay you a second visit; but my friends, I fancy, by this time wonder at my stay, so let me have the money immediately." Trulliber then put on a stern look, and cried out, "Thou dost not intend to rob me?" At which the wife, bursting into tears, fell on her knees, and roared out, "O dear sir! for heaven's sake, don't rob my master; we are but poor people." "Get up for a fool as thou art, and go about thy business," said Trulliber; "dost think the man will venture his life? he is a beggar, and no robber." "Very true, indeed," answered Adams. "I wish, with all my heart, the tithing-man was here," cries Trulliber; "I would have thee punished as a vagabond for thy impudence. Fourteen shillings indeed! I won't give thee a farthing. I believe thou art no more a clergyman than the woman there (pointing to his wife); but if thou art, dost deserve to have thy gown stripped over thy shoulders for running about the country in such a manner." "I forgive your suspicions," says Adams, "but suppose I am not a clergyman, I am nevertheless thy brother, and thou, as a Christian, much more as a clergyman, art obliged to relieve my distress." "Dost preach to me?" replied Trulliber; "dost pretend to instruct me in my duty?" "Ifacks, a good story," cries Mrs. Trulliber, "to preach to my master." "Silence, woman," cries Trulliber. "I would have thee know, friend" (addressing himself to Adams), "I shall not learn my duty from such as thee. I know what charity is better than to give to vagabonds." "Besides, if we were inclined, the poor's rate obliges us to give so much charity," cries the wife. "Pugh! thou art a fool. Poor's rate! Hold thy nonsense," answered Trulliber; and then turning to Adams, he told him he would give him nothing. "I am sorry," answered Adams, "that you do not know what charity is, since you practise it no better: I must tell you, if you trust to your knowledge for your justification, you will find yourself deceived, though you should add faith to it, without good works." "Fellow," cries Trulliber, "dost thou speak against faith in my house? Get out of my doors: I will no longer remain under the same roof with a wretch who speaks wantonly of faith and the Scriptures." "Name not the Scriptures," says Adams. "How! not name the Scriptures! Do you disbelieve the Scriptures?" cries Trulliber. "No, but you do," answered Adams, "if I may reason from your practise, for their commands are so explicit, and their rewards and punishments so immense, that it is impossible a man should steadfastly believe without obeying. Now, there is no command more express, no duty more frequently enjoined, than charity. Whoever, therefore, is void of charity, I make no scruple of pronouncing that he is no Christian." "I would not advise thee," says Trulliber, "to say that I am no Christian: I won't take it of you, for I believe I am as good a man as thyself" (and indeed, though he was now rather too corpulent for athletic exercises, he had, in his youth, been one of the best boxers and cudgel-players in the county). His wife, seeing him clench his fist, interposed and begged him not to fight, but show himself a true Christian and take the law of him. As nothing could provoke Adams to strike but an absolute assault on himself or his friend, he smiled at the angry look and gestures of Trulliber, and, telling him he was sorry to see such men in orders, departed without further ceremony.

CHAPTER XV: *An adventure, the consequence of a new instance which Parson Adams gave of his forgetfulness.*

WHEN he came back to the inn, he found Joseph and Fanny sitting together. They were so far from thinking his absence long, as he had feared they would, that they never once missed or thought of him. Indeed, I have been often assured by both that they spent these hours in a most delightful conversation, but, as I never could prevail on either to relate it, so I cannot communicate it to the reader.

Adams acquainted the lovers with the ill success of his enterprise. They were all greatly confounded, none being able to propose any method of departing, till Joseph at last advised calling in the hostess and desiring her to trust them, which Fanny said she despaired of her doing, as she was one of the sourest-faced women she had ever beheld.

But she was agreeably disappointed, for the hostess was no sooner asked the question than she readily agreed, and, with a curtsey and smile, wished them a good journey. However, lest Fanny's skill in physiognomy should be called in question, we will venture to assign one reason which might probably incline her to this confidence and good humour. When Adams said he was going to visit his brother, he had unwittingly imposed on Joseph and Fanny, who both believed he meant his natural brother and not his brother in divinity, and had so informed the hostess, on her inquiry after him. Now Mr. Trulliber had, by his professions of piety, by his gravity, austerity, reserve, and the opinion of his great wealth, so great an authority in his parish, that they all lived in the utmost fear and apprehension of him. It was therefore no wonder that the hostess, who knew it was in his option whether she should ever sell another mug of drink, did not dare to affront his supposed brother by denying him credit.

They were now just on their departure, when Adams recollected he had left his great-coat and hat at Mr. Trulliber's. As he was not desirous of renewing his visit, the hostess herself, having no servant at home, offered to fetch it.

This was an unfortunate expedient, for the hostess was soon undeceived in the opinion she had entertained of Adams, whom Trulliber abused in the grossest terms, especially when he heard he had had the assurance to pretend to be his near relation.

At her return, therefore, she entirely changed her note. She said folks might be ashamed of travelling about and pretending to be what they were not. That taxes were high, and for her part she was obliged to pay for what she had; she could not therefore possibly, nor would she, trust anybody, no, not her own father. That money was never scarcer, and she wanted to make up a sum. That she expected, therefore, they should pay their reckoning before they left the house.

Adams was now greatly perplexed, but as he knew that he could easily have borrowed such a sum in his own parish, and as he knew he would have lent it himself to any mortal in distress, so he took fresh courage and sallied out all round the parish, but to no purpose; he returned as penniless as he went, groaning and lamenting that it was possible, in a country professing Christianity, for a wretch to starve in the midst of his fellow-creatures who abounded.

Whilst he was gone, the hostess, who stayed as a sort of guard with Joseph and Fanny, entertained them with the goodness of Parson Trulliber. And, indeed, he had not only a very good character as to other qualities in the neighbourhood, but was reputed a man of great charity, for though he never gave a farthing, he had always that word in his mouth.

Adams was no sooner returned the second time than the storm grew exceeding high, the hostess declaring, among other things, that if they offered to stir without paying her she would soon overtake them with a warrant.

Plato and Aristotle, or somebody else, hath said that *when the most exquisite cunning fails, chance often hits the mark, and that by means the least expected.* Vergil expresses this very boldly:

> *Turne, quod optanti divum promittere nemo*
> *Auderet, volvenda dies, en! attulit ultro.*[1]

I would quote more great men if I could, but my memory not permitting me, I will proceed to exemplify these observations by the following instance.

There chanced (for Adams had not cunning enough to contrive it) to be at that time in the ale-house a fellow who had been formerly a drummer in an Irish regiment, and now travelled the country as a pedlar. This man having attentively listened to the discourse of the hostess, at last took Adams aside and asked him what the sum was for which they were detained. As soon as he was informed, he sighed, and said he was sorry it was so much, for that he had no more than six shillings and sixpence in his pocket, which he would lend them with all his heart. Adams gave a caper, and cried out it would do, for that he had sixpence himself. And thus these poor people, who could not engage the compassion of riches and piety were at length delivered out of their distress by the charity of a poor pedlar.

I shall refer it to my reader to make what observations he pleases on this incident: it is sufficient for me to inform him, that, after Adams and his companions had returned him a thousand thanks, and told him where he might call to be repaid, they all sallied out of the house without any compliments from their hostess, or indeed without paying her any, Adams declaring he would take particular care never to call there again, and she, on her side, assuring them she wanted no such guests.

CHAPTER XVI: *A very curious adventure, in which Mr. Adams gave a much greater instance of the honest simplicity of his heart than of his experience in the ways of this world.*

OUR travellers had walked about two miles from that inn, which they had more reason to have mistaken for a castle than Don Quixote ever had any of those in which he sojourned, seeing they had met with such difficulty in escaping out of its walls, when they came to a parish, and beheld a sign of invitation hanging out. A gentleman sat smoking a pipe at the door, of whom Adams inquired the road and received so courteous and obliging an answer, accompanied with so smiling a countenance, that the good parson, whose heart was naturally disposed to love and affection, began to ask several other questions, particularly the name of the parish and who was the owner of a large house whose front they then had in prospect. The gentleman answered as obligingly as before, and as to the house, acquainted him it was his own. He then proceeded in the following manner: "Sir, I presume by your habit you are a clergyman, and as you are travelling on foot, I suppose a glass of good beer will not be disagreeable to you, and I can recommend my landlord's within as some of the best in all this county. What say you, will you halt a little and let us take a pipe together? There is no better tobacco in the kingdom." This proposal was not displeasing to Adams, who had allayed his thirst that day with no better liquor than what Mrs. Trulliber's cellar had produced, and which was indeed little superior, either in richness or flavour, to that which distilled from those grains her generous husband bestowed on his hogs. Having therefore abundantly thanked the gentleman for his kind invitation, and bid Joseph and Fanny follow him, he entered the ale-house, where a large loaf and cheese and a pitcher of beer, which truly answered the character given of it, being set before them, the three travellers fell to eating with appetites infinitely more voracious than are to be found at the most exquisite eating-houses in the parish of St. James's.

The gentleman expressed great delight in the hearty and cheerful behaviour of Adams, and particularly in the familiarity with which he conversed with Joseph and Fanny, whom he often called his children, a term he explained to mean no more than his parishioners, saying he looked on all those whom God had entrusted to his cure to stand to him in that relation. The gentleman, shaking him by the hand, highly applauded those sentiments. "They are, indeed," says he, "the true principles of a Christian divine, and I heartily wish they were universal, but, on the contrary, I am sorry to say the parson of our parish, instead of esteeming his poor parishioners as a part of his family seems rather to consider them as not of the same species with himself. He seldom speaks to any, unless some few of the richest of us; nay, indeed, he will not move his hat to the others. I often laugh when I behold him on Sundays strutting along the church-yard like a turkey-cock through rows of his parishioners, who bow to him with as much submission and are as unregarded as a set of servile courtiers by the proudest prince in Christendom. But if such temporal pride is ridiculous, surely the spiritual is odious and detestable; if such a puffed-up empty human bladder strutting in princely robes justly moves one's derision, surely in the habit of a priest it must raise our scorn."

"Doubtless," answered Adams, "your opinion is right, but I hope such examples are rare. The clergy whom I have the honour to know maintain a different behaviour, and you will allow me, sir, that the readiness which too many of the laity show to condemn the order may be one reason of their avoiding too much humility." "Very true, indeed," says the gentleman; "I find, sir, you are a man of excellent sense, and am happy in this opportunity of knowing you; perhaps our accidental meeting may not be disadvantageous to you neither. At present, I shall only say to you that the incumbent of this living is old and infirm, and that it is in my gift. Doctor, give me your hand, and assure yourself of it at his decease." Adams told him he was never more confounded in his life, than at his utter incapacity to make any return to such noble and unmerited generosity. "A mere trifle, sir," cries the gentleman, "scarce worth your acceptance—a little more than three hundred a year. I wish it was double the value for your sake." Adams bowed, and cried from the emotions of his gratitude, when the other asked him if he was married, or had any children, besides those in the spiritual sense he had mentioned. "Sir," replied the parson, "I have a wife and six at your service." "That is unlucky," says the gentleman, "for I would otherwise have taken you into my own house as my chaplain; however, I have another in the parish (for the parsonage-house is not good enough) which I will furnish for you. Pray, does your wife understand a dairy?" "I can't profess she does," says Adams. "I am sorry for it," quoth the gentleman; "I would have given you half a dozen cows, and very good grounds to have maintained them." "Sir," said Adams, in an ecstasy, "you are too liberal; indeed you are." "Not at all," cries the gentleman: "I esteem riches only as they give me an opportunity of doing good, and I never saw one whom I had a greater inclination to serve." At which words he shook him heartily by the hand and told him he had sufficient room in his house to entertain him and his friends. Adams begged he might give him no such trouble, that they could be very well accommodated in the house where they were, forgetting that they had not a six-penny piece among them. The gentleman would not be denied, and, informing himself how far they were travelling, he said it was too long a journey to take on foot, and begged that they would favour him by suffering him to lend them a servant and horses, adding withal that if they would do him the pleasure of their company only two days, he would furnish them with his coach and six. Adams turning to Joseph, said, "How lucky is this gentleman's goodness to you, who I am afraid would be scarce able to hold out on your lame leg," and then addressing the person who made him these liberal promises, after much bowing, he cried out, "Blessed be the hour which first introduced me to a man of your charity; you are indeed a Christian of the true primitive kind, and an honour to the country wherein you live. I would willingly have taken a pilgrimage to the Holy Land to have beheld you, for the advantages which we draw from your goodness give me little pleasure in comparison of what I enjoy for your own sake, when I consider the treasures you are by these means laying up for yourself in a country that passeth not away. We will therefore, most generous sir, accept your goodness, as well the entertainment you have so kindly offered us at your house this evening, as the accommodation of your horses tomorrow morning." He then began to search for his hat, as did Joesph for his, and both they and Fanny were in order of departure when the gentleman stopping short, and, seeming to meditate by himself for the space of about a minute, exclaimed thus: "Sure never anything was so unlucky; I had forgot that my housekeeper was gone abroad and hath locked up all my rooms;

indeed, I would break them open for you, but shall not be able to furnish you with a bed, for she has likewise put away all my linen. I am glad it entered into my head before I had given you the trouble of walking there; besides, I believe you will find better accommodations here than you expected. Landlord, you can provide good beds for these people, can't you?" "Yes, and please your worship," cries the host, "and such as no lord or justice of the peace in the kingdom need be ashamed to lie in." "I am heartily sorry," says the gentleman, "for this disappointment. I am resolved I will never suffer her to carry away the keys again." "Pray, sir, let it not make you uneasy," cries Adams; "we shall do very well here, and the loan of your horses is a favour we shall be incapable of making any return to." "Aye!" said the Squire, "the horses shall attend you here, at what hour in the morning you please." And now, after many civilities too tedious to enumerate, many squeezes by the hand with most affectionate looks and smiles at each other, and after appointing the horses at seven the next morning, the gentleman took his leave of them and departed to his own house. Adams and his companions returned to the table, where the parson smoked another pipe and then they all retired to rest.

Mr. Adams rose very early and called Joseph out of his bed, between whom a very fierce dispute ensued whether Fanny should ride behind Joseph or behind the gentleman's servant, Joseph insisting on it that he was perfectly recovered, and was as capable of taking care of Fanny as any other person could be. But Adams would not agree to it, and declared he would not trust her behind him, for that he was weaker than he imagined himself to be.

This dispute continued a long time, and had begun to be very hot, when a servant arrived from their good friend to acquaint them that he was unfortunately prevented from lending them any horses, for that his groom had, unknown to him, put his whole stable under a course of physic.

This advice presently struck the two disputants dumb. Adams cried out, "Was ever anything so unlucky as this poor gentleman? I protest I am more sorry on his account than my own. You see, Joseph, how this good-natured man is treated by his servants; one locks up his linen, another physics his horses, and I suppose, by his being at this house last night, the butler had locked up his cellar. Bless us! how good nature is used in this world! I protest I am more concerned on his account than my own." "So am not I," cries Joseph; "not that I am much troubled about walking on foot—all my concern is, how we shall get out of the house, unless God sends another pedlar to redeem us. But certainly this gentleman has such an affection for you that he would lend you a larger sum than we owe here, which is not above four or five shillings." "Very true, child," answered Adams; "I will write a letter to him and will even venture to solicit him for three half-crowns; there will be no harm in having two or three shillings in our pockets; as we have full forty miles to travel, we may possibly have occasion for them."

Fanny being now risen, Joseph paid her a visit and left Adams to write his letter, which having finished, he despatched a boy with it to the gentleman, and then seated himself by the door, lighted his pipe, and betook himself to meditation.

The boy staying longer than seemed to be necessary, Joseph, who with Fanny was now returned to the parson, expressed some apprehensions that the gentleman's steward had locked up his purse too. To which Adams answered, "It might very possibly be; and he should wonder at no liberties which the devil might put into the head of a wicked servant to take with so worthy a master," but added that as the sum was so small, so noble a gentleman would be easily able to procure it in the parish, though he had it not in his own pocket. "Indeed," says he, "if it was four or five guineas, or any such large quantity of money, it might be a different matter."

They were now sat down to breakfast, over some toast and ale, when the boy returned and informed them that the gentleman was not at home. "Very well!" cries Adams, "but why, child, did you not stay till his return? Go back again, my good boy, and wait for his coming home: he cannot be gone far, as his horses are all sick, and besides, he had no intention to go abroad, for he invited us to spend this day and tomorrow at his house. Therefore go back, child, and tarry till his return home." The messenger departed and was back again with great expedition, bringing an account that the gentleman was gone a long journey and would not be at home again this month. At these words Adams seemed greatly confounded, saying, "This must be a sudden accident, as the sickness or death of a relation, or some such unforeseen misfortune," and then turning to Joseph, cried, "I wish you had reminded me to have borrowed this money last night." Joseph, smiling, answered he was very much deceived if the gentleman would not have found some excuse to avoid lending it. "I own," says he, "I was never much pleased with his professing so much kindness for you at first sight, for I have heard the gentlemen of our cloth in London tell many such stories of their masters. But when the boy brought the message back of his not being at home, I presently knew what would follow; for whenever a man of fashion doth not care to fulfil his promises, the custom is to order his servants that he will never be at home to the person so promised. In London they call it denying him. I have myself denied Sir Thomas Booby about a hundred times, and when the man hath danced attendance for about a month, or sometimes longer, he is acquainted in the end that the gentleman is gone out of town, and could do nothing in the business." "Good Lord!" says Adams, "what wickedness is there in the Christian world? I profess almost equal to what I have read of the heathens. But surely, Joseph, your suspicions of this gentleman must be unjust, for what a silly fellow must he be who would do the devil's work for nothing, and canst thou tell me any interest he could possibly propose to himself by deceiving us in his professions?" "It is not for me," answered Joseph, "to give reasons for what men do to a gentleman of your learning." "You say right," quoth Adams; "knowledge of men is only to be learnt from books; Plato and Seneca for that, and those are authors, I am afraid, child, you never read." "Not I, sir, truly," answered Joseph; "all I know is, it is a maxim among the gentlemen of our cloth that those masters who promise the most, perform the least, and I have often heard them say they have found the largest vails in those families where they were not promised any. But, sir, instead of considering any farther these matters, it would be our wisest way to contrive some method of getting out of this house, for the generous gentleman, instead of doing us any service, hath left us the whole reckoning to pay." Adams was going to answer, when their host came in, and, with a kind of jeering smile, said, "Well, masters! the Squire hath not sent his horses to you yet. Laud help me! how easily some folks make promises!" "How!" says Adams, "have you ever known him to do anything of this kind before?" "Aye! marry have I," answered the host; "it is no business of mine, you know, sir, to say anything to a gentleman to his face, but now he is not here I will assure you he hath not his fellow within the three next market-towns. I own I could not help laughing when I heard him offer you the living, for thereby hangs a good jest. I thought he would have offered you my house next, for one is no more his to dispose of than the other." At these words Adams, blessing himself, declared, "he had never read of such a monster. But what vexes me most," says he, "is, that he hath decoyed us into running up a long debt with you which we are not able to pay, for we have no money about us, and what is worse, live at such a distance that, if you should trust us, I am afraid you would lose your money for want of our finding any conveniency of sending it." "Trust you, master!" says the host, "that I will with all my heart. I honour the clergy too much to deny trusting one of them for such a trifle; besides, I like your fear of never paying me. I have lost many a debt in my life-time; but was promised to be paid them all in a very short time. I will score this reckoning for the novelty of it. It is the first, I do assure you, of its kind. But what say you, master, shall we have t'other pot before we part? It will waste but a little chalk more, and if you never pay me a shilling the loss will not ruin me." Adams liked the invitation very well, especially as it was delivered with so hearty an accent. He shook his host by the hand, and, thanking him, said he would tarry another pot, rather for the pleasure of such worthy company than for the liquor, adding he was glad to find some Christians left in the kingdom, for that he almost began to suspect that he was sojourning in a country inhabited only by Jews and Turks.

The kind host produced the liquor, and Joseph with Fanny retired into the garden, where while they solaced themselves with amorous discourse, Adams sat down with his host; and, both filling their glasses and lighting their pipes, they began that dialogue which the reader will find in the next chapter.

CHAPTER XVII: *A dialogue between Mr. Abraham Adams and his host, which, by the disagreement in their opinions, seemed to threaten an unlucky catastrophe, had it not been timely prevented by the return of the lovers.*

"Sir," said the host, "I assure you you are not the first to whom our Squire hath promised more than he hath performed. He is so famous for this practise that his word will not be taken for much by those who know him. I remember a young fellow whom he promised his parents to make an exciseman. The poor people, who could ill afford it, bred their son to writing and accounts and other learning to qualify him for the place, and the boy held up his head above his condition with these hopes, nor would he go to plough nor to any other kind of work, and went constantly dressed as fine as could be, with two clean Holland shirts a week, and this for several years, till at last he followed the Squire up to London, thinking there to mind him of his promises, but he could never get sight of him. So that, being out of money and business, he fell into evil company and wicked courses, and in the end came to a sentence of transportation, the news of which broke the mother's heart. I will tell you another true story of him: There was a neighbour of mine, a farmer, who had two sons whom he bred up to the business. Pretty lads they were. Nothing would serve the Squire but that the youngest must be made a parson. Upon which, he persuaded the father to send him to school, promising that he would afterwards maintain him at the university, and, when he was of a proper age, give him a living. But after the lad had been seven years at school, and his father had brought him to the Squire with a letter from his master that he was fit for the university, the Squire, instead of minding his promise or sending him thither at his expense, only told his father that the young man was a fine scholar, and it was pity he could not afford to keep him at Oxford for four or five years more, by which time, if he could get him a curacy, he might have him ordained. The farmer said he was not a man sufficient to do any such thing. 'Why then,' answered the Squire, 'I am very sorry you have given him so much learning, for if he cannot get his living by that, it will rather spoil him for anything else, and your other son, who can hardly write his name, will do more at ploughing and sowing, and is in a better condition, than he.' And indeed so it proved, for the poor lad, not finding friends to maintain him in his learning as he had expected, and being unwilling to work, fell to drinking, though he was a very sober lad before, and in a short time, partly with grief, and partly with good liquor, fell into a consumption and died. Nay, I can tell you more still: There was another, a young woman, and the handsomest in all this neighbourhood, whom he enticed up to London, promising to make her a gentlewoman to one of your women of quality, but instead of keeping his word, we have since heard, after having a child by her himself, she became a common whore, then kept a coffee-house in Covent Garden, and a little after died of the French distemper in a gaol. I could tell you many more stories, but how do you imagine he served me myself? You must know, sir, I was bred a seafaring man, and have been many voyages, till at last I came to be a master of a ship myself, and was in a fair way of making a fortune, when I was attacked by one of those cursed guarda-costas who took our ships before the beginning of the war, and after a fight wherein I lost the greater part of my crew, my rigging being all demolished, and two shots received between wind and water, I was forced to strike. The villains carried off my ship, a brigantine of 150 tons—a pretty creature she was—and put me, a man, and a boy into a little bad pink, in which, with much ado, we at last made Falmouth, though I believe the Spaniards did not imagine she could possibly live a day at sea. Upon my return hither, where my wife, who was of this country, then lived, the Squire told me he was so pleased with the defence I had made against the enemy that he did not fear getting me promoted to a lieutenancy of a man-of-war if I would accept of it, which I thankfully assured him I would. Well, sir, two or three years passed, during which I had many repeated promises not only from the Squire, but (as he told me) from the Lords of the Admiralty. He never returned from London but I was assured I might be satisfied now, for I was certain of the first vacancy, and what surprised me still, when I reflect on it, these assurance were given me with no less confidence, after so many disappointments, than at first. At last, sir, growing weary, and somewhat suspicious after so much delay, I wrote a friend in London who I knew had some acquaintance at the best house in the Admiralty, and desired him to back the Squire's interest, for indeed I feared he had solicited the affair with more coldness than he pretended. And what answer do you think my friend sent me? Truly, sir, he acquainted me that the Squire had never mentioned my name at the Admiralty in his life, and, unless I had much faithfuller interest, advised me to give over my pretensions; which I immediately did, and, with the concurrence of my wife, resolved to set up an ale-house, where you are heartily welcome; and so my service to you, and may the Squire, and all such sneaking rascals, go to the devil together." "Oh fie!" says Adams, "Oh fie! He is indeed a wicked man; but G— will, I hope, turn his heart to repentance. Nay, if he could but once see the meanness of this detestable vice—would he but once reflect that he is one of the most scandalous as well as pernicious liars—sure he must despise himself to so intolerable a degree that it would be impossible for him to continue a moment in such a course. And to confess the truth, notwithstanding the baseness of his character, which he hath too well deserved, he hath in his countenance sufficient symptoms of that *bona indoles,* that sweetness of disposition, which furnishes out a good Christian." "Ah! master, master," says the host, "if you had travelled as far as I have, and conversed with the many nations where I have traded, you would not give any credit to a man's countenance. Symptoms in his countenance, quotha! I would look there, perhaps, to see whether a man had had the small-pox, but for nothing else." He spoke this with so little regard to the parson's observation that it a good deal nettled him, and, taking the pipe hastily from his mouth, he thus answered: "Master of mine, perhaps I have travelled a great deal farther than you, without the assistance of a ship. Do you imagine sailing by different cities or countries is travelling? No.

"Coelum non animum mutant qui trans mare currunt.[1]

I can go farther in an afternoon than you in a twelve-month. What, I suppose you have seen the Pillars of Hercules, and perhaps the walls of Carthage. Nay, you may have heard Scylla, and seen Charybdis; you may have entered the closet where Archimedes was found at the taking Syracuse. I suppose you have sailed among the Cyclades, and passed the famous straits which take their name from the unfortunate Helle, whose fate is sweetly described by Apollonius Rhodius; you have passed the very spot, I conceive, where Daedalus fell into that sea, his waxen wings being melted by the sun; you have traversed the Euxine Sea I make no doubt, nay, you may have been on the banks of the Caspian and called at Colchis to see if there is ever another golden fleece." "Not I, truly, master," answered the host: "I never touched at any of these places." "But I have been at all these," replied Adams. "Then, I suppose," cries the host, "you have been at the East Indies, for there are no such, I will be sworn, either in the West or the Levant?" "Pray, where's the Levant?" quoth Adams; "that should be in the East Indies by right." "Oho! you are a pretty traveller," cries the host, "and not know the Levant. My service to you, master; you must not talk of these things with me! you must not tip us the traveller; it won't go here." "Since thou art so dull to misunderstand me still," quoth Adams, "I will inform thee the travelling I mean is in books, the only way of travelling by which any knowledge is to be acquired. From them I learn what I asserted just now, that nature generally imprints such a portraiture of the mind in the countenance that a skilful physiognomist will rarely be deceived. I presume you have never read the story of Socrates to this purpose, and therefore I will tell it you. A certain physiognomist asserted of Socrates that he plainly discovered by his features that he was a rogue in his nature. A character so contrary to the tenor of all this great man's actions, and the generally received opinion concerning him, incensed the boys of Athens so that they threw stones at the physiognomist, and would have demolished him for his ignorance, had not Socrates himself prevented them by confessing the truth of his observations, and acknowledging, that, though he corrected his disposition by philosophy, he was indeed naturally as inclined to vice as had been predicated of him. Now, pray, resolve me—how should a man know this story, if he had not read it?" "Well, master," said the host, "and what signifies it whether a man knows it or no? He who goes abroad as I have done will always have opportunities enough of knowing the world, without troubling his head with Socrates, or any such fellows." "Friend," cries Adams, "if a man should sail round the world, and anchor in every harbour of it, without learning, he would return home as ignorant as he went out." "Lord help you," answered the host, "there was my boatswain, poor fellow! he could scarce either write or read, and yet he would navigate a ship with any master of a man of war; and a very pretty knowledge of trade he had too." "Trade," answered Adams, "as Aristotle proves in his first chapter of Politics, is below a philosopher, and unnatural as it is managed now." The host looked steadfastly at Adams and after a minute's silence asked him if he was one of the writers of the Gazetteers. "For I have heard," says he, "they are writ by parsons." "Gazetteers!" answered Adams. "What is that?" "It is a dirty newspaper," replied the host, "which hath been given away all over the nation for these many years to abuse trade and honest men, which I would not suffer to lie on my table, though it hath been offered me for nothing." "Not I truly," said Adams; "I never write anything but sermons, and I assure you I am no enemy to trade, whilst it is consistent with honesty; nay, I have always looked on the tradesman as a very valuable member of society, and, perhaps, inferior to none but the man of learning." "No, I believe he is not, nor to him neither," answered the host. "Of what use would learning be in a country without trade! What would all you parsons do to clothe your backs and feed your bellies? Who fetches you your silks, and your linens, and your wines, and all the other necessaries of life? I speak chiefly with regard to the sailors." "You should say the extravagances of life," replied the parson; "but admit they were the necessaries, there is something more necessary than life itself, which is provided by learning; I mean the learning of the clergy. Who clothes you with piety, meekness, humility, charity, patience, and all the other Christian virtues? Who feeds your souls with the milk of brotherly love, and diets them with all the dainty food of holiness, which at once cleanses them of all impure carnal affections and fattens them with the truly rich Spirit of grace? Who doth this?" "Aye, who indeed!" cries the host, "for I do not remember ever to have seen any such clothing or such feeding. And so in the meantime, master, my service to you." Adams was going to answer with some severity, when Joseph and Fanny returned and pressed his departure so eagerly that he would not refuse them, and so, grasping his crab-stick, he took leave of his host (neither of them being so well pleased with each other as they had been at their first sitting down together), and with Joseph and Fanny, who both expressed much impatience, departed, and now all together renewed their journey.

BOOK THREE

CHAPTER I: *Matter prefatory in praise of biography.*

NOTWITHSTANDING the preference which may be vulgarly given to the authority of those romance-writers who entitle their books, "The History of England, the History of France, of Spain, etc." it is most certain that truth is to be found only in the works of those who celebrate the lives of great men, and are commonly called biographers, as the others should indeed be termed topographers, or chorographers—words which might well mark the distinction between them; it being the business of the latter chiefly to describe countries and cities, which, with the assistance of maps, they do pretty justly, and may be depended upon; but as to the actions and characters of men their writings are not quite so authentic, of which there needs no other proof than those eternal contradictions occurring between two topographers who undertake the history of the same country, for instance, between my lord Clarendon and Mr. Whitlock, between Mr. Echard and Rapin, and many others, where, facts being set forth in a different light, every reader believes as he pleases, and, indeed, the more judicious and suspicious very justly esteem the whole as no other than a romance in which the writer hath indulged a happy and fertile invention. But though these widely differ in the narrative of facts, some ascribing victory to the one, and others to the other party; some representing the same man as a rogue, while others give him a great and honest character; yet all agree in the scene where the fact is supposed to have happened, and where the person, who is both a rogue and an honest man, lived. Now with us biographers the case is different; the facts we deliver may be relied on, though we often mistake the age and country wherein they happened: for though it may be worth the examination of critics whether the shepherd Chrysostom, who, as Cervantes informs us, died for love of the fair Marcella, who hated him, was ever in Spain, will anyone doubt but that such a silly fellow hath really existed?

Is there in the world such a sceptic as to disbelieve the madness of Cardenio, the perfidy of Ferdinand, the impertinent curiosity of Anselmo, the weakness of Camilla, the irresolute friendship of Lothario—though perhaps, as to the time and place where those several persons lived, that good historian may be deplorably deficient. But the most known instance of this kind is in the true history of Gil Blas, where the inimitable biographer hath made a notorious blunder in the country of Dr. Sangrado, who used his patients as a vintner doth his wine-vessels, by letting out their blood and filling them up with water. Doth not everyone who is the least versed in physical history know that Spain was not the country in which this doctor lived? The same writer hath likewise erred in the country of his archbishop, as well as that of those great personages whose understandings were too sublime to taste anything but tragedy, and in many others. The same mistakes may likewise be observed in Scarron, the *Arabian Nights,* the history of *Marianne* and *Le Paysan Parvenu,* and perhaps some few other writers of this class, whom I have not read or do not at present recollect, for I would by no means be thought to comprehend those persons of surprising genius, the authors of immense romances, or the modern novel and Atalantis writers, who, without any assistance from nature or history, record persons who never were, or will be, and facts which never did, nor possibly can, happen, whose heroes are of their own creation and their brains the chaos whence all the materials are selected. Not that such writers deserve no honour; so far otherwise that perhaps they merit the highest: for what can be nobler than to be as an example of the wonderful extent of human genius! One may apply to them what Balzac says of Aristotle, that they are a second nature (for they have no communication with the first), by which authors of an inferior class, who cannot stand alone, are obliged to support themselves as with crutches; but these of whom I am now speaking seem to be possessed of those stilts which the excellent Voltaire tells us, in his letters, "carry the genius far off, but with an irregular pace." Indeed, far out of the sight of the reader,

Beyond the realm of Chaos and old Night.[1]

But, to return to the former class, who are contented to copy nature instead of forming originals from the confused heap of matter in their own brains; is not such a book as that which records the achievements of the renowned Don

Quixote more worthy the name of a history than even Mariana's; for whereas the latter is confined to a particular period of time, and to a particular nation, the former is the history of the world in general, at least that part which is polished by laws, arts, and sciences, and of that from the time it was first polished to this day—nay, and forwards as long as it shall so remain.

I shall now proceed to apply these observations to the work before us; for indeed I have set them down principally to obviate some constructions which the good nature of mankind, who are always forward to see their friends' virtues recorded, may put to particular parts. I question not but several of my readers will know the lawyer in the stage-coach the moment they hear his voice. It is likewise odds but the wit and the prude meet with some of their acquaintance, as well as all the rest of my characters. To prevent, therefore, any such malicious applications, I declare here once for all I describe not men, but manners; not an individual, but a species. Perhaps it will be answered, Are not the characters then taken from life? To which I answer in the affirmative; nay, I believe I might aver that I have writ little more than I have seen. The lawyer is not only alive, but hath been so these four thousand years, and I hope G— will indulge his life as many yet to come. He hath not indeed confined himself to one profession, one religion, or one country; but when the first mean selfish creature appeared on the human stage who made self the centre of the whole creation, would give himself no pain, incur no danger, advance no money, to assist or preserve his fellow-creatures, then was our lawyer born, and whilst such a person as I have described exists on earth, so long shall he remain upon it. It is therefore doing him little honour to imagine he endeavours to mimic some little obscure fellow, because he happens to resemble him in one particular feature, or perhaps in his profession, whereas his appearance in the world is calculated for much more general and noble purposes; nor to expose one pitiful wretch to the small and contemptible circle of his acquaintance, but to hold the glass to thousands in their closets, that they may contemplate their deformity and endeavour to reduce it, and thus by suffering private mortification may avoid public shame. This places the boundary between, and distinguishes the satirist from, the libeller; for the former privately corrects the fault for the benefit of the person, like a parent; the latter publicly exposes the person himself as an example to others, like an executioner.

There are, besides, little circumstances to be considered, as the draper of a picture, which, though fashion varies at different times, the resemblance of the countenance is not by those means diminished. Thus I believe we may venture to say Mrs. Tow-wouse is coeval with our lawyer, and though perhaps, during the changes which so long an existence must have passed through, she may in her turn have stood behind the bar at an inn, I will not scruple to affirm she hath likewise in the revolution of ages sat on a throne. In short, where extreme turbulency of temper, avarice, and an insensibility of human misery, with a degree of hypocrisy, have united in a female composition, Mrs. Tow-wouse was that woman; and where a good inclination, eclipsed by a poverty of spirit and understanding, hath glimmered forth in a man, that man hath been no other than her sneaking husband.

I shall detain my reader no longer than to give him one caution more of an opposite kind, for as in most of our particular characters we mean not to lash individuals, but all of the like sort, so, in our general descriptions we mean not universals, but would be understood with many exceptions: for instance, in our description of high people we cannot be intended to include such as, whilst they are an honour to their high rank, by a well-guided condescension make their superiority as easy as possible to those whom fortune chiefly hath placed below them. Of this number I could name a peer no less elevated by nature than by fortune who, whilst he wears the noblest ensigns of honour on his person, bears the truest stamp of dignity on his mind, adorned with greatness, enriched with knowledge, and embellished with genius. I have seen this man relieve with generosity while he hath conversed with freedom, and be to the same person a patron and a companion. I could name a commoner, raised higher above the multitude by superior talents than is in the power of his prince to exalt him, whose behaviour to those he hath obliged is more amiable than the obligation itself, and who is so great a master of affability that, if he could divest himself of an inherent greatness in his manner, would often make the lowest of his acquaintance forget who was the master of that palace in which they are so courteously entertained. These are pictures which must be, I believe, known: I declare they are taken from the life, and not intended to exceed it. By those high people, therefore, whom I have described, I mean a set of wretches, who, while they are a disgrace to their ancestors, whose honours and fortunes they inherit (or perhaps a greater to their mother, for such degeneracy is scarce credible), have the insolence to treat those with disregard who are at least equal to the founders of their own splendour. It is, I fancy, impossible to conceive a spectacle more worthy of our indignation than that of a fellow who is not only a blot in the escutcheon of a great family but a scandal to the human species, maintaining a supercilious behaviour to men who are an honour to their nature and a disgrace to their fortune.

And now reader, taking these hints along with you, you may, if you please, proceed to the sequel of this our true history.

CHAPTER II: *A night-scene, wherein several wonderful adventures befell Adams and his fellow-travellers.*

It was so late when our travellers left the inn or ale-house (for it might be called either), that they had not travelled many miles before night overtook them, or met them, which you please. The reader must excuse me if I am not particular as to the way they took, for as we are now drawing near the seat of the Boobys, and as that is a ticklish name, which malicious persons may apply, according to their evil inclinations, to several worthy country squires, a race of men whom we look upon as entirely inoffensive, and for whom we have an adequate regard, we shall lend no assistance to any such malicious purposes.

Darkness had now overspread the hemisphere when Fanny whispered Joseph that she begged to rest herself a little for that she was so tired she could walk no farther. Joseph immediately prevailed with Parson Adams, who was as brisk as a bee, to stop. He had no sooner seated himself than he lamented the loss of his dear Aeschylus, but was a little comforted when reminded that if he had it in his possession he could not see to read.

The sky was so clouded that not a star appeared. It was indeed, according to Milton, darkness visible. This was a circumstance, however, very favourable to Joseph, for Fanny, not suspicious of being overseen by Adams, gave a loose to her passion which she had never done before, and, reclining her head on his bosom, threw her arm carelessly round him and suffered him to lay his cheek close to hers. All this infused such happiness into Joseph that he would not have changed his turf for the finest down in the finest palace in the universe.

Adams sat at some distance from the lovers, and, being unwilling to disturb them, applied himself to meditation, in which he had not spent much time before he discovered a light at some distance that seemed approaching towards him. He immediately hailed it, but, to his sorrow and surprise, it stopped for a moment and then disappeared. He then called to Joseph, asking him if he had not seen the light. Joseph answered he had. "And did you not mark how it vanished?" returned he; "though I am not afraid of ghosts, I do not absolutely disbelieve them."

He then entered into a meditation on those unsubstantial beings, which was soon interrupted by several voices, which he thought almost at his elbow, though in fact they were not so extremely near. However, he could distinctly hear them agree on the murder of anyone they met. And a little after heard one of them say he had killed a dozen since that day fortnight.

Adams now fell on his knees and committed himself to the care of Providence, and poor Fanny, who likewise heard those terrible words, embraced Joseph so closely that had not he, whose ears were also open, been apprehensive on her account, he would have thought no danger which threatened only himself too dear a price for such embraces.

Joseph now drew forth his pen-knife, and Adams, having finished his ejaculations, grasped his crab-stick, his only weapon, and, coming up to Joseph, would have had him quit Fanny and place her in the rear; but his advice was fruitless, she clung closer to him, not at all regarding the presence of Adams, and in a soothing voice declared she would die in his arms. Joseph, clasping her with inexpressible eagerness, whispered her that he preferred death in hers to life out of them. Adams, brandishing his crab-stick, said he despised death as much as any man, and then repeated aloud,

Est hic, est animus lucis contemptor et illum
Qui vita bene credat emi quo tendis, honorem.[1]

Upon this the voices ceased for a moment, and then one of them called out, "D—n you, who is there?" To which Adams was prudent enough to make no reply, and of a sudden he observed half a dozen lights, which seemed to rise all at once from the ground and advance briskly towards him. This he immediately concluded to be an apparition, and now beginning to conceive that the voices were of the same kind, he called out, "In the name of the L—d, what wouldst thou have?" He had no sooner spoke than he heard one of the voices cry out, "D—n them, here they come," and soon after heard several hearty blows, as if a number of men had been engaged at quarterstaff. He was just advancing towards the place of combat when Joseph, catching him by the skirts, begged him that they might take the opportunity of the dark to convey away Fanny from the danger which threatened her. He presently complied, and Joseph lifting up Fanny, they all three made the best of their way, and, without looking behind them or being overtaken, they had travelled full two miles, poor Fanny not once complaining of being tired, when they saw far off several lights scattered at a small distance from each other and at the same time found themselves on the descent of a very steep hill. Adams's foot slipping, he instantly disappeared, which greatly frightened both Joseph and Fanny; indeed, if the light had permitted them to see it, they would scarce have refrained laughing to see the parson rolling down the hill, which he did from top to bottom, without receiving any harm. He then halloed as loud as he could to inform them of his safety and relieve them from the fears which they had conceived for him. Joseph and Fanny halted some time, considering what to do; at last they advanced a few paces, where the declivity seemed least steep, and then Joseph, taking his Fanny in his arms, walked firmly down the hill, without making a false step, and at length landed her at the bottom, where Adams soon came to them.

Learn hence, my fair countrywomen, to consider your own weakness, and the many occasions on which the strength of a man may be useful to you, and duly weighing this, take care that you match not yourselves with the spindle-shanked beaux and *petit-maîtres* of the age, who, instead of being able, like Joseph Andrews, to carry you in lusty arms through the rugged ways and downhill steeps of life, will rather want to support their feeble limbs with your strength and assistance.

Our travellers now moved forwards where the nearest light presented itself, and having crossed a common field, they came to a meadow, where they seemed to be at a very little distance from the light, when, to their grief, they arrived at the banks of a river. Adams here made a full stop and declared he could swim, but doubted how it was possible to get Fanny over; to which Joseph answered, if they walked along its banks they might be certain of soon finding a bridge, especially as by the number of lights they might be assured a parish was near. "Odso, that's true indeed," said Adams; "I did not think of that."

Accordingly, Joseph's advice being taken, they passed over two meadows and came to a little orchard, which led them to a house. Fanny begged of Joseph to knock at the door, assuring him she was so weary that she could hardly stand on her feet. Adams, who was foremost, performed this ceremony, and, the door being immediately opened, a plain kind of man appeared at it. Adams acquainted him that they had a young woman with them who was so tired with her journey that he should be much obliged to him if he would suffer her to come in and rest herself. The man, who saw Fanny by the light of the candle which he held in his hand, perceiving her innocent and modest look, and having no apprehensions, from the civil behaviour of Adams, presently answered that the young woman was very welcome to rest herself in his house, and so were her company. He then ushered them into a very decent room where his wife was sitting at a table; she immediately rose up and assisted them in setting forth chairs and desired them to sit down, which they had no sooner done than the man of the house asked them if they would have anything to refresh themselves with. Adams thanked him and answered he should be obliged to him for a cup of his ale, which was likewise chosen by Joseph and Fanny. Whilst he was gone to fill a very large jug with this liquor, his wife told Fanny she seemed greatly fatigued and desired her to take something stronger than ale, but she refused with many thanks, saying it was true she was very much tired, but a little rest she hoped would restore her. As soon as the company were all seated, Mr. Adams, who had filled himself with ale, and by public permission had lighted his pipe, turned to the master of the house, asking him if evil spirits did not use to walk in that neighbourhood, to which receiving no answer, he began to inform him of the adventure which they had met with on the downs, nor had he proceeded far in his story when somebody knocked very hard at the door. The company expressed some amazement, and Fanny and the good woman turned pale; her husband went forth, and whilst he was absent, which was some time, they all remained silent, looking at one another, and heard several voices discoursing pretty loudly. Adams was fully persuaded that spirits were abroad, and began to meditate some exorcisms; Joseph a little inclined to the same opinion; Fanny was more afraid of men; and the good woman herself began to suspect her guests and imagined those without were rogues belonging to their gang. At length the master of the house returned, and, laughing, told Adams he had discovered his apparition; that the murderers were sheep-stealers, and the twelve persons murdered were no other than twelve sheep, adding that the shepherds had got the better of them, had secured two, and were proceeding with them to a justice of peace. This account greatly relieved the fears of the whole company; but Adams muttered to himself he was convinced of the truth of apparitions for all that.

They now sat cheerfully round the fire till the master of the house, having surveyed his guests, and conceiving that the cassock, which having fallen down appeared under Adams's great-coat, and the shabby livery on Joseph Andrews, did not well suit with the familiarity between them, began to entertain some suspicions not much to their advantage; addressing himself therefore to Adams, he said he perceived he was a clergyman by his dress, and supposed that honest man was his footman. "Sir," answered Adams, "I am a clergyman at your service, but as to that young man, whom you have rightly termed honest, he is at present in nobody's service; he never lived in any other family than that of Lady Booby, from whence he was discharged, I assure you for no crime." Joseph said he did not wonder the gentleman was surprised to see one of Mr. Adams's character condescend to so much goodness with a poor man. "Child," said Adams, "I should be ashamed of my cloth if I thought a poor man who is honest, below my notice or my familiarity. I know not how those who think otherwise can profess themselves followers and servants of Him who made no distinction, unless, peradventure, by preferring the poor to the rich.—Sir," said he, addressing himself to the gentleman, "these two poor young people are my parishioners, and I look on them and love them as my children. There is something singular enough in their history, but I have not now time to recount it." The master of the house, notwithstanding the simplicity which discovered itself in Adams, knew too much of the world to give a hasty belief to professions. He was not yet quite certain that Adams had any more of the clergyman in him than his cassock. To try him therefore further, he asked him if Mr. Pope had lately published anything new. Adams answered he had heard great commendations of that poet, but that he had never read, nor knew, any of his works. "Ho! ho!" says the gentleman to himself, "have I caught you?—What," said he, "have you never seen his Homer?" Adams answered he had never read any translation of the classics. "Why truly," replied the gentleman, "there is a dignity in the Greek language which I think no modern tongue can reach." "Do you understand Greek, sir?" said Adams hastily. "A little sir," answered the gentleman. "Do you know, sir," cried Adams, "where I can buy an Aeschylus? an unlucky misfortune lately happened to mine." Aeschylus was beyond the gentleman, though he knew him very well by name; he therefore returning back to Homer, asked Adams what part of the *Iliad* he thought most excellent? Adams returned, his question would be properer, what kind of beauty was the chief in poetry? for that Homer was equally excellent in them all. "And, indeed," continued he, "what Cicero says of a complete orator, may well be applied to a great poet: 'He ought to comprehend all perfections.' Homer did this in the most excellent degree; it is not without reason therefore, that the philosopher, in the twenty-second chapter of his Poetics, mentions him by no other appellation than that of The Poet. He was the father of the drama as well as the epic; not of tragedy only, but of comedy also, for his *Margites,* which is deplorably lost, bore, says Aristotle, the same analogy to comedy as his *Odyssey* and *Iliad* to tragedy. To him, therefore, we owe Aristophanes as well as Euripides, Sophocles, and my poor Aeschylus. But if you please we will confine ourselves (at least for the present) to the *Iliad,* his noblest work, though neither Aristotle nor Horace give it the preference, as I remember, to the *Odyssey.* First, then, as to his subject, can anything be more simple and at the same time more noble? He is rightly praised by the first of those judicious critics, for not choosing the whole war, which, though he says it hath a complete beginning and end, would have been too great for the understanding to comprehend at one view. I have therefore often wondered why so correct a writer as Horace should, in his epistle to Lollius, call him the *Trojani belli scriptorem.* Secondly, his action, termed by Aristotle *pragmaton systasis:* is it possible for the mind of man to conceive an idea of such perfect unity and at the same time so replete with greatness? And here I must observe, what I do not remember to have seen noted by any, the *harmotton,* that agreement of his action to his subject, for as the subject is anger, how agreeable is his action, which is war? from which every incident arises, and to which every episode immediately relates. Thirdly, his manners, which Aristotle places second in his description of the several parts of tragedy and which he says are included in the action; I am at a loss whether I should rather admire the exactness of his judgement in the nice distinction, or the immensity of his imagination in their variety. For, as to the former of these, how accurately is the sedate, injured resentment of Achilles distinguished from the hot, insulting passion of Agamemnon! How widely doth the brutal courage of Ajax differ from the amiable bravery of Diomedes; and the wisdom of Nestor, which is the result of long reflection and experience, from the cunning of Ulysses, the effect of art and subtlety only! If we consider their variety, we may cry out, with Aristotle in his twenty-fourth chapter, that no part of this divine poem is destitute of manners. Indeed, I might affirm that there is scarce a character in human nature untouched in some part or other. And as there is no passion which he is not able to describe, so is there none in his reader which he cannot raise. If he hath any superior excellence to the rest, I have been inclined to fancy it is in the pathetic. I am sure I never read with dry eyes the two episodes where Andromache is introduced, in the former lamenting the danger, and in the latter the death, of Hector. The images are so extremely tender in these that I am convinced the poet hath the worthiest and best heart imaginable. Nor can I help observing how Sophocles falls short of the beauties of the original in that imitation of the dissuasive speech of Andromache which he hath put into the mouth of Tecmessa. And yet Sophocles was the greatest genius who ever wrote tragedy, nor have any of his successors in that art, that is to say, neither Euripides nor Seneca the tragedian, been able to come near him. As to his sentiments and diction, I need say nothing: the former are particularly remarkable for the utmost perfection on that head, namely, propriety; and as to the latter, Aristotle, whom doubtless you have read over and over, is very diffuse. I shall mention but one thing more, which that great critic in his division of tragedy calls *opsis,* or the scenery, and which is as proper to the epic as to the drama, with this difference, that in the former it falls to the share of the poet, and in the latter to that of the painter. But did ever painter imagine a scene like that in the thirteenth and fourteenth *Iliads?* where the reader sees at one view the prospect of Troy with the army drawn up before it: the Grecian Army, camp, and fleet; Jupiter sitting on Mount Ida, with his head wrapped in a cloud and a thunderbolt in his hand, looking towards Thrace; Neptune driving through the sea, which divides on each side to permit his passage, and then seating himself on Mount Samos: the heavens opened, and the deities all seated on their thrones. This is sublime! This is poetry!" Adams then rapped out a hundred Greek verses, and with such a voice, emphasis, and action, that he almost frightened the women, and as for the gentleman, he was so far from entertaining any further suspicion of Adams that he now doubted whether he had not a bishop in his house. He ran into the most extravagant encomiums on his learning, and the goodness of his heart began to dilate to all the strangers. He said he had great compassion for the poor young woman, who looked pale and faint with her journey, and in truth he conceived a much higher opinion of her quality than it deserved. He said he was sorry he could not accommodate them all but if they were content with his fire-side, he would sit up with the men, and the young woman might, if she pleased, partake his wife's bed, which he advised her to, for that they must walk upwards of a mile to any house of entertainment, and that not very good neither. Adams, who liked his seat, his ale, his tobacco, and his company, persuaded Fanny to accept this kind proposal, in which solicitation he was seconded by Joseph. Nor was she very difficultly prevailed on, for she had slept little the last night and not at all the preceding, so that love itself was scarce able to keep her eyes open any longer. The offer therefore being kindly accepted, the good woman produced everything eatable in her house on the table, and the guests, being heartily invited, as heartily regaled themselves, especially Parson Adams. As to the other two, they were examples of the truth of that physical observation that love, like other sweet things, is no whetter of the stomach.

Supper was no sooner ended than Fanny, at her own request, retired, and the good woman bore her company. The man of the house, Adams, and Joseph, who would modestly have withdrawn had not the gentleman insisted on the contrary, drew round the fire-side, where Adams (to use his own words) replenished his pipe and the gentleman produced a bottle of excellent beer, being the best liquor in his house.

The modest behaviour of Joseph, with the gracefulness of his person, the character which Adams gave of him, and the friendship he seemed to entertain for him, began to work on the gentleman's affections and raised in him a curiosity to know the singularity which Adams had mentioned in his history. This curiosity Adams was no sooner informed of than, with Joseph's consent, he agreed to gratify it, and accordingly related all he knew, with as much tenderness as was possible for the character of Lady Booby, and concluded with the long, faithful, and mutual passion between him and Fanny, not concealing the meanness of her birth and education. These latter circumstances entirely cured a jealousy which had lately risen in the gentleman's mind that Fanny was the daughter of some person of fashion, and that Joseph had run away with her and Adams was concerned in the plot. He was now enamoured of his guests, drank their healths with great cheerfulness, and returned many thanks to Adams, who had spent much breath, for he was a circumstantial teller of a story.

Adams told him it was now in his power to return that favour, for his extraordinary goodness, as well as that fund of literature he was master of, * which he did not expect to find under such a roof, had raised in him more curiosity than he had ever known. "Therefore," said he, "if it be not too troublesome, sir, your history, if you please."

The gentleman answered he could not refuse him what he had so much right to insist on, and after some of the common apologies which are the usual preface to a story, he thus began.

CHAPTER III: *In which the gentleman relates the history of his life.*

"SIR, I am descended of a good family, and was born a gentleman. My education was liberal, and at a public school, in which I proceeded so far as to become master of the Latin, and to be tolerably versed in the Greek language. My father died when I was sixteen, and left me master of myself. He bequeathed me a moderate fortune, which he intended I should not receive till I attained the age of twenty-five, for he constantly asserted that was full early enough to give up any man entirely to the guidance of his own discretion. However, as this intention was so obscurely worded in his will that the lawyers advised me to contest the point with my trustees, I own I paid so little regard to the inclinations of my dead father, which were sufficiently certain to me, that I followed their advice and soon succeeded, for the trustees did not contest the matter very obstinately on their side." "Sir," said Adams, "may I crave the favour of your name?" The gentleman answered his name was Wilson, and then proceeded.

"I stayed a very little while at school after his death, for, being a forward youth, I was extremely impatient to be in the world, for which I thought my parts, knowledge, and manhood thoroughly qualified me. And to this early introduction into life without a guide I impute all my future misfortunes, for, besides the obvious mischiefs which attend this, there is one which hath not been so generally observed: the first impression which mankind receives of you will be very difficult to eradicate. How unhappy, therefore, must it be to fix your character in life before you can possibly know its value or weigh the consequences of those actions which are to establish your future reputation?

"A little under seventeen I left my school and went to London, with no more than six pounds in my pocket—a great sum, as I then conceived, and which I was afterwards surprised to find so soon consumed.

"The character I was ambitious of attaining was that of a fine gentleman, the first requisites to which, I apprehended, were to be supplied by a tailor, a periwig-maker, and some few more tradesmen who deal in furnishing out the human body. Notwithstanding the lowness of my purse I found credit with them more easily than I expected and was soon equipped to my wish. This I own then agreeably surprised me, but I have since learned that it is a maxim among many tradesmen at the polite end of the town to deal as largely as they can, reckon as high as they can, and arrest as soon as they can.

"The next qualifications, namely, dancing, fencing, riding the great horse, and music, came into my head, but, as they required expense and time, I comforted myself, with regard to dancing, that I had learned a little in my youth, and could walk a minuet genteelly enough; as to fencing, I thought my good humour would preserve me from the danger of a quarrel; as to the horse, I hoped it would not be thought of; and for music, I imagined I could easily acquire the reputation of it, for I had heard some of my school-fellows pretend to knowledge in operas without being able to sing or play on the fiddle.

"Knowledge of the town seemed another ingredient; this I thought I should arrive at by frequenting public places. Accordingly I paid constant attendance to them all, by which means I was soon master of the fashionable phrases, learned to cry up the fashionable diversions, and knew the names and faces of the most fashionable men and women.

"Nothing now seemed to remain but an intrigue, which I was resoved to have immediately—I mean the reputation of it

—and indeed I was so successful that in a very short time I had half a dozen with the finest women in town."

At these words Adams fetched a deep groan and then, blessing himself, cried out, "Good Lord! what wicked times these are!"

"Not so wicked as you imagine," continued the gentleman, "for I assure you they were all Vestal Virgins for anything which I knew to the contrary. The reputation of intriguing with them was all I sought, and was what I arrived at; and perhaps I only flattered myself even in that, for very probably the persons to whom I showed their billets knew as well as I that they were counterfeits and that I had written them to myself." "Write letters to yourself!" said Adams, staring. "Oh sir," answered the gentleman, "it is the very error of the times. Half our modern plays have one of these characters in them. It is incredible the pains I have taken, and the absurd methods I employed, to traduce the character of women of distinction. When another had spoken in raptures of anyone, I have answered, 'D—n her, she! We shall have her at H——d's[1] very soon.' When he hath replied he thought her virtuous, I have answered, 'Aye, thou wilt always think a woman virtuous till she is in the streets; but you and I, Jack or Tom (turning to another in company), know better.' At which I have drawn a paper out of my pocket, perhaps a tailor's bill, and kissed it, crying at the same time, 'By Gad I was once fond of her.' "

"Proceed, if you please, but do not swear any more," said Adams.

"Sir," said the gentleman, "I ask your pardon. Well, sir, in this course of life I continued full three years." "What course of life?" answered Adams; "I do not remember you have mentioned any." "Your remark is just," said the gentleman, smiling; "I should rather have said, in this course of doing nothing. I remember some time afterwards I wrote the journal of one day, which would serve, I believe, as well for any other during the whole time. I will endeavour to repeat it to you.

"In the morning I arose, took my great stick, and walked out in my green frock, with my hair in papers (a groan from Adams), and sauntered about till ten. Went to the auction; told Lady —— she had a dirty face; laughed heartily at something Captain —— said, I can't remember what, for I did not very well hear it; whispered Lord ——; bowed to the Duke of ——; and was going to bid for a snuff-box, but did not, for fear I should have had it.

"From 2 to 4, dressed myself. *A groan.*
4 to 6, dined. *A groan.*
6 to 8, coffee-house.
8 to 9, Drury-Lane play-house.
9 to 10, Lincoln's Inn Fields.
10 to 12, Drawing-room. *A great groan.*

"At all which places nothing happened worth remark."

At which Adams said, with some vehemence, "Sir, this is below the life of an animal, hardly above vegetation, and I am surprised what could lead a man of your sense into it." "What leads us into more follies than you imagine, Doctor," answered the gentleman "—vanity: for as contemptible a creature as I was, and I assure you yourself cannot have more contempt for such a wretch than I now have, I then admired myself, and should have despised a person of your present appearance (you will pardon me), with all your learning and those excellent qualities which I have remarked in you." Adams bowed, and begged him to proceed. "After I had continued two years in this course of life," said the gentleman, "an accident happened which obliged me to change the scene. As I was one day at St. James's coffee-house making very free with the character of a young lady of quality, an officer of the guards, who was present, thought proper to give me the lie. I answered I might possibly be mistaken, but I intended to tell no more than the truth. To which he made no reply but by a scornful sneer. After this I observed a strange coldness in all my acquaintance; none of them spoke to me first, and very few returned me even the civility of a bow. The company I used to dine with left me out, and within a week I found myself in as much solitude at St. James's as if I had been in a desert. An honest elderly man, with a great hat and long sword, at last told me he had a compassion for my youth and therefore advised me to show the world I was not such a rascal as they thought me to be. I did not at first understand him; but he explained himself, and ended with telling me, if I would write a challenge to the captain, he would, out of pure charity, go to him with it." "A very charitable person, truly!" cried Adams. "I desired till the next day," continued the gentleman, "to consider on it, and, retiring to my lodgings, I weighed the consequences on both sides as fairly as I could. On the one, I saw the risk of this alternative—either losing my own life, or having on my hands the blood of a man with whom I was not in the least angry. I soon determined that the good which appeared on the other was not worth this hazard. I therefore resolved to quit the scene, and presently retired to the Temple, where I took chambers. Here I soon got a fresh set of acquaintance, who knew nothing of what had happened to me. Indeed they were not greatly to my approbation, for the beaux of the Temple are only the shadows of the others. They are the affectation of affectation. The vanity of these are still more ridiculous, if possible, than of the others. Here I met with smart fellows who drank with lords they did not know and intrigued with women they never saw. Covent Garden was now the farthest stretch of my ambition, where I shone forth in the balconies at the playhouses, visited whores, made love to orange-wenches, and damned plays. This career was soon put a stop to by my surgeon, who convinced me of the necessity of confining myself to my room for a month. At the end of which, having had leisure to reflect, I resolved to quit all farther conversation with beaux and smarts of every kind and to avoid, if possible, any occasion of returning to this place of confinement." "I think," said Adams, "the advice of a month's retirement and reflection was very proper; but I should rather have expected it from a divine than a surgeon." The gentleman smiled at Adams's simplicity, and, without explaining himself farther on such an odious subject, went on thus: "I was no sooner perfectly restored to health than I found my passion for women, which I was afraid to satisfy as I had done, made me very uneasy; I determined, therefore, to keep a mistress. Nor was I long before I fixed my choice on a young woman who had before been kept by two gentlemen, and to whom I was recommended by a celebrated bawd. I took her home to my chambers and made her a settlement during cohabitation. This would, perhaps, have been very ill paid, however, she did not suffer me to be perplexed on that account; for, before quarter-day, I found her at my chambers in too familiar conversation with a young fellow who was dressed like an officer but was indeed a city apprentice. Instead of excusing her inconstancy, she rapped out half a dozen oaths, and, snapping her fingers at me, swore she scorned to confine herself to the best man in England. Upon this we parted, and the same bawd presently provided her another keeper. I was not so much concerned at our separation as I found within a day or two I had reason to be for our meeting, for I was obliged to pay a second visit to my surgeon. I was now forced to do penance for some weeks, during which time I contracted an acquaintance with a beautiful young girl, the daughter of a gentleman, who, after having been forty years in the army and in all the campaigns under the Duke of Marlborough, died a lieutenant on half-pay and had left a widow with this only child, in very distressed circumstances; they had only a small pension from the government with what little the daughter could add to it by her work, for she had great excellence at her needle. This girl was, at my first acquaintance with her, solicited in marriage by a young fellow in good circumstances. He was apprentice to a linen-draper and had a little fortune, sufficient to set up his trade. The mother was greatly pleased with this match, as indeed she had sufficient reason. However, I soon prevented it. I represented him in so low a light to his mistress, and made so good an use of flattery, promises, and presents, that, not to dwell longer on this subject than is necessary, I prevailed with the poor girl and conveyed her away from her mother! In a word, I debauched her." (At which words Adams started up, fetched three strides cross the room, and then replaced himself in his chair.) "You are not more affected with this part of my story than myself—I assure you it will never be sufficiently repented of in my own opinion—but if you already detest it, how much more will your indignation be raised when you hear the fatal consequences of this barbarous, this villainous action? If you please, therefore, I will here desist." "By no means," cries Adams. "Go on, I beseech you, and Heaven grant you may sincerely repent of this and many other things you have related." "I was now," continued the gentleman, "as happy as the possession of a fine young creature, who had a good education and was endued with many agreeable qualities, could make me. We lived some months with vast fondness together, without any company or conversation more than we found in one another; but this could not continue always, and though I still preserved great affection for her I began more and more to want the relief of other company, and consequently to leave her by degrees, at last, whole days to herself. She failed not to testify some uneasiness on these occasions, and complained of the melancholy life she led, to remedy which, I introduced her into the acquaintance of some other kept mistresses, with whom she used to play at cards and frequent plays and other diversions. She had not lived long in this intimacy before I perceived a visible alteration in her behaviour; all her modesty and innocence vanished by degrees, till her mind became thoroughly tainted. She affected the company of rakes, gave herself all manner of airs, was never easy but abroad or when she had a party at my chambers. She was rapacious of money, extravagant to excess, loose in her conversation, and if ever I demurred to any of her demands, oaths, tears, and fits were the immediate consequences. As the first raptures of fondness were long since over, this behaviour soon estranged my affections from her; I began to reflect with pleasure that she was not my wife and to conceive an intention of parting with her, of which having given her a hint, she took care to prevent me the pains of turning her out of doors and accordingly departed herself, having first broken open my escritoire and taken with her all she could find, to the amount of about £200. In the first heat of my resentment I resolved to pursue her with all the vengeance of the law, but, as she had the good luck to escape me during that ferment, my passion afterwards cooled, and, having reflected that I had been the first aggressor and had done her an injury for which I could make her no reparation by robbing her of the innocence of her mind, and hearing at the same time that the poor old woman her mother had broke her heart on her daughter's elopement from her, I, concluding myself her murderer" ("As you very well might," cries Adams, with a groan), "was pleased that God Almighty had taken this method of punishing me, and resolved quietly to submit to the loss. Indeed, I could wish I had never heard more of the poor creature, who became in the end an abandoned profligate, and after being some years a common prostitute, at last ended her miserable life in Newgate." Here the gentleman fetched a deep sigh, which Mr. Adams echoed very loudly; and both continued silent, looking on each other for some minutes. At last the gentleman proceeded thus: "I had been perfectly constant to this girl during the whole time I kept her, but she had scarce departed before I discovered more marks of her infidelity to me than the loss of my money. In short, I was forced to make a third visit to my surgeon, out of whose hands I did not get a hasty discharge.

"I now forswore all future dealings with the sex, complained loudly that the pleasure did not compensate the pain, and railed at the beautiful creatures in as gross language as Juvenal himself formerly reviled them in. I looked on all the town-harlots with a detestation not easy to be conceived; their persons appeared to me as painted palaces inhabited by Disease and Death, nor could their beauty make them more desirable objects in my eyes than gilding could make me covet a pill or golden plates a coffin. But though I was no longer the absolute slave, I found some reasons to own myself still the subject of love. My hatred for women decreased daily, and I am not positive but time might have betrayed me again to some common harlot had I not been secured by a passion for the charming Sapphira, which having once entered upon, made a violent progress in my heart. Sapphira was wife to a man of fashion and gallantry, and one who seemed, I own, every way worthy of her affections, which, however, he had not the reputation of having. She was indeed a coquette *achevée*." "Pray, sir," says Adams, "what is a coquette? I have met with the word in French authors, but never could assign any idea to it. I believe it is the same with *une sotte, Anglice,* a fool." "Sir," answered the gentleman, "perhaps you are not much mistaken, but as it is a particular kind of folly, I will endeavour to describe it. Were all creatures to be ranked in the order of creation according to their usefulness, I know few animals that would not take the place of a coquette, nor indeed hath this creature much pretence to anything beyond instinct, for though sometimes we might imagine it was animated by the passion of vanity, yet far the greater part of its actions fall beneath even that low motive; for instance, several absurd gestures and tricks, infinitely more foolish than what can be observed in the most ridiculous birds and beasts, and which would persuade the beholder that the silly wretch was aiming at our contempt. Indeed its characteristic is affectation, and this led and governed by whim only, for as beauty, wisdom, wit, good nature, politeness, and health are sometimes affected by this creature, so are ugliness, folly, nonsense, ill-nature, ill-breeding, and sickness likewise put on by it in their turn. Its life is one constant lie, and the only rule by which you can form any judgement of them is that they are never what they seem. If it was possible for a coquette to love (as it is not, for if ever it attains this passion the coquette ceases instantly), it would wear the face of indifference, if not of hatred, to the beloved object; you may therefore be assured, when they endeavour to persuade you of their liking, that they are indifferent to you at least. And indeed this was the case of my Sapphira, who no sooner saw me in the number of her admirers than she gave me what is commonly called encouragement: she would often look at me, and when she perceived me meet her eyes would instantly take them off, discovering at the same time as much surprise and emotion as possible. These arts failed not of the success she intended, and as I grew more particular to her than the rest of her admirers, she advanced, in proportion, more directly to me than to the others. She affected the low voice, whisper, lisp, sigh, start, laugh, and many other indications of passion which daily deceive thousands. When I played at whist with her, she would look earnestly at me, and at the same time lose deal or revoke, then burst into a ridiculous laugh, and cry, 'La! I can't imagine what I was thinking of.' To detain you no longer, after I had gone through a sufficient course of gallantry, as I thought, and was thoroughly convinced I had raised a violent passion in my mistress, I sought an opportunity of coming to an *eclaircissement* with her. She avoided this as much as possible; however, great assiduity at length presented me one. I will not describe all the particulars of this interview; let it suffice that, till she could no longer pretend not to see my drift, she first affected a violent surprise and immediately after as violent a passion; she wondered what I had seen in her conduct which could induce me to affront her in this manner, and, breaking from me the first moment she could, told me I had no other way to escape the consequence of her resentment than by never seeing, or at least speaking to her, more. I was not contented with this answer; I still pursued her, but to no purpose, and was at length convinced that her husband had the sole possession of her person, and that neither he nor any other had made any impression on her heart. I was taken off from following this *ignis fatuus* by some advances which were made me by the wife of a citizen, who, though neither very young nor handsome, was yet too agreeable to be rejected by my amorous constitution. I accordingly soon satisfied her that she had not cast away her hints on a barren or cold soil; on the contrary, they instantly produced her an eager and desiring lover. Nor did she give me any reason to complain; she met the warmth she had raised with equal ardour. I had no longer a coquette to deal with, but one who was wiser than to prostitute the noble passion of love to the ridiculous lust of vanity. We presently understood one another, and as the pleasures we sought lay in a mutual gratification, we soon found and enjoyed them. I thought myself at first greatly happy in the possession of this new mistress, whose fondness would have quickly surfeited a more sickly appetite, but it had a different effect on mine: she carried my passion higher by it than youth or beauty had been able. But my happiness could not long continue uninterrupted. The apprehensions we lay under from the jealousy of her husband gave us great uneasiness." "Poor wretch! I pity him," cried Adams. "He did indeed deserve it," said the gentleman, "for he loved his wife with great tenderness, and, I assure you, it is a great satisfaction to me that I was not the man who first seduced her affections from him. These apprehensions appeared also too well grounded, for in the end he discovered us and procured witnesses of our caresses. He then prosecuted me at law and recovered £3,000 damages, which much distressed my fortune to pay, and what was worse, his wife, being divorced, came upon my hands. I led a very uneasy life with her, for, besides that my passion was now much abated, her excessive jealousy was very troublesome. At length death rid me of an inconvenience which the consideration of my having been the author of her misfortunes would never suffer me to take any other method of discarding.

"I now bade adieu to love and resolved to pursue other less dangerous and expensive pleasures. I fell into the acquaintance of a set of jolly companions, who slept all day and drank all night, fellows who might rather be said to consume time than to live. Their best conversation was nothing but noise: singing, halloing, wrangling, drinking, toasting, sp—wing, smoking, were the chief ingredients of our entertainment. And yet, bad as they were, they were more tolerable than our graver scenes, which were either excessive tedious narratives of dull common matters of fact, or hot disputes about trifling matters, which commonly ended in a wager. This way of life the first serious reflection put a period to; and I became member of a club frequented by young men of great abilities. The bottle was now only called in to the assistance of our conversation, which rolled on the deepest points of philosophy. These gentlemen were engaged in a search after truth, in the pursuit of which they threw aside all the prejudices of education and governed themselves only by the infallible guide of human reason. This great guide, after having shown them the falsehood of that very ancient but simple tenet, that there is such a being as a Deity in the universe, helped them to establish in his stead a certain rule of right, by adhering to which they all arrived at the utmost purity of morals. Reflection made me as much delighted with this society as it had taught me to despise and detest the former. I began now to esteem myself a being of a higher order than I had ever before conceived, and was the more charmed with this rule of right as I really found in my own nature nothing repugnant to it. I held in utter contempt all persons who wanted any other inducement to virtue besides her intrinsic beauty and excellence, and had so high an opinion of my present companions with regard to their morality that I would have trusted them with whatever was nearest and dearest to me. Whilst I was engaged in this delightful dream, two or three accidents happened successively which at first much surprised me, for one of our greatest philosophers, or rule-of-right men, withdrew himself from us, taking with him the wife of one of his most intimate friends. Secondly, another of the same society left the club without remembering to take leave of his bail. A third, having borrowed a sum of money of me for which I received no security, when I asked him to repay it, absolutely denied the loan. These several practises, so inconsistent with our golden rule, made me begin to suspect its infallibility, but when I communicated my thoughts to one of the club, he said there was nothing absolutely good or evil in itself, that actions were denominated good or bad by the circumstances of the agent. That possibly the man who ran away with his neighbour's wife might be one of very good inclinations but overprevailed on by the violence of an unruly passion, and, in other particulars, might be a very worthy member of society; that, if the beauty of any woman created in him an uneasiness, he had a right, from nature, to relieve himself—with many other things, which I then detested so much that I took leave of the society that very evening and never returned to it again. Being now reduced to a state of solitude, which I did not like, I became a great frequenter of the play-houses, which indeed was always my favourite diversion, and most evenings passed away two or three hours behind the scenes, where I met with several poets, with whom I made engagements at the taverns. Some of the players were likewise of our parties. At these meetings we were generally entertained by the poets with reading their performances, and by the players with repeating their parts, upon which occasions I observed the gentleman who furnished our entertainment was commonly the best pleased of the company, who, though they were pretty civil to him to his face, seldom failed to take the first opportunity of his absence to ridicule him. Now I made some remarks, which probably are too obvious to be worth relating." "Sir," says Adams, "your remarks if you please." "First then," says he, "I concluded that the general observation that wits are most inclined to vanity, is not true. Men are equally vain of riches, strength, beauty, honours, etc. But these appear of themselves to the eyes of the beholders, whereas the poor wit is obliged to produce his performance to show you his perfection, and on his readiness to do this that vulgar opinion I have before mentioned is grounded: but doth not the person who expends vast sums in the furniture of his house or the ornaments of his person, who consumes much time and employs great pains in dressing himself, or who thinks himself paid for self-denial, labour, or even villainy, by a title or a ribbon sacrifice as much to vanity as the poor wit who is desirous to read you his poem or his play? My second remark was that vanity is the worst of passions, and more apt to contaminate the mind than any other: for as selfishness is much more general than we please to allow it; so it is natural to hate and envy those who stand between us and the good we desire. Now, in lust and ambition these are few, and even in avarice we find many who are no obstacles to our pursuits, but the vain man seeks pre-eminence, and everything which is excellent or praiseworthy in another renders him the mark of his antipathy." Adams now began to fumble in his pockets and soon cried out, "Oh, la! I have it not about me." Upon this the gentleman asking him what he was searching for, he said he searched after a sermon, which he thought his masterpiece, against vanity. "Fie upon it, fie upon it!" cries he, "why do I ever leave that sermon out of my pocket? I wish it was within five miles; I would willingly fetch it, to read it you." The gentleman answered that there was no need, for he was cured of the passion. "And for that very reason," quoth Adams, "I would read it, for I am confident you would admire it; indeed, I have never been a greater enemy to any passion than that silly one of vanity." The gentleman smiled, and proceeded. "From this society I easily passed to that of the gamesters, where nothing remarkable happened but the finishing my fortune, which those gentlemen soon helped me to the end of. This opened scenes of life hitherto unknown: poverty and distress, with their horrid train of duns, attorneys, bailiffs, haunted me day and night. My clothes grew shabby, my credit bad, my friends and acquaintance of all kinds cold. In this situation, the strangest thought imaginable came into my head, and what was this but to write a play? for I had sufficient leisure: fear of bailiffs confined me every day to my room; and having always had a little inclination, and something of a genius that way, I set myself to work, and within a few months produced a piece of five acts which was accepted of at the theatre. I remembered to have formerly taken tickets of other poets for their benefits long before the appearance of their performances, and, resolving to follow a precedent which was so well suited to my present circumstances, I immediately provided myself with a large number of little papers. Happy indeed would be the state of poetry would these tickets pass current at the bake-house, the ale-house, and the chandler's shop, but alas! far otherwise: no tailor will take them in payment for buckram, canvas, stay-tape, nor no bailiff for civility-money. They are, indeed, no more than a passport to beg with; a certificate that the owner wants five shillings, which induces well-disposed Christians to charity. I now experienced what is worse than poverty, or rather what is the worst consequence of poverty—I mean attendance and dependence on the great. Many a morning have I waited hours in the cold parlours of men of quality, where, after seeing the lowest rascals in lace and embroidery, the pimps and buffoons in fashion, admitted, I have been sometimes told, on sending in my name, that my lord could not possibly see me this morning: a sufficient assurance that I should never more get entrance into that house. Sometimes I have been at last admitted, and the great man hath thought proper to excuse himself by telling me he was tied up." "Tied up," says Adams, "pray what's that?" "Sir," says the gentleman, "the profit which book-sellers allowed authors for the best works was so very small that certain men of birth and fortune some years ago, who were the patrons of wit and learning, thought fit to encourage them farther by entering into voluntary subscriptions for their encouragement. Thus Prior, Rowe, Pope, and some other men of genius received large sums for their labours from the public. This seemed so easy a method of getting money that many of the lowest scribblers of the times ventured to publish their works in the same way, and many had the assurance to take in subscriptions for what was not writ, nor even intended. Subscriptions in this manner growing infinite, and a kind of tax on the public, some persons, finding it not so easy a task to discern good from bad authors or to know what genius was worthy encouragement and what was not, to prevent the expense of subscribing to so many, invented a method to excuse themselves from all subscriptions whatever, and this was to receive a small sum of money in consideration of giving a large one if ever they subscribed, which many have done, and many more have pretended to have done in order to silence all solicitation. The same method was likewise taken with play-house tickets, which were no less a public grievance, and this is what they call being tied up from subscribing." "I can't say but the term is apt enough, and somewhat typical," said Adams, "for a man of large fortune who ties himself up, as you call it, from the encouragement of men of merit, ought to be tied up in reality." "Well, sir," says the gentleman, "to return to my story. Sometimes I have received a guinea from a man of quality, given with as ill a grace as alms are generally to the meanest beggar, and purchased too with as much time spent in attendance as, if it had been spent in honest industry, might have brought me more profit with infinitely more satisfaction. After about two months spent in this disagreeable way, with the utmost mortification, when I was pluming my hopes on the prospect of a plentiful harvest from my play, upon applying to the prompter to know when it came into rehearsal, he informed me he had received orders from the managers to return me the play again, for that they could not possibly act it that season, but, if I would take it and revise it against the next, they would be glad to see it again. I snatched it from him with great indignation and retired to my room, where I threw myself on the bed in a fit of despair." "You should rather have thrown yourself on your knees," says Adams, "for despair is sinful." "As soon," continued the gentleman, "as I had indulged the first tumult of my passion, I began to consider coolly what course I should take, in a situation without friends, money, credit, or reputation of any kind. After revolving many things in my mind, I could see no other possibility of furnishing myself with the miserable necessaries of life than to retire to a garret near the Temple and commence hackney-writer to the lawyers, for which I was well qualified, being an excellent penman. This purpose I resolved on, and immediately put it in execution. I had an acquaintance with an attorney who had formerly transacted affairs for me, and to him I applied, but instead of furnishing me with any business he laughed at my undertaking and told me he was afraid I should turn his deeds into plays and he should expect to see them on the stage. Not to tire you with instances of this kind from others, I found that Plato himself did not hold poets in greater abhorrence than these men of business do. Whenever I durst venture to a coffee-house, which was on Sundays [2] only, a whisper ran round the room, which was constantly attended with a sneer, 'That's poet Wilson'; for I know not whether you have observed it, but there is a malignity in the nature of man which, when not weeded out, or at least covered by a good education and politeness, delights in making another uneasy or dissatisfied with himself. This abundantly appears in all assemblies except those which are filled by people of fashion, and especially among the younger people of both sexes whose birth and fortunes place them just without the polite circles; I mean the lower class of the gentry and the higher of the mercantile world, who are, in reality, the worst bred part of mankind. Well, sir, whilst I continued in this miserable state, with scarce sufficient business to keep me from starving, the reputation of a poet being my bane, I accidentally became acquainted with a book-seller, who told me it was pity a man of my learning and genius should be obliged to such a method of getting his livelihood; that he had a compassion for me, and if I would engage with him, he would undertake to provide handsomely for me. A man in my circumstances, as he very well knew, had no choice. I accordingly accepted his proposal with his conditions, which were none of the most favourable, and fell to translating with all my might. I had no longer reason to lament the want of business, for he furnished me with so much that in half a year I almost writ myself blind. I likewise contracted a distemper by my sedentary life, in which no part of my body was exercised but my right arm, which rendered me incapable of writing for a long time. This unluckily happening to delay the publication of a work, and my last performance not having sold well, the book-seller declined any further engagement, and aspersed me to his brethern as a careless, idle fellow. I had, however, by having half-worked and half-starved myself to death during the time I was in his service, saved a few guineas, with which I bought a lottery ticket, resolving to throw myself into Fortune's lap and try if she would make me amends for the injuries she had done me at the gaming-table. This purchase being made left me almost penniless, when, as if I had not been sufficiently miserable, a bailiff in woman's clothes got admittance to my chamber, whither he was directed by the book-seller. He arrested me at my tailor's suit for thirty-five pounds, a sum for which I could not procure bail and was therefore conveyed to his house, where I was locked up in an upper chamber. I had now neither health (for I was scarce recovered from my indisposition), liberty, money, or friends; and had abandoned all hopes, and even the desire of life." "But this could not last long," said Adams, "for doubtless the tailor released you the moment he was truly acquainted with your affairs, and knew that your circumstances would not permit you to pay him." "Oh, sir," answered the gentleman, "he knew that before he arrested me; nay, he knew that nothing but incapacity could prevent me paying my debts, for I had been his customer many years, had spent vast sums of money with him, and had always paid most punctually in my prosperous days: but when I reminded him of this, with assurances that if he would not molest my endeavours I would pay him all the money I could by my utmost labour and industry procure, reserving only what was sufficient to preserve me alive, he answered his patience was worn out; that I had put him off from time to time; that he wanted the money; that he had put it into a lawyer's hands; and if I did not pay him immediately, or find security, I must lie in jail, and expect no mercy." "He may expect mercy," cries Adams, starting from his chair, "where he will find none! How can such a wretch repeat the Lord's prayer, where the word which is translated, I know not for what reason, 'trespasses,' is, in the original, 'debts'! And as surely as we do not forgive others their debts when they are unable to pay them, so surely shall we ourselves be unforgiven, when we are in no condition of paying." He ceased, and the gentleman proceeded. "While I was in this deplorable situation, a former acquaintance to whom I had communicated my lottery ticket found me out, and, making me a visit, with great delight in his countenance, shook me heartily by the hand, and wished me joy of my good fortune, for, says he, your ticket is come up a prize of £3,000." Adams snapped his fingers at these words in an ecstasy of joy, which, however, did not continue long for the gentleman thus proceeded: "Alas! sir, this was only a trick of fortune to sink me the deeper, for I had disposed of this lottery ticket two days before to a relation who refused lending me a shilling without it, in order to procure myself bread. As soon as my friend was acquainted with my unfortunate sale, he began to revile me, and remind me of all the ill conduct and miscarriages of my life. He said I was one whom Fortune could not save if she would; that I was now ruined without any hopes of retrieval, nor must expect any pity from my friends; that it would be extreme weakness to compassionate the misfortunes of a man who ran headlong to his own destruction. He then painted to me, in as lively colours as he was able, the happiness I should have now enjoyed had I not foolishly disposed of my ticket. I urged the plea of necessity, but he made no answer to that and began again to revile me till I could bear it no longer and desired him to finish his visit. I soon exchanged the bailiff's house for a prison, where, as I had not money sufficient to procure me a separate apartment, I was crowded in with a great number of miserable wretches, in common with whom I was destitute of every convenience of life, even that which all the brutes enjoy, wholesome air. In these dreadful circumstances, I applied by letter to several of my old acquaintance, and such to whom I had formerly lent money without any great prospect of its being returned, for their assistance; but in vain. An excuse, instead of a denial, was the gentlest answer I received.—Whilst I languished in a condition too horrible to be described, and which, in a land of humanity, and what is much more, Christianity, seems a strange punishment for a little inadvertency and indiscretion, whilst I was in this condition, a fellow came into the prison, and, inquiring me out, delivered me the following letter:

" 'SIR—My father, to whom you sold your ticket in the last lottery, died the same day in which it came up a prize, as you have possibly heard, and left me sole heiress of all his fortune. I am so much touched with your present circumstances, and the uneasiness you must feel at having been driven to dispose of what might have made you happy, that I must desire your acceptance of the inclosed, and am

" 'Your humble servant,

" 'HARRIET HEARTY.'

"And what do you think was inclosed?" "I don't know," cried Adams; "not less than a guinea, I hope." "Sir, it was a bank-note for £200." "£200!" says Adams, in a rapture. "No less, I assure you," answered the gentleman; "a sum I was not half so delighted with, as with the dear name of the generous girl that sent it me, and who was not only the best but the handsomest creature in the universe, and for whom I had long had a passion which I never durst disclose to her. I kissed her name a thousand times, my eyes overflowing with tenderness and gratitude; I repeated——But not to detain you with these raptures, I immediately acquired my liberty, and, having paid all my debts, departed, with upwards of fifty pounds in my pocket, to thank my kind deliverer. She happened to be then out of town, a circumstance which, upon reflection, pleased me, for by that means I had an opportunity to appear before her in a more decent dress. At her return to town within a day or two, I threw myself at her feet with the most ardent acknowledgements, which she rejected with an unfeigned greatness of mind and told me I could not oblige her more than by never mentioning, or if possible thinking on, a circumstance which must bring to my mind an accident that might be grievous to me to think on. She proceeded thus: 'What I have done is in my own eyes a trifle, and perhaps infinitely less than would have become me to do. And if you think of engaging in any business where a larger sum may be serviceable to you, I shall not be overrigid either as to the security or interest.' I endeavoured to express all the gratitude in my power to this profusion of goodness, though perhaps it was my enemy, and began to afflict my mind with more agonies than all the miseries I had underwent; it affected me with severer reflections than poverty, distress, and prisons united had been able to make me feel, for, sir, these acts and professions of kindness, which were sufficient to have raised in a good heart the most violent passion of friendship to one of the same, or to age and ugliness in a different, sex, came to me from a woman, a young and beautiful woman, one whose perfections I had long known and for whom I had long conceived a violent passion, though with a despair which made me endeavour rather to curb and conceal than to nourish or acquaint her with it. In short, they came upon me united with beauty, softness, and tenderness, such bewitching smiles—oh, Mr. Adams, in that moment I lost myself, and, forgetting our different situations, not considering what return I was making to her goodness by desiring her, who had given me so much, to bestow her all, I laid gently hold on her hand, and, conveying it to my lips, I pressed it with inconceivable ardour, then, lifting up my swimming eyes, I saw her face and neck overspread with one blush; she offered to withdraw her hand, yet not so as to deliver it from mine, though I held it with the gentlest force. We both stood trembling, her eyes cast on the ground, and mine steadfastly fixed on her. Good G—d, what was then the condition of my soul! burning with love, desire, admiration, gratitude, and every tender passion, all bent on one charming object. Passion at last got the better of both reason and respect, and, softly letting go her hand, I offered madly to clasp her in my arms, when, a little recovering herself, she started from me, asking me with some show of anger if she had any reason to expect this treatment from me. I then fell prostrate before her and told her, if I had offended, my life was absolutely in her power, which I would in any manner lose for her sake. 'Nay, madam,' said I, 'you shall not be so ready to punish me as I to suffer. I own my guilt. I detest the reflection that I would have sacrificed your happiness to mine. Believe me, I sincerely repent my ingratitude; yet, believe me too, it was my passion, my unbounded passion for you, which hurried me so far: I have loved you long and tenderly, and the goodness you have shown me hath innocently weighed down a wretch undone before. Acquit me of all mean, mercenary views, and, before I take my leave of you forever, which I am resolved instantly to do, believe me that Fortune could have raised me to no height to which I could not have gladly lifted you. Oh, curst be Fortune!' 'Do not,' says she, interrupting me with the sweetest voice, 'do not curse Fortune, since she hath made me happy; and, if she hath put your happiness in my power, I have told you you shall ask nothing in reason which I will refuse.' 'Madam,' said I, 'you mistake me if you imagine, as you seem, my happiness is in the power of Fortune now. You have obliged me too much already; if I have any wish, it is for some blessed accident by which I may contribute with my life to the least augmentation of your felicity. As for myself, the only happiness I can ever have will be hearing of yours, and if Fortune will make that complete, I will forgive her all her wrongs to me.' 'You may indeed,' answered she smiling, 'for your own happiness must be included in mine. I have long known your worth; nay, I must confess,' said she blushing, 'I have long discovered that passion for me you profess, notwithstanding those endeavours, which I am convinced were unaffected, to conceal it, and if all I can give with reason will not suffice, —take reason away—and now I believe you cannot ask me what I will deny.'——She uttered these words with a sweetness not to be imagined. I immediately started; my blood, which lay freezing at my heart, rushed tumultuously through every vein. I stood for a moment silent; then, flying to her, I caught her in my arms, no longer resisting, and softly told her she must give me then herself. Oh, sir—can I describe her look? She remained silent, and almost motionless, several minutes. At last, recovering herself a little, she insisted on my leaving her, and in such a manner that I instantly obeyed. You may imagine, however, I soon saw her again.—But I ask pardon: I fear I have detained you too long in relating the particulars of the former interview." "So far otherwise," said Adams, licking his lips, "that I could willingly hear it over again." "Well, sir," continued the gentleman, "to be as concise as possible, within a week she consented to make me the happiest of mankind. We were married shortly after, and when I came to examine the circumstances of my wife's fortune (which, I do assure you, I was not presently at leisure enough to do), I found it amounted to about six thousand pounds, most part of which lay in effects, for her father had been a wine-merchant, and she seemed willing, if I liked it, that I should carry on the same trade. I readily, and too inconsiderately, undertook it, for, not having been bred up to the secrets of the business, and endeavouring to deal with the utmost honesty and uprightness, I soon found our fortune in a declining way, and my trade decreasing by little and little, for my wines, which I never adulterated after their importation, and were sold as neat as they came over, were universally decried by the vintners, to whom I could not allow them quite as cheap as those who gained double the profit by a less price. I soon began to despair of improving our fortune by these means; nor was I at all easy at the visits and familiarity of many who had been my acquaintance in my prosperity but denied and shunned me in my adversity, and now very forwardly renewed their acquaintance with me. In short, I had sufficiently seen that the pleasures of the world are chiefly folly, and the business of it mostly knavery; and both nothing better than vanity—the men of pleasure tearing one another to pieces from the emulation of spending money, and the men of business from envy in getting it. My happiness consisted entirely in my wife, whom I loved with an inexpressible fondness, which was perfectly returned; and my prospects were no other than to provide for our growing family, for she was now big of her second child. I therefore took an opportunity to ask her opinion of entering into a retired life, which, after hearing my reasons, and perceiving my affection for it, she readily embraced. We soon put our small fortune, now reduced under three thousand pounds, into money, with part of which we purchased this little place, whither we retired soon after her delivery, from a world full of bustle, noise, hatred, envy, and ingratitude, to ease, quiet, and love. We have here lived almost twenty years, with little other conversation than our own, most of the neighbourhood taking us for very strange people; the Squire of the parish representing me as a madman, and the parson as a Presbyterian, because I will not hunt with the one, nor drink with the other." "Sir," says Adams, "Fortune hath, I think, paid you all her debts in this sweet retirement." "Sir," replied the gentleman, "I am thankful to the great Author of all things for the blessings I here enjoy. I have the best of wives, and three pretty children for whom I have the true tenderness of a parent. But no blessings are pure in this world: within three years of my arrival here I lost my eldest son." (Here he sighed bitterly.) "Sir," said Adams, "we must submit to Providence, and consider death as common to all." "We must submit, indeed," answered the gentleman; "and, if he had died, I could have borne the loss with patience, but alas! sir, he was stolen away from my door by some wicked travelling people, whom they call Gipsies; nor could I ever with the most diligent search recover him. Poor child! he had the sweetest look, the exact picture of his mother—" at which some tears unwittingly dropped from his eyes, as did likewise from those of Adams, who always sympathized with his friends on those occasions. "Thus, sir," said the gentleman, "I have finished my story, in which, if I have been too particular, I ask your pardon; and now, if you please, I will fetch you another bottle," which proposal the parson thankfully accepted.

CHAPTER IV: *A description of Mr. Wilson's way of living. The tragical adventure of the dog, and other grave matters.*

THE gentleman returned with the bottle, and Adams and he sat some time silent, when the former started up and cried, "No, that won't do." The gentleman inquired into his meaning; he answered he had been considering that it was possible the late famous King Theodore might have been the very son whom he had lost, but added that his age could not answer that imagination. "However," says he, "G— disposes all things for the best, and very probably he may be some great man, or duke, and may, one day or other, revisit you in that capacity." The gentleman answered he should know him amongst ten thousand, for he had a mark on his left breast of a strawberry, which his mother had given him by longing for that fruit.

That beautiful young lady the Morning now rose from her bed, and with a countenance blooming with fresh youth and sprightliness, like Miss ——,* with soft dews hanging on her pouting lips, began to take her early walk over the eastern hills, and presently after, that gallant person the Sun stole softly from his wife's chamber to pay his addresses to her, when the gentleman asked his guest if he would walk forth and survey his little garden, which he readily agreed to, and Joseph at the same time awaking from a sleep in which he had been two hours buried, went with them. No parterres, no fountains, no statues, embellished this little garden. Its only ornament was a short walk, shaded on each side by a filbert-hedge with a small alcove at one end, whither in hot weather the gentleman and his wife used to retire and divert themselves with their children, who played in the walk before them. But though vanity had no votary in this little spot, here was variety of fruit and everything useful for the kitchen, which was abundantly sufficient to catch the admiration of Adams, who told the gentleman he had certainly a good gardener. "Sir," answered he, "that gardener is now before you: whatever you see here is the work solely of my own hands. Whilst I am providing necessaries for my table, I likewise procure myself an appetite for them. In fair seasons, I seldom pass less than six hours of the twenty-four in this place, where I am not idle, and by these means I have been able to preserve my health ever since my arrival here without assistance from physic. Hither I generally repair at the dawn, and exercise myself whilst my wife dresses her children and prepares our breakfast, after which we are seldom asunder during the residue of the day, for, when the weather will not permit them to accompany me here, I am usually within with them; for I am neither ashamed of conversing with my wife nor of playing with my children: to say the truth, I do not perceive that inferiority of understanding which the levity of rakes, the dulness of men of business, or the austerity of the learned, would persuade us of in women. As for my woman, I declare I have found none of my own sex capable of making juster observations on life, or of delivering them more agreeably, nor do I believe anyone possessed of a faithfuller or braver friend. And sure as this friendship is sweetened with more delicacy and tenderness, so is it confirmed by dearer pledges than can attend the closest male alliance, for what union can be so fast as our common interest in the fruits of our embraces? Perhaps, sir, you are not yourself a father; if you are not, be assured you cannot conceive the delight I have in my little ones. Would you not despise me if you saw me stretched on the ground and my children playing round me?" "I should reverence the sight," quoth Adams; "I myself am now the father of six, and have been of eleven, and I can say I never scourged a child of my own, unless as his schoolmaster, and then have felt every stroke on my own posteriors. And, as to what you say concerning women, I have often lamented my own wife did not understand Greek." The gentleman smiled and answered, he would not be apprehended to insinuate that his own had an understanding above the care of her family. "On the contrary," says he, "my Harriet, I assure you, is a notable housewife, and few gentlemen's housekeepers understand cookery or confectionery better—but these are arts which she hath no great occasion for now; however, the wine you commended so much last night at supper was of her own making, as is indeed all the liquor in my house except my beer, which falls to my province." "And I assure you it is as excellent," quoth Adams, "as ever I tasted." "We formerly kept a maid-servant, but since my girls have been growing up she is unwilling to indulge them in idleness, for as the fortunes I shall give them will be very small, we intend not to breed them above the rank they are likely to fill hereafter, nor to teach them to despise or ruin a plain husband. Indeed, I could wish a man of my own temper, and a retired life, might fall to their lot; for I have experienced that calm serene happiness which is seated in content is inconsistent with the hurry and bustle of the world." He was proceeding thus, when the little things, being just risen, ran eagerly towards him and asked him blessing. They were shy to the strangers, but the eldest acquainted her father that her mother and the young gentlewoman were up, and that breakfast was ready. They all went in, where the gentleman was surprised at the beauty of Fanny, who had now recovered herself from her fatigue and was entirely clean dressed, for the rogues who had taken away her purse had left her her bundle. But if he was so much amazed at the beauty of this young creature, his guests were no less charmed at the tenderness which appeared in the behaviour of the husband and wife to each other and to their children, and at the dutiful and affectionate behaviour of these to their parents. These instances pleased the well-disposed mind of Adams, equally with the readiness which they expressed to oblige their guests and their forwardness to offer them the best of everything in their house, and what delighted him still more was an instance or two of their charity, for, whilst they were at breakfast, the good woman was called forth to assist her sick neighbour, which she did with some cordials made for the public use, and the good man went into his garden at the same time to supply another with something which he wanted thence, for they had nothing which those who wanted it were not welcome to. These good people were in the utmost cheerfulness, when they heard the report of a gun, and immediately afterwards a little dog, the favourite of the eldest daughter, came limping in all bloody and laid himself at his mistress's feet; the poor girl, who was about eleven years old, burst into tears at the sight, and presently one of the neighbours came in and informed them that the young Squire, the son of the lord of the manor, had shot him as he passed by, swearing at the same time he would prosecute the master of him for keeping a spaniel, for that he had given notice that he would not suffer one in the parish. The dog, whom his mistress had taken into her lap, died in a few minutes, licking her hand. She expressed great agony at his loss, and the other children began to cry for their sister's misfortune, nor could Fanny herself refrain. Whilst the father and mother attempted to comfort her, Adams grasped his crabstick and would have sallied out after the Squire had not Joseph withheld him. He could not, however, bridle his tongue—he pronounced the word "rascal" with great emphasis, said he deserved to be hanged more than a highwayman, and wished he had the scourging him. The mother took her child, lamenting and carrying the dead favourite in her arms, out of the room, when the gentleman said this was the second time this Squire had endeavoured to kill the little wretch, and had wounded him smartly once before, adding, he could have no motive but ill-nature, for the little thing, which was not near as big as one's fist, had never been twenty yards from the house in the six years his daughter had had it. He said he had done nothing to deserve this usage, but his father had too great a fortune to contend with; that he was as absolute as any tyrant in the universe, and had killed all the dogs and taken away all the guns in the neighbourhood; and not only that but he trampled down hedges and rode over corn and gardens with no more regard than if they were the highway. "I wish I could catch him in my garden," said Adams; "though I would rather forgive him riding through my house than such an ill-natured act as this."

The cheerfulness of the conversation being interrupted by this accident, in which the guests could be of no service to their kind entertainer; and as the mother was taken up in administering consolation to the poor girl, whose disposition was too good hastily to forget the sudden loss of her little favourite, which had been fondling with her a few minutes before; and as Joseph and Fanny were impatient to get home and begin those previous ceremonies to their happiness which Adams had insisted on, they now offered to take their leave. The gentleman importuned them much to stay dinner, but when he found their eagerness to depart, he summoned his wife, and accordingly, having performed all the usual ceremonies of bows and curtseys, more pleasant to be seen than to be related, they took their leave, the gentleman and his wife heartily wishing them a good journey and they as heartily thanking them for their kind entertainment. They then departed, Adams declaring that this was the manner in which the people had lived in the golden age.

CHAPTER V: *A disputation on schools, held on the road between Mr. Abraham Adams and Joseph, and a discovery not unwelcome to them both.*

OUR travellers, having well refreshed themselves at the gentleman's house, Joseph and Fanny with sleep, and Mr. Abraham Adams with ale and tobacco, renewed their journey with great alacrity, and, pursuing the road in which they were directed, travelled many miles before they met with any adventure worth relating. In this interval, we shall present our readers with a very curious discourse, as we apprehend it, concerning public schools, which passed between Mr. Joseph Andrews and Mr. Abraham Adams.

They had not gone far before Adams, calling to Joseph, asked him if he had attended to the gentleman's story; he answered, "To all the former part." "And don't you think," says he, "he was a very unhappy man in his youth?" "A very unhappy man, indeed," answered the other. "Joseph," cries Adams, screwing up his mouth, "I have found it; I have discovered the cause of all the misfortunes which befell him: a public school, Joseph, was the cause of all the calamities which he afterwards suffered. Public schools are the nurseries of all vice and immorality. All the wicked fellows whom I remember at the university were bred at them. Ah, Lord! I can remember, as well as if it was but yesterday, a knot of them; they called them King's Scholars, I forget why ——very wicked fellows! Joseph, you may thank the Lord you were not bred at a public school: you would never have preserved your virtue as you have. The first care I always take is of a boy's morals; I had rather he should be a blockhead than an atheist or a Presbyterian. What is all the learning of the world compared to his immortal soul? What shall a man take in exchange for his soul! But the masters of great schools trouble themselves about no such thing. I have known a lad of eighteen at the university who hath not been able to say his catechism, but for my own part I always scourged a lad sooner for missing that than any other lesson. Believe me, child, all that gentleman's misfortunes arose from his being educated at a public school."

"It doth not become me," answered Joseph, "to dispute anything, sir, with you, especially a matter of this kind, for to be sure you must be allowed by all the world to be the best teacher of a school in all our county." "Yes, that," said Adams, "I believe is granted me; that I may without much vanity pretend to—nay, I believe I may go to the next county too—but *gloriari non est meum*."[1] "However, sir, as you are pleased to bid me speak," says Joseph, "you know my late master, Sir Thomas Booby, was bred at a public school, and he was the finest gentleman in all the neighbourhood. And I have often heard him say, if he had a hundred boys he would breed them all at the same place. It was his opinion, and I have often heard him deliver it, that a boy taken from a public school and carried into the world will learn more in one year there than one of a private education will in five. He used to say the school itself initiated him a great way (I remember that was his very expression), for great schools are little societies, where a boy of any observation may see in epitome what he will afterwards find in the world at large." "*Hinc illae lachrymae:*[2] for that very reason," quoth Adams, "I prefer a private school, where boys may be kept in innocence and ignorance; for, according to that fine passage in the play of *Cato*,[3] the only English tragedy I ever read,

"If knowledge of the world must make men villains,
May Juba ever live in ignorance.

Who would not rather preserve the purity of his child than wish him to attain the whole circle of arts and sciences; which, by-the-bye, he may learn in the classes of a private school; for I would not be vain, but I esteem myself to be second to none, *nulli secundum,* in teaching these things; so that a lad may have as much learning in a private as in a public education." "And, with submission," answered Joseph, "he may get as much vice: witness several country gentlemen who were educated within five miles of their own houses and are as wicked as if they had known the world from their infancy. I remember, when I was in the stable, if a young horse was vicious in his nature, no correction would make him otherwise; I take it to be equally the same among men: if a boy be of a mischievous, wicked inclination, no school, though ever so private, will ever make him good; on the contrary, if he be of a righteous temper, you may trust him to London, or wherever else you please, he will be in no danger of being corrupted. Besides, I have often heard my master say that the discipline practised in public schools was much better than that in private." "You talk like a jackanapes," says Adams, "and so did your master. Discipline indeed! Because one man scourges twenty or thirty boys more in a morning than another, is he therefore a better disciplinarian? I do presume to confer in this point with all who have taught from Chiron's time to this day, and, if I was master of six boys only, I would preserve as good discipline amongst them as the master of the greatest school in the world. I say nothing, young man; remember, I say nothing, but if Sir Thomas himself had been educated nearer home, and under the tuition of somebody, remember, I name nobody, it might have been better for him—but his father must institute him in the knowledge of the world. *Nemo mortalium omnibus horis sapit.*" [4] Joseph, seeing him run on in this manner, asked pardon many times, assuring him he had no intention to offend. "I believe you had not, child," said he, "and I am not angry with you, but for maintaining good discipline in a school, for this"—and then he ran on as before, named all the masters who are recorded in old books and preferred himself to them all. Indeed, if this good man had an enthusiasm, or what the vulgar call a blind side, it was this: he thought a schoolmaster the greatest character in the world, and himself the greatest of all schoolmasters, neither of which points he would have given up to Alexander the Great at the head of his army.

Adams continued his subject till they came to one of the beautifullest spots of ground in the universe. It was a kind of natural amphitheatre formed by the winding of a small rivulet, which was planted with thick woods, and the trees rose gradually above each other, by the natural ascent of the ground they stood on; which ascent as they hid with their boughs, they seemed to have been disposed by the design of the most skilful planter. The soil was spread with a verdure which no paint could imitate, and the whole place might have raised romantic ideas in older minds than those of Joseph and Fanny, without the assistance of love.

Here they arrived about noon, and Joseph proposed to Adams that they should rest a while in this delightful place, and refresh themselves with some provisions which the good nature of Mrs. Wilson had provided them with. Adams made no objection to the proposal, so down they sat, and, pulling out a cold fowl and a bottle of wine, they made a repast with a cheerfulness which might have attracted the envy of more splendid tables. I should not omit that they found among their provision a little paper containing a piece of gold, which Adams, imagining had been put there by mistake, would have returned back to restore it; but he was at last convinced by Joseph that Mr. Wilson had taken this handsome way of furnishing them with a supply for their journey, on his having related the distress which they had been in when they were relieved by the generosity of the pedlar. Adams said he was glad to see such an instance of goodness, not so much for the conveniency which it brought them, as for the sake of the doer, whose reward would be great in heaven. He likewise comforted himself with a reflection that he should shortly have an opportunity of returning it him, for the gentleman was within a week to make a journey into Somersetshire, to pass through Adams's parish, and had faithfully promised to call on him; a circumstance which we thought too immaterial to mention before, but which those who have as great an affection for that gentleman as ourselves will rejoice at, as it may give them hopes of seeing him again. Then Joseph made a speech on charity which the reader, if he is so disposed, may see in the next chapter, for we scorn to betray him into any such reading without first giving him warning.

CHAPTER VI: *Moral reflections by Joseph Andrews, with the hunting adventure, and Parson Adams's miraculous escape.*

"I HAVE often wondered, sir," said Joseph, "to observe so few instances of charity among mankind, for though the goodness of a man's heart did not incline him to relieve the distress of his fellow-creatures, methinks the desire of honour should move him to it. What inspires a man to build fine houses, to purchase fine furniture, pictures, clothes, and other things, at a great expense, but an ambition to be respected more than other people? Now, would not one great act of charity, one instance of redeeming a poor family from all the miseries of poverty, restoring an unfortunate tradesman by a sum of money to the means of procuring a livelihood by his industry, discharging an undone debtor from his debts or a gaol, or any such-like example of goodness, create a man more honour and respect than he could acquire by the finest house, furniture, pictures, or clothes that were ever beheld? For not only the object himself, who was thus relieved, but all who heard the name of such a person must, I imagine, reverence him infinitely more than the possessor of all those other things, which when we so admire, we rather praise the builder, the workman, the painter, the lace-maker, the tailor, and the rest, by whose ingenuity they are produced, than the person who by his money makes them his own. For my own part, when I have waited behind my lady in a room hung with fine pictures, while I have been looking at them I have never once thought of their owner, nor hath anyone else, as I ever observed, for when it has been asked whose picture that was, it was never once answered, the master's of the house, but Ammyconni, Paul Varnish, Hannibal Scratchi, or Hogarthi, which I suppose were the names of the painters; but if it was asked, Who redeemed such a one out of prison? Who lent such a ruined tradesman money to set up? Who clothed that family of poor small children? it is very plain what must be the answer. And besides, these great folks are mistaken if they imagine they get any honour at all by these means; for I do not remember I ever was with my lady at any house where she commended the house or furniture but I have heard her at her return home make sport and jeer at whatever she had before commended, and I have been told by other gentlemen in livery that it is the same in their families: but I defy the wisest man in the world to turn a true good action into ridicule. I defy him to do it. He who should endeavour it would be laughed at himself, instead of making others laugh. Nobody scarce doth any good, yet they all agree in praising those who do. Indeed, it is strange that all men should consent in commending goodness and no man endeavour to deserve that commendation, whilst, on the contrary, all rail at wickedness and all are as eager to be what they abuse. This I know not the reason of, but it is as plain as daylight to those who converse in the world, as I have done these three years." "Are all the great folks wicked, then?" says Fanny. "To be sure there are some exceptions," answered Joseph. "Some gentlemen of our cloth report charitable actions done by their lords and masters, and I have heard Squire Pope, the great poet, at my lady's table, tell stories of a man that lived at a place called Ross, and another at the Bath, one Al—Al— [1] I forget his name, but it is in the book of verses. This gentleman hath built up a stately house too, which the Squire likes very well, but his charity is seen farther than his house, though it stands on a hill, aye, and brings him more honour too. It was his charity that put him in the book, where the Squire says he puts all those who deserve it, and, to be sure, as he lives among all the great people, if there were any such he would know them."—This was all of Mr. Joseph Andrews's speech which I could get him to recollect, which I have delivered as near as was possible in his own words, with a very small embellishment. But I believe the reader hath not been a little surprised at the long silence of Parson Adams, especially as so many occasions offered themselves to exert his curiosity and observation. The truth is, he was fast asleep, and had so been from the beginning of the preceding narrative; and, indeed, if the reader considers that so many hours had passed since he had closed his eyes, he will not wonder at his repose, though even Henley [2] himself, or as great an orator (if any such be), had been in his rostrum or tub before him.

Joseph, who whilst he was speaking had continued in one attitude, with his head reclining on one side, and his eyes cast on the ground, no sooner perceived, on looking up, the position of Adams, who was stretched on his back and snored louder than the usual braying of the animal with long ears, than he turned towards Fanny, and, taking her by the hand, began a dalliance, which, though consistent with the purest innocence and decency, neither he would have attempted nor she permitted before any witness. Whilst they amused themselves in this harmless and delightful manner, they heard a pack of hounds approaching in full cry towards them, and presently afterwards saw a hare pop forth from the wood, and, crossing the water, land within a few yards of them in the meadows. The hare was no sooner on shore than it seated itself on its hinder legs and listened to the sound of the pursuers. Fanny was wonderfully pleased with the little wretch and eagerly longed to have it in her arms, that she might preserve it from the dangers which seemed to threaten it; but the rational part of the creation do not always aptly distinguish their friends from their foes —what wonder then if this silly creature, the moment it beheld her, fled from the friend who would have protected it, and traversing the meadows again, passed the little rivulet on the opposite side. It was, however, so spent and weak that it fell down twice or thrice in its way. This affected the tender heart of Fanny, who exclaimed with tears in her eyes against the barbarity of worrying a poor innocent defenceless animal out of its life and putting it to the extremest torture for diversion. She had not much time to make reflections of this kind, for on a sudden the hounds rushed through the wood, which resounded with their throats and the throats of their retinue, who attended on them on horseback. The dogs now passed the rivulet and pursued the footsteps of the hare; five horsemen attempted to leap over, three of whom succeeded, and two were in the attempt thrown from their saddles into the water; their companions, and their own horses too, proceeded after their sport, and left their friends and riders to invoke the assistance of Fortune, or employ the more active means of strength and agility for their deliverance. Joseph, however, was not so unconcerned on this occasion; he left Fanny for a moment to herself and ran to the gentlemen, who were immediately on their legs, shaking their ears, and easily, with the help of his hand, obtained the bank (for the rivulet was not at all deep), and without staying to thank their kind assister, ran dripping across the meadow, calling to their brother sportsmen to stop their horses; but they heard them not.

The hounds were now very little behind their poor, reeling, staggering prey, which, fainting almost at every step, crawled through the wood, and had almost got round to the place where Fanny stood when it was overtaken by its enemies, and, being driven out of the covert, was caught, and instantly tore to pieces before Fanny's face, who was unable to assist it with any aid more powerful than pity, nor could she prevail on Joseph, who had been himself a sportsman in his youth, to attempt anything contrary to the laws of hunting in favour of the hare, which he said was killed fairly.

The hare was caught within a yard or two of Adams, who lay asleep at some distance from the lovers, and the hounds, in devouring it and pulling it backwards and forwards, had drawn it so close to him that some of them (by mistake perhaps for the hare's skin) laid hold of the skirts of his cassock; others at the same time applying their teeth to his wig, which he had with a handkerchief fastened to his head, began to pull him about, and had not the motion of his body had more effect on him than seemed to be wrought by the noise they must certainly have tasted his flesh, which delicious flavour might have been fatal to him; but being roused by these tuggings, he instantly awaked, and with a jerk delivering his head from his wig, he with most admirable dexterity recovered his legs, which now seemed the only members he could entrust his safety to. Having, therefore, escaped likewise from at least a third part of his cassock, which he willingly left as his *exuviae* or spoils to the enemy, he fled with the utmost speed he could summon to his assistance. Nor let this be any detraction from the bravery of his character: let the number of the enemies, and the surprise in which he was taken, be considered, and if there be any modern so outrageously brave that he cannot admit of flight in any circumstance whatever, I say (but I whisper that softly, and I solemnly declare without any intention of giving offence to any brave man in the nation), I say, or rather I whisper, that he is an ignorant fellow, and hath never read Homer, nor Vergil, nor knows he anything of Hector or Turnus, nay, he is unacquainted with the history of some great men living, who, though as brave as lions, aye, as tigers, have run away, the Lord knows how far, and the Lord knows why, to the surprise of their friends and the entertainment of their enemies. But if persons of such heroic disposition are a little offended at the behaviour of Adams, we assure them they shall be as much pleased with what we shall immediately relate of Joseph Andrews. The master of the pack was just arrived, or, as the sportsmen call it, come in, when Adams set out, as we have before mentioned. This gentleman was generally said to be a great lover of humour, but, not to mince the matter, especially as we are upon this subject, he was a great hunter of men; indeed, he had hitherto followed the sport only with dogs of his own species, for he kept two or three couple of barking curs for that use only. However, as he thought he had now found a man nimble enough, he was willing to indulge himself with other sport, and accordingly crying out, stole away, encouraged the hounds to pursue Mr. Adams, swearing it was the largest jack-hare he ever saw, at the same time hallooing and hooping as if a conquered foe was flying before him, in which he was imitated by these two or three couple of human or rather two-legged curs on horseback which we have mentioned before.

Now Thou, whoever Thou art, whether a muse, or by what other name soever Thou choosest to be called, who presidest over biography, and hast inspired all the writers of lives in these our times: Thou who didst infuse such wonderful humour into the pen of immortal Gulliver; who hast carefully guided the judgement, whilst Thou hast exalted the nervous manly style of thy Mallet: Thou who hadst no hand in that dedication and preface, or the translations, which

Thou wouldst willingly have struck out of the life of Cicero: lastly Thou who, without the assistance of the least spice of literature, and even against his inclination, hast, in some pages of his book, forced Colley Cibber to write English; do Thou assist me in what I find myself unequal to. Do Thou introduce on the plain, the young, the gay, the brave Joseph Andrews, whilst men shall view him with admiration and envy, tender virgins with love and anxious concern for his safety.

No sooner did Joseph Andrews perceive the distress of his friend, when first the quick-scenting dogs attacked him, than he grasped his cudgel in his right hand, a cudgel which his father had of his grandfather, to whom a mighty strong man of Kent had given it for a present in that day when he broke three heads on the stage. It was a cudgel of mighty strength and wonderful art, made by one of Mr. Deard's best workmen, whom no other artificer can equal and who hath made all those sticks which the beaux have lately walked with about the Park in the morning; but this was far his master-piece. On its head was engraved a nose and chin which might have been mistaken for a pair of nut-crackers. The learned have imagined it designed to represent the Gorgon, but it was in fact copied from the face of a certain long English baronet, of infinite wit, humour, and gravity. He did intend to have engraved here many histories, as the first night of Captain B——'s play, where you would have seen critics in embroidery transplanted from the boxes to the pit, whose ancient inhabitants were exalted to the galleries, where they played on catcalls. He did intend to have painted an auction-room, where Mr. Cock would have appeared aloft in his pulpit, trumpeting forth the praises of a China basin, and with astonishment wondering that, "Nobody bids more for that fine, that superb"—he did intend to have engraved many other things, but was forced to leave all out for want of room.

No sooner had Joseph grasped this cudgel in his hands than lightning darted from his eyes and the heroic youth, swift of foot, ran with the utmost speed to his friend's assistance. He overtook him just as Rockwood had laid hold of the skirt of his cassock, which being torn, hung to the ground. Reader, we would make a simile on this occasion, but for two reasons: the first is, it would interrupt the description, which should be rapid in this part; but that doth not weigh much, many precedents occurring for such an interruption; the second, and much the greater, reason is that we could find no simile adequate to our purpose, for, indeed, what instance could we bring to set before our reader's eyes at once the idea of friendship, courage, youth, beauty, strength, and swiftness, all which blazed in the person of Joseph Andrews. Let those therefore that describe lions and tigers, and heroes fiercer than both, raise their poems or plays with the simile of Joseph Andrews, who is himself above the reach of any simile.

Now Rockwood had laid fast hold on the parson's skirts, and stopped his flight; which Joseph no sooner perceived than he levelled his cudgel at his head and laid him sprawling. Jowler and Ringwood then fell on his great-coat and had undoubtedly brought him to the ground had not Joseph, collecting all his force, given Jowler such a rap on the back that, quitting his hold, he ran, howling over the plain. A harder fate remained for thee, O Ringwood, Ringwood, the best hound that ever pursued a hare, who never threw his tongue but where the scent was undoubtedly true; good at trailing, and sure in a highway; no babbler, no overrunner; respected by the whole pack, who, whenever he opened, knew the game was at hand. He fell by the stroke of Joseph. Thunder and Plunder, and Wonder and Blunder, were the next victims of his wrath, and measured their lengths on the ground. Then Fairmaid, a bitch which Mr. John Temple had bred up in his house and fed at his own table, and lately sent the Squire fifty miles for a present, ran fiercely at Joseph and bit him by the leg: no dog was ever fiercer than she, being descended from an Amazonian breed, and had worried bulls in her own country and now waged an unequal fight, and had shared the fate of those we have mentioned before had not Diana (the reader may believe or not if he pleases) in that instant interposed, and, in the shape of the huntsman, snatched her favourite up in her arms.

The parson now faced about and with his crab-stick felled many to the earth and scattered others, till he was attacked by Caesar and pulled to the ground. Then Joseph flew to his rescue and with such might fell on the victor that, O eternal blot to his name! Caesar ran yelping away.

The battle now raged with the most dreadful violence, when, lo! the huntsman, a man of years and dignity, lifted his voice, and called his hounds from the fight, telling them, in a language they understood, that it was in vain to contend longer, for that fate had decreed the victory to their enemies.

Thus far the muse hath with her usual dignity related this

prodigious battle, a battle, we apprehend, never equalled by any poet, romance- or life-writer whatever, and, having brought it to a conclusion, she ceased; we shall therefore proceed in our ordinary style with the continuation of this history. The Squire and his companions, whom the figure of Adams and the gallantry of Joseph had at first thrown into a violent fit of laughter, and who had hitherto beheld the engagement with more delight than any chase, shooting-match, race, cock-fighting, bull- or bear-baiting had ever given them, began now to apprehend the danger of their hounds, many of which lay sprawling in the fields. The Squire, therefore, having first called his friends about him, as guards for the safety of his person, rode manfully up to the combatants, and, summoning all the terror he was master of into his countenance, demanded with an authoritative voice of Joseph, what he meant by assaulting his dogs in that manner. Joseph answered with great intrepidity that they had first fallen on his friend, and if they had belonged to the greatest man in the kingdom he would have treated them in the same way, for, whilst his veins contained a single drop of blood, he would not stand idle by and see that gentleman (pointing to Adams) abused either by man or beast; and having so said, both he and Adams brandished their wooden weapons, and put themselves into such a posture, that the Squire and his company thought proper to preponderate before they offered to revenge the cause of their four-footed allies.

At this instant Fanny, whom the apprehension of Joseph's danger had alarmed so much that, forgetting her own, she had made the utmost expedition, came up. The Squire and all the horsemen were so surprised with her beauty that they immediately fixed both their eyes and thoughts solely on her, everyone declaring he had never seen so charming a creature. Neither mirth nor anger engaged them a moment longer, but all sat in silent amaze. The huntsman only was free from her attraction, who was busy in cutting the ears of the dogs and endeavouring to recover them to life, in which he succeeded so well that only two of no great note remained slaughtered on the field of action. Upon this the huntsman declared 'twas well it was no worse; for his part he could not blame the gentleman, and wondered his master would encourage the dogs to hunt Christians; that it was the surest way to spoil them, to make them follow vermin instead of sticking to a hare.

The Squire, being informed of the little mischief that had

been done, and perhaps having more mischief of another kind in his head, accosted Mr. Adams with a more favourable aspect than before: he told him he was sorry for what had happened, that he had endeavoured all he could to prevent it the moment he was acquainted with his cloth, and greatly commended the courage of his servant, for so he imagined Joseph to be. He then invited Mr. Adams to dinner, and desired the young woman might come with him. Adams refused a long while, but the invitation was repeated with so much earnestness and courtesy that at length he was forced to accept it. His wig and hat, and other spoils of the field, being gathered together by Joseph (for otherwise probably they would have been forgotten) he put himself into the best order he could, and then the horse and foot moved forward in the same pace towards the Squire's house, which stood at a very little distance.

Whilst they were on the road, the lovely Fanny attracted the eyes of all: they endeavoured to outvie one another in encomiums on her beauty, which the reader will pardon my not relating, as they had not anything new or uncommon in them; so must he likewise my not setting down the many curious jests which were made on Adams, some of them declaring, that parson-hunting was the best sport in the world; others commending his standing at bay, which they said he had done as well as any badger; with such-like merriment, which, though it would ill become the dignity of this history, afforded much laughter and diversion to the Squire and his facetious companions.

CHAPTER VII: *A scene of roasting very nicely adapted to the present taste and times.*

THEY arrived at the Squire's house just as his dinner was ready. A little dispute arose on the account of Fanny, whom the Squire, who was a bachelor, was desirous to place at his own table, but she would not consent, nor would Mr. Adams permit her to be parted from Joseph, so that she was at length with him consigned over to the kitchen, where the servants were ordered to make him drunk, a favour which was likewise intended for Adams; which design being executed, the Squire thought he should easily accomplish what he had, when he first saw her, intended to perpetrate with Fanny.

It may not be improper, before we proceed farther, to open a little the character of this gentleman, and that of his friends. The master of this house, then, was a man of a very considerable fortune, a bachelor, as we have said, and about forty years of age; he had been educated (if we may use the expression) in the country, and at his own home, under the care of his mother and a tutor, who had orders never to correct him, nor to compel him to learn more than he liked, which it seems was very little, and that only in his childhood, for from the age of fifteen he addicted himself entirely to hunting and other rural amusements, for which his mother took care to equip him with horses, hounds, and all other necessaries, and his tutor, endeavouring to ingratiate himself with his young pupil, who would he knew, be able handsomely to provide for him, became his companion, not only at these exercises, but likewise over a bottle, which the young Squire had a very early relish for. At the age of twenty, his mother began to think she had not fulfilled the duty of a parent; she therefore resolved to persuade her son, if possible, to that which she imagined would well supply all that he might have learned at a public school or university. This is what they commonly call travelling, which, with the help of the tutor, who was fixed on to attend him, she easily succeeded in. He made in three years the tour of Europe, as they term it, and returned home well furnished with French clothes, phrases, and servants, with a hearty contempt for his own country, especially which had any savour of the plain spirit and honesty of our ancestors. His mother greatly applauded herself at his return. And now being master of his own fortune, he soon procured himself a seat in Parliament and was in the common opinion one of the finest gentlemen of his age; but what distinguished him chiefly was a strange delight which he took in everything which is ridiculous, odious, and absurd in his own species; so that he never chose a companion without one or more of these ingredients, and those who were marked by nature in the most eminent degree with them, were most his favourites. If he ever found a man who either had not, or endeavoured to conceal, these imperfections, he took great pleasure in inventing methods of forcing him into absurdities which were not natural to him, or in drawing forth and exposing those that were, for which purpose he was always provided with a set of fellows, whom we have before called curs, and who did, indeed, no great honour to the canine kind. Their business was to hunt out and display everything that had any savour of the above-mentioned qualities, and especially in the gravest and best characters, but if they failed in their search, they were to turn even virtue and wisdom themselves into ridicule, for the diversion of their master and feeder. The gentlemen of curlike disposition who were now at his house, and whom he had brought with him from London, were an old half-pay officer, a player, a dull poet, a quack doctor, a scraping fiddler, and a lame German dancing-master.

As soon as dinner was served, while Mr. Adams was saying grace the captain conveyed his chair from behind him, so that when he endeavoured to seat himself, he fell down on the ground, and thus completed joke the first to the great entertainment of the whole company. The second joke was performed by the poet, who sat next him on the other side, and took an opportunity, while poor Adams was respectfully drinking to the master of the house, to overturn a plate of soup into his breeches, which, with the many apologies he made, and the parson's gentle answers, caused much mirth in the company. Joke the third was served up by one of the waiting-men, who had been ordered to convey a quantity of gin into Mr. Adams's ale, which he declared to be the best liquor he ever drank, but rather too rich of the malt, contributed again to their laughter. Mr. Adams, from whom we had most of this relation, could not recollect all the jests of this kind practised on him, which the inoffensive disposition of his own heart made him slow in discovering; and indeed, had it not been for the information which we received from a servant of the family, this part of our history, which we take to be none of the least curious, must have been deplorably imperfect, though we must own it probable that some more jokes were (as they call it) cracked during their dinner, but we have by no means been able to come at the knowledge of them. When dinner was removed, the poet began to repeat some verses, which, he said, were made extempore. The following is a copy of them, procured with the greatest difficulty.

An extempore poem on Parson Adams.

Did ever mortal such a parson view;
His cassock old, his wig not overnew?
Well might the hounds have him for fox mistaken,
*In smell more like to that than rusty bacon:**
But would it not make any mortal stare,
To see this parson taken for a hare?

Could Phoebus err thus grossly, even he
For a good player might have taken thee.

At which words the bard whipped off the player's wig and received the approbation of the company, rather perhaps for the dexterity of his hand than his head. The player, instead of retorting the jest on the poet, began to display his talents on the same subject. He repeated many scraps of wit out of plays, reflecting on the whole body of the clergy, which were received with great acclamations by all present. It was now the dancing-master's turn to exhibit his talents; he therefore, addressing himself to Adams in broken English, told him he was a man ver well made for de dance, and he suppose by his walk dat he had learn of some great master. He said it was ver pretty quality in clergyman to dance, and concluded with desiring him to dance a minuet, telling him his cassock would serve for petticoats, and that he would himself be his partner. At which words, without waiting for an answer, he pulled out his gloves and the fiddler was preparing his fiddle. The company all offered the dancing-master wagers that the parson outdanced him, which he refused, saying he believed so too; for he had never seen any man in his life who looked de dance so well as de gentleman. He then stepped forwards to take Adams by the hand, which the latter hastily withdrew, and at the same time clenching his fist advised him not to carry the jest too far, for he would not endure being put upon. The dancing-master no sooner saw the fist than he prudently retired out of its reach and stood aloof, mimicking Adams, whose eyes were fixed on him, not guessing what he was at but to avoid his laying hold on him, which he had once attempted. In the meanwhile, the captain, perceiving an opportunity, pinned a cracker or devil to the cassock, and then lighted it with their little smoking-candle. Adams, being a stranger to this sport, and believing he had been blown up in reality, started from his chair and jumped about the room, to the infinite joy of the beholders, who declared he was the best dancer in the universe. As soon as the devil had done tormenting him, and he had a little recovered his confusion, he returned to the table, standing up in the posture of one who intended to make a speech. They all cried out, Hear him, hear him, and he then spoke in the following manner: "Sir, I am sorry to see one to whom Providence hath been so bountiful in bestowing his favours make so ill and ungrateful a return for them, for, though you have not insulted me yourself, it is visible you have delighted in those that do it, nor have once discouraged the many rudenesses which have been shown towards me—indeed, towards yourself, if you rightly understood them, for I am your guest, and by the laws of hospitality entitled to your protection. One gentleman had thought proper to produce some poetry upon me, of which I shall only say that I had rather be the subject than the composer. He hath pleased to treat me with disrespect as a parson. I apprehend my order is not the object of scorn, nor that I can become so unless by being a disgrace to it, which I hope poverty will never be called. Another gentleman indeed, hath repeated some sentences where the order itself is mentioned with contempt. He says they are taken from plays. I am sure such plays are a scandal to the government which permits them, and cursed will be the nation where they are represented. How others have treated me, I need not observe; they themselves, when they reflect, must allow the behaviour to be as improper to my years as to my cloth. You found me, sir, travelling with two of my parishioners (I omit your hounds falling on me, for I have quite forgiven it, whether it proceeded from the wantonness or negligence of the huntsman); my appearance might very well persuade you that your invitation was an act of charity, though in reality we were well provided; yes, sir, if we had had an hundred miles to travel, we had sufficient to bear our expenses in a noble manner." At which words he produced the half-guinea which was found in the basket. "I do not show you this out of ostentation of riches, but to convince you I speak truth. Your seating me at your table was an honour which I did not ambitiously affect. When I was here, I endeavoured to behave towards you with the utmost respect; if I have failed, it was not with design, nor could I, certainly, so far be guilty as to deserve the insults I have suffered. If they were meant, therefore, either to my order or my poverty (and you see I am not very poor), the shame doth not lie at my door, and I heartily pray that the sin may be averted from yours." He thus finished, and received a general clap from the whole company. Then the gentleman of the house told him he was sorry for what had happened; that he could not accuse him of any share in it; that the verses were, as himself had well observed, so bad that he might easily answer them; and for the serpent, it was undoubtedly a very great affront done him by the dancing-master, for which if he well threshed him, as he deserved, he should be very much pleased to see it (in which probably he spoke truth). Adams answered whoever had done it, it was not his profession to punish him that way but, for the person whom he had accused, "I am a witness," says he, "of his innocence, for I had my eye on him all the while. Whoever he was, God forgive him, and bestow on him a little more sense as well as humanity." The captain answered with a surly look and accent that he hoped he did not mean to reflect upon him; d—n him, he had as much imanity as another, and, if any man said he had not, he would convince him of his mistake by cutting his throat. Adams, smiling, said he believed he had spoke right by accident. To which the captain returned, "What do you mean by my speaking right? If you was not a parson, I would not take these words; but your gown protects you. If any man who wears a sword had said so much, I had pulled him by the nose before this." Adams replied if he attempted any rudeness to his person he would not find any protection for himself in his gown, and, clenching his fist, declared he had threshed many a stouter man. The gentleman did all he could to encourage this warlike disposition in Adams, and was in hopes to have produced a battle, but he was disapppointed, for the captain made no other answer than, "It is very well you are a parson," and so drinking off a bumper to old mother Church, ended the dispute.

Then the doctor, who had hitherto been silent, and who was the gravest but most mischievous dog of all, in a very pompous speech highly applauded what Adams had said, and as much discommended the behaviour to him. He proceeded to encomiums on the Church and poverty, and lastly recommended forgiveness of what had passed to Adams; who immediately answered that everything was forgiven, and in the warmth of his goodness he filled a bumper of strong beer (a liquor he preferred to wine), and drank a health to the whole company, shaking the captain and the poet heartily by the hand and addressing himself with great respect to the doctor; who, indeed, had not laughed outwardly at anything that passed, as he had a perfect command of his muscles and could laugh inwardly without betraying the least symptoms in his countenance. The doctor now began a second formal speech, in which he declaimed against all levity of conversation, and what is usually called mirth. He said there were amusements fitted for persons of all ages and degrees, from the rattle to the discussing a point of philosophy, and that men discovered themselves in nothing more than in the choice of their amusements, "for," says he, "as it must greatly raise our expectation of the future conduct in life of boys whom in their tender years we perceive, instead of taw or balls, or other childish playthings, to choose, at their leisure hours, to exercise their genius in contentions of wit, learning, and such-like, so must it inspire one with equal contempt of a man if we should discover him playing at taw or other childish play." Adams highly commended the doctor's opinion, and said he had often wondered at some passages in ancient authors, where Scipio, Laelius, and other great men were represented to have passed many hours in amusements of the most trifling kind. The doctor replied he had by him an old Greek manuscript where a favourite diversion of Socrates was recorded. "Aye!" says the parson eagerly, "I should be most infinitely obliged to you for the favour of perusing it." The doctor promised to send it him and farther said that he believed he could describe it. "I think," says he, "as near as I can remember, it was like this: there was a throne erected, on one side of which sat a king, and on the other a queen, with their guards and attendants ranged on both sides; to them was introduced an ambassador, which part Socrates always used to perform himself, and when he was led up to the footsteps of the throne, he addressed himself to the monarchs in some grave speech, full of virtue, and goodness, and morality, and such-like. After which he was seated between the king and queen, and royally entertained. This I think was the chief part. Perhaps I may have forgot some particulars; for it is long since I read it." Adams said it was indeed a diversion worthy the relaxation of so great a man and thought something resembling it should be instituted among our great men, instead of cards and other idle pastime, in which, he was informed, they trifled away too much of their lives. He added, the Christian religion was a nobler subject for these speeches than any Socrates could have invented. The gentleman of the house approved what Mr. Adams said, and declared he resolved to perform the ceremony this very evening. To which the doctor objected, as no one was prepared with a speech, "unless," said he (turning to Adams with a gravity of countenance which would have deceived a more knowing man), "you have a sermon about you, Doctor." "Sir," says Adams, "I never travel without one, for fear of what may happen." He was easily prevailed on by his worthy friend, as he now called the doctor, to undertake the part of the ambassador, so that the gentleman sent immediate orders to have the throne erected, which was performed before they had drank two bottles. And perhaps the reader will hereafter have no great reason to admire the nimbleness of the servants. Indeed, to confess the truth, the throne was no more than this; there was a great tub of water provided, on each side of which were placed two stools raised higher than the surface of the tub, and over the whole was laid a blanket; on these stools were placed the king and queen, namely, the master of the house and the captain. And now the ambassador was introduced between the poet and the doctor, who, having read his sermon to the great entertainment of all present, was led up to his place, and seated between their majesties. They immediately rose up, when the blanket, wanting its supports at either end, gave way, and soused Adams over head and ears in the water. The captain made his escape, but, unluckily, the gentleman himself not being as nimble as he ought, Adams caught hold of him before he descended from his throne and pulled him in with him, to the entire secret satisfaction of all the company. Adams, after ducking the Squire twice or thrice, leaped out of the tub and looked sharp for the doctor, whom he would certainly have conveyed to the same place of honour, but he had wisely withdrawn; he then searched for his crab-stick, and having found that, as well as his fellow-travellers, he declared he would not stay a moment longer in such a house. He then departed, without taking leave of his host, whom he had exacted a more severe revenge on than he intended; for as he did not use sufficient care to dry himself in time, he caught a cold by the accident, which threw him into a fever that had like to have cost him his life.

CHAPTER VIII: *Which some readers will think too short, others too long.*

ADAMS and Joseph, who was no less enraged than his friend at the treatment he met with, went out with their sticks in their hands and carried off Fanny, notwithstanding the opposition of the servants, who did all, without proceeding to violence, in their power to detain them. They walked as fast as they could, not so much from any apprehension of being pursued, as that Mr. Adams might by exercise prevent any harm from the water. The gentleman, who had given such orders to his servants concerning Fanny that he did not in the least fear her getting away no sooner heard that she was gone than he began to rave and immediately despatched several with orders either to bring her back or never return. The poet, the player, and all but the dancing-master and doctor, went on this errand.

The night was very dark in which our friends began their journey; however, they made such expedition that they soon arrived at an inn which was at seven miles' distance. Here they unanimously consented to pass the evening, Mr. Adams being now as dry as he was before he had set out on his embassy.

This inn, which indeed we might call an ale-house had not the words THE NEW INN been writ on the sign, afforded them no better provision than bread and cheese and ale; on which, however, they made a very comfortable meal, for hunger is better than a French cook.

They had no sooner supped than Adams, returning thanks to the Almighty for his food, declared he had ate his homely commons with much greater satisfaction than his splendid dinner; and expressed great contempt for the folly of mankind, who sacrificed their hopes of heaven to the acquisition of vast wealth, since so much comfort was to be found in the humblest state and the lowest provision. "Very true, sir," says a grave man who sat smoking his pipe by the fire, and who was a traveller as well as himself. "I have often been as much surprised as you are when I consider the value which mankind in general set on riches, since every day's experience shows us how little is in their power; for what, indeed, truly desirable can they bestow on us? Can they give beauty to the deformed, strength to the weak, or health to the infirm? Surely if they could we should not see so many ill-favoured faces haunting the assemblies of the great, nor would such numbers of feeble wretches languish in their coaches and palaces. No, not the wealth of a kingdom can purchase any paint to dress pale Ugliness in the bloom of that young maiden, nor any drugs to equip Disease with the vigour of that young man. Do not riches bring us solicitude instead of rest, envy instead of affection, and danger instead of safety? Can they prolong their own possession, or lengthen his days who enjoys them? So far otherwise that the sloth, the luxury, the care, which attend them, shorten the lives of millions, and bring them with pain and misery to an untimely grave. Where then is their value if they can neither embellish nor strengthen our forms, sweeten nor prolong our lives? Again: Can they adorn the mind more than the body? Do they not rather swell the heart with vanity, puff up the cheeks with pride, shut our ears to every call of virtue, and our bowels to every motive of compassion?" "Give me your hand, brother," said Adams in a rapture, "for I suppose you are a clergyman." "No truly," answered the other (indeed, he was a priest of the church of Rome; but those who understand our laws will not wonder he was not overready to own it). "Whatever you are," cries Adams, "you have spoken my sentiments: I believe I have preached every syllable of your speech twenty times over, for it hath always appeared to me easier for a cable rope (which by the way is the true rendering of that word we have translated 'camel') to go through the eye of a needle, than for a rich man to get into the kingdom of heaven." "That, sir," said the other, "will be easily granted you by divines, and is deplorably true, but as the prospect of our good at a distance doth not so forcibly affect us it might be of some service to mankind to be made thoroughly sensible, which I think they might be with very little serious attention, that even the blessings of this world are not to be purchased with riches—a doctrine, in my opinion, not only metaphysically, but, if I may so say, mathematically demonstrable, and which I have been always so perfectly convinced of that I have a contempt for nothing so much as for gold." Adams now began a long discourse, but as most which he said occurs among many authors who have treated this subject, I shall omit inserting it. During its continuance Joseph and Fanny retired to rest, and the host likewise left the room. When the English parson had concluded, the Romish resumed the discourse, which he continued with great bitterness and invective, and at last ended by desiring Adams to lend him eighteen pence to pay his reckoning, promising, if he never paid him, he might be assured of his prayers. The good man answered that eighteen pence would be too little to carry him any very long journey; that he had half a guinea in his pocket, which he would divide with him. He then fell to searching his pockets but could find no money, for indeed the company with whom he dined had passed one jest upon him which we did not then enumerate, and had picked his pocket of all that treasure which he had so ostentatiously produced.

"Bless me," cried Adams, "I have certainly lost it; I can never have spent it. Sir, as I am a Christian, I had a whole half-guinea in my pocket this morning, and have not now a single halfpenny of it left. Sure the devil must have taken it from me!" "Sir," answered the priest smiling, "you need make no excuses; if you are not willing to lend me the money, I am contented." "Sir," cries Adams, "if I had the greatest sum in the world, aye, if I had ten pounds about me, I would bestow it all to rescue any Christian from distress. I am more vexed at my loss on your account than my own. Was ever anything so unlucky? because I have no money in my pocket, I shall be suspected to be no Christian." "I am more unlucky," quoth the other, "if you are as generous as you say; for really a crown would have made me happy and conveyed me in plenty to the place I am going, which is not above twenty miles off and where I can arrive by tomorrow night. I assure you I am not accustomed to travel penniless. I am but just arrived in England, and we were forced by a storm in our passage to throw all we had overboard. I don't suspect but this fellow will take my word for the trifle I owe him, but I hate to appear so mean as to confess myself without a shilling to such people; for these, and indeed too many others, know little difference in their estimation between a beggar and a thief." However, he thought he should deal better with the host that evening than the next morning; he therefore resolved to set out immediately, notwithstanding the darkness, and accordingly, as soon as the host returned, he communicated to him the situation of his affairs, upon which the host, scratching his head, answered, "Why, I do not know, master; if it be so, and you have no money, I must trust, I think, though I had rather always have ready money if I could; but, marry, you look like so honest a gentleman that I don't fear your paying me, if it was twenty times as much." The priest made no reply, but, taking leave of him and Adams as fast as he could, not without confusion, and perhaps with some distrust of Adams's sincerity, departed.

He was no sooner gone than the host fell a-shaking his head, and declared if he had suspected the fellow had no money, he would not have drawn him a single drop of drink, saying he despaired of ever seeing his face again, for that he looked like a confounded rogue. "Rabbit the fellow," cries he, "I thought by his talking so much about riches that he had a hundred pounds at least in his pocket." Adams chid him for his suspicions, which he said were not becoming a Christian, and then, without reflecting on his loss, or considering how he himself should depart in the morning, he retired to a very homely bed, as his companions had before; however, health and fatigue gave them a sweeter repose than is often in the power of velvet and down to bestow.

CHAPTER IX: *Containing as surprising and bloody adventures as can be found in this or perhaps any other authentic history.*

IT WAS almost morning when Joseph Andrews, whose eyes the thoughts of his dear Fanny had opened, as he lay fondly meditating on that lovely creature, heard a violent knocking at the door over which he lay. He presently jumped out of bed, and, opening the window, was asked if there were no travellers in the house, and presently by another voice if two young men and a young woman had not taken up there their lodging that night? Though he knew not the voices, he began to entertain a suspicion of the truth, for indeed he had received some information from one of the servants of the Squire's house of his design, and answered in the negative. One of the servants, who knew the host well, called out to him by his name, just as he had opened another window, and asked him the same question, to which he answered in the affirmative. "O ho!" said another, "have we found you?" and ordered the host to come down and open his door. Fanny, who was as wakeful as Joseph, no sooner heard all this, than she leaped from her bed, and, hastily putting on her gown and petticoats, ran as fast as possible to Joseph's room, who then was almost dressed. He immediately let her in, and, embracing her with the most passionate tenderness, bid her fear nothing, for he would die in her defence. "Is that a reason why I should not fear," says she, "when I should lose what is dearer to me than the whole world?" Joseph then, kissing her hand, said he could almost thank the occasion which had extorted from her a tenderness she would never indulge him with before. He then ran and waked his bed-fellow Adams, who was yet fast asleep, notwithstanding many calls from Joseph, but was no sooner made sensible of their danger than he leaped from his bed, without considering the presence of Fanny, who hastily turned her face from him, and enjoyed a double benefit from the dark, which, as it would have prevented any offence to an innocence less pure or a modesty less delicate, so it concealed even those blushes which were raised in her.

Adams had soon put on all his clothes but his breeches,

which in the hurry he forgot; however, they were pretty well supplied by the length of his other garments, and now, the house-door being opened, the captain, the poet, the player, and three servants came in. The captain told the host that two fellows who were in his house had run away with a young woman, and desired to know in which room she lay. The host, who presently believed the story, directed them, and instantly the captain and poet, jostling one another, ran up. The poet, who was the nimblest, entering the chamber first, searched the bed and every other part, but to no purpose; the bird was flown, as the impatient reader, who might otherwise have been in pain for her, was before advertised. They then inquired where the man lay, and were approaching the chamber when Joseph roared out in a loud voice that he would shoot the first man who offered to attack the door. The captain inquired what fire-arms they had, to which the host answered he believed they had none; nay, he was almost convinced of it, for he heard one ask the other in the evening what they should have done if they had been overtaken, when they had no arms, to which the other answered they would have defended themselves with their sticks as long as they were able, and God would assist a just cause. This satisfied the captain but not the poet, who prudently retreated downstairs, saying it was his business to record great actions, and not to do them. The captain was no sooner well satisfied that there were no fire-arms than, bidding defiance to gun-powder, and swearing he loved the smell of it, he ordered the servants to follow him, and, marching boldly up, immediately attempted to force the door, which the servants soon helped him to accomplish. When it was opened, they discovered the enemy drawn up three deep, Adams in the front, and Fanny in the rear. The captain told Adams that if they would go all back to the house again they should be civilly treated, but unless they consented he had orders to carry the young lady with him, whom there was great reason to believe they had stolen from her parents, for, notwithstanding her disguise, her air, which she could not conceal, sufficiently discovered her birth to be infinitely superior to theirs. Fanny, bursting into tears, solemnly assured him he was mistaken, that she was a poor helpless foundling, and had no relation in the world which she knew of, and, throwing herself on her knees, begged that he would not attempt to take her from her friends, who she was convinced would die before they would lose her, which Adams confirmed with words not far from amounting to an oath. The captain swore he had no leisure to talk, and bidding them thank themselves for what happened, he ordered the servants to fall on, at the same time endeavouring to pass by Adams, in order to lay hold on Fanny; but the parson interrupting him, received a blow from one of them, which, without considering whence it came, he returned to the captain, and gave him so dexterous a knock in that part of the stomach which is vulgarly called the pit, that he staggered some paces backwards. The captain, who was not accustomed to this kind of play, and who wisely apprehended the consequence of such another blow, two of them seeming to him equal to a thrust through the body, drew forth his hanger, as Adams approached him, and was levelling a blow at his head which would probably have silenced the preacher forever had not Joseph in that instant lifted up a certain huge stone pot of the chamber with one hand, which six beaux could not have lifted with both, and discharged it, together with the contents, full in the captain's face. The uplifted hanger dropped from his hand and he fell prostrated on the floor with a lumpish noise, and his halfpence rattled in his pocket; the red liquor which his veins contained, and the white liquor which the pot contained, ran in one stream down his face and his clothes. Nor had Adams quite escaped, some of the water having in its passage shed its honours on his head, and began to trickle down the wrinkles or rather furrows of his cheeks, when one of the servants, snatching a mop out of a pail of water which had already done its duty in washing the house, pushed it in the parson's face; yet could not he bear him down, for the parson, wresting the mop from the fellow with one hand, with his other brought the enemy as low as the earth, having given him a stroke over that part of the face where, in some men of pleasure, the natural and artificial noses are conjoined.

Hitherto Fortune seemed to incline the victory on the travellers' side, when, according to her custom, she began to show the fickleness of her disposition; for now the host entering the field, or rather chamber, of battle, flew directly at Joseph, and darting his head into his stomach (for he was a stout fellow, and an expert boxer) almost staggered him; but Joseph, stepping one leg back, did with his left hand so chuck him under the chin that he reeled. The youth was pursuing his blow with his right hand, when he received from one of the servants such a stroke with a cudgel on his temples that it instantly deprived him of sense, and he measured his length on the ground.

Fanny rent the air with her cries, and Adams was coming to the assistance of Joseph, but the two serving-men and the host now fell on him and soon subdued him, though he fought like a madman, and looked so black with the impressions he had received from the mop that Don Quixote would certainly have taken him for an enchanted Moor. But now follows the most tragical part; for the captain was risen again, and, seeing Joseph on the floor, and Adams secured, he instantly laid hold on Fanny, and, with the assistance of the poet and player, who, hearing the battle was over were now come up, dragged her, crying and tearing her hair, from the sight of her Joseph, and, with a perfect deafness to all her entreaties, carried her downstairs by violence and fastened her on the player's horse; and the captain, mounting his own and leading that on which this poor miserable wretch was, departed, without any more consideration of her cries than a butcher hath of those of a lamb, for indeed his thoughts were entertained only with the degree of favour which he promised himself from the Squire on the success of this adventure.

The servants, who were ordered to secure Adams and Joseph as safe as possible, that the Squire might receive no interruption to his design on poor Fanny, immediately, by the poet's advice, tied Adams to one of the bed-posts, as they did Joseph on the other side, as soon as they could bring him to himself, and then leaving them together, back to back, and desiring the host not to set them at liberty nor to go near them till he had further orders, they departed towards their master, but happened to take a different road from that which the captain had fallen into.

CHAPTER X: *A discourse between the poet and the player, of no other use in this history but to divert the reader.*

BEFORE we proceed any farther in this tragedy we shall leave Mr. Joseph and Mr. Adams to themselves, and imitate the wise conductors of the stage, who in the midst of a grave action entertain you with some excellent piece of satire or humour called a dance. Which piece indeed is therefore danced, and not spoke, as it is delivered to the audience by persons whose thinking faculty is by most people held to lie in their heels, and to whom, as well as heroes, who think with their hands, Nature hath only given heads for the sake of conformity, and as they are of use in dancing, to hang their hats on.

The poet, addressing the player, proceeded thus: "As I was saying" (for they had been at this discourse all the time of the engagement above-stairs), "the reason you have no good new plays is evident; it is from your discouragement of authors. Gentlemen will not write, sir, they will not write, without the expectation of fame or profit, or perhaps both. Plays are like trees, which will not grow without nourishment, but, like mushrooms, they shoot up spontaneously, as it were, in a rich soil. The muses, like vines, may be pruned, but not with a hatchet. The town, like a peevish child, knows not what it desires, and is always best pleased with a rattle. A farce-writer hath indeed some chance for success: but they have lost all taste for the sublime. Though I believe one reason of their depravity is the badness of the actors. If a man writes like an angel, sir, those fellows know not how to give a sentiment utterance." "Not so fast," says the player; "the modern actors are as good at least as their authors, nay, they come nearer their illustrious predecessors; and I expect a Booth on the stage again sooner than a Shakespeare or an Otway; and indeed I may turn your observation against you, and with truth say that the reason no actors are encouraged is because we have no good new plays." "I have not affirmed the contrary," said the poet, "but I am surprised you grow so warm: you cannot imagine yourself interested in this dispute; I hope you have a better opinion of my taste than to apprehend I squinted at yourself. No, sir, if we had six such actors as you, we should soon rival the Bettertons and Sandfords of former times, for, without a compliment to you, I think it impossible for anyone to have excelled you in most of your parts. Nay, it is solemn truth, and I have heard many, and all great judges, express as much; and you will pardon me if I tell you, I think, every time I have seen you lately, you have constantly acquired some new excellence, like a snow-ball. You have deceived me in my estimation of perfection, and have outdone what I thought inimitable." "You are as little interested," answered the player, "in what I have said of other poets; for d—n me if there are not many strokes, aye, whole scenes, in your last tragedy, which at least equal Shakespeare. There is a delicacy of sentiment, a dignity of expression, in it which I will own many of our gentlemen did not do adequate justice to. To confess the truth, they are bad enough, and I pity an author who is present at the murder of his works." "Nay, it is but seldom that it can happen," returned the poet; "the works of most modern authors, like dead-born children, cannot be murdered. It is such wretched, half-begotten, half-writ, lifeless, spiritless, low, grovelling stuff that I almost pity the actor who is obliged to get it by heart, which must be almost as difficult to remember as words in a language you do not understand." "I am sure," said the player, "if the sentences have little meaning when they are writ, when they are spoken they have less. I know scarce one who ever lays an emphasis right, and much less adapts his action to his character. I have seen a tender lover in an attitude of fighting with his mistress, and a brave hero suing to his enemy with his sword in his hand. I don't care to abuse my profession, but rot me if in my heart I am not inclined to the poet's side." "It is rather generous in you than just," said the poet; "and though I hate to speak ill of any person's production—nay, I never do it, nor will—but yet to do justice to the actors, what could Booth or Betterton have made of such horrible stuff as Fenton's Mariamne, Frowde's Philotas, or Mallet's Eurydice, or those low, dirty, last-dying speeches, which a fellow in the city of Wapping, your Dillo or Lillo, what was his name, called tragedies?" "Very well," says the player; "and pray what do you think of such fellows as Quin and Delane, or that face-making puppy young Cibber, that ill-looked dog Macklin, or that saucy slut Mrs. Clive? What work would they make with your Shakespeares, Otways, and Lees? How would those harmonious lines of the last come from their tongues?

"———*No more; for I disdain*
All pomp when thou art by—far be the noise
Of kings and crowns from us, whose gentle souls
Our kinder fates have steered another way.
Free as the forest birds we'll pair together,
Without rememb'ring who our fathers were:
Fly to the arbours, grots, and flow'ry meads,
There in soft murmurs interchange our souls,
Together drink the crystal of the stream,
Or taste the yellow fruit which autumn yields.
And when the golden evening calls us home,
Wing to our downy nests, and sleep till morn.[1]

"Or how would this disdain of Otway—

"*Who'd be that foolish sordid thing called man?*"[2]

"Hold, hold, hold," said the poet. "Do repeat that tender speech in the third act of my play which you made such a figure in." "I would willingly," said the player, "but I have forgot it." "Aye, you was not quite perfect enough in it when you played it," cries the poet, "or you would have had such an applause as was never given on the stage, an applause I was extremely concerned for your losing." "Sure," said the player, "if I remember, that was hissed more than any passage in the whole play." "Aye, your speaking it was hissed," said the poet. "My speaking it!" said the player. "I mean your not speaking it," said the poet. "You was out, and then they hissed." "They hissed, and then I was out, if I remember," answered the player; "and I must say this for myself, that the whole audience allowed I did your part justice, so don't lay the damnation of your play to my account." "I don't know what you mean by damnation," replied the poet. "Why, you know it was acted but one night," cried the player. "No," said the poet, "you and the whole town were enemies; the pit were all my enemies, fellows that would cut my throat if the fear of hanging did not restrain them. All tailors, sir, all tailors." "Why should the tailors be so angry with you?" cries the player. "I suppose you don't employ so many in making your clothes." "I admit your jest," answered the poet; "but you remember the affair as well as myself; you know there was a party in the pit and upper gallery would not suffer it to be given out again; though much, aye, infinitely the majority, all the boxes in particular, were desirous of it, nay, most of the ladies swore they never would come to the house till it was acted again. Indeed, I must own their policy was good, in not letting it be given out a second time, for the rascals knew if it had gone a second night it would have run fifty, for if ever there was distress in a tragedy—I am not fond of my own performance; but if I should tell you what the best judges said of it—— Nor was it entirely owing to my enemies, neither, that it did not succeed on the stage as well as it hath since among the polite readers, for you can't say it had justice done it by the performers." "I think," answered the player, "the performers did the distress of it justice, for I am sure we were in distress enough, who were pelted with oranges all the last act: we all imagined it would have been the last act of our lives."

The poet, whose fury was now raised, had just attempted to answer, when they were interrupted and an end put to their discourse by an accident, which if the reader is impatient to know, he must skip over the next chapter, which is a sort of counterpart to this, and contains some of the best and gravest matters in the whole book, being a discourse between Parson Abraham Adams and Mr. Joseph Andrews.

CHAPTER XI: *Containing the exhortations of Parson Adams to his friend in affliction, calculated for the instruction and improvement of the reader.*

Joseph no sooner came perfectly to himself than, perceiving his mistress gone, he bewailed her loss with groans which would have pierced any heart but those which are possessed by some people, and are made of a certain composition not unlike flint in its hardness and other properties; for you may strike fire from them which will dart through the eyes, but they can never distil one drop of water the same way. His own, poor youth, was of a softer composition, and at those words, "O my dear Fanny! O my love! shall I never, never see thee more?" his eyes overflowed with tears which would have become anything but a hero. In a word, his despair was more easy to be conceived than related.

Mr. Adams, after many groans, sitting with his back to Joseph, began thus in a sorrowful tone: "You cannot imagine, my good child, that I entirely blame these first agonies of your grief, for when misfortunes attack us by surprise, it must require infinitely more learning than you are master of to resist them; but it is the business of a man and a Christian to summon reason as quickly as he can to his aid, and she will presently teach him patience and submission. Be comforted, therefore, child; I say be comforted. It is true you have lost the prettiest, kindest, loveliest, sweetest young woman, one with whom you might have expected to have lived in happiness, virtue, and innocence, by whom you might have promised yourself many little darlings, who would have been the delight of your youth, and the comfort of your age. You have not only lost her, but have reason to fear the utmost violence which lust and power can inflict upon her. Now, indeed, you may easily raise ideas of horror, which might drive you to despair." "Oh, I shall run mad," cries Joseph. "Oh, that I could but command my hands to tear my eyes out, and my flesh off." "If you would use them to such purposes, I am glad you can't," answered Adams. "I have stated your misfortune as strong as I possibly can, but, on the other side, you are to consider you are a Christian, that no accident happens to us without the divine permission, and that it is the duty of a man and a Christian to submit.

We did not make ourselves, but the same power which made us, rules over us, and we are absolutely at his disposal; he may do with us what he pleases, nor have we any right to complain. A second reason against our complaint is our ignorance, for as we know not future events, so neither can we tell to what purpose any accident tends, and that which at first threatens us with evil may in the end produce our good. I should indeed have said our ignorance is twofold (but I have not at present time to divide properly), for as we know not to what purpose any event is ultimately directed; so neither can we affirm from what cause it originally sprung. You are a man, and consequently a sinner, and this may be a punishment to you for your sins; indeed in this sense it may be esteemed as a good, yea, as the greatest good, which satisfies the anger of heaven and averts that wrath which cannot continue without our destruction. Thirdly, our impotency in relieving ourselves demonstrates the folly and absurdity of our complaints, for whom do we resist, or against whom do we complain, but a power from whose shafts no armour can guard us, no speed can fly? a power which leaves us no hope but in submission." "Oh sir," cried Joseph, "all this is very true and very fine, and I could hear you all day, if I was not so grieved at heart as now I am." "Would you take physic," says Adams, "when you are well, and refuse it when you are sick? Is not comfort to be administered to the afflicted, and not to those who rejoice, or those who are at ease?" "Oh, you have not spoken one word of comfort to me yet," returned Joseph. "No!" cries Adams. "What am I then doing? what can I say to comfort you?" "Oh, tell me," cries Joseph, "that Fanny will escape back to my arms, that they shall again inclose that lovely creature with all her sweetness, all her untainted innocence about her." "Why, perhaps you may," cries Adams; "but I can't promise you what's to come. You must with perfect resignation wait the event; if she be restored to you again, it is your duty to be thankful, and so it is if she be not. Joseph, if you are wise, and truly know your own interest, you will peaceably and quietly submit to all the dispensations of Providence, being thoroughly assured that all the misfortunes, how great soever, which happen to the righteous, happen to them for their own good. Nay, it is not your interest only, but your duty, to abstain from immoderate grief, which if you indulge, you are not worthy the name of a Christian." He spoke these last words with an accent a little severer than usual, upon which Joseph begged him not to be angry, saying he mistook him if he thought he denied it was his duty, for he had known that long ago. "What signifies knowing your duty if you do not perform it?" answered Adams. "Your knowledge increases your guilt. Oh Joseph, I never thought you had this stubbornness in your mind." Joseph replied he fancied he misunderstood him, "which I assure you," says he, "you do if you imagine I endeavour to grieve; upon my soul I don't." Adams rebuked him for swearing, and then proceeded to enlarge on the folly of grief, telling him all the wise men and philosophers, even among the heathens, had written against it, quoting several passages from Seneca, and the *Consolation,* which, though it was not Cicero's, was, he said, as good almost as any of his works, and concluded all by hinting that immoderate grief in this case might incense that power which alone could restore him his Fanny. This reason, or indeed rather the idea which it raised of the restoration of his mistress, had more effect than all which the parson had said before, and for a moment abated his agonies; but when his fears sufficiently set before his eyes the danger that poor creature was in his grief returned again with repeated violence, nor could Adams in the least assuage it, though it may be doubted, in his behalf, whether Socrates himself could have prevailed any better.

They remained some time in silence, and groans and signs issued from them both; at length Joseph burst out into the following soliloquy:

"Yes, I will bear my sorrows like a man,
But I must also feel them as a man.
I cannot but remember such things were,
And were most dear to me."

Adams asked him what stuff that was he repeated. To which he answered, they were some lines he had gotten by heart out of a play.—"Aye, there is nothing but heathenism to be learned from plays," replied he. "I never heard of any plays fit for a Christian to read but *Cato* and the *Conscious Lovers,*[1] and I must own in the latter there are some things almost solemn enough for a sermon." But we shall now leave them a little, and inquire after the subject of their conversation.

CHAPTER XII: *More adventures, which we hope will as much please as surprise the reader.*

NEITHER the facetious dialogue which passed between the poet and the player nor the grave and truly solemn discourse of Mr. Adams will, we conceive, make the reader sufficient amends for the anxiety which he must have felt on the account of poor Fanny, whom we left in so deplorable a condition. We shall therefore now proceed to the relation of what happened to that beautiful and innocent virgin after she fell into the wicked hands of the captain.

The man of war having conveyed his charming prize out of the inn a little before day, made the utmost expedition in his power towards the Squire's house, where this delicate creature was to be offered up a sacrifice to the lust of a ravisher. He was not only deaf to all her bewailings and entreaties on the road, but accosted her ears with impurities, which, having been never before accustomed to them, she happily for herself very little understood. At last he changed this note, and attempted to soothe and mollify her, by setting forth the splendour and luxury which would be her fortune with a man who would have the inclination, and power too, to give her whatever her utmost wishes could desire, and told her he doubted not but she would soon look kinder on him, as the instrument of her happiness, and despise that pitiful fellow, whom her ignorance could only make her fond of. She answered she knew not whom he meant; she never was fond of any pitiful fellow. "Are you affronted, madam," says he, "at my calling him so? But what better can be said of one in a livery, notwithstanding your fondness for him?" She returned that she did not understand him, that the man had been her fellow-servant and she believed was as honest a creature as any alive, but as for fondness for men——"I warrant ye," cries the captain, "we shall find means to persuade you to be fond; and I advise you to yield to gentle ones, for you may be assured that it is not in your power, by any struggles whatever, to preserve your virginity two hours longer. It will be your interest to consent; for the Squire will be much kinder to you if he enjoys you willingly than by force." At which words she began to call aloud for assistance (for it was now open day), but, finding none, she lifted her eyes to heaven and supplicated the divine assistance to preserve her innocence. The captain told her if she persisted in her vociferation he would find a means of stopping her mouth. And now the poor wretch perceiving no hopes of succour, abandoned herself to despair, and sighing out the name of Joseph! Joseph! a river of tears ran down her lovely cheeks and wet the handkerchief which covered her bosom. A horseman now appeared in the road, upon which the captain threatened her violently if she complained; however, the moment they approached each other, she begged him, with the utmost earnestness, to relieve a distressed creature who was in the hands of a ravisher. The fellow stopped at those words, but the captain assured him it was his wife and that he was carrying her home from her adulterer, which so satisfied the fellow, who was an old one (and perhaps a married one too), that he wished him a good journey and rode on. He was no sooner passed than the captain abused her violently for breaking his commands, and threatened to gag her, when two more horsemen, armed with pistols, came into the road just before them. She again solicited their assistance, and the captain told the same story as before. Upon which one said to the other. "That's a charming wench, Jack; I wish I had been in the fellow's place, whoever he is." But the other, instead of answering him, cried out, "Zounds, I know her," and then turning to her, said, "Sure you are not Fanny Goodwill." "Indeed, indeed I am," she cried. "Oh, John, I know you now—Heaven hath sent you to my assistance, to deliver me from this wicked man, who is carrying me away for his vile purposes—oh, for God's sake, rescue me from him!" A fierce dialogue immediately ensued between the captain and these two men, who being both armed with pistols, and the chariot which they attended being now arrived, the captain saw both force and stratagem were vain, and endeavoured to make his escape, in which however he could not succeed. The gentleman who rode in the chariot ordered it to stop, and with an air of authority examined into the merits of the cause; of which being advertised by Fanny, whose credit was confirmed by the fellow who knew her, he ordered the captain, who was all bloody from his encounter at the inn, to be conveyed as a prisoner behind the chariot, and very gallantly took Fanny into it; for, to say the truth, this gentleman (who was no other than the celebrated Mr. Peter Pounce, and who preceded the Lady Booby only a few miles by setting out earlier in the morning) was a very gallant person, and loved a pretty girl better than anything, besides his own money or the money of other people.

The chariot now proceeded towards the inn, which, as Fanny was informed, lay in their way, and where it arrived at that very time while the poet and player were disputing below-stairs, and Adams and Joseph were discoursing back to back above: just at that period to which we brought them both in the two preceding chapters, the chariot stopped at the door and in an instant Fanny, leaping from it, ran up to her Joseph. Oh, reader, conceive if thou canst the joy which fired the breasts of these lovers on this meeting; and if thy own heart doth not sympathetically assist thee in this conception, I pity thee sincerely from my own; for let the hard-hearted villain know this, that there is a pleasure in a tender sensation beyond any which he is capable of tasting.

Peter, being informed by Fanny of the presence of Adams, stopped to see him and receive his homage, for, as Peter was an hypocrite, a sort of people whom Mr. Adams never saw through, the one paid that respect to his seeming goodness which the other believed to be paid to his riches; hence Mr. Adams was so much his favourite that he once lent him four pounds thirteen shillings and sixpence, to prevent his going to gaol, on no greater security than a bond and judgement, which probably he would have made no use of though the money had not been (as it was) paid exactly at the time.

It is not perhaps easy to describe the figure of Adams: he had risen in such a hurry that he had on neither breeches, garters, nor stockings, nor had he taken from his head a red spotted handkerchief, which by night bound his wig, turned inside out around his head. He had on his torn cassock and his great-coat, but as the remainder of his cassock hung down below his great-coat, so did a small stripe of white, or rather whitish, linen, appear below that; to which we may add the several colours which appeared on his face, where a long piss-burnt beard served to retain the liquor of the stone pot, and that of a blacker hue which distilled from the mop.—This figure, which Fanny had delivered from his captivity, was no sooner spied by Peter, than it disordered the composed gravity of his muscles; however, he advised him immediately to make himself clean, nor would accept his homage in that pickle.

The poet and player no sooner saw the captain in captivity, than they began to consider of their own safety, of which flight presented itself as the only means; they therefore both of them mounted the poet's horse and made the most expeditious retreat in their power.

The host, who well knew Mr. Pounce, and Lady Booby's livery, was not a little surprised at this change of the scene, nor was his confusion much helped by his wife, who was now just risen, and, having heard from him the account of what had passed, comforted him with a decent number of fools and blockheads; asked him why he did not consult her; and told him he would never leave following the nonsensical dictates of his own numskull till she and her family were ruined.

Joseph being informed of the captain's arrival, and seeing his Fanny now in safety, quitted her a moment, and, running downstairs, went directly to him, and stripping off his coat, challenged him to fight, but the captain refused, saying he did not understand boxing. He then grasped a cudgel in one hand, and, catching the captain by the collar with the other, gave him a most severe drubbing and ended with telling him he had now had some revenge for what his dear Fanny had suffered.

When Mr. Pounce had a little regaled himself with some provision which he had in his chariot, and Mr. Adams had put on the best appearance his clothes would allow him, Pounce ordered the captain into his presence, for he said he was guilty of felony and the next justice of peace should commit him, but the servants (whose appetite for revenge is soon satisfied) being sufficiently contented with the drubbing which Joseph had inflicted on him, and which was indeed of no very moderate kind, had suffered him to go off, which he did threatening a severe revenge against Joseph, which I have never heard he thought proper to take.

The mistress of the house made her voluntary appearance before Mr. Pounce, and with a thousand curtseys told him she hoped His Honour would pardon her husband, who was a very nonsense man, for the sake of his poor family; that indeed, if he could be ruined alone, she should be very willing of it, for because as why, His Worship very well knew he deserved it, but she had three poor small children who were not capable to get their own living and if her husband was sent to gaol they must all come to the parish, for she was a poor weak woman, continually a-breeding, and had no time to work for them. She therefore hoped His Honour would take it into His Worship's consideration, and forgive her husband this time, for she was sure he never intended any harm to man, woman, or child, and, if it was not for that blockhead of his own, the man in some things was well enough, for she had had three children by him in less than three years, and was almost ready to cry out the fourth time. She would have proceeded in this manner much longer had not Peter stopped her tongue by telling her he had nothing to say to her husband nor her neither. So, as Adams and the rest had assured her of forgiveness, she cried and curtseyed out of the room.

Mr. Pounce was desirous that Fanny should continue her journey with him in the chariot but she absolutely refused, saying she would ride behind Joseph on a horse which one of Lady Booby's servants had equipped him with. But, alas! when the horse appeared, it was found to be no other than that identical beast which Mr. Adams had left behind him at the inn, and which these honest fellows, who knew him, had redeemed. Indeed, whatever horse they had provided for Joseph, they would have prevailed with him to mount none, no not even to ride before his beloved Fanny, till the parson was supplied, much less would he deprive his friend of the beast which belonged to him, and which he knew the moment he saw, though Adams did not; however, when he was reminded of the affair, and told that they had brought the horse with them which he left behind, he answered—"Bless me! and so I did."

Adams was very desirous that Joseph and Fanny should mount this horse, and declared he could very easily walk home. "If I walked alone," says he, "I would wage a shilling that the pedestrian outstripped the equestrian travellers, but as I intend to take the company of a pipe, peradventure I may be an hour later." One of the servants whispered Joseph to take him at his word, and suffer the old put to walk if he would. This proposal was answered with an angry look and a peremptory refusal by Joseph, who, catching Fanny up in his arms, averred he would rather carry her home in that manner than take away Mr. Adams's horse and permit him to walk on foot.

Perhaps, reader, thou hast seen a contest between two gentlemen or two ladies quickly decided, though they have both asserted they would not eat such a nice morsal, and each insisted on the other's accepting it, but in reality both were very desirous to swallow it themselves. Do not therefore conclude hence that this dispute would have come to a speedy decision, for here both parties were heartily in earnest, and it is very probable they would have remained in the inn-yard to this day had not the good Peter Pounce put a stop to it;

for finding he had no longer hopes of satisfying his old appetite with Fanny, and being desirous of having someone to whom he might communicate his grandeur, he told the parson he would convey him home in his chariot. This favour was by Adams, with many bows and acknowledgements, accepted, though he afterwards said he ascended the chariot rather that he might not offend than from any desire of riding in it, for that in his heart he preferred the pedestrian even to the vehicular expedition. All matters being now settled, the chariot, in which rode Adams and Pounce, moved forwards and Joseph, having borrowed a pillion from the host, Fanny had just seated herself thereon, and had laid hold of the girdle which her lover wore for that purpose, when the wise beast, who concluded that one at a time was sufficient, that two to one were odds, etc., discovered much uneasiness at his double load and began to consider his hinder as his fore legs, moving the direct contrary way to that which is called forwards. Nor could Joseph, with all his horsemanship, persuade him to advance; but without having any regard to the lovely part of the lovely girl which was on his back, he used such agitations that had not one of the men come immediately to her assistance, she had, in plain English, tumbled backwards on the ground. This inconvenience was presently remedied by an exchange of horses, and then Fanny, being again placed on her pillion, on a better-natured, and somewhat a better-fed beast, the parson's horse finding he had no longer odds to contend with, agreed to march, and the whole procession set forwards for Booby Hall, where they arrived in a few hours without anything remarkable happening on the road, unless it was a curious dialogue between the parson and the steward, which, to use the language of a late apologist, a pattern to all biographers, "waits for the reader in the next chapter."

CHAPTER XIII: *A curious dialogue which passed between Mr. Abraham Adams and Mr. Peter Pounce, better worth reading than all the works of Colley Cibber and many others.*

THE chariot had not proceeded far before Mr. Adams observed it was a very fine day. "Aye, and a very fine country too," answered Pounce. "I should think so more," returned Adams, "if I had not lately travelled over the Downs, which I take to exceed this and all other prospects in the universe."

"A fig for prospects," answered Pounce; "one acre here is worth ten there, and for my own part I have no delight in the prospect of any land but my own." "Sir," said Adams, "you can indulge yourself with many fine prospects of that kind." "I thank God I have a little," replied the other, "with which I am content, and envy no man; I have a little, Mr. Adams, with which I do as much good as I can." Adams answered that riches without charity were nothing worth, for that they were a blessing only to him who made them a blessing to others. "You and I," said Peter, "have different notions of charity. I own, as it is generally used, I do not like the word, nor do I think it becomes one of us gentlemen; it is a mean parsonlike quality, though I would not infer many parsons have it neither." "Sir," said Adams, "my definition of charity is a generous disposition to relieve the distressed." "There is something in that definition," answered Peter, "which I like well enough; it is, as you say, a disposition, and does not so much consist in the act as in the disposition to do it; but, alas, Mr. Adams, who are meant by the distressed? Believe me, the distresses of mankind are mostly imaginary, and it would be rather folly than goodness to relieve them." "Sure, sir," replied Adams, "hunger and thirst, cold and nakedness, and other distresses which attend the poor, can never be said to be imaginary evils." "How can any man complain of hunger," said Peter, "in a country where such excellent salads are to be gathered in almost every field? or of thirst, where every river and stream produces such delicious potations? And as for cold and nakedness, they are evils introduced by luxury and custom. A man naturally wants clothes no more than a horse or any other animal, and there are whole nations who go without them; but these are things perhaps which you, who do not know the world——" "You will pardon me, sir," returned Adams; "I have read of the Gymnosophists." "A plague of your Jehosaphats," cried Peter; "the greatest fault in our constitution is the provision made for the poor, except that perhaps made for some others. Sir, I have not an estate which doth not contribute almost as much again to the poor as to the land-tax, and I do assure you I expect to come myself to the parish in the end." To which Adams giving a dissenting smile, Peter thus proceeded: "I fancy, Mr. Adams, you are one of those who imagine I am a lump of money, for there are many who, I fancy, believe that not only my pockets but my whole clothes are lined with bank-bills; but I assure you, you are all mistaken; I am not the man the world esteems me. If I can hold my head above water, it is all I can. I have injured myself by purchasing. I have been too liberal of my money. Indeed, I fear my heir will find my affairs in a worse situation than they are reputed to be. Ah! he will have reason to wish I had loved money more, and land less. Pray, my good neighbour, where should I have that quantity of riches the world is so liberal to bestow on me? Where could I possibly, without I had stole it, acquire such a treasure?" "Why, truly," says Adams, "I have been always of your opinion; I have wondered as well as yourself with what confidence they could report such things of you, which have to me appeared as mere impossibilities; for you know, sir, and I have often heard you say it, that your wealth is of your own acquisition, and can it be credible that in your short time you should have amassed such a heap of treasure as these people will have you worth? Indeed, had you inherited an estate like Sir Thomas Booby, which had descended in your family for many generations, they might have had a colour for their assertions." "Why, what do they say I am worth?" cries Peter with a malicious sneer. "Sir," answered Adams, "I have heard some aver you are not worth less than twenty thousand pounds." At which Peter frowned. "Nay, sir," said Adams, "you ask me only the opinion of others; for my own part I have always denied it, nor did I ever believe you could possibly be worth half that sum." "However, Mr. Adams," said he, squeezing him by the hand, "I would not sell them all I am worth for double that sum, and as to what you believe, or they believe, I care not a fig, no not a fart. I am not poor because you think me so, nor because you attempt to undervalue me in the country. I know the envy of mankind very well; but I thank heaven I am above them. It is true, my wealth is of my own acquisition. I have not an estate like Sir Thomas Booby, that has descended in my family through many generations, but I know heirs of such estates who are forced to travel about the country like some people in torn cassocks, and might be glad to accept of a pitiful curacy, for what I know. Yes, sir, as shabby fellows as yourself, whom no man of my figure, without that vice of a good nature about him, would suffer to ride in a chariot with him." "Sir," said Adams, "I value not your chariot of a rush, and if I had known you had intended to affront me I would have walked to the world's end on foot ere I would have accepted a place in it. However, sir, I will soon rid you of that inconvenience," and so saying he opened the chariot-door, without calling to the coachman, and leapt out into the highway, forgetting to take his hat along with him, which, however, Mr. Pounce threw after him with great violence. Joseph and Fanny stopped to bear him company the rest of the way, which was not above a mile.

BOOK FOUR

CHAPTER I: *The arrival of Lady Booby and the rest at Booby Hall.*

THE coach and six, in which Lady Booby rode, overtook the other travellers as they entered the parish. She no sooner saw Joseph than her cheeks glowed with red, and immediately after became as totally pale. She had in her surprise almost stopped her coach, but recollected herself timely enough to prevent it. She entered the parish amidst the ringing of bells and the acclamations of the poor, who were rejoiced to see their patroness returned after so long an absence, during which time all her rents had been drafted to London without a shilling being spent among them, which tended not a little to their utter impoverishing; for, if the court would be severely missed in such a city as London, how much more must the absence of a person of great fortune be felt in a little country village, for whose inhabitants such a family finds a constant employment and supply and with the offals of whose table the infirm, aged, and infant poor are abundantly fed, with a generosity which hath scarce a visible effect on their benefactors' pockets?

But if their interest inspired so public a joy into every countenance, how much more forcibly did the affection which they bore Parson Adams operate upon all who beheld his return? They flocked about him like dutiful children round an indulgent parent, and vied with each other in demonstrations of duty and love. The parson on his side shook everyone by the hand, inquired heartily after the healths of all that were absent, of their children and relations; and expressed a satisfaction in his face which nothing but benevolence made happy by its objects could infuse.

Nor did Joseph and Fanny want a hearty welcome from all who saw them. In short, no three persons could be more kindly received, as, indeed, none ever more deserved to be universally beloved.

Adams carried his fellow-travellers home to his house,

where he insisted on their partaking whatever his wife, whom, with his children, he found in health and joy, could provide—where we shall leave them enjoying perfect happiness over a homely meal, to view scenes of greater splendour but infinitely less bliss.

Our more intelligent readers will doubtless suspect by this second appearance of Lady Booby on the stage that all was not ended by the dismission of Joseph; and, to be honest with them, they are in the right: the arrow had pierced deeper than she imagined, nor was the wound so easily to be cured. The removal of the object soon cooled her rage, but it had a different effect on her love; that departed with his person, but this remained lurking in her mind with his image. Restless, interrupted slumbers, and confused horrible dreams, were her portion the first night. In the morning, fancy painted her a more delicious scene, but to delude, not delight her, for before she could reach the promised happiness, it vanished, and left her to curse, not bless, the vision.

She started from her sleep, her imagination being all on fire with the phantom, when her eyes accidentally glancing towards the spot where yesterday the real Joseph had stood, that little circumstance raised his idea in the liveliest colours in her memory. Each look, each word, each gesture, rushed back on her mind with charms which all his coldness could not abate. Nay, she imputed that to his youth, his folly, his awe, his religion, to everything but what would instantly have produced contempt, want of passion for the sex, or that which would have roused her hatred, want of liking to her.

Reflection then hurried her farther and told her she must see this beautiful youth no more, nay, suggested to her, that she herself had dismissed him for no other fault than probably that of too violent an awe and respect for herself, and which she ought rather to have esteemed a merit, the effects of which were, besides, so easily and surely to have been removed; she then blamed, she cursed, the hasty rashness of her temper; her fury was vented all on herself, and Joseph appeared innocent in her eyes. Her passion at length grew so violent that it forced her on seeking relief, and now she thought of recalling him; but pride forbade that: pride, which soon drove all softer passions from her soul and represented to her the meanness of him she was fond of. That thought soon began to obscure his beauties; contempt succeeded next, and then disdain, which presently introduced her hatred of the creature who had given her so much uneasiness.

These enemies of Joseph had no sooner taken possession of her mind than they insinuated to her a thousand things in his disfavour; everything but dislike of her person, a thought which, as it would have been intolerable to bear, she checked the moment it endeavoured to arise. Revenge came now to her assistance; and she considered her dismission of him, stripped, and without a character, with the utmost pleasure. She rioted in the several kinds of misery which her imagination suggested to her might be his fate; and with a smile composed of anger, mirth, and scorn, viewed him in the rags in which her fancy had dressed him.

Mrs. Slipslop, being summoned, attended her mistress, who had now in her own opinion totally subdued this passion. Whilst she was dressing, she asked if that fellow had been turned away according to her orders. Slipslop answered she had told her ladyship so (as indeed she had).—"And how did he behave?" replied the lady. "Truly, madam," cries Slipslop, "in such a manner that infected everybody who saw him. The poor lad had but little wages to receive, for he constantly allowed his father and mother half his income, so that when your ladyship's livery was stripped off he had not wherewithal to buy a coat, and must have gone naked if one of the footmen had not incommodated him with one; and whilst he was standing in his shirt (and to say the truth he was an amorous figure), being told that your ladyship would not give him a character, he sighed and said he had done nothing willingly to offend; that, for his part, he should always give your ladyship a good character wherever he went; and he prayed God to bless you, for you was the best of ladies, though his enemies had set you against him. I wish you had not turned him away, for I believe you have not a faithfuller servant in the house." "How came you then," replied the lady, "to advise me to turn him away?" "I, madam!" said Slipslop; "I am sure you will do me the justice to say I did all in my power to prevent it; but I saw your ladyship was angry, and it is not the business of us upper-servants to hinterfere on those occasions." "And was it not you, audacious wretch," cried the lady, "who made me angry? Was it not your tittle-tattle, in which I believe you belied the poor fellow, which incensed me against him? He may thank you for all that hath happened, and so may I for the loss of a good servant, and one who probably had more merit than all of you. Poor fellow! I am charmed with his goodness to his parents. Why did not you tell me of that, but suffer me to dismiss so good a creature without a character? I see the reason of your whole behaviour now, as well as your complaint; you was jealous of the wenches." "I jealous!" said Slipslop; "I assure you, I look upon myself as his betters; I am not meat for a footman, I hope." These words threw the lady into a violent passion, and she sent Slipslop from her presence, who departed tossing her nose, and crying, "Marry come up! there are some people more jealous than I, I believe." Her lady affected not to hear the words, though in reality she did, and understood them too. Now ensued a second conflict, so like the former that it might savour of repetition to relate it minutely. It may suffice to say, that Lady Booby found good reason to doubt whether she had so absolutely conquered her passion as she had flattered herself, and, in order to accomplish it quite, took a resolution, more common than wise, to retire immediately into the country. The reader hath long ago seen the arrival of Mrs. Slipslop, whom no pertness could make her mistress resolve to part with; lately, that of Mr. Pounce, her forerunners; and lastly, that of the lady herself.

The morning after her arrival, being Sunday, she went to church, to the great surprise of everybody, who wondered to see her ladyship, being no very constant church-woman, there so suddenly upon her journey. Joseph was likewise there, and I have heard it was remarked that she fixed her eyes on him much more than on the parson; but this I believe to be only a malicious rumour. When the prayers were ended, Mr. Adams stood up and with a loud voice pronounced: "'I publish the banns of marriage between Joseph Andrews and Frances Goodwill, both of this parish," etc. Whether this had any effect on Lady Booby or no, who was then in her pew, which the congregation could not see into, I could never discover, but certain it is that in about a quarter of an hour she stood up and directed her eyes to that part of the church where the women sat, and persisted in looking that way during the remainder of the sermon in so scrutinizing a manner, and with so angry a countenance, that most of the women were afraid she was offended at them. The moment she returned home she sent for Slipslop into her chamber and told her, she wondered what that impudent fellow Joseph did in that parish? Upon which Slipslop gave her an account of her meeting Adams with him on the road, and likewise the adventure with Fanny. At the relation of which, the lady often changed her countenance, and when she had heard all, she ordered Mr. Adams into her presence, to whom she behaved as the reader will see in the next chapter.

CHAPTER II: *A dialogue between Mr. Abraham Adams and the Lady Booby.*

MR. ADAMS was not far off, for he was drinking her ladyship's health below in a cup of her ale. He no sooner came before her than she began in the following manner: "I wonder, sir, after the many great obligations you have had to this family" (with all which the reader hath, in the course of this history, been minutely acquainted), "that you will ungratefully show any respect to a fellow who hath been turned out of it for his misdeeds. Nor doth it, I can tell you, sir, become a man of your character to run about the country with an idle fellow and wench. Indeed, as for the girl, I know no harm of her. Slipslop tells me she was formerly bred up in my house, and behaved as she ought, till she hankered after this fellow, and he spoiled her. Nay, she may still, perhaps, do very well, if he will let her alone. You are therefore doing a monstrous thing in endeavouring to procure a match between these two people, which will be the ruin of them both." "Madam," says Adams, "if your ladyship will but hear me speak, I protest I never heard any harm of Mr. Joseph Andrews; if I had, I should have corrected him for it, for I never have, nor will, encourage the faults of those under my cure. As for the young woman, I assure your ladyship I have as good an opinion of her as your ladyship yourself or any other can have. She is the sweetest-tempered, honestest, worthiest, young creature; indeed, as to her beauty, I do not commend her on that account, though all men allow she is the handsomest woman, gentle or simple, that ever appeared in the parish." "You are very impertinent," says she, "to talk such fulsome stuff to me. It is mighty becoming truly in a clergyman to trouble himself about handsome women, and you are a delicate judge of beauty, no doubt. A man who hath lived all his life in such a parish as this is a rare judge of beauty. Ridiculous! Beauty indeed, a country-wench a beauty. I shall be sick whenever I hear beauty mentioned again. And so this wench is to stock the parish with beauties, I hope. But, sir, our poor is numerous enough already; I will have no more vagabonds settled here." "Madam," says Adams, "your ladyship is offended with me, I protest, without any reason. This couple were desirous to consummate long ago, and I dissuaded them from it; nay, I may venture to say, I believe I was the sole cause of their delaying it." "Well," says she, "and you did very wisely and honestly too, notwithstanding she is the greatest beauty in the parish." "And now, madam," continued he, "I only perform my office to Mr. Joseph." "Pray, don't mister such fellows to me," cries the lady. "He," said the parson, "with the consent of Fanny, before my face put in the banns. "Yes," answered the lady, "I suppose the slut is forward enough; Slipslop tells me how her head runs upon fellows; that is one of her beauties, I suppose. But, if they have put in the banns, I desire you will publish them no more without my orders." "Madam," cries Adams, "if anyone puts in sufficient caution, and assigns a proper reason against them, I am willing to surcease." "I tell you a reason," says she: "he is a vagabond, and he shall not settle here and bring a nest of beggars into the parish; it will make us but little amends that they will be beauties." "Madam," answered Adams, "with the utmost submission to your ladyship, I have been informed by lawyer Scout that any person who serves a year gains a settlement in the parish where he serves." "Lawyer Scout," replied the lady, "is an impudent coxcomb; I will have no lawyer Scout interfere with me. I repeat to you again, I will have no more incumbrances brought on us: so I desire you will proceed no farther." "Madam," returned Adams, "I would obey your ladyship in everything that is lawful, but surely the parties being poor is no reason against their marrying. God forbid there should be any such law. The poor have little share enough of this world already; it would be barbarous indeed to deny them the common privileges, and innocent enjoyments, which nature indulges to the animal creation." "Since you understand yourself no better," cries the lady, "nor the respect due from such as you to a woman of my distinction, than to affront my ears by such loose discourse, I shall mention but one short word: it is my orders to you, that you publish these banns no more, and if you dare, I will recommend it to your master, the doctor, to discard you from his service. I will, sir, notwithstanding your poor family, and then you and the greatest beauty in the parish may go and beg together." "Madam," answered Adams, "I know not what your ladyship means by the terms master and service. I am in the service of a master who will never discard me for doing my duty; and if the doctor (for indeed I have never been able to pay for a licence) thinks proper to turn me from my cure, God will provide me, I hope, another. At least my family, as well as myself, have hands, and he will prosper, I doubt not, our endeavours to get our bread honestly with them. Whilst my conscience is pure, I shall never fear what man can do unto me." "I condemn my humility," said the lady, "for demeaning myself to converse with you so long. I shall take other measures, for I see you are a confederate with them. But the sooner you leave me the better, and I shall give orders that my doors may no longer be open to you. I will suffer no parsons who run about the country with beauties to be entertained here." "Madam," said Adams, "I shall enter into no persons' doors against their will; but I am assured when you have inquired farther into this matter you will applaud, not blame, my proceeding; and so I humbly take my leave," which he did with many bows, or at least many attempts at a bow.

CHAPTER III: *What passed between the lady and Lawyer Scout.*

In the afternoon the lady sent for Mr. Scout, whom she attacked most violently for intermeddling with her servants, which he denied, and indeed with truth, for he had only asserted accidentally, and perhaps rightly, that a year's service gained a settlement, and so far he owned he might have formerly informed the parson, and believed it was law. "I am resolved," said the lady, "to have no discarded servants of mine settled here; and so, if this be your law, I shall send to another lawyer." Scout said if she sent to a hundred lawyers not one or all of them could alter the law. The utmost that was in the power of a lawyer was to prevent the law's taking effect, and that he himself could do for her ladyship as well as any other. "And I believe," says he, "madam, your ladyship not being conversant in these matters, hath mistaken a difference, for I asserted only that a man who served a year was settled. Now there is a material difference between being settled in law and settled in fact, and as I affirmed generally he was settled, and law is preferable to fact, my settlement must be understood in law, and not in fact. And suppose, madam, we admit he was settled in law, what use will they make of it, how doth that relate to fact? He is not settled in fact, and if he be not settled in fact, he is not an inhabitant; and if he is not an inhabitant, he is not of this parish; and then undoubtedly he ought not to be published here, for Mr. Adams hath told me your ladyship's pleasure and the reason, which is a very good one, to prevent burdening us with the poor; we have too many already, and I think we ought to have an act to hang or transport half of them. If we can prove in evidence that he is not settled in fact, it is another matter. What I said to Mr. Adams was on a supposition that he was settled in fact; and indeed, if that was the case, I should doubt——" "Don't tell me your facts and your ifs," said the lady, "I don't understand your gibberish; you take too much upon you, and are very impertinent, in pretending to direct in this parish; and you shall be taught better, I assure you you shall. But as to the wench, I am resolved she shall not settle here; I will not suffer such beauties as these to produce children for us to keep." "Beauties, indeed! your ladyship is pleased to be merry," answered Scout. "Mr. Adams described her so to me," said the lady. "Pray what sort of dowdy is it, Mr. Scout?" "The ugliest creature almost I ever beheld; a poor dirty drab; your ladyship never saw such a wretch." "Well, but dear Mr. Scout, let her be what she will, these ugly women will bring children, you know, so that we must prevent the marriage." "True, madam," replied Scout, "for the subsequent marriage, co-operating with the law, will carry law into fact. When a man is married he is settled in fact, and then he is not removable. I will see Mr. Adams, and I make no doubt of prevailing with him. His only objection is, doubtless, that he shall lose his fee, but that being once made easy, as it shall be, I am confident no farther objection will remain. No, no, it is impossible; but your ladyship can't discommend his unwillingness to depart from his fee. Every man ought to have a proper value for his fee. As to the matter in question, if your ladyship pleases to employ me in it, I will venture to promise you success. The laws of this land are not so vulgar to permit a mean fellow to contend with one of your ladyship's fortune. We have one sure card, which is to carry him before Justice Frolick, who, upon hearing your ladyship's name, will commit him without any farther questions. As for the dirty slut, we shall have nothing to do with her, for if we get rid of the fellow, the ugly jade will——" "Take what measures you please, good Mr. Scout," answered the lady, "but I wish you could rid the parish of both, for Slipslop tells me such stories of this wench that I abhor the thoughts of her, and though you say she is such an ugly slut yet you know, dear Mr. Scout, these forward creatures who run after men will always find some as forward as themselves, so that, to prevent the increase of beggars, we must get rid of her." "Your ladyship is very much in the right," answered Scout, "but I am afraid the law is a little deficient in giving us any such power of prevention; however, the justice will stretch it as far as he is able, to oblige your ladyship. To say truth, it is a great blessing to the country that he is in the commission, for he hath taken several poor off our hands that the law would never lay hold on. I know some justices who make as much of committing a man to Bridewell as his lordship at 'size would of hanging him; but it would do a man good to see his worship, our justice, commit a fellow to Bridewell, he takes so much pleasure in it; and when once we ha'um there, we seldom hear any more o'um. He's either starved or eat up by vermin in a month's time." Here the arrival of a visitor put an end to the conversation, and Mr. Scout, having undertaken the cause and promised it success, departed.

This Scout was one of those fellows who, without any knowledge of the law or being bred to it, take upon them, in defiance of an act of Parliament, to act as lawyers in the country, and are called so. They are the pests of society, and a scandal to a profession, to which indeed they do not belong, and which owes to such kind of rascallions the ill-will which weak persons bear towards it. With this fellow, to whom a little before she would not have condescended to have spoken, did a certain passion for Joseph, and the jealousy and the disdain of poor innocent Fanny, betray the Lady Booby into a familiar discourse, in which she inadvertently confirmed many hints, with which Slipslop, whose gallant he was, had preacquainted him, and whence he had taken an opportunity to assert those severe falsehoods of little Fanny which possibly the reader might not have been well able to account for if we had not thought proper to give him this information.

CHAPTER IV: *A short chapter, but very full of matter; particularly the arrival of Mr. Booby and his lady.*

ALL that night and the next day the Lady Booby passed with the utmost anxiety; her mind was distracted, and her soul tossed up and down by many turbulent and opposite passions. She loved, hated, pitied, scorned, admired, despised the same person by fits, which changed in a very short interval. On Tuesday morning, which happened to be a holiday, she went to church, where, to her surprise, Mr. Adams published the banns again with as audible a voice as before. It was lucky for her that, as there was no sermon, she had an immediate opportunity of returning home to vent her rage, which she could not have concealed from the congregation five minutes; indeed, it was not then very numerous, the assembly consisting of no more than Adams, his clerk, his wife, the lady, and one of her servants. At her return she met Slipslop, who accosted her in these words: "O meam, what doth your ladyship think? To be sure, Lawyer Scout hath carried Joseph and Fanny both before the justice. All the parish are in tears, and say they will certainly be hanged, for nobody knows what it is for." "I suppose they deserve it," says the lady. "Why dost thou mention such wretches to me?" "O dear madam," answered Slipslop, "is it not a pity such a graceless young man should die a virulent death? I hope the judge will take commensuration on his youth. As for Fanny, I don't think it signifies much what becomes of her, and if poor Joseph hath done anything, I could venture to swear she traduced him to it: few men ever come to fragrant punishment but by those nasty creatures, who are a scandal to our sect." The lady was no more pleased at this news, after a moment's reflection, than Slipslop herself; for though she wished Fanny far enough, she did not desire the removal of Joseph, especially with her. She was puzzled how to act, or what to say on this occasion, when a coach and six drove into the court and a servant acquainted her with the arrival of her nephew Booby and his lady. She ordered them to be conducted into a drawing-room, whither she presently repaired, having composed her countenance as well as she could, and being a little satisfied that the wedding would by these means be at least interrupted, and that she should have an opportunity to execute any resolution she might take, for which she saw herself provided with an excellent instrument in Scout.

The Lady Booby apprehended her servant had made a mistake when he mentioned Mr. Booby's lady, for she had never heard of his marriage, but how great was her surprise when, at her entering the room, her nephew presented his wife to her, saying, "Madam, this is that charming Pamela, of whom I am convinced you have heard so much." The lady received her with more civility than he expected, indeed with the utmost, for she was perfectly polite, nor had any vice inconsistent with good breeding. They passed some little time in ordinary discourse, when a servant came and whispered Mr. Booby, who presently told the ladies he must desert them a little on some business of consequence, and, as their discourse during his absence would afford little improvement or entertainment to the reader, we will leave them for a while to attend Mr. Booby.

CHAPTER V: *Containing justice business: curious precedents of depositions, and other matters necessary to be perused by all justices of the peace and their clerks.*

THE young Squire and his lady were no sooner alighted from their coach than the servants began to inquire after Mr. Joseph, from whom they said their lady had not heard a word, to her great surprise, since he had left Lady Booby's. Upon this they were instantly informed of what had lately happened, with which they hastily acquainted their master, who took an immediate resolution to go himself and endeavour to restore his Pamela her brother before she even knew she had lost him.

The justice before whom the criminals were carried, and who lived within a short mile of the lady's house, was luckily Mr. Booby's acquaintance, by his having an estate in his neighbourhood. Ordering therefore his horses to his coach, he set out for the judgement-seat, and arrived when the justice had almost finished his business. He was conducted into a hall, where he was acquainted that his worship would wait on him in a moment, for he had only a man and a woman to commit to Bridewell first. As he was now convinced he had not a minute to lose, he insisted on the servant's introducing him directly into the room where the justice was then executing his office, as he called it. Being brought thither, and the first compliments being passed between the Squire and his worship, the former asked the latter what crime those two young people had been guilty of. "No great crime," answered the justice; "I have only ordered them to Bridewell for a month." "But what is their crime?" repeated the Squire. "Larceny, an't please Your Honour," said Scout. "Aye," says the justice, "a kind of felonious larcenous thing. I believe I must order them a little correction too, a little stripping and whipping." (Poor Fanny, who had hitherto supported all with the thoughts of Joseph's company, trembled at that sound; but, indeed, without reason, for none but the devil himself would have executed such a sentence on her.) "Still," said the Squire, "I am ignorant of the crime, the fact I mean." "Why, there it is in peaper," answered the justice, showing him a deposition which, in the absence of his clerk, he had writ himself, of which we have with great difficulty procured an authentic copy, and here it follows *verbatim et literatim:*

The depusition of James Scout, layer, and Thomas Trotter, yeoman, taken before me, one of his magesty's justasses of the piece for Zumersetshire.

"THESE deponants saith, and first Thomas Trotter for himself saith, that on the   of this instant October being Sabbath-day, between the ours of 2 and 4 in the afternoon, he zeed Joseph Andrews and Francis Goodwill walk akross a certane felde belunging to layer Scout, and out of the path which ledes thru the said felde, and there he zede Joseph Andrews with a nife cut one hasel-twig, of the value, as he believes, of 3 half-pence, or thereabouts; and he saith that the said Francis Goodwill was likewise walking on the grass out of the said path in the said felde, and did receive and karry in her hand the said twig, and so was comfarting, eading, and abating to the said Joseph therein. And the said James Scout for himself says that he verily believes the said twig to be his own proper twig," &c.

"Jesu!" said the Squire, "would you commit two persons to Bridewell for a twig?" "Yes," said the lawyer, "and with great lenity too; for if we had called it a young tree, they would have been both hanged." "Harkee," says the justice, taking aside the Squire, "I should not have been so severe on this occasion but Lady Booby desires to get them out of the parish, so Lawyer Scout will give the constable orders to let them run away, if they please; but it seems they intend to marry together, and the lady hath no other means, as they are legally settled there, to prevent their bringing an incumbrance on her own parish." "Well," said the Squire, "I will take care my aunt shall be satisfied in this point, and likewise I promise you Joseph here shall never be any incumbrance on her. I shall be obliged to you, therefore, if, instead of Bridewell, you will commit them to my custody." "Oh, to be sure, sir, if you desire it," answered the justice, and without more ado Joseph and Fanny were delivered over to Squire Booby, whom Joseph very well knew, but little guessed how nearly he was related to him. The justice burnt his mittimus; the constable was sent about his business; the lawyer made no complaint for want of justice; and the prisoners, with exulting hearts, gave a thousand thanks to his honour Mr. Booby, who did not intend their obligations to him should cease here, for, ordering his man to produce a cloak-bag, which he had caused to be brought from Lady Booby's on purpose, he desired the justice that he might have Joseph with him into a room, where, ordering a servant to take out a suit of his own clothes, with linen and other necessaries, he left Joseph to dress himself, who, not yet knowing the cause of all this civility, excused his accepting such a favour as long as decently he could. Whilst Joseph was dressing, the Squire repaired to the justice, whom he found talking with Fanny, for during the examination she had flopped her hat over her eyes, which were also bathed in tears, and had by that means concealed from his worship what might perhaps have rendered the arrival of Mr. Booby unnecessary, at least for herself. The justice no sooner saw her countenance cleared up, and her bright eyes shining through her tears, than he secretly cursed himself for having once thought of Bridewell for her. He would willingly have sent his own wife thither, to have had Fanny in her place. And conceiving almost at the same instant desires and schemes to accomplish them, he employed the minutes whilst the Squire was absent with Joseph in assuring her how sorry he was for having treated her so roughly before he knew her merit, and told her that, since Lady Booby was unwilling that she should settle in her parish, she was heartily welcome to his, where he promised her his protection, adding that he would take Joseph and her into his own family, if she liked; which assurance he confirmed with a squeeze by the hand. She thanked him very kindly, and said she would acquaint Joseph with the offer, which he would certainly be glad to accept, for that Lady Booby was angry with them both though she did not know either had done anything to offend her, but imputed it to Madam Slipslop, who had always been her enemy.

The Squire now returned and prevented any farther continuance of this conversation; and the justice, out of a pretended respect to his guest, but in reality from an apprehension of a rival (for he knew nothing of his marriage), ordered Fanny into the kitchen, whither she gladly retired, nor did the Squire, who declined the trouble of explaining the whole matter, oppose it.

It would be unnecessary, if I was able, which indeed I am not, to relate the conversation between these two gentlemen, which rolled, as I have been informed, entirely on the subject of horse-racing. Joseph was soon dressed in the plainest dress he could find, which was a blue coat and breeches, with a gold edging, and a red waistcoat with the same: and as this suit, which was rather too large for the Squire, exactly fitted him, so he became it so well, and looked so genteel, that no person would have doubted its being as well adapted to his quality as his shape; nor have suspected, as one might, when my Lord ——, or Sir ——, or Mr. —— appear in lace or embroidery, that the tailor's man wore those clothes home on his back which he should have carried under his arm.

The Squire now took leave of the justice, and, calling for Fanny, made her and Joseph, against their wills, get into the coach with him, which he then ordered to drive to Lady Booby's. It had moved a few yards only when the Squire asked Joseph if he knew who that man was crossing the field, for, added he, I never saw one take such strides before. Joseph answered eagerly, "Oh, sir, it is Parson Adams!" "Oh, la, indeed and so it is," said Fanny; "poor man, he is coming to do what he could for us. Well, he is the worthiest best-natured creature." "Aye," said Joseph; "God bless him, for there is not such another in the universe." "The best creature living sure," cries Fanny. "Is he?" says the Squire; "then I am resolved to have the best creature living in my coach," and so saying he ordered it to stop, whilst Joseph, at his request, halloed to the parson, who, well knowing his voice, made all the haste imaginable and soon came up with them. He was desired by the master, who could scarce refrain from laughter at his figure, to mount into the coach, which he with many thanks refused, saying he could walk by its side, and he'd warrant he kept up with it, but he was at length overprevailed on. The Squire now acquainted Joseph with his marriage, but he might have spared himself that labour, for his servant, whilst Joseph was dressing, had performed that office before. He continued to express the vast happiness he enjoyed in his sister, and the value he had for all who belonged to her. Joseph made many bows, and expressed as many acknowledgements, and Parson Adams, who now first perceived Joseph's new apparel, burst into tears with joy, and fell to rubbing his hands and snapping his fingers as if he had been mad.

They were now arrived at the Lady Booby's, and the Squire, desiring them to wait a moment in the court, walked in to his aunt, and, calling her out from his wife, acquainted her with Joseph's arrival; saying, "Madam, as I have married a virtuous and worthy woman, I am resolved to own her relations, and show them all proper respect; I shall think myself therefore infinitely obliged to all mine who will do the same. It is true, her brother hath been your servant, but he is now become my brother; and I have one happiness that neither his character, his behaviour or appearance give me any reason to be ashamed of calling him so. In short, he is now below, dressed like a gentleman, in which light I intend he shall hereafter be seen; and you will oblige me beyond expression, if you will admit him to be of our party, for I know it will give great pleasure to my wife, though she will not mention it."

This was a stroke of fortune beyond the Lady Booby's hopes or expectation; she answered him eagerly, "Nephew, you know how easily I am prevailed on to do anything which Joseph Andrews desires—Phoo, I mean which you desire me; and as he is now your relation, I cannot refuse to entertain him as such." The Squire told her he knew his obligation to her for her compliance, and, going three steps, returned and told her he had one more favour, which he believed she would easily grant as she had accorded him the former. "There is a young woman——"—"Nephew," says she, "don't let my good nature make you desire, as is too commonly the case, to impose on me. Nor think, because I have with so much condescension agreed to suffer your brother-in-law to come to my table, that I will submit to the company of all my own servants, and all the dirty trollops in the country." "Madam," answered the Squire, "I believe you never saw this young creature. I never beheld such sweetness and innocence joined with such beauty, and withal so genteel." "Upon my soul I won't admit her," replied the lady in a passion; "the whole world shan't prevail on me: I resent even the desire as an affront, and——" The Squire, who knew her inflexibility, interrupted her by asking pardon, and promising not to mention it more. He then returned to Joseph, and she to Pamela. He took Joseph aside and told him he would carry him to his sister, but could not prevail as yet for Fanny. Joseph begged that he might see his sister alone and then be with his Fanny, but the Squire, knowing the pleasure his wife would have in her brother's company, would not admit it, telling Joseph there would be nothing in so short an absence from Fanny whilst he was assured of her safety, adding he hoped he could not easily quit a sister whom he had not seen so long, and who so tenderly loved him. Joseph immediately complied, for indeed no brother could love a sister more, and, recommending Fanny, who rejoiced that she was not to go before Lady Booby, to the care of Mr. Adams, he attended the Squire upstairs, whilst Fanny repaired with the parson to his house, where she thought herself secure of a kind reception.

CHAPTER VI: *Of which you are desired to read no more than you like.*

THE meeting between Joseph and Pamela was not without tears of joy on both sides, and their embraces were full of tenderness and affection. They were, however, regarded with much more pleasure by the nephew than by the aunt, to whose flame they were fuel only; and being assisted by the addition of dress, which was indeed not wanted to set off the lively colours in which Nature had drawn health, strength, comeliness, and youth. In the afternoon Joseph, at their request, entertained them with an account of his adventures, nor could Lady Booby conceal her dissatisfaction at those parts in which Fanny was concerned, especially when Mr. Booby launched forth into such rapturous praises of her beauty. She said, applying to her niece, that she wondered her nephew, who had pretended to marry for love, should think such a subject proper to amuse his wife with, adding that, for her part, she should be jealous of a husband who spoke so warmly in praise of another woman. Pamela answered, indeed she thought she had cause, but it was an instance of Mr. Booby's aptness to see more beauty in women than they were mistresses of. At which words both the women fixed their eyes on two looking-glasses and Lady Booby replied that men were, in the general, very ill judges of beauty, and then, whilst both contemplated only their own faces, they paid a cross compliment to each other's charms. When the hour of rest approached, which the lady of the house deferred as long as decently she could, she informed Joseph (whom for the future we shall call Mr. Joseph, he having as good a title to that appellation as many others; I mean that incontested one of good clothes) that she had ordered a bed to be provided for him. He declined this favour to his utmost, for his heart had long been with his Fanny, but she insisted on his accepting it, alleging that the parish had no proper accommodation for such a person as he was now to esteem himself. The Squire and his lady both joining with her, Mr. Joseph was at last forced to give over his design of visiting Fanny that evening, who, on her side, as impatiently expected him till midnight, when, in complacence to Mr. Adams's family, who had sat up two hours out of respect to her, she retired to bed, but not to sleep; the thoughts of her love kept her waking, and his not returning according to his promise filled her with uneasiness, of which, however, she could not assign any other cause than merely that of being absent from him.

Mr. Joseph rose early in the morning and visited her in whom his soul delighted. She no sooner heard his voice in the parson's parlour than she leapt from her bed, and, dressing herself in a few minutes, went down to him. They passed two hours with inexpressible happiness together, and then having appointed Monday, by Mr. Adams's permission, for their marriage, Mr. Joseph returned, according to his promise, to breakfast at the Lady Booby's, with whose behaviour since the evening we shall now acquaint the reader.

She was no sooner retired to her chamber than she asked Slipslop what she thought of this wonderful creature her nephew had married. "Madam," said Slipslop, not yet sufficiently understanding what answer she was to make. "I ask you," answered the lady, "what you think of the dowdy, my niece, I think I am to call her?" Slipslop wanting no further hint, began to pull her to pieces, and so miserably defaced her that it would have been impossible for anyone to have known the person. The lady gave her all the assistance she could and ended with saying, "I think, Slipslop, you have done her justice; but yet, bad as she is, she is an angel compared to this Fanny." Slipslop then fell on Fanny, whom she hacked and hewed in the like barbarous manner, concluding with an observation that there was always something in those low-life creatures which must eternally extinguish them from their betters. "Really," said the lady, "I think there is one exception to your rule; I am certain you may guess who I mean." "Not I, upon my word, madam," said Slipslop. "I mean a young fellow; sure you are the dullest wretch," said the lady. "Oh, la, I am indeed. Yes, truly, madam, he is an accession," answered Slipslop. "Aye, is he not, Slipslop?" returned the lady. "Is he not so genteel that a prince might, without a blush, acknowledge him for his son? His behaviour is such that would not shame the best education. He borrows from his station a condescension in everything to his superiors, yet unattended by that mean servility which is called good behaviour in such persons. Everything he doth hath no mark of the base motive of fear, but visibly shows some respect and gratitude, and carries with it the persuasion of love. And then for his virtues: such piety to his parents, such tender affection to his sister, such integrity in his friendship, such bravery, such goodness, that if he had been born a gentleman his wife would have possessed the most invaluable blessing." "To be sure, ma'am," says Slipslop. "But as he is," answered the lady, "if he had a thousand more good qualities, it must render a woman of fashion contemptible even to be suspected of thinking of him; yes, I should despise myself for such a thought." "To be sure, ma'am," said Slipslop. "And why to be sure?" replied the lady; "thou art always one's echo. Is he not more worthy of affection than a dirty country clown, though born of a family as old as the flood, or an idle worthless rake, or little puisny beau of quality? And yet these we must condemn ourselves to, in order to avoid the censure of the world; to shun the contempt of others, we must ally ourselves to those we despise; we must prefer birth, title, and fortune to real merit. It is a tyranny of custom, a tyranny we must comply with, for we people of fashion are the slaves of custom." "Marry come up!" said Slipslop, who now well knew which party to take, "if I was a woman of your ladyship's fortune and quality, I would be a slave to nobody." "Me," said the lady; "I am speaking, if a young woman of fashion, who had seen nothing of the world, should happen to like such a fellow. Me, indeed; I hope thou dost not imagine——" "No, ma'am, to be sure," cries Slipslop. "No! what no?" cried the lady. "Thou art always ready to answer before thou hast heard one. So far I must allow, he is a charming fellow. Me, indeed! No, Slipslop, all thoughts of men are over with me. I have lost a husband, who—but if I should reflect, I should run mad. My future ease must depend upon forgetfulness. Slipslop, let me hear some of thy nonsense, to turn my thoughts another way. What dost thou think of Mr. Andrews?" "Why I think," says Slipslop, "he is the handsomest, most properest man I ever saw, and if I was a lady of the greatest degree, it would be well for some folks. Your ladyship may talk of custom, if you please, but I am confidous there is no more comparison between young Mr. Andrews and most of the young gentlemen who come to your ladyship's house in London—a parcel of whipper-snapper sparks: I would sooner marry our old Parson Adams. Never tell me what people say whilst I am happy in the arms of him I love. Some folks rail against other folks, because other folks have what some folks would be glad of." "And so," answered the lady, "if you was a woman of condition, you would really marry Mr. Andrews?" "Yes, I assure your ladyship," replied Slipslop, "if he would have me." "Fool, idiot," cries the lady; "if he would have a woman of fashion! is that a question?" "No, truly, madam," said Slipslop, "I believe it would be none if Fanny was out of the way, and I am confidous, if I was in your ladyship's place, and liked Mr. Joseph Andrews, she should not stay in the parish a moment. I am sure Lawyer Scout would send her a-packing if your ladyship would but say the word." This last speech of Slipslop raised a tempest in the mind of her mistress. She feared Scout had betrayed her, or rather that she had betrayed herself. After some silence, and a double change of her complexion, first to pale and then to red, she thus spoke: "I am astonished at the liberty you give your tongue. Would you insinuate that I employed Scout against this wench on the account of the fellow?" "La, ma'am," said Slipslop, frighted out of her wits, "I assassinate such a thing!" "I think you dare not," answered the lady; "I believe my conduct may defy malice itself to assert so cursed a slander. If I had ever discovered any wantonness, any lightness in my behaviour; if I had followed the example of some whom thou hast, I believe, seen, in allowing myself indecent liberties, even with a husband—but the dear man who is gone" (here she began to sob), "was he alive again" (then she produced tears), "could not upbraid me with any one act of tenderness or passion. No, Slipslop, all the time I cohabited with him he never obtained even a kiss from me without my expressing reluctance in the granting it. I am sure he himself never suspected how much I loved him. Since his death, thou knowest, though it is almost six weeks (it wants but a day) ago, I have not admitted one visitor till this fool my nephew arrived. I have confined myself quite to one party of friends. And can such a conduct as this fear to be arraigned? To be accused, not only of a passion which I have always despised, but of fixing it on such an object, a creature so much beneath my notice." "Upon my word, ma'am," says Slipslop, "I do not understand your ladyship, nor know I anything of the matter." "I believe indeed thou dost not understand me. Those are delicacies which exist only in superior minds; thy coarse ideas cannot comprehend them. Thou art a low creature, of the Andrews breed, a reptile of a lower order, a weed that grows in the common garden of the creation." "I assure your ladyship," says Slipslop, whose passions were almost of as high an order as her lady's, "I have no more to do with Common Garden than other folks. Really, your ladyship talks of servants as if they were not born of the Christian specious. Servants have flesh and blood as well as quality, and Mr. Andrews himself is a proof that they have as good, if not better. And for my own part, I can't perceive my dears * are coarser than other people's; and I am sure, if Mr. Andrews was a dear of mine, I should not be ashamed of him in company with gentlemen; for whoever hath seen him in his new clothes must confess he looks as much like a gentleman as anybody. Coarse, quotha! I can't bear to hear the poor young fellow run down neither, for I will say this, I never heard him say an ill word of anybody in his life. I am sure his coarseness doth not lie in his heart, for he is the best-natured man in the world, and as for his skin, it is no coarser than other people's, I am sure. His bosom when a boy was as white as driven snow, and, where it is not covered with hairs, is so still. 'Ifackins! if I was Mrs. Andrews, with a hundred a year, I should not envy the best she who wears a head. A woman that could not be happy with such a man ought never to be so, for if he can't make a woman happy, I never yet beheld the man who could. I say again, I wish I was a great lady for his sake. I believe when I had made a gentleman of him he'd behave so that nobody should deprecate what I had done, and I fancy few would venture to tell him he was no gentleman to his face, nor to mine neither." At which words, taking up the candles, she asked her mistress, who had been some time in her bed, if she had any farther commands; who mildly answered she had none, and, telling her she was a comical creature, bid her good night.

CHAPTER VII: *Philosophical reflections, the like not to be found in any light French romance. Mr. Booby's grave advice to Joseph, and Fanny's encounter with a beau.*

HABIT, my good reader, hath so vast a prevalence over the human mind that there is scarce anything too strange or too strong to be asserted of it. The story of the miser, who, from long accustoming to cheat others, came at last to cheat himself, and with great delight and triumph picked his own pocket of a guinea to convey to his hoard, is not impossible or improbable. In like manner it fares with the practisers of deceit, who, from having long deceived their acquaintance, gain at last a power of deceiving themselves, and acquire that very opinion (however false) of their own abilities, excellencies, and virtues, into which they have for years perhaps endeavoured to betray their neighbours. Now, reader, to apply this observation to my present purpose, thou must know that as the passion generally called love exercises most of the talents of the female or fair world, so in this they now and then discover a small inclination to deceit; for which thou wilt not be angry with the beautiful creatures when thou hast considered, that at the age of seven, or something earlier, miss is instructed by her mother that master is a very monstrous kind of animal who will, if she suffers him to come too near her, infallibly eat her up, and grind her to pieces; that, so far from kissing or toying with him on her own accord, she must not admit him to kiss or toy with her; and, lastly, that she must never have any affection towards him, for if she should, all her friends in petticoats would esteem her a traitress, point at her, and hunt her out of their society. These impressions being first received, are farther and deeper inculcated by their schoolmistresses and companions, so that by the age of ten they have contracted such a dread and abhorrence of the above-named monster, that, whenever they see him, they fly from him as the innocent hare doth from the greyhound. Hence, to the age of fourteen or fifteen, they entertain a mighty antipathy to master; they resolve, and frequently profess, that they will never have any commerce with him, and entertain fond hopes of passing their lives out of his reach, of the possibility of which they have so visible an example in their good maiden aunt. But when they arrive at this period, and have now passed their second climacteric, when their wisdom, grown riper, begins to see a little farther, and, from almost daily falling in master's way, to apprehend the great difficulty of keeping out of it; and when they observe him look often at them, and sometimes very eagerly and earnestly too (for the monster seldom takes any notice of them till at this age), they then begin to think of their danger; and as they perceive they cannot easily avoid him, the wiser part bethink themselves of providing by other means for their security. They endeavour, by all the methods they can invent, to render themselves so amiable in his eyes that he may have no inclination to hurt them; in which they generally succeed so well that his eyes, by frequent languishing, soon lessen their idea of his fierceness, and so far abate their fears that they venture to parley with him; and when they perceive him so different from what he hath been described, all gentleness, softness, kindness, tenderness, fondness, their dreadful apprehensions vanish in a moment; and now (it being usual with the human mind to skip from one extreme to its opposite, as easily, and almost as suddenly, as a bird from one bough to another) love instantly succeeds to fear; but as it happens to persons who have in their infancy been thoroughly frightened with certain no-persons called ghosts that they retain their dread of those beings after they are convinced that there are no such things, so these young ladies, though they no longer apprehend devouring, cannot so entirely shake off all that hath been instilled into them; they still entertain the idea of that censure which was so strongly imprinted on their tender minds, to which the declarations of abhorrence they every day hear from their companions greatly contribute. To avoid this censure, therefore, is now their only care; for which purpose they still pretend the same aversion to the monster, and, the more they love him, the more ardently they counterfeit the antipathy. By the continual and constant practise of which deceit on others, they at length impose on themselves, and really believe they hate what they love. Thus, indeed, it happened to Lady Booby, who loved Joseph long before she knew it, and now loved him much more than she suspected. She had, indeed, from the time of his sister's arrival in the quality of her niece, and from the instant she viewed him in the dress and character of a gentleman, began to conceive secretly a design which love had concealed from herself, till a dream betrayed it to her.

She had no sooner risen, than she sent for her nephew. When he came to her, after many compliments on his choice she told him he might perceive in her condescension to admit her own servant to her table that she looked on the family of Andrews as his relations, and indeed hers; that as he had married into such a family, it became him to endeavour by all methods to raise it as much as possible. At length she advised him to use all his art to dissuade Joseph from his intended match, which would still enlarge their relation to meanness and poverty; concluding that, by a commission in the army, or some other genteel employment, he might soon put young Mr. Andrews on the foot of a gentleman, and that being once done, his accomplishments might quickly gain him an alliance which would not be to their discredit.

Her nephew heartily embraced this proposal, and finding Mr. Joseph with his wife, at his return to her chamber, he immediately began thus: "My love to my dear Pamela, brother, will extend to all her relations, nor shall I show them less respect than if I had married into the family of a duke. I hope I have given you some early testimonies of this, and shall continue to give you daily more. You will excuse me therefore, brother, if my concern for your interest makes me mention what may be, perhaps, disagreeable to you to hear, but I must insist upon it that, if you have any value for my alliance or my friendship, you will decline any thoughts of engaging farther with a girl who is, as you are a relation of mine, so much beneath you. I know there may be at first some difficulty in your compliance, but that will daily diminish; and you will in the end sincerely thank me for my advice. I own, indeed, the girl is handsome; but beauty alone is a poor ingredient, and will make but an uncomfortable marriage." "Sir," said Joseph, "I assure you her beauty is her least perfection, nor do I know a virtue which that young creature is not possessed of." "As to her virtues," answered Mr. Booby, "you can be yet but a slender judge of them; but if she had never so many, you will find her equal in these among her superiors in birth and fortune, which now you are to esteem on a footing with yourself; at least I will take care they shall shortly be so, unless you prevent me by degrading yourself with such a match, a match I have hardly patience to think of, and which would break the hearts of your parents, who now rejoice in the expectation of seeing you make a figure in the world." "I know not," replied Joseph, "that my parents have any power over my inclinations, nor am I obliged to sacrifice my happiness to their whim or ambition; besides, I shall be very sorry to see that the unexpected advancement of my sister should so suddenly inspire them with this wicked pride and make them despise their equals. I am resolved on no account to quit my dear Fanny; no, though I could raise her as high above her present station as you have raised my sister." "Your sister, as well as myself," said Booby, "are greatly obliged to you for the comparison, but, sir, she is not worthy to be compared in beauty to my Pamela, nor hath she half her merit. And besides, sir, as you civilly throw my marriage with your sister in my teeth, I must teach you the wide difference between us: my fortune enabled me to please myself, and it would have been as overgrown a folly in me to have omitted it, as in you to do it." "My fortune enables me to please myself likewise," said Joseph, "for all my pleasure is centered in Fanny, and whilst I have health, I shall be able to support her with my labour in that station to which she was born and with which she is content." "Brother," said Pamela, "Mr. Booby advises you as a friend; and no doubt my papa and mamma will be of his opinion, and will have great reason to be angry with you for destroying what his goodness hath done and throwing down our family again after he hath raised it. It would become you better, brother, to pray for the assistance of grace against such a passion than to indulge it." "Sure, sister, you are not in earnest; I am sure she is your equal, at least." "She was my equal," answered Pamela, "but I am no longer Pamela Andrews; I am now this gentleman's lady, and, as such, am above her. I hope I shall never behave with an unbecoming pride: but, at the same time, I shall always endeavour to know myself, and question not the assistance of grace to that purpose." They were now summoned to breakfast and thus ended their discourse for the present, very little to the satisfaction of any of the parties.

Fanny was now walking in an avenue at some distance from the house, where Joseph had promised to take the first opportunity of coming to her. She had not a shilling in the world, and had subsisted, ever since her return, entirely on the charity of Parson Adams. A young gentleman, attended by many servants, came up to her and asked her if that was not the Lady Booby's house before him? This, indeed, he well knew, but had framed the question for no other reason than to make her look up, and discover if her face was equal to the delicacy of her shape. He no sooner saw it than he was struck with amazement. He stopped his horse and swore she was the most beautiful creature he ever beheld. Then instantly alighting, and delivering his horse to his servant, he rapped out half a dozen oaths that he would kiss her; to which she at first submitted, begging he would not be rude, but he was not satisfied with the civility of a salute, nor even with the rudest attack he could make on her lips, but caught her in his arms, and endeavoured to kiss her breasts, which with all her strength she resisted, and, as our spark was not of the Herculean race, with some difficulty prevented. The young gentleman, being soon out of breath in the struggle, quitted her, and, remounting his horse, called one of his servants to him, whom he ordered to stay behind with her and make her any offers whatever to prevail on her to return home with him in the evening and to assure her he would take her into keeping. He then rode on with his other servants and arrived at the lady's house, to whom he was a distant relation and was come to pay a visit.

The trusty fellow, who was employed in an office he had been long accustomed to, discharged his part with all the fidelity and dexterity imaginable, but to no purpose. She was entirely deaf to his offers, and rejected them with the utmost disdain. At last the pimp, who had perhaps more warm blood about him than his master, began to solicit for himself; he told her, though he was a servant, he was a man of some fortune, which he would make her mistress of—and this without any insult to her virtue, for that he would marry her. She answered, if his master himself, or the greatest lord in the land, would marry her, she would refuse him. At last, being weary with persuasions, and on fire with charms which would have almost kindled a flame in the bosom of an ancient philosopher or modern divine, he fastened his horse to the ground and attacked her with much more force than the gentleman had exerted. Poor Fanny would not have been able to resist his rudeness a short time, but the deity who presides over chaste love sent her Joseph to her assistance. He no sooner came within sight, and perceived her struggling with a man, than like a cannon ball, or like lightning, or anything that is swifter, if anything be, he ran towards her, and coming up just as the ravisher had torn her handkerchief from her breast, before his lips had touched that seat of innocence and bliss, he dealt him so lusty a blow in that part of his neck which a rope would have become with the utmost propriety that the fellow staggered backwards, and, perceiving that he had to do with something rougher than the little, tender, trembling hand of Fanny, he quitted her, and, turning about, saw his rival, with fire flashing from his eyes, again ready to assail him; and, indeed, before he could well defend himself, or return the first blow, he received a second, which, had it fallen on that part of the stomach to which it was directed, would have been probably the last he would have had any occasion for, but the ravisher lifting up his hand, drove the blow upwards to his mouth, whence it dislodged three of his teeth; and now not conceiving any extraordinary affection for the beauty of Joseph's person, nor being extremely pleased with this method of salutation, he collected all his force, and aimed a blow at Joseph's breast, which he artfully parried with one fist so that it lost its force entirely in the air, and stepping one foot backward he darted his fist so fiercely at his enemy that had he not caught it in his hand (for he was a boxer of no inferior fame) it must have tumbled him on the ground. And now the ravisher meditated another blow, which he aimed at that part of the breast where the heart is lodged; Joseph did not catch it as before, yet so prevented its aim that it fell directly on his nose, but with abated force. Joseph then moving both fist and foot forwards at the same time, threw his head so dexterously into the stomach of the ravisher that he fell a lifeless lump on the field, where he lay many minutes breathless and motionless.

When Fanny saw her Joseph receive a blow in his face, and blood running in a stream from him, she began to tear her hair, and invoke all human and divine power to his assistance. She was not, however, long under this affliction before Joseph, having conquered his enemy, ran to her and assured her he was not hurt; she then instantly fell on her knees and thanked God that he had made Joseph the means of her rescue and at the same time preserved him from being injured in attempting it. She offered with her handkerchief to wipe his blood from his face, but he, seeing his rival attempting to recover his legs, turned to him and asked him if he had enough. To which the other answered he had, for he believed he had fought with the devil instead of a man, and, loosening his horse, said he should not have attempted the wench if he had known she had been so well provided for.

Fanny now begged Joseph to return with her to Parson Adams and to promise that he would leave her no more. These were propositions so agreeable to Joseph that, had he heard them, he would have given an immediate assent; but indeed his eyes were now his only sense, for you may remember, reader, that the ravisher had tore her handkerchief from Fanny's neck, by which he had discovered such a sight that Joseph had declared all the statues he ever beheld were so much inferior to it in beauty that it was more capable of converting a man into a statue, than of being imitated by the greatest master of that art. This modest creature, whom no warmth in summer could ever induce to expose her charms to the wanton sun, a modesty to which perhaps they owed their inconceivable whiteness, had stood many minutes bare-necked in the presence of Joseph, before her apprehension of his danger, and the horror of seeing his blood, would suffer her once to reflect on what concerned herself; till at last, when the cause of her concern had vanished, an admiration at his silence, together with observing the fixed position of his eyes, produced an idea in the lovely maid which brought more blood into her face than had flowed from Joseph's nostrils. The snowy hue of her bosom was likewise exchanged to vermilion, at the instant when she clapped her handkerchief around her neck. Joseph saw the uneasiness she suffered, and immediately removed his eyes from an object in surveying which he had felt the greatest delight which the organs of sight were capable of conveying to his soul—so great was his fear of offending her, and so truly did his passion for her deserve the noble name of love.

Fanny, being recovered from her confusion, which was almost equalled by what Joseph had felt from observing it, again mentioned her request; this was instantly and gladly complied with, and together they crossed two or three fields, which brought them to the habitation of Mr. Adams.

CHAPTER VIII: *A discourse which happened between Mr. Adams, Mrs. Adams, Joseph, and Fanny, with some behaviour of Mr. Adams, which will be called by some few readers very low, absurd, and unnatural.*

THE parson and his wife had just ended a long dispute when the lovers came to the door. Indeed, this young couple had been the subject of the dispute, for Mrs. Adams was one of those prudent people who never do anything to injure their families, or perhaps one of those good mothers who would even stretch their conscience to serve their children. She had long entertained hopes of seeing her eldest daughter succeed Mrs. Slipslop, and of making her second son an exciseman by Lady Booby's interest. These were expectations she could not endure the thought of quitting, and was therefore very uneasy to see her husband so resolute to oppose the lady's intention in Fanny's affair. She told him it behoved every man to take the first care of his family; that he had a wife and six children, the maintaining and providing for whom would be business enough for him, without intermeddling in other folks' affairs; that he had always preached up submission to superiors and would do ill to give an example of the contrary behaviour in his own conduct; that if Lady Booby did wrong, she must answer for it herself, and the sin would not lie at their door; that Fanny had been a servant, and bred up in the lady's own family, and consequently she must have known more of her than they did, and it was very improbable, if she had behaved herself well, that the lady would have been so bitterly her enemy; that perhaps he was too much inclined to think well of her, because she was handsome, but handsome women were often no better than they should be; that G— made ugly women as well as handsome ones, and that if a woman had virtue, it signified nothing whether she had beauty or no. For all which reasons she concluded he should oblige the lady, and stop the future publication of the banns. But all these excellent arguments had no effect on the parson, who persisted in doing his duty without regarding the consequence it might have on his worldly interest. He endeavoured to answer her as well as he could, to which she had just finished her reply (for she had always the last word everywhere but at church), when Joseph and Fanny entered their kitchen, where the parson and his wife then sat at breakfast over some bacon and cabbage. There was a coldness in the civility of Mrs. Adams which persons of accurate speculation might have observed but escaped her present guests; indeed, it was a good deal covered by the heartiness of Adams, who no sooner heard that Fanny had neither eat nor drank that morning than he presented her a bone of bacon he had just been gnawing, being the only remains of his provision, and then ran nimbly to the tap and produced a mug of small beer, which he called ale; however, it was the best in his house. Joseph, addressing himself to the parson, told him the discourse which had passed between Squire Booby, his sister, and himself concerning Fanny; he then acquainted him with the dangers whence he had rescued her and communicated some apprehensions on her account. He concluded that he should never have an easy moment till Fanny was absolutely his, and begged that he might be suffered to fetch a licence, saying he could easily borrow the money. The parson answered that he had already given his sentiments concerning a licence, and that a very few days would make it unnecessary. "Joseph," says he, "I wish this haste doth not arise rather from your impatience than your fear, but as it certainly springs from one of these causes, I will examine both. Of each of these therefore in their turn, and first, for the first of these, namely, impatience. Now, child, I must inform you that if, in your purposed marriage with this young woman, you have no intention but the indulgence of carnal appetites, you are guilty of a very heinous sin. Marriage was ordained for nobler purposes, as you will learn when you hear the service provided on that occasion read to you. Nay, perhaps, if you are a good lad, I, child, shall give you a sermon *gratis,* wherein I shall demonstrate how little regard ought to be had to the flesh on such occasions. The text will be, child, Matthew the 5th, and part of the 28th verse, 'Whosoever looketh on a woman so as to lust after her.' The latter part I shall omit, as foreign to my purpose. Indeed, all such brutal lusts and affections are to be greatly subdued, if not totally eradicated, before the vessel can be said to be consecrated to honour. To marry with a view of gratifying those inclinations is a prostitution of that holy ceremony, and must entail a curse on all who so lightly undertake it. If, therefore, this haste arises from impatience, you are to correct, and not give way to it. Now, as to the second head which I proposed to speak to, namely, fear: It argues a diffidence highly criminal of that Power in which alone we should put our trust, seeing we may be well assured that He is able, not only to defeat the designs of our enemies, but even to turn their hearts. Instead of taking, therefore, any unjustifiable or desperate means to rid ourselves of fear, we should resort to prayer only on these occasions, and we may be then certain of obtaining what is best for us. When any accident threatens us, we are not to despair, nor, when it overtakes us, to grieve; we must submit in all things to the will of Providence, and set our affections so much on nothing here, that we cannot quit it without reluctance. You are a young man, and can know but little of this world; I am older, and have seen a great deal. All passions are criminal in their excess; and even love itself, if it is not subservient to our duty, may render us blind to it. Had Abraham so loved his son Isaac as to refuse the sacrifice required, is there any of us who would not condemn him? Joseph, I know your many good qualities, and value you for them, but, as I am to render an account of your soul, which is committed to my cure, I cannot see any fault without reminding you of it. You are too much inclined to passion, child, and have set your affections so absolutely on this young woman that, if G— required her at your hands, I fear you would reluctantly part with her. Now, believe me, no Christian ought so to set his heart on any person or thing in this world but that, whenever it shall be required or taken from him in any manner by divine Providence, he may be able, peaceably, quietly, and contentedly to resign it." At which words one came hastily in and acquainted Mr. Adams, that his youngest son was drowned. He stood silent a moment, and soon began to stamp about the room and deplore his loss with the bitterest agony. Joseph, who was overwhelmed with concern likewise, recovered himself sufficiently to endeavour to comfort the parson, in which attempt he used many arguments that he had at several times remembered out of his own discourses, both in private and public (for he was a great enemy to the passions, and preached nothing more than the conquest of them by reason and grace), but he was not at leisure now to hearken to his advice. "Child, child," said he, "do not go about impossibilities. Had it been any other of my children, I could have borne it with patience, but my little prattler, the darling and comfort of my old age—the little wretch, to be snatched out of life just at his entrance into it, the sweetest, best-tempered boy, who never did a thing to offend me. It was but this morning I gave him his first lesson in *Quae Genus.*[1] This was the very book he learnt; poor child! it is of no further use to thee now. He would have made the best scholar and have been an ornament to the church—such parts, and such goodness, never met in one so young." "And the handsomest lad too," says Mrs. Adams, recovering from a swoon in Fanny's arms. "My poor Jacky, shall I never see thee more?" cries the parson. "Yes, surely," says Joseph, "and in a better place, you will meet again never to part more." I believe the parson did not hear these words, for he paid little regard to them but went on lamenting, whilst the tears trickled down into his bosom. At last he cried out, "Where is my little darling?" and was sallying out, when, to his great surprise and joy, in which I hope the reader will sympathize, he met his son, in a wet condition indeed, but alive, and running towards him. The person who brought the news of his misfortune had been a little too eager, as people sometimes are, from, I believe, no very good principle, to relate ill news, and seeing him fall into the river, instead of running to his assistance directly ran to acquaint his father of a fate which he had concluded to be inevitable, but whence the child was relieved by the same poor pedlar who had relieved his father before from a less distress. The parson's joy was now as extravagant as his grief had been before; he kissed and embraced his son a thousand times, and danced about the room like one frantic, but as soon as he discovered the face of his old friend the pedlar, and heard the fresh obligation he had to him, what were his sensations? Not those which two courtiers feel in one another's embraces; not those with which a great man receives the vile treacherous engines of his wicked purposes; not those with which a worthless younger brother wishes his elder joy of a son, or a man congratulates his rival on his obtaining a mistress, a place, or an honour. No, reader, he felt the ebullition, the overflowings, of a full, honest, open heart towards the person who had conferred a real obligation, and of which, if thou canst not conceive an idea within, I will not vainly endeavour to assist thee.

When these tumults were over, the parson, taking Joseph aside, proceeded thus: "No, Joseph, do not give too much way to thy passions, if thou dost expect happiness." The patience of Joseph, nor perhaps of Job, could bear no longer; he interrupted the parson, saying it was easier to give advice than take it, nor did he perceive he could so entirely conquer himself when he apprehended he had lost his son, or when he found him recovered. "Boy," replied Adams, raising his voice, "it doth not become green heads to advise grey hairs. Thou art ignorant of the tenderness of fatherly affection: when thou art a father, thou wilt be capable then only of knowing what a father can feel. No man is obliged to impossibilities; and the loss of a child is one of those great trials where our grief may be allowed to become immoderate." "Well, sir," cries Joseph, "and if I love a mistress as well as you your child, surely her loss would grieve me equally." "Yes, but such love is foolishness, and wrong in itself, and ought to be conquered," answered Adams; "it savours too much of the flesh." "Sure, sir," says Joseph, "it is not sinful to love my wife, no, not even to dote on her to distraction!" "Indeed but it is," says Adams. "Every man ought to love his wife, no doubt—we are commanded so to do—but we ought to love her with moderation and discretion." "I am afraid I shall be guilty of some sin in spite of all my endeavours," says Joseph, "for I shall love without any moderation, I am sure." "You talk foolishly and childishly," cries Adams. "Indeed," says Mrs. Adams, who had listened to the latter part of their conversations, "you talk more foolishly yourself. I hope, my dear, you will never preach any such doctrines as that husbands can love their wives too well. If I knew you had such a sermon in the house, I am sure I would burn it, and I declare, if I had not been convinced you had loved me as well as you could, I can answer for myself, I should have hated and despised you. Marry come up! Fine doctrine, indeed! A wife hath a right to insist on her husband's loving her as much as ever he can, and he is a sinful villain who doth not. Doth he not promise to love her, and to comfort her, and to cherish her, and all that? I am sure I remember it all as well as if I had repeated it over but yesterday, and shall never forget it. Besides, I am certain you do not preach as you practise, for you have been a loving and a cherishing husband to me, that's the truth on't, and why you should endeavour to put such wicked nonsense into this young man's head I cannot devise. Don't hearken to him, Mr. Joseph; be as good a husband as you are able, and love your wife with all your body and soul too." Here a violent rap at the door put an end to their discourse, and produced a scene which the reader will find in the next chapter.

CHAPTER IX: *A visit which the good Lady Booby and her polite friend paid to the parson.*

THE Lady Booby had no sooner had an account from the gentleman of his meeting a wonderful beauty near her house, and perceived the raptures with which he spoke of her, than, immediately concluding it must be Fanny, she began to meditate a design of bringing them better acquainted, and to entertain hopes that the fine clothes, presents, and promises of this youth would prevail on her to abandon Joseph; she therefore proposed to her company a walk in the fields before dinner, when she led them towards Mr. Adams's house, and, as she approached it, told them if they pleased she would divert them with one of the most ridiculous sights they had ever seen, which was an old foolish parson, who, she said laughing, kept a wife and six brats on a salary of about twenty pounds a year, adding, that there was not such another ragged family in the parish. They all readily agreed to this visit, and arrived whilst Mrs. Adams was declaiming as in the last chapter. Beau Didapper, which was the name of the young gentleman we have seen riding towards Lady Booby's, with his cane mimicked the rap of a London footman at the door. The people within, namely, Adams, his wife, and three children, Joseph, Fanny, and the pedlar, were all thrown into confusion by this knock, but Adams went directly to the door, which being opened, the Lady Booby and her company walked in and were received by the parson with about two hundred bows, and by his wife with as many curtseys; the latter telling the lady she was ashamed to be seen in such a pickle, and that her house was in such a litter, but that if she had expected such an honour from her ladyship she should have found her in a better manner. The parson made no apologies, though he was in his half cassock, and a flannel night-cap. He said they were heartily welcome to his poor cottage, and, turning to Mr. Didapper, cried out, "*Non mea renidet in domo lacunar.*" [1] The beau answered he did not understand Welsh, at which the parson stared and made no reply.

Mr. Didapper, or Beau Didapper, was a young gentleman of about four foot five inches in height. He wore his own hair, though the scarcity of it might have given him sufficient excuse for a periwig. His face was thin and pale; the shape of his body and legs none of the best, for he had very narrow shoulders, and no calf; and his gait might more properly be called hopping than walking. The qualifications of his mind were well adapted to his person. We shall handle them first negatively. He was not entirely ignorant; for he could talk a little French, and sing two or three Italian songs; he had lived too much in the world to be bashful, and too much at court to be proud; he seemed not much inclined to avarice, for he was profuse in his expenses, nor had he all the features of prodigality, for he never gave a shilling; no hater of women, for he always dangled after them, yet so little subject to lust that he had, among those who knew him best, the character of great moderation in his pleasures. No drinker of wine, nor so addicted to passion but that a hot word or two from an adversary made him immediately cool.

Now, to give him only a dash or two on the affirmative side: though he was born to an immense fortune, he chose, for the pitiful and dirty consideration of a place of little consequence, to depend entirely on the will of a fellow whom they call a great man, who treated him with the utmost disrespect and exacted of him a plenary obedience to his commands, which he implicitly submitted to at the expense of his conscience, his honour, and of his country, in which he had himself so very large a share. And to finish his character, as he was entirely well satisfied with his own person and parts, so he was very apt to ridicule and laugh at any imperfection in another. Such was the little person, or rather thing, that hopped after Lady Booby into Mr. Adams's kitchen.

The parson and his company retreated from the chimney-side where they had been seated to give room to the lady and hers. Instead of returning any of the curtseys or extraordinary civility of Mrs. Adams, the lady, turning to Mr. Booby, cried out, "*Quelle bête! Quel animal!*" And presently after discovering Fanny (for she did not need the circumstance of her standing by Joseph to assure the identity of her person), she asked the beau whether he did not think her a pretty girl. "Begad, madam," answered he, " 'tis the very same I met." "I did not imagine," replied the lady, "you had so good a taste." "Because I never liked you, I warrant," cries the beau. "Ridiculous!" said she: "you knew you was always my aversion." "I would never mention aversion," answered the beau, "with that face; * dear Lady Booby, wash your face before you mention aversion, I beseech you." He then laughed, and turned about to coquet it with Fanny.

Mrs. Adams had been all this time begging and praying the ladies to sit down, a favour which she at last obtained. The little boy to whom the accident had happened still keeping his place by the fire, was chid by his mother for not being more mannerly, but Lady Booby took his part, and, commending his beauty, told the parson he was his very picture. She then, seeing a book in his hand, asked if he could read. "Yes," cried Adams, "a little Latin, madam: he is just got into *Quae Genus.*" "A fig for quere genius," answered she, "let me hear him read a little English." "*Lege,* Dick, *lege,*" said Adams, but the boy made no answer till he saw the parson knit his brows, and then cried, "I don't understand you, Father." "How, boy!" says Adams; "what doth *lego* make in the imperative mood? *Legito,* doth it not?" "Yes," answered Dick. "And what besides?" says the father. "*Lege,*" quoth the son, after some hesitation. "A good boy," says the father. "And now, child, what is the English of *lego?*" To which the boy, after long puzzling, answered, he could not tell. "How," cries Adams, in a passion, "what, hath the water washed away your learning? Why, what is Latin for the English verb, read? Consider before you speak." The child considered some time, and then the parson cried twice or thrice "*Le—, le—.*" Dick answered, "*Lego.*" "Very well; and then what is the English," says the parson, "of the verb *lego?*" "To read," cried Dick. "Very well," said the parson; "a good boy; you can do well if you will take pains. I assure your ladyship he is not much above eight years old, and is out of his *Propria quae Maribus*[2] already. Come, Dick, read to her ladyship," which she again desiring, in order to give the beau time and opportunity with Fanny, Dick began as in the following chapter.

CHAPTER X: *The history of two friends, which may afford an useful lesson to all those persons who happen to take up their residence in married families.*

"LEONARD and Paul were two friends." "Pronounce it Lennard, child," cried the parson. "Pray, Mr. Adams," says Lady Booby, "let your son read without interruption." Dick then proceeded. "Lennard and Paul were two friends, who, having been educated together at the same school, commenced a friendship which they preserved a long time for each other. It was so deeply fixed in both their minds that a long absence, during which they had maintained no correspondence, did not eradicate nor lessen it, but it revived in all its force at their first meeting, which was not till after fifteen years' absence, most of which time Lennard had spent in the East Indi-es." "Pronounce it short, Indies," says Adams. "Pray, sir, be quiet," says the lady. The boy repeated, "in the East Indies, whilst Paul had served his king and country in the army. In which different services they had found such different success that Lennard was now married and retired with a fortune of thirty thousand pound, and Paul was arrived to the degree of a lieutenant of foot and was not worth a single shilling.

"The regiment in which Paul was stationed happened to be ordered into quarters within a small distance from the estate which Lennard had purchased, and where he was settled. This latter, who was now become a country gentleman, and a justice of peace, came to attend the quarter-sessions in the town where his old friend was quartered, soon after his arrival. Some affair in which a soldier was concerned occasioned Paul to attend the justices. Manhood, and time, and the change of climate, had so much altered Lennard that Paul did not immediately recollect the features of his old acquaintance, but it was otherwise with Lennard. He knew Paul the moment he saw him, nor could he contain himself from quitting the bench and running hastily to embrace him. Paul stood at first a little surprised, but had soon sufficient information from his friend, whom he no sooner remembered than he returned his embrace with a passion which made many of the spectators laugh and gave to some few a much higher and more agreeable sensation.

"Not to detain the reader with minute circumstances, Lennard insisted on his friend's returning with him to his house that evening, which request was complied with, and leave for a month's absence for Paul obtained of the commanding officer.

"If it was possible for any circumstance to give any addition to the happiness which Paul proposed in this visit, he received that additional pleasure by finding, on his arrival at his friend's house, that his lady was an old acquaintance which he had formerly contracted at his quarters, and who had always appeared to be of a most agreeable temper; a character she had ever maintained among her intimates, being of that number every individual of which is called quite the best sort of woman in the world.

"But, good as this lady was, she was still a woman, that is to say, an angel, and not an angel." "You must mistake, child," cries the parson, "for you read nonsense." "It is so in the book," answered the son. Mr. Adams was then silenced by authority, and Dick proceeded. "For though her person was of that kind to which men attribute the name of angel, yet in her mind she was perfectly woman. Of which a great degree of obstinacy gave the most remarkable and perhaps most pernicious instance.

"A day or two passed after Paul's arrival before any instances of this appeared, but it was impossible to conceal it long. Both she and her husband soon lost all apprehension from their friend's presence and fell to their disputes with as much vigour as ever. These were still pursued with the utmost ardour and eagerness, however trifling the causes were whence they first arose. Nay, however incredible it may seem, the little consequence of the matter in debate was frequently given as a reason for the fierceness of the contention, as thus: 'If you loved me, sure you would never dispute with me such a trifle as this.' The answer to which is very obvious, for the argument would hold equally on both sides, and was constantly retorted with some addition, as: 'I am sure I have much more reason to say so, who am in the right.' During all these disputes, Paul always kept strict silence and preserved an even countenance, without showing the least visible inclination to either party. One day, however, when madam had left the room in a violent fury, Lennard could not refrain from referring his cause to his friend. 'Was ever anything so unreasonable,' says he, 'as this woman? What shall I do with her? I dote on her to distraction, nor have I any cause to complain of more than this obstinacy in her temper; whatever she asserts, she will maintain against all the reason and conviction in the world. Pray give me your advice.' 'First,' says Paul, 'I will give my opinion, which is, flatly, that you are in the wrong; for supposing she is in the wrong, was the subject of your contention any ways material? What signified it whether you was married in a red or yellow waistcoat? for that was your dispute. Now suppose she was mistaken, as you love her you say so tenderly, and I believe she deserves it, would it not have been wiser to have yielded, though you certainly knew yourself in the right, than to give either her or yourself any uneasiness? For my own part, if ever I marry, I am resolved to enter into an agreement with my wife that in all disputes (especially about trifles), that party who is most convinced they are right, shall always surrender the victory, by which means we shall both be forward to give up the cause.' 'I own,' said Lennard, 'my dear friend,' shaking him by the hand, 'there is great truth and reason in what you say; and I will for the future endeavour to follow your advice.' They soon after broke up the conversation, and Lennard, going to his wife, asked her pardon and told her his friend had convinced him he had been in the wrong. She immediately began a vast encomium on Paul, in which he seconded her, and both agreed he was the worthiest and wisest man upon earth. When next they met, which was at supper, though she had promised not to mention what her husband told her, she could not forbear casting the kindest and most affectionate looks on Paul, and asked him with the sweetest voice whether she should help him to some potted woodcock? 'Potted partridge, my dear, you mean,' says the husband. 'My dear,' says she, 'I ask your friend if he will eat any potted woodcock, and I am sure I must know, who potted it.' 'I think I should know too who shot them,' replied the husband, 'and I am convinced that I have not seen a woodcock this year; however, though I know I am in the right, I submit, and the potted partridge is potted woodcock, if you desire to have it so.' 'It is equal to me,' says she, 'whether it is one or the other; but you would persuade one out of one's senses; to be sure, you are always in the right in your own opinion, but your friend, I believe, knows which he is eating.' Paul answered nothing, and the dispute continued, as usual, the greatest part of the evening. The next morning the lady accidentally meeting Paul, and being convinced he was her friend and of her side, accosted him thus: 'I am certain, sir, you have long since wondered at the unreasonableness of my husband. He is indeed, in other respects, a good sort of man, but so positive that no woman but one of my complying temper could possibly live with him. Why, last night, now, was ever any creature so unreasonable? I am certain you must condemn him. Pray, answer me, was he not in the wrong?' Paul, after a short silence, spoke as follows: 'I am sorry, madam, that as good manners obliges me to answer against my will, so an adherence to truth forces me to declare myself of a different opinion. To be plain and honest, you was entirely in the wrong; the cause I own not worth disputing, but the bird was undoubtedly a partridge.' 'Oh, sir!' replied the lady, 'I cannot possibly help your taste.' 'Madam,' returned Paul, 'that is very little material, for had it been otherwise, a husband might have expected submission.' 'Indeed! sir,' says she, 'I assure you!' 'Yes, madam,' cried he, 'he might, from a person of your excellent understanding; and pardon me for saying, such a condescension would have shown a superiority of sense even to your husband himself.' 'But, dear sir,' said she, 'why should I submit when I am in the right?' 'For that very reason,' answered he, 'it would be the greatest instance of affection imaginable; for can anything be a greater object of our compassion than a person we love in the wrong?' 'Aye, but I should endeavour,' said she, 'to set him right.' 'Pardon me, madam,' answered Paul: 'I will apply to your own experience, if you ever found your arguments had that effect. The more our judgements err, the less we are willing to own it; for my own part, I have always observed the persons who maintain the worst side in any contest are the warmest.' 'Why,' says she, 'I must confess there is truth in what you say, and I will endeavour to practise it.' The husband then coming in, Paul departed. And Lennard, approaching his wife with an air of good humour, told her he was sorry for their foolish dispute the last night but he was now convinced of his error. She answered, smiling, she believed she owed his condescension to his complacence; that she was ashamed to think a word had passed on so silly an occasion, especially as she was satisfied she had been mistaken. A little contention followed, but with the utmost good will to each other, and was concluded by her asserting that Paul had thoroughly convinced her she had been in the wrong. Upon which they both united in the praises of their common friend.

"Paul now passed his time with great satisfaction, these disputes being much less frequent, as well as shorter than usual; but the devil, or some unlucky accident in which perhaps the devil had no hand, shortly put an end to his happiness. He was now eternally the private referee of every difference, in which, after having perfectly, as he thought, established the doctrine of submission, he never scrupled to assure both privately that they were in the right in every argument, as before he had followed the contrary method. One day a violent litigation happened in his absence and both parties agreed to refer it to his decision. The husband professing himself sure the decision would be in his favour, the wife answered he might be mistaken; for she believed his friend was convinced how seldom she was to blame—and that if he knew all——The husband replied: 'My dear, I have no desire of any retrospect, but I believe, if you knew all too, you would not imagine my friend so entirely on your side.' 'Nay,' says she, 'since you provoke me, I will mention one instance. You may remember our dispute about sending Jacky to school in cold weather, which point I gave up to you from mere compassion, knowing myself to be in the right, and Paul himself told me afterwards he thought me so.' 'My dear,' replied the husband, 'I will not scruple your veracity, but I assure you solemnly, on my applying to him, he gave it absolutely on my side and said he would have acted in the same manner.' They then proceeded to produce numberless other instances, in all which Paul had, on vows of secrecy, given his opinion on both sides. In the conclusion, both believing each other, they fell severely on the treachery of Paul, and agreed that he had been the occasion of almost every dispute which had fallen out between them. They then became extremely loving, and so full of condescension on both sides that they vied with each other in censuring their own conduct, and jointly vented their indignation on Paul, whom the wife, fearing a bloody consequence, earnestly entreated her husband to suffer quietly to depart the next day, which was the time fixed for his return to quarters, and then drop his acquaintance.

"However ungenerous this behaviour in Lennard may be esteemed, his wife obtained a promise from him (though with difficulty) to follow her advice; but they both expressed such unusual coldness that day to Paul that he, who was quick of apprehension, taking Lennard aside, pressed him so home that he at last discovered the secret. Paul acknowledged the truth, but told him the design with which he had done it. To which the other answered he would have acted more friendly to have let him into the whole design, for that he might have assured himself of his secrecy. Paul replied, with some indignation, he had given him a sufficient proof how capable he was of concealing a secret from his wife. Lennard returned with some warmth; he had more reason to upbraid him, for that he had caused most of the quarrels between them by his strange conduct, and might (if they had not discovered the affair to each other) have been the occasion of their separation. Paul then said."—But something now happened which put a stop to Dick's reading, and of which we shall treat in the next chapter.

CHAPTER XI: *In which the history is continued.*

JOSEPH ANDREWS had borne with great uneasiness the impertinence of Beau Didapper to Fanny, who had been talking pretty freely to her, and offering her settlements, but the respect to the company had restrained him from interfering whilst the beau confined himself to the use of his tongue only; but the said beau, watching an opportunity whilst the ladies' eyes were disposed another way, offered a rudeness to her with his hands, which Joseph no sooner perceived than he presented him with so sound a box on the ear that it conveyed him several paces from where he stood. The ladies immediately screamed out, rose from their chairs; and the beau, as soon as he recovered himself, drew his hanger, which Adams observing, snatched up the lid of a pot in his left hand, and covering himself with it as with a shield, without any weapon of offence in his other hand, stepped in before Joseph and exposed himself to the enraged beau, who threatened such perdition and destruction that it frighted the women, who were all got in a huddle together, out of their wits even to hear his denunciations of vengeance. Joseph was of a different complexion, and begged Adams to let his rival come on, for he had a good cudgel in his hand and did not fear him. Fanny now fainted into Mrs. Adams's arms and the whole room was in confusion, when Mr. Booby, passing by Adams, who lay snug under the pot-lid, came up to Didapper and insisted on his sheathing the hanger, promising he should have satisfaction; which Joseph declared he would give him and fight him at any weapon whatever. The beau now sheathed his hanger, and, taking out a pocket-glass, and vowing vengeance all the time, readjusted his hair; the parson deposited his shield; and Joseph, running to Fanny, soon brought her back to life. Lady Booby chid Joseph for his insult on Didapper; but he answered he would have attacked an army in the same cause.

"What cause?" said the lady. "Madam," answered Joseph, "he was rude to that young woman." "What," says the lady, "I suppose he would have kissed the wench, and is a gentleman to be struck for such an offer? I must tell you, Joseph, these airs do not become you." "Madam," said Mr. Booby, "I saw the whole affair, and I do not commend my brother, for I cannot perceive why he should take upon him to be this girl's champion." "I can commend him," says Adams: "he is a brave lad, and it becomes any man to be the champion of the innocent; and he must be the basest coward who would not vindicate a woman with whom he is on the brink of marriage." "Sir," says Mr. Booby, "my brother is not a proper match for such a young woman as this."—"No," says Lady Booby, "nor do you, Mr. Adams, act in your proper character by encouraging any such doings, and I am very much surprised you should concern yourself in it. I think your wife and family your properer care." "Indeed, madam, your ladyship says very true," answered Mrs. Adams: "he talks a pack of nonsense, that the whole parish are his children. I am sure I don't understand what he means by it; it would make some women suspect he had gone astray, but I acquit him of that; I can read Scripture as well as he, and I never found that the parson was obliged to provide for other folks' children; and besides, he is but a poor curate, and hath little enough, as your ladyship knows, for me and mine." "You say very well, Mrs. Adams," quoth the Lady Booby, who had not spoken a word to her before; "you seem to be a very sensible woman, and I assure you your husband is acting a very foolish part and opposing his own interest, seeing my nephew is violently set against this match, and, indeed, I can't blame him; it is by no means one suitable to our family." In this manner the lady proceeded with Mrs. Adams, whilst the beau hopped about the room shaking his head, partly from pain and partly from anger, and Pamela was chiding Fanny for her assurance in aiming at such a match as her brother. Poor Fanny answered only with her tears, which had long since begun to wet her handkerchief; which Joseph perceiving, took her by the arm, and, wrapping it in his, carried her off, swearing he would own no relation to anyone who was an enemy to her he loved more than all the world. He went out with Fanny under his left arm, brandishing a cudgel in his right, and neither Mr. Booby nor the beau thought proper to oppose him. Lady Booby and her company made a very short stay behind him, for the lady's bell now summoned them to dress, for which they had just time before dinner.

Adams seemed now very much dejected, which his wife perceiving, began to apply some matrimonial balsam. She told him he had reason to be concerned, for that he had probably ruined his family with his tricks almost—but perhaps he was grieved for the loss of his two children, Joseph and Fanny. His eldest daughter went on: "Indeed, Father, it is very hard to bring strangers here to eat your children's bread out of their mouths. You have kept them ever since they came home, and for anything I see to the contrary may keep them a month longer: are you obliged to give her meat, tho'f she was never so handsome? But I don't see she is so much handsomer than other people. If people were to be kept for their beauty, she would scarce fare better than her neighbours, I believe. As for Mr. Joseph, I have nothing to say; he is a young man of honest principles, and will pay some time or other for what he hath. But for the girl—why doth she not return to her place she ran away from? I would not give such a vagabond slut a halfpenny, though I had a million of money; no, though she was starving." "Indeed but I would," cries little Dick, "and Father, rather than poor Fanny shall be starved, I will give her all this bread and cheese"—(offering what he held in his hand). Adams smiled on the boy, and told him he rejoiced to see he was a Christian, and that if he had a halfpenny in his pocket, he would have given it him, telling him it was his duty to look upon all his neighbours as his brothers and sisters, and love them accordingly. "Yes, Papa," says he, "I love her better than my sisters; for she is handsomer than any of them." "Is she so, sauce-box?" says the sister, giving him a box on the ear; which the father would probably have resented had not Joseph, Fanny, and the pedlar at that instant returned together. Adams bid his wife prepare some food for their dinner; she said, Truly she could not, she had something else to do. Adams rebuked her for disputing his commands, and quoted many texts of Scripture to prove that the husband is the head of the wife, and she is to submit and obey. The wife answered it was blasphemy to talk Scripture out of church; that such things were very proper to be said in the pulpit, but that it was profane to talk them in common discourse. Joseph told Mr. Adams he was not come with any design to give him or Mrs. Adams any trouble but to desire the favour of all their company to the George (an alehouse in the parish), where he had bespoke a piece of bacon and greens for their dinner. Mrs. Adams, who was a very good sort of woman, only rather too strict in economics, readily accepted this invitation, as did the parson himself by her example, and away they all walked together, not omitting little Dick, to whom Joseph gave a shilling when he heard of his intended liberality to Fanny.

CHAPTER XII: *Where the good-natured reader will see something which will give him no great pleasure.*

THE pedlar had been very inquisitive from the time he had first heard that the great house in this parish belonged to the Lady Booby, and had learnt that she was the widow of Sir Thomas, and that Sir Thomas had bought Fanny, at about the age of three or four years, of a travelling woman; and, now their homely, but hearty meal was ended, he told Fanny he believed he could acquaint her with her parents. The whole company, especially she herself, started at this offer of the pedlar's. He then proceeded thus, while they all lent their strictest attention: "Though I am now contented with this humble way of getting my livelihood, I was formerly a gentleman, for so all those of my profession are called. In a word, I was a drummer in an Irish regiment of foot. Whilst I was in this honourable station, I attended an officer of our regiment into England, a-recruiting. In our march from Bristol to Froome (for since the decay of the woollen trade, the clothing towns have furnished the army with a great number of recruits) we overtook on the road a woman who seemed to be about thirty years old or thereabouts, not very handsome, but well enough for a soldier. As we came up to her she mended her pace, and, falling into discourse with our ladies (for every man of the party, namely, a sergeant, two private men, and a drum, were provided with their women except myself), she continued to travel on with us. I, perceiving she must fall to my lot, advanced presently to her, made love to her in our military way, and quickly succeeded to my wishes. We struck a bargain within a mile, and lived together as man and wife to her dying day." "I suppose," says Adams, interrupting him, "you were married with a licence, for I don't see how you could contrive to have the banns published while you were marching from place to place." "No, sir," said the pedlar, "we took a licence to go to bed together without any banns, "Aye! aye!" said the parson:

"*ex necessitate,* a licence may be allowable enough; but surely, surely, the other is the more regular and eligible way." The pedlar proceeded thus: "She returned with me to our regiment and removed with us from quarters to quarters, till at last, whilst we lay at Galway, she fell ill of a fever, and died. When she was on her death-bed she called me to her, and, crying bitterly, declared she could not depart this world without discovering a secret to me which, she said, was the only sin which sat heavy on her heart. She said she had formerly travelled in a company of Gipsies, who had made a practise of stealing away children; that, for her own part, she had been only once guilty of the crime, which, she said, she lamented more than all the rest of her sins, since probably it might have occasioned the death of the parents: 'for,' added she, 'it is almost impossible to describe the beauty of the young creature, which was about a year and a half old when I kidnapped it. We kept her (for she was a girl) above two years in our company, when I sold her myself, for three guineas, to Sir Thomas Booby, in Somersetshire.' Now, you know whether there are any more of that name in this county." "Yes," says Adams, "there are several Boobys who are squires, but I believe no baronet now alive; besides, it answers so exactly in every point, there is no room for doubt; but you have forgot to tell us the parents from whom the child was stolen." "Their name," answered the pedlar, "was Andrews. They lived about thirty miles from the Squire, and she told me that I might be sure to find them out by one circumstance, for that they had a daughter of a very strange name, Paměla, or Pamēla; some pronounced it one way, and some the other." Fanny, who had changed colour at the first mention of the name, now fainted away; Joseph turned pale, and poor Dicky began to roar; the parson fell on his knees, and ejaculated many thanksgivings that this discovery had been made before the dreadful sin of incest was committed; and the pedlar was struck with amazement, not being able to account for all this confusion, the cause of which was presently opened by the parson's daughter, who was the only unconcerned person (for the mother was chafing Fanny's temples, and taking the utmost care of her), and indeed, Fanny was the only creature whom the daughter would not have pitied in her situation; wherein, though we compassionate her ourselves, we shall leave her for a little while and pay a short visit to Lady Booby.

CHAPTER XIII: *The history, returning to the Lady Booby, gives some account of the terrible conflict in her breast between love and pride, with what happened on the present discovery.*

THE lady sat down with her company to dinner, but ate nothing. As soon as her cloth was removed, she whispered Pamela that she was taken a little ill, and desired her to entertain her husband and Beau Didapper. She then went up into her chamber, sent for Slipslop, threw herself on the bed in the agonies of love, rage, and despair, nor could she conceal these boiling passions longer without bursting. Slipslop now approached her bed and asked how her ladyship did; but instead of revealing her disorder, as she intended, she entered into a long encomium on the beauty and virtues of Joseph Andrews, ending at last with expressing her concern that so much tenderness should be thrown away on so despicable an object as Fanny. Slipslop, well knowing how to humour her mistress's frenzy, proceeded to repeat, with exaggeration if possible, all her mistress had said, and concluded with a wish that Joseph had been a gentleman, and that she could see her lady in the arms of such a husband. The lady then started from the bed, and, taking a turn or two cross the room, cried out with a deep sigh, "Sure, he would make any woman happy." "Your ladyship," says she, "would be the happiest woman in the world with him. A fig for custom and nonsense. What vails what people say? Shall I be afraid of eating sweetmeats because people may say I have a sweet tooth? If I had a mind to marry a man, all the world should not hinder me. Your ladyship hath no parents to tutelar your infections; besides, he is of your ladyship's family now, and as good a gentleman as any in the country, and why should not a woman follow her mind as well as a man? Why should not your ladyship marry the brother as well as your nephew the sister? I am sure if it was a fragrant crime I would not persuade your ladyship to it." "But, dear Slipslop," answered the lady, "if I could prevail on myself to commit such a weakness, there is that cursed Fanny in the way, whom the idiot—oh, how I hate and despise him!" "She, a little ugly minx," cries Slipslop; "leave her to me. I suppose your ladyship hath heard of Joseph's fitting with one of Mr. Didapper's servants about her; and his master hath ordered them to carry her away by force this evening. I'll take care they shall not want assistance. I was talking with this gentleman, who was below just when your ladyship sent for me." "Go back," says the Lady Booby, "this instant, for I expect Mr. Didapper will soon be going. Do all you can, for I am resolved this wench shall not be in our family; I will endeavour to return to the company, but let me know as soon as she is carried off." Slipslop went away and her mistress began to arraign her own conduct in the following manner:

"What am I doing? How do I suffer this passion to creep imperceptibly upon me! How many days are passed since I could have submitted to ask myself the question? Marry a footman! Distraction! Can I afterwards bear the eyes of my acquaintance? But I can retire from them; retire with one, in whom I propose more happiness than the world without him can give me! Retire—to feed continually on beauties, which my inflamed imagination sickens with eagerly gazing on; to satisfy every appetite, every desire, with their utmost wish. Ha! and do I dote thus on a footman! I despise, I detest my passion.—Yet why? Is he not generous, gentle, kind? —Kind to whom? to the meanest wretch, a creature below my consideration. Doth he not?—yes, he doth prefer her. Curse his beauties, and the little low heart that possesses them, which can basely descend to this despicable wench and be ungratefully deaf to all the honours I do him. And can I then love this monster? No, I will tear his image from my bosom, tread on him, spurn him. I will have those pitiful charms, which now I despise, mangled in my sight; for I will not suffer the little jade I hate to riot in the beauties I condemn. No, though I despise him myself; though I would spurn him from my feet, was he to languish at them, no other shall taste the happiness I scorn. Why do I say happiness? To me, it would be misery. To sacrifice my reputation, my character, my rank in life, to the indulgence of a mean and a vile appetite. How I detest the thought! How much more exquisite is the pleasure resulting from the reflection of virtue and prudence than the faint relish of what flows from vice and folly! Whither did I suffer this improper, this mad passion to hurry me, only by neglecting to summon the aids of reason to my assistance? Reason, which hath now set before me my desires in their proper colours, and immediately helped me to expel them. Yes, I thank Heaven and my pride, I have now perfectly conquered this unworthy passion, and if there was no obstacle in its way, my pride would disdain any pleasures which could be the consequence of so base, so mean, so vulgar——" Slipslop returned at this instant in a violent hurry, and with the utmost eagerness cried out, "Oh, madam, I have strange news. Tom the footman is just come from the George, where it seems Joseph and the rest of them are a-jinketting, and he says, there is a strange man who hath discovered that Fanny and Joseph are brother and sister." "How, Slipslop!" cries the lady in a surprise. "I had not time, madam," cries Slipslop, "to inquire about particles, but Tom says it is most certainly true."

This unexpected account entirely obliterated all those admirable reflections which the supreme power of reason had so wisely made just before. In short, when despair, which had more share in producing the resolutions of hatred we have seen taken, began to retreat, the lady hesitated a moment, and then, forgetting all the purport of her soliloquy, dismissed her woman again with orders to bid Tom attend her in the parlour, whither she now hastened to acquaint Pamela with the news. Pamela said she could not believe it, for she had never heard that her mother had lost any child, or that she had ever had any more than Joseph and herself. The lady flew into a violent rage with her, and talked of upstarts and disowning relations who had so lately been on a level with her. Pamela made no answer, but her husband, taking up her cause, severely reprimanded his aunt for her behaviour to his wife: he told her if it had been earlier in the evening she should not have stayed a moment longer in her house; that he was convinced, if this young woman could be proved her sister, she would readily embrace her as such, and he himself would do the same. He then desired the fellow might be sent for and the young woman with him; which Lady Booby immediately ordered, and, thinking proper to make some apology to Pamela for what she had said, it was readily accepted and all things reconciled.

The pedlar now attended, as did Fanny and Joseph, who would not quit her; the parson likewise was induced, not only by curiosity, of which he had no small portion, but his duty, as he apprehended it, to follow them, for he continued all the way to exhort them, who were now breaking their hearts, to offer up thanksgivings and be joyful for so miraculous an escape.

When they arrived at Booby Hall, they were presently called into the parlour, where the pedlar repeated the same story he had told before and insisted on the truth of every circumstance, so that all who heard him were extremely well satisfied of the truth except Pamela, who imagined, as she had never heard either of her parents mention such an accident, that it must be certainly false, and except the Lady Booby, who suspected the falsehood of the story from her ardent desire that it should be true, and Joseph, who feared its truth, from his earnest wishes that it might prove false.

Mr. Booby now desired them all to suspend their curiosity and absolute belief or disbelief till the next morning, when he expected old Mr. Andrews and his wife to fetch himself and Pamela home in his coach, and then they might be certain of certainly knowing the truth or falsehood of this relation, in which, he said, as there were many strong circumstances to induce their credit, so he could not perceive any interest the pedlar could have in inventing it, or in endeavouring to impose such a falsehood on them.

The Lady Booby, who was very little used to such company, entertained them all, *viz.*, her nephew, his wife, her brother and sister, the beau, and the parson, with great good humour at her own table. As to the pedlar, she ordered him to be made as welcome as possible by her servants. All the company in the parlour except the disappointed lovers, who sat sullen and silent, were full of mirth, for Mr. Booby had prevailed on Joseph to ask Mr. Didapper's pardon, with which he was perfectly satisfied. Many jokes passed between the beau and the parson, chiefly on each other's dress; these afforded much diversion to the company. Pamela chid her brother Joseph for the concern which he expressed at discovering a new sister. She said if he loved Fanny as he ought, with a pure affection, he had no reason to lament being related to her. Upon which Adams began to discourse on Platonic love, whence he made a quick transition to the joys in the next world, and concluded with strongly asserting that there was no such thing as pleasure in this. At which Pamela and her husband smiled on one another. This happy pair proposing to retire (for no other person gave the least symptom of desiring rest), they all repaired to several beds provided for them in the same house, nor was Adams himself suffered to go home, it being a stormy night. Fanny indeed often begged she might go home with the parson, but her stay was so strongly insisted on that she at last, by Joseph's advice, consented.

CHAPTER XIV: *Containing several curious night-adventures, in which Mr. Adams fell into many hairbreadth 'scapes, partly owing to his goodness, and partly to his inadvertency.*

ABOUT an hour after they had all separated (it being now past three in the morning) Beau Didapper, whose passion for Fanny permitted him not to close his eyes but had employed his imagination in contrivances how to satisfy his desires, at last hit on a method by which he hoped to effect it. He had ordered his servant to bring him word where Fanny lay, and had received his information; he therefore arose, put on his breeches and night-gown, and stole softly along the gallery which led to her apartment, and being come to the door, as he imagined it, he opened it with the least noise possible and entered the chamber. A savour now invaded his nostrils which he did not expect in the room of so sweet a young creature, and which might have probably had no good effect on a cooler lover. However, he groped out the bed with difficulty, for there was not a glimpse of light, and opening the curtains he whispered in Joseph's voice (for he was an excellent mimic), "Fanny, my angel, I am come to inform thee that I have discovered the falsehood of the story we last night heard. I am no longer thy brother, but thy lover, nor will I be delayed the enjoyment of thee one moment longer. You have sufficient assurances of my constancy not to doubt my marrying you, and it would be want of love to deny me the possession of thy charms." So saying, he disencumbered himself from the little clothes he had on, and, leaping into bed, embraced his angel, as he conceived her, with great rapture. If he was surprised at receiving no answer, he was no less pleased to find his hug returned with equal ardour. He remained not long in this sweet confusion, for both he and his paramour presently discovered their error. Indeed it was no other than the accomplished Slipslop whom he had engaged, but though she immediately knew the person whom she had mistaken for Joseph, he was at a loss to guess at the representative of Fanny. He had so little seen or taken notice of this gentlewoman that light itself would have afforded him no assistance in his conjecture. Beau Didapper no sooner had perceived his mistake than he attempted to escape from the bed with much greater haste than he had made to it, but the watchful Slipslop prevented him. For that prudent woman, being disappointed of those delicious offerings which her fancy had promised her pleasure, resolved to make an immediate sacrifice to her virtue. Indeed, she wanted an opportunity to heal some wounds which her late conduct had, she feared, given her reputation, and as she had a wonderful presence of mind she conceived the person of the unfortunate beau to be luckily thrown in her way to restore her lady's opinion of her impregnable chastity. At that instant, therefore, when he offered to leap from the bed, she caught fast hold of his shirt, at the same time roaring out, "O thou villain! who hast attacked my chastity, and, I believe, ruined me in my sleep; I will swear a rape against thee, I will prosecute thee with the utmost vengeance." The beau attempted to get loose, but she held him fast, and when he struggled, she cried out, "Murder! murder! rape! robbery! ruin!" At which words Parson Adams, who lay in the next chamber wakeful and meditating on the pedlar's discovery, jumped out of bed and without staying to put a rag of clothes on hastened into the apartment whence the cries proceeded. He made directly to the bed in the dark, where laying hold of the beau's skin (for Slipslop had torn his shirt almost off), and finding his skin extremely soft, and hearing him in a low voice begging Slipslop to let him go, he no longer doubted but this was the young woman in danger of ravishing, and immediately falling on the bed, and laying hold on Slipslop's chin, where he found a rough beard, his belief was confirmed; he therefore rescued the beau, who presently made his escape, and then, turning towards Slipslop, received such a cuff on his chops that, his wrath kindling instantly, he offered to return the favour so stoutly that had poor Slipslop received the fist, which in the dark passed by her and fell on the pillow, she would most probably have given up the ghost.—Adams, missing his blow, fell directly on Slipslop, who cuffed and scratched as well as she could; nor was he behindhand with her in his endeavours, but happily the darkness of the night befriended her.—She then cried, she was a woman; but Adams answered, she was rather the devil, and if she was, he would grapple with him; and being again irritated by another stroke on his chops, he gave her such a remembrance in the guts that she began to roar loud enough to be heard all over the house. Adams then seizing her by the hair (for her double-clout had fallen off in the scuffle) pinned her head down to the bolster, and then both called for lights together. The Lady Booby, who was as wakeful as any of her guests, had been alarmed from the beginning; and, being a woman of a bold spirit, she slipped on a night-gown, petticoat, and slippers, and taking a candle which always burnt in her chamber in her hand, she walked undauntedly to Slipslop's room, where she entered just at the instant as Adams had discovered, by the two mountains which Slipslop carried before her, that he was concerned with a female. He then concluded her to be a witch, and said he fancied those breasts gave suck to a legion of devils. Slipslop, seeing Lady Booby enter the room, cried, "Help! or I am ravished," with a most audible voice, and Adams, perceiving the light, turned hastily and saw the lady (as she did him) just as she came to the feet of the bed, nor did her modesty, when she found the naked condition of Adams, suffer her to approach farther. She then began to revile the parson as the wickedest of all men, and particularly railed at his impudence in choosing her house for the scene of his debaucheries, and her own woman for the object of his bestiality. Poor Adams had before discovered the countenance of his bed-fellow, and, now first recollecting he was naked, he was no less confounded than Lady Booby herself, and immediately whipped under the bed-clothes, whence the chaste Slipslop endeavoured in vain to shut him out. Then putting forth his head, on which, by way of ornament, he wore a flannel night-cap, he protested his innocence and asked ten thousand pardons of Mrs. Slipslop for the blows he had struck her, vowing he had mistaken her for a witch. Lady Booby then casting her eyes on the ground, observed something sparkle with great lustre, which, when she had taken it up, appeared to be a very fine pair of diamond buttons for the sleeves. A little farther, she saw lie the sleeve itself of a shirt with laced ruffles. "Heydey!" says she, "what is the meaning of this?" "Oh, madam!" says Slipslop, "I don't know what hath happened, I have been so terrified. Here may have been a dozen men in the room." "To whom belongs this laced shirt and jewels?" says the lady. "Undoubtedly," cries the parson, "to the young gentleman whom I mistook for a woman on coming into the room, whence proceeded all the subsequent mistakes; for if I had suspected him for a man, I would have seized him, had he been another Hercules, though, indeed, he seems rather to resemble Hylas." He then gave an account of the reason of his rising from bed, and the rest, till the lady came into the room; at which, and the figures of Slipslop and her gallant, whose heads only were visible at the opposite corners of the bed, she could not refrain from laughter; nor did Slipslop persist in accusing the parson of any motions towards a rape. The lady therefore desired him to return to his bed as soon as she was departed, and then ordering Slipslop to rise and attend her in her own room, she returned herself thither. When she was gone, Adams renewed his petitions for pardon to Mrs. Slipslop, who, with a most Christian temper, not only forgave, but began to move with much courtesy towards him, which he taking as a hint to begin, immediately quitted the bed and made the best of his way towards his own; but unluckily, instead of turning to the right, he turned to the left, and went to the apartment where Fanny lay, who (as the reader may remember) had not slept a wink the preceding night, and who was so hagged out with what had happened to her in the day that, notwithstanding all thoughts of her Joseph, she was fallen into so profound a sleep that all the noise in the adjoining room had not been able to disturb her. Adams groped out the bed, and, turning the clothes down softly, a custom Mrs. Adams had long accustomed him to, crept in, and deposited his carcase on the bed-post, a place which that good woman had always assigned him.

As the cat or lap-dog of some lovely nymph for whom ten thousand lovers languish lies quietly by the side of the charming maid, and, ignorant of the scene of delight on which they repose, meditates the future capture of a mouse or surprisal of a plate of bread and butter, so Adams lay by the side of Fanny, ignorant of the paradise to which he was so near, nor could the emanation of sweets which flowed from her breath overpower the fumes of tobacco which played in the parson's nostrils. And now sleep had not overtaken the good man when Joseph, who had secretly appointed Fanny to come to her at the break of day, rapped softly at the chamber door, which, when he had repeated twice, Adams cried, "Come in, whoever you are." Joseph thought he had mistaken the door, though she had given him the most exact directions; however, knowing his friend's voice, he opened it, and saw some female vestments lying on a chair. Fanny waking at the same instant, and stretching out her hand on Adams's beard, she cried out, "O heavens! where am I?" "Bless me, where am I?" said the parson. Then Fanny screamed, Adams leapt out of bed, and Joseph stood, as the tragedians call it, like the statue of Surprise. "How came she into my room?" cried Adams. "How came you into hers?" cried Joseph, in an astonishment. "I know nothing of the matter," answered Adams, "but that she is a vestal for me. As I am a Christian, I know not whether she is a man or woman. He is an infidel who doth not believe in witchcraft. They as surely exist now as in the days of Saul. My clothes are bewitched away too, and Fanny's brought into their place." For he still insisted he was in his own apartment; but Fanny denied it vehemently and said his attempting to persuade Joseph of such a falsehood convinced her of his wicked designs. "How!" said Joseph in a rage, "hath he offered any rudeness to you?" She answered she could not accuse him of any more than villainously stealing to bed to her, which she thought rudeness sufficient, and what no man would do without a wicked intention.

Joseph's great opinion of Adams was not easily to be staggered, and when he heard from Fanny that no harm had happened he grew a little cooler; yet still he was confounded, and, as he knew the house, and that the women's apartments were on this side Mrs. Slipslop's room, and the men's on the other, he was convinced that he was in Fanny's chamber. Assuring Adams therefore of this truth, he begged him to give some account how he came there. Adams then, standing in his shirt, which did not offend Fanny, as the curtains of the bed were drawn, related all that had happened; and when he had ended, Joseph told him it was plain he had mistaken by turning to the right instead of the left. "Odso!" cries Adams, "that's true: as sure as sixpence, you have hit on the very thing." He then traversed the room, rubbing his hands, and begged Fanny's pardon, assuring her he did not know whether she was a man or woman. That innocent creature, firmly believing all he said, told him she was no longer angry, and begged Joseph to conduct him into his own apartment, where he should stay himself till she had put her clothes on. Joseph and Adams accordingly departed, and the latter soon was convinced of the mistake he had committed; however, whilst he was dressing himself he often asserted he believed in the power of witchcraft notwithstanding, and did not see how a Christian could deny it.

CHAPTER XV: *The arrival of Gaffer and Gammer Andrews, with another person not much expected, and a perfect solution of the difficulties raised by the pedlar.*

As soon as Fanny was dressed Joseph returned to her, and they had a long conversation together, the conclusion of which was that, if they found themselves to be really brother and sister, they vowed a perpetual celibacy, and to live together all their days, and indulge a Platonic friendship for each other.

The company were all very merry at breakfast, and Joseph and Fanny rather more cheerful than the preceding night. The Lady Booby produced the diamond button, which the beau most readily owned and alleged that he was very subject to walk in his sleep. Indeed, he was far from being ashamed of his amour, and rather endeavoured to insinuate that more than was really true had passed between him and the fair Slipslop.

Their tea was scarce over when news came of the arrival of old Mr. Andrews and his wife. They were immediately introduced and kindly received by the Lady Booby, whose heart went now pit-a-pat, as did those of Joseph and Fanny. They felt perhaps little less anxiety in this interval than Oedipus himself whilst his fate was revealing.

Mr. Booby first opened the cause by informing the old gentleman that he had a child in the company more than he knew of, and, taking Fanny by the hand, told him this was that daughter of his who had been stolen away by Gipsies in her infancy. Mr. Andrews, after expressing some astonishment, assured his honour that he had never lost a daughter by Gipsies, nor ever had any other children than Joseph and Pamela. These words were a cordial to the two lovers, but had a different effect on Lady Booby. She ordered the pedlar to be called, who recounted his story as he had done before. At the end of which old Mrs. Andrews, running to Fanny, embraced her, crying out, "She is, she is my child!" The company were all amazed at this disagreement between the man and his wife; and the blood had now forsaken the cheeks of the lovers, when the old woman, turning to her husband, who was more surprised than all the rest, and having a little recovered her own spirits, delivered herself as follows: "You may remember, my dear, when you went a sergeant to Gibraltar, you left me big with child; you stayed abroad, you know, upwards of three years. In your absence I was brought to bed, I verily believe, of this daughter; whom I am sure I have reason to remember, for I suckled her at this very breast till the day she was stolen from me. One afternoon, when the child was about a year or a year and a half old, or thereabouts, two Gipsy women came to the door and offered to tell my fortune. One of them had a child in her lap. I showed them my hand, and desired to know if you was ever to come home again, which I remember as well as if it was but yesterday: they faithfully promised me you should. I left the girl in the cradle and went to draw them a cup of liquor, the best I had; when I returned with the pot (I am sure I was not absent longer than whilst I am telling it to you), the women were gone. I was afraid they had stolen something, and looked and looked, but to no purpose, and heaven knows I had very little for them to steal. At last, hearing the child cry in the cradle, I went to take it up—but, O the living! how was I surprised to find, instead of my own girl that I had put into the cradle, who was as fine a fat thriving child as you shall see in a summer's day, a poor sickly boy that did not seem to have an hour to live. I ran out, pulling my hair off, and crying like any mad after the women, but never could hear a word of them from that day to this. When I came back, the poor infant (which is our Joseph there, as stout as he now stands) lifted up its eyes upon me so piteously that, to be sure, notwithstanding my passion, I could not find in my heart to do it any mischief. A neighbour of mine happening to come in at the same time, and hearing the case, advised me to take care of this poor child, and God would perhaps one day restore me my own. Upon which I took the child up, and suckled it, to be sure, all the world as if it had been born of my own natural body, and as true as I am alive, in a little time I loved the boy all to nothing as if it had been my own girl.—Well, as I was saying, times growing very hard, I, having two children and nothing but my own work, which was little enough, God knows, to maintain them, was obliged to ask relief of the parish; but instead of giving it me, they removed me, by justices' warrants, fifteen miles, to the place where I now live, where I had not been long settled before you came home. Joseph (for that was the name I gave him myself—the Lord knows whether he was baptized or no, or by what name), Joseph, I say, seemed to me about five years old when you returned; for I believe he is two or three years older than our daughter here (for I am thoroughly convinced she is the same); and when you saw him, you said he was a chopping boy, without ever minding his age; and so I, seeing you did not suspect anything of the matter, thought I might e'en as well keep it to myself, for fear you should not love him as well as I did. And all this is veritably true, and I will take my oath of it before any justice in the kingdom."

The pedlar, who had been summoned by the order of Lady Booby, listened with the utmost attention to Gammer Andrews's story, and, when she had finished, asked her if the suppositious child had no mark on its breast? To which she answered yes, he had as fine a strawberry as ever grew in a garden. This Joseph acknowledged, and, unbuttoning his coat at the intercession of the company, showed to them. "Well," says Gaffer Andrews, who was a comical sly old fellow and very likely desired to have no more children than he could keep, "you have proved, I think, very plainly, that this boy doth not belong to us; but how are you certain that the girl is ours?" The parson then brought the pedlar forward and desired him to repeat the story which he had communicated to him the preceding day at the ale-house; which he complied with, and related what the reader, as well as Mr. Adams, hath seen before. He then confirmed, from his wife's report, all the circumstances of the exchange, and of the strawberry on Joseph's breast. At the repetition of the word "strawberry," Adams, who had seen it without any emotion, started, and cried, "Bless me! something comes into my head." But before he had time to bring anything out, a servant called him forth. When he was gone, the pedlar assured Joseph that his parents were persons of much greater circumstances than those he had hitherto mistaken for such; for that he had been stolen from a gentleman's house by those whom they call Gipsies, and had been kept by them during a whole year, when, looking on him as in a dying condition, they had exchanged him for the other healthier child, in the manner before related. He said as to the name of his father, his wife had either never known or forgot it, but that she had acquainted him he lived about forty miles from the place where the exchange had been made, and which way, promising to spare no pains in endeavouring with him to discover the place.

But Fortune, which seldom doth good or ill, or makes men happy or miserable by halves, resolved to spare him this labour. The reader may please to recollect that Mr. Wilson had intended a journey to the west, in which he was to pass through Mr. Adams's parish, and had promised to call on him. He was now arrived at the Lady Booby's gates for that purpose, being directed thither from the parson's house, and had sent in the servant whom we have above seen call Mr. Adams forth. This had no sooner mentioned the discovery of a stolen child, and had uttered the word "strawberry," than Mr. Wilson, with wildness in his looks, and the utmost eagerness in his words, begged to be showed into the room, where he entered without the least regard to any of the company but Joseph, and, embracing him with a complexion all pale and trembling, desired to see the mark on his breast; the parson followed him capering, rubbing his hands, and crying out, *Hic est quem quaeris; inventus est,* [1] *etc.* Joseph complied with the request of Mr. Wilson, who no sooner saw the mark than, abandoning himself to the most extravagant rapture of passion, he embraced Joseph with inexpressible ecstasy, and cried out in tears of joy, "I have discovered my son, I have him again in my arms!" Joseph was not sufficiently apprised yet to taste the same delight with his father (for so in reality he was); however, he returned some warmth to his embraces; but he no sooner perceived, from his father's account, the agreement of every circumstance, of person, time, and place, then he threw himself at his feet, and, embracing his knees, with tears begged his blessing, which was given with much affection, and received with such respect, mixed with such tenderness on both sides, that it affected all present—but none so much as Lady Booby, who left the room in an agony, which was but too much perceived, and not very charitably accounted for by some of the company.

CHAPTER XVI: *Being the last. In which this true history is brought to a happy conclusion.*

FANNY was very little behind her Joseph in the duty she expressed towards her parents, and the joy she evidenced in discovering them. Gammer Andrews kissed her, and said she was heartily glad to see her, but for her part she could never love anyone better than Joseph. Gaffer Andrews testified no remarkable emotion: he blessed and kissed her, but complained bitterly that he wanted his pipe, not having had a whiff that morning.

Mr. Booby, who knew nothing of his aunt's fondness, imputed her abrupt departure to her pride, and disdain of the family into which he was married; he was therefore desirous to be gone with the utmost celerity, and now, having congratulated Mr. Wilson and Joseph on the discovery, he saluted Fanny, called her sister, and introduced her as such to Pamela, who behaved with great decency on the occasion.

He now sent a message to his aunt, who returned that she wished him a good journey, but was too disordered to see any company. He therefore prepared to set out, having invited Mr. Wilson to his house, and Pamela and Joseph both so insisted on his complying that he at last consented, having first obtained a messenger from Mr. Booby to acquaint his wife with the news; which, as he knew it would render her completely happy, he could not prevail on himself to delay a moment in acquainting her with.

The company were ranged in this manner: the two old people, with their two daughters, rode in the coach; the Squire, Mr. Wilson, Joseph, Parson Adams, and the pedlar, proceeded on horseback.

In their way, Joseph informed his father of his intended match with Fanny, to which, though he expressed some reluctance at first, on the eagerness of his son's instances he consented, saying, if she was so good a creature as she appeared, and he described her, he thought the disadvantages of birth and fortune might be compensated. He however insisted on the match being deferred till he had seen his mother, in which Joseph perceiving him positive, with great duty obeyed him, to the great delight of Parson Adams, who by these means saw an opportunity of fulfilling the church forms and marrying his parishioners without a licence.

Mr. Adams greatly exulting on this occasion (for such ceremonies were matters of no small moment with him), accidentally gave spurs to his horse, which the generous beast disdaining—for he was of high mettle, and had been used to more expert riders than the gentleman who at present bestrode him, for whose horsemanship he had perhaps some contempt—immediately ran away full speed, and played so many antic tricks that he tumbled the parson from his back, which Joseph perceiving, came to his relief.

This accident afforded infinite merriment to the servants, and no less frighted poor Fanny, who beheld him as he passed by the coach; but the mirth of the one and terror of the other were soon determined when the parson declared he had received no damage.

The horse having freed himself from his unworthy rider, as he probably thought him, proceeded to make the best of his way, but was stopped by a gentleman and his servants, who were travelling the opposite way and were now at a little distance from the coach. They soon met; and as one of the servants delivered Adams his horse, his master hailed him, and Adams, looking up, presently recollected he was the justice of peace before whom he and Fanny had made their appearance. The parson presently saluted him very kindly; and the justice informed him that he had found the fellow who attempted to swear against him and the young woman the very next day, and had committed him to Salisbury gaol, where he was charged with many robberies.

Many compliments having passed between the parson and the justice, the latter proceeded on his journey; and the former, having with some disdain refused Joseph's offer of changing horses, and declared he was as able a horseman as any in the kingdom, remounted his beast; and now the company again proceeded, and happily arrived at their journey's end, Mr. Adams, by good luck rather than by good riding, escaping a second fall.

The company, arriving at Mr. Booby's house, were all received by him in the most courteous and entertained in the most splendid manner, after the custom of the old English hospitality, which is still preserved in some very few families in the remote parts of England. They all passed that day with the utmost satisfaction, it being perhaps impossible to find any set of people more solidly and sincerely happy. Joseph and Fanny found means to be alone upwards of two hours, which were the shortest but the sweetest imaginable.

In the morning, Mr. Wilson proposed to his son to make a visit with him to his mother, which, notwithstanding his dutiful inclinations, and a longing desire he had to see her, a little concerned him, as he must be obliged to leave his Fanny. But the goodness of Mr. Booby relieved him; for he proposed to send his own coach and six for Mrs. Wilson, whom Pamela so very earnestly invited that Mr. Wilson at length agreed with the entreaties of Mr. Booby and Joseph and suffered the coach to go empty for his wife.

On Saturday night the coach returned with Mrs. Wilson, who added one more to this happy assembly. The reader may imagine much better and quicker too than I can describe the many embraces and tears of joy which succeeded her arrival. It is sufficient to say she was easily prevailed with to follow her husband's example, in consenting to the match.

On Sunday Mr. Adams performed the service at the Squire's parish church, the curate of which very kindly exchanged duty and rode twenty miles to the Lady Booby's parish so to do, being particularly charged not to omit publishing the banns, being the third and last time.

At length the happy day arrived which was to put Joseph in the possession of all his wishes. He arose, and dressed himself in a neat but plain suit of Mr. Booby's, which exactly fitted him, for he refused all finery; as did Fanny likewise, who could be prevailed on by Pamela to attire herself in nothing richer than a white dimity night-gown. Her shift indeed, which Pamela presented her, was of the finest kind, and had an edging of lace round the bosom. She likewise equipped her with a pair of fine white thread stockings, which were all she would accept; for she wore one of her own short round-eared caps, and over it a little straw hat lined with cherry-coloured silk, and tied with a cherry-coloured ribbon. In this dress she came forth from her chamber, blushing and breathing sweets; and was by Joseph, whose eyes sparkled fire, led to church, the whole family attending, where Mr. Adams performed the ceremony; at which nothing was so remarkable, as the extraordinary and unaffected modesty of Fanny, unless the true Christian piety of Adams, who publicly rebuked Mr. Booby and Pamela for laughing in so sacred a place, and on so solemn an occasion. Our parson would have done no less to the highest prince on earth, for though he paid all submission and deference to his superiors in other matters, where the least spice of religion intervened he immediately lost all respect of persons. It was his maxim that he was a servant of the Highest, and could not, without departing from his duty, give up the least article of his honour or of his cause to the greatest earthly potentate. Indeed, he always asserted that Mr. Adams at church with his surplice on, and Mr. Adams without that ornament, in any other place, were two very different persons.

When the church rites were over, Joseph led his blooming bride back to Mr. Booby's (for the distance was so very little they did not think proper to use a coach); the whole company attended them likewise on foot; and now a most magnificent entertainment was provided, at which Parson Adams demonstrated an appetite surprising, as well as surpassing everyone present. Indeed the only persons who betrayed any deficiency on this occasion were those on whose account the feast was provided. They pampered their imaginations with the much more exquisite repast which the approach of night promised them, the thoughts of which filled both their minds, though with different sensations, the one all desire, while the other had her wishes tempered with fears.

At length, after a day passed with the utmost merriment, corrected by the strictest decency, in which, however, Parson Adams, being well filled with ale and pudding, had given a loose to more facetiousness than was usual to him, the happy, the blessed moment arrived when Fanny retired with her mother, her mother-in-law, and her sister.

She was soon undressed, for she had no jewels to deposit

in their caskets, nor fine laces to fold with the nicest exactness. Undressing to her was properly discovering, not putting off, ornaments, for as all her charms were the gifts of nature, she could divest herself of none. How, reader, shall I give thee an adequate idea of this lovely young creature! the bloom of roses and lilies might a little illustrate her complexion, or their smell her sweetness; but to comprehend her entirely, conceive youth, health, bloom, neatness, and innocence, in her bridal bed; conceive all these in their utmost perfection, and you may place the charming Fanny's picture before your eyes.

Joseph no sooner heard she was in bed than he fled with the utmost eagerness to her. A minute carried him into her arms, where we shall leave this happy couple to enjoy the private rewards of their constancy, rewards so great and sweet, that I apprehend Joseph neither envied the noblest duke nor Fanny the finest duchess, that night.

The third day, Mr. Wilson and his wife, with their son and daughter, returned home; where they now live together in a state of bliss scarce ever equalled. Mr. Booby hath with unprecedented generosity given Fanny a fortune of two thousand pounds, which Joseph hath laid out in a little estate in the same parish with his father, which he now occupies (his father having stocked it for him); and Fanny presides with most excellent management in his dairy, where, however, she is not at present very able to bustle much, being, as Mr. Wilson informs me in his last letter, extremely big with her first child.

Mr. Booby hath presented Mr. Adams with a living of one hundred and thirty pounds a year. He at first refused it, resolving not to quit his parishioners, with whom he had lived so long; but, on recollecting he might keep a curate at this living, he hath been lately inducted into it.

The pedlar, besides several handsome presents both from Mr. Wilson and Mr. Booby, is, by the latter's interest, made an exciseman, a trust which he discharges with such justice, that he is greatly beloved in his neighbourhood.

As for the Lady Booby, she returned to London in a few days, where a young captain of dragoons, together with eternal parties at cards, soon obliterated the memory of Joseph.

Joseph remains blessed with his Fanny, whom he dotes on with the utmost tenderness, which is all returned on her side. The happiness of this couple is a perpetual fountain of pleasure to their fond parents, and, what is particularly remarkable, he declares he will imitate them in their retirement, nor will be prevailed on by any book-sellers, or their authors, to make his appearance in high-life.

NOTES

The following notes, keyed to the text by page number, will aid in the reader's comprehension of *Joseph Andrews.* Those indicated by an asterisk are Fielding's own. The others, numbered consecutively within chapters, have been prepared especially for this edition.

Note

Page v, Number 1. *Joseph Andrews* was originally published in 2 volumes 12 mo.

Page x, Number 1. William Congreve, in "Of Pleasing."

Page 21, Number *. In English, sprung from a dunghill.

Page 24, Number 1. In full, *modus decimandi,* an arrangement by which, instead of paying tithes in kind, one paid the money value, which might, in subsequent years, be worth much less than the produce it originally stood for.

Page 27, Number *. It may seem an absurdity that Tattle should visit, as she actually did, to spread a known scandal, but the reader may reconcile this by supposing with me that notwithstanding what she says, this was her first acquaintance with it.

Page 35, Number 1. The inventor of the English pantomime, John Rich (1682–1761), is referred to here as a symbol of debasement of public taste.

Page 37, Number 1. Actors of Fielding's time, who had acted in his plays.

Page 57, Number 1. Correctly, *venienti occurrite morbo* (Persius, *Satires,* iii, 64): "meet the disease as it comes."

Page 57, Number 2. These high-sounding, but unrelated, Greek phrases are from Homer.

Page 62, Number 1. "With all his might of the converse view."

Page 66, Number 1. He was saving up for a payment due.

Page 66, Number *. To blink is a term used to signify the dog's passing by a bird without pointing at it.

Page 71, Number 1. The date of Charles I's execution; sermons on the anniversary were often more popular than pious.

Page 79, Number 1. I.e., serially, by installments.

Page 81, Number 1. "So to say."

Page 81, Number 2. Fielding's translation of "the sole cause" into Greek.

Page 92, Number *. This letter was written by a young lady on reading the former.

Page 99, Number 1. "Your most humble servant . . . I understand you perfectly well."

Page 101, Number 2. *Tout-brilliant* may be translated "most gleaming"; *ruelle*, "bedside"; *hardiesse*, "boldness"; *Avec tout le respecte*, "with all the respect"; *dévoté*, "devoted."

Page 105, Number 1. The foreign words here are rather more Italianized English than Italian, and may be taken to mean: *disgracia*, "disgrace"; *accustomata*, "used"; *cuffardo*, "punching"; *bastonza*, "cudgeling"; *uno insipido del nullo senso*, "a senseless idiot"; *Damnata di me*, "I'll be dashed"; *spectaculo*, "sight."

Page 106, Number 2. "I see very well that all is peace"—in mixed French and Italian.

Page 111, Number 1. "Anyone else."

Page 112, Number 2. *Charmante*, "charming"; *politesse*, "courtesy"; *triste*, "sad"; *A jamais! Coeur! Ange! Au diable!* "Never! Dear heart! Angel! The devil with it!"; *dans le monde*, "in the world."

Page 116, Number 1. "Not even a word, so to say."

Page 117, Number 2. "We cannot all accomplish all" (Virgil, *Eclogues*, viii, 63).

Page 122, Number 1. "Heigh, you!"

Page 125, Number 2. Jack Sheppard, hanged in 1724 at the age of twenty-two, as a highwayman, was the subject of a biography by Defoe.

Page 127, Number 1. By the play on words, Fielding associates Dick Turpin, the highwayman (1706-39), with Latin *turpis*, "shame."

Page 127, Number 2. The one challenged is supposed to supply a classical quotation beginning with the same letter as the one just given ends with. "The witty fellow" not only misquotes Ovid in his first and second offering, but gives what is not properly a quotation in his third, which is a mnemonic for the genders of Latin nouns.

Page 129, Number 3. I.e., Fathers of the Church. The two Greek words he reads aloud show that this is not a catechism but *Seven Against Thebes.*

Page 132, Number 1. "What you ask for is nowhere" (Ovid, *Metamorphoses,* iii, 433).

Page 132, Number 2. "In our stupidity we ask for the sky itself" (Horace, *Odes,* I, iii, 38).

Page 141, Number 1. "I have naught to do with swine."

Page 147, Number 1. "Lo, Turnus, what not even a god would have dared to promise in fulfillment of your hopes, the passage of time has brought to itself" (Vergil, Aeneid, ix, 6).

Page 157, Number 1. "They change their clime, not mind, who rush across the sea" (Horace, *Epistles,* I, xi, 27).

Page 161, Number 1. Properly:

> . . . beyond
> Frightened the Reign of *Chaos* and old Night

(Milton, *Paradise Lost,* I, 539-40).

Page 165, Number 1. "This is a soul that values life little and willingly yields it for the sake of that honor you follow" (Vergil, *Aeneid,* ix, 205-06).

Page 172, Number *. The Author hath by some been represented to have made a blunder here, for Adams had indeed shown some learning (say they), perhaps all the Author had; but the gentleman hath shown none, unless his approbation of Mr. Adams be such, but surely it would be preposterous in him to call it so. I have, however, notwithstanding this criticism, which I am told came from the mouth of a great orator in a public coffee-house, left this blunder as it stood in the first edition. I will not have the vanity to apply to anything in this work the observation which Mme. Dacier makes in her preface to her Aristophanes: *Je tiens pour une maxime constante, qu'une beauté mediocre plait plus généralemente qu'une beauté sans default.* Mr. Congreve hath made such another blunder in his *Love for Love,* where Tattle tells Miss Prue, "She should admire him as much for the beauty he commends in her as if he himself was possessed of it."

Page 174, Number 1. A London brothel of that time.

Page 185, Number 2. Persons were immune from arrest for debt on Sundays.

Page 192, Number *. Whoever the reader pleases.

Page 197, Number 1. "It is not for me to boast."

Page 197, Number 2. "Hence those tears" (Horace, *Epistles*, I, xix, 41).

Page 197, Number 3. By Joseph Addison.

Page 198, Number 4. "No mortal always knows what is right."

Page 200, Number 1. The former is John Kyrle, "the Man of Ross" in Pope's *Moral Essays*, iii; the latter, Ralph Allen, in Pope's *Epilogues to the Satires*, Dialogue i.

Page 201, Number 2. John Henley (1692–1756), known as "Orator Henley," a preacher who figures in Pope's *Dunciad* as the "zany of his age."

Page 209, Number *. All hounds that will hunt fox or other vermin will hunt a piece of rusty bacon trailed on the ground.

Page 223, Number 1. From Nathanael Lee's *Theodosius*, II, i.

Page 223, Number 2. From Thomas Otway's *The Orphan*, I, i.

Page 227, Number 1. A play by Sir Richard Steele.

Page 256, Number *. Meaning perhaps ideas.

Page 266, Number 1. The section of Latin grammar dealing with the genders of words.

Page 269, Number 1. "No carved ceiling [of ivory or gold] glitters in my house" (Horace, *Odes*, II, xviii, 1-2).

Page 270, Number *. Lest this should appear unnatural to some readers, we think proper to acquaint them that it is taken verbatim from very polite conversation.

Page 270, Number 2. I.e., he has completed the study of proper nouns in Latin.

Page 293, Number 1. "Here is he you are looking for; he is found."

A NOTE ON THE TEXT

Joseph Andrews was first published serially in 1742, and in book form later that year. Fielding made piece-meal, but not wholly inconsequential, changes in it until his death, in 1754. These changes were all included in the first collected edition of his works in 1762.

The present text is based on the 1762 edition. In removing errors and inconsistencies found there, the 1742 edition, with which this has been compared word for word, has occasionally been relied on. The spelling has been brought into conformity with contemporary British practice, and the punctuation, in so far as Fielding's syntax permits, has been modernized.

The VICAR of WAKEFIELD

by
Oliver Goldsmith

Sperate miseri, cavete foelices

CONTENTS

ADVERTISEMENT

There are an hundred faults in this Thing, and an hundred things might be said to prove them beauties. But it is needless. A book may be amusing with numerous errors, or it may be very dull without a single absurdity. The hero of this piece unites in himself the three greatest characters upon earth; he is a priest, an husbandman, and the father of a family. He is drawn as ready to teach and ready to obey, as simple in affluence and majestic in adversity. In this age of opulence and refinement whom can such a character please? Such as are fond of high life will turn with disdain from the simplicity of his country fireside. Such as mistake ribaldry for humour will find no wit in his harmless conversation; and such as have been taught to deride religion will laugh at one whose chief stores of comfort are drawn from futurity.

OLIVER GOLDSMITH

CHAPTER I

THE DESCRIPTION OF THE FAMILY OF WAKEFIELD, IN WHICH A KINDRED LIKENESS PREVAILS AS WELL OF MINDS AS OF PERSONS

I was ever of opinion that the honest man who married and brought up a large family did more service than he who continued single and only talked of population. From this motive, I had scarce taken orders a year before I began to think seriously of matrimony, and chose my wife as she did her wedding gown, not for a fine glossy surface, but such qualities as would wear well. To do her justice, she was a good-natured notable woman; and as for breeding, there were few country ladies who at that time could show more. She could read any English book without much spelling; and for pickling, preserving, and cookery, none could excel her. She prided herself much also upon being an excellent contriver in house-keeping; yet I could never find that we grew richer with all her contrivances.

However, we loved each other tenderly, and our fondness increased with age. There was in fact nothing that could make us angry with the world or each other. We had an elegant house, situated in a fine country and a good neighbourhood. The year was spent in moral or rural amusements, in visiting our rich neighbours, or relieving such as were poor. We had no revolutions to fear, nor fatigues to undergo; all our adventures were by the fire-side, and all our migrations from the blue bed to the brown.

As we lived near the road, we often had the traveller or

stranger come to taste our gooseberry wine, for which we had great reputation; and I profess with the veracity of an historian that I never knew one of them find fault with it. Our cousins too, even to the fortieth remove, all remembered their affinity, without any help from the herald's office, and came very frequently to see us. Some of them did us no great honour by these claims of kindred; for literally speaking, we had the blind, the maimed, and the halt amongst the number. However, my wife always insisted that as they were the same *flesh and blood* with us, they should sit with us at the same table. So that if we had not very rich, we generally had very happy friends about us; for this remark will hold good thro' life, that the poorer the guest, the better pleased he ever is with being treated; and as some men gaze with admiration at the colours of a tulip, and others are smitten with the wing of a butterfly, so I was by nature an admirer of happy human faces. However, when any one of our relations was found to be a person of very bad character, a troublesome guest, or one we desired to get rid of, upon his leaving my house for the first time, I ever took care to lend him a riding coat, or a pair of boots, or sometimes an horse of small value, and I always had the satisfaction of finding he never came back to return them. By this the house was cleared of such as we did not like; but never was the family of Wakefield known to turn the traveller or the poor dependant out of doors.

Thus we lived several years in a state of much happiness, not but that we sometimes had those little rubs which Providence sends to enhance the value of its other favours. My orchard was often robbed by school-boys, and my wife's custards plundered by the cats or the children. The Squire would sometimes fall asleep in the most pathetic parts of my sermon, or his lady return my wife's civilities at church with a mutilated curtsey. But we soon got over the uneasiness caused by such accidents, and usually in three or four days we began to wonder how they vext us.

My children, the offspring of temperance, as they were educated without softness, so they were at once well formed and healthy; my sons hardy and active, my daughters dutiful and blooming. When I stood in the midst of the little circle, which promised to be the supports of my declining age, I could not avoid repeating the famous story of Count Abensberg, who, in Henry II's progress through Germany, when other courtiers came with their treasures, brought his thirty-two children and presented them to his sovereign as the most valuable offering he had to bestow. In this manner, though I had but six, I considered them as a very valuable present made to my country, and consequently looked upon it as my debtor. Our eldest son was named George, after his uncle, who left us ten thousand pounds. Our second child, a girl, I intended to call after her aunt Grissel; but my wife, who during her pregnancy had been reading romances, insisted upon her being called Olivia. In less than another year we had a daughter again, and now I was determined that Grissel should be her name; but a rich relation taking a fancy to stand godmother, the girl was, by her directions, called Sophia; so that we had two romantic names in the family; but I solemnly protest I had no hand in it. Moses was our next, and after an interval of twelve years, we had two sons more.

It would be fruitless to deny my exultation when I saw my little ones about me; but the vanity and the satisfaction of my wife were even greater than mine. When our visitors would usually say, "Well, upon my word, Mrs. Primrose, you have the finest children in the whole country."——"Ay, neighbour," she would answer, "they are as heaven made them, handsome enough, if they be good enough; for handsome is that handsome does." And then she would bid the girls hold up their heads; who, to conceal nothing, were certainly very handsome. Mere outside is so very trifling a circumstance with me that I should scarce have remembered to mention it, had it not been a general topic of conversation in the country. Olivia, now about eighteen, had that luxuriancy of beauty with which painters generally draw Hebe; open, sprightly, and commanding. Sophia's features were not so striking at first, but often did more certain execution; for they were soft, modest, and alluring. The one vanquished by a single blow, the other by efforts successfully repeated.

The temper of a woman is generally formed from the turn of her features; at least it was so with my daughters. Olivia wished for many lovers, Sophia to secure one. Olivia was often affected from too great a desire to please. Sophia even represt excellence from her fears to offend. The one entertained me with her vivacity when I was gay, the other with her sense when I was serious. But these qualities were never carried to excess in either, and I have often seen them exchange characters for a whole day together. A suit of mourning has transformed my coquette into a prude, and a new set of ribands given her younger sister more than natural vivacity. My eldest son George was bred at Oxford, as I intended him for one of the learned professions. My second boy Moses, whom I designed for business, received a sort of miscellaneous education at home. But it would be needless to attempt describing the particular characters of young people that had seen but very little of the world. In short, a family likeness prevailed through all, and properly speaking, they had but one character, that of being all equally generous, credulous, simple, and inoffensive.

CHAPTER II

FAMILY MISFORTUNES. THE LOSS OF FORTUNE ONLY SERVES TO INCREASE THE PRIDE OF THE WORTHY

The temporal concerns of our family were chiefly committed to my wife's management, as to the spiritual I took them entirely under my own direction. The profits of my living, which amounted to but thirty-five pounds a year, I gave to the orphans and widows of the clergy of our diocese; for having a sufficient fortune of my own, I was careless of temporalities and felt a secret pleasure in doing my duty without reward. I also set a resolution of keeping no curate, and of being acquainted with every man in the parish, exhorting the married men to temperance and the bachelors to matrimony; so that in a few years it was a common saying that there were three strange wants at Wakefield, a parson wanting pride, young men wanting wives, and alehouses wanting customers.

Matrimony was always one of my favourite topics, and I wrote several sermons to prove its utility and happiness: but there was a peculiar tenet which I made a point of supporting; for I maintained with Whiston that it was unlawful for a priest of the church of England, after the death of his first wife, to take a second, or to express it in one word, I valued myself upon being a strict monogamist.

I was early initiated into this important dispute, on which so many laborious volumes have been written. I published some tracts upon the subject myself, which, as they never sold, I have the consolation of thinking are read only by the happy *Few*. Some of my friends called this my weak side; but alas! they had not like me made it the subject of long contemplation. The more I reflected upon it, the more important it appeared. I even went a step beyond Whiston in displaying my principles: as he had engraven upon his wife's tomb that she was the *only* wife of William Whiston, so I wrote a similar epitaph for my wife, though still living, in which I extolled her prudence, economy, and obedience till death; and having got it copied fair, with an elegant frame, it was placed over the chimney-piece, where it answered several very useful purposes. It admonished my wife of her duty to me, and my fidelity to her; it inspired her with a passion for fame, and constantly put her in mind of her end.

It was thus, perhaps, from hearing marriage so often recommended, that my eldest son, just upon leaving college, fixed his affections upon the daughter of a neighbouring clergyman, who was a dignitary in the church, and in circumstances to give her a large fortune, but fortune was her smallest accomplishment. Miss Arabella Wilmot was allowed by all (except my two daughters), to be completely pretty. Her youth, health, and innocence were still heightened by a complexion so transparent, and such an happy sensibility of look, that even age could not gaze on with indifference. As Mr. Wilmot knew that I could make a very handsome settlement on my son, he was not averse to the match; so both families lived together in all that harmony which generally precedes an expected alliance. Being convinced by experience that the days of courtship are the most happy of our lives, I was willing enough to lengthen the period; and the various amusements which the young couple every day shared in each other's company seemed to increase their passion. We were generally awaked in the morning by music, and on fine days rode a-hunting. The hours between breakfast and dinner the ladies devoted to dress and study: they usually read a page, and then gazed at themselves in the glass, which even philosophers might own often presented the page of greatest beauty. At dinner my wife took the lead; for as she always insisted upon carving every thing herself, it being her mother's way, she gave us upon these occasions the history of every dish. When we had dined, to prevent the ladies leaving us, I generally ordered the table to be removed; and sometimes, with the music master's assistance, the girls would give us a very agreeable concert. Walking out, drinking tea, country dances, and forfeits shortened the rest of the day, without the assistance of cards, as I hated all manner of gaming, except backgammon, at which my old friend and I sometimes took a two-penny hit. Nor can I here pass over an ominous circumstance that happened the last time we played together: I only wanted to fling a quatre, and yet I threw deuce ace five times running.

Some months were elapsed in this manner, till at last it was thought convenient to fix a day for the nuptials of the young couple, who seemed earnestly to desire it. During the preparations for the wedding, I need not describe the busy importance of my wife, nor the sly looks of my daughters; in fact, my attention was fixed on another object, the completing a tract which I intended shortly to publish in defence of monogamy. As I looked upon this as a masterpiece both for argument and style, I could not in the pride of my heart avoid showing it to my old friend Mr. Wilmot, as I made no doubt of receiving his approbation; but too late I discovered that he was most violently attached to the contrary opinion, and with good reason; for he was at that time actually courting a fourth wife. This, as may be expected, produced a dispute attended with some acrimony, which threatened to interrupt our intended alliance; but on the day before that appointed for the ceremony, we agreed to discuss the subject at large.

It was managed with proper spirit on both sides: he asserted that I was heterodox, I retorted the charge: he replied, and I rejoined. In the meantime, while the controversy was hottest, I was called out by one of my relations, who, with a face of concern, advised me to give up the dispute and allow the old gentleman to be a husband if he could, at least till my son's wedding was over. "How," cried I, "relinquish the cause of truth, and let him be an husband, already driven to the very verge of absurdity. You might as well advise me to give up my fortune as my argument."——"That fortune," returned my friend, "I am now sorry to inform you, is almost nothing. Your merchant in town, in whose hands your money was lodged, has gone off, to avoid a statute of bankruptcy, and it is thought has not left a shilling in the pound. I was unwilling to shock you or the family with the account till after the wedding, but now it may serve to moderate your warmth in the argument; for, I suppose, your own prudence will enforce the necessity of dissembling at least till your son has the young lady's fortune secure."——"Well," returned I, "if what you tell me be true, and if I am to be a beggar, it shall never make me a rascal, or induce me to disavow my principles. I'll go this moment and inform the company of my circumstances; and as for the argument, I even here retract my former concessions in the old gentleman's favour, nor will I allow him now to be an husband either de jure, de facto, or in any sense of the expression."

It would be endless to describe the different sensations of both families when I divulged the news of my misfortunes; but what others felt was slight to what the young lovers appeared to endure. Mr. Wilmot, who seemed before sufficiently inclined to break off the match, was by this blow soon determined: one virtue he had in perfection, which was prudence, too often the only virtue that is left us unimpaired at seventy-two.

CHAPTER III

A MIGRATION. THE FORTUNATE CIRCUMSTANCES OF OUR LIVES ARE GENERALLY FOUND AT LAST TO BE OF OUR OWN PROCURING

The only hope of our family now was that the report of our misfortunes might be malicious or premature; but a letter from my agent in town soon came with a confirmation of every particular. The loss of fortune to myself alone would have been trifling; the only uneasiness I felt was for my family, who were to be humble without such an education as could render them callous to contempt.

Near a fortnight passed away before I attempted to restrain their affliction; for premature consolation is but the remembrancer of sorrow. During this interval, my thoughts were employed on some future means of supporting them; and at last a small cure of fifteen pounds a year was offered me in a distant neighbourhood, where I could still enjoy my principles without molestation. With this proposal I joyfully closed, having determined to increase my salary by managing a little farm.

Having taken this resolution, my next care was to get together the wrecks of my fortune; and all debts collected and paid, out of fourteen thousand pounds we had now but four hundred remaining. My chief attention therefore was next to bring down the pride of my family to their circumstances; for I well knew that aspiring beggary is wretchedness itself. "You can't be ignorant, my children," cried I, "that no prudence of ours could have prevented our late misfortune; but prudence may do much in disappointing its effects. We are now poor, my fondlings, and wisdom bids us conform to our humble situation. Let us then, without repining, give up those splendours with which numbers are wretched, and seek in humbler circumstances that peace with which all may be happy. The poor live pleasantly without our help, and we are not so imperfectly formed as to be incapable of living without theirs. No, my children, let us from this moment give up all pretensions to gentility; we have still enough left for happiness if we are wise, and let us draw upon content for the deficiencies of fortune."

As my eldest son was bred a scholar, I determined to send him to town, where his abilities might contribute to our support and his own. The separation of friends and families is, perhaps, one of the most distressful circumstances attendant on penury. The day soon arrived on which we were to disperse for the first time. My son, after taking leave of his mother and the rest, who mingled their tears with their kisses, came to ask a blessing from me. This I gave him from my heart, and which, added to five guineas, was all the patrimony I had now to bestow. "You are going, my boy," cried I, "to London on foot, in the manner Hooker, your great ancestor, travelled there before you. Take from me the same horse that was given him by the good bishop Jewel, this staff, and take this book too, it will be your comfort on the way; these two lines in it are worth a million—*I have been young, and now am old; yet never saw I the righteous man forsaken, or his seed begging their bread*. Let this be your consolation as you travel on. Go, my boy, whatever be thy fortune let me see thee once a year; still keep a good heart, and farewell." As he was possest of integrity and honour, I was under no apprehensions from throwing him naked into the amphitheatre of life; for I knew he would act a good part whether he rose or fell.

His departure only prepared the way for our own, which arrived a few days afterwards. The leaving a neighbourhood in which we had enjoyed so many hours of tranquility was not without a tear, which scarce fortitude itself could suppress. Besides, a journey of seventy miles to a family that had hitherto never been above ten from home filled us with apprehension, and the cries of the poor, who followed us for some miles, contributed to increase it. The first day's journey brought us in safety within thirty miles of our future retreat, and we put up for the night at an obscure inn in a village by the way. When we were shown a room, I desired the landlord, in my usual way, to let us have his company, with which he complied, as what he drank would increase the bill next morning. He knew, however, the whole neighbourhood to which I was removing, particularly Squire Thornhill, who was to be my landlord, and who lived within a few miles of the place. This gentleman he described as one who desired to know little more of the world than the pleasures it afforded, being particularly remarkable for his attachment to the fair sex. He observed that no virtue was able to resist his arts and assiduity, and that scarce a farmer's daughter within ten miles round but what had found him successful and faithless. Though this account gave me some pain, it had a very different effect upon my daughters, whose features seemed to brighten with the expectation of an approaching triumph, nor was my wife less pleased and confident of their allurements and virtue. While our thoughts were thus employed, the hostess entered the room to inform her husband that the strange gentleman, who had been two days in the house, wanted money, and could not satisfy them for his reckoning. "Want money!" replied the host, "that must be impossible; for it was no later than yesterday he paid three guineas to our beadle to spare an old broken soldier that was to be whipped through the town for dog-stealing." The hostess, however, still persisting in her first assertion, he was preparing to leave the room, swearing that he would be satisfied one way or another, when I begged the landlord would introduce me to a stranger of so much charity as he described. With this he complied, showing in a gentleman who seemed to be about thirty, drest in clothes that once were laced. His person was well formed, though his face was marked with the lines of thinking. He had something short and dry in his address, and seemed not to understand ceremony, or to despise it. Upon the landlord's leaving the room, I could not avoid expressing my concern to the stranger at seeing a gentleman in such circumstances, and offered him my purse to satisfy the present demand. "I take it with all my heart, sir," replied he, "and am glad that a late oversight in giving what money I had about me has shown me that there is still some benevolence left among us. I must, however, previously entreat being informed of the name and residence of my benefactor, in order to remit it as soon as possible." In this I satisfied him fully, not only mentioning my name and late misfortunes, but the place to which I was going to remove. "This," cried he, "happens still more luckily than I hoped for, as I am going the same way myself, having been detained here two days by the floods, which, I hope, by to-morrow will be found passable." I testified the pleasure I should have in his company, and my wife and daughters joining in entreaty, he was prevailed upon to stay supper. The stranger's conversation, which was at once pleasing and instructive, induced me to wish for a continuance of it; but it was now high time to retire and take refreshment against the fatigues of the following day.

The next morning we all set forward together: my family on horseback, while Mr. Burchell, our new companion, walked along the foot-path by the road-side, observing, with a smile, that as we were ill mounted, he would be too generous to attempt leaving us behind. As the floods were not yet subsided, we were obliged to hire a guide, who trotted on before, Mr. Burchell and I bringing up the rear. We lightened the fatigues of the road with philosophical disputes, which he seemed perfectly to understand. But what surprised me most was that though he was a money-borrower, he defended his opinions with as much obstinacy as if he had been my patron. He now and then also informed me to whom the different seats belonged that lay in our view as we travelled the road. "That," cried he, pointing to a very magnificent house which stood at some distance, "belongs to Mr. Thornhill, a young gentleman who enjoys a large fortune, though entirely dependant on the will of his uncle, Sir William Thornhill, a gentleman who, content with a little himself, permits his nephew to enjoy the rest, and chiefly resides in town."—"What!" cried I, "is my young landlord then the nephew of a man whose virtues, generosity, and singularities are so universally known? I have heard Sir William Thornhill represented as one of the most generous, yet whimsical, men in the kingdom; a man of consummate benevolence."——"Something, perhaps, too much so," replied Mr. Burchell; "at least he carried benevolence to an excess when young; for his passions were then strong, and as they all were upon the side of virtue, they led it up to a romantic extreme. He early began to aim at the qualifications of the soldier and scholar, was soon distinguished in the army, and had some reputation among men of learning. Adulation ever follows the ambitious; for such alone receive most pleasure from flattery. He was surrounded with crowds, who showed him only one side of their character; so that he began to lose a regard for private interest in universal sympathy. He loved all mankind; for fortune prevented him from knowing that there were rascals. Physicians tell us of a disorder in which the whole body is so exquisitely sensible that the slightest touch gives pain: what some have thus suffered in their persons this gentleman felt in his mind. The slightest distress, whether real or fictitious, touched him to the quick, and his soul laboured under a sickly sensibility of the miseries of others. Thus disposed to relieve, it will be easily conjectured he found numbers disposed to solicit: his profusions began to impair his fortune, but not his good-nature; that, indeed, was seen to increase as the other seemed to decay; he grew improvident as he grew poor; and though he talked like a man of sense, his actions were those of a fool. Still, however, being surrounded with importunity, and no longer able to satisfy every request that was made him, instead of *money* he gave *promises*. They were all he had to bestow, and he had not resolution enough to give any man pain by a denial. By this means he drew round him crowds of dependants whom he was sure to disappoint, yet wished to relieve. These hung upon him for a time, and left him with merited reproaches and contempt. But in proportion as he became contemptible to others, he became despicable to himself. His mind had leaned upon their adulation, and that support taken away, he could find no pleasure in the applause of his heart, which he had never learnt to reverence itself. The world now began to wear a different aspect; the flattery of his friends began to dwindle into simple approbation that soon took the more friendly form of advice, and advice when rejected ever begets reproaches. He now found that such friends as benefits had gathered round him were by no means the most estimable: it was now found that a man's own heart must be ever given to gain that of another. I now found that—but I forget what I was going to observe: in short, sir, he resolved to respect himself, and laid down a plan of restoring his shattered fortune. For this purpose, in his own whimsical manner, he travelled through Europe on foot, and before he attained the age of thirty, his circumstances were more affluent than ever. At present, therefore, his bounties are more rational and moderate than before; but still he preserves the character of an humourist, and finds most pleasure in eccentric virtues."

My attention was so much taken up by Mr. Burchell's account that I scarce looked forward as we went along, till we were alarmed by the cries of my family, when, turning, I perceived my youngest daughter in the midst of a rapid stream, thrown from her horse, and struggling with the torrent. She had sunk twice, nor was it in my power to disengage myself in time to bring her relief. My sensations were even too violent to permit my attempting her rescue: she would have certainly perished had not my companion, perceiving her danger, instantly plunged in to her relief, and, with some difficulty, brought her in safety to the opposite shore. By taking the current a little farther up, the rest of the family got safely over, where we had an opportunity of joining our acknowledgments to hers. Her gratitude may be more readily imagined than described: she thanked her deliverer more with looks than words, and continued to lean upon his arm, as if still willing to receive assistance. My wife also hoped one day to have the pleasure of returning his kindness at her own house. Thus, after we were all refreshed at the next inn, and had dined together, as he was going to a different part of the country, he took leave; and we pursued our journey. My wife observing as we went that she liked Mr. Burchell extremely, and protesting that if he had birth and fortune to entitle him to match into such a family as ours, she knew no man she would sooner fix upon. I could not but smile to hear her talk in this strain: one almost at the verge of beggary thus to assume language of the most insulting affluence might excite the ridicule of ill-nature; but I was never much displeased with those innocent delusions that tend to make us more happy.

CHAPTER IV

A PROOF THAT EVEN THE HUMBLEST FORTUNE MAY GRANT HAPPINESS AND DELIGHT, WHICH DEPEND NOT ON CIRCUMSTANCE, BUT CONSTITUTION

The place of our new retreat was in a little neighbourhood consisting of farmers who tilled their own grounds and were equal strangers to opulence and poverty. As they had almost all the conveniences of life within themselves, they seldom visited towns or cities in search of superfluity. Remote from the polite, they still retained a primeval simplicity of manners, and frugal by long habit, scarce knew that temperance was a virtue. They wrought with cheerfulness on days of labour, but observed festivals as intervals of idleness and pleasure. They kept up the Christmas carol, sent true love-knots on Valentine morning, ate pancakes on Shrovetide, showed their wit on the first of April, and religiously cracked nuts on Michaelmas eve. Being apprized of our approach, the whole neighbourhood came out to meet their minister, drest in their finest clothes, and preceded by a pipe and tabor: also a feast was provided for our reception, at which we sat cheerfully down; and what the conversation wanted in wit, we made up in laughter.

Our little habitation was situated at the foot of a sloping hill, sheltered with a beautiful underwood behind, and a prattling river before; on one side a meadow, on the other a green. My farm consisted of about twenty acres of excellent land, having given an hundred pound for my predecessor's good-will. Nothing could exceed the neatness of my little enclosures, the elms and hedge rows appearing with inexpressible beauty. My house consisted of but one story, and was covered with thatch, which gave it an air of great snugness; the walls on the inside were nicely white-washed, and my daughters undertook to adorn them with pictures of their own designing. Though the same room served us for parlour and kitchen, that only made it the warmer. Besides, as it was kept with the utmost neatness, the dishes, plates, and coppers being well scoured and all disposed in bright rows on the shelves, the eye was agreeably relieved, and did not seem to want rich furniture. There were three other apartments, one for my wife and me, another for our two daughters within our own, and the third, with two beds, for the rest of my children.

The little republic to which I gave laws was regulated in the following manner: by sun-rise we all assembled in our common apartment, the fire being previously kindled by the servant. After we had saluted each other with proper ceremony, for I always thought fit to keep up some mechanical forms of good breeding, without which freedom ever destroys friendship, we all bent in gratitude to that Being who gave us another day. This duty being performed, my son and I went to pursue our usual industry abroad, while my wife and daughters employed themselves in providing breakfast, which was always ready at a certain time. I allowed half an hour for this meal, and an hour for dinner; which time was taken up in innocent mirth between my wife and daughters, and in philosophical arguments between my son and me.

As we rose with the sun, so we never pursued our labours after it was gone down, but returned home to the expecting family, where smiling looks, a neat hearth, and pleasant fire were prepared for our reception. Nor were we without other guests: sometimes farmer Flamborough, our talkative neighbour, and often the blind piper, would pay us a visit and taste our gooseberry wine, for the making of which we had lost neither the receipt nor the reputation. These harmless people had several ways of being good company; while one played the pipes, another would sing some soothing ballad, *Johnny Armstrong's Last Good Night*, or *The Cruelty of Barbara Allen*. The night was concluded in the manner we began the morning, my youngest boys being appointed to read the lessons of the day; and he that read loudest, distinctest, and best was to have an halfpenny on Sunday to put in the poor's box.

When Sunday came, it was indeed a day of finery, which all my sumptuary edicts could not restrain. How well so ever I fancied my lectures against pride had conquered the vanity of my daughters, yet I still found them secretly attached to all their former finery: they still loved laces, ribands, bugles, and catgut; my wife herself retained a passion for her crimson paduasoy, because I formerly happened to say it became her.

The first Sunday in particular their behaviour served to mortify me. I had desired my girls the preceding night to be drest early the next day; for I always loved to be at church a good while before the rest of the congregation. They punctually obeyed my directions; but when we were to assemble in the morning at breakfast, down came my wife and daughters, drest out in all their former splendour: their hair plastered up with pomatum, their faces patched to taste, their trains bundled up into an heap behind, and rustling at every motion. I could not help smiling at their vanity, particularly that of my wife, from whom I expected more discretion. In this exigence, therefore, my only resource was to order my son, with with an important air, to call our coach. The girls were amazed at the command; but I repeated it with more solemnity than before. "Surely, my dear, you jest," cried my wife; "we can walk it perfectly well: we want no coach to carry us now."—"You mistake, child," returned I, "we do want a coach; for if we walk to church in this trim, the very children in the parish will hoot after us for a show."——"Indeed," replied my wife, "I always imagined that my Charles was fond of seeing his children neat and handsome about him."——"You may be as neat as you please," interrupted I, "and I shall love you the better for it; but all this is not neatness, but frippery. These rufflings, and pinkings, and patchings will only make us hated by all the wives of all our neighbours. No, my children," continued I, more gravely, "those gowns may be altered into something of a plainer cut; for finery is very unbecoming in us, who want the means of decency. I don't know whether such flouncing and shredding is becoming even in the rich, if we consider, upon a moderate calculation, that the nakedness of the indigent world may be clothed from the trimmings of the vain."

This remonstrance had the proper effect; they went with great composure, that very instant, to change their dress; and the next day I had the satisfaction of finding my daughters, at their own request, employed in cutting up their trains into Sunday waistcoats for Dick and Bill, the two little ones, and what was still more satisfactory, the gowns seemed improved by being thus curtailed.

CHAPTER V

A NEW AND GREAT ACQUAINTANCE INTRODUCED. WHAT WE PLACE MOST HOPES UPON GENERALLY PROVES MOST FATAL

At a small distance from the house my predecessor had made a seat, overshaded by an hedge of hawthorn and honeysuckle. Here, when the weather was fine, and our labour soon finished, we usually all sat together, to enjoy an extensive landscape, in the calm of the evening. Here too we drank tea, which now was become an occasional banquet; and as we had it but seldom, it diffused a new joy, the preparations for it being made with no small share of bustle and ceremony. On these occasions, our two little ones always read for us, and they were regularly served after we had done. Sometimes, to give a variety to our amusements, the girls sung to the guitar; and while they thus formed a little concert, my wife and I would stroll down the sloping field, that was embellished with blue-bells and centaury, talk of our children with rapture, and enjoy the breeze that wafted both health and harmony.

In this manner we began to find that every situation in life might bring its own peculiar pleasures; every morning waked us to a repetition of toil, but the evening repaid it with vacant hilarity.

It was about the beginning of autumn, on a holiday, for I kept such as intervals of relaxation from labour, that I had drawn out my family to our usual place of amusement, and our young musicians began their usual concert. As we were thus engaged, we saw a stag bound nimbly by, within about twenty paces of where we were sitting, and by its panting, it seemed prest by the hunters. We had not much time to reflect upon the poor animal's distress, when we perceived the dogs and horsemen come sweeping along at some distance behind, and making the very path it had taken. I was instantly for returning in with my family; but either curiosity or surprise, or some more hidden motive, held my wife and daughters to their seats. The huntsman, who rode foremost, past us with great swiftness, followed by four or five persons more, who seemed in equal haste. At last, a young gentleman of a more genteel appearance than the rest came forward, and for a while regarding us, instead of pursuing the chase, stopt short, and giving his horse to a servant who attended, approached us with a careless superior air. He seemed to want no introduction, but was going to salute my daughters as one certain of a kind reception; but they had early learnt the lesson of looking presumption out of countenance. Upon which he let us know that his name was Thornhill, and that he was owner of the estate that lay for some extent round us. He again, therefore, offered to salute the female part of the family; and such was the power of fortune and fine clothes that he found no second repulse. As his address, though confident, was easy, we soon became more familiar; and perceiving musical instruments lying near, he begged to be favoured with a song. As I did not approve of such disproportioned acquaintances, I winked upon my daughters in order to prevent their compliance; but my hint was counteracted by one from their mother, so that with a cheerful air they gave us a favourite song of Dryden's. Mr. Thornhill seemed highly delighted with their performance and choice, and then took up the guitar himself. He played but very indifferently; however, my eldest daughter repaid his former applause with interest, and assured him that his tones were louder than even those of her master. At this compliment he bowed, which she returned with a curtsey. He praised her taste, and she commended his understanding: an age could not have made them better acquainted. While the fond mother too, equally happy, insisted upon her landlord's stepping in and tasting a glass of her gooseberry. The whole family seemed earnest to please him: my girls attempted to entertain him with topics they thought most modern, while Moses, on the contrary, gave him a question or two from the ancients, for which he had the satisfaction of being laughed at; for he always ascribed to his wit that laughter which was lavished at his simplicity: my little ones were no less busy, and fondly stuck close to the stranger. All my endeavours could scarce keep their dirty fingers from handling and tarnishing the lace on his clothes and lifting up the flaps of his pocket-holes to see what was there. At the approach of evening he took leave; but not till he had requested permission to renew his visit, which, as he was our landlord, we most readily agreed to.

As soon as he was gone, my wife called a council on the conduct of the day. She was of opinion that it was a most fortunate hit; for that she had known even stranger things at last brought to bear. She hoped again to see the day in which we might hold up our heads with the best of them; and concluded, she protested she could see no reason why the two Miss Wrinklers should marry great fortunes, and her children get none. As this last argument was directed to me, I protested I could see no reason for it neither, nor why one got the ten thousand pound prize in the lottery and another sat down with a blank. "But those," added I, "who either aim at husbands greater than themselves or at the ten thousand pound prize have been fools for their ridiculous claims, whether successful or not." —"I protest, Charles," cried my wife, "this is the way you always damp my girls and me when we are in spirits. Tell me, Sophy, my dear, what do you think of our new visitor? Don't you think he seemed to be good-natured?"—"Immensely so, indeed, mamma," replied she. "I think he has a great deal to say upon every thing, and is never at a loss; and the more trifling the subject, the more he has to say; and what is more, I protest he is very handsome."——"Yes," cried Olivia, "he is well enough for a man; but for my part, I don't much like him, he is so extremely impudent and familiar; but on the guitar he is shocking." These two last speeches I interpreted by contraries. I found by this that Sophia internally despised as much as Olivia secretly admired him. "Whatever may be your opinions of him, my children," cried I, "to confess a truth, he has not prepossest me in his favour. Disproportioned friendships ever terminate in disgust; and I thought, notwithstanding all his ease, that he seemed perfectly sensible of the distance between us. Let us keep to companions of our own rank. There is no character among men more contemptible than that of a fortune-hunter; and I can see no reason why fortune-hunting women should not be contemptible too. Thus, at best, it will be contempt if his views are honourable; but if they are otherwise! I should shudder but to think of that; for though I have no apprehensions from the conduct of my children, I think there are some from his character." I would have proceeded, but for the interruption of a servant from the Squire, who, with his compliments, sent us a side of venison and a promise to dine with us some days after. This well-timed present pleaded more powerfully in his favour than any thing I had to say could obviate. I therefore continued silent, satisfied with just having pointed out danger, and leaving it to their own discretion to avoid it. That virtue which requires to be ever guarded is scarce worth the sentinel.

CHAPTER VI

THE HAPPINESS OF A COUNTRY FIRE-SIDE

As we carried on the former dispute with some degree of warmth, in order to accommodate matters, it was universally concluded upon that we should have a part of the venison for supper, and the girls undertook the task with alacrity. "I am sorry," cried I, "that we have no neighbour or stranger to take a part in this good cheer: feasts of this kind acquire a double relish from hospitality."——"Bless me," cried my wife, "here comes our good friend Mr. Burchell, that saved our Sophia, and that run you down fairly in the argument."——"Confute me in argument, child!" cried I. "You mistake there, my dear. I believe there are but few that can do that. I never dispute your abilities at making a goose-pie, and I beg you'll leave argument to me." As I spoke, poor Mr. Burchell entered the house, and was welcomed by the family, who shook him heartily by the hand, while little Dick officiously reached him a chair.

I was pleased with the poor man's friendship for two reasons: because I knew that he wanted mine, and I knew him to be friendly as far as he was able. He was known in our neighbourhood by the character of the poor gentleman that would do no good when he was young, though he was not yet above thirty. He would at intervals talk with great good sense; but in general he was fondest of the company of children, whom he used to call harmless little men. He was famous, I found, for singing them ballads and telling them stories, and seldom went without something in his pockets for them, a piece of gingerbread or a halfpenny whistle. He generally came into our neighbourhood once a year and lived upon the neighbours' hospitality. He sat down to supper among us, and my wife was not sparing of her gooseberry wine. The tale went round; he sung us old songs, and gave the children the story of the Buck of Beverland, with the history of Patient Grissel. The adventures of Catskin next entertained them, and then Fair Rosamond's bower. Our cock, which always crew at eleven, now told us it was time for repose; but an unforeseen difficulty started about lodging the stranger: all our beds were already taken up, and it was too late to send him to the next alehouse. In this dilemma, little Dick offered him his part of the bed, if his brother Moses would let him lie with him. "And I," cried Bill, "will give Mr. Burchell my part, if my sisters will take me to theirs."——"Well done, my good children," cried I, "hospitality is one of the first Christian duties. The beast retires to its shelter, and the bird flies to its nest; but helpless man can only find refuge from his fellow creature. The greatest stranger in this world was he that came to save it. He never had an house, as if willing to see what hospitality was left remaining amongst us. Deborah, my dear," cried I to my wife, "give those boys a lump of sugar each, and let Dick's be the largest, because he spoke first."

In the morning early I called out my whole family to help at saving an after-growth of hay, and our guest offering his assistance, he was accepted among the number. Our labours went on lightly, we turned the swath to the wind, I went foremost, and the rest followed in due succession. I could not avoid, however, observing the assiduity of Mr. Burchell in assisting my daughter Sophia in her part of the task. When he had finished his own, he would join in hers, and enter into a close conversation: but I had too good an opinion of Sophia's understanding, and was too well convinced of her ambition, to be under any uneasiness from a man of broken fortune. When we were finished for the day, Mr. Burchell was invited as on the night before; but he refused, as he was to lie that night at a neighbour's, to whose child he was carrying a whistle. When gone, our conversation at supper turned upon our late unfortunate guest. "What a strong instance," said I, "is that poor man of the miseries attending a youth of levity and extravagance. He by no means wants sense, which only serves to aggravate his former folly. Poor forlorn creature, where are now the revellers, the flatterers, that he could once inspire and command! Gone, perhaps, to attend the bagnio pander, grown rich by his extravagance. They once praised him, and now they applaud the pander: their former raptures at his wit are now converted into sarcasms at his folly: he is poor, and perhaps deserves poverty; for he has neither the ambition to be independent, nor the skill to be useful." Prompted, perhaps, by some secret reasons, I delivered this observation with too much acrimony, which my Sophia gently reproved. "Whatsoever his former conduct may be, pappa, his circumstances should exempt him from censure now. His present indigence is a sufficient punishment for former folly; and I have heard my pappa himself say that we should never strike our unnecessary blow at a victim over whom providence already holds the scourge of its resentment."——"You are right, Sophy," cried my son Moses, "and one of the ancients finely represents so malicious a conduct, by the attempts of a rustic to flay Marsyas, whose skin, the fable tells us, had been wholly stript off by another. Besides, I don't know if this poor man's situation be so bad as my father would represent it. We are not to judge of the feelings of others by what we might feel if in their place. However dark the habitation of the mole to our eyes, yet the animal itself finds the apartment sufficiently lightsome. And to confess a truth, this man's mind seems fitted to his station; for I never heard any one more sprightly than he was to-day, when he conversed with you." This was said without the least design; however, it excited a blush, which she strove to cover by an affected laugh, assuring him that she scarce took any notice of what he said to her, but that she believed he might once have been a very fine gentleman. The readiness with which she undertook to vindicate herself, and her blushing, were symptoms I did not internally approve; but I represt my suspicions.

As we expected our landlord the next day, my wife went to make the venison pasty: Moses sat reading, while I taught the little ones; my daughters seemed equally busy with the rest; and I observed them for a good while cooking something over the fire. I at first supposed they were assisting their mother; but little Dick informed me in a whisper that they were making a *wash* for the face. Washes of all kinds I had a natural antipathy to; for I knew that instead of mending the complexion they spoiled it. I therefore approached my chair by sly degrees to the fire, and grasping the poker, as if it wanted mending, seemingly by accident overturned the whole composition, and it was too late to begin another.

CHAPTER VII

A TOWN WIT DESCRIBED. THE DULLEST FELLOWS MAY LEARN TO BE COMICAL FOR A NIGHT OR TWO

When the morning arrived on which we were to entertain our young landlord, it may be easily supposed what provisions were exhausted to make an appearance. It may also be conjectured that my wife and daughters expanded their gayest plumage upon this occasion. Mr. Thornhill came with a couple of friends, his chaplain and feeder. The servants, who were numerous, he politely ordered to the next ale-house: but my wife, in the triumph of her heart, insisted on entertaining them all; for which, by the bye, the family was pinched for three weeks after. As Mr. Burchell had hinted to us the day before that he was making some proposals of marriage to Miss Wilmot, my son George's former mistress, this a good deal damped the heartiness of his reception: but accident, in some measure, relieved our embarrassment; for one of the company happening to mention her name, Mr. Thornhill observed with an oath, that he never knew any thing more absurd than calling such a fright a beauty: "For strike me ugly," continued he, "if I should not find as much pleasure in choosing my mistress by the information of a lamp under the clock at St. Dunstan's." At this he laughed, and so did we: the jests of the rich are ever successful. Olivia too could not avoid whispering, loud enough to be heard, that he had an infinite fund of humour.

After dinner, I began with my usual toast, the church; for this I was thanked by the chaplain, as he said the church was the only mistress of his affections. "Come, tell us honestly, Frank," said the Squire, with his usual archness, "suppose the church, your present mistress, drest in lawn sleeves, on one hand, and Miss Sophia, with no lawn about her, on the other, which would you be for?" —"For both, to be sure," cried the chaplain.——"Right, Frank," cried the Squire; "for may this glass suffocate me but a fine girl is worth all the priestcraft in the nation. For what are tithes and tricks but an imposition, all a confounded imposture, and I can prove it." ——"I wish you would," cried my son Moses, "and I think," continued he, "that I should be able to combat in the opposition."——"Very well, sir," cried the Squire, who immediately smoked him, and winking on the rest of the company, to prepare us for the sport, "if you are for a cool argument upon that subject, I am ready to accept the challenge. And first, whether are you for managing it analogically or dialogically?"—"I am for managing it rationally," cried Moses, quite happy at being permitted to dispute.—"Good again," cried the Squire, "and firstly, of the first. I hope you'll not deny that whatever is, is. If you don't grant me that, I can go no further."——"Why," returned Moses, "I think I may grant that, and make the best of it."——"I hope too," returned the other, "you'll grant that a part is less than the whole."—"I grant that too," cried Moses, "It is but just and reasonable."——"I hope," cried the Squire, "you will not deny that the two angles of a triangle are equal to two right ones."——"Nothing can be plainer," returned t'other, and looked round with his usual importance.——"Very well," cried the Squire, speaking very quick, "the premises being thus settled, I proceed to observe that the concatenation of self-existences, proceeding in a reciprocal duplicate ratio, naturally produce a problematical dialogism, which in some measure proves that the essence of spirituality may be referred to the second predicable"——"Hold, hold," cried the other, "I deny that. Do you think I can thus tamely submit to such heterodox doctrines?"——"What," replied the Squire, as if in a passion, "not submit! Answer me one plain question: Do you think Aristotle right when he says that relatives are related?"—"Undoubtedly," replied the other.——"If so then," cried the Squire, "answer me directly to what I propose: Whether do you judge the analytical investigation of the first part of my enthymem deficient secundum quoad, or quoad minus, and give me your reasons too; give me your reasons, I say, directly."——"I protest," cried Moses, "I don't rightly comprehend the force of your reasoning; but if it be reduced to one simple proposition, I fancy it may then have an answer."——"O, sir," cried the Squire, "I am your most humble servant, I find you want me to furnish you with argument and intellects both. No, sir, there I protest you are too hard for me." This effectually raised the laugh against poor Moses, who sat the only dismal figure in a group of merry faces: nor did he offer a single syllable more during the whole entertainment.

But though all this gave me no pleasure, it had a very different effect upon Olivia, who mistook this humour, which was a mere act of the memory, for real wit. She thought him therefore a very fine gentleman; and such as consider what powerful ingredients a good figure, fine clothes, and fortune are in that character will easily forgive her. Mr. Thornhill, notwithstanding his real ignorance, talked with ease, and could expatiate upon the common topics of conversation with fluency. It is not surprising then that such talents should win the affections of a girl who by education was taught to value an appearance in herself, and consequently to set a value upon it when found in another.

Upon his departure, we again entered into a debate upon the merits of our young landlord. As he directed his looks and conversation to Olivia, it was no longer doubted but that she was the object that induced him to be our visitor. Nor did she seem to be much displeased at the innocent raillery of her brother and sister upon this occasion. Even Deborah herself seemed to share the glory of the day, and exulted in her daughter's victory as if it were her own. "And now, my dear," cried she to me, "I'll fairly own that it was I that instructed my girls to encourage our landlord's addresses. I had always some ambition, and you now see that I was right; for who knows how this may end?"—"Ay, who knows that indeed," answered I, with a groan: "for my part I don't much like it; and I could have been better pleased with one that was poor and honest than this fine gentleman with his fortune and infidelity; for depend on't, if he be what I suspect him, no free-thinker shall ever have a child of mine."

"Sure, father," cried Moses, "you are too severe in this; for heaven will never arraign him for what he thinks, but for what he does. Every man has a thousand vicious thoughts, which arise without his power to suppress. Thinking freely of religion may be involuntary with this gentleman: so that allowing his sentiments to be wrong, yet as he is purely passive in their reception, he is no more to be blamed for their incursions than the governor of a city without walls for the shelter he is obliged to afford an invading enemy."

"True, my son," cried I; "but if the governor invites the enemy, there he is justly culpable. And such is always the case with those who embrace error. The vice does not lie in assenting to the proofs they see; but in being blind to many of the proofs that offer. Like corrupt judges on a bench, they determine right on that part of the evidence they hear; but they will not hear all the evidence. Thus, my son, though our erroneous opinions be involuntary when formed, yet as we have been wilfully corrupt, or very negligent in forming them, we deserve punishment for our vice, or contempt for our folly."

My wife now kept up the conversation, though not the argument: she observed that several very prudent men of our acquaintance were free-thinkers and made very good husbands; and she knew some sensible girls that had skill enough to make converts of their spouses. "And who knows, my dear," continued she, "what Olivia may be able to do. The girl has a great deal to say upon every subject, and to my knowledge is very well skilled in controversy."

"Why, my dear, what controversy can she have read?" cried I. "It does not occur to my memory that I ever put such books into her hands; you certainly over-rate her merit."—"Indeed, pappa," replied Olivia, "she does not;

I have read a great deal of controversy. I have read the disputes between Thwackum and Square; the controversy between Robinson Crusoe and Friday the savage, and I am now employed in reading the controversy in Religious courtship."——"Very well," cried I, "that's a good girl. I find you are perfectly qualified for making converts, and so go help your mother to make the gooseberry-pie."

CHAPTER VIII

AN AMOUR, WHICH PROMISES LITTLE GOOD FORTUNE, YET MAY BE PRODUCTIVE OF MUCH

The next morning we were again visited by Mr. Burchell, though I began, for certain reasons, to be displeased with the frequency of his return; but I could not refuse him my company and fire-side. It is true his labour more than requited his entertainment; for he wrought among us with vigour, and either in the meadow or at the hay-rick put himself foremost. Besides, he had always something amusing to say that lessened our toil, and was at once so out of the way and yet so sensible that I loved, laughed at, and pitied him. My only dislike arose from an attachment he discovered to my daughter; he would, in a jesting manner, call her his little mistress, and when he bought each of the girls a set of ribands, hers was the finest. I knew not how, but he every day seemed to become more amiable, his wit to improve, and his simplicity to assume the superior airs of wisdom.

Our family dined in the field, and we sat, or rather reclined, round a temperate repast, our cloth spread upon the hay, while Mr. Burchell seemed to give cheerfulness to the feast. To heighten our satisfaction two blackbirds answered each other from opposite hedges, the familiar redbreast came and pecked the crumbs from our hands, and every sound seemed but the echo of tranquillity. "I never sit thus," says Sophia, "but I think of the two lovers, so sweetly described by Mr. Gay, who were struck dead in each other's arms under a barley mow. There is something so pathetic in the description that I have read it an hundred times with new rapture."——"In my opinion," cried my son, "the finest strokes in that description are much below those in the Acis and Galatea of Ovid. The Roman poet understands the use of *contrast* better, and upon that figure artfully managed all strength in the pathetic depends."——"It is remarkable," cried Mr. Burchell, "that both the poets you mention have equally contributed to introduce a false taste into their respective countries, by loading all their lines with epithet. Men of little genius found them most easily imitated in their defects, and English poetry, like that in the latter empire of Rome, is nothing at present but a combination of luxuriant images without plot or connexion; a string of epithets that improve the sound without carrying on the sense. But perhaps, madam, while I thus reprehend others, you'll think it just that I should give them an opportunity to retaliate, and indeed I have made this remark only to have an opportunity of introducing to the company a ballad which, whatever be its other defects, is I think at least free from those I have mentioned."

A BALLAD

"Turn, gentle hermit of the dale,
 And guide my lonely way,
To where yon taper cheers the vale,
 With hospitable ray.

"For here forlorn and lost I tread,
 With fainting steps and slow;
Where wilds immeasurably spread,
 Seem lengthening as I go."

"Forbear, my son," the hermit cries,
 "To tempt the dangerous gloom;
For yonder phantom only flies
 To lure thee to thy doom.

"Here to the houseless child of want,
My door is open still;
And tho' my portion is but scant,
I give it with good will.

"Then turn to-night, and freely share
Whate'er my cell bestows;
My rushy couch, and frugal fare,
My blessing and repose.

"No flocks that range the valley free,
To slaughter I condemn:
Taught by that power that pities me,
I learn to pity them.

"But from the mountain's grassy side
A guiltless feast I bring;
A scrip with herbs and fruits supplied,
And water from the spring.

"Then, pilgrim, turn, thy cares forego;
For earth-born cares are wrong:
Man wants but little here below,
Nor wants that little long."

Soft as the dew from heav'n descends,
His gentle accents fell:
The grateful stranger lowly bends,
And follows to the cell.

Far shelter'd in a glade obscure
The modest mansion lay;
A refuge to the neighbouring poor
And strangers led astray.

No stores beneath its humble thatch
Requir'd a master's care;
The door just opening with a latch,
Receiv'd the harmless pair.

And now when worldly crowds retire
  To revels or to rest,
The hermit trimm'd his little fire,
  And cheer'd his pensive guest;

And spread his vegetable store,
  And gayly prest, and smil'd,
And skill'd in legendary lore,
  The lingering hours beguil'd.

Around in sympathetic mirth
  Its tricks the kitten tries,
The cricket chirrups in the hearth;
  The crackling faggot flies.

But nothing could a charm impart
  To soothe the stranger's woe;
For grief was heavy at his heart,
  And tears began to flow.

His rising cares the hermit spied,
  With answering care opprest:
"And whence, unhappy youth," he cried,
  "The sorrows of thy breast?

"From better habitations spurn'd,
  Reluctant dost thou rove;
Or grieve for friendship unreturn'd,
  Or unregarded love?

"Alas! the joys that fortune brings
  Are trifling and decay;
And those who prize the paltry things,
  More trifling still than they.

"And what is friendship but a name,
  A charm that lulls to sleep;
A shade that follows wealth or fame,
  But leaves the wretch to weep?

"And love is still an emptier sound,
The haughty fair one's jest;
On earth unseen, or only found
To warm the turtle's nest.

"For shame, fond youth, thy sorrows hush,
And spurn the sex," he said:
But while he spoke a rising blush
The bashful guest betray'd.

He sees unnumber'd beauties rise,
Expanding to the view;
Like clouds that deck the morning skies,
As bright, as transient too.

Her looks, her lips, her panting breast
Alternate spread alarms:
The lovely stranger stands confest
A maid in all her charms.

"And, ah, forgive a stranger rude,
A wretch forlorn," she cried;
"Whose feet unhallowed thus intrude
Where heaven and you reside.

"But let a maid thy pity share,
Whom love has taught to stray;
Who seeks for rest, but finds despair
Companion of her way.

"My father liv'd beside the Tyne,
A wealthy Lord was he;
And all his wealth was mark'd as mine,
He had but only me.

"To win me from his tender arms,
Unnumber'd suitors came;
Who prais'd me for imputed charms,
And felt or feign'd a flame.

"Each morn the gay phantastic crowd
With richest proffers strove:
Among the rest young Edwin bow'd,
But never talk'd of love.

"In humble simplest habit clad,
No wealth nor power had he;
A constant heart was all he had,
But that was all to me.

"The blossom opening to the day,
The dews of heaven refin'd,
Could nought of purity display,
To emulate his mind.

"The dew, the blossom on the tree,
With charms inconstant shrine;
Their charms were his, but woe to me,
Their constancy was mine.

"For still I tried each fickle art,
Importunate and vain;
And while his passion touch'd my heart,
I triumph'd in his pain.

"Till quite dejected with my scorn,
He left me to my pride;
And sought a solitude forlorn,
In secret where he died.

"But mine the sorrow, mine the fault,
And well my life shall pay;
I'll seek the solitude he sought,
And stretch me where he lay.

"And there forlorn despairing hid,
I'll lay me down and die:
'Twas so for me that Edwin did,
And so for him will I."

"Thou shalt not thus," the hermit cried,
And clasp'd her to his breast:
The wondering fair one turn'd to chide,
'Twas Edwin's self that prest.

"Turn, Angelina, ever dear,
My charmer, turn to see,
Thy own, thy long-lost Edwin here,
Restor'd to love and thee.

"Thus let me hold thee to my heart,
And ev'ry care resign:
And shall we never, never part,
O thou—my all that's mine.

"No, never, from this hour to part,
We'll live and love so true;
The sigh that rends thy constant heart,
Shall break thy Edwin's too."

While this ballad was reading, Sophia seemed to mix an air of tenderness with her approbation. But our tranquillity was soon disturbed by the report of a gun just by us, and immediately after a man was seen bursting through the hedge to take up the game he had killed. This sportsman was the Squire's chaplain, who had shot one of the blackbirds that so agreeably entertained us. So loud a report, and so near, startled my daughters; and I could perceive that Sophia in the fright had thrown herself into Mr. Burchell's arms for protection. The gentleman came up and asked pardon for having disturbed us, affirming that he was ignorant of our being so near. He therefore sat down by my youngest daughter, and, sportsman like, offered her what he had killed that morning. She was going to refuse, but a private look from her mother soon induced her to correct the mistake and accept his present, though with some reluctance. My wife, as usual, discovered her pride in a whisper, observing that Sophy had made a conquest of the chaplain as well as her sister had of the Squire. I suspected, however, with more probability, that her affections were placed upon a different object. The chaplain's errand was to inform us that Mr. Thornhill had provided music and refreshments, and intended that night giving the young ladies a ball by moonlight on the grass-plot before our door. "Nor can I deny," continued he, "but I have an interest in being first to deliver this message, as I expect for my reward to be honoured with Miss Sophy's hand as a partner." To this my girl replied that she should have no objection, if she could do it with honour. "But here," continued she, "is a gentleman," looking at Mr. Burchell, "who has been my companion in the task for the day, and it is fit he should share in its amusements." Mr. Burchell returned her a compliment for her intentions, but resigned her up to the chaplain, adding that he was to go that night five miles, being invited to an harvest supper. His refusal appeared to me a little extraordinary, nor could I conceive how so sensible a girl as my youngest could thus prefer a middle-aged man of broken fortune to a sprightly young fellow of twenty-two. But as men are most capable of distinguishing merit in women, so the ladies often form the truest judgments upon us. The two sexes seem placed as spies upon each other, and are furnished with different abilities, adapted for mutual inspection.

CHAPTER IX

TWO LADIES OF GREAT DISTINCTION INTRODUCED. SUPERIOR FINERY EVER SEEMS TO CONFER SUPERIOR BREEDING

Mr. Burchell had scarce taken leave, and Sophia consented to dance with the chaplain, when my little ones came running out to tell us that the Squire was come with a crowd of company. Upon our return, we found our landlord with a couple of under gentlemen and two young ladies richly drest, whom he introduced as women of very great distinction and fashion from town. We happened not to have chairs enough for the whole company; but Mr. Thornhill immediately proposed that every gentleman should sit in a lady's lap. This I positively objected to, notwithstanding a look of disapprobation from my wife. Moses was therefore dispatched to borrow a couple of chairs; and as we were in want of ladies also to make up a set at country dances, the two gentlemen went with him in quest of a couple of partners. Chairs and partners were soon provided. The gentlemen returned with my neighbour Flamborough's rosy daughters, flaunting with red top-knots. But there was an unlucky circumstance which was not adverted to; though the Miss Flamboroughs were reckoned the very best dancers in the parish, and understood the jig and the roundabout to perfection, yet they were totally unacquainted with country dances. This at first discomposed us; however, after a little shoving and dragging, they began to go merrily on. Our music consisted of two fiddles, with a pipe and tabor. The moon shone bright. Mr. Thornhill and my eldest daughter led up the ball, to the great delight of the spectators; for the neighbours hearing what was going forward came flocking about us. My girl moved with so much grace and vivacity that my wife could not avoid discovering the pride of her heart, by assuring me that though the little chit did it so cleverly, all the steps were stolen from herself. The ladies of the town strove hard to be equally easy, but without success. They swam, sprawled, languished, and frisked; but all would not do: the gazers indeed owned that it was fine; but neighbour Flamborough observed that Miss Livy's feet seemed as pat to the music as its echo. After the dance had continued about an hour, the two ladies, who were apprehensive of catching cold, moved to break up the ball. One of them, I thought, expressed her sentiments upon this occasion in a very coarse manner, when she observed, that by the *living jingo,* she was all of a muck of sweat. Upon our return to the house, we found a very elegant cold supper, which Mr. Thornhill had ordered to be brought with him. The conversation at this time was more reserved than before. The two ladies threw my girls quite into the shade; for they would talk of nothing but high life and high-lived company, with other fashionable topics, such as pictures, taste, Shakespear, and the musical glasses. 'Tis true they once or twice mortified us sensibly by slipping out an oath; but that appeared to me as the surest symptom of their distinction (tho' I am since informed swearing is now perfectly unfashionable). Their finery, however, threw a veil over any grossness in their conversation. My daughters seemed to regard their superior accomplishments with envy, and what appeared amiss was ascribed to tip-top quality breeding. But the condescension of the ladies was still superior to their other accomplishments. One of them observed that had Miss Olivia seen a little more of the world, it would greatly improve her. To which the other added that a single winter in town would make her little Sophia quite another thing. My wife warmly assented to both; adding that there was nothing she more ardently wished than to give her girls a single winter's polishing. To this I could not help replying that their breeding was already superior to their fortune; and that greater refinement would only serve to make their poverty ridiculous and give them a taste for pleasures they had no right to possess. "And what pleasures," cried Mr. Thornhill, "do they not deserve, who have so much in their power to bestow? As for my part," continued he, "my fortune is pretty large; love, liberty, and pleasure are my maxims; but curse me if a settlement of half my estate could give my charming Olivia pleasure, it should be hers; and the only favour I would ask in return would be to add myself to the benefit." I was not such a stranger to the world as to be ignorant that this was the fashionable cant to disguise the insolence of the basest proposal; but I made an effort to suppress my resentment. "Sir," cried I, "the family which you now condescend to favour with your company has been bred with as nice a sense of honour as you. Any attempts to injure that may be attended with very dangerous consequences. Honour, sir, is our only possession at present, and of that last treasure we must be particularly careful." I was soon sorry for the warmth with which I had spoken this, when the young gentleman, grasping my hand, swore he commended my spirit, though he disapproved my suspicions. "As to your present hint," continued he, "I protest nothing was farther from my heart than such a thought. No, by all that's tempting, the virtue that will stand a regular siege was never to my taste; for all my amours are carried by a coup de main."

The two ladies, who affected to be ignorant of the rest, seemed highly displeased with this last stroke of freedom, and began a very discreet and serious dialogue upon virtue; in this my wife, the chaplain, and I soon joined; and the Squire himself was at last brought to confess a sense of sorrow for his former excesses. We talked of the pleasures of temperance, and the sun-shine in the mind unpolluted with guilt. I was well pleased that my little ones were kept up beyond the usual time to be edified by such good conversation. Mr. Thornhill even went beyond me, and demanded if I had any objection to giving prayers. I joyfully embraced the proposal, and in this manner the night was passed in a most comfortable way, till at last the company began to think of returning. The ladies seemed very unwilling to part from my daughters, for whom they had conceived a particular affection, and joined in a request to have the pleasure of their company home. The Squire seconded the proposal, and my wife added her entreaties: the girls too looked upon me as if they wished to go. In this perplexity I made two or three excuses, which my daughters as readily removed; so that at last I was obliged to give a peremptory refusal, for which we had nothing but sullen looks and short answers the whole day ensuing.

CHAPTER X

THE FAMILY ENDEAVORS TO COPE WITH THEIR BETTERS. THE MISERIES OF THE POOR WHEN THEY ATTEMPT TO APPEAR ABOVE THEIR CIRCUMSTANCES

I now began to find that all my long and painful lectures upon temperance, simplicity, and contentment were entirely disregarded. The distinctions lately paid us by our betters awaked that pride which I had laid asleep, but not removed. Our windows now again, as formerly, were filled with washes for the neck and face. The sun was dreaded an an enemy to the skin without doors, and the fire as a spoiler of the complexion within. My wife observed that rising too early would hurt her daughters' eyes, that working after dinner would redden their noses, and convinced me that the hands never looked so white as when they did nothing. Instead therefore of finishing George's shirts, we now had them new modelling their old gauzes, or flourishing upon catgut. The poor Miss Flamboroughs, their former gay companions, were cast off as mean acquaintance, and the whole conversation ran upon high life and high lived company, with pictures, taste, Shakespear, and the musical glasses.

But we could have borne all this, had not a fortune-telling gypsy come to raise us into perfect sublimity. The tawny sybil no sooner appeared than my girls came running to me for a shilling a piece to cross her hand with silver. To say the truth, I was tired of being always wise, and could not help gratifying their request, because I loved to see them happy. I gave each of them a shilling; though, for the honour of the family, it must be observed that they never went without money themselves, as my wife always generously let them have a guinea each to keep in their pockets, but with strict injunctions never to change it. After they had been closeted up with the fortune-teller for some time, I knew by their looks, upon their returning, that they had been promised something great. "Well, my girls, how have you sped? Tell me, Livy, has the fortune-teller given thee a pennyworth?"——"I protest, pappa," says the girl, with a serious face, "I believe she deals with some body that's not right; for she positively declared that I am to be married to a great Squire in less than a twelvemonth?"——"Well now, Sophy, my child," said I, "and what sort of a husband are you to have?"—"Sir," replied she, "I am to have a Lord soon after my sister has been married to the Squire."——"How," cried I, "is that all you are to have for your two shillings! Only a Lord and a Squire for two shillings! You fools, I could have promised you a Prince and a Nabob for half the money."

This curiosity of theirs, however, was attended with very serious effects: we now began to think ourselves designed by the stars for something exalted, and already anticipated our future grandeur.

It has been a thousand times observed, and I must observe it once more, that the hours we pass with happy prospects in view are more pleasing than those crowned with fruition. In the first case we cook the dish to our own appetite; in the latter nature cooks it for us. It is impossible to repeat the train of agreeable reveries we called up for our entertainment. We looked upon our fortunes as once more rising; and as the whole parish asserted that the Squire was in love with my daughter, she was actually so with him; for they persuaded her into passion. In this agreeable interval, my wife had the most lucky dreams in the world, which she took care to tell us every morning with great solemnity and exactness. It was one night a coffin and cross bones, the sign of an approaching wedding; at another time she imagined her daughters' pockets filled with farthings, a certain sign of their being one day stuffed with gold. The girls had their omens too: they felt strange kisses on their lips; they saw rings in the candle, purses bounced from the fire, and true love-knots lurked at the bottom of every tea-cup.

Towards the end of the week we received a card from the town ladies; in which, with their compliments, they hoped to see all our family at church the Sunday following. All Saturday morning I could perceive, in consequence of this, my wife and daughters in close conference together, and now and then glancing at me with looks that betrayed a latent plot. To be sincere, I had strong suspicions that some absurd proposal was preparing for appearing with splendour the next day. In the evening they began their operations in a very regular manner, and my wife undertook to conduct the siege. After tea, when I seemed in spirits, she began thus. "I fancy, Charles, my dear, we shall have a great deal of good company at our church to-morrow."——"Perhaps we may, my dear," returned I; "though you need be under no uneasiness about that, you shall have a sermon whether there be or not." ——"That is what I expect," returned she; "but I think, my dear, we ought to appear there as decently as possible, for who knows what may happen?"—"Your precautions," replied I, "are highly commendable. A decent behaviour and appearance in church is what charms me. We should be devout and humble, cheerful and serene."——"Yes," cried she, "I know that; but I mean we should go there in as proper a manner as possible; not altogether like the scrubs about us."— "You are quite right, my dear," returned I, "and I was going to make the very same proposal. The proper manner of going is to go there as early as possible, to have time for meditation before the service begins."——"Phoo, Charles," interrupted she, "all that is very true; but not what I would be at. I mean, we should go there genteelly. You know the church is two miles off, and I protest I don't like to see my daughters trudging up to their pew all blowzed and red with walking, and looking for all the world as if they had been winners at a smock race. Now, my dear, my proposal is this: there are our two plow horses, the colt that has been in our family these nine years and his companion Blackberry, that have scarce done an earthly thing for this month past and are both grown fat and lazy. Why should not they do something as well as we? And let me tell you, when Moses has trimmed them a little, they will not be so contemptible."

To this proposal I objected that walking would be twenty times more genteel than such a paltry conveyance, as Blackberry was wall-eyed and the colt wanted a tail; that they had never been broke to the rein, but had an hundred vicious tricks; and that we had but one saddle and pillion in the whole house. All these objections, however, were over-ruled, so that I was obliged to comply. The next morning I perceived them not a little busy in collecting such materials as might be necessary for the expedition; but as I found it would be a business of much time, I walked on to the church before, and they promised speedily to follow. I waited near an hour in the reading desk for their arrival; but not finding them come as expected, I was obliged to begin, and went through the service, not without some uneasiness at finding them absent. This was increased when all was finished and no appearance of the family. I therefore walked back by the horse-way, which was five miles round, tho' the footway was but two, and when got about half way home, perceived the procession marching slowly forward towards the church; my son, my wife, and the two little ones exalted upon one horse, and my two daughters upon the other. I demanded the cause of their delay; but I soon found by their looks they had met with a thousand misfortunes on the road. The horses had at first refused to move from the door, till Mr. Burchell was kind enough to beat them forward for about two hundred yards with his cudgel. Next the straps of my wife's pillion broke down, and they were obliged to stop to repair them before they could proceed. After that, one of the horses took it into his head to stand still, and neither blows nor entreaties could prevail with him to proceed. It was just recovering from this dismal situation that I found them; but perceiving every thing safe, I own their present mortification did not much displease me, as it might give me many opportunities of future triumph, and teach my daughters more humility.

CHAPTER XI

THE FAMILY STILL RESOLVE TO HOLD UP THEIR HEADS

Michaelmas-eve happening on the next day, we were invited to burn nuts and play tricks at neighbour Flamborough's. Our late mortifications had humbled us a little, or it is probable we might have rejected such an invitation with contempt; however, we suffered ourselves to be happy. Our honest neighbour's goose and dumplings were fine, and the lamb's-wool, even in the opinion of my wife, who was a connoisseur, was thought excellent. It is true, his manner of telling stories was not quite so well. They were very long, and very dull, and all about himself, and we had laughed at them ten times before; however, we were kind enough to laugh at them once more.

Mr. Burchell, who was of the party, was always fond of seeing some innocent amusement going forward, and set the boys and girls to blind man's buff. My wife too was persuaded to join in the diversion, and it gave me pleasure to think she was not yet too old. In the meantime, my neighbour and I looked on, laughed at every feat, and praised our own dexterity when we were young. Hot cockles succeeded next, questions and commands followed that, and last of all they sat down to hunt the slipper. As every person may not be acquainted with this primeval pastime, it may be necessary to observe that the company at this play plant themselves in a ring upon the ground, all except one who stands in the middle, whose business it is to catch a shoe, which the company shove about under their hams from one to another, something like a weaver's shuttle. As it is impossible, in this case, for the lady who is up to face all the company at once, the great beauty of the play lies in hitting her a thump with the heel of the shoe on that side least capable of making a defence. It was in this manner that my eldest daughter was hemmed in, and thumped about, all blowzed, in spirits, and bawling for fair play, fair play, with a voice that might deafen a ballad singer, when confusion on confusion, who should enter the room but our two great acquaintances from town, Lady Blarney and Miss Carolina Wilelmina Amelia Skeggs! Description would but beggar, therefore it is unnecessary to describe this new mortification. Death! To be seen by ladies of such high breeding in such vulgar attitudes! Nothing better could ensue from such a vulgar play of Mr. Flamborough's proposing. We seemed stuck to the ground for some time, as if actually petrified with amazement.

The two ladies had been at our house to see us, and finding us from home, came after us hither, as they were uneasy to know what accident could have kept us from church the day before. Olivia undertook to be our prolocutor and delivered the whole in a summary way, only saying, "We were thrown from our horses." At which account the ladies were greatly concerned; but being told the family received no hurt, they were extremely glad; but being informed that we were almost killed by the fright, they were vastly sorry; but hearing that we had a very good night, they were extremely glad again. Nothing could exceed their complaisance to my daughters; their professions the last evening were warm, but now they were ardent. They protested a desire of having a more lasting acquaintance. Lady Blarney was particularly attached to Olivia; Miss Carolina Wilelmina Amelia Skeggs (I love to give the whole name) took a greater fancy to her sister. They supported the conversation between themselves, while my daughters sat silent, admiring their exalted breeding. But as every reader, however beggarly himself, is fond of high-lived dialogues, with anecdotes of Lords, Ladies, and Knights of the Garter, I must beg leave to give him the concluding part of the present conversation.

"All that I know of the matter," cried Miss Skeggs, "is this, that it may be true, or it may not be true: but this I can assure your Ladyship, that the whole rout was in amaze; his Lordship turned all manner of colours, my Lady fell into a swoon; but Sir Tomkyn, drawing his sword, swore he was hers to the last drop of his blood."

"Well," replied our Peeress, "this I can say, that the Duchess never told me a syllable of the matter, and I believe her Grace would keep nothing a secret from me. But this you may depend upon as fact, that the next morning my Lord Duke cried out three times to his valet de chambre, Jernigan, Jernigan, Jernigan, bring me my garters."

But previously I should have mentioned the very impolite behaviour of Mr. Burchell, who, during this discourse, sat with his face turned to the fire, and at the conclusion of every sentence would cry out *fudge,* an expression which displeased us all, and in some measure damped the rising spirit of the conversation.

"Besides, my dear Skeggs," continued our Peeress, "there is nothing of this in the copy of verses that Dr. Burdock made upon the occasion."

"I am surprised at that," cried Miss Skeggs; "for he seldom leaves any thing out, as he writes only for his own amusement. But can your Ladyship favour me with a sight of them?"

"My dear creature," replied our Peeress, "do you think I carry such things about me? Though they are very fine to be sure, and I think myself something of a judge; at least I know what pleases myself. Indeed I was ever an admirer of all Dr. Burdock's little pieces; for except what he does, and our dear Countess at Hanover-Square, there's nothing comes out but the most lowest stuff in nature; not a bit of high life among them."

"Your Ladyship should except," says t'other, "your own things in the Lady's Magazine. I hope you'll say there's nothing low lived there? But I suppose we are to have no more from that quarter?"

"Why, my dear," says the Lady, "you know my reader and companion has left me, to be married to Captain Roach, and as my poor eyes won't suffer me to write myself, I have been for some time looking out for another. A proper person is no easy matter to find, and to be sure thirty pounds a year is a small stipend for a well-bred girl of character that can read, write, and behave in company; as for the chits about town, there is no bearing them about one."

"That I know," cried Miss Skeggs, "by experience. For of the three companions I had this last half year, one of them refused to do plain-work an hour in the day, another thought twenty-five guineas a year too small a salary, and I was obliged to send away the third, because I suspected an intrigue with the chaplain. Virtue, my dear Lady Blarney, virtue is worth any price; but where is that to be found?"

My wife had been for a long time all attention to this discourse, but was particularly struck with the latter part of it. Thirty pounds and twenty-five guineas a year made fifty-six pounds five shillings English money, all which was in a manner going a-begging, and might easily be secured in the family. She for a moment studied my looks for approbation; and, to own a truth, I was of opinion that two such places would fit our two daughters exactly. Besides, if the Squire had any real affection for my eldest daughter, this would be the way to make her every way qualified for her fortune. My wife therefore was resolved that we should not be deprived of such advantages for want of assurance, and undertook to harangue for the family. "I hope," cried she, "your Ladyships will pardon my present presumption. It is true we have no right to pretend to such favours; but yet it is natural for me to wish putting my children forward in the world. And I will be bold to say my two girls have had a pretty good education, and capacity, at least the country can't show better. They can read, write, and cast accounts; they understand their needle, broadstitch, cross and change, and all manner of plain-work; they can pink, point, and frill; and know something of music; they can do up small clothes, work upon catgut; my eldest can cut paper and my youngest has a very pretty manner of telling fortunes upon the cards."

When she had delivered this pretty piece of eloquence, the two ladies looked at each other a few minutes in silence, with an air of doubt and importance. At last

Miss Carolina Wilelmina Amelia Skeggs condescended to observe that the young ladies, from the opinion she could form of them from so slight an acquaintance, seemed very fit for such employments. "But a thing of this kind, madam," cried she, addressing my spouse, "requires a thorough examination into characters and a more perfect knowledge of each other. Not, madam," continued she, "that I in the least suspect the young ladies' virtue, prudence, and discretion; but there is a form in these things, madam, there is a form."

My wife approved her suspicions very much, observing that she was very apt to be suspicious herself; but referred her to all the neighbours for a character; but this our Peeress declined as unnecessary, alleging that her cousin Thornhill's recommendation would be sufficient, and upon this we rested our petition.

CHAPTER XII

FORTUNE SEEMS RESOLVED TO HUMBLE THE FAMILY OF WAKEFIELD. MORTIFICATIONS ARE OFTEN MORE PAINFUL THAN REAL CALAMITIES

When we were returned home, the night was dedicated to schemes of future conquest. Deborah exerted much sagacity in conjecturing which of the two girls was likely to have the best place, and most opportunities of seeing good company. The only obstacle to our preferment was in obtaining the Squire's recommendation; but he had already shown us too many instances of his friendship to doubt of it now. Even in bed my wife kept up the usual theme: "Well, faith, my dear Charles, between ourselves, I think we have made an excellent day's work of it."——"Pretty well," cried I, not knowing what to say.——"What, only pretty well!" returned she. "I think it is very well. Suppose the girls should come to make acquaintances of taste in town! And this I am assured of, that London is the only place in the world for all manner of husbands. Besides, my dear, stranger things happen every day; and as ladies of quality are so taken with my daughters, what will not men of quality be! Entre nous, I protest I like my Lady Blarney vastly, so very obliging. However, Miss Carolina Wilelmina Amelia Skeggs has my warm heart. But yet, when they came to talk of places in town, you saw at once how I nailed them. Tell me, my dear, don't you think I did for my children there?"——"Ay," returned I, not knowing well what to think of the matter, "heaven grant they may be both the better for it this day three months!" This was one of those observations I usually made to impress my wife with an opinion of my sagacity; for if the girls succeeded, then it was a pious wish fulfilled; but if any thing unfortunate ensued, then it might be looked upon as a prophecy. All this conversation, however, was only preparatory to another scheme, and indeed I dreaded as much. This was nothing less than that as we were now to hold up our heads a little higher in the world, it would be proper to sell the colt, which was grown old, at a neighbouring fair, and buy us an horse that would carry single or double upon an occasion, and make a pretty appearance at church or upon a visit. This at first I opposed stoutly; but it was as stoutly defended. However, as I weakened, my antagonist gained strength, till at last it was resolved to part with him.

As the fair happened on the following day, I had intentions of going myself; but my wife persuaded me that I had got a cold, and nothing could prevail upon her to permit me from home. "No, my dear," said she, "our son Moses is a discreet boy, and can buy and sell to very good advantage; you know all our great bargains are of his purchasing. He always stands out and higgles, and actually tires them till he gets a bargain."

As I had some opinion of my son's prudence, I was willing enough to entrust him with this commission; and the next morning I perceived his sisters mighty busy in fitting out Moses for the fair; trimming his hair, brushing his buckles, and cocking his hat with pins. The business of the toilet being over, we had at last the satisfaction of seeing him mounted upon the colt, with a deal box before him to bring home groceries in. He had on a coat made of that cloth they call thunder and lightning, which, though grown too short, was much too good to be thrown away. His waistcoat was of gosling green, and his sisters had tied his hair with a broad black riband. We all followed him several paces from the door, bawling after him good luck, good luck, till we could see him no longer.

He was scarce gone, when Mr. Thornhill's butler came to congratulate us upon our good fortune, saying that he overheard his young master mention our names with great commendations.

Good fortune seemed resolved not to come alone. Another footman from the same family followed, with a card for my daughters, importing that the two ladies had received such a pleasing account from Mr. Thornhill of us all, that after a few previous enquiries more, they hoped to be perfectly satisfied. "Ay," cried my wife, "I now see it is no easy matter to get into the families of the great; but when one once gets in, then, as Moses says, they may go sleep." To this piece of humour, for she intended it for wit, my daughters assented with a loud laugh of pleasure. In short, such was her satisfaction at this message that she actually put her hand to her pocket and gave the messenger seven-pence halfpenny.

This was to be our visiting-day. The next that came was Mr. Burchell, who had been at the fair. He brought my little ones a pennyworth of gingerbread each, which my wife undertook to keep for them, and give them by letters at a time. He brought my daughters also a couple of boxes in which they might keep wafers, snuff, patches, or even money, when they got it. My wife was usually fond of a weasel-skin purse, as being the most lucky; but this by the bye. We had still a regard for Mr. Burchell, though his late rude behaviour was in some measure displeasing; nor could we now avoid communicating our happiness to him and asking his advice: although we seldom followed advice, we were all ready enough to ask it. When he read the note from the two ladies, he shook his head and observed that an affair of this sort demanded the utmost circumspection. This air of diffidence highly displeased my wife. "I never doubted, sir," cried she, "your readiness to be against my daughters and me. You have more circumspection than is wanted. However, I fancy when we come to ask advice, we will apply to persons who seem to have made use of it themselves."——"Whatever my own conduct may have been, madam," replied he, "is not the present question; tho' as I have made no use of advice myself, I should in conscience give it to those that will." As I was apprehensive this answer might draw on a repartee, making up by abuse what it wanted in wit, I changed the subject by seeming to wonder what could keep our son so long at the fair, as it was now almost nightfall. "Never mind our son," cried my wife; "depend upon it he knows what he is about. I'll warrant we'll never see him sell his hen of a rainy day. I have seen him buy such bargains as would amaze one. I'll tell you a good story about that, that will make you split your sides with laughing. But as I live, yonder comes Moses, without an horse, and the box at his back."

As she spoke, Moses came slowly on foot, and sweating under the deal box, which he had strapt round his shoulders. "Welcome, welcome, Moses; well, my boy, what have you brought us from the fair?"——"I have brought you myself," cried Moses, with a sly look, and resting the box on the dresser.——"Ay, Moses," cried my wife, "that we know, but where is the horse?"—"I have sold him," cried Moses, "for three pounds five shillings and two-pence."——"Well done, my good boy," returned she; "I knew you would touch them off. Between ourselves, three pounds five shillings and two-pence is no bad day's work. Come, let us have it then."——"I have brought back no money," cried Moses again. "I have laid it all out in a bargain, and here it is," pulling out a bundle from his breast: "here they are; a gross of green spectacles, with silver rims and shagreen cases."——"A gross of green spectacles!" repeated my wife in a faint voice. "And you have parted with the colt, and brought us back nothing but a gross of green paltry spectacles!"——"Dear mother," cried the boy, "why won't you listen to reason? I had them a dead bargain, or I should not have bought them. The silver rims alone will sell for double the money."——"A fig for the silver rims," cried my wife, in a passion: "I dare swear they won't sell for above half the money at the rate of broken silver, five shillings an ounce."——"You need be under no uneasiness," cried I, "about selling the rims; for I perceive they are only copper varnished over."——"What," cried my wife, "not silver, the rims not silver!"—"No," cried I, "no more silver than your sauce-pan."——"And so," returned she, "we have parted with the colt, and have only got a gross of green spectacles, with copper rims and shagreen cases! A murrain take such trumpery. The blockhead has been imposed upon, and should have known his company better."——"There, my dear," cried I, "you are wrong, he should not have known them at all."——"Marry, hang the idiot," returned she again, "to bring me such stuff; if I had them, I would throw them in the fire."—"There again you are wrong, my dear," cried I; "for though they be copper, we will keep them by us, as copper spectacles, you know, are better than nothing."

By this time the unfortunate Moses was undeceived. He now saw that he had indeed been imposed upon by a prowling sharper, who, observing his figure, had marked him for an easy prey. I therefore asked the circumstances of his deception. He sold the horse, it seems, and walked the fair in search of another. A reverend-looking man brought him to a tent, under a pretence of having one to sell. "Here," continued Moses, "we met another man, very well drest, who desired to borrow twenty pounds upon these, saying that he wanted money, and would dispose of them for a third of the value. The first gentleman, who pretended to be my friend, whispered me to buy them, and cautioned me not to let so good an offer pass. I sent for Mr. Flamborough, and they talked him up as finely as they did me, and so at last we were persuaded to buy the two gross between us."

CHAPTER XIII

MR. BURCHELL IS FOUND TO BE AN ENEMY, FOR HE HAS THE CONFIDENCE TO GIVE DISAGREEABLE ADVICE

Our family had now made several attempts to be fine; but some unforeseen disaster demolished each as soon as projected. I endeavoured to take the advantage of every disappointment, to improve their good sense in proportion as they were frustrated in ambition. "You see, my children," cried I, "how little is to be got by attempts to impose upon the world, in coping with our betters. Such as are poor and will associate with none but the rich are hated by those they avoid and despised by those they follow. Unequal combinations are always disadvantageous to the weaker side; the rich having the pleasure and the poor the inconveniences that result from them. But come, Dick, my boy, and repeat the fable that you were reading to-day, for the good of the company."

"Once upon a time," cried the child, "a Giant and a Dwarf were friends, and kept together. They made a bargain that they would never forsake each other, but go seek adventures. The first battle they fought was with two Saracens, and the Dwarf, who was very courageous, dealt one of the champions a most angry blow. It did the Saracen but very little injury, who lifting up his sword, fairly struck off the poor Dwarf's arm. He was now in a woeful plight; but the Giant, coming to his assistance, in a short time left the two Saracens dead on the plain, and the Dwarf cut off the dead man's head out of spite. They then travelled on to another adventure. This was against three bloody-minded Satyrs, who were carrying away a damsel in distress. The Dwarf was not quite so fierce now as before; but for all that struck the first blow, which was returned by another that knocked out his eye; but the Giant was soon up with them, and had they not fled, would certainly have killed them every one. They were all very joyful for this victory, and the damsel who was relieved fell in love with the Giant and married him. They now travelled far, and farther than I can tell, till they met with a company of robbers. The Giant, for the first time, was foremost now; but the Dwarf was not far behind. The battle was stout and long. Wherever the Giant came all fell before him; but the Dwarf had like to have been killed more than once. At last the victory declared for the two adventurers; but the Dwarf lost his leg. The Dwarf was now without an arm, a leg, and an eye, while the Giant, who was without a single wound cried out to him, 'Come on, my little hero; this is glorious sport; let us get one victory more, and then we shall have honour for ever.'—'No,' cries the Dwarf, who was by this time grown wiser, 'no, I declare off; I'll fight no more; for I find in every battle that you get all the honour and rewards, but all the blows fall upon me.' "

I was going to moralize this fable, when our attention was called off to a warm dispute between my wife and Mr. Burchell, upon my daughters' intended expedition to town. My wife very strenuously insisted upon the advantages that would result from it. Mr. Burchell, on the contrary, dissuaded her with great ardour, and I stood neuter. His present dissuasions seemed but the second part of those which were received with so ill a grace in the morning. The dispute grew high, while poor Deborah, instead of reasoning stronger, talked louder, and at last was obliged to take shelter from a defeat in clamour. The conclusion of her harangue, however, was highly displeasing to us all: she knew, she said, of some who had their own secret reasons for what they advised; but, for her part, she wished such to stay away from her house for the future. "Madam," cried Burchell, with looks of great composure, which tended to inflame her the more, "as for secret reasons, you are right; I have secret reasons, which I forbear to mention because you are not able to answer those of which I make no secret. But I find my visits here are become troublesome; I'll take my leave therefore now, and perhaps come once more to take a final farewell when I am quitting the country." Thus saying, he took up his hat, nor could the attempts of Sophia, whose looks seemed to upbraid his precipitancy, prevent his going.

When gone, we all regarded each other for some minutes with confusion. My wife, who knew herself to be the cause, strove to hide her concern with a forced smile and an air of assurance, which I was willing to reprove: "How, woman," cried I to her, "is it thus we treat strangers? Is it thus we return their kindness? Be assured, my dear, that these were the harshest words and to me the most unpleasing that ever escaped your lips!"——"Why would he provoke me then," replied she; "but I know the motives of his advice perfectly well. He would prevent my girls from going to town, that he may have the pleasure of my youngest daughter's company here at home. But whatever happens, she shall choose better company than such low-lived fellows as he."——"Low-lived, my dear, do you call him," cried I; "it is very possible we may mistake this man's character: for he seems upon some occasions the most finished gentleman I ever knew. Tell me, Sophia, my girl, has he ever given you any secret instances of his attachment?"——"His conversation with me, sir," replied my daughter, "has ever been sensible, modest, and pleasing. As to aught else, no, never. Once, indeed, I remember to have heard him say he never knew a woman who could find merit in a man that seemed poor."—"Such, my dear," cried I, "is the common cant of all the unfortunate or idle. But I hope you have been taught to judge properly of such men, and that it would be even madness to expect happiness from one who has been so very bad an economist of his own. Your mother and I have now better prospects for you. The next winter, which you will probably spend in town, will give you opportunities of making a more prudent choice."

What Sophia's reflections were upon this occasion, I can't pretend to determine; but I was not displeased at the bottom that we were rid of a guest from whom I had much to fear. Our breach of hospitality went to my conscience a little; but I quickly silenced that monitor by two or three specious reasons, which served to satisfy and reconcile me to myself. The pain which conscience gives the man who has already done wrong is soon got over. Conscience is a coward, and those faults it has not strength enough to prevent, it seldom has justice enough to punish by accusing.

CHAPTER XIV

FRESH MORTIFICATIONS, OR A DEMONSTRATION THAT SEEMING CALAMITIES MAY BE REAL BLESSINGS

The journey of my daughters to town was now resolved upon, Mr. Thornhill having kindly promised to inspect their conduct himself, and inform us by letter of their behaviour. But it was thought indispensably necessary that their appearance should equal the greatness of their expectations, which could not be done without some expence. We debated therefore in full council what were the easiest methods of raising money, or, more properly speaking, what we could most conveniently sell. The deliberation was soon finished: it was found that our remaining horse was utterly useless for the plow without his companion, and equally unfit for the road as wanting an eye; it was therefore determined that we should dispose of him for the purposes above-mentioned, at the neighbouring fair, and, to prevent imposition, that I should go with him myself. Though this was one of the first mercantile transactions of my life, yet I had no doubt about acquitting myself with reputation. The opinion a man forms of his own prudence is measured by that of the company he keeps, and as mine was mostly in the family way, I had conceived no unfavourable sentiments of my worldly wisdom. My wife, however, next morning at parting, after I had got some paces from the door, called me back to advise me, in a whisper, to have all my eyes about me.

I had, in the usual forms, when I came to the fair, put my horse through all his paces; but for some time had no bidders. At last a chapman approached, and, after he had for a good while examined the horse round, finding him blind of one eye, would have nothing to say to him; a second came up, but observing he had a spavin, declared he would not take him for the driving home; a third perceived he had a windgall, and would bid no money; a fourth knew by his eye that he had the botts: a fifth, more impertinent than all the rest, wondered what a plague I could do to the fair with a blind, spavined, galled hack that was only fit to be cut up for a dog kennel. By this time I began to have a most hearty contempt for the poor animal myself, and was almost ashamed at the approach of every new customer; for though I did not entirely believe all the fellows told me, yet I reflected that the number of witnesses was a strong presumption they were right, and St. Gregory, upon good works, professes himself to be of the same opinion.

I was in this mortifying situation, when a brother clergyman, an old acquaintance, who had also business to the fair, came up, and shaking me by the hand, proposed adjourning to a public-house and taking a glass of whatever we could get. I readily closed with the offer, and entering an ale-house, we were shown into a little back room, where there was only a venerable old man, who sat wholly intent over a large book, which he was reading. I never in my life saw a figure that prepossessed me more favourably. His locks of silver grey venerably shaded his temples, and his green old age seemed to be the result of health and benevolence. However, his presence did not interrupt our conversation; my friend and I discoursed on the various turns of fortune we had met: the Whistonian controversy, my last pamphlet, the archdeacon's reply, and the hard measure that was dealt me. But our attention was in a short time taken off by the appearance of a youth who, entering the room, respectfully said something softly to the old stranger. "Make no apologies, my child," said the old man; "to do good is a duty we owe to all our fellow creatures; take this, I wish it were more; but five pounds will relieve your distress, and you are welcome." The modest youth shed tears of gratitude, and yet his gratitude was scarce equal to mine. I could have hugged the good old man in my arms, his benevolence pleased me so. He continued to read, and we resumed our conversation, until my companion, after some time, recollecting that he had business to transact in the fair, promised to be soon back, adding that he always desired to have as much of Dr. Primrose's company as possible. The old gentleman, hearing my name mentioned, seemed to look at me with attention, and when my friend was gone, most respectfully demanded if I was any way related to the great Primrose, that courageous monogamist, who had been the bulwark of the church. Never did my heart feel sincerer rapture than at that moment. "Sir," cried I, "the applause of so good a man, as I am sure you are, adds to that happiness in my breast which your benevolence has already excited. You behold before you, sir, that Dr. Primrose, the monogamist, whom you have been pleased to call great. You here see that unfortunate Divine who has so long, and it would ill become me to say successfully, fought against the deuterogamy of the age." —"Sir," cried the stranger, struck with awe, "I fear I have been too familiar; but you'll forgive my curiosity, sir: I beg pardon."—"Sir," cried I, grasping his hand, "you are so far from displeasing me by your familiarity that I must beg you'll accept my friendship, as you already have all my esteem."——"Then with gratitude I accept the offer," cried he, squeezing me by the hand, "thou glorious pillar of unshaken orthodoxy; and do I behold—" I hereto interrupted what he was going to say; for tho', as an author, I could digest no small share of flattery, yet now my modesty would permit no more. However, no lovers in romance ever cemented a more instantaneous friendship. We talked upon several subjects: at first I thought he seemed rather devout than learned, and began to think he despised all human doctrines as dross. Yet this no way lessened him in my esteem; for I had for some time begun privately to harbour such an opinion myself. I therefore took occasion to observe that the world in general began to be blameably indifferent as to doctrinal matters, and followed human speculations too much. "Ay, sir," replied he, as if he had reserved all his learning to that moment, "ay, sir, the world is in its dotage, and yet the cosmogony or creation of the world has puzzled philosophers of all ages. What a medley of opinions have they not broached upon the creation of the world? Sanconiathon, Manetho, Berosus, and Ocellus Lucanus have all attempted it in vain. The latter has these words, *Anarchon ara kai atelutaion to pan,* which imply that all things have neither beginning nor end. Manetho also, who lived about the time of Nebuchadon-Asser, Asser being a Syriac word usually applied as a surname to the kings of that country, as Teglat Phael-Asser, Nabon-Asser, he, I say, formed a conjecture equally absurd; for as we usually say *ek to biblion kubernetes,* which implies that books will never teach the world; so he attempted to investigate—But, sir, I ask pardon, I am straying from the question." That he actually was; nor could I for my life see how the creation of the world had any thing to do with the business I was talking of; but it was sufficient to show me that he was a man of letters, and I now reverenced him the more. I was resolved therefore to bring him to the touchstone; but he was too mild and too gentle to contend for victory. Whenever I made any observation that looked like a challenge to controversy, he would smile, shake his head, and say nothing; by which I understood he could say much, if he thought proper. The subject therefore insensibly changed from the business of antiquity to that which brought us both to the fair; mine I told him was to sell an horse, and very luckily, indeed, his was to buy one for one of his tenants. My horse was soon produced, and in fine we struck a bargain. Nothing now remained but to pay me, and he accordingly pulled out a thirty pound note, and bid me change it. Not being in a capacity of complying with his demand, he ordered the landlady to call up his footman, who made his appearance in a very genteel livery. "Here, Abraham," cried he, "go and get gold for this; you'll do it at neighbour Jackson's, or any where." While the fellow was gone, he entertained me with a pathetic harangue on the great scarcity of silver, which I undertook to improve, by deploring also the great scarcity of gold; and by the time Abraham returned, we had both agreed that money was never so hard to be come at as now. Abraham returned to inform us that he had been over the whole fair and could not get change, tho' he had offered half a crown for doing it. This was a very great disappointment to us all; but the old gentleman having paused a little, asked me if I knew one Solomon Flamborough in my part of the country: upon replying that he was my next door neighbour, "If that be the case then," returned he, "I believe we shall deal. You shall have a draught upon him, payable at sight; and let me tell you he is as warm a man as any within five miles round him. Honest Solomon and I have been acquainted for many years together. I remember I always beat him at three jumps; but he could hop upon one leg farther than I." A draught upon my neighbour was to me the same as money; for I was sufficiently convinced of his ability: the draught was signed and put into my hands, and Mr. Jenkinson, the old gentleman, his man Abraham, and my horse, old Blackberry, trotted off very well pleased with each other.

Being now left to reflection, I began to recollect that I had done wrong in taking a draught from a stranger, and so prudently resolved upon having back my horse and following the purchaser. But this was now too late. I therefore made directly homewards, resolving to get the draught changed into money at my friend's as fast as possible. I found my honest neighbour smoking his pipe at his own door, and informing him that I had a small bill upon him, he read it twice over. "You can read the name, I suppose," cried I, "Ephraim Jenkinson."—"Yes," returned he, "the name is written plain enough, and I know the gentleman too, the greatest rascal under the canopy of heaven. This is the very same rogue who sold us the spectacles. Was he not a venerable-looking man, with grey hair, and no flaps to his pocket-holes? And did he not talk a long string of learning about Greek and cosmogony and the world?" To this I replied with a groan. "Ay," continued he, "he has but one piece of learning in the world, and he always talks it away whenever he finds a scholar in company; but I know the rogue, and will catch him yet."

Though I was already sufficiently mortified, my greatest struggle was to come in facing my wife and daughters. No truant was ever more afraid of returning to school, there to behold the master's sweet visage, than I was of going home. I was determined, however, to anticipate their fury by first falling into a passion myself.

But, alas! upon entering, I found the family no way disposed for battle. My wife and girls were all in tears, Mr. Thornhill having been there that day to inform them that their journey to town was entirely over. The two ladies having heard reports of us from some malicious person about us were that day set out for London. He could neither discover the tendency, nor the author of these, but whatever they might be, or whoever might have broached them, he continued to assure our family of his friendship and protection. I found, therefore, that they bore my disappointment with great resignation, as it was eclipsed in the greatness of their own. But what perplexed us most was to think who could be so base as to asperse the character of a family so harmless as ours, too humble to excite envy, and too inoffensive to create disgust.

CHAPTER XV

ALL MR. BURCHELL'S VILLAINY AT ONCE DETECTED. THE FOLLY OF BEING OVER-WISE

That evening and a part of the following day was employed in fruitless attempts to discover our enemies; scarce a family in the neighbourhood but incurred our suspicions, and each of us had reasons for our opinion best known to ourselves. As we were in this perplexity, one of our little boys, who had been playing abroad, brought in a letter-case, which he found on the green. It was quickly known to belong to Mr. Burchell, with whom it had been seen, and, upon examination, contained some hints upon different subjects; but what particularly engaged our attention was a sealed note, superscribed, *the copy of a letter to be sent to the two ladies at Thornhill-castle*. It instantly occurred that he was the base informer, and we deliberated whether the note should not be broke open. I was against it; but Sophia, who said she was sure that of all men he would be the last to be guilty of so much baseness, insisted upon its being read. In this she was seconded by the rest of the family, and, at their joint solicitation, I read as follows:

"LADIES,—The bearer will sufficiently satisfy you as to the person from whom this comes: one at least the friend of innocence, and ready to prevent its being seduced. I am informed for a truth that you have some intentions of bringing two young ladies to town, whom I have some knowledge of, under the character of companions. As I would neither have simplicity imposed upon, nor virtue contaminated, I must offer it as my opinion that the impropriety of such a step will be attended with dangerous consequences. It has never been my way to treat the infamous or the lewd with severity; nor should I now have taken this method of explaining myself, or reproving folly, did it not aim at guilt. Take therefore the admonition of a friend, and seriously reflect on the consequences of introducing infamy and vice into retreats where peace and innocence have hitherto resided."

Our doubts were now at an end. There seemed indeed something applicable to both sides in this letter, and its censures might as well be referred to those to whom it was written, as to us; but the malicious meaning was obvious, and we went no further. My wife had scarce patience to hear me to the end, but railed at the writer with unrestrained resentment. Olivia was equally severe, and Sophia seemed perfectly amazed at his baseness. As for my part, it appeared to me one of the vilest instances of unprovoked ingratitude I had met with. Nor could I account for it in any other manner than by imputing it to his desire of detaining my youngest daughter in the country, to have the more frequent opportunities of an interview. In this manner we all sat ruminating upon schemes of vengeance, when our other little boy came running in to tell us that Mr. Burchell was approaching at the other end of the field. It is easier to conceive than describe the complicated sensations which are felt from the pain of a recent injury, and the pleasure of approaching revenge. Tho' our intentions were only to upbraid him with his ingratitude, yet it was resolved to do it in a manner that would be perfectly cutting. For this purpose we agreed to meet him with our usual smiles, to chat in the beginning with more than ordinary kindness, to amuse him a little; but then in the midst of the flattering calm to burst upon him like an earthquake, and overwhelm him with the sense of his own baseness. This being resolved upon, my wife undertook to manage the business herself, as she really had some talents for such an undertaking. We saw him approach, he entered, drew a chair, and sat down. "A fine day, Mr. Burchell."

—"A very fine day, Doctor; though I fancy we shall have some rain by the shooting of my corns."—"The shooting of your horns," cried my wife, in a loud fit of laughter, and then asked pardon for being fond of a joke.—"Dear madam," replied he, "I pardon you with all my heart; for I protest I should not have thought it a joke till you told me."—"Perhaps not, sir," cried my wife, winking at us, "and yet I dare say you can tell us how many jokes go to an ounce."—"I fancy, madam," returned Burchell, "you have been reading a jest book this morning, that ounce of jokes is so very good a conceit; and yet, madam, I had rather see half an ounce of understanding."—"I believe you might," cried my wife, still smiling at us, though the laugh was against her; "and yet I have seen some men pretend to understanding that have very little."—"And no doubt," replied her antagonist, "you have known ladies set up for wit that had none." I quickly began to find that my wife was likely to gain but little at this business; so I resolved to treat him in a style of more severity myself. "Both wit and understanding," cried I, "are trifles, without integrity; it is that which gives value to every character. The ignorant peasant, without fault, is greater than the philosopher with many; for what is genius or courage without an heart? *An honest man is the noblest work of God.*"

"I always held that favourite maxim of Pope," returned Mr. Burchell, "as very unworthy a man of genius, and a base desertion of his own superiority. As the reputation of books is raised not by their freedom from defect, but the greatness of their beauties, so should that of men be prized not for their exemption from fault, but the size of those virtues they are possessed of. The scholar may want prudence, the statesman may have pride, and the champion ferocity; but shall we prefer to these men the low mechanic, who laboriously plods on through life without censure or applause? We might as well prefer the tame correct paintings of the Flemish school to the erroneous, but sublime animations of the Roman pencil."

"Sir," replied I, "your present observation is just, when there are shining virtues and minute defects; but when it appears that great vices are opposed in the same mind to as extraordinary virtues, such a character deserves contempt."

"Perhaps," cried he, "there may be some such monsters as you describe, of great vices joined to great virtues; yet in my progress through life, I never yet found one instance of their existence: on the contrary, I have ever perceived that where the mind was capacious, the affections were good. And indeed Providence seems kindly our friend in this particular, thus to debilitate the understanding where the heart is corrupt, and diminish the power where there is the will to do mischief. This rule seems to extend even to other animals: the little vermin race are ever treacherous, cruel, and cowardly, whilst those endowed with strength and power are generous, brave, and gentle."

"These observations sound well," returned I, "and yet it would be easy this moment to point out a man," and I fixed my eye steadfastly upon him, "whose head and heart form a most detestable contrast. Ay, sir," continued I, raising my voice, "and I am glad to have this opportunity of detecting him in the midst of his fancied security. Do you know this, sir, this pocket-book?"——"Yes, sir," returned he, with a face of impenetrable assurance, "that pocket-book is mine, and I am glad you have found it."——"And do you know," cried I, "this letter? Nay, never falter, man; but look me full in the face. I say, do you know this letter?"——"That letter," returned he, "yes, it was I that wrote that letter."——"And how could you," said I, "so basely, so ungratefully presume to write this letter?"——"And how came you," replied he, with looks of unparalleled effrontery, "so basely to presume to break open this letter? Don't you know, now, I could hang you all for this? All that I have to do is to swear at the next justice's that you have been guilty of breaking open the lock of my pocket-book, and so hang you all up at his door." This piece of unexpected insolence raised me to such a pitch that I could scarce govern my passion. "Ungrateful wretch, begone, and no longer pollute my dwelling with thy baseness. Begone, and never let me see thee again: go from my doors, and the only punishment I wish thee is an alarmed conscience, which will be a sufficient tormentor!" So saying, I threw him his pocket-book, which he took up with a smile, and shutting the clasps with the utmost composure, left us quite astonished at the serenity of his assurance. My wife was particularly enraged that nothing could make him angry or make him seem ashamed of his villainies. "My dear," cried I, willing to calm those passions that had been raised too high among us, "we are not to be surprised that bad men want shame; they only blush at being detected in doing good, but glory in their vices.

"Guilt and shame, says the allegory, were at first companions, and in the beginning of their journey inseparably kept together. But their union was soon found to be disagreeable and inconvenient to both; guilt gave shame frequent uneasiness, and shame often betrayed the secret conspiracies of guilt. After long disagreement, therefore, they at length consented to part for ever. Guilt boldly walked forward alone to overtake fate, that went before in the shape of an executioner; but shame, being naturally timorous, returned back to keep company with virtue, which, in the beginning of their journey, they had left behind. Thus, my children, after men have travelled through a few stages in vice, they no longer continue to have shame at doing evil, and shame attends only upon their virtues."

CHAPTER XVI

THE FAMILY USE ART, WHICH IS OPPOSED WITH STILL GREATER

Whatever might have been Sophia's sensations, the rest of the family was easily consoled for Mr. Burchell's absence by the company of our landlord, whose visits now became more frequent and longer. Though he had been disappointed in procuring my daughters the amusements of the town, as he designed, he took every opportunity of supplying them with those little recreations which our retirement would admit of. He usually came in the morning, and while my son and I followed our occupations abroad, he sat with the family at home and amused them by describing the town, with every part of which he was particularly acquainted. He could repeat all the observations that were retailed in the atmosphere of the play-houses, and had all the good things of the high wits by rote long before they made way into the jest-books. The intervals between conversation were employed in teaching my daughters piquet, or sometimes in setting my two little ones to box to make them *sharp,* as he called it; but the hopes of having him for a son-in-law in some measure blinded us to all his defects. It must be owned that my wife laid a thousand schemes to entrap him, or, to speak it more tenderly, used every art to magnify the merit of her daughter. If the cakes at tea ate short and crisp, they were made by Olivia; if the gooseberry wine was well knit, the gooseberries were of her gathering; it was her fingers gave the pickles their peculiar green; and in the composition of a pudding, her judgment was infallible. Then the poor woman would sometimes tell the Squire that she thought him and Olivia extremely like each other, and would bid both stand up to see which was tallest. These instances of cunning, which she thought impenetrable, yet which every body saw through, were very pleasing to our benefactor, who gave every day some new proofs of his passion, which though they had not arisen to proposals of marriage, yet we thought fell but little short of it; and his slowness was attributed sometimes to native bashfulness, and sometimes to his fear of offending a rich uncle. An occurrence, however, which happened soon after, put it beyond a doubt that he designed to become one of the family; my wife even regarded it as an absolute promise.

My wife and daughters happening to return a visit to neighbour Flamborough's found that family had lately got their pictures drawn by a limner, who travelled the country, and did them for fifteen shillings a head. As this family and ours had long a sort of rivalry in point of taste, our spirit took the alarm at this stolen march upon us, and notwithstanding all I could say, and I said much, it was resolved that we should have our pictures done too. Having therefore, engaged the limner, for what could I do? our next deliberation was to show the superiority of our taste in the attitudes. As for our neighbour's family, there were seven of them and they were drawn with seven oranges, a thing quite out of taste, no variety in life, no composition in the world. We desired to have something done in a brighter style, and, after many debates, at length came to an unanimous resolution to be drawn together, in one large historical family piece. This would be cheaper, since one frame would serve for all, and it would be infinitely more genteel; for all families of any taste were now drawn in the same manner. As we did not immediately recollect an historical subject to hit us, we were contented each with being drawn as independent historical figures. My wife desired to be represented as Venus, with a stomacher richly set with diamonds, and her two little ones as Cupids by her side, while I, in my gown and band, was to present her with my books on the Whistonian controversy. Olivia would be drawn as an Amazon, sitting upon a bank of flowers, drest in a green joseph laced with gold, and a whip in her hand. Sophia was to be a shepherdess, with as many sheep as the painter could spare; and Moses was to be drest out with an hat and white feather. Our taste so much pleased the Squire that he insisted on being put in as one of the family in the character of Alexander the Great, at Olivia's feet. This was considsidered by us all as an indication of his desire to be introduced into the family in reality, nor could we refuse his request. The painter was therefore set to work, and as he wrought with assiduity and expedition, in less than four days the whole was completed. The piece was large, and it must be owned he did not spare his colours; for which my wife gave him great encomiums. We were all perfectly satisfied with his performance; but an unfortunate circumstance had not occurred till the picture was finished, which now struck us with dismay. It was so very large that we had no place in the house to fix it. How we all came to disregard so material a point is inconceivable; but certain it is, we were this time all greatly overseen. Instead therefore of gratifying our vanity, as we hoped, there it leaned, in a most mortifying manner, against the kitchen wall, where the canvas was stretched and painted, much too large to be got through any of the doors, and the jest of all our neighbours. One compared it to Robinson Crusoe's long-boat, too large to be removed; another thought it more resembled a reel in a bottle; some wondered how it should be got out, and still more were amazed how it ever got in.

But though it excited the ridicule of some, it effectually raised more ill-natured suggestions in many. The Squire's portrait being found united with ours was an honour too great to escape envy. Malicious whispers began to circulate at our expence, and our tranquillity continually to be disturbed by persons who came as friends to tell us what was said of us by enemies. These reports we always resented with becoming spirit; but scandal ever improves by opposition. We again therefore entered into a consultation upon obviating the malice of our enemies, and at last came to a resolution which had too much cunning to give me entire satisfaction. It was this: as our principal object was to discover the honour of Mr. Thornhill's addresses, my wife undertook to sound him, by pretending to ask his advice in the choice of an husband for her eldest daughter. If this was not found sufficient to induce him to a declaration, it was then fixed upon to terrify him with a rival, which it was thought would compel him, though never so refractory. To this last step, however, I would by no means give my consent, till Olivia gave me the most solemn assurances that she would marry the person provided to rival him upon this occasion, if Mr. Thornhill did not prevent it by taking her himself. Such was the scheme laid, which though I did not strenuously oppose, I did not entirely approve.

The next time, therefore, that Mr. Thornhill came to see us, my girls took care to be out of the way, in order to give their mamma an opportunity of putting her scheme in execution; but they only retired to the next room, from whence they could over-hear the whole conversation, which my wife artfully introduced by observing that one of the Miss Flamboroughs was like to have a very good match of it in Mr. Spanker. To this the Squire assenting, she proceeded to remark that they who had warm fortunes were always sure of getting good husbands: "But heaven help," continued she, "the girls that have none. What signifies beauty, Mr. Thornhill? or what signifies all the virtue, and all the qualifications in the world, in this age of self-interest? It is not, what is she? but what has she? is all the cry."

"Madam," returned he, "I highly approve the justice, as well as the novelty, of your remarks, and if I were a king, it should be otherwise. It would then, indeed, be fine times with the girls without fortunes; our two young ladies should be the first for whom I would provide."

"Ah, sir!" returned my wife, "you are pleased to be facetious; but I wish I were a queen, and then I know where they should look for an husband. But now that you have put it into my head, seriously, Mr. Thornhill, can't you recommend me a proper husband for my eldest girl? She is now nineteen years old, well grown and well educated, and, in my humble opinion, does not want for parts."

"Madam," replied he, "if I were to choose, I would find out a person possessed of every accomplishment that can make an angel happy. One with prudence, fortune, taste, and sincerity; such, madam, would be, in my opinion, the proper husband."—"Ay, sir," said she, "but do you know of any such person?"——"No, madam," returned he, "it is impossible to know any person that deserves to be her husband: she's too great a treasure for one man's possession: she's a goddess. Upon my soul, I speak what I think, she's an angel."——"Ah, Mr. Thornhill, you only flatter my poor girl: but we have been thinking of marrying her to one of your tenants, whose mother is lately dead, and who wants a manager; you know whom I mean, farmer Williams; a warm man, Mr. Thornhill, able to give her good bread; ay, and who has several times made her proposals" (which was actually the case): "but, sir," concluded she, "I should be glad to have your approbation of our choice."——"How, madam," replied he, "my approbation! My approbation of such a choice! Never. What! Sacrifice so much beauty, and sense, and goodness, to a creature insensible of the blessing! Excuse me, I can never approve of such a piece of injustice! And I have my reasons!"——"Indeed, sir," cried Deborah, "if you have your reasons, that's another affair; but I should be glad to know those reasons."——"Excuse me, madam," returned he, "they lie too deep for discovery" (laying his hand upon his bosom); "they remain buried, rivetted here."

After he was gone, upon general consultation, we could not tell what to make of these fine sentiments. Olivia considered them as instances of the most exalted passion; but I was not quite so sanguine: it seemed to me pretty plain that they had more of love than matrimony in them: yet, whatever they might portend, it was resolved to prosecute the scheme of farmer Williams, who, since my daughter's first appearance in the country, had paid her his addresses.

CHAPTER XVII

SCARCE ANY VIRTUE FOUND TO RESIST THE POWER OF LONG AND PLEASING TEMPTATION

As I only studied my child's real happiness, the assiduity of Mr. Williams pleased me, as he was in easy circumstances, prudent, and sincere. It required but very little encouragement to revive his former passion; so that in an evening or two after, he and Mr. Thornhill met at our house, and surveyed each other for some time with looks of anger: but Williams owed his landlord no rent, and little regarded his indignation. Olivia, on her side, acted the coquette to perfection, if that might be called acting which was her real character, pretending to lavish all her tenderness on her new lover. Mr. Thornhill appeared quite dejected at this preference, and with a pensive air took leave, though I own it puzzled me to find him so much in pain as he appeared to be, when he had it in his power so easily to remove the cause, by declaring an honourable passion. But whatever uneasiness he seemed to endure, it could easily be perceived that Olivia's anguish was still greater. After any of these interviews between her lovers, of which there were several, she usually retired to solitude, and there indulged her grief. It was in such a situation I found her one evening, after she had been for some time supporting a fictitious gayety. "You now see, my child," said I, "that your confidence in Mr. Thornhill's passion was all a dream: he permits the rivalry of another, every way his inferior, though he knows it lies in his power to secure you by a candid declaration himself."——"Yes, pappa," returned she, "but he has his reasons for this delay. I know he has. The sincerity of his looks and words convince me of his real esteem. A short time, I hope, will discover the generosity of his sentiments, and convince you that my opinion of him has been more just than yours."——"Olivia, my darling," returned I, "every scheme that has been hitherto pursued to compel him to a declaration has been proposed and planned by yourself, nor can you in the least say that I have constrained you. But you must not suppose, my dear, that I will be ever instrumental in suffering his honest rival to be the dupe of your ill-placed passion. Whatever time you require to bring your fancied admirer to an explanation shall be granted; but at the expiration of that term, if he is still regardless, I must absolutely insist that honest Mr. Williams shall be rewarded for his fidelity. The character which I have hitherto supported in life demands this from me, and my tenderness, as a parent, shall never influence my integrity as a man. Name then your day, let it be as distant as you think proper, and in the meantime take care to let Mr. Thornhill know the exact time on which I design delivering you up to another. If he really loves you, his own good sense will readily suggest that there is but one method alone to prevent his losing you for ever." This proposal, which she could not avoid considering as perfectly just, was readily agreed to. She again renewed her most positive promise of marrying Mr. Williams, in case of the other's insensibility; and at the next opportunity, in Mr. Thornhill's presence, that day month was fixed upon for her nuptials with his rival.

Such vigorous proceedings seemed to redouble Mr. Thornhill's anxiety; but what Olivia really felt gave me some uneasiness. In this struggle between prudence and passion, her vivacity quite forsook her, and every opportunity of solitude was sought, and spent in tears. One week passed away; but her lover made no efforts to restrain her nuptials. The succeeding week he was still assiduous; but not more open. On the third he discontinued his visits entirely, and instead of my daughter testifying any impatience, as I expected, she seemed to retain a pensive tranquillity, which I looked upon as resignation. For my own part, I was now sincerely pleased with thinking that my child was going to be secured in a continuance of competence and peace, and frequently applauded her resolution. It was within about four days of her intended nuptials that my little family at night were gathered round a charming fire, telling stories of the past, and laying schemes for the future; busied in forming a thousand projects, and laughing at whatever folly came uppermost. "Well, Moses," cried I, "we shall soon, my boy, have a wedding in the family; what is your opinion of matters and things in general?"——"My opinion, father, is that all things go on very well; and I was just now thinking, that when sister Livy is married to farmer Williams, we shall then have the loan of his cider-press and brewing tubs for nothing."——"That we shall, Moses," cried I, "and he will sing us *Death and the Lady* to raise our spirits into the bargain."——"He has taught that song to our Dick," cried Moses; "and I think he goes thro' it very prettily."——"Does he so?" cried I, "then let us have it: where's little Dick? let him up with it boldly."——"My brother Dick," cried Bill my youngest, "is just gone out with sister Livy; but Mr. Williams has taught me two songs, and I'll sing them for you, pappa. Which song do you choose, *The Dying Swan,* or the *Elegy on the Death of a Mad Dog?"*—"The elegy, child, by all means," said I; "I never heard that yet; and Deborah, my life, grief you know is dry, let us have a bottle of the best gooseberry wine, to keep up our spirits. I have wept so much at all sorts of elegies of late that without an enlivening glass I am sure this will overcome me; and Sophy, love, take your guitar, and thrum in with the boy a little."

AN ELEGY ON THE DEATH OF A MAD DOG

Good people all, of every sort,
  Give ear unto my song;
And if you find it wond'rous short,
  It cannot hold you long.

In Isling town there was a man,
  Of whom the world might say,
That still a goodly race he ran,
  Whene'er he went to pray.

A kind and gentle heart he had,
  To comfort friends and foes;
The naked every day he clad,
  When he put on his clothes.

And in that town a dog was found,
  As many dogs there be,
Both mongrel, puppy, whelp, and hound,
  And curs of low degree.

This dog and man at first were friends;
  But when a pique began,
The dog, to gain his private ends,
  Went mad and bit the man.

Around from all the neighbouring streets,
  The wondering neighbours ran,
And swore the dog had lost his wits,
  To bite so good a man.

The wound it seem'd both sore and sad,
  To every Christian eye;
And while they swore the dog was mad,
  They swore the man would die.

But soon a wonder came to light,
  That show'd the rogues they lied,
The man recovered of the bite,
  The dog it was that died.

"A very good boy, Bill, upon my word, and an elegy that may truly be called tragical. Come, my children, here's Bill's health, and may he one day be a bishop."

"With all my heart," cried my wife; "and if he but preaches as well as he sings, I make no doubt of him. The most of his family, by the mother's side, could sing a good song: it was a common saying in our country, that the family of the Blenkinsops could never look straight before them, nor the Hugginses blow out a candle; that there were none of the Grograms but could sing a song, or of the Marjorams but could tell a story."——"However that be," cried I, "the most vulgar ballad of them all generally pleases me better than the fine modern odes and things that petrify us in a single stanza, productions that we at once detest and praise. Put the glass to your brother, Moses. The great fault of these elegists is that they are in despair for griefs that give the sensible part of mankind very little pain. A lady loses her lap-dog, and so the silly poet runs home to versify the disaster."

"That may be the mode," cried Moses, "in sublimer compositions; but the Ranelagh songs that come down to us are perfectly familiar, and all cast in the same mold: Colin meets Dolly, and they hold a dialogue together; he gives her a fairing to put in her hair, and she presents him with a nosegay; and then they go together to church, where they give good advice to young nymphs and swains to get married as fast as they can."

"And very good advice too," cried I, "and I am told there is not a place in the world where advice can be given with so much propriety as there; for, as it persuades us to marry, it also furnishes us with a wife; and surely that must be an excellent market, my boy, where we are told what we want and supplied with it when wanting."

"Yes, sir," returned Moses, "and I know but of two such markets for wives in Europe, Ranelagh in England and Fontarabia in Spain. The Spanish market is open once a year, but our English wives are saleable every night."

"You are right, my boy," cried his mother. "Old England is the only place in the world for husbands to get wives."—"And for wives to manage their husbands," interrupted I. "It is a proverb abroad, that if a bridge were built across the sea, all the ladies of the Continent would come over to take pattern from ours; for there are no such wives in Europe as our own.

"But let us have one bottle more, Deborah, my life, and Moses give us a good song. What thanks do we not owe to heaven for thus bestowing tranquillity, health, and competence. I think myself happier now than the greatest monarch upon earth. He has no such fire-side, nor such pleasant faces about it. Yes, Deborah, my dear, we are now growing old; but the evening of our life is likely to be happy. We are descended from ancestors that knew no stain, and we shall leave a good and virtuous race of children behind us. While we live they will be our support and our pleasure here, and when we die they will transmit our honour untainted to posterity. Come, my son, we wait for your song; let us have a chorus. But where is my darling Olivia? That little cherub's voice is always sweetest in the concert." Just as I spoke Dick came running in. "O pappa, pappa, she is gone from us, she is gone from us, my sister Livy is gone from us for ever."—"Gone, child?"—"Yes, she is gone off with two gentlemen in a post-chaise, and one of them kissed her, and said he would die for her; and she cried very much, and was for coming back; but he persuaded her again, and she went into the chaise, and said, 'O what will my poor pappa do when he knows I am undone!' "—

"Now then," cried I, "my children, go and be miserable; for we shall never enjoy one hour more. And O may heaven's everlasting fury light upon him and his! Thus to rob me of my child! And sure it will, for taking back my sweet innocent that I was leading up to heaven. Such sincerity as my child was possest of. But all our earthly happiness is now over! Go, my children, go, and be miserable and infamous; for my heart is broken within me!"——"Father," cried my son, "is this your fortitude?" ——"Fortitude, child! Yes, he shall see I have fortitude! Bring me my pistols. I'll pursue the traitor. While he is on earth I'll pursue him. Old as I am, he shall find I can sting him yet. The villain! The perfidious villain!" I had by this time reached down my pistols, when my poor wife, whose passions were not so strong as mine, caught me in her arms. "My dearest, dearest husband," cried she, "the Bible is the only weapon that is fit for your old hands now. Open that, my love, and read our anguish into patience, for she has vilely deceived." Her sorrow represt the rest in silence. "Indeed, sir," resumed my son, after a pause, "your rage is too violent and unbecoming. You should be my mother's comforter, and you increase her pain. It ill suited you and your reverend character thus to curse your greatest enemy; you should not have curst the wretch, villain as he is."——"I did not curse him, child, did I?"——"Indeed, sir, you did; you curst him twice."——"Then may heaven forgive me and him if I did. And now, my son, I see it was more than human benevolence that first taught us to bless our enemies! Blest be his holy name for all the good he has given, and for that he has taken away. But it is not, it is not, a small distress that can wring tears from these old eyes, that have not wept for so many years. My child!—to undo my darling! May confusion seize—Heaven forgive me, what am I about to say! You may remember, my love, how good she was, and how charming; till this vile moment all her care was to make us happy. Had she but died! But she is gone, the honour of our family contaminated, and I must look out for happiness in other worlds than here. But my child, you saw them go off: perhaps he forced her away? If he forced her, she may yet be innocent."——"Ah no, sir!" cried the child; "he only kissed her, and called her his angel, and she wept very much, and leaned upon his arm, and they drove off very fast."——"She's an ungrateful creature," cried my wife, who could scarce speak for weeping, "to use us thus. She never had the least constraint put upon her affections. The vile strumpet has basely deserted her parents without any provocation, thus to bring your grey hairs to the grave, and I must shortly follow."

In this manner that night, the first of our real misfortunes, was spent in the bitterness of complaint, and ill supported sallies of enthusiasm. I determined, however, to find out our betrayer, wherever he was, and reproach his baseness. The next morning we missed our wretched child at breakfast, where she used to give life and cheerfulness to us all. My wife, as before, attempted to ease her heart by reproaches. "Never," cried she, "shall that vilest stain of our family again darken these harmless doors. I will never call her daughter more. No, let the strumpet live with her vile seducer: she may bring us to shame, but she shall never more deceive us."

"Wife," said I, "do not talk thus hardly: my detestation of her guilt is as great as yours; but ever shall this house and this heart be open to a poor returning repentant sinner. The sooner she returns from her transgression, the more welcome shall she be to me. For the first time the very best may err; art may persuade, and novelty spread out its charm. The first fault is the child of simplicity; but every other the offspring of guilt. Yes, the wretched creature shall be welcome to this heart and this house, tho' stained with ten thousand vices. I will again hearken to the music of her voice, again will I hang fondly on her bosom, if I find but repentance there. My son, bring hither my Bible and my staff; I will pursue her, wherever she is, and tho' I cannot save her from shame, I may prevent the continuance of iniquity."

CHAPTER XVIII

THE PURSUIT OF A FATHER TO RECLAIM A LOST CHILD TO VIRTUE

Tho' the child could not describe the gentleman's person who handed his sister into the post-chaise, yet my suspicions fell entirely upon our young landlord, whose character for such intrigues was but too well known. I therefore directed my steps towards Thornhill-castle, resolving to upbraid him, and, if possible, to bring back my daughter; but before I had reached his seat, I was met by one of my parishioners, who said he saw a young lady resembling my daughter in a post-chaise with a gentleman whom, by the description, I could only guess to be Mr. Burchell, and that they drove very fast. This information, however, did by no means satisfy me. I therefore went to the young Squire's, and though it was yet early, insisted upon seeing him immediately; he soon appeared with the most open familiar air, and seemed perfectly amazed at my daughter's elopement, protesting upon his honour that he was quite a stranger to it. I now therefore condemned my former suspicions, and could turn them only on Mr. Burchell, who I recollected had of late several private conferences with her; but the appearance of another witness left me no room to doubt of his villainy, who averred, that he and my daughter were actually gone towards the wells, about thirty miles off, where there was a great deal of company. Hearing this, I resolved to pursue them there. I walked along with earnestness, and enquired of several by the way; but received no accounts, till entering the town, I was met by a person on horseback whom I remembered to have seen at the Squire's, and he assured me that if I followed them to the races, which were but thirty miles farther, I might depend upon overtaking them; for he had seen them dance there the night before, and the whole assembly seemed charmed with my daughter's performance. Early the next day I walked forward to the races, and about four in the afternoon I came upon the course. The company made a very brilliant appearance, all earnestly employed in one pursuit, that of pleasure; how different from mine, that of reclaiming a lost child to virtue! I thought I perceived Mr. Burchell at some distance from me; but, as if he dreaded an interview, upon my approaching him, he mixed among a crowd, and I saw him no more. I now reflected that it would be to no purpose to continue my pursuit farther, and resolved to return home to an innocent family, who wanted my assistance. But the agitations of my mind, and the fatigues I had undergone, threw me into a fever, the symptoms of which I perceived before I came off the course. This was another unexpected stroke, as I was more than seventy miles distant from home; however, I retired to a little ale-house by the road-side, and in this place, the usual retreat of indigence and frugality, I laid me down patiently to wait the issue of my disorder. I languished here for near three weeks; but at last my constitution prevailed, though I was unprovided with money to defray the expences of my entertainment. It is possible the anxiety from this last circumstance alone might have brought on a relapse, had I not been supplied by a traveller, who stopt to take a cursory refreshment. This person was no other than the philanthropic bookseller in St. Paul's church-yard, who has written so many little books for children: he called himself their friend; but he was the friend of all mankind. He was no sooner alighted, but he was in haste to be gone; for he was ever on business of the utmost importance, and was at that time actually compiling materials for the history of one Mr. Thomas Trip. I immediately recollected this good-natured man's red pimpled face; for he had published for me against the Deuterogamists of the age, and from him I borrowed a few pieces to be paid at my return. Leaving the inn, therefore, as I was yet but weak, I resolved to return home by easy journies of ten miles a day. My health and usual tranquillity were almost restored, and I now condemned that pride which had made me refractory to the hand of correction. Man little knows what calamities are beyond his patience to bear till he tries them; as in ascending the heights of ambition, which look bright from below, every step we rise shows us some new prospect of hidden disappointment; so in our descent to the vale of wretchedness, which, from the summits of pleasure, appears dark and gloomy, the busy mind, still attentive to its own amusement, finds something to flatter and surprise it. Still as we descend, the objects appear to brighten, unexpected prospects amuse, and the mental eye becomes adapted to its gloomy situation.

I now proceeded forwards, and had walked about two hours, when I perceived what appeared at a distance like the waggon, which I was resolved to overtake; but when I came up with it, found it to be a strolling company's cart that was carrying their scenes and other theatrical furniture to the next village, where they were to exhibit. The cart was attended only by the person who drove it and one of the company, as the rest of the players were to follow the ensuing day. Good company upon the road, says the proverb, is always the shortest cut. I therefore entered into conversation with the poor player; and as I once had some theatrical powers myself, I disserted on such topics with my usual freedom: but as I was pretty much unacquainted with the present state of the stage, I demanded who were the present theatrical writers in vogue, who the Drydens and Otways of the day. "I fancy, sir," cried the player, "few of our modern dramatists would think themselves much honoured by being compared to the writers you mention. Dryden and Row's manner, sir, are quite out of fashion; our taste has gone back a whole century, Fletcher, Ben Jonson, and all the plays of Shakespear, are the only things that go down." ——"How," cried I, "is it possible the present age can be pleased with that antiquated dialect, that obsolete humour, those over-charged characters, which abound in the works you mention?"——"Sir," returned my companion, "the public think nothing about dialect, or humour, or character; for that is none of their business, they only go to be amused, and find themselves happy when they can enjoy a pantomime under the sanction of Jonson's or Shakespear's name."——"So then, I suppose," cried I, "that our modern dramatists are rather imitators of Shakespear than of nature."——"To say the truth," returned my companion, "I don't know that they imitate any thing at all; nor indeed does the public require it of them: it is not the composition of the piece, but the number of starts and attitudes that may be introduced into it that elicits applause. I have known a piece with not one jest in the whole shrugged into popularity, and another saved by the poet's throwing in a fit of the gripes. No, sir, the works of Congreve and Farquhar have too much wit in them for the present taste; our modern dialogue is much more natural."

By this time the equipage of the strolling company was arrived at the village, which, it seems, had been apprized of our approach and was come out to gaze at us; for my companion observed that strollers always have more spectators without doors than within. I did not consider the impropriety of my being in such company till I saw a mob gathered about me. I therefore took shelter, as fast as possible, in the first ale-house that offered, and being shown into the common room, was accosted by a very well-drest gentleman who demanded whether I was the real chaplain of the company or whether it was only to be my masquerade character in the play. Upon informing him of the truth, and that I did not belong to the company, he was condescending enough to desire me and the player to partake in a bowl of punch, over which he discussed modern politics with great earnestness and seeming interest. I set him down in my own mind for nothing less than a parliament-man at least; but was almost confirmed in my conjectures, when upon my asking what there was in the house for supper, he insisted that the player and I should sup with him at his house, with which request, after some entreaties, I was prevailed on to comply.

CHAPTER XIX

THE DESCRIPTION OF A PERSON DISCONTENTED WITH THE PRESENT GOVERNMENT, AND APPREHENSIVE OF THE LOSS OF OUR LIBERTIES

The house where we were to be entertained, lying at a small distance from the village, our inviter observed that as the coach was not ready, he would conduct us on foot, and we soon arrived at one of the most magnificent mansions I had seen in the country. The apartment into which we were shown was perfectly elegant and modern; he went to give orders for supper, while the player, with a wink, observed that we were perfectly in luck. Our entertainer soon returned, an elegant supper was brought in, two or three ladies, in an easy deshabille, were introduced, and the conversation began with some sprightliness. Politics, however, was the subject on which our entertainer chiefly expatiated; for he asserted that liberty was at once his boast and his terror. After the cloth was removed, he asked me if I had seen the last Monitor, to which replying in the negative, "What, nor the Auditor, I suppose?" cried he.—"Neither, sir," returned I.—"That's strange, very strange," replied my entertainer. "Now, I read all the politics that come out. The Daily, the Public, the Ledger, the Chronicle, the London Evening, the Whitehall Evening, the seventeen magazines, and the two reviews; and though they hate each other, I love them all. Liberty, sir, liberty is the Briton's boast, and by all my coal mines in Cornwall, I reverence its guardians."—"Then it is to be hoped," cried I, "you reverence the king."—"Yes," returned my entertainer, "when he does what we would have him; but if he goes on as he has done of late, I'll never trouble myself more with his matters. I say nothing. I think only. I could have directed some things better. I don't think there has been a sufficient number of advisers: he should advise with every person willing to give him advice, and then we should have things done in another manner."

"I wish," cried I, "that such intruding advisers were fixed in the pillory. It should be the duty of honest men to assist the weaker side of our constitution, that sacred power that has for some years been every day declining, and losing its due share of influence in the state. But these ignorants still continue the cry of liberty, and if they have any weight, basely throw it into the subsiding scale."

"How," cried one of the ladies, "do I live to see one so base, so sordid, as to be an enemy to liberty and a defender of tyrants? Liberty, that sacred gift of heaven, that glorious privilege of Britons!"

"Can it be possible," cried our entertainer, "that there should be any found at present advocates for slavery? Any who are for meanly giving up the privileges of Britons? Can any, sir, be so abject?"

"No, sir," replied I, "I am for liberty, that attribute of Gods! Glorious liberty! that theme of modern declamation. I would have all men kings. I would be a king myself. We have all naturally an equal right to the throne: we are all originally equal. This is my opinion, and was once the opinion of a set of honest men who were called Levellers. They tried to erect themselves into a community, where all should be equally free. But, alas! it would never answer; for there were some among them stronger, and some more cunning than others, and these became masters of the rest; for as sure as your groom rides your horses, because he is a cunninger animal than they, so surely will the animal that is cunninger or stronger than he sit upon his shoulders in turn. Since then it is entailed upon humanity to submit, and some are born to command and others to obey, the question is, as there must be tyrants, whether it is better to have them in the same house with us, or in the same village, or still farther off, in the metropolis. Now, sir, for my own part, as I naturally hate the face of a tyrant, the farther off he is removed from me, the better pleased am I. The generality of mankind also are of my way of thinking, and have unanimously created one king, whose election at once diminishes the number of tyrants, and puts tyranny at the greatest distance from the greatest number of people. Now those who were tyrants themselves before the election of one tyrant are naturally averse to a power raised over them, and whose weight must ever lean heaviest on the subordinate orders. It is the interest of the great, therefore, to diminish kingly power as much as possible; because whatever they take from it is naturally restored to themselves; and all they have to do in a state is to undermine the single tyrant, by which they resume their primeval authority. Now, a state may be so constitutionally circumstanced, its laws may be so disposed, and its men of opulence so minded, as all to conspire to carry on this business of undermining monarchy. If the circumstances of the state be such, for instance, as to favour the accumulation of wealth, and make the opulent still more rich, this will increase their strength and their ambition. But an accumulation of wealth must necessarily be the consequence in a state when more riches flow in from external commerce than arise from internal industry, for external commerce can only be managed to advantage by the rich, and they have also at the same time all the emoluments arising from internal industry; so that the rich, in such a state, have two sources of wealth, whereas the poor have but one. Thus wealth in all commercial states is found to accumulate, and such have hitherto in time become aristocratical. Besides this, the very laws of a country may contribute to the accumulation of wealth; as when those natural ties that bind the rich and poor together are broken, and it is ordained that the rich shall only marry among each other; or when the learned are held unqualified to serve their country as counsellors merely from a defect of opulence, and wealth is thus made the object of a wise man's ambition; by these means, I say, and such means as these, riches will accumulate. The possessor of accumulated wealth, when furnished with the necessaries and pleasures of life, can employ the superfluity of fortune only in purchasing power. That is, differently speaking, in making dependents, in purchasing the liberty of the needy or the venal, of men who are willing to bear the mortification of contiguous tyranny for bread. Thus each very opulent man generally gathers round him a circle of the poorest of the people; and the polity abounding in accumulated wealth may be compared to a Cartesian system, each orb with a vortex of its own. Those, however, who are willing to move in a great man's vortex are only such as must be slaves, the rabble of mankind, whose souls and whose education are adapted to servitude, and who know nothing of liberty except the name. But there must still be a large number of the people without the sphere of the opulent man's influence, namely, that order of men which subsists between the very rich and the very rabble; those men who are possest of too large fortunes to submit to the neighbouring man in power, and yet are too poor to set up for tyranny themselves. In this middle order of mankind are generally to be found all the arts, wisdom, and virtues of society. This order alone is known to be the true preserver of freedom, and may be called the People. Now it may happen that this middle order of mankind may lose all its influence in a state, and its voice be in a manner drowned in that of the rabble; for if the fortune sufficient for qualifying a person at present to give his voice in state affairs be ten times less than was judged sufficient upon forming the constitution, it is evident that greater numbers of the rabble will thus be introduced into the political system, and they ever moving in the vortex of the great will follow where greatness shall direct. In such a state, therefore, all that the middle order has left is to preserve the prerogative and privileges of the one principal tyrant with the most sacred circumspection. For he divides the power of the rich, and calls off the great from falling with tenfold weight on the middle order placed beneath them. The middle order may be compared to a town of which the opulent are forming the siege, and which the tyrant is hastening to relieve. While the besiegers are in dread of the external enemy, it is but natural to offer the townsmen the most specious terms, to flatter them with sounds and amuse them with privileges; but if they once defeat the tyrant, the walls of the town will be but a small defence to its inhabitants. What they may then expect may be seen by turning our eyes to Holland, Genoa, or Venice, where the laws govern the poor, and the rich govern the law. I am then for, and would die for, monarchy, sacred monarchy; for if there be any thing sacred amongst men, it must be the anointed sovereign of his people, and every diminution of his power in war or in peace is an infringement upon the real liberties of the subject. The sounds of liberty, patriotism, and Britons have already done *much;* it is to be hoped that the true sons of freedom will prevent their ever doing more. I have known many of those bold champions for liberty in my time, yet do I not remember one that was not in his heart and in his family a tyrant."

My warmth, I found, had lengthened this harangue beyond the rules of good breeding; but the impatience of my entertainer, who often strove to interrupt it, could be restrained no longer. "What," cried he, "then I have been all this while entertaining a Jesuit in parson's clothes; but by all the coal mines of Cornwall, out he shall pack, if my name be Wilkinson." I now found I had gone too far, and asked pardon for the warmth with which I had spoken. "Pardon," returned he in a fury; "I think such principles demand ten thousand pardons. What, give up liberty, property, and, as the Gazetteer says, lie down to be saddled with wooden shoes! Sir, I insist upon your marching out of this house immediately, to prevent worse consequences. Sir, I insist upon it." I was going to repeat my remonstrances; but just then we heard a footman's rap at the door, and the two ladies cried out, "As sure as death there is our master and mistress come home." It seems my entertainer was all this while only the butler, who, in his master's absence, had a mind to cut a figure and be for a while the gentleman himself; and, to say the truth, he talked politics as well as most country gentlemen do. But nothing could now exceed my confusion upon seeing the gentleman with his lady enter, nor was their surprise at finding such company and good cheer less than ours. "Gentlemen," cried the real master of the house to me and my companion, "I am your most humble servant; but I protest this is so unexpected a favour that I almost sink under the obligation." However unexpected our company might be to him, his, I am sure, was still more so to us, and I was struck dumb with the apprehensions of my own absurdity, when whom should I next see enter the room but my dear Miss Arabella Wilmot, who was formerly designed to be married to my son George, but whose match was broken off, as already related. As soon as she saw me, she flew to my arms with the utmost joy. "My dear sir," cried she, "to what happy accident is it that we owe so unexpected a visit? I am sure my uncle and aunt will be in raptures when they find they have the good Dr. Primrose for their guest." Upon hearing my name, the old gentleman and lady very politely stept up, and welcomed me with most cordial hospitality. Nor could they forbear smiling upon being informed of the nature of my present visit; but the unfortunate butler, whom they at first seemed disposed to turn away, was, at my intercession, forgiven.

Mr. Arnold and his lady, to whom the house belonged, now insisted upon having the pleasure of my stay for some days, and as their niece, my charming pupil, whose mind in some measure had been formed under my own instructions, joined in their entreaties, I complied. That night I was shown to a magnificent chamber, and the next morning early Miss Wilmot desired to walk with me in the garden, which was decorated in the modern manner. After some time spent in pointing out the beauties of the place, she enquired, with seeming unconcern, when last I had heard from my son George. "Alas! madam," cried I, "he has now been near three years absent, without ever writing to his friends or me. Where he is I know not; perhaps I shall never see him or happiness more. No, my dear madam, we shall never more see such pleasing hours as were once spent by our fire-side at Wakefield. My little family are now dispersing very fast, and poverty has brought not only want, but infamy upon us." The good-natured girl let fall a tear at this account; but as I saw her possessed of too much sensibility, I forbore a more minute detail of our sufferings. It was, however, some consolation to me to find that time had made no alteration in her affections, and that she had rejected several matches that had been made her since our leaving her part of the country. She led me round all the extensive improvements of the place, pointing to the several walks and arbours, and at the same time catching from every object a hint for some new question relative to my son. In this manner we spent the forenoon, till the bell summoned us in to dinner, where we found the manager of the strolling company, who was come to dispose of tickets for the Fair Penitent, which was to be acted that evening, the part of Horatio by a young gentleman who had never appeared on any stage before. He seemed to be very warm in the praises of the new performer, and averred that he never saw any who bid so fair for excellence. Acting, he observed, was not learned in a day; "but this gentleman," continued he, "seems born to tread the stage. His voice, his figure, and attitude are all admirable. We caught him up accidentally in our journey down." This account, in some measure, excited our curiosity, and, at the entreaty of the ladies, I was prevailed upon to accompany them to the playhouse, which was no other than a barn. As the company with which I went was incontestably the chief of the place, we were received with the greatest respect and placed in the front seat of the theatre, where we sat for some time with no small impatience to see Horatio make his appearance. The new performer advanced at last, and I found it was my unfortunate son. He was going to begin, when, turning his eyes upon the audience, he perceived us, and stood at once speechless and immovable. The actors behind the scene, who ascribed this pause to his natural timidity, attempted to encourage him; but instead of going on, he burst into a flood of tears and retired off the stage. I don't know what were the sensations I felt, for they succeeded with too much rapidity for description; but I was soon awakened from this disagreeable reverie by Miss Wilmot, who, pale and with a trembling voice, desired me to conduct her back to her uncle's. When we got home, Mr. Arnold, who was as yet a stranger to our extraordinary behaviour, being informed that the new performer was my son, sent his coach and an invitation for him; and as he persisted in his refusal to appear again upon the stage, the players put another in his place, and we soon had him with us. Mr. Arnold gave him the kindest reception, and I received him with my usual transport; for I could never counterfeit false resentment. Miss Wilmot's reception was mixed with seeming neglect, and yet I could perceive she acted a studied part. The tumult in her mind seemed not yet abated; she said twenty giddy things that looked like joy, and then laughed loud at her own want of meaning. At intervals she would take a sly peep at the glass, as if happy in the consciousness of unresisting beauty, and often would ask questions, without giving any manner of attention to the answers.

CHAPTER XX

THE HISTORY OF A PHILOSOPHIC VAGABOND, PURSUING NOVELTY, BUT LOSING CONTENT

After we had supped, Mrs. Arnold politely offered to send a couple of her footmen for my son's baggage, which he at first seemed to decline; but upon her pressing the request, he was obliged to inform her that a stick and a wallet were all the movable things upon this earth that he could boast of. "Why, ay, my son," cried I, "you left me but poor, and poor I find you are come back; and yet I make no doubt you have seen a great deal of the world." ——"Yes, sir," replied my son, "but travelling after fortune, is not the way to secure her; and, indeed, of late I have desisted from the pursuit."——"I fancy, sir," cried

Mrs. Arnold, "that the account of your adventures would be amusing: the first part of them I have often heard from my niece; but could the company prevail for the rest, it would be an additional obligation."—— "Madam," replied my son, "I can promise you the pleasure you have in hearing will not be half so great as my vanity in the recital; and yet in the whole narrative I can scarce promise you one adventure, as my account is not of what I did, but what I saw. The first misfortune of my life, which you all know, was great; but tho' it distrest, it could not sink me. No person ever had a better knack at hoping than I. The less kind I found fortune then, the more I expected from her another time, and being now at the bottom of her wheel, every new revolution might lift, but could not depress me. I proceeded, therefore, towards London in a fine morning, no way uneasy about to-morrow, but cheerful as the birds that carolled by the road. I comforted myself with various reflections, that London was the true mart where abilities of every kind were sure of meeting distinction and reward.

"Upon my arrival in town, sir, my first care was to deliver your letter of recommendation to our cousin, who was himself in little better circumstances than me. My first scheme, you know, sir, was to be usher at an academy, and I asked his advice on the affair. Our cousin received the proposal with a true sardonic grin. 'Ay,' cried he, 'this is a pretty career, indeed, that has been chalked out for you. I have been once an usher at a boarding school myself; and may I die by an anodyne necklace, but I had rather be an under turnkey in Newgate. I was up early and late. I was brow-beat by the master, hated for my ugly face by the mistress, worried by the boys within, and never permitted to stir out to meet civility abroad. But are you sure you are fit for a school? Let me examine you a little. Have you been bred apprentice to the business? No. Then you won't do for a school. Can you dress the boys' hair? No. Then you won't do for a school. Have you had the small-pox? No. Then you won't do for a school. Can you lie three in a bed? No. Then you will never do for a school. Have you got a good stomach? Yes. Then you will by no means do for a school. No, sir, if you are for a genteel easy profession, bind yourself seven years as an apprentice to turn a cutler's wheel; but avoid a school by any means. But come,' continued he, 'I see you are a lad of spirit and some learning, what do you think of commencing author, like me? You have read in books, no doubt, of men of genius starving at the trade; but at present I'll show you forty very dull fellows about town that live by it in opulence. All honest jogg-trot men, who go on smoothly and dully, and write history and politics, and are praised; and who, had they been bred cobblers, would all their lives have only mended shoes, but never made them.'

"Finding that there was no great degree of gentility affixed to the character of an usher, I resolved to accept his proposal; and having the highest respect for literature, I hailed the antiqua mater of Grub Street with reverence. I thought it my glory to pursue a track which Dryden and Otway trod before me. In fact, I considered the goddess of this region as the parent of excellence; and however an intercourse with the world might give us good sense, the poverty she granted was the nurse of genius! Big with these reflections, I sat down, and finding that the best things remained to be said on the wrong side, I resolved to write a book that should be wholly new. I therefore drest up three paradoxes with some ingenuity. They were false, indeed, but they were new. The jewels of truth have been so often imported by others that nothing was left for me to import but some splendid things that at a distance looked every bit as well. Witness, you powers, what fancied importance sat perched upon my quill while I was writing. The whole learned world, I made no doubt, would rise to oppose my systems; but then I was prepared to oppose the whole learned world. Like the porcupine I sat self-collected, with a quill pointed against every opposer."

"Well said, my boy," cried I, "and what subject did you treat upon? I hope you did not pass over the importance of hierarchal monogamy. But I interrupt, go on; you published your paradoxes; well, and what did the learned world say to your paradoxes?"

"Sir," replied my son, "the learned world said nothing to my paradoxes; nothing at all, sir. Every man of them was employed in praising his friends and himself, or condemning his enemies; and, unfortunately, as I had neither, I suffered the cruellest mortification, neglect.

"As I was meditating one day in a coffee-house on the fate of my paradoxes, a little man happening to enter the room placed himself in the box before me, and after some preliminary discourse, finding me to be a scholar, drew out a bundle of proposals, begging me to subscribe to a new edition he was going to give the world of Propertius, with notes. This demand necessarily produced a reply that I had no money; and that concession led him on to enquire into the nature of my expectations. Finding that my expectations were just as great as my purse, 'I see,' cried he, 'you are unacquainted with the town. I'll teach you a part of it. Look at these proposals; upon these very proposals I have subsisted very comfortably for twelve years. The moment a nobleman returns from his travels, a Creolian arrives from Jamaica, or a dowager from her country seat, I strike for a subscription. I first besiege their hearts with flattery, and then pour in my proposals at the breach. If they subscribe readily the first time, I renew my request to beg a dedication fee. If they let me have that, I smite them once more for engraving their coat of arms at the top. Thus,' continued he, 'I live by vanity, and laugh at it. But between ourselves, I am now too well known. I should be glad to borrow your face a bit: a nobleman of distinction has just returned from Italy; my face is familiar to his porter; but if you bring this copy of verses, my life for it you succeed, and we divide the spoil.' "

"Bless us, George," cried I, "and is that the employment of poets now! Do men of their exalted talents thus stoop to beggary! Can they so far disgrace their calling as to make a vile traffic of praise for bread?"

"O no, sir," returned he, "a true poet can never be so base; for wherever there is genius there is pride. The creatures I now describe are only beggars in rhyme. The real poet, as he braves every hardship for fame, so he is equally a coward to contempt, and none but those who are unworthy protection condescend to solicit it.

"Having a mind too proud to stoop to such indignities, and yet a fortune too humble to hazard a second attempt for fame, I was now obliged to take a middle course and write for bread. But I was unqualified for a profession where mere industry alone could ensure success. I could not suppress my lurking passion for applause; but usually consumed that time in efforts after excellence which takes up but little room, when it should have been more advantageously employed in the diffusive productions of fruitful mediocrity. My little piece would come forth in the mist of periodical publication, unnoticed and unknown. The public were more importantly employed than to observe the easy simplicity of my style, or the harmony of my periods. Sheet after sheet was thrown off to oblivion. My essays were buried among the essays upon liberty, eastern tales, and cures for the bite of a mad dog; while Philautos, Philalethes, Philelutheros, and Philanthropos all wrote better, because they wrote faster, than I.

"Now, therefore, I began to associate with none but disappointed authors, like myself, who praised, deplored, and despised each other. The satisfaction we found in every celebrated writer's attempts was inversely as their merits. I found that no genius in another could please me. My unfortunate paradoxes had entirely dried up that source of comfort. I could neither read nor write with satisfaction; for excellence in another was my aversion, and writing was my trade.

"In the midst of these gloomy reflections, as I was one day sitting on a bench in St. James's park, a young gentleman of distinction, who had been my intimate acquaintance at the university, approached me. We saluted each other with some hesitation, he almost ashamed of being known to one who made so shabby an appearance, and I afraid of a repulse. But my suspicions soon vanished; for Ned Thornhill was at the bottom a very good-natured fellow."

"What did you say, George?" interrupted I. "Thornhill, was not that his name? It can certainly be no other than my landlord."——"Bless me," cried Mrs. Arnold, "is Mr. Thornhill so near a neighbour of yours? He has long been a friend in our family, and we expect a visit from him shortly."

"My friend's first care," continued my son, "was to alter my appearance by a very fine suit of his own clothes, and then I was admitted to his table upon the footing of half-friend, half-underling. My business was to attend him at auctions, to put him in spirits when he sat for his picture, to take the left hand in his chariot when not filled by another, and to assist at tattering a kip, as the phrase was, when he had a mind for a frolic. Beside this, I had twenty other little employments in the family. I was to do many small things without bidding: to carry the cork screw; to stand godfather to all the butler's children; to sing when I was bid; to be never out of humour; always to be humble, and, if I could, to be happy.

"In this honourable post, however, I was not without a rival. A captain of marines, who seemed formed for the place by nature, opposed me in my patron's affections. His mother had been laundress to a man of quality, and thus he early acquired a taste for pimping and pedigree. As this gentleman made it the study of his life to be acquainted with lords, though he was dismissed from several for his stupidity, yet he found many of them who permitted his assiduities, being as dull as himself. As flattery was his trade, he practised it with the easiest address imaginable; but it came awkward and stiff from me; and as every day my patron's desire of flattery increased, so every hour being better acquainted with his defects, I became more unwilling to give it. Thus I was once more fairly going to give up the field to the captain, when my friend found occasion for my assistance. This was nothing less than to fight a duel for him with a gentleman whose sister it was pretended he had used ill. I readily complied with his request, and tho' I see you are displeased at my conduct, yet as it was a debt indispensably due to friendship, I could not refuse. I undertook the affair, disarmed my antagonist, and soon after had the pleasure of finding that the lady was only a woman of the town and the fellow her bully and a sharper. This piece of service was repaid with the warmest professions of gratitude; but as my friend was to leave town in a few days, he knew no other method to serve me, but by recommending me to his uncle Sir William Thornhill and another nobleman of great distinction, who enjoyed a post under the government. When he was gone, my first care was to carry his recommendatory letter to his uncle, a man whose character for every virtue was universal, yet just. I was received by his servants with the most hospitable smiles; for the looks of the domestics ever transmit their master's benevolence. Being shown into a grand apartment, where Sir William soon came to me, I delivered my message and letter, which he read, and after pausing some minutes, 'Pray, sir,' cried he, 'inform me what you have done for my kinsman, to deserve this warm recommendation? But I suppose, sir, I guess at your merits, you have fought for him; and so you would expect a reward from me, for being the instrument of his vices. I wish, sincerely wish, that my present refusal may be some punishment for your guilt; but still more, that it may be some inducement to your repentance.' The severity of this rebuke I bore patiently, because I knew it was just. My whole expectations now, therefore, lay in my letter to the great man. As the doors of the nobility are almost ever beset with beggars all ready to thrust in some sly petition, I found it no easy matter to gain admittance. However, after bribing the servants with half my worldly fortune, I was at last shown into a spacious apartment, my letter being previously sent up for his lordship's inspection. During this anxious interval I had full time to look round me. Every thing was grand, and of happy contrivance: the paintings, the furniture, the gildings, petrified me with awe and raised my idea of the owner. Ah, thought I to myself, how very great must the possessor of all these things be, who carries in his head the business of the state, and whose house displays half the wealth of a kingdom: sure his genius must be unfathomable! During these awful reflections I heard a step come heavily forward. Ah, this is the great man himself! No, it was only a chambermaid. Another foot was heard soon after. This must be He! No, it was only the great man's valet de chambre. At last his lordship actually made his appearance. 'Are you,' cried he, 'the bearer of this here letter?' I answered with a bow. 'I learn by this,' continued he, 'as how that —' But just at that instant a servant delivered him a card, and without taking further notice, he went out of the room and left me to digest my own happiness at leisure. I saw no more of him, till told by a footman that his lordship was going to his coach at the door. Down I immediately followed and joined my voice to that of three or four more, who came, like me, to petition for favours. His lordship, however, went too fast for us and was gaining his chariot door with large strides, when I hallooed out to know if I was to have any reply. He was by this time got in and muttered an answer, half of which only I heard, the other half was lost in the rattling of his chariot wheels. I stood for some time with my neck stretched out, in the posture of one that was listening to catch the glorious sounds, till looking round me, I found myself alone at his lordship's gate.

"My patience," continued my son, "was now quite exhausted: stung with the thousand indignities I had met with, I was willing to cast myself away, and only wanted the gulf to receive me. I regarded myself as one of those vile things that nature designed should be thrown by into her lumber room, there to perish in unpitied obscurity. I had still, however, half a guinea left, and of that I thought fortune herself should not deprive me; but in order to be sure of this, I was resolved to go instantly and spend it while I had it, and then trust to occurrences for the rest. As I was going along with this resolution, it happened that Mr. Cripse's office seemed invitingly open to give me a welcome reception. In this office Mr. Cripse kindly offers all his majesty's subjects a generous promise of thirty pounds a year, for which promise all they give in return is their liberty for life and permission to let him transport them to America as slaves. I was happy at finding a place where I could lose my fears in desperation, and therefore entered this cell; for it had the appearance of one, being dark, damp, and dirty. Here I found a number of poor creatures, all in circumstances like myself, expecting the arrival of Mr. Cripse, presenting a true epitome of English impatience. Each untractable soul at variance with fortune wreaked her injuries on their own hearts: but Mr. Cripse at last came down, and all our murmurs were hushed. He deigned to regard me with an air of peculiar approbation, and indeed he was the first man who for a month past talked to me with smiles. After a few questions, he found I was fit for every thing in the world. He paused a while upon the properest means of providing for me, and slapping his forehead, as if he had found it, assured me that there was at that time an embassy talked of from the synod of Pennsylvania to the Chickasaw Indians, and that he would use his interest to get me made secretary. I knew in my own heart that the fellow lied, and yet his promise gave me pleasure, there was something so magnificent in the sound. I fairly, therefore, divided my half guinea, one half of which went to be added to his thirty thousand pound, and with the other half I resolved to go to the next tavern, to be there more happy than he.

"As I was going out with that resolution, I was met at the door by the captain of a ship with whom I had formerly some little acquaintance, and he agreed to be my companion over a bowl of punch. As I never chose to make a secret of my circumstances, he assured me that I was upon the very point of ruin in listening to the office-keeper's promises; for that he only designed to sell me to the plantations. 'But,' continued he, 'I fancy you might, by a much shorter voyage, be very easily put into a genteel way of bread. Take my advice. My ship sails to-morrow for Amsterdam. What if you go in her as a passenger? The moment you land all you have to do is to teach the Dutchmen English, and I'll warrant you'll get pupils and money enough. I suppose you understand English,' added he, 'by this time, or the deuce is in it.' I confidently assured him of that, but expressed a doubt whether the Dutch would be willing to learn English. He affirmed with an oath that they were fond of it to distraction; and upon that affirmation I agreed with his proposal and embarked the next day to teach the Dutch English in Holland. The wind was fair, our voyage short, and after having paid my passage with half my movables, I found myself, fallen as if from the skies, a stranger in one of the principal streets of Amsterdam. In this situation I was unwilling to let any time pass unemployed in teaching. I addressed myself therefore to two or three of those I met, whose appearance seemed most promising; but it was impossible to make ourselves mutually understood. It was not till this very moment I recollected that, in order to teach Dutchmen English, it was necessary that they should first teach me Dutch. How I came to overlook so obvious an objection is to me amazing; but certain it is I overlooked it.

"This scheme thus blown up, I had some thoughts of fairly shipping back to England again; but happening into company with an Irish student, who was returning from Louvain, our conversation turning upon topics of literature (for by the way it may be observed that I always forgot the meanness of my circumstances when I could converse upon such subjects), from him I learned that there were not two men in his whole university who understood Greek. This amazed me. I instantly resolved to travel to Louvain, and there live by teaching Greek; and in this design I was heartened by my brother student, who threw out some hints that a fortune might be got by it.

"I set boldly forward the next morning. Every day lessened the burden of my movables, like Æsop and his basket of bread; for I paid them for my lodgings to the Dutch as I travelled on. When I came to Louvain, I was resolved not to go sneaking to the lower professors, but openly tendered my talents to the principal himself. I went, had admittance, and offered him my service as a master of the Greek language, which I had been told was a desideratum in his university. The principal seemed at first to doubt of my abilities; but of these I offered to convince him, by turning a part of any Greek author he should fix upon into Latin. Finding me perfectly earnest in my proposal, he addressed me thus: 'You see me, young man,' continued he. 'I never learned Greek, and I don't find that I ever missed it. I have had a doctor's cap and gown without Greek: I have ten thousand florins a year without Greek; and I eat heartily without Greek. In short,' continued he, 'I don't know Greek, and I do not believe there is any use in it.'

"I was now too far from home to think of returning; so I resolved to go forward. I had some knowledge of music, with a tolerable voice, and now turned what was once my amusement into a present means of bare subsistence. I passed among the harmless peasants of Flanders, and among such of the French as were poor enough to be very merry; for I ever found them sprightly in proportion to their wants. Whenever I approached a peasant's house towards night-fall, I played one of my most merry tunes, and that procured me not only a lodging, but subsistence for the next day. I once or twice attempted to play for people of fashion; but they still thought my performance odious, and never rewarded me even with a trifle. This was to me the more extraordinary, as whenever I used formerly to play for company, when playing was my amusement, my music never failed to throw them into raptures, and the ladies especially; but as it was now my only means, it was received with contempt: a proof how ready the world is to under-rate those talents which a man lives by.

"In this manner I proceeded to Paris, with no design but just to look about me, and then to go forward. The people of Paris are much fonder of strangers that have money, than of those that have wit. You may imagine then, as I could not boast much of either, that I was no great favourite. After I had walked about the town four or five days, and seen the outsides of the best houses, I was preparing to leave this retreat of venal hospitality, when passing through one of the principal streets, whom should I meet but our cousin, to whom you first recommended me. This meeting was very agreeable to me, and I believe not displeasing to him. He enquired into the nature of my journey to Paris and informed me of his business there, which was to collect pictures, medals, intaglios, and antiques of all kinds for a gentleman in

London who had just stept into taste and a large fortune. I was still more surprised at seeing our cousin pitched upon for this office, as himself had often assured me he knew nothing of the matter. Upon my asking how he had been taught the art of a *cognoscente* so very suddenly, he assured me that nothing was more easy. The whole secret consisted in a strict adherence to two rules: the one always to observe that the picture might have been better if the painter had taken more pains; and the other, to praise the works of Pietro Perugino. 'But,' says he, 'as I once taught you how to be an author in London, I'll now undertake to instruct you in the art of picture buying at Paris.'

"With this proposal I very readily closed, as it was a living, and now all my ambition was to live. I went therefore to his lodgings, improved my dress by his assistance, and after some time, accompanied him to auctions of pictures, where the English gentry were expected to be purchasers. I was not a little surprised at his intimacy with people of the best fashion, who referred themselves to his judgment upon every picture or medal, as to an unerring standard of taste. He made very good use of my assistance upon these occasions; for when asked his opinion, he would gravely take me aside and ask mine, shrug, look wise, return, and assure the company that he could give no opinion upon an affair of so much importance. Yet there was sometimes an occasion for a more supported assurance. I remember to have seen him, after giving his opinion that the colouring of a picture was not mellow enough, very deliberately take a brush with brown varnish, that was accidentally lying in the place, and rub it over the piece with great composure before all the company, and then ask if he had not improved the tints.

"When he had finished his commission in Paris, he left me strongly recommended to several men of distinction, as a person very proper for a travelling tutor; and I was after some time employed in that capacity by a gentleman who brought his ward to Paris, in order to set him forward on his tour through Europe. I was to be the young gentleman's governor, with this injunction, that he should always be permitted to direct himself. My pupil in fact understood the art of guiding in money concerns much better than me. He was heir to a fortune of about two hundred thousand pounds, left him by an uncle in the West Indies; and his guardians, to qualify him for the management of it, had bound him apprentice to an attorney. Thus avarice was his prevailing passion; all his questions on the road were how money might be saved: which was the least expensive course of travel; whether any thing could be bought that would turn to account when disposed of again in London. Such curiosities on the way as could be seen for nothing he was ready enough to look at; but if the sight was to be paid for, he usually asserted that he had been told it was not worth seeing. He never paid a bill that he would not observe how amazingly expensive travelling was, and all this though he was not yet come to the age of twenty-one. When arrived at Leghorn, as we took a walk to look at the port and shipping, he enquired the expence of the passage by sea home to England. This he was informed was but a trifle, compared to his returning by land; he was therefore unable to withstand the temptation; so paying me the small part of my salary that was then due, he took leave and embarked with only one attendant for London.

"I now therefore was left once more upon the world at large, but then it was a thing I was used to. However, my skill in music could avail me nothing in a country where every peasant was a better musician than I; but by this time I had acquired another talent, which answered my purpose as well, and this was a skill in disputation. In all the foreign universities and convents, there are upon certain days philosophical theses maintained against every adventitious disputant; for which, if the champion opposes with any dexterity, he can claim a gratuity in money, a dinner, and a bed for one night. In this manner therefore I fought my way towards England, walked along from city to city, examined mankind more nearly, and, if I may so express it, saw both sides of the picture. My remarks, however, were few: I found that monarchy was the best government for the poor to live in, and commonwealths for the rich. I found that riches in general were in every country another name for freedom; and that no man is so fond of freedom himself that he would not choose to subject the will of some individuals of society to his own.

"Upon my arrival in England, I resolved to pay my respects first to you, and then to enlist as a volunteer in the first expedition that was sent out; but on my journey down my resolutions were changed by meeting an old acquaintance, who I found belonged to a company of comedians that were going to make a summer campaign in the country. The company seemed not much to disapprove of me for an associate. They all, however, apprized me of the importance of the task at which I aimed; that the public was a many headed monster, and that only such as had very good heads could please it; that acting was not to be learnt in a day; and that without some traditional shrugs, which had been on the stage, and only on the stage, these hundred years, I could never pretend to please. The next difficulty was in fitting me with parts, as almost every character was in keeping. I was driven for some time from one character to another, till at last Horatio was fixed upon, which the presence of the present company happily hindered me from acting."

CHAPTER XXI

THE SHORT CONTINUANCE OF FRIENDSHIP AMONGST THE VICIOUS, WHICH IS COEVAL ONLY WITH MUTUAL SATISFACTION

My son's account was too long to be delivered at once; the first part of it was begun that night, and he was concluding the rest after dinner the next day, when the appearance of Mr. Thornhill's equipage at the door seemed to make a pause in the general satisfaction. The butler, who was now become my friend in the family, informed me with a whisper that the Squire had already made some overtures to Miss Wilmot, and that her aunt and uncle seemed highly to approve the match. Upon Mr. Thornhill's entering, he seemed, at seeing my son and me, to start back; but I readily imputed that to surprise, and not displeasure. However, upon our advancing to salute him, he returned our greeting with the most apparent candour; and after a short time his presence seemed only to increase the general good humour.

After tea he called me aside, to enquire after my daughter; but upon my informing him that my enquiry was unsuccessful, he seemed greatly surprised; adding that he had been since frequently at my house, in order to comfort the rest of my family, whom he left perfectly well. He then asked if I had communicated her misfortune to Miss Wilmot or my son; and upon my replying that I had not told them as yet, he greatly approved my prudence and precaution, desiring me by all means to keep it a secret: "For at best," cried he, "it is but divulging one's own infamy; and perhaps Miss Livy may not be so guilty as we all imagine." We were here interrupted by a servant, who came to ask the Squire in, to stand up at country dances; so that he left me quite pleased with the interest he seemed to take in my concerns. His addresses, however, to Miss Wilmot were too obvious to be mistaken; and yet she seemed not perfectly pleased, but bore them rather in compliance to the will of her aunt than from real inclination. I had even the satisfaction to see her lavish some kind looks upon my unfortunate son, which the other could neither extort by his fortune nor assiduity. Mr. Thornhill's seeming composure, however, not a little surprised me: we had now continued here a week, at the pressing instances of Mr. Arnold; but each day the more tenderness Miss Wilmot showed my son, Mr. Thornhill's friendship seemed proportionably to increase for him.

He had formerly made us the most kind assurances of using his interest to serve the family; but now his generosity was not confined to promises alone: the morning I designed for my departure, Mr. Thornhill came to me with looks of real pleasure to inform me of a piece of service he had done for his friend George. This was nothing less than his having procured him an ensign's commission in one of the regiments that was going to the West Indies, for which he had promised but one hundred pounds, his interest having been sufficient to get an abatement of the other two. "As for this trifling piece of service," continued the young gentleman, "I desire no other reward but the pleasure of having served my friend; and as for the hundred pound to be paid, if you are unable to raise it yourselves, I will advance it, and you shall repay me at your leisure." This was a favour we wanted words to express our sense of. I readily therefore gave my bond for the money, and testified as much gratitude as if I never intended to pay.

George was to depart for town the next day to secure his commission, in pursuance of his generous patron's directions, who judged it highly expedient to use dispatch, lest in the meantime another should step in with more advantageous proposals. The next morning, therefore, our young soldier was early prepared for his departure, and seemed the only person among us that was not affected by it. Neither the fatigues and dangers he was going to encounter, nor the friends and mistress, for Miss Wilmot actually loved him, he was leaving behind, any way damped his spirits. After he had taken leave of the rest of the company, I gave him all I had, my blessing. "And now, my boy," cried I, "thou art going to fight for thy country, remember how thy brave grandfather fought for his sacred king, when loyalty among Britons was a virtue. Go, my boy, and imitate him in all but his misfortunes, if it was a misfortune to die with Lord Falkland. Go, my boy, and if you fall, tho' distant, exposed and unwept by those that love you, the most precious tears are those with which heaven bedews the unburied head of a soldier."

The next morning I took leave of the good family that had been kind enough to entertain me so long, not without several expressions of gratitude to Mr. Thornhill for his late bounty. I left them in the enjoyment of all that happiness which affluence and good breeding procure, and returned towards home, despairing of ever finding my daughter more, but sending a sigh to heaven to spare and to forgive her. I was now come within about twenty miles of home, having hired an horse to carry me, as I was yet but weak, and comforted myself with the hopes of soon seeing all I held dearest upon earth. But the night coming on, I put up at a little public-house by the roadside, and asked for the landlord's company over a pint of wine. We sat beside his kitchen fire, which was the best room in the house, and chatted on politics and the news of the country. We happened, among other topics, to talk of young Squire Thornhill, whom the host assured me was hated as much as an uncle of his, who sometimes came down to the country, was loved. He went on to observe that he made it his whole study to betray the daughters of such as received him to their houses, and after a fortnight or three weeks possession, he turned them out unrewarded and abandoned to the world. As we continued our discourse in this manner, his wife, who had been out to get change, returned, and perceiving that her husband was enjoying a pleasure in which she was not a sharer, she asked him, in an angry tone, what he did there, to which he only replied in an ironic way, by drinking her health. "Mr. Symmonds," cried she, "you use me very ill, and I'll bear it no longer. Here three parts of the business is left for me to do, and the fourth left unfinished; while you do nothing but soak with the guests all day long, whereas if a spoonful of liquor were to cure me of a fever, I never touch a drop." I now found what she would be at, and immediately poured her out a glass, which she received with a curtsey, and drinking towards my good health, "Sir," resumed she, "it is not so much for the value of the liquor I am angry, but one cannot help it, when the house is going out of the windows. If the customers or guests are to be dunned, all the burden lies upon my back; he'd as lief eat that glass as budge after them himself. There now above stairs, we have a young woman who has come to take up her lodgings here, and I don't believe she has got any money by her over-civility. I am certain she is very slow of payment, and I wish she were put in mind of it."——

"What signifies minding her," cried the host, "if she be slow, she is sure."——"I don't know that," replied the wife; "but I know that I am sure she has been here a fortnight, and we have not yet seen the cross of her money." ——"I suppose, my dear," cried he, "we shall have it all in a lump."——"In a lump!" cried the other, "I hope we may get it any way; and that I am resolved we shall this very night, or out she tramps, bag and baggage." ——"Consider, my dear," cried the husband, "she is a gentlewoman, and deserves more respect."——"As for the matter of that," returned the hostess, "gentle or simple, out she shall pack with a sassarara. Gentry may be good things where they take; but for my part I never saw much good of them at the sign of the Harrow." Thus saying, she ran up a narrow flight of stairs that went from the kitchen to a room overhead, and I soon perceived by the loudness of her voice, and the bitterness of her reproaches, that no money was to be had from her lodger. I could hear her remonstrances very distinctly: "Out I say, pack out this moment; tramp, thou infamous strumpet, or I'll give thee a mark thou won't be the better for this three months. What! you trumpery, to come and take up an honest house, without cross or coin to bless yourself with; come along, I say."——"O dear madam," cried the stranger, "pity me, pity a poor abandoned creature for one night, and death will soon do the rest." I instantly knew the voice of my poor ruined child, Olivia. I flew to her rescue, while the woman was dragging her along by the hair, and caught the dear forlorn wretch in my arms. "Welcome, any way welcome, my dearest lost one, my treasure, to your poor old father's bosom. Tho' the vicious forsake thee, there is yet one in the world that will never forsake thee; tho' thou hadst ten thousand crimes to answer for, he will forget them all."——"O my own dear"—for minutes she could no more—"my own dearest good pappa! Could angels be kinder! How do I deserve so much! The villain, I hate him and myself, to be a reproach to such goodness. You can't forgive me. I know you cannot."——"Yes, my child, from my heart I do forgive thee! Only repent, and we both shall yet be happy. We shall see many pleasant days yet, my Olivia!"——"Ah! never, sir, never. The rest of my wretched life must be infamy abroad and shame at home. But, alas! pappa, you look much paler than you used to do. Could such a thing as I am give you so much uneasiness? Sure you have too much wisdom to take the miseries of my guilt upon yourself." ——"Our wisdom, young woman," replied I.——"Ah, why so cold a name, pappa?" cried she. "This is the first time you ever called me by so cold a name."——"I ask pardon, my darling," returned I; "but I was going to observe that wisdom makes but a slow defence against trouble, though at last a sure one."

The landlady now returned to know if we did not choose a more genteel apartment, to which assenting, we were shown a room where we could converse more freely. After we had talked ourselves into some degree of tranquillity, I could not avoid desiring some account of the gradations that led to her present wretched situation. "That villain, sir," said she, "from the first day of our meeting made me honourable, though private, proposals."

"Villain indeed," cried I; "and yet it in some measure surprises me how a person of Mr. Burchell's good sense and seeming honour could be guilty of such deliberate baseness, and thus step into a family to undo it."

"My dear pappa," returned my daughter, "you labour under a strange mistake. Mr. Burchell never attempted to deceive me. Instead of that he took every opportunity of privately admonishing me against the artifices of Mr. Thornhill, whom now I find was even worse than he represented him."——"Mr. Thornhill," interrupted I; "can it be?"——"Yes, sir," returned she, "it was Mr. Thornhill who seduced me, who employed the two ladies, as he called them, but who, in fact, were abandoned women of the town, without breeding or pity, to decoy us up to London. Their artifices, you may remember, would have certainly succeeded, but for Mr. Burchell's letter, who directed those reproaches at them, which we all applied to ourselves. How he came to have so much influence as to defeat their intentions still remains a secret to me; but I am convinced he was ever our warmest, sincerest friend."

"You amaze me, my dear," cried I; "but now I find my first suspicions of Mr. Thornhill's baseness were too well grounded: but he can triumph in security; for he is rich and we are poor. But tell me, my child, sure it was no small temptation that could thus obliterate all the impressions of such an education, and so virtuous a disposition as thine?"

"Indeed, sir," replied she, "he owes all his triumph to the desire I had of making him, and not myself, happy. I knew that the ceremony of our marriage, which was privately performed by a popish priest, was no way binding, and that I had nothing to trust to but his honour."—"What," interrupted I, "and were you indeed married by a priest, and in orders?"——"Indeed, sir, we were," replied she, "though we were both sworn to conceal his name."——"Why then, my child, come to my arms again, and now you are a thousand times more welcome than before; for you are now his wife to all intents and purposes; nor can all the laws of man, tho' written upon tables of adamant, lessen the forces of that sacred connexion."

"Alas, pappa," replied she, "you are but little acquainted with his villainies: he has been married already, by the same priest, to six or eight wives more, whom, like me, he has deceived and abandoned."

"Has he so?" cried I, "then we must hang the priest, and you shall inform against him to-morrow."——"But, sir," returned she, "will that be right, when I am sworn to secrecy?"——"My dear," I replied, "if you have made such a promise, I cannot, nor will not, tempt you to break it. Even tho' it may benefit the public, you must not inform against him. In all human institutions a smaller evil is allowed to procure a greater good; as in politics, a province may be given away to secure a kingdom; in medicine, a limb may be lopt off to preserve the body. But in religion the law is written, and inflexible, *never* to do evil. And this law, my child, is right; for otherwise, if we commit a smaller evil to procure a greater good, certain guilt would be thus incurred in expectation of contingent advantage. And though the advantage should certainly follow, yet the interval between commission and advantage, which is allowed to be guilty, may be that in which we are called away to answer for the things we have done, and the volume of human actions is closed for ever. But I interrupt you, my dear; go on."

"The very next morning," continued she, "I found what little expectations I was to have from his sincerity. That very morning he introduced me to two unhappy women more, whom, like me, he had deceived, but who lived in contented prostitution. I loved him too tenderly to bear such rivals in his affections, and strove to forget my infamy in a tumult of pleasures. With this view, I danced, dressed, and talked; but still was unhappy. The gentlemen who visited there told me every moment of the power of my charms, and this only contributed to increase my melancholy, as I had thrown all their power quite away. Thus each day I grew more pensive, and he more insolent, till at last the monster had the assurance to offer me to a young Baronet of his acquaintance. Need I describe, sir, how his ingratitude stung me. My answer to this proposal was almost madness. I desired to part. As I was going he offered me a purse; but I flung it at him with indignation, and burst from him in a rage, that for a while kept me insensible of the miseries of my situation. But I soon looked round me and saw myself a vile, abject, guilty thing, without one friend in the world to apply to.

"Just in that interval, a stage-coach happening to pass by, I took a place, it being my only aim to be driven at a distance from a wretch I despised and detested. I was set down here, where, since my arrival, my own anxiety and this woman's unkindness have been my only companions. The hours of pleasure that I have passed with my mamma and sister now grow painful to me. Their sorrows are much; but mine is greater than theirs; for mine is guilt and infamy."

"Have patience, my child," cried I, "and I hope things will yet be better. Take some repose to-night, and to-morrow I'll carry you home to your mother and the rest of the family, from whom you will receive a kind reception. Poor woman, this has gone to her heart: but she loves you still, Olivia, and will forget it."

CHAPTER XXII

OFFENCES ARE EASILY PARDONED WHERE THERE IS LOVE AT BOTTOM

The next morning I took my daughter behind me, and set out on my return home. As we travelled along, I strove, by every persuasion, to calm her sorrows and fears, and to arm her with resolution to bear the presence of her offended mother. I took every opportunity, from the prospect of a fine country through which we passed, to observe how much kinder heaven was to us than we were to each other, and that the misfortunes of nature's making were very few. I assured her that she should never perceive any change in my affections, and that during my life, which yet might be long, she might depend upon a guardian and an instructor. I armed her against the censures of the world, showed her that books were sweet unreproaching companions to the miserable, and that if they could not bring us to enjoy life, they would teach us to endure it.

The hired horse that we rode was to be put up that night at an inn by the way, within about five miles from my house, and as I was willing to prepare my family for my daughter's reception, I determined to leave her that night at the inn, and to come for her, accompanied by my daughter Sophia, early the next morning. It was night before we reached our appointed stage; however, after seeing her provided with a decent apartment, and having ordered the hostess to prepare proper refreshments, I kissed her and proceeded towards home. My heart caught new sensations of pleasure the nearer I approached that peaceful mansion. As a bird that has been frighted from its nest, my affections out-went my haste, and hovered round my little fire-side with all the rapture of expectation. I called up the many fond things I had to say, and anticipated the welcome I was to receive. I already felt my wife's tender embrace, and smiled at the joy of my little ones. As I walked but slowly, the night waned apace. The labourers of the day were all retired to rest; the lights were out in every cottage; no sounds were heard but of the shrilling cock and the deepmouthed watch-dog, at hollow distance. I approached my little abode of pleasure, and before I was within a furlong of the place, our honest mastiff came running to welcome me.

It was now near mid-night that I came to knock at my door; all was still and silent; my heart dilated with unutterable happiness, when, to my amazement, the house was bursting out in a blaze of fire and every apperture was red with conflagration! I gave a loud convulsive outcry, and fell upon the pavement insensible. This alarmed my son, who, perceiving the flames, instantly waked my wife and daughter, and all running out, naked, and wild with apprehension, recalled me to life with their anguish. But it was only to objects of new terror; for the flames had, by this time, caught the roof of our dwelling, part after part continuing to fall in, while the family stood, with silent agony, looking on as if they enjoyed the blaze. I gazed upon them and upon it by turns, and then looked round me for my two little ones; but they were not to be seen. O misery! "Where," cried I, "where are my little ones?"——"They are burnt to death in the flames," says my wife calmly, "and I will die with them." That moment I heard the cry of the babes within, who were just awaked by the fire, and nothing could have stopped me. "Where, where, are my children?" cried I, rushing through the flames and bursting the door of the chamber in which they were confined. "Where are my little ones?"——"Here, dear pappa, here we are," cried they together, while the flames were just catching the bed where they lay. I caught them both in my arms and snatched them through the fire as fast as possible, while just as I was got out, the roof sunk in. "Now," cried I, holding up my children, "now let the flames burn on, and all my possessions perish. Here they are, I have saved my treasure. Here, my dearest, here are our treasures, and we shall yet be happy." We kissed our little darlings a thousand times, they clasped us round the neck, and seemed to share our transports, while their mother laughed and wept by turns.

I now stood a calm spectator of the flames, and after some time, began to perceive that my arm to the shoulder was scorched in a terrible manner. It was therefore out of my power to give my son any assistance, either in attempting to save our goods or preventing the flames spreading to our corn. By this time, the neighbours were alarmed, and came running to our assistance; but all they could do was to stand, like us, spectators of the calamity. My goods, among which were the notes I had reserved for my daughters' fortunes, were entirely consumed, except a box with some papers that stood in the kitchen and two or three things more of little consequence, which my son brought away in the beginning. The neighbours contributed, however, what they could to lighten our distress. They brought us clothes and furnished one of our out-houses with kitchen-utensils; so that by day-light we had another, tho' a wretched, dwelling to retire to. My honest next neighbour and his children were not the least assiduous in providing us with everything necessary and offering whatever consolation untutored benevolence could suggest.

When the fears of my family had subsided, curiosity to know the cause of my long stay began to take place; having therefore informed them of every particular, I proceeded to prepare them for the reception of our lost one, and tho' we had nothing but wretchedness now to impart, yet to procure her a welcome to what we had. This task would have been more difficult but for our recent calamity, which had humbled my wife's pride and blunted it by more poignant afflictions. Being unable to go for my poor child myself, as my arm now grew very painful, I sent my son and daughter, who soon returned, supporting the wretched delinquent, who had not courage to look up at her mother, whom no instructions of mine could persuade to a perfect reconciliation; for women have a much stronger sense of female error than men. "Ah, madam," cried her mother, "this is but a poor place you are come to after so much finery. My daughter Sophy and I can afford but little entertainment to persons who have kept company only with people of distinction. Yes, Miss Livy, your poor father and I have suffered very much of late; but I hope heaven will forgive you." During this reception, the unhappy victim stood pale and trembling, unable to weep or to reply; but I could not continue a silent spectator of her distress; wherefore assuming a degree of severity in my voice and manner, which was ever followed with instant submission, "I entreat, woman, that my words may be now marked once for all: I have here brought you back a poor deluded wanderer; her return to duty demands the revival of our tenderness. The real hardships of life are now coming fast upon us; let us not therefore increase them by dissention among each other. If we live harmoniously together, we may yet be contented, as there are enough of us here to shut out the censuring world and keep each other in countenance. The kindness of heaven is promised to the penitent, and let ours be directed by the example. Heaven, we are assured, is much more pleased to view a repentant sinner, than many persons who have supported a course of undeviating rectitude. And this is right; for that single effort by which we stop short in the down-hill path to perdition is itself a greater exertion of virtue than an hundred acts of justice."

CHAPTER XXIII

NONE BUT THE GUILTY CAN BE LONG AND COMPLETELY MISERABLE

Some assiduity was now required to make our present abode as convenient as possible, and we were soon again qualified to enjoy our former serenity. Being disabled myself from assisting my son in our usual occupations, I read to my family from the few books that were saved, and particularly from such as, by amusing the imagination, contributed to ease the heart. Our good neighbours too came every day with the kindest condolence, and fixed a time in which they were all to assist at repairing my former dwelling. Honest farmer Williams was not last among these visitors, but heartily offered his friendship. He would even have renewed his addresses to my daughter; but she rejected them in such a manner as totally represt his future solicitations. Her grief seemed formed for continuing, and she was the only person of our little society that a week did not restore to cheerfulness. She now lost that unblushing innocence which once taught her to respect herself and to seek pleasure by pleasing. Anxiety now had taken strong possession of her mind, her beauty began to be impaired with her constitution, and neglect still more contributed to diminish it. Every tender epithet bestowed on her sister brought a pang to her heart and a tear to her eye; and as one vice, tho' cured, almost ever plants others where it has been, so her former guilt, tho' driven out by repentance, left jealousy and envy behind. I strove a thousand ways to lessen her care, and even forgot my own pain in a concern for hers, collecting such amusing passages of history as a strong memory and some reading could suggest. "Our happiness, my dear," I would say, "is in the power of one who can bring it about a thousand unforseen ways that mock our foresight. If example be necessary to prove this, I'll give you a story, my child, told us by a grave, tho' sometimes a romancing, historian.

"Matilda was married very young to a Neapolitan nobleman of the first quality, and found herself a widow and a mother at the age of fifteen. As she stood one day caressing her infant son in the open window of an apartment, which hung over the river Volturna, the child, with a sudden spring, leaped from her arms into the flood below and disappeared in a moment. The mother, struck with instant surprise, and making an effort to save him, plunged in after; but, far from being able to assist the infant, she herself with great difficulty escaped to the opposite shore, just when some French soldiers were plundering the country on that side, who immediately made her their prisoner.

"As the war was then carried on between the French and Italians with the utmost inhumanity, they were going at once to perpetrate those two extremes, suggested by appetite and cruelty. This base resolution, however, was opposed by a young officer who, tho' their retreat required the utmost expedition, placed her behind him and brought her in safety to his native city. Her beauty at first caught his eye, her merit soon after his heart. They were married; he rose to the highest posts; they lived long together and were happy. But the felicity of a soldier can never be called permanent; after an interval of several years, the troops which he commanded having met with a repulse, he was obliged to take shelter in the city where he had lived with his wife. Here they suffered a siege, and the city at length was taken. Few histories can produce more various instances of cruelty than those which the French and Italians at that time exercised upon each other. It was resolved by the victors upon this occasion to put all the French prisoners to death; but particularly the husband of the unfortunate Matilda, as he was principally instrumental in protracting the siege. Their determinations were, in general, executed almost as soon as resolved upon. The captive soldier was led forth, and the executioner, with his sword, stood ready, while the spectators in gloomy silence awaited the fatal blow, which was only suspended till the general, who presided as judge, should give the signal. It was in this interval of anguish and expectation that Matilda came to take her last farewell of her husband and deliverer, deploring her wretched situation and the cruelty of fate that had saved her from perishing by a premature death in the river Volturna, to be the spectator of still greater calamities. The general, who was a young man, was struck with surprise at her beauty, and pity at her distress; but with still stronger emotions when he heard her mention her former dangers. He was her son, the infant for whom she had encountered so much danger. He acknowledged her at once as his mother and fell at her feet. The rest may be easily supposed: the captive was set free, and all the happiness that love, friendship, and duty could confer on each were united."

In this manner I would attempt to amuse my daughter, but she listened with divided attention; for her own misfortunes engrossed all the pity she once had for those of another, and nothing gave her ease. In company she dreaded contempt, and in solitude she only found anxiety. Such was the colour of her wretchedness when we received certain information that Mr. Thornhill was going to be married to Miss Wilmot, for whom I always suspected he had a real passion, tho' he took every opportunity before me to express his contempt both of her person and fortune. This news only served to increase poor Olivia's affliction; such a flagrant breach of fidelity was more than her courage could support. I was resolved, however, to get more certain information, and to defeat, if possible, the completion of his designs by sending my son to old Mr. Wilmot's with instructions to know the truth of the report, and to deliver Miss Wilmot a letter intimating Mr. Thornhill's conduct in my family. My son went, in pursuance of my directions, and in three days returned, assuring us of the truth of the account; but that he had found it impossible to deliver the letter, which he was therefore obliged to leave, as Mr. Thornhill and Miss Wilmot were visiting round the country. They were to be married, he said, in a few days, having appeared together at church the Sunday before he was there, in great splendour, the bride attended by six young ladies drest in white and he by as many gentlemen. Their approaching nuptials filled the whole country with rejoicing, and they usually rode out together in the grandest equipage that had been seen in the country for many years. All the friends of both families, he said, were there, particularly the Squire's uncle, Sir William Thornhill, who bore so good a character. He added that nothing but mirth and feasting were going forward, that all the country praised the young bride's beauty and the bridegroom's fine person, and that they were immensely fond of each other, concluding that he could not help thinking Mr. Thornhill one of the most happy men in the world.

"Why let him if he can," returned I, "but, my son, observe this bed of straw and unsheltering roof, those mouldering walls and humid floor, my wretched body thus disabled by fire and my children weeping round me for bread; you have come home, my child, to all this; yet here, even here, you see a man that would not for a thousand worlds exchange situations. O, my children, if you could but learn to commune with your own hearts and know what noble company you can make them, you would little regard the elegance and splendours of the worthless. Almost all men have been taught to call life a passage, and themselves the travellers. The similitude still may be improved when we observe that the good are joyful and serene, like travellers that are going towards home; the wicked but by intervals happy, like travellers that are going into exile."

My compassion for my poor daughter, overpowered by this new disaster, interrupted what I had further to observe. I bade her mother support her, and after a short time she recovered. She appeared from this time more calm, and I imagined had gained a new degree of resolution; but appearances deceived me, for her tranquillity was the langour of over-wrought resentment. A supply of provisions, charitably sent us by my kind parishioners, seemed to diffuse cheerfulness amongst the rest of the family, nor was I displeased at seeing them once more sprightly and at ease. It would have been unjust to damp their satisfactions, merely to condole with resolute melancholy, or to burden them with a sadness they did not feel. Once more, therefore, the tale went round and the song was demanded, and cheerfulness condescended to hover round our little habitation.

CHAPTER XXIV

FRESH CALAMITIES

The next morning the sun arose with peculiar warmth for the season; so that we agreed to breakfast together at the honey-suckle bank, where, while we sat, my youngest daughter, at my request, joined her voice to the concert on the trees about us. It was here my poor Olivia first met her seducer, and every object served to recall her sadness. But that melancholy which is excited by objects of pleasure or inspired by sounds of harmony soothes the heart instead of corroding it. Her mother too, upon this occasion, felt a pleasing distress, and wept, and loved her daughter as before. "Do, my pretty Olivia," cried she, "let us have that little melancholy air your pappa was so fond of; your sister Sophy has already obliged us. Do child, it will please your old father." She complied in a manner so exquisitely pathetic as moved me.

When lovely woman stoops to folly,
  And finds too late that men betray,
What charm can soothe her melancholy,
  What art can wash her guilt away?

The only art her guilt to cover,
To hide her shame from every eye,
To give repentance to her lover,
And wring his bosom—is to die.

As she was concluding the last stanza, to which an interruption in her voice from sorrow gave peculiar softness, the appearance of Mr. Thornhill's equipage at a distance alarmed us all, but particularly increased the uneasiness of my eldest daughter, who, desirous of shunning her betrayer, returned to the house with her sister. In a few minutes he was alighted from his chariot, and making up to the place where I was still sitting, enquired after my health with his usual air of familiarity. "Sir," replied I, "your present assurance only serves to aggravate the baseness of your character; and there was a time when I would have chastised your insolence for presuming thus to appear before me. But now you are safe; for age has cooled my passions, and my calling restrains them."

"I vow, my dear sir," returned he, "I am amazed at all this; nor can I understand what it means! I hope you don't think your daughter's late excursion with me had any thing criminal in it."

"Go," cried I, "thou art a wretch, a poor, pitiful wretch, and every way a liar; but your meanness secures you from my anger! Yet, sir, I am descended from a family that would not have borne this! And so, thou vile thing, to gratify a momentary passion thou hast made one poor creature wretched for life, and polluted a family that had nothing but honor for their portion."

"If she or you," returned he, "are resolved to be miserable, I cannot help it. But you may still be happy; and whatever opinion you may have formed of me, you shall ever find me ready to contribute to it. We can readily marry her to another, and what is more, she may keep her lover beside; for I protest I shall ever continue to have a true regard for her."

I found all my passions awakened at this new degrading proposal; for though the mind may often be calm under great injuries, little villainy can at any time get within the soul and sting it into rage. "Avoid my sight, thou reptile," cried I, "nor continue to insult me with thy presence. Were my brave son at home, he would not suffer this; but I am old, and disabled, and every way undone."

"I find," cried he, "you are bent upon obliging me to talk in an harsher manner than I intended. But as I have shown you what may be hoped from my friendship, it may not be improper to represent what may be the consequences of my resentment. My attorney, to whom your late bond has been transferred, threatens hard, nor do I know how to prevent the course of justice, except by paying the money myself, which, as I have been at some expences lately, previous to my intended marriage, it is not so easy to be done. And then my steward talks of driving for the rent; it is certain he knows his duty, for I never trouble myself with affairs of that nature. Yet still I could wish to serve you, and even to have you and your daughter present at my marriage, which is shortly to be solemnized with Miss Wilmot; it is even the request of my charming Arabella herself, whom I hope you will not refuse."

"Mr. Thornhill," replied I, "hear me once for all: as to your marriage with any but my daughter, that I never will consent to; and though your friendship could raise me to a throne, or your resentment sink me to the grave, yet would I despise both. Thou hast once woefully, irreparably, deceived me. I reposed my heart upon thine honour and have found its baseness. Never more, therefore, expect friendship from me. Go, and possess what fortune has given thee, beauty, riches, health, and pleasure. Go, and leave me to want, infamy, disease, and sorrow. Yet humbled as I am, shall my heart still vindicate its dignity, and though thou hast my forgiveness, thou shalt ever have my contempt."

"If so," returned he, "depend upon it you shall feel the effects of this insolence, and we shall shortly see which is the fittest object of scorn, you or me." Upon which he departed abruptly.

My wife and son, who were present at this interview, seemed terrified with the apprehension. My daughters also, finding that he was gone, came out to be informed of the result of our conference, which, when known, alarmed them not less than the rest. But as to myself, I disregarded the utmost stretch of his malevolence; he had already struck the blow, and now I stood prepared to repel every new effort, like one of those instruments used in the art of war, which, however thrown, still presents a point to receive the enemy.

We soon, however, found that he had not threatened in vain; for the very next day his steward came to demand my annual rent, which, by the train of accidents already related, I was unable to pay. The consequence of my incapacity was his driving my cattle that evening, and their being appraised and sold the next day for less than half their value. My wife and children now therefore entreated me to comply upon any terms, rather than incur certain destruction. They even begged of me to admit his visits once more, and used all their little eloquence to paint the calamities I was going to endure: the terrors of a prison, in so rigorous a season as the present, with the danger that threatened my health from the late accident that happened by the fire. But I continued inflexible.

"Why, my treasures," cried I, "why will you thus attempt to persuade me to the thing that is not right! My duty has taught me to forgive him; but my conscience will not permit me to approve. Would you have me applaud to the world what my heart must internally condemn? Would you have me tamely sit down and flatter our infamous betrayer; and to avoid a prison continually suffer the more galling bonds of mental confinement! No, never. If we are to be taken from this abode, only let us hold to the right, and wherever we are thrown, we can still retire to a charming apartment and look round our own hearts with intrepidity and with pleasure!"

In this manner we spent that evening. Early the next morning, as the snow had fallen in great abundance in the night, my son was employed in clearing it away and opening a passage before the door. He had not been thus engaged long, when he came running in, with looks all pale, to tell us that two strangers, whom he knew to be officers of justice, were making towards the house.

Just as he spoke they came in, and approaching the

bed where I lay, after previously informing me of their employment and business, made me their prisoner, bidding me prepare to go with them to the county gaol, which was eleven miles off.

"My friends," said I, "this is severe weather on which you have come to take me to a prison; and it is particularly unfortunate at this time, as one of my arms has lately been burnt in a terrible manner, and it has thrown me into a slight fever, and I want clothes to cover me, and I am now too weak and old to talk far in such deep snow: but if it must be so, I'll try to obey you."

I then turned to my wife and children and directed them to get together what few things were left us, and to prepare immediately for leaving this place. I entreated them to be expeditious, and desired my son to assist his elder sister, who, from a consciousness that she was the cause of all our calamities, was fallen and had lost anguish in insensibility. I encouraged my wife, who, pale and trembling, clasped our affrighted little ones in her arms, that clung to her bosom in silence, dreading to look round at the strangers. In the meantime my youngest daughter prepared for our departure, and as she received several hints to use dispatch, in about an hour we were ready to depart.

CHAPTER XXV

NO SITUATION, HOWEVER WRETCHED IT SEEMS, BUT HAS SOME SORT OF COMFORT ATTENDING IT

We set forward from this peaceful neighbourhood, and walked on slowly. My eldest daughter being enfeebled by a slow fever, which had begun for some days to undermine her constitution, one of the officers, who had an horse, kindly took her behind him; for even these men cannot entirely divest themselves of humanity. My son led one of the little ones by the hand, and my wife the other, while I leaned upon my youngest girl, whose tears fell not for her own but my distresses.

We were now got from my late dwelling about two miles, when we saw a crowd running and shouting behind us, consisting of about fifty of my poorest parishioners. These, with dreadful imprecations, soon seized upon the two officers of justice, and swearing they would never see their minister go to gaol while they had a drop of blood to shed in his defence, were going to use them with great severity. The consequence might have been fatal, had I not immediately interposed, and with some difficulty rescued the officers from the hands of the enraged multitude. My children, who looked upon my delivery now as certain, appeared transported with joy and were incapable of containing their raptures. But they were soon undeceived upon hearing me address the poor deluded people, who came, as they imagined, to do me service.

"What! my friends," cried I, "and is this the way you love me? Is this the manner you obey the instructions I have given you from the pulpit? Thus to fly in the face of justice and bring down ruin on yourselves and me! Which is your ringleader? Show me the man that has thus seduced you. As sure as he lives he shall feel my resentment. Alas! my dear deluded flock, return back to the duty you owe to God, to your country, and to me. I shall yet perhaps one day see you in greater felicity here and contribute to make your lives more happy. But let it at least be my comfort when I pen my fold for immortality, that not one here shall be wanting."

They now seemed all repentance, and melting into tears, came one after the other to bid me farewell. I shook each tenderly by the hand, and leaving them my blessing, proceeded forward without meeting any further interruption. Some hours before night we reached the town, or rather village; for it consisted but of a few mean houses, having lost all its former opulence, and retaining no marks of its ancient superiority but the gaol.

Upon entering, we put up at an inn, where we had such

refreshments as could most readily be procured, and I supped with my family with my usual cheerfulness. After seeing them properly accommodated for that night, I next attended the sheriff's officers to the prison, which had formerly been built for the purposes of war and consisted of one large apartment, strongly grated and paved with stone, common to both felons and debtors at certain hours in the four and twenty. Besides this, every prisoner had a separate cell, where he was locked in for the night.

I expected upon my entrance to find nothing but lamentations and various sounds of misery; but it was very different. The prisoners seemed all employed in one common design, that of forgetting thought in merriment or clamour. I was apprized of the usual perquisite required upon these occasions, and immediately complied with the demand, though the little money I had was very near being all exhausted. This was immediately sent away for liquor, and the whole prison soon was filled with riot, laughter, and profaneness.

"How," cried I to myself, "shall men so very wicked be cheerful, and shall I be melancholy? I feel only the same confinement with them, and I think I have more reason to be happy."

With such reflections I laboured to become cheerful; but cheerfulness was never yet produced by effort, which is itself painful. As I was sitting therefore in a corner of the gaol, in a pensive posture, one of my fellow prisoners came up, and sitting by me, entered into conversation. It was my constant rule in life never to avoid the conversation of any man who seemed to desire it: for if good, I might profit by his instruction; if bad, he might be assisted by mine. I found this to be a knowing man, of strong unlettered sense, but a thorough knowledge of the world, as it is called, or, more properly speaking, of human nature on the wrong side. He asked me if I had taken care to provide myself with a bed, which was a circumstance I had never once attended to.

"That's unfortunate," cried he, "as you are allowed here nothing but straw, and your apartment is very large and cold. However, you seem to be something of a gentleman, and as I have been one myself in my time, part of my bed-clothes are heartily at your service."

I thanked him, professing my surprise at finding such humanity in a gaol in misfortunes; adding, to let him see that I was a scholar, "That the sage ancient seemed to understand the value of company in affliction, when he said, *Ton kosmon aire, ei dos ton etairon;* and in fact," continued I, "what is the world if it affords only solitude?"

"You talk of the world, sir," returned my fellow prisoner; "the world is in its dotage, and yet the cosmogony or creation of the world has puzzled the philosophers of every age. What a medley of opinions have they not broached upon the creation of the world. Sanconiathon, Manetho, Berosus, and Ocellus Lucanus have all attempted it in vain. The latter has these words, *Anarchon ara kai atelutaion to pan,* which implies——" "I ask pardon, sir," cried I, "for interrupting so much learning; but I think I have heard all this before. Have I not had the pleasure of once seeing you at Welbridge fair, and is not your name Ephraim Jenkinson?" At this demand he only sighed. "I suppose you must recollect," resumed I, "one Dr. Primrose, from whom you bought a horse."

He now at once recollected me; for the gloominess of the place and the approaching night had prevented his distinguishing my features before. "Yes, sir," returned Mr. Jenkinson, "I remember you perfectly well. I bought an horse, but forgot to pay for him. Your neighbour Flamborough is the only prosecutor I am any way afraid of at the next assizes, for he intends to swear positively against me as a coiner. I am heartily sorry, sir, I ever deceived you, or indeed any man; for you see," continued he, showing his shackles, "what my tricks have brought me to."

"Well, sir," replied I, "your kindness in offering me assistance, when you could expect no return, shall be repaid with my endeavours to soften or totally suppress Mr. Flamborough's evidence, and I will send my son to him for that purpose the first opportunity; nor do I in the least doubt but he will comply with my request, and as to my own evidence, you need be under no uneasiness about that."

"Well, sir," cried he, "all the return I can make shall be yours. You shall have more than half my bed-clothes to-night, and I'll take care to stand your friend in the prison, where I think I have some influence."

I thanked him, and could not avoid being surprised at the present youthful change in his aspect; for at the time I had seen him before he appeared at least sixty. "Sir," answered he, "you are little acquainted with the world; I had at that time false hair, and have learnt the art of counterfeiting every age from seventeen to seventy. Ah, sir, had I but bestowed half the pains in learning a trade, that I have in learning to be a scoundrel, I might have been a rich man at this day. But rogue as I am, still I may be your friend, and that perhaps when you least expect it."

We were now prevented from further conversation by the arrival of the gaoler's servants, who came to call over the prisoner's names and lock up for the night. A fellow also, with a bundle of straw for my bed attended, who led me along a dark narrow passage into a room paved like the common prison, and in one corner of this I spread my bed and the clothes given me by my fellow prisoner; which done, my conductor, who was civil enough, bade me a good-night. After my usual meditations, and having praised my heavenly corrector, I laid myself down and slept with the utmost tranquillity till morning.

CHAPTER XXVI

A REFORMATION IN THE GAOL. TO MAKE LAWS COMPLETE, THEY SHOULD REWARD AS WELL AS PUNISH

The next morning early I was awakened by my family, whom I found in tears at my bed-side. The gloomy strength of every thing about us, it seems, had daunted them. I gently rebuked their sorrow, assuring them I had never slept with greater tranquillity, and next enquired after my eldest daughter, who was not among them. They informed me that yesterday's uneasiness and fatigue had increased her fever, and it was judged proper to leave her behind. My next care was to send my son to procure a room or two to lodge the family in, as near the prison as conveniently could be found. He obeyed, but could only find one apartment, which was hired at a small expence, for his mother and sisters, the gaoler with humanity consenting to let him and his two little brothers lie in the prison with me. A bed was therefore prepared for them in a corner of the room, which I thought answered very conveniently. I was willing, however, previously to know whether my little children chose to lie in a place which seemed to fright them upon entrance.

"Well," cried I, "my good boys, how do you like your bed? I hope you are not afraid to lie in this room, dark as it appears."

"No, pappa," says Dick, "I am not afraid to lie any where where you are."

"And I," says Bill, who was yet but four years old, "love every place best that my pappa is in."

After this, I allotted to each of the family what they were to do. My daughter was particularly directed to watch her declining sister's health; my wife was to attend me; my little boys were to read to me: "And as for you, my son," continued I, "it is by the labour of your hands we must all hope to be supported. Your wages, as a day-labourer, will be full sufficient, with proper frugality, to maintain us all, and comfortably too. Thou art now sixteen years old, and hast strength, and it was given thee, my son, for very useful purposes; for it must save from famine your helpless parents and family. Prepare then this evening to look out for work against to-morrow, and bring home every night what money you earn, for our support."

Having thus instructed him and settled the rest, I walked down to the common prison, where I could enjoy more air and room. But I was not long there when the execrations, lewdness, and brutality that invaded me on every side drove me back to my apartment again. Here I sat for some time, pondering upon the strange infatuation of wretches, who finding all mankind in open arms against them were, however, labouring to make themselves a future and a tremendous enemy.

Their insensibility excited my highest compassion and blotted my own uneasiness a while from my mind. It even appeared as a duty incumbent upon me to attempt to reclaim them. I resolved therefore once more to return, and in spite of their contempt to give them my advice and conquer them by perseverance. Going therefore among them again, I informed Mr. Jenkinson of my design, at which he laughed, but communicated it to the rest. The proposal was received with the greatest good-humour, as it promised to afford a new fund of entertainment to persons who had now no other resource for mirth, but what could be derived from ridicule or debauchery.

I therefore read them a portion of the service with a loud unaffected voice, and found my audience perfectly merry upon the occasion. Lewd whispers, groans of contrition burlesqued, winking, and coughing alternately excited laughter. However, I continued with my natural solemnity to read on, sensible that what I did might amend some, but could itself receive no contamination from any.

After reading, I entered upon my exhortation, which was rather calculated at first to amuse them than to reprove. I previously observed that no other motive but their welfare could induce me to this; that I was their fellow prisoner, and now gained nothing by preaching. I was sorry, I said, to hear them so very profane; because they got nothing by it, but might lose a great deal: "For be assured, my friends," cried I, "for you are my friends, however the world may disclaim your friendship, though you swore twelve thousand oaths in a day, it would not put one penny in your purse. Then what signifies calling every moment upon the devil and courting his friendship, since you find how scurvily he uses you. He has given you nothing here, you find, but a mouthful of oaths and an empty belly; and by the best accounts I have of him, he will give you nothing that's good hereafter.

"If used ill in our dealings with one man, we naturally go elsewhere. Were it not worth your while then, just to try how you may like the usage of another master, who gives you fair promises at least to come to him. Surely, my friends, of all stupidity in the world, his must be greatest, who, after robbing an house, runs to the thief-takers for protection. And yet how are you more wise? You are all seeking comfort from him that has already betrayed you, applying to a more malicious being than any thieftaker of them all; for they only decoy and then hang you; but he decoys and hangs, and what is worst of all, will not let you loose after the hangman has done."

When I had concluded, I received the compliments of my audience, some of whom came and shook me by the hand, swearing that I was a very honest fellow, and that they desired my further acquaintance. I therefore promised to repeat my lecture next day, and actually conceived some hopes of making a reformation here; for it had ever been my opinion that no man was past the hour of amendment, every heart lying open to the shafts of reproof, if the archer could but take a proper aim. When I had thus satisfied my mind, I went back to my apartment, where my wife had prepared a frugal meal, while

Mr. Jenkinson begged leave to add his dinner to ours and partake of the pleasure, as he was kind enough to express it, of my conversation. He had not yet seen my family; for as they came to my apartment by a door in the narrow passage, already described, by this means they avoided the common prison. Jenkinson at the first interview therefore seemed not a little struck with the beauty of my youngest daughter, which her pensive air contributed to heighten, and my little ones did not pass unnoticed.

"Alas, Doctor," cried he, "these children are too handsome and too good for such a place as this!"

"Why, Mr. Jenkinson," replied I, "thank heaven my children are pretty tolerable in morals, and if they be good, it matters little for the rest."

"I fancy, sir," retruned my fellow prisoner, "that it must give you great comfort to have this little family about you."

"A comfort, Mr. Jenkinson," replied I, "yes, it is indeed a comfort, and I would not be without them for all the world; for they can make a dungeon seem a palace. There is but one way in this life of wounding my happiness, and that is by injuring them."

"I am afraid then, sir," cried he, "that I am in some measure culpable; for I think I see here" (looking at my son Moses) "one that I have injured, and by whom I wish to be forgiven."

My son immediately recollected his voice and features, though he had before seen him in disguise, and taking him by the hand, with a smile forgave him. "Yet," continued he, "I can't help wondering at what you could see in my face, to think me a proper mark for deception."

"My dear sir," returned the other, "it was not your face, but your white stockings and the black riband in your hair, that allured me. But no disparagement to your parts, I have deceived wiser men than you in my time; and yet, with all my tricks, the blockheads have been too many for me at last."

"I suppose," cried my son, "that the narrative of such a life as yours must be extremely instructive and amusing."

"Not much of either," returned Mr. Jenkinson. "Those relations which describe the tricks and vices only of mankind, by increasing our suspicion in life, retard our success. The traveller that distrusts every person he meets, and turns back upon the appearance of every man that looks like a robber, seldom arrives in time to his journey's end.

"Indeed, I think from my own experience I may say that the knowing one is the silliest fellow under the sun. I was thought cunning from my very childhood; when but seven years old the ladies would say that I was a perfect little man; at fourteen I knew the world, cocked my hat, and loved the ladies; at twenty, though I was perfectly honest, yet every one thought me so cunning that not one would trust me. Thus I was at last obliged to turn sharper in my own defence, and have lived ever since, my head throbbing with schemes to deceive, and my heart palpitating with fears of detection.

"I used often to laugh at your honest simple neighbour Flamborough, and one way or another generally cheated him once a year. Yet still the honest man went forward without suspicion and grew rich, while I still continued tricksy and cunning, and was poor without the consolation of being honest.

"However," continued he, "let me know your case, and what has brought you here; perhaps, though I have not skill to avoid a gaol myself, I may extricate my friends."

In compliance with his curiosity, I informed him of the whole train of accidents and follies that had plunged me into my present troubles, and my utter inability to get free.

After hearing my story and pausing some minutes, he slapt his forehead, as if he had hit upon something material, and took his leave, saying he would try what could be done.

CHAPTER XXVII

THE SAME SUBJECT CONTINUED

The next morning I communicated to my wife and children the scheme I had planned of reforming the prisoners, which they received with universal disapprobation, alleging the impossibility and impropriety of it; adding that my endeavours would no way contribute to their amendment, but might probably disgrace my calling.

"Excuse me," returned I, "these people, however fallen, are still men, and that is a very good title to my affections. Good counsel rejected returns to enrich the giver's bosom; and though the instruction I communicate may not mend them, yet it will assuredly mend myself. If these wretches, my children, were princes, there would be thousands ready to offer their ministry; but, in my opinion, the heart that is buried in a dungeon is as precious as that seated upon a throne. Yes, my treasures, if I can mend them I will; perhaps they will not all despise me. Perhaps I may catch up even one from the gulf, and that will be great gain; for is there upon earth a gem so precious as the human soul?"

Thus saying, I left them, and descended to the common prison, where I found the prisoners very merry, expecting my arrival, and each prepared with some gaol trick to play upon the doctor. Thus, as I was going to begin, one turned my wig awry, as if by accident, and then asked my pardon. A second, who stood at some distance, had a knack of spitting through his teeth, which fell in showers upon my book. A third would cry amen in such an affected tone as gave the rest great delight. A fourth had slily picked my pocket of my spectacles. But there was one whose trick gave more universal pleasure than all the rest; for observing the manner in which I had disposed my books on the table before me, he very dexterously displaced one of them, and put an obscene jest-book of his own in the place. However, I took no notice of all that this mischievous group of little beings could do; but went on, perfectly sensible that what was ridiculous in my attempt would excite mirth only the first or second time, while what was serious would be permanent. My design succeeded, and in less than six days some were penitent, and all attentive.

It was now that I applauded my perseverance and address at thus giving sensibility to wretches divested of every moral feeling, and now began to think of doing them temporal services also, by rendering their situation somewhat more comfortable. Their time had hitherto been divided between famine and excess, tumultuous riot and bitter repining. Their only employment was quarrelling among each other, playing cribbage, and cutting tobacco stoppers. From this last mode of idle industry I took the hint of setting such as chose to work at cutting pegs for tobacconists and shoemakers, the proper wood being bought by a general subscription, and when manufactured, sold by my appointment; so that each earned something every day: a trifle indeed, but sufficient to maintain him.

I did not stop here, but instituted fines for the punishment of immorality, and rewards for peculiar industry. Thus, in less than a fortnight, I had formed them into something social and humane, and had the pleasure of regarding myself as a legislator, who had brought men from their native ferocity into friendship and obedience.

And it were highly to be wished that legislative power would thus direct the law rather to reformation than severity; that it would appear convinced that the work of eradicating crimes is not by making punishments familiar, but formidable. Instead of our present prisons, which find or make men guilty, which enclose wretches for the commission of one crime, and return them, if returned alive, fitted for the perpetuation of thousands, it were to be wished we had, as in other parts of Europe, places of penitence and solitude, where the accused might be attended by such as could give them repentance if guilty, or new motives to virtue if innocent. And this, but not the increasing punishments, is the way to mend a state: nor can I avoid even questioning the validity of that right which social combinations have assumed of capitally punishing offences of a slight nature. In cases of murder their right is obvious, as it is the duty of us all, from the law of self-defence, to cut off that man who has shown a disregard for the life of another. Against such, all nature rises in arms; but it is not so against him who steals my property. Natural law gives me no right to take away his life, as by that the horse he steals is as much his property as mine. If then I have any right, it must be from a compact made between us that he who deprives the other of his horse shall die. But this is a false compact, because no man has a right to barter his life, no more than to take it away, as it is not his own. And next, the compact is inadequate and would be set aside even in a court of modern equity, as there is a great penalty for a very trifling convenience, since it is far better that two men should live than that one man should ride. But a compact that is false between two men is equally so between an hundred, or an hundred thousand; for as ten millions of circles can never make a square, so the united voice of myriads cannot lend the smallest foundation to falsehood. It is thus that reason speaks, and untutored nature says the same thing. Savages that are directed nearly by natural law alone are very tender of the lives of each other; they seldom shed blood but to retaliate former cruelty.

Our Saxon ancestors, fierce as they were in war, had but few executions in times of peace; and in all commencing governments that have the print of nature still strong upon them, scarce any crime is held capital.

It is among the citizens of a refined community that penal laws, which are in the hands of the rich, are laid upon the poor. Government, while it grows older, seems to acquire the moroseness of age; and as if our possessions were become dearer in proportion as they increased, as if the more enormous our wealth, the more extensive our fears, our possessions are paled up with new edicts every day, and hung round with gibbets to scare every invader.

Whether is it from the number of our penal laws or the licentiousness of our people that this country should show more convicts in a year than half the dominions of Europe united? Perhaps it is owing to both; for they mutually produce each other. When by indiscriminate penal laws a nation beholds the same punishment affixed to dissimilar degrees of guilt, from perceiving no distinction in the penalty, the people are led to lose all sense of distinction in the crime, and this distinction is the bulwark of all morality: thus the multitude of laws produce new vices, and new vices call for fresh restraints.

It were to be wished then that power, instead of contriving news laws to punish vice, instead of drawing hard the cords of society till a convulsion come to burst them, instead of cutting away wretches as useless before we have tried their utility, instead of converting correction into vengeance, it were to be wished that we tried the restrictive arts of government, and made law the protector but not the tyrant of the people. We should then find that creatures whose souls are held as dross only wanted the hand of a refiner; we should then find that wretches, now stuck up for long tortures, lest luxury should feel a momentary pang, might, if properly treated, serve to sinew the state in times of danger; that, as their faces are like ours, their hearts are so too; that few minds are so base as that perseverance cannot amend; that a man may see his last crime without dying for it; and that very little blood will serve to cement our security.

CHAPTER XXVIII

HAPPINESS AND MISERY RATHER THE RESULT OF PRUDENCE THAN OF VIRTUE IN THIS LIFE. TEMPORAL EVILS OR FELICITIES BEING REGARDED BY HEAVEN AS THINGS MERELY IN THEMSELVES TRIFLING AND UNWORTHY ITS CARE IN THE DISTRIBUTION

I had now been confined more than a fortnight, but had not since my arrival been visited by my dear Olivia, and I greatly longed to see her. Having communicated my wishes to my wife, the next morning the poor girl entered my apartment, leaning on her sister's arm. The change which I saw in her countenance struck me. The numberless graces that once resided there were now fled, and the hand of death seemed to have molded every feature to alarm me. Her temples were sunk, her forehead was tense, and a fatal paleness sat upon her cheek.

"I am glad to see thee, my dear," cried I; "but why this dejection, Livy? I hope, my love, you have too great a regard for me to permit disappointment thus to undermine a life which I prize as my own. Be cheerful, child, and we may yet see happier days."

"You have ever, sir," replied she, "been kind to me, and it adds to my pain that I shall never have an opportunity of sharing that happiness you promise. Happiness, I fear, is no longer reserved for me here; and I long to be rid of a place where I have only found distress. Indeed, sir, I wish you would make a proper submission to Mr. Thornhill; it may, in some measure, induce him to pity you, and it will give me relief in dying."

"Never, child," replied I, "I never shall be brought to acknowledge my daughter a prostitute; for tho' the world may look upon your offence with scorn, let it be mine to regard it as a mark of credulity, not of guilt. My dear, I am no way miserable in this place, however dismal it may seem, and be assured that while you continue to bless me by living, he shall never have my consent to make you more wretched by marrying another."

After the departure of my daughter, my fellow prisoner, who was by at this interview, sensibly enough expostulated upon my obstinacy in refusing a submission which promised to give me freedom. He observed that the rest of my family was not to be sacrificed to the peace of one child alone, and she the only one who had offended me. "Beside," added he, "I don't know if it be just thus to obstruct the union of man and wife, which you do at present, by refusing to consent to a match which you cannot hinder, but may render unhappy."

"Sir," replied I, "you are unacquainted with the man that oppresses us. I am very sensible that no submission I can make could procure me liberty even for an hour. I am told that even in this very room a debtor of his, no later than last year, died for want. But though my submission and approbation could transfer me from hence to the most beautiful apartment he is possessed of, yet I would grant neither, as something whispers me that it would be giving a sanction to adultery. While my daughter lives, no other marriage of his shall ever be legal in my eye. Were she removed, indeed, I should be the basest of men, from any resentment of my own, to attempt putting asunder those who wish for an union. No, villain as he is, I could then wish him married, to prevent the consequences of his future debaucheries. But should I not now be the most cruel of all fathers, to sign an instrument which must send my child to the grave, merely to avoid a prison myself; and thus to escape one pang, break my child's heart with a thousand?"

He acquiesced in the justice of this answer, but could not avoid observing that he feared my daughter's life was already too much wasted to keep me long a prisoner. "However," continued he, "though you refuse to submit to the nephew, I hope you have no objections to laying your case before the uncle, who has the first character in the kingdom of every thing that is just and good. I would advise you to send him a letter by the post, intimating all his nephew's ill usage, and my life for it that in three days you shall have an answer." I thanked him for the hint and instantly set about complying; but I wanted paper, and unluckily all our money had been laid out that morning in provisions; however, he supplied me.

For the three ensuing days I was in a state of anxiety, to know what reception my letter might meet with; but in the meantime was frequently solicited by my wife to submit to any conditions rather than remain here, and every hour received repeated accounts of the decline of my daughter's health. The third day and the fourth arrived, but I received no answer to my letter; the complaints of a stranger against a favourite nephew were no way likely to succeed, so that these hopes soon vanished like all my former. My mind, however, still supported itself, though confinement and bad air began to make a visible alteration in my health, and my arm that had suffered in the fire grew worse. But my children still sat by me, and while I was stretched on my straw, read to me by turns, or listened and wept at my instructions. But my daughter's health declined faster than mine; every message from her contributed to increase my apprehensions and pain. The fifth morning after I had written the letter which was sent to Sir William Thornhill, I was alarmed with an account that she was speechless. Now it was that confinement was truly painful to me; my soul was bursting from its prison to be near the pillow of my child, to comfort, to strengthen her, to receive her last wishes, and teach her soul the way to heaven! Another account came. She was expiring, and yet I was debarred the small comfort of weeping by her. My fellow prisoner, some time after, came with the last account. He bade me be paitent. She was dead!—The next morning he returned and found me with my two little ones, now my only companions, who were using all their innocent efforts to comfort me. They entreated to read to me, and bid me not to cry, for I was now too old to weep. "And is not my sister an angel, now, pappa," cried the eldest, "and why then are you sorry for her? I wish I were an angel out of this frightful place, if my pappa were with me."—"Yes," added my youngest darling, "heaven, where my sister is, is a finer place than this, and there are none but good people there, and the people here are very bad."

Mr. Jenkinson interrupted their harmless prattle by observing that now my daughter was no more, I should seriously think of the rest of my family and attempt to save my own life, which was every day declining for want of necessaries and wholesome air. He added that it was now incumbent on me to sacrifice any pride or resentment of my own to the welfare of those who depended on me for support; and that I was now, both by reason and justice, obliged to try to reconcile my landlord.

"Heaven be praised," replied I, "there is no pride left me now. I should detest my own heart if I saw either pride or resentment lurking there. On the contrary, as my oppressor has been once my parishioner, I hope one day to present him up an unpolluted soul at the eternal tribunal. No, sir, I have no resentment now, and though he has taken from me what I held dearer than all his treasures, though he has wrung my heart, for I am sick almost to fainting, very sick, my fellow prisoner; yet that shall never inspire me with vengeance. I am now willing to approve his marriage, and if this submission can do him any pleasure, let him know that if I have done him any injury, I am sorry for it." Mr. Jenkinson took pen and ink, and wrote down my submission nearly as I have exprest it, to which I signed my name. My son was employed to carry the letter to Mr. Thornhill, who was then at his seat in the country. He went, and in about six hours returned with a verbal answer. He had some difficulty, he said, to get a sight of his landlord, as the servants were insolent and suspicious; but he accidentally saw him as he was going out upon business, preparing for his marriage, which was to be in three days. He continued to inform us that he stept up in the humblest manner and delivered the letter, which, when Mr. Thornhill had read, he said that all submission was now too late and unnecessary; that he had heard of our application to his uncle, which met with the contempt it deserved; and as for the rest, that all future applications should be directed to his attorney, not to him. He observed, however, that as he had a very good opinion of the discretion of the two young ladies, they might have been the most agreeable intercessors.

"Well, sir," said I to my fellow prisoner, "you now discover the temper of the man that oppresses me. He can at once be facetious and cruel; but let him use me as he will, I shall soon be free, in spite of all his bolts to restrain me. I am now drawing towards an abode that looks brighter as I approach it; this expectation cheers my afflictions, and though I shall leave an helpless family of orphans behind me, yet they will not be utterly forsaken; some friend, perhaps, will be found to assist them for the sake of their poor father, and some may charitably relieve them for the sake of their heavenly father."

Just as I spoke, my wife, whom I had not seen that day before, appeared with looks of terror, and making efforts, but unable to speak. "Why, my love," cried I, "why will you thus increase my affliction by your own? What though no submissions can return our severe master, tho' he has doomed me to die in this place of wretchedness, and though we have lost a darling child, yet still you will find comfort in your other children when I shall be no more."—"We have indeed lost," returned she, "a darling child. My Sophia, my dearest, is gone, snatched from us, carried off by ruffians!"

"How, madam," cried my fellow prisoner, "Miss Sophia carried off by villains! Sure it cannot be?"

She could only answer with a fixed look and a flood of tears. But one of the prisoner's wives, who was present, and came in with her, gave us a more distinct account; she informed us that as my wife, my daughter, and herself were taking a walk together on the great road a little way out of the village, a post-chaise and four drove up to them and instantly stopt. Upon which, a well-drest man, but not Mr. Thornhill, stepping out, clasped my daughter round the waist, and forcing her in, bid the postillion drive on, so that they were out of sight in a moment.

"Now," cried I, "the sum of my miseries is made up, nor is it in the power of any thing on earth to give me another pang. What! not one left! not to leave me one!

the monster! the child that was next to my heart! she had the beauty of an angel and almost the wisdom of an angel. But support that woman, nor let her fall. Not to leave me one!"——"Alas! my husband," said my wife, "you seem to want comfort even more than I. Our distresses are great; but I could bear this and more, if I saw you but easy. They may take away my children and all the world, if they leave me but you."

My son, who was present, endeavoured to moderate our grief; he bade us take comfort, for he hoped that we might still have reason to be thankful. "My child," cried I, "look round the world and see if there be any happiness left me now. Is not every ray of comfort shut out; while all our bright prospects only lie beyond the grave?"——"My dear father," returned he, "I hope there is still something that will give you an interval of satisfaction; for I have a letter from my brother George." ——"What of him, child," interrupted I, "does he know of our misery? I hope my boy is exempt from any part of what his wretched family suffers."——"Yes, sir," returned he, "he is perfectly gay, cheerful, and happy. His letter brings nothing but good news; he is the favourite of his colonel, who promises to procure him the very next lieutenacy that becomes vacant!"

"And are you sure of all this," cried my wife, "are you sure that nothing ill has befallen my boy?"——"Nothing indeed, madam," returned my son; "you shall see the letter, which will give you the highest pleasure; and if any thing can produce you comfort, I am sure that will." —"But are you sure," still repeated she, "that the letter is from himself, and that he is really so happy?"—— "Yes, madam," replied he, "it is certainly his, and he will one day be the credit and the support of our family!" ——"Then I thank providence," cried she, "that my last letter to him has miscarried. Yes, my dear," continued she, turning to me, "I will now confess that though the hand of heaven is sore upon us in other instances, it has been favourable here. By the last letter I wrote my son, which was in the bitterness of anger, I desired him, upon his mother's belssing, and if he had the heart of a man, to see justice done his father and sister, and avenge our cause. But thanks be to him that directs all things, it has miscarried, and I am at rest."—"Woman," cried I, "thou hast done very ill, and at another time my reproaches might have been more severe. Oh! what a tremendous gulf hast thou escaped, that would have buried both thee and him in endless ruin. Providence, indeed, has here been kinder to us than we to ourselves. It has reserved that son to be the father and protector of my children when I shall be away. How unjustly did I complain of being stript of every comfort, when still I hear that he is happy and insensible of our afflictions, still kept in reserve to support his widowed mother, to protect his brothers and sisters. But what sisters has he left, he has no sisters now, they are all gone, robbed from me, and I am undone."——"Father," interrupted my son, "I beg you will give me leave to read his letter. I know it will please you." Upon which, with my permission, he read as follows:

"HONOURED SIR,—I have called off my imagination a few moments from the pleasures that surround me to fix it upon objects that are still more pleasing, the dear little fire-side at home. My fancy draws that harmless group as listening to every line of this with great composure. I view those faces with delight which never felt the deforming hand of ambition or distress! But whatever your happiness may be at home, I am sure it will be some addition to it to hear that I am perfectly pleased with my situation, and every way happy here.

"Our regiment is countermanded and is not to leave the kingdom; the colonel, who professes himself my friend, takes me with him to all companies where he is acquainted, and after my first visit I generally find myself received with increased respect upon repeating it. I danced last night with Lady G——, and could I forget you know whom, I might be perhaps successful. But it is my fate still to remember others, while I am myself forgotten by most of my absent friends, and in this number, I fear, sir, that I must consider you; for I have long expected the pleasure of a letter from home to no purpose. Olivia and Sophia, too, promised to write, but seem to have forgotten me. Tell them they are two arrant little baggages, and that I am this moment in a most violent passion with them: yet still, I know not how, tho' I want to bluster a little, my heart is respondent only to softer emotions. Then tell them, sir, that after all, I love them affectionately, and be assured of my ever remaining—

YOUR DUTIFUL SON."

"In all our miseries," cried I, "what thanks have we not to return, that one at least of our family is exempted from what we suffer. Heaven be his guard, and keep my boy thus happy to be the supporter of his widowed mother, and the father of these two babes, which is all the patrimony I can now bequeath him. May he keep their innocence from the temptations of want, and be their conductor in the paths of honour." I had scarce said these words, when a noise, like that of a tumult, seemed to proceed from the prison below; it died away soon after, and a clanking of fetters was heard along the passage that led to my apartment. The keeper of the prison entered, holding a man all bloody, wounded and fettered with the heaviest irons. I looked with compassion on the wretch as he approached me, but with horror when I found it was my own son. "My George! My George! and do I behold thee thus! Wounded! Fettered! Is this thy happiness! Is this the manner you return to me! O that this sight could break my heart at once and let me die!"

"Where, sir, is your fortitude?" returned my son with an intrepid voice. "I must suffer, my life is forfeited, and let them take it; it is my last happiness that I have committed no murder, tho' I have lost all hopes of pardon."

I tried to restrain my passions for a few minutes in silence, but I thought I should have died with the effort. "O my boy, my heart weeps to behold thee thus, and I cannot, cannot help it. In the moment that I thought thee blest, and prayed for thy safety, to behold thee thus again! Chained, wounded. And yet the death of the youthful is happy. But I am old, a very old man, and have lived to see this day. To see my children all untimely falling about me, while I continue a wretched survivor in the midst of ruin! May all the curses that ever sunk a soul fall heavy upon the murderer of my children. May he live, like me, to see——"

"Hold, sir," replied my son, "or I shall blush for thee. How, sir, forgetful of your age, your holy calling, thus to arrogate the justice of heaven and fling those curses upward that must soon descend to crush thy own grey head with destruction! No, sir, let it be your care now to fit me for that vile death I must shortly suffer, to arm me with hope and resolution, to give me courage to drink of that bitterness which must shortly be my portion."

"My child, you must not die. I am sure no offence of thine can deserve so vile a punishment. My George could never be guilty of any crime to make his ancestors ashamed of him."

"Mine, sir," returned my son, "is, I fear, an unpardonable one. I have sent a challenge, and that is death by a late act of parliament. When I received my mother's letter from home, I immediately came down, determined to punish the betrayer of our honour, and sent him an order to meet me, which he answered, not in person, but by his dispatching four of his domestics to seize me. I wounded one, but the rest made me their prisoner. The coward is determined to put the law in execution against me; the proofs are undeniable, and as I am the first transgressor upon the statute, I see no hopes of pardon. But you have often charmed me with the lessons of fortitude; let me now, sir, find them in your example."

"And, my son, you shall find them. I am now raised above this world and all the pleasures it can produce. From this moment I break from my heart all the ties that held it down to earth, and will prepare to fit us both for eternity. Yes, my son, I will point out the way, and my soul shall guide yours in the ascent, for we will take our flight together. I now see and am convinced you can expect no pardon here, and I can only exhort you to seek it at that greatest tribunal where we both shall shortly answer. But let us not be niggardly in our exhortation, but let all our fellow prisoners have a share: good gaoler, let them be permitted to stand here, while I attempt to improve them." Thus saying, I made an effort to rise from my straw, but wanted strength, and was able only to recline against the wall. The prisoners assembled according to my directions, for they loved to hear my counsel; my son and his mother supported me on either side; I looked and saw that none were wanting, and then addressed them with the following exhortation.

CHAPTER XXIX

THE EQUAL DEALINGS OF PROVIDENCE DEMONSTRATED WITH REGARD TO THE HAPPY AND THE MISERABLE HERE BELOW. THAT FROM THE NATURE OF PLEASURE AND PAIN, THE WRETCHED MUST BE REPAID THE BALANCE OF THEIR SUFFERINGS IN THE LIFE HEREAFTER

"My friends, my children, and fellow sufferers, when I reflect on the distribution of good and evil here below, I find that much has been given man to enjoy, yet still more to suffer. Though we should examine the whole world, we shall not find one man so happy as to have nothing left to wish for; but we daily see thousands who by suicide show us they have nothing left to hope. In this life then it appears that we cannot be entirely blest; but yet we may be completely miserable!

"Why man should thus feel pain, why our wretchedness should be requisite in the formation of universal felicity, why, when all other systems are made perfect only by the perfection of their subordinate parts, the great system should require for its perfection, parts that are not only subordinate to others, but imperfect in themselves? These are questions that never can be explained, and might be useless if known. On this subject providence has thought fit to elude our curiosity, satisfied with granting us motives to consolation.

"In this situation man has called in the friendly assistance of philosophy, and heaven, seeing the incapacity of that to console him, has given him the aid of religion. The consolations of philosophy are very amusing, but often fallacious. It tells us that life is filled with comforts, if we will but enjoy them; and on the other hand, that though we unavoidably have miseries here, life is short, and they will soon be over. Thus do these consolations destroy each other; for if life is a place of comfort, its shortness must be misery, and if it be long, our griefs are protracted. Thus philosophy is weak; but religion comforts in an higher strain. Man is here, it tells us, fitting up his mind and preparing it for another abode. When the good man leaves the body and is all a glorious mind, he will find he has been making himself a heaven of happiness here, while the wretch that has been maimed and contaminated by his vices shrinks from his body with terror, and finds that he has anticipated the vengeance of heaven. To religion then we must hold in every circumstance of life for our truest comfort; for if already we are happy, it is a pleasure to think that we can make that happiness unending, and if we are miserable, it is very consoling to think that there is a place of rest. Thus to the fortunate religion holds out a continuance of bliss, to the wretched a change from pain.

"But though religion is very kind to all men, it has promised peculiar reward to the unhappy; the sick, the naked, the houseless, the heavy-laden, and the prisoner have ever most frequent promises in our sacred law. The author of our religion every where professes himself the wretch's friend, and unlike the false ones of this world, bestows all his caresses upon the forlorn. The unthinking have censured this as partiality, as a preference without merit to deserve it. But they never reflect that it is not in the power even of heaven itself to make the offer of unceasing felicity as great a gift to the happy as to the miserable. To the first eternity is but a single blessing, since at most it but increases what they already possess. To the latter it is a double advantage; for it diminishes their pain here and rewards them with heavenly bliss hereafter.

"But providence is in another respect kinder to the poor than the rich; for as it thus makes the life after death more desirable, so it smooths the passage there. The wretched have long familiarity with every face of terror. The man of sorrows lays himself quietly down; he has no possessions to regret, and but few ties to stop his departure: he feels only nature's pang in the final separation, and this is no way greater than he has often fainted under before; for after a certain degree of pain, every new breach that death opens in the constitution nature kindly covers with insensibility.

"Thus providence has given the wretched two advantages over the happy in this life, greater felicity in dying, and in heaven all that superiority of pleasure which arises from contrasted enjoyment. And this superiority, my friends, is no small advantage, and seems to be one of the pleasures of the poor man in the parable; for though he was already in heaven, and felt all the raptures it could give, yet it was mentioned as an addition to his happiness that he had once been wretched and now was comforted, that he had known what it was to be miserable, and now felt what it was to be happy.

"Thus, my friends, you see religion does what philosophy could never do: it shows the equal dealings of heaven to the happy and the unhappy, and levels all human enjoyments to nearly the same standard. It gives to both rich and poor and the same happiness hereafter, and equal hopes to aspire after it; but if the rich have the advantage of enjoying pleasure here, the poor have the endless satisfaction of knowing what it was once to be miserable, when crowned with endless felicity hereafter; and even though this should be called a small advantage, yet being an eternal one, it must make up by duration what the temporal happiness of the great may have exceeded by intenseness.

"These are therefore the consolations which the wretched have peculiar to themselves, and in which they are above the rest of mankind; in other respects they are below them. They who would know the miseries of the poor must see life and endure it. To declaim on the temporal advantages they enjoy is only repeating what none either believe or practise. The men who have the necessaries of living are not poor, and they who want them must be miserable. Yes, my friends, we must be miserable. No vain efforts of a refined imagination can soothe the wants of nature, can give elastic sweetness to the dank vapour of a dungeon, or ease to the throbbings of a woe-worn heart. Let the philosopher from his couch of softness tell us that we can resist all these. Alas! the effort by which we resist them is still the greatest pain! Death is slight, and any man may sustain it; but torments are dreadful, and these no man can endure.

"To us then, my friends, the promises of happiness in heaven should be peculiarly dear; for if our reward be in this life alone, we are then indeed of all men the most miserable. When I look round these gloomy walls, made to terrify as well as to confine us, this light that only serves to show the horrors of the place, those shackles that tyranny has imposed or crime made necessary, when I survey these emaciated looks, and hear those groans, O my friends, what a glorious exchange would heaven be for these. To fly through regions unconfined as air, to bask in the sunshine of eternal bliss, to carrol over endless hymns of praise, to have no master to threaten or insult us, but the form of goodness himself for ever in our eyes, when I think of these things, death becomes the messenger of very glad tidings; when I think of these things, his sharpest arrow becomes the staff of my support; when I think of these things, what is there in life worth having; when I think of these things, what is there that should not be spurned away: kings in their palaces should groan for such advantages; but we, humbled as we are, should yearn for them.

"And shall these things be ours? Ours they will certainly be if we but try for them; and what is a comfort, we are shut out from many temptations that would retard our pursuit. Only let us try for them, and they will certainly be ours, and what is still a comfort, shortly too; for if we look back on past life, it appears but a very short span, and whatever we may think of the rest of life, it will yet be found of less duration; as we grow older, the days seem to grow shorter, and our intimacy with time ever lessens the perception of his stay. Then let us take comfort now, for we shall soon be at our journey's end; we shall soon lay down the heavy burden laid by heaven upon us, and though death, the only friend of the wretched, for a little while mocks the weary traveller with the view, and like his horizon, still flies before him, yet the time will certainly and shortly come, when we shall cease from our toil; when the luxurious great ones of the world shall no more tread us to the earth; when we shall think with pleasure on our sufferings below; when we shall be surrounded with all our friends, or such as deserved our friendship; when our bliss shall be unutterable, and still, to crown all, unending."

CHAPTER XXX

HAPPIER PROSPECTS BEGIN TO APPEAR. LET US BE INFLEXIBLE, AND FORTUNE WILL AT LAST CHANGE IN OUR FAVOUR

When I had thus finished and my audience was retired, the gaoler, who was one of the most humane of his profession, hoped I would not be displeased, as what he did was but his duty, observing that he must be obliged to remove my son into a stronger cell, but that he should be permitted to revisit me every morning. I thanked him for his clemency, and grasping my boy's hand, bade him farewell and be mindful of the great duty that was before him.

I again, therefore, laid me down, and one of my little ones sat by my bedside reading, when Mr. Jenkinson entering, informed me that there was news of my daughter; for that she was seen by a person about two hours before in a strange gentleman's company, and that they had stopt at a neighbouring village for refreshment and seemed as if returning to town. He had scarce delivered this news, when the gaoler came with looks of haste and pleasure to inform me that my daughter was found. Moses came running in a moment after, crying out that his sister Sophy was below and coming up with our old friend Mr. Burchell.

Just as he delivered this news my dearest girl entered, and with looks almost wild with pleasure, ran to kiss me in a transport of affection. Her mother's tears and silence also showed her pleasure. "Here, pappa," cried the charming girl, "here is the brave man to whom I owe my delivery; to this gentleman's intrepidity I am indebted for my happiness and safety—" A kiss from Mr. Burchell, whose pleasure seemed even greater than hers, interrupted what she was going to add.

"Ah, Mr. Burchell," cried I, "this is but a wretched habitation you now find us in; and we are now very different from what you last saw us. You were ever our friend; we have long discovered our errors with regard to you, and repented of our ingratitude. After the vile usage you then received at my hands, I am almost ashamed to behold your face; yet I hope you'll forgive me, as I was deceived by a base ungenerous wretch who, under the mask of friendship, has undone me."

"It is impossible," replied Mr. Burchell, "that I should forgive you, as you never deserved my resentment. I partly saw your delusion then, and as it was out of my power to restrain, I could only pity it!"

"It was ever my conjecture," cried I, "that your mind was noble; but now I find it so. But tell me, my dear child, how hast thou been relieved, or who the ruffians were who carried thee away?"

"Indeed, sir," replied she, "as to the villain who brought me off, I am yet ignorant. For as my mamma and I were walking out, he came behind us, and almost before I could call for help, forced me into the post-chaise, and in an instant the horses drove away. I met several on the road to whom I cried out for assistance; but they disregarded my entreaties. In the meantime the ruffian himself used every art to hinder me from crying out: he flattered and threatened by turns, and swore that if I continued but silent, he intended no harm. In the meantime I had broken the canvas that he had drawn up, and whom should I perceive at some distance but your old friend Mr. Burchell, walking along with his usual swiftness, with the great stick for which we used so much to ridicule him. As soon as we came within hearing, I called out to him by name and entreated his help. I repeated my exclamations several times, upon which, with a very loud voice, he bid the postillion stop; but the boy took no notice, but drove on with still greater speed. I now thought he could never overtake us, when in less than a minute I saw Mr. Burchell come running up by the side of the horses, and with one blow knock the postillion to the ground. The horses when he was fallen soon stopt of themselves, and the ruffian stepping out, with oaths and menaces drew his sword, and ordered him at his peril to retire; but Mr. Burchell running up, shivered his sword to pieces, and then pursued him for near a quarter of a mile; but he made his escape. I was at this time come out myself, willing to assist my deliverer; but he soon returned to me in triumph. The postillion, who was recovered, was going to make his escape too; but Mr. Burchell ordered him at his peril to mount again and drive back to town. Finding it impossible to resist, he reluctantly complied, though the wound he had received seemed, to me at least, to be dangerous. He continued to complain of the pain as we drove along, so that he at last excited Mr. Burchell's compassion, who, at my request, exchanged him for another at an inn where we called on our return."

"Welcome then," cried I, "my child, and thou her gallant deliverer, a thousand welcomes. Though our cheer is but wretched, yet our hearts are ready to receive you. And now, Mr. Burchell, as you have delivered my girl, if you think her a recompence she is yours; if you can stoop to an alliance with a family so poor as mine, take her, obtain her consent, as I know you have her heart, and you have mine. And let me tell you, sir, that I give you no small treasure; she has been celebrated for beauty it is true, but that is not my meaning. I give you up a treasure in her mind."

"But I suppose, sir," cried Mr. Burchell, "that you are

apprized of my circumstances, and of my incapacity to support her as she deserves?"

"If your present objection," replied I, "be meant as an evasion of my offer, I desist; but I know no man so worthy to deserve her as you; and if I could give her thousands, and thousands sought her from me, yet my honest brave Burchell should be my dearest choice."

To all this his silence alone seemed to give a mortifying refusal, and without the least reply to my offer, he demanded if we could not be furnished with refreshments from the next inn, to which being answered in the affirmative, he ordered them to send in the best dinner that could be provided upon such short notice. He bespoke also a dozen of their best wine and some cordials for me. Adding, with a smile, that he would stretch a little for once, and tho' in a prison, asserted he was never better disposed to be merry. The waiter soon made his appearance with preparations for dinner, a table was lent us by the gaoler, who seemed remarkably assiduous, the wine was disposed in order, and two very well-drest dishes were brought in.

My daughter had not yet heard of her poor brother's melancholy situation, and we all seemed unwilling to damp her cheerfulness by the relation. But it was in vain that I attempted to appear cheerful; the circumstances of my unfortunate son broke through all efforts to dissemble, so that I was at last obliged to damp our mirth by relating his misfortunes, and wishing that he might be permitted to share with us in this little interval of satisfaction. After my guests were recovered from the consternation my account had produced, I requested also that Mr. Jenkinson, a fellow prisoner, might be admitted, and the gaoler granted my request with an air of unusual submission. The clanking of my son's irons was no sooner heard along the passage than his sister ran impatiently to meet him, while Mr. Burchell, in the meantime, asked me if my son's name were George, to which replying in the affirmative, he still continued silent. As soon as my boy entered the room, I could perceive he regarded Mr. Burchell with a look of astonishment and reverence. "Come on," cried I, "my son, though we are fallen very low, yet providence has been pleased to grant us some small relaxation from pain. Thy sister is restored to us, and there is her deliverer; to that brave man it is that I am indebted for yet having a daughter; give him, my boy, the hand of friendship, he deserves our warmest gratitude."

My son seemed all this while regardless of what I said, and still continued fixed at respectful distance. "My dear brother," cried his sister, "why don't you thank my good deliverer? the brave should ever love each other."

He still continued his silence and astonishment, till our guest at last perceived himself to be known, and assuming all his native dignity, desired my son to come forward. Never before had I seen any thing so truly majestic as the air he assumed upon this occasion. The greatest object in the universe, says a certain philosopher, is a good man struggling with adversity; yet there is still a greater, which is the good man that comes to relieve it. After he had regarded my son for some time with a superior air, "I again find," said he, "unthinking boy, that the same crime—" But here he was interrupted by one of the gaoler's servants, who came to inform us that a person of distinction, who had driven into town with a chariot and several attendants, sent his respects to the gentleman that was with us, and begged to know when he should think proper to be waited upon. "Bid the fellow wait," cried our guest, "till I shall have leisure to receive him"; and then turning to my son, "I again find, sir," proceeded he, "that you are guilty of the same offence for which you once had my reproof, and for which the law is now preparing its justest punishments. You imagine, perhaps, that a contempt for your own life gives you a right to take that of another; but where, sir, is the difference between a duelist who hazards a life of no value and the murderer who acts with greater security? Is it any diminution of the gamester's fraud when he alleges that he has staked a counter?"

"Alas, sir," cried I, "whoever you are, pity the poor misguided creature; for what he has done was in obedience to a deluded mother, who in the bitterness of her resentment required him upon her blessing to avenge her quarrel. Here, sir, is the letter, which will serve to convince you of her imprudence and diminish his guilt."

He took the letter, and hastily read it over. "This," says he, "though not a perfect excuse, is such a palliation of his fault as induces me to forgive him. And now, sir," continued he, kindly, taking my son by the hand, "I see you are surprised at finding me here; but I have often visited prisons upon occasions less interesting. I am now come to see justice done a worthy man, for whom I have the most sincere esteem. I have long been a disguised spectator of thy father's benevolence. I have at his little dwelling enjoyed respect uncontaminated by flattery, and have received that happiness that courts could not give, from the amusing simplicity round his fire-side. My nephew has been apprized of my intentions of coming here, and I find is arrived; it would be wronging him and you to condemn him without examination: if there be injury, there shall be redress; and this I may say without boasting, that none have ever taxed the injustice of Sir William Thornhill."

We now found the personage whom we had so long entertained as an harmless amusing companion was no other than the celebrated Sir William Thornhill, to whose virtues and singularities scarce any were strangers. The poor Mr. Burchell was in reality a man of large fortune and great interest, to whom senates listened with applause, and whom party heard with conviction; who was the friend of his country, but loyal to his kin. My poor wife, recollecting her former familiarity, seemed to shrink with apprehension; but Sophia, who a few moments before thought him her own, now perceiving the immense distance to which he was removed by fortune, was unable to conceal her tears.

"Ah, sir," cried my wife, with a piteous aspect, "how is it possible that I can ever have your forgiveness; the slights you received from me the last time I had the honour of seeing you at our house, and the jokes which I audaciously threw out, these jokes, sir, I fear can never be forgiven."

"My dear good lady," returned he with a smile, "if you had your joke, I had my answer. I'll leave it to all the company if mine were not as good as yours. To say the truth, I know no body whom I am disposed to be angry with at present but the fellow who so frighted my little girl here. I had not even time to examine the rascal's person so as to describe him in an advertisement. Can you tell me, Sophia, my dear, whether you should know him again?"

"Indeed, sir," replied she, "I can't be positive; yet now I recollect he had a large mark over one of his eye-brows."—"I ask pardon, madam," interrupted Jenkinson, who was by, "but be so good as to inform me if the fellow wore his own red hair?"——"Yes, I think so," cried Sophia.——"And did your honour," continued he, turning to Sir William, "observe the length of his legs?"——"I can't be sure of their length," cried the Baronet, "but I am convinced of their swiftness; for he out-ran me, which is what I thought few men in the kingdom could have done."——"Please your honour," cried Jenkinson, "I know the man: it is certainly the same; the best runner in England; he has beaten Pinwire of Newcastle, Timothy Baxter is his name, I know him perfectly, and the very place of his retreat this moment. If your honour will bid Mr. Gaoler let two of his men go with me, I'll engage to produce him to you in an hour at farthest." Upon this the gaoler was called, who instantly appearing, Sir William demanded if he knew him. "Yes, please your honour," replied the gaoler, "I know Sir William Thornhill well, and every body that knows any thing of him will desire to know more of him."——"Well then," said the Baronet, "my request is that you will permit this man and two of your servants to go upon a message by my authority, and as I am in the commission of the peace, I undertake to secure you."——"Your promise is sufficient," replied the other, "and you may at a minute's warning send them over England whenever your honour thinks fit."

In pursuance of the gaoler's compliance, Jenkinson was dispatched in search of Timothy Baxter, while we were amused with the assiduity of our youngest boy Bill, who had just come in and climbed up to Sir William's neck in order to kiss him. His mother was immediately going to chastise his familiarity, but the worthy man prevented her; and taking the child, all ragged as he was, upon his knee, "What, Bill, you chubby rogue," cried he, "do you remember your old friend Burchell? And Dick too, my honest veteran, are you here? You shall find I have not forgot you." So saying, he gave each a large piece of gingerbread, which the poor fellows ate very heartily, as they had got that morning but a very scanty breakfast.

We now sat down to dinner, which was almost cold; but previously, my arm still continuing painful, Sir William wrote a prescription, for he had made the study of physic his amusement and was more than moderately skilled in the profession; this being sent to an apothecary who lived in the place, my arm was dressed, and I found almost instantaneous relief. We were waited upon at dinner by the gaoler himself, who was willing to do our guest all the honour in his power. But before we had well dined, another message was brought from his nephew, desiring permission to appear in order to vindicate his innocence and honour, with which request the Baronet complied, and desired Mr. Thornhill to be introduced.

CHAPTER XXXI

FORMER BENEVOLENCE NOW REPAID WITH UNEXPECTED INTEREST

Mr. Thornhill made his entrance with a smile, which he seldom wanted, and was going to embrace his uncle, which the other repulsed with an air of disdain. "No fawning, sir, at present," cried the Baronet with a look of severity; "the only way to my heart is by the road of honour; but here I only see complicated instances of falsehood, cowardice, and oppression. How is it, sir, that this poor man, for whom I know you professed a friendship, is used thus hardly? His daughter vilely seduced, as a recompence for his hospitality, and he himself thrown into a prison perhaps but for resenting the insult? His son too, whom you feared to face as a man——"

"Is it possible, sir," interrupted his nephew, "that my uncle could object that as a crime which his repeated instructions alone have persuaded me to avoid?"

"Your rebuke," cried Sir William, "is just; you have acted in this instance prudently and well, though not quite as your father would have done: my brother indeed was the soul of honour, but thou—yes, you have acted in this instance perfectly right, and it has my warmest approbation."

"And I hope," said his nephew, "that the rest of my conduct will not be found to deserve censure. I appeared, sir, with this gentleman's daughter at some places of public amusement; thus what was levity, scandal called by a harsher name, and it was reported that I had debauched her. I waited on her father in person, willing to clear the thing to his satisfaction, and he received me only with insult and abuse. As for the rest, with regard to his being here, my attorney and steward can best inform you, as I commit the management of business entirely to them. If he has contracted debts and is unwilling or even unable to pay them, it is their business to proceed in this manner, and I see no hardship or injustice in pursuing the most legal means of redress."

"If this," cried Sir William, "be as you have stated it, there is nothing unpardonable in your offence; and though your conduct might have been more generous in not suffering this gentleman to be oppressed by subordinate tyranny, yet it has been at least equitable."

"He cannot contradict a single particular," replied the Squire; "I defy him to do so, and several of my servants are ready to attest what I say. Thus, sir," continued he, finding that I was silent, for in fact I could not contradict him, "thus, sir, my own innocence is vindicated; but though at your entreaty I am ready to forgive this gentleman every other offence, yet his attempts to lessen me in your esteem excite a resentment that I cannot govern. And this too at a time when his son was actually preparing to take away my life; this, I say, was such guilt that I am determined to let the law take its course. I have here the challenge that was sent me and two witnesses to prove it; and even though my uncle himself should dissuade me, which I know he will not, yet I will see public justice done, and he shall suffer for it."

"Thou monster," cried my wife, "hast thou not had vengeance enough already, but must my poor boy feel thy cruelty? I hope that good Sir William will protect us, for my son is as innocent as a child; I am sure he is, and never did harm to man."

"Madam," replied the good man, "your wishes for his safety are not greater than mine; but I am sorry to find his guilt too plain; and if my nephew persists—" But the appearance of Jenkinson and the gaoler's two servants now called off our attention, who entered, haling in a tall man, very genteely drest, and answering the description already given of the ruffian who had carried off my daughter. "Here," cried Jenkinson, pulling him in, "here we have him, and if ever there was a candidate for Tyburn, this is one."

The moment Mr. Thornhill perceived the prisoner and Jenkinson, who had him in custody, he seemed to shrink back with terror. His face became pale with conscious guilt, and he would have withdrawn; but Jenkinson, who perceived his design, stopt him. "What, Squire," cried he, "are you ashamed of your two old acquaintances, Jenkinson and Baxter? But this is the way that all great men forget their friends, though I am resolved we will not forget you. Our prisoner, please your honour," continued he, turning to Sir William, "has already confessed all. He declares that it was Mr. Thornhill who first put him upon this affair, that he gave him the clothes he now wears to appear like a gentleman, and furnished him with the post-chaise. The plan was laid between them that he should carry off the young lady to a place of safety, and that there he should threaten and terrify her; but Mr. Thornhill was to come in in the meantime, as if by accident, to her rescue, and that they should fight awhile and then he was to run off, by which Mr. Thornhill would have the better opportunity of gaining her affections himself under the character of her defender."

Sir William remembered the coat to have been frequently worn by his nephew, and all the rest the prisoner himself confirmed by a more circumstantial account, concluding that Mr. Thornhill had often declared to him that he was in love with both sisters at the same time.

"Heavens," cried Sir William, "what a viper have I been fostering in my bosom! And so fond of public justice too as he seemed to be. But he shall have it; secure him, Mr. Gaoler—yet hold, I fear there is not legal evidence to detain him."

Upon this, Mr. Thornhill, with the utmost humility, entreated that two such abandoned wretches might not be admitted as evidences against him, but that his servants should be examined. "Your servants," replied Sir William, "wretch, call them yours no longer; but come let us hear what those fellows have to say; let his butler be called."

When the butler was introduced, he soon perceived by his former master's looks that all his power was now over. "Tell me," cried Sir William sternly, "have you ever seen your master and that fellow drest up in his clothes in company together?"—"Yes, please your honour," cried the butler, "a thousand times; he was the man that always brought him his ladies."——"How," interrupted young Mr. Thornhill, "this to my face!"——"Yes," replied the butler, "or to any man's face. To tell you a truth, Master Thornhill, I never either loved you or liked you, and I don't care if I tell you now a piece of my mind."——"Now then," cried Jenkinson, "tell his honour whether you know any thing of me."——"I can't say," replied the butler, "that I know much good of you. The night that gentleman's daughter was deluded to our house, you were one of them."——"So then," cried Sir William, "I find you have brought a very fine witness to prove your innocence: thou stain to humanity! to associate with such wretches!" (But continuing his examination) "You tell me, Mr. Butler, that this was the person who brought him this old gentleman's daughter?"

——"No, please your honour," replied the butler, "he did not bring her, for the Squire himself undertook that business; but he brought the priest that pretended to marry them."——"It is but too true," cried Jenkinson, "I cannot deny it; that was the employment assigned me, and I confess it to my confusion."

"Good heavens!" exclaimed the Baronet, "how every new discovery of his villainy alarms me. All his guilt is now too plain, and I find his present prosecution was dictated by tyranny, cowardice, and revenge; at my request, Mr. Gaoler, set this young officer, now your prisoner, free, and trust to me for the consequences. I'll make it my business to set the affair in a proper light to my friend the magistrate who has committed him. But where is the unfortunate young lady herself? Let her appear to confront this wretch; I long to know by what arts he has seduced her honour. Entreat her to come in. Where is she?"

"Ah, sir," said I, "that question stings me to the heart. I was once indeed happy in a daughter, but her miseries—" Another interruption here prevented me; for who should make her appearance but Miss Arabella Wilmot, who was next day to have been married to Mr. Thornhill. Nothing could equal her surprise at seeing Sir William and his nephew here before her, for her arrival was quite accidental. It happened that she and the old gentleman, her father, were passing through the town on their way to her aunt's, who had insisted that her nuptials with Mr. Thornhill should be consummated at her house; but stopping for refreshment, they put up at an inn at the other end of the town. It was there from the window that the young lady happened to observe one of my little boys playing in the street, and instantly sending a footman to bring the child to her, she learnt from him some account of our misfortunes, but was still kept ignorant of young Mr. Thornhill's being the cause. Though her father made several remonstrances on the impropriety of going to a prison to visit us, yet they were ineffectual; she desired the child to conduct her, which he did, and it was thus she surprised us at a juncture so unexpected.

Nor can I go on without a reflection on those accidental

meetings which, though they happen every day, seldom excite our surprise but upon some extraordinary occasion. To what a fortuitous concurrence do we not owe every pleasure and convenience of our lives. How many seeming accidents must unite before we can be clothed or fed. The peasant must be disposed to labour, the shower must fall, the wind fill the merchant's sail, or numbers must want the usual supply.

We all continued silent for some moments, while my charming pupil, which was the name I generally gave this young lady, united in her looks compassion and astonishment, which gave new finishings to her beauty. "Indeed, my dear Mr. Thornhill," cried she to the Squire, who she supposed was come here to succour and not to oppress us, "I take it a little unkindly that you should come here without me, or never inform me of the situation of a family so dear to us both; you know I should take as much pleasure in contributing to the relief of my reverend old master here, whom I shall ever esteem, as you can. But I find that, like your uncle, you take a pleasure in doing good in secret."

"He find pleasure in doing good!" cried Sir William, interrupting her. "No, my dear, his pleasures are as base as he is. You see in him, madam, as complete a villain as ever disgraced humanity. A wretch, who after having deluded this poor man's daughter, after plotting against the innocence of her sister, has thrown the father into prison and the eldest son into fetters, because he had courage to face his betrayer. And give me leave, madam, now to congratulate you upon an escape from the embraces of such a monster."

"O goodness," cried the lovely girl, "how have I been deceived! Mr. Thornhill informed me for certain that this gentleman's eldest son, Captain Primrose, was gone off to America with his new-married lady."

"My sweetest miss," cried my wife, "he has told you nothing but falsehoods. My son George never left the kingdom nor never was married. Tho' you have forsaken him, he has always loved you too well to think of any body else; and I have heard him say he would die a bachelor for your sake." She then proceeded to expatiate upon the sincerity of her son's passion; she set his duel with Mr. Thornhill in a proper light; from thence she made a rapid digression to the Squire's debaucheries, his pretended marriages, and ended with a most insulting picture of his cowardice.

"Good heavens!" cried Miss Wilmot, "how very near have I been to the brink of ruin! But how great is my pleasure to have escaped it! Ten thousand falsehoods has this gentleman told me! He had at last art enough to persuade me that my promise to the only man I esteemed was no longer binding, since he had been unfaithful. By his falsehoods I was taught to detest one equally brave and generous!"

But by this time my son was freed from the incumbrances of justice. Mr. Jenkinson also, who had acted as his valet de chambre, had dressed up his hair and furnished him with whatever was necessaary to make a genteel appearance. He now therefore entered, handsomely drest in his regimentals, and, without vanity (for I am above it), he appeared as handsome a fellow as ever wore a military dress. As he entered, he made Miss Wilmot a modest and distant bow, for he was not as yet acquainted with the change which the eloquence of his mother had wrought in his favour. But no decorums could restrain the impatience of his blushing mistress to be forgiven. Her tears, her looks, all contributed to discover the real sensations of her heart for having forgotten her former promise and having suffered herself to be deluded by an impostor. My son appeared amazed at her condescension and could scarce believe it real. "Sure, madam," cried he, "this is but delusion! I can never have merited this! To be blest thus is to be too happy." ——"No, sir," replied she, "I have been deceived, basely deceived, else nothing could have ever made me unjust to my promise. You know my friendship, you have long known it; but forget what I have done, and as you once had my warmest vows of constancy, you shall now have them repeated; and be assured that if your Arabella cannot be yours, she shall never be another's."——"And no other's you shall be," cried Sir William, "if I have any influence with your father."

This hint was sufficient for my son Moses, who immediately flew to the inn where the old gentleman was, to inform him of every circumstance that had happened. But in the meantime the Squire, perceiving that he was on every side undone, now finding that no hopes were left from flattery or dissimulation, concluded that his wisest way would be to turn and face his pursuers. Thus laying aside all shame, he appeared the open hardy villain. "I find then," cried he, "that I am to expect no justice here; but I am resolved it shall be done me. You shall know, sir," turning to Sir William, "I am no longer a poor dependant upon your favours. I scorn them. Nothing can keep Miss Wilmot's fortune from me, which, I thank her father's assiduity, is pretty large. The articles, and a bond for her fortune, are signed and safe in my possession. It was her fortune, not her person, that induced me to wish for this match, and possessed of the one, let who will take the other."

This was an alarming blow. Sir William was sensible of the justice of his claims, for he had been instrumental in drawing up the marriage articles himself. Miss Wilmot therefore perceiving that her fortune was irretrievably lost, turning to my son, she asked if the loss of fortune could lessen her value to him. "Though fortune," said she, "is out of my power, at least I have my hand to give."

"And that, madam," cried her real lover, "was indeed all that you ever had to give; at least all that I ever thought worth the acceptance. And I now protest, my Arabella, by all that's happy, your want of fortune this moment increases my pleasure, as it serves to convince my sweet girl of my sincerity."

Mr. Wilmot now entering, he seemed not a little pleased at the danger his daughter had just escaped, and readily consented to a dissolution of the match. But finding that her fortune, which was secured to Mr. Thornhill by bond, would not be given up, nothing could exceed his disappointment. He now saw that his money must all go to enrich one who had no fortune of his own. He could bear his being a rascal; but to want an equivalent to his daughter's fortune was wormwood. He sat therefore for some minutes employed in the most mortifying speculations, till Sir William attempted to lessen his anxiety. "I must confess, sir," cried he, "that your present disappointment does not entirely displease me. Your immoderate passion for wealth is now justly punished. But tho' the young lady cannot be rich, she has still a competence sufficient to give content. Here you see an honest young soldier, who is willing to take her without fortune; they have long loved each other, and for the friendship I bear his father, my interest shall not be wanting for his promotion. Leave then that ambition which disappoints you, and for once admit happiness which courts your acceptance."

"Sir William," replied the old gentleman, "be assured I never yet forced her inclinations, nor will I now. If she still continues to love this young gentleman, let her have him with all my heart. There is still, thank heaven, some fortune left, and your promise will make it something more. Only let my old friend here" (meaning me) "give me a promise of settling six thousand pounds upon my girl, if ever he should come to his fortune, and I am ready this night to be the first to join them together."

As it now remained with me to make the young couple happy, I readily gave a promise of making the settlement he required, which, to one who had such little expectations as I, was no great favour. We had now therefore the satisfaction of seeing them fly into each other's arms in a transport. "After all my misfortunes," cried my son George, "to be thus rewarded! Sure this is more than I could ever have presumed to hope for. To be possessed of all that's good, and after such an interval of pain! My warmest wishes could never rise so high!"——"Yes, my George," returned his lovely bride, "now let the wretch take my fortune; since you are happy without it so am I. O what an exchange have I made from the basest of men to the dearest best! Let him enjoy our fortune, I now can be happy even in indigence."——"And I promise you," cried the Squire, with a malicious grin, "that I shall be very happy with what you despise." ——"Hold, hold, sir," cried Jenkinson, "there are two words to that bargain. As for that lady's fortune, sir, you shall never touch a single stiver of it. Pray your honour," continued he to Sir William, "can the Squire have this lady's fortune if he be married to another?"——"How can you make such a simple demand?" replied the Baronet; "undoubtedly he cannot."——"I am sorry for that," cried Jenkinson; "for as this gentleman and I have been old fellow sporters, I have a friendship for him. But I must declare, well as I love him, that his contract is not worth a tobacco stopper, for he is married already."——"You lie, like a rascal," returned the Squire, who seemed roused by this insult; "I never was legally married to any woman."——"Indeed, begging your honour's pardon," replied the other, "you were; and I hope you will show a proper return of friendship to your own honest Jenkinson, who brings you a wife, and if the company restrains their curiosity a few minutes, they shall see her." So saying he went off with his usual celerity, and left us all unable to form any probable conjecture as to his design. "Ay, let him go," cried the Squire; "whatever else I may have done I defy him there. I am too old now to be frightened with squibs."

"I am surprised," said the Baronet, "what the fellow can intend by this. Some low piece of humour, I suppose!"——"Perhaps, sir," replied I, "he may have a more serious meaning. For when we reflect on the various schemes this gentleman laid to seduce innocence, perhaps some one more artful than the rest has been found able to deceive him. When we consider what numbers he has ruined, how many parents now feel with anguish the infamy and the contamination which he has brought into their families, it would not surprise me if some one of them—Amazement! Do I see my lost daughter! Do I hold her! It is, it is my life, my happiness. I thought thee lost, my Olivia, yet still I hold thee—and still shalt thou live to bless me." The warmest transports of the fondest lover were not greater than mine when I saw him introduce my child, and held my daughter in my arms, whose silence only spoke her raptures. "And art thou returned to me, my darling," cried I, "to be my comfort in age!"——"That she is," cried Jenkinson, "and make much of her, for she is your own honourable child, and as honest a woman as any in the whole room, let the other be who she will. And as for you, Squire, as sure as you stand there, this young lady is your lawful wedded wife. And to convince you that I speak nothing but truth, here is the licence by which you were married together." So saying, he put the licence into the Baronet's hands, who read it and found it perfect in every respect. "And now, gentlemen," continued he, "I find you are surprised at all this; but a few words will explain the difficulty. That there Squire of renown, for whom I have a great friendship, but that's between ourselves, has often employed me in doing odd little things for him. Among the rest, he commissioned me to procure him a false licence and a false priest, in order to deceive this young lady. But as I was very much his friend, what did I do but went and got a true licence and a true priest, and married them both as fast as the cloth could make them. Perhaps you'll think it was generosity that made me do all this. But no. To my shame I confess it, my only design was to keep the licence and let the Squire know that I could prove it upon him whenever I thought proper, and so make him come down whenever I wanted money." A burst of pleasure now seemed to fill the whole apartment; our joy reached even to the common room, where the prisoners themselves sympathized,

And shook their chains
In transport and rude harmony.

Happiness expanded upon every face, and even Olivia's cheek seemed flushed with pleasure. To be thus restored to reputation, to friends and fortune at once, was a rapture sufficient to stop the progress of decay and restore former health and vivacity. But perhaps among all there was not one who felt sincerer pleasure than I. Still holding the dear-loved child in my arms, I asked my heart if these transports were not delusion. "How could you," cried I, turning to Mr. Jenkinson, "how could you add to my miseries by the story of her death! But it matters not; my pleasure at finding her again is more than a recompence for the pain."

"As to your question," replied Jenkinson, "that is

easily answered. I thought the only probable means of freeing you from prison was by submitting to the Squire and consenting to his marriage with the other young lady. But these you had vowed never to grant while your daughter was living; there was therefore no other method to bring things to bear but by persuading you that she was dead. I prevailed on your wife to join in the deceit, and we have not had a fit opportunity of undeceiving you till now."

In the whole assembly now there only appeared two faces that did not glow with transport. Mr. Thornhill's assurance had entirely forsaken him; he now saw the gulf of infamy and want before him, and trembled to take the plunge. He therefore fell on his knees before his uncle, and in a voice of piercing misery implored compassion. Sir William was going to spurn him away, but at my request he raised him, and after pausing a few moments, "Thy vices, crimes, and ingratitude," cried he, "deserve no tenderness; yet thou shalt not be entirely forsaken, a bare competence shall be supplied, to support the wants of life, but not its follies. This young lady, thy wife, shall be put in possession of a third part of that fortune which once was thine, and from her tenderness alone thou art to expect any extraordinary supplies for the future." He was going to express his gratitude for such kindness in a set speech; but the Baronet prevented him by bidding him not aggravate his meanness, which was already but too apparent. He ordered him at the same time to be gone, and from all his former domestics to choose one such as he should think proper, which was all that should be granted to attend him.

As soon as he left us, Sir William very politely stept up to his new niece with a smile and wished her joy. His example was followed by Miss Wilmot and her father; my wife too kissed her daughter with much affection, as, to use her own expression, she was now made an honest woman of. Sophia and Moses followed in turn, and even our benefactor Jenkinson desired to be admitted to that honour. Our satisfaction seemed scarce capable of increase. Sir William, whose greatest pleasure was in doing good, now looked round with a countenance open as the sun and saw nothing but joy in the looks of all except that of my daughter Sophia, who, for some reasons we could not comprehend, did not seem perfectly satisfied. "I think now," cried he, with a smile, "that all the company, except one or two, seem perfectly happy. There only remains an act of justice for me to do. You are sensible, sir," continued he, turning to me, "of the obligations we both owe Mr. Jenkinson for his late assiduity in detecting a scoundrel. It is but just we should both reward him for it. Your youngest daughter, Miss Sophia, will, I am sure, make him very happy, and he shall have from me five hundred pounds as her fortune, and upon this I am sure they can live very comfortably together. Come, Miss Sophia, what say you to this match of my making? Will you have him?" My poor girl seemed almost sinking into her mother's arms at the hideous proposal. "Have him, sir!" cried she faintly. "No, sir, never."—— "What," cried he again, "not have Mr. Jenkinson, your benefactor, an handsome young fellow, with five hundred pounds and good expectations!"——"I beg, sir," returned she, scarce able to speak, "that you'll desist, and not make me so very wretched."——"Was ever such obstinacy known," cried he again, "to refuse a man whom the family has such infinite obligations to, who has preserved your sister. What! not have him!"——"No, sir, never," replied she angrily, "I'd sooner die first."——"If that be the case then," cried he, "if you will not have him—I think I must have you myself." And so saying, he caught her to his breast with ardour. "My loveliest, my most sensible of girls," cried he, "how could you ever think your own Burchell could deceive you, or that Sir William Thornhill could ever cease to admire a mistress that loved him for himself alone? I have for some years sought for a woman who, a stranger to my fortune, could think that I had merit as a man. After having tried in vain, even amongst the pert and the ugly, how great at last must be my rapture to have made a conquest over such sense and such heavenly beauty." Then turning to Jenkinson, "As I cannot, sir, part with this young lady myself, for she has taken a fancy to the cut of my face, all the recompence I can make is to give you her fortune, and you may call upon my steward to-morrow for five hundred pounds." Thus we had all our compliments to repeat, and Lady Thornhill underwent the same round of ceremony that her sisters had done before. In the meantime Sir William's gentleman appeared to tell us that the equipages were ready to carry us to the inn, where every thing was prepared for our reception. My wife and I led the van and left those gloomy mansions of sorrow. The generous Baronet ordered forty pounds to be distributed among the prisoners, and Mr. Wilmot, induced by his example, gave half that sum. We were received below by the shouts of the villagers, and I saw and shook by the hand two or three of my honest parishioners, who were among the number. They attended us to our inn, where a sumptuous entertainment was provided, and coarser provisions distributed in great quantities among the populace.

After supper, as my spirits were exhausted by the alternation of pleasure and pain which they had sustained during the day, I asked permission to withdraw, and leaving the company in the midst of their mirth, as soon as I found myself alone, I poured out my heart in gratitude to the giver of joy as well as of sorrow, and then slept undisturbed till morning.

CHAPTER XXXII

THE CONCLUSION

The next morning, as soon as I awaked, I found my eldest son sitting by my bedside, who came to increase my joy with another turn of fortune in my favour. First having released me from the settlement that I had made the day before in his favour, he let me know that my merchant who had failed in town was arrested at Antwerp, and there had given up effects to a much greater amount than what was due to his creditors. My boy's generosity pleased me almost as much as this unlooked for good fortune. But I had some doubts whether I ought in justice to accept his offer. While I was pondering upon this, Sir William entered the room, to whom I communicated my doubts. His opinion was that as my son was already possessed of a very affluent fortune by his marriage, I might accept his offer without any hesitation. His business, however, was to inform me that as he had the night before sent for the licences and expected them every hour, he hoped that I would not refuse my assistance in making all the company happy that morning. A footman entered while we were speaking to tell us that the messenger was returned, and as I was by this time ready, I went down, where I found the whole company as merry as affluence and innocence could make them. However, as they were now preparing for a very solemn ceremony, their laughter entirely displeased me. I told them of the grave, becoming, and sublime deportment they should assume upon this mystical occasion, and read them two homilies and a thesis of my own composing, in order to prepare them. Yet they still seemed perfectly refractory and ungovernable. Even as we were going along to church, to which I led the way, all gravity had quite forsaken them, and I was often tempted to turn back in indignation. In church a new dilemma arose, which promised no easy solution. This was, which couple should be married first; my son's bride warmly insisted that Lady Thornhill (that was to be) should take the lead; but this the other refused with equal ardour, protesting she would not be guilty of such rudeness for the world. The argument was supported for some time between both with equal obstinacy and good breeding. But as I stood all this time with my book ready, I was at last quite tired of the contest, and shutting it, "I perceive," cried I, "that none of you have a mind to be married, and I think we had as good go back again; for I suppose there will be no business done here to-day." This at once reduced them to reason. The Baronet and his Lady were first married, and then my son and his lovely partner.

I had previously that morning given orders that a coach should be sent for my honest neighbour Flamborough and his family, by which means, upon our return to the inn, we had the pleasure of finding the two Miss Flamboroughs alighted before us. Mr. Jenkinson gave his hand to the eldest and my son Moses led up the other (and I have since found that he has taken a real liking to the girl, and my consent and bounty he shall have whenever he thinks proper to demand them). We were no sooner returned to the inn, but numbers of my parishioners, hearing of my success, came to congratulate me; but among the rest were those who rose to rescue me, and whom I formerly rebuked with such sharpness. I told the story to Sir William, my son-in-law, who went out and reproved them with great severity; but finding them quite disheartened by his harsh reproof, he gave them half a guinea a piece to drink his health and raise their dejected spirits.

Soon after this we were called to a very genteel entertainment, which was drest by Mr. Thornhill's cook. And it may not be improper to observe with respect to that gentleman that he now resides in quality of companion at a relation's house, being very well liked and seldom sitting at the side-table, except when there is no room at the other; for they make no stranger of him. His time is pretty much taken up in keeping his relation, who is a little melancholy, in spirits, and in learning to blow the French-horn. My eldest daughter, however, still remembers him with regret; and she has even told me, though I make a great secret of it, that when he reforms she may be brought to relent. But to return, for I am not apt to digress thus, when we were to sit down to dinner our ceremonies were going to be renewed. The question was whether my eldest daughter, as being a matron, should not sit above the two young brides, but the debate was cut short by my son George, who proposed that the company should sit indiscriminately, every gentleman by his lady. This was received with great approbation by all, excepting my wife, who I could perceive was not perfectly satisfied, as she expected to have had the pleasure of sitting at the head of the table and carving all the meat for all the company. But notwithstanding this, it is impossible to describe our good humour. I can't say whether we had more wit amongst us now than usual; but I am certain we had more laughing, which answered the end as well. One jest I particularly remember: old Mr. Wilmot drinking to Moses, whose head was turned another way, my son replied, "Madam, I thank you." Upon which the old gentleman, winking upon the rest of the company, observed that he was thinking of his mistress. At which jest I thought the two Miss Flamboroughs would have died with laughing. As soon as dinner was over, according to my old custom, I requested that the table might be taken away, to have the pleasure of seeing all my family assembled once more by a cheerful fire-side. My two little ones sat upon each knee, the rest of the company by their partners. I had nothing now on this side of the grave to wish for, all my cares were over, my pleasure was unspeakable. It now only remained that my gratitude in good fortune should exceed my former submission in adversity.

FINIS

A Note on the Text

The text is based on the first edition of *The Vicar of Wakefield*, published in two volumes in London in 1766. Typographical errors have been corrected, and archaic spelling and punctuation have been brought into conformity with modern British usage.

Selected Bibliography

Works by Daniel Defoe

There is no complete edition of Defoe's voluminous writings. The most significant are to be found in:

Defoe, Daniel. *The Best of Defoe's Review,* ed. William L. Payne, New York: Columbia University Press, 1951.

———. *Conjugal Lewdness, or Matrimonial Whoredom* Gainesville, Florida: Scholars' Facsimiles & Reprints, 1967.

———. *An Essay upon Projects.* Menston, England: The Scolar Press, 1969.

———. *The Novels and Selected Writings.* Oxford: Basil Blackwell, 1927-28, 14 vols. (The Shakespeare Head Edition).

Lee, William. *Daniel Defoe; His Life, and Recently Discovered Writings. London: J. C. Hotten, 1869, 3 vols.*

A Journal of the Plague Year (CW 927), *Moll Flanders* (CW 1170), and *Robinson Crusoe* (CW1052) are available in Signet Classic editions.

Works About Daniel Defoe

Dobrée, Bonamy. *English Literature in the Early Eighteenth Century, 1700-1740.* (Vol. VII, *Oxford History of English Literature*). Oxford: Clarendon Press, 1959.

McKillop, Alan Dugald. *The Early Masters of English Fiction.* Lawrence: University of Kansas Press, 1956.

Moore, John Robert. *Daniel Defoe: Citizen of the Modern World.* Chicago: University of Chicago Press, 1958.

Novak, Maximilian E. *Defoe and the Nature of Man.* London: Oxford University Press, 1963.

Richetti, John J. *Defoe's Narratives: Situations and Structures.* London: Oxford University Press, 1975.

Rogers, Katharine M. "The Feminism of Daniel Defoe," *Woman in the 18th Century and Other Essays,* ed. Paul Fritz and Richard Morton. Toronto: Hakkert, 1976.

Sutherland, James. *Defoe.* London: Methuen, 1950.

Watt, Ian. *The Rise of the Novel: Studies in Defoe, Richardson, and Fielding.* Berkeley: University of California Press, 1957.

Woolf, Virginia. "Defoe," *The Common Reader, First Series.* New York: Harcourt, Brace & Co., 1925.

Work by Henry Fielding

The Temple Beau, 1730 Play
Tom Thumb, A Tragedy, 1730 Play
The Coffee-House Politician, 1730 Play
The Grub-Street Opera, 1731 Play
The Miser, 1733 Play
Don Quixote in England, 1734 Play
The Virgin Unmask'd, 1735 Play
Pasquin, 1736 Play
Shamela, 1741 Satire
Joseph Andrews, 1742 Novel (Signet Classic CJ1358)
Jonathan Wild, 1743 Novel (Signet Classic CY1069)
Tom Jones, 1749 Novel (Signet Classic CE1451)
Amelia, 1751 Novel
Journey of a Voyage to Lisbon, 1755 Travel

Works About Henry Fielding

Alter, Robert. *Fielding and the Nature of the Novel.* Cambridge, Mass.: Harvard University Press, 1968.

Battestin, Martin C. *The Moral Basis of Fielding's Art: A Study of Joseph Andrews.* Middleton, Ct.: Wesleyan University Press, 1959.

Butt, John. *Fielding*. London: Longmans, Green, 1954.

Cross, W. L. *The History of Henry Fielding.* 3 vols. New Haven: Yale University Press, 1918.

Golden, Morris. *Fielding's Moral Psychology.* Boston: University of Massachuetts Press, 1966.

Harrison, Bernard. *Henry Fielding's Tom Jones: The Novelist as Moral Philosopher.* London: Chatto & Windus, 1975.

Hatfield, Glenn W. *Henry Fielding and the Language of Irony.* Chicago: University of Chicago Press, 1968.

Hutchens, Eleanor. *Irony in Tom Jones.* University: University of Alabama Press, 1965.

Johnson, Maurice. *Fielding's Art of Fiction.* Philadelphia: University of Pennsylvania Press, 1961.

Levine, George R. *Henry Fielding and the Dry Mock: A Study of the Techniques of Irony in His Early Works.* The Hague: Moulton, 1967.

McKillop, A. D. "Henry Fielding." In *The Early Masters of English Fiction.* Lawrence: University of Kansas Press, 1956.

Miller, Henry Knight. *Essays on Fielding's Miscellanies: A Commentary on Volume One*. Princeton, N.J.: Princeton University Press, 1961.

Paulson, Ronald, ed. *Fielding: A Collection of Critical Essays*. Englewood Cliffs, N.J.: Prentice-Hall, 1962.

——— and Thomas Lockwood, eds. *Fielding: The Critical Heritage*. London: Routledge & Kegan Paul; New York: Barnes & Noble, 1969.

Preston, John. *The Reader's Role in Eighteenth-Century Fiction*. London: Heinemann, 1970.

Rawson, Claude J. *Henry Fielding and the Augustan Ideal under Stress*. London: Routledge & Kegan Paul, 1972.

Sacks, Sheldon. *Fiction and the Shape of Belief*. Berkeley: University of California Press, 1964.

Watt, Ian. *The Rise of the Novel: Studies in Deofe, Richardson, and Fielding*. Berkeley: University of California Press, 1957.

Wright, Andrew. *Henry Fielding: Mask and Feast*. Berkeley: University of California Press, 1965.

Works by Oliver Goldsmith

The Bee, 1759 Essays

An Enquiry into the Present State of Polite Learning in Europe, 1759 Essay

The Citizen of the World, 1762 Essays

The Traveller, 1764 Poem

Asem, an Eastern Tale, 1765 Story

The Good Natur'd Man, 1768 Play

The Deserted Village, 1770 Poem

The Beauties of the Magazines, 1772 Essays

She Stoops to Conquer, 1773 Play

Works About Oliver Goldsmith

Balderston, Katherine C. *The History and Sources of Percy's Memoir of Goldsmith*. New York: The Macmillan Company, 1926.

Lucas, Frank L. *Search for Good Sense: Four 18th Century Characters: Johnson, Chesterfield, Boswell and Goldsmith*. New York: The Macmillan Company, 1959.

Neal, Minnie Mills. *Oliver Goldsmith*. Los Angeles: Pageant Publishers, 1955.

Percy, Thomas. *Memoir of Goldsmith*. Ed. by K. C. Balderston. New York: Oxford University Press, 1926.

Scott, Macaulay, and Thackeray. *Essays on Goldsmith*. New York: Oxford University Press, 1918.

Scott, Temple. *Oliver Goldsmith Bibliographically and Biographically Considered*. New York: W. E. Rudge, 1928.

Wardle, Ralph M. *Oliver Goldsmith*. Lawrence, Kansas: University of Kansas Press, 1957.